Outward Bound

Books by Robert A. Heinlein

Novels

Beyond This Horizon (1948)
Sixth Column (1949)
The Puppet Masters (1951)
Double Star (1956)
The Door Into Summer (1957)
Methuselah's Children (1958)
Starship Troopers (1959)
Stranger in a Strange Land (1961)
Glory Road (1963)
Orphans of the Sky (1963)
Farnham's Freehold (1964)
The Moon Is a Harsh Mistress (1966)
I Will Fear No Evil (1970)
Time Enough for Love (1973)
The Number of the Beast (1980)
Friday (1982)
Job: A Comedy of Justice (1984)
The Cat Who Walks Through Walls (1985)
To Sail Beyond the Sunset (1987)
For Us, The Living (2003)

Juvenile Novels

Rocket Ship Galileo (1947)
Space Cadet (1948)
Red Planet (1949)
Farmer in the Sky (1950)
Between Planets (1951)
The Rolling Stones (1952)
Starman Jones (1953)
The Star Beast (1954)
Tunnel in the Sky (1955)
Time for the Stars (1956)
Citizen of the Galaxy (1957)
Have Space Suit—Will Travel (1958)
Podkayne of Mars (1963)

Short Fiction & Miscellaneous

The Man Who Sold the Moon (1950)
Waldo and Magic, Inc. (1950)
The Green Hills of Earth (1951)
Revolt in 2100 (1953)
Assignment in Eternity (1953)
The Menace From Earth (1959)
The Unpleasant Profession of
   Jonathan Hoag (1959)
The Worlds of Robert A. Heinlein
   (1966)
The Past Through Tomorrow (1967)
Expanded Universe (1980)
Grumbles from the Grave (1989)
Requiem: New Collected Works (1992)
Tramp Royale (1992)
The Fantasies of Robert A. Heinlein
   (1999)

Outward Bound

HAVE SPACE SUIT—WILL TRAVEL
STARSHIP TROOPERS
PODKAYNE OF MARS

Robert A. Heinlein

SF
BC
SCIENCE
FICTION

HAVE SPACE SUIT—WILL TRAVEL   Copyright © 1958 by
   Robert A. Heinlein
STARSHIP TROOPERS   Copyright © 1959 by Robert A. Heinlein
PODKAYNE OF MARS   Copyright © 1963 by Robert A. Heinlein
   Postlude to *Podkayne of Mars*, original version © 1989 by
   Robert A. & Virginia Heinlein Trust UDT 20 June 1983

First SFBC Science Fiction printing: June 2006.

Visit The SFBC at http://www.sfbc.com

ISBN-10: 0-7394-6891-X
ISBN-13: 978-0-7394-6891-3

Printed in the United States of America.

Contents

HAVE SPACE SUIT— WILL TRAVEL

For Harry and Barbara Stine

Chapter 1

You see, I had this space suit.

How it happened was this way:

"Dad," I said, "I want to go to the Moon."

"Certainly," he answered and looked back at his book. It was Jerome K. Jerome's *Three Men in a Boat,* which he must know by heart.

I said, "Dad, please! I'm serious."

This time he closed the book on a finger and said gently, "I said it was all right. Go ahead."

"Yes . . . but *how?*"

"Eh?" He looked mildly surprised. "Why, that's your problem, Clifford."

Dad was like that. The time I told him I wanted to buy a bicycle he said, "Go right ahead," without even glancing up—so I had gone to the money basket in the dining room, intending to take enough for a bicycle. But there had been only eleven dollars and forty-three cents in it, so about a thousand miles of mowed lawns later I bought a bicycle. I hadn't said any more to Dad because if money wasn't in the basket, it wasn't anywhere; Dad didn't bother with banks—just the money basket and one next to it marked "UNCLE SAM," the contents of which he bundled up and mailed to the government once a year. This caused the Internal Revenue Service considerable headache and once they sent a man to remonstrate with him.

First the man demanded, then he pleaded. "But, Dr. Russell, we know your background. You've no excuse for not keeping proper records."

"But I do," Dad told him. "Up here." He tapped his forehead. "The law requires written records."

"Look again," Dad advised him. "The law can't even require a man to read and write. More coffee?"

The man tried to get Dad to pay by check or money order. Dad read him the fine print on a dollar bill, the part about "legal tender for all debts, public and private."

In a despairing effort to get *something* out of the trip he asked Dad *please* not to fill in the space marked "occupation" with "Spy."

"Why not?"

"What? Why, because you *aren't*—and it upsets people."

"Have you checked with the F.B.I.?"

"Eh? No."

"They probably wouldn't answer. But you've been very polite. I'll mark it 'Unemployed Spy.' Okay?"

The tax man almost forgot his brief case. Nothing fazed Dad, he meant what he said, he wouldn't argue and he never gave in. So when he told me I could go to the Moon but the means were up to me, he meant just that. I could go tomorrow—provided I could wangle a billet in a space ship.

But he added meditatively, "There must be a number of ways to get to the Moon, son. Better check 'em all. Reminds me of this passage I'm reading. They're trying to open a tin of pineapple and Harris has left the can opener back in London. They try several ways." He started to read aloud and I sneaked out—I had heard that passage five hundred times. Well, three hundred.

I went to my workshop in the barn and thought about ways. One way was to go to the Air Academy at Colorado Springs—if I got an appointment, if I graduated, *if* I managed to get picked for the Federation Space Corps, there was a chance that someday I would be ordered to Lunar Base, or at least one of the satellite stations.

Another way was to study engineering, get a job in jet propulsion, and buck for a spot that would get me sent to the Moon. Dozens, maybe hundreds, of engineers had been to the Moon, or were still there—for all sorts of work: electronics, cryogenics, metallurgy, ceramics, air conditioning, as well as rocket engineering.

Oh, yes! Out of a million engineers a handful got picked for the Moon. Shucks, I rarely got picked even playing post office.

Or a man could be an M.D., or a lawyer, or geologist, or tool-maker, and wind up on the Moon at a fat salary—provided they wanted him and nobody else. I didn't care about salary—but how do you arrange to be number one in your specialty?

And there was the straightforward way: trundle in a wheelbarrow of money and buy a ticket.

This I would never manage—I had eighty-seven cents at that moment—but it had caused me to think about it steadily. Of the boys in our school half admitted that they wanted to space, half pretended not to care, knowing how feeble the chances were—plus a handful of creeps who wouldn't leave Earth for any reason. But we talked about it and some of us were determined to go. I didn't break into a rash until American Express and Thos. Cook & Son announced tourist excursions.

I saw their ads in *National Geographic* while waiting to have my teeth cleaned. After that I never was the same.

The idea that any rich man could simply lay cash on the line and *go* was more than I could stand. I just *had* to go. I would never be able to pay for it—or, at least, that was so far in the future there was no use thinking about it. So what could I do to be *sent?*

You see stories about boys, poor-but-honest, who go to the top because they're smarter than anyone in the county, maybe the state. But they're not talking about me. I was in the top quarter of my graduating class but they do not give scholarships to M.I.T. for that—not from Centerville High. I am stating a fact; our high school isn't very good. It's great to go to—we're league champions in basketball and our square-dance team is state runner-up and we have a swell sock hop every Wednesday. Lots of school spirit.

But not much studying.

The emphasis is on what our principal, Mr. Hanley, calls "preparation for life" rather than on trigonometry. Maybe it does prepare you for life; it certainly doesn't prepare you for CalTech.

I didn't find this out myself. Sophomore year I brought home a questionnaire cooked up by our group project in "Family Living" in social studies. One question read: "How is your family council organized?"

At dinner I said, "Dad, how is our family council organized?"

Mother said, "Don't disturb your father, dear."

Dad said, "Eh? Let me see that."

He read it, then told me to fetch my textbooks. I had not brought them home, so he sent me to school to get them. Fortunately the building was open—rehearsals for the Fall Blow-Out. Dad rarely gave orders but when he did he expected results.

I had a swell course that semester—social study, commercial arithmetic, applied English (the class had picked "slogan writing" which was fun), handicrafts (we were building sets for the Blow-Out), and gym—which was basketball practice for me; I wasn't tall enough for first team but a reliable substitute gets his varsity letter his senior year. All in all, I was doing well in school and knew it.

Dad read all my textbooks that night; he is a fast reader. In social study I reported that our family was an informal democracy; it got by—the class was arguing whether the chairmanship of a council should rotate or be elective, and whether a grandparent living in the home was eligible. We decided that a grandparent was a member but should not be chairman, then we formed committees to draw up a constitution for an ideal family organization, which we would present to our families as the project's findings.

Dad was around school a good bit the next few days, which worried me—when parents get overactive they are always up to something.

The following Saturday evening Dad called me into his study. He had a stack of textbooks on his desk and a chart of Centerville High School's curriculum, from American Folk Dancing to Life Sciences. Marked on it was my course, not only for that semester but for junior and senior years the way my faculty advisor and I had planned it.

Dad stared at me like a gentle grasshopper and said mildly, "Kip, do you intend to go to college?"

"Huh? Why, certainly, Dad!"

"With what?"

I hesitated. I knew it cost money. While there had been times when dollar bills spilled out of the basket onto the floor, usually it wouldn't take long to count what was in it. "Uh, maybe I'll get a scholarship. Or I could work my way."

He nodded. "No doubt . . . if you want to. Money problems can always be solved by a man not frightened by them. But when I said, 'With what?' I was talking about up *here*." He tapped his skull.

I simply stared. "Why, I'll graduate from high school, Dad. That'll get me into college."

"So it will. Into our State University, or the State Aggie, or State Normal. But, Kip, do you know that they are flunking out 40 per cent of each freshman class?"

"I wouldn't flunk!"

"Perhaps not. But you will if you tackle any serious subject—engineering, or science, or pre-med. You would, that is to say, if your preparation were based on *this*." He waved a hand at the curriculum.

I felt shocked. "Why, Dad, Center is a swell school." I remembered things they had told us in P.T.A. Auxiliary. "It's run along the latest, most scientific lines, approved by psychologists, and—"

"—and paying excellent salaries," he interrupted, "for a staff highly trained in modern pedagogy. Study projects emphasize practical human problems to orient the child in democratic social living, to fit him for the vital, meaningful tests of adult life in our complex modern culture. Excuse me, son; I've talked with Mr. Hanley. Mr. Hanley is sincere—and to achieve these noble purposes we are spending more per student than is any other state save California and New York."

"Well . . . what's wrong with that?"

"What's a dangling participle?"

I didn't answer. He went on, "Why did Van Buren fail of re-election? How do you extract the cube root of eighty-seven?"

Van Buren had been a president; that was all I remembered. But I could answer the other one. "If you want a cube root, you look in a table in the back of the book."

Dad sighed. "Kip, do you think that table was brought down from on high by an archangel?" He shook his head sadly. "It's my fault, not yours. I should have looked into this years ago—but I had assumed, simply because you liked to read and were quick at figures and clever with your hands, that you were getting an education."

"You think I'm not?"

"I know you are not. Son, Centerville High is a delightful place, well equipped, smoothly administered, beautifully kept. Not a 'blackboard jungle,' oh, no!—I think you kids love the place. You should. But *this*—" Dad slapped the curriculum chart angrily. "Twaddle! Beetle tracking! Occupational therapy for morons!"

I didn't know what to say. Dad sat and brooded. At last he said, "The law declares that you must attend school until you are eighteen or have graduated from high school."

"Yes, sir."

"The school you are in is a waste of time. The toughest course we can pick won't stretch your mind. But it's either this school, or send you away."

I said, "Doesn't that cost a lot of money?"

He ignored my question. "I don't favor boarding schools, a
teen-ager belongs with his family. Oh, a tough prep school back
east can drill you so that you can enter Stanford, or Yale, or any of
the best—but you can pick up false standards, too—nutty ideas
about money and social position and the right tailor. It took me
years to get rid of ones I acquired that way. Your mother and I did
not pick a small town for your boyhood unpurposefully. So you'll
stay in Centerville High."

I looked relieved.

"Nevertheless you intend to go to college. Do you intend to
become a professional man? Or will you look for snap courses in
more elaborate ways to make bayberry candles? Son, your life is
yours, to do with as you wish. But if you have any thought of going to a good university and studying anything of importance,
then we must consider how to make best use of your next three
years."

"Why, gosh, Dad, of course I want to go to a good—"

"See me when you've thought it over. Good night."

I did for a week. And, you know, I began to see that Dad was
right. Our project in "Family Living" was twaddle. What did
those kids know about running a family? Or Miss Finchley?—
unmarried and no kids. The class decided unanimously that every
child should have a room of his own, and be given an allowance
"to teach him to handle money." Great stuff . . . but how about
the Quinlan family, nine kids in a five-room house? Let's not be
foolish.

Commercial arithmetic wasn't silly but it was a waste of time.
I read the book through the first week; after that I was bored.

Dad switched me to algebra, Spanish, general science, English
grammar and composition; the only thing unchanged was gym. I
didn't have it too tough catching up; even those courses were wa-
tered down. Nevertheless, I started to learn, for Dad threw a lot of
books at me and said, "Clifford, you would be studying these if
you were not in overgrown kindergarten. If you soak up what is in
them, you should be able to pass College Entrance Board Examinations. Possibly."

After that he left me alone; he meant it when he said that it
was my choice. I almost bogged down—those books were *hard,*
not the predigested pap I got in school. Anybody who thinks that
studying Latin by himself is a snap should try it.

I got discouraged and nearly quit—then I got mad and leaned
into it. After a while I found that Latin was making Spanish easier

and vice versa. When Miss Hernandez, my Spanish teacher, found out I was studying Latin, she began tutoring me. I not only worked my way through Virgil, I learned to speak Spanish like a Mexicano.

Algebra and plane geometry were all the math our school offered; I went ahead on my own with advanced algebra and solid geometry and trigonometry and might have stopped so far as College Boards were concerned—but math is worse than peanuts. Analytical geometry seems pure Greek until you see what they're driving at—then, if you know algebra, it bursts on you and you race through the rest of the book. Glorious!

I had to sample calculus and when I got interested in electronics I needed vector analysis. General science was the only science course the school had and pretty general it was, too—about Sunday supplement level. But when you read about chemistry and physics you want to do it, too. The barn was mine and I had a chem lab and a darkroom and an electronics bench and, for a while, a ham station. Mother was perturbed when I blew out the windows and set fire to the barn—just a small fire—but Dad was not. He simply suggested that I not manufacture explosives in a frame building.

When I took the College Boards my senior year I passed them.

It was early March my senior year that I told Dad I wanted to go to the Moon. The idea had been made acute by the announcement of commercial flights but I had been "space happy" ever since the day they announced that the Federation Space Corps had established a lunar base. Or earlier. I told Dad about my decision because I felt that he would know the answer. You see, Dad always found ways to do anything he decided to do.

When I was little we lived lots of places—Washington, New York, Los Angeles, I don't know where—usually in hotel apartments. Dad was always flying somewhere and when he was home there were visitors; I never saw him much. Then we moved to Centerville and he was always home, his nose in a book or working at his desk. When people wanted to see him they had to come to him. I remember once, when the money basket was empty, Dad told Mother that "a royalty was due." I hung around that day because I had never seen a king (I was eight) and when a visitor showed up I was disappointed because he didn't wear a crown. There was money in the basket the next day so I decided that he had been incognito (I was reading *The Little Lame Prince*) and had tossed Dad a purse of gold—it was at least a year before I found out that a "royalty" could be money from a patent or a book or business stock, and some of the glamour went out of life. But this visitor, though not king, thought he could make Dad do what he wanted rather than what Dad wanted:

"Dr. Russell, I concede that Washington has an atrocious climate. But you will have air-conditioned offices."

"With clocks, no doubt. And secretaries. And soundproofing."

"Anything you want, Doctor."

"The point is, Mr. Secretary, I don't want them. This household has no clocks. Nor calendars. Once I had a large income and a larger ulcer; I now have a small income and no ulcer. I stay here."

"But the job needs *you*."

"The need is not mutual. Do have some more meat loaf."

Since Dad did not want to go to the Moon, the problem was mine. I got down college catalogs I had collected and started listing engineering schools. I had no idea how I could pay tuition or even eat—but the first thing was to get myself accepted by a tough school with a reputation.

If not, I could enlist in the Air Force and try for an appointment. If I missed, I could become an enlisted specialist in electronics; Lunar Base used radar and astrar techs. One way or another, I was going.

Next morning at breakfast Dad was hidden behind the *New York Times* while Mother read the *Herald-Trib*. I had the *Centerville Clarion* but it's fit only for wrapping salami. Dad looked over his paper at me. "Clifford, here's something in your line."

"Huh?"

"Don't grunt; that is an uncouth privilege of seniors. This." He handed it to me.

It was a soap ad.

It announced that tired old gimmick, a gigantic super-colossal prize contest. This one promised a thousand prizes down to a last hundred, each of which was a year's supply of Skyway Soap.

Then I spilled cornflakes in my lap. The first prize was—

"—AN ALL-EXPENSE TRIP TO THE MOON!!!"

That's the way it read, with three exclamation points—only to me there were a dozen, with bursting bombs and a heavenly choir.

Just complete this sentence in twenty-five words or less: "I use Skyway Soap because . . ."

(And send in the usual soap wrapper or reasonable facsimile.)
There was more about "—joint management of American Express and Thos. Cook—" and "—with the cooperation of the United States Air Force—" and a list of lesser prizes. But all I saw, while milk and soggy cereal soaked my pants, was:

"—TRIP TO THE MOON!!!"

Chapter 2

First I went sky-high with excitement . . . then as far down with
depression. I didn't win contests—why, if I bought a box of
Cracker Jack, I'd get one they forgot to put a prize in. I had been
cured of matching pennies. If I ever—

"Stop it," said Dad.

I shut up.

"There is no such thing as luck; there is only adequate or in-
adequate preparation to cope with a statistical universe. Do you
intend to enter this?"

"Do I!"

"I assume that to be affirmative. Very well, make a systematic
effort."

I did and Dad was helpful—he didn't just offer me more meat
loaf. But he saw to it I didn't go to pieces; I finished school and
sent off applications for college and kept my job—I was working
after school that semester at Charton's Pharmacy—soda jerk, but
also learning about pharmacy. Mr. Charton was too conscientious
to let me touch anything but packaged items, but I learned—
materia medica and nomenclature and what various antibiotics
were for and why you had to be careful. That led into organic
chemistry and biochemistry and he lent me *Walker, Boyd and
Asimov*—biochemistry makes atomic physics look simple, but
presently it begins to make sense.

Mr. Charton was an old widower and pharmacology was his
life. He hinted that someone would have to carry on the pharmacy
someday—some young fellow with a degree in pharmacy and devotion to the profession. He said that he might be able to help such

a person get through school. If he had suggested that I could someday run the dispensary at Lunar Base, I might have taken the bait. I explained that I was dead set on spacing, and engineering looked like my one chance.

He didn't laugh. He said I was probably right—but that I shouldn't forget that wherever Man went, to the Moon, on Mars, or the farthest stars, pharmacists and dispensaries would go along. Then he dug out books for me on space medicine—Strughold and Haber and Stapp and others. "I once had ideas along that line, Kip," he said quietly, "but now it's too late."

Even though Mr. Charton was not really interested in anything but drugs, we sold everything that drugstores sell, from bicycle tires to home permanent kits.

Including soap, of course.

We were selling darned little Skyway Soap; Centerville is conservative about new brands—I'll bet some of them made their own soap. But when I showed up for work that day I had to tell Mr. Charton about it. He dug out two dust-covered boxes and put them on the counter. Then he phoned his jobber in Springfield.

He really did right by me. He marked Skyway Soap down almost to cost and pushed it—and he almost always got the wrappers before he let the customer go. Me, I stacked a pyramid of Skyway Soap on each end of the fountain and every coke was accompanied by a spiel for good old Skyway, the soap that washes cleaner, is packed with vitamins, and improves your chances of Heaven, not to mention its rich creamy lather, finer ingredients, and refusal to take the Fifth Amendment. Oh, I was shameless! Anybody who got away without buying was deaf or fast on his feet.

If he bought soap without leaving the wrappers with me he was a magician. Adults I talked out of it; kids, if I had to, I paid a penny for each wrapper. If they brought in wrappers from around town, I paid a dime a dozen and threw in a cone. The rules permitted a contestant to submit any number of entries as long as each was written on a Skyway Soap wrapper or reasonable facsimile.

I considered photographing one and turning out facsimiles by the gross, but Dad advised me not to. "It is within the rules, Kip, but I've never yet known a skunk to be welcome at a picnic."

So I used soap. And I sent in wrappers with slogans:
"I use Skyway Soap because—
—it makes me feel so *clean*."
—highway or byway, there's no soap like Skyway!"
—its quality is sky-high."

—it is pure as the Milky Way."
—it is pure as Interstellar Space."
—it leaves me fresh as a rain-swept sky."
And so on endlessly, until I tasted soap in my dreams.

Not just my own slogans either; Dad thought them up, and so did Mother and Mr. Charton. I kept a notebook and wrote them down in school or at work or in the middle of the night. I came home one evening and found that Dad had set up a card file for me and after that I kept them alphabetically to avoid repeating. A good thing, too, for toward the last I sent in as many as a hundred a day. Postage mounted, not to mention having to buy some wrappers.

Other kids in town were in the contest and probably some adults, but they didn't have the production line I had. I'd leave work at ten o'clock, hurry home with the day's slogans and wrappers, pick up more slogans from Dad and Mother, then use a rubber stamp on the inside of each wrapper: "I use Skyway Soap because—" with my name and address. As I typed, Dad filled out file cards. Each morning I mailed the bunch on my way to school.

I got laughed at but the adults most inclined to kid me were quickest to let me have their wrappers.

All but one, an oaf called "Ace" Quiggle. I shouldn't class Ace as an adult; he was an over-age juvenile delinquent. I guess every town has at least one Ace. He hadn't finished Centerville High, a distinction since Mr. Hanley believed in promoting everybody "to keep age groups together." As far back as I remember Ace hung around Main Street, sometimes working, mostly not.

He specialized in "wit." He was at our fountain one day, using up two dollars' worth of space and time for one thirty-five-cent malt. I had just persuaded old Mrs. Jenkins to buy a dozen cakes and had relieved her of the wrappers. As she left, Ace picked one off my counter display and said, "You're selling these, Space Cadet?"

"That's right, Ace. You'll never find such a bargain again."

"You expect to go to the Moon, just selling soap, Captain? Or should I say 'Commodore'? Yuk yuk yukkity yuk!" That's how Ace laughed, like a comic strip.

"I'm trying," I said politely. "How about some?"

"You're sure it's good soap?"

"Positive."

"Well, I'll tell you. Just to help you out—I'll buy one bar."

A plunger. But this might be the winning wrapper. "Sure thing, Ace. Thanks a lot." I took his money, he slipped the cake into his pocket and started to leave. "Just a second, Ace. The wrapper. Please?"

He stopped. "Oh, yes." He took out the bar, peeled it, held up the wrapper. "You want this?"

"Yes, Ace. Thanks."

"Well, I'll show you how to get the best use of it." He reached across to the cigar lighter on the tobacco counter and set fire to it, lit a cigarette with it, let the wrapper burn almost to his fingers, dropped it and stepped on it.

Mr. Charton watched from the window of the dispensary.

Ace grinned. "Okay, Space Cadet?"

I was gripping the ice-cream scoop. But I answered, "Perfectly okay, Ace. It's your soap."

Mr. Charton came out and said, "I'll take the fountain, Kip. There's a package to deliver."

That was almost the only wrapper I missed. The contest ended May 1 and both Dad and Mr. Charton decided to stock up and cleaned out the last case in the store. It was almost eleven before I had them written up, then Mr. Charton drove me to Springfield to get them postmarked before midnight.

I had sent in five thousand seven hundred and eighty-two slogans. I doubt if Centerville was ever so scrubbed.

The results were announced on the Fourth of July. I chewed my nails to the elbows in those nine weeks. Oh, other things happened. I graduated and Dad and Mother gave me a watch and we paraded past Mr. Hanley and got our diplomas. It felt good, even though what Dad had persuaded me to learn beat what I learned at dear old Center six ways from zero. Before that was Sneak Day and Class Honeymoon and Senior Prom and the Class Play and the Junior-Senior Picnic and all the things they do to keep the animals quiet. Mr. Charton let me off early if I asked, but I didn't ask often as my mind wasn't on it and I wasn't going steady anyhow. I had been earlier in the year, but she—Elaine McMurty—wanted to talk boys and clothes and I wanted to talk space and engineering so she put me back into circulation.

After graduation I worked for Mr. Charton full time. I still didn't know how I was going to college. I didn't think about it; I just dished sundaes and held my breath until the Fourth of July.

It was to be on television at 8 P.M. We had a TV—a black and white flat-image job—but it hadn't been turned on in months; after I built it I lost interest. I dug it out, set it up in the living room and tested the picture. I killed a couple of hours adjusting it, then spent the rest of the day chewing nails. I couldn't eat dinner. By seven-thirty I was in front of the set, not-watching a comedy team and fiddling with my file cards. Dad came in, looked sharply at me, and said, "Take a grip on yourself, Kip. Let me remind you again that the chances are against you."

I gulped. "I know, Dad."

"Furthermore, in the long run it won't matter. A man almost always gets what he wants badly enough. I am sure you will get to the Moon someday, one way or another."

"Yes, sir. I just wish they would get it over with."

"They will. Coming, Emma?"

"Right away, dearest," Mother called back. She came in, patted my hand and sat down.

Dad settled back. "Reminds me of election nights."

Mother said, "I'm glad you're no longer up to your ears in *that*."

"Oh, come now, sweetheart, you enjoyed every campaign."

Mother sniffed.

The comics went back where comics go, cigarettes did a can-can, then dived into their packs while a soothing voice assured us that carcinogenous factors were unknown in Coronets, the safe, Safe, SAFE smoke with the true tobacco flavor. The program cut to the local station; we were treated to a thrilling view of Center Lumber & Hardware and I started pulling hairs out of the back of my hand.

The screen filled with soap bubbles; a quartet sang that this was the Skyway Hour, as if we didn't know. Then the screen went blank and sound cut off and I swallowed my stomach.

The screen lighted up with: "Network Difficulty—Do Not Adjust Your Sets."

I yelped, "Oh, they can't do that! They can't!"

Dad said, "Stop it, Clifford."

I shut up. Mother said, "Now, dearest, he's just a boy."

Dad said, "He is not a boy; he is a man. Kip, how do you expect to face a firing squad calmly if this upsets you?"

I mumbled; he said, "Speak up." I said I hadn't really planned on facing one.

"You may need to, someday. This is good practice. Try the Springfield channel; you may get a skip image."

I tried, but all I got was snow and the sound was like two cats in a sack. I jumped back to our local station.

"—jor General Bryce Gilmore, United States Air Force, our guest tonight, who will explain to us, later in this program, some hitherto unreleased pictures of Federation Lunar Base and the infant Luna City, the fastest growing little city on the Moon. Immediately after announcing the winners we will attempt a television linkage with Lunar Base, through the cooperation of the Space Corps of the—"

I took a deep breath and tried to slow my heartbeat, the way you steady down for a free-throw in a tie game. The gabble dragged on while celebrities were introduced, the contest rules were explained, an improbably sweet young couple explained to each other why they always used Skyway Soap. My own sales talks were better.

At last they got to it. Eight girls paraded out; each held a big card over her head. The M.C. said in an awe-struck voice: "And now . . . and *now*—the winning Skyway slogan for the . . . FREE TRIP TO THE MOON!"

I couldn't breathe.

The girls sang, "I like Skyway Soap because—" and went on, each turning her card as a word reached her: "—it . . . is . . . as . . . pure . . . as . . . the . . . sky . . . itself!"

I was fumbling cards. I thought I recognized it but couldn't be sure—not after more than five thousand slogans. Then I found it—and checked the cards the girls were holding.

"Dad! Mother! I've won, I've *won!*"

Chapter 3

"Hold it, Kip!" Dad snapped. "Stop it."

Mother said, "Oh, *dear!*"

I heard the M.C. saying, "—present the lucky winner, Mrs. Xenia Donahue, of Great Falls, Montana. . . . Mrs. *Donahue!*"

To a fanfare a little dumpy woman teetered out. I read the cards again. They still matched the one in my hand. I said, "Dad, what happened? That's *my* slogan."

"You didn't listen."

"They've cheated me!"

"Be quiet and listen."

"—as we explained earlier, in the event of duplicate entries, priority goes to the one postmarked first. Any remaining tie is settled by time of arrival at the contest office. Our winning slogan was submitted by eleven contestants. To them go the first eleven prizes. Tonight we have with us the six top winners—for the trip to the Moon, the weekend in a satellite space station, the jet flight around the world, the flight to Antarctica, the—"

"Beaten by a postmark. A *postmark!*"

"—sorry we can't have every one of the winners with us tonight. To the rest this comes as a surprise." The M.C. looked at his watch. "Right this minute, in a thousand homes across the land . . . right this *second*—there is a lucky knock on a lucky door of some loyal friend of Skyway—"

There was a knock on *our* door.

I fell over my feet. Dad answered. There were three men, an enormous crate, and a Western Union messenger singing about

Skyway Soap. Somebody said, "Is this where Clifford Russell lives?"

Dad said, "Yes."

"Will you sign for this?"

"What is it?"

"It just says 'This Side Up.' Where do you want it?"

Dad passed the receipt to me and I signed, somehow. Dad said, "Will you put it in the living room, please?"

They did and left and I got a hammer and sidecutters. It looked like a coffin and I could have used one.

I got the top off. A lot of packing got all over Mother's rugs. At last we were down to it.

It was a space suit.

Not much, as space suits go these days. It was an obsolete model that Skyway Soap had bought as surplus material—the tenth-to-hundredth prizes were all space suits. But it was a real one, made by Goodyear, with air conditioning by York and auxiliary equipment by General Electric. Its instruction manual and maintenance-and-service log were with it and it had racked up more than eight hundred hours in rigging the second satellite station.

I felt better. This was no phony, this was no toy. It had been out in space, even if I had not. But I would!—someday. I'd learn to use it and someday I'd wear it on the naked face of the Moon.

Dad said, "Maybe we'd better carry this to your workshop. Eh, Kip?"

Mother said, "There's no rush, dearest. Don't you want to try it on, Clifford?"

I certainly did. Dad and I compromised by toting the crate and packing out to the barn. When we came back, a reporter from the *Clarion* was there with a photographer—the paper had known I was a winner before I did, which didn't seem right.

They wanted pictures and I didn't mind.

I had an awful time getting into it—dressing in an upper berth is a cinch by comparison. The photographer said, "Just a minute, kid. I've seen 'em do it at Wright Field. Mind some advice?"

"Uh? No. I mean, yes, tell me."

"You slide in like an Eskimo climbing into a kayak. Then wiggle your right arm in—"

It was fairly easy that way, opening front gaskets wide and sitting down in it, though I almost dislocated a shoulder. There were straps to adjust for size but we didn't bother; he stuffed me into it, zippered the gaskets, helped me to my feet and shut the helmet.

It didn't have air bottles and I had to live on the air inside while he got three shots. By then I knew that the suit had seen service; it smelled like dirty socks. I was glad to get the helmet off.

Just the same, it made me feel good to wear it. Like a spacer.

They left and presently we went to bed, leaving the suit in the living room.

About midnight I catfooted down and tried it on again.

The next morning I moved it out to my shop before I went to work. Mr. Charton was diplomatic; he just said he'd like to see my space suit when I had time. Everybody knew about it—my picture was on the front page of the *Clarion* along with the Pikes Peak Hill Climb and the holiday fatalities. The story had been played for laughs, but I didn't mind. I had never really *believed* I would win—and I had an honest-to-goodness space suit, which was more than my classmates had.

That afternoon Dad brought me a special delivery letter from Skyway Soap. It enclosed a property title to one suit, pressure, serial number so-and-so, ex-US-AF. The letter started with congratulations and thanks but the last paragraphs meant something:

> Skyway Soap realizes that your prize may not be of immediate use to you. Therefore, as mentioned in paragraph 4 (a) of the rules, Skyway offers to redeem it for a cash premium of five hundred dollars ($500.00). To avail yourself of this privilege you should return the pressure suit via express collect to Goodyear Corporation (Special Appliances Division, attn: Salvage), Akron, Ohio, on or before the 15th of September.
>
> Skyway Soap hopes that you have enjoyed our Grand Contest as much as we have enjoyed having you and hopes that you will retain your prize long enough to appear with it on your local television station in a special Skyway Jubilee program. A fee of fifty dollars ($50.00) will be paid for this appearance. Your station manager will be in touch with you. We hope that you will be our guest.
>
> All good wishes from Skyway, the Soap as Pure as the Sky Itself.

I handed it to Dad. He read it and handed it back.

I said, "I suppose I should."

He said, "I see no harm. Television leaves no external scars."

"Oh, that. Sure, it's easy money. But I meant I really ought to sell the suit back to them." I should have felt happy since I needed money, while I needed a space suit the way a pig needs a pipe organ. But I didn't, even though I had never had five hundred dollars in my life.

"Son, any statement that starts 'I really ought to—' is suspect. It means you haven't analyzed your motives."

"But five hundred dollars is tuition for a semester, almost."

"Which has nothing to do with the case. Find out what you want to do, then do it. Never talk yourself into doing something you don't want. Think it over." He said good-bye and left.

I decided it was foolish to burn my bridges before I crossed them. The space suit was mine until the middle of September even if I did the sensible thing—by then I might be tired of it.

But I didn't get tired of it; a space suit is a marvelous piece of machinery—a little space station with everything miniaturized. Mine was a chrome-plated helmet and shoulder yoke which merged into a body of silicone, asbestos, and glass-fibre cloth. This hide was stiff except at the joints. They were the same rugged material but were "constant volume"—when you bent a knee a bellows arrangement increased the volume over the knee cap as much as the space back of the knee was squeezed. Without this a man wouldn't be able to move; the pressure inside, which can add up to several tons, would hold him rigid as a statue. These volume compensators were covered with dural armor; even the finger joints had little dural plates over the knuckles.

It had a heavy glass-fibre belt with clips for tools, and there were the straps to adjust for height and weight. There was a back pack, now empty, for air bottles, and zippered pockets inside and out, for batteries and such.

The helmet swung back, taking a bib out of the yoke with it, and the front opened with two gasketed zippers; this left a door you could wiggle into. With helmet clamped and zippers closed it was impossible to open the suit with pressure inside.

Switches were mounted on the shoulder yoke and on the helmet; the helmet was monstrous. It contained a drinking tank, pill dispensers six on each side, a chin plate on the right to switch radio from "receive" to "send," another on the left to increase or decrease flow of air, an automatic polarizer for the face lens, microphone and earphones, space for radio circuits in a bulge back of the head, and an instrument board arched over the head. The instrument dials read backwards because they were reflected in an inside mirror in front of the wearer's forehead at an effective fourteen inches from the eyes.

Above the lens or window there were twin headlights. On top were two antennas, a spike for broadcast and a horn that squirted microwaves like a gun—you aimed it by facing the receiving station. The horn antenna was armored except for its open end.

This sounds as crowded as a lady's purse but everything was beautifully compact; your head didn't touch anything when you looked out the lens. But you could tip your head back and see reflected instruments, or tilt it down and turn it to work chin controls, or simply turn your neck for water nipple or pills. In all remaining space sponge-rubber padding kept you from banging your head no matter what.

My suit was like a fine car, its helmet like a Swiss watch.

But its air bottles were missing; so was radio gear except for built-in antennas; radar beacon and emergency radar target were gone, pockets inside and out were empty, and there were no tools on the belt. The manual told what it ought to have—it was like a stripped car.

I decided I just had to make it work right.

First I swabbed it out with Clorox to kill the locker-room odor. Then I got to work on the air system.

It's a good thing they included that manual; most of what I thought I knew about space suits was wrong.

A man uses around three pounds of oxygen a day—pounds mass, not pounds per square inch. You'd think a man could carry oxygen for a month, especially out in space where mass has no weight, or on the Moon where three pounds weigh only half a pound. Well, that's okay for space stations or ships or frogmen; they run air through soda lime to take out carbon dioxide, and breathe it again. But not space suits.

Even today people talk about "the bitter cold of outer space"—but space is vacuum and if vacuum were cold, how could a Thermos jug keep hot coffee hot? Vacuum is *nothing*—it has no temperature, it just insulates.

Three-fourths of your food turns into heat—a lot of heat, enough each day to melt fifty pounds of ice and more. Sounds preposterous, doesn't it? But when you have a roaring fire in the furnace, you are *cooling* your body; even in the winter you keep a room about thirty degrees cooler than your body. When you turn up a furnace's thermostat, you are picking a more comfortable rate for cooling. Your body makes so much heat you have to get rid of it, exactly as you have to cool a car's engine.

Of course, if you do it too fast, say in a sub-zero wind, you can freeze—but the usual problem in a space suit is to keep from being boiled like a lobster. You've got vacuum all around you and it's *hard* to get rid of heat.

Some radiates away but not enough, and if you are in sunlight, you pick up still more—this is why space ships are polished like mirrors.

So what can you do?

Well, you can't carry fifty-pound blocks of ice. You get rid of heat the way you do on Earth, by convection and evaporation—you keep air moving over you to evaporate sweat and cool you off. Oh, they'll learn to build space suits that recycle like a space ship but today the practical way is to let used air escape from the suit, flushing away sweat and carbon dioxide and excess heat—while wasting most of the oxygen.

There are other problems. The fifteen pounds per square inch around you includes three pounds of oxygen pressure. Your lungs can get along on less than half that, but only an Indian from the high Andes is likely to be comfortable on less than two pounds oxygen pressure. Nine-tenths of a pound is the limit. Any less than nine-tenths of a pound won't force oxygen into blood—this is about the pressure at the top of Mount Everest.

Most people suffer from hypoxia (oxygen shortage) long before this, so better use two p.s.i. of oxygen. Mix an inert gas with it, because pure oxygen can cause a sore throat or make you drunk or even cause terrible cramps. Don't use nitrogen (which you've breathed all your life) because it will bubble in your blood if pressure drops and cripple you with "bends." Use helium which doesn't. It gives you a squeaky voice, but who cares?

You can die from oxygen shortage, be poisoned by too much oxygen, be crippled by nitrogen, drown in or be acid-poisoned by carbon dioxide, or dehydrate and run a killing fever. When I finished reading that manual I didn't see how anybody could stay alive anywhere, much less in a space suit.

But a space suit was in front of me that had protected a man for hundreds of hours in empty space.

Here is how you beat those dangers. Carry steel bottles on your back; they hold "air" (oxygen and helium) at a hundred and fifty atmospheres, over 2000 pounds per square inch; you draw from them through a reduction valve down to 150 p.s.i. and through still another reduction valve, a "demand" type which keeps pressure in your helmet at three to five pounds per square inch—two pounds of it oxygen. Put a silicone-rubber collar around your neck and put tiny holes in it, so that the pressure in the body of your suit is less, the air movement still faster; then evaporation and cooling will be increased while the effort of bending is decreased. Add exhaust valves, one at each wrist and ankle—these have to pass water as well as gas because you may be ankle deep in sweat.

The bottles are big and clumsy, weighing around sixty pounds apiece, and each holds only about five mass pounds of air even at that enormous pressure; instead of a month's supply you will have only a few hours—my suit was rated at eight hours for the bottles it used to have. But you will be okay for those hours—if everything works right. You can stretch time, for you don't die from overheating very fast and can stand too much carbon dioxide even longer—but let your oxygen run out and you die in about seven minutes. Which gets us back where we started—it takes oxygen to stay alive.

To make darn sure that you're getting enough (your nose can't tell) you clip a little photoelectric cell to your ear and let it see the color of your blood; the redness of the blood measures the oxygen it carries. Hook this to a galvanometer. If its needle gets into the danger zone, start saying your prayers.

I went to Springfield on my day off, taking the suit's hose fittings, and shopped. I picked up, second hand, two thirty-inch steel bottles from a welding shop—and got myself disliked by insisting on a pressure test. I took them home on the bus, stopped at Pring's Garage and arranged to buy air at fifty atmospheres. Higher pressures, or oxygen or helium, I could get from the Springfield airport, but I didn't need them yet.

When I got home I closed the suit, empty, and pumped it with a bicycle pump to two atmospheres absolute, or one relative, which gave me a test load of almost four to one compared with space conditions. Then I tackled the bottles. They needed to be mirror bright, since you can't afford to let them pick up heat from the Sun. I stripped and scraped and wire-brushed, and buffed and polished, preparatory to nickel-plating.

Next morning, Oscar the Mechanical Man was limp as a pair of long johns.

Getting that old suit not just airtight but helium-tight was the worst headache. Air isn't bad but the helium molecule is so small and agile that it migrates right through ordinary rubber—and I wanted this job to be *right*, not just good enough to perform at home but okay for space. The gaskets were shot and there were slow leaks almost impossible to find.

I had to get new silicone-rubber gaskets and patching compound and tissue from Goodyear; small-town hardware stores don't handle such things. I wrote a letter explaining what I wanted and why—and they didn't even charge me. They sent me some mimeographed sheets elaborating on the manual.

It still wasn't easy. But there came a day when I pumped Oscar full of pure helium at two atmospheres absolute.

A week later he was still tight as a six-ply tire.

That day I wore Oscar as a self-contained environment. I had already worn him many hours without the helmet, working around the shop, handling tools while hampered by his gauntlets, getting height and size adjustments right. It was like breaking in new ice skates and after a while I was hardly aware I had it on—once I came to supper in it. Dad said nothing and Mother has the social restraint of an ambassador; I discovered my mistake when I picked up my napkin.

Now I wasted helium to the air, mounted bottles charged with air, and suited them. Then I clamped the helmet and dogged the safety catches.

Air sighed softly into the helmet, its flow through the demand valve regulated by the rise and fall of my chest—I could reset it to speed up or slow down by the chin control. I did so, watching the gauge in the mirror and letting it mount until I had twenty pounds absolute inside. That gave me five pounds more than the pressure around me, which was as near as I could come to space conditions without being in space.

I could feel the suit swell and the joints no longer felt loose and easy. I balanced the cycle at five pounds differential and tried to move—

And almost fell over. I had to grab the workbench.

Suited up, with bottles on my back, I weighed more than twice what I do stripped. Besides that, although the joints were constant-volume, the suit didn't work as freely under pressure. Dress yourself in heavy fishing waders, put on an overcoat and boxing gloves and a bucket over your head, then have somebody strap two sacks of cement across your shoulders and you will know what a space suit feels like under one gravity.

But ten minutes later I was handling myself fairly well and in half an hour I felt as if I had worn one all my life. The distributed weight wasn't too great (and I knew it wouldn't amount to much on the Moon). The joints were just a case of getting used to more effort. I had had more trouble learning to swim.

It was a blistering day: I went outside and looked at the Sun. The polarizer cut the glare and I was able to look at it. I looked away; polarizing eased off and I could see around me.

I stayed cool. The air, cooled by semi-adiabatic expansion (it said in the manual), cooled my head and flowed on through the suit, washing away body heat and used air through the exhaust valves. The manual said that heating elements rarely cut in, since the usual problem was to get rid of heat; I decided to get dry ice and force a test of thermostat and heater.

I tried everything I could think of. A creek runs back of our place and beyond is a pasture. I sloshed through the stream, lost my footing and fell—the worst trouble was that I could never see where I was putting my feet. Once I was down I lay there a while, half floating but mostly covered. I didn't get wet, I didn't get hot, I didn't get cold, and my breathing was as easy as ever even though water shimmered over my helmet.

I scrambled heavily up the bank and fell again, striking my helmet against a rock. No damage, Oscar was built to take it. I pulled my knees under me, got up, and crossed the pasture, stumbling on rough ground but not falling. There was a haystack there and I dug into it until I was buried.

Cool fresh air . . . no trouble, no sweat.

After three hours I took it off. The suit had relief arrangements like any pilot's outfit but I hadn't rigged it yet, so I had come out before my air was gone. When I hung it in the rack I had built, I patted the shoulder yoke. "Oscar, you're all right," I told it. "You and I are partners. We're going places."

I would have sneered at five thousand dollars for Oscar.

While Oscar was taking his pressure tests I worked on his electrical and electronic gear. I didn't bother with a radar target or beacon; the first is childishly simple, the second is fiendishly expensive. But I did want radio for the space-operations band of the spectrum—the antennas suited only those wavelengths. I could have built an ordinary walkie-talkie and hung it outside—but I would have been kidding myself with a wrong frequency and gear that might not stand vacuum. Changes in pressure and temperature and humidity do funny things to electronic circuits; that is why the radio was housed inside the helmet.

The manual gave circuit diagrams, so I got busy. The audio and modulating circuits were no problem, just battery-operated transistor circuitry which I could make plenty small enough. But the microwave part—

It was a two-headed calf, each with transmitter and receiver—one centimeter wavelength for the horn and three octaves lower at eight centimeters for the spike in a harmonic relationship, one crystal controlling both. This gave more signal on broadcast and better aiming when squirting out the horn and also meant that only part of the rig had to be switched in changing antennas. The output of a variable-frequency oscillator was added to the crystal frequency in tuning the receiver. The circuitry was simple—on paper.

But microwave circuitry is never easy; it takes precision machining and a slip of a tool can foul up the impedance and ruin a mathematically calculated resonance.

Well, I tried. Synthetic precision crystals are cheap from surplus houses and some transistors and other components I could vandalize from my own gear. And I made it work, after the fussiest pray-and-try-again I have ever done. But the consarned thing simply would *not* fit into the helmet.

Call it a moral victory—I've never done better work.

I finally bought one, precision made and embedded in plastic, from the same firm that sold me the crystal. Like the suit it was made for, it was obsolete and I paid a price so low that I merely screamed. By then I would have mortgaged my soul—I wanted that suit to *work*.

The only thing that complicated the rest of the electrical gear was that everything had to be either "fail-safe" or "no-fail"; a man in a space suit can't pull into the next garage if something goes wrong—the stuff *has* to keep on working or he becomes a vital statistic. That was why the helmet had twin headlights; the second cut in if the first failed—even the peanut lights for the dials over my head were twins. I didn't take short cuts; every duplicate circuit I kept duplicate and tested to make sure that automatic changeover always worked.

Mr. Charton insisted on filling the manual's list on those items a drugstore stocks—maltose and dextrose and amino tablets, vitamins, dexedrine, dramamine, aspirin, antibiotics, antihistamines, codeine, almost any pill a man can take to help him past a hump that might kill him. He got Doc Kennedy to write prescriptions so that I could stock Oscar without breaking laws.

When I got through Oscar was in as good shape as he had ever been in Satellite Two. It had been more fun than the time I helped Jake Bixby turn his heap into a hotrod.

But summer was ending and it was time I pulled out of my daydream. I still did not know where I was going to school, or how—or if. I had saved money but it wasn't nearly enough. I had spent a little on postage and soap wrappers but I got that back and more by one fifteen-minute appearance on television and I hadn't spent a dime on girls since March—too busy. Oscar cost surprisingly little; repairing Oscar had been mostly sweat and screwdriver. Seven dollars out of every ten I had earned was sitting in the money basket.

But it wasn't enough.

I realized glumly that I was going to have to sell Oscar to get through the first semester. But how would I get through the rest of the year? Joe Valiant the all-American boy always shows up on the campus with fifty cents and a heart of gold, then in the last chapter is tapped for Skull-and-Bones and has money in the bank. But I wasn't Joe Valiant, not by eight decimal places. Did it make sense to start if I was going to have to drop out about Christmas? Wouldn't it be smarter to stay out a year and get acquainted with a pick and shovel?

Did I have a choice? The only school I was sure of was State U.—and there was a row about professors being fired and talk that State U. might lose its accredited standing. Wouldn't it be comical to spend years slaving for a degree and then have it be worthless because your school wasn't recognized?

State U. wasn't better than a "B" school in engineering even before this fracas.

Rensselaer and CalTech turned me down the same day—one with a printed form, the other with a polite letter saying it was impossible to accept all qualified applicants.

Little things were getting my goat, too. The only virtue of that television show was the fifty bucks. A person looks foolish wearing a space suit in a television studio and our announcer milked it for laughs, rapping the helmet and asking me if I was still in there. Very funny. He asked me what I wanted with a space suit and when I tried to answer he switched off the mike in my suit and patched in a tape with nonsense about space pirates and flying saucers. Half the people in town thought it was my voice.

It wouldn't have been hard to live down if Ace Quiggle hadn't turned up. He had been missing all summer, in jail maybe, but the day after the show he took a seat at the fountain, stared at me and said in a loud whisper, "Say, ain't you the famous space pirate and television star?"

I said, "What'll you have, Ace?"

"Gosh! Could I have your autograph? I ain't never seen a real live space pirate before!"

"Give me your order, Ace. Or let someone else use that stool."

"A choc malt, Commodore—and leave out the soap."

Ace's "wit" went on every time he showed up. It was a dreadfully hot summer and easy to get tempery. The Friday before Labor Day weekend the store's cooling system went sour, we couldn't get a repairman and I spent three bad hours fixing it, ruining my second-best pants and getting myself reeking. I was back at the fountain and wishing I could go home for a bath when Ace swaggered in, greeting me loudly with "Why, if it isn't Commander Comet, the Scourge of the Spaceways! Where's your blaster gun, Commander? Ain't you afraid the Galactic Emperor will make you stay in after school for running around bare-nekkid? Yuk yuk yukkity yuk!"

A couple of girls at the fountain giggled.

"Lay off, Ace," I said wearily. "It's a hot day."

"That's why you're not wearing your rubber underwear?" The girls giggled again.

Ace smirked. He went on: "Junior, seein' you got that clown suit, why don't you put it to work? Run an ad in the *Clarion:* 'Have Space Suit—Will Travel.' Yukkity yuk! Or you could hire out as a scarecrow."

The girls snickered. I counted ten, then again in Spanish, and in Latin, and said tensely, "Ace, just tell me what you'll have."

"My usual. And snap it up—I've got a date on Mars."

Mr. Charton came out from behind his counter, sat down and asked me to mix him a lime cooler, so I served him first. It stopped the flow of wit and probably saved Ace's life.

The boss and I were alone shortly after. He said quietly, "Kip, a reverence for life does not require a man to respect Nature's obvious mistakes."

"Sir?"

"You need not serve Quiggle again. I don't want his trade."

"Oh, I don't mind. He's harmless."

"I wonder how harmless such people are? To what extent civilization is retarded by the laughing jackasses, the empty-minded belittlers? Go home; you'll want to make an early start tomorrow."

I had been invited to the Lake of the Forest for the long Labor Day weekend by Jake Bixby's parents. I wanted to go, not only to get away from the heat but also to chew things over with Jake. But I answered, "Shucks, Mr. Charton, I ought not to leave you stuck."

"The town will be deserted over the holiday; I may not open the fountain. Enjoy yourself. This summer has worn you a bit fine, Kip."

I let myself be persuaded but I stayed until closing and swept up. Then I walked home, doing some hard thinking.

The party was over and it was time to put away my toys. Even the village half-wit knew that I had no sensible excuse to have a space suit. Not that I cared what Ace thought . . . but I did have no use for it—and I needed money. Even if Stanford and M.I.T. and Carnegie and the rest turned me down, I was going to start this semester. State U. wasn't the best—but neither was I and I had learned that more depended on the student than on the school.

Mother had gone to bed and Dad was reading. I said hello and went to the barn, intending to strip my gear off Oscar, pack him into his case, address it, and in the morning phone the express office to pick it up. He'd be gone before I was back from the Lake of the Forest. Quick and clean.

He was hanging on his rack and it seemed to me that he grinned hello. Nonsense, of course. I went over and patted his shoulder. "Well, old fellow, you've been a real chum and it's been nice knowing you. See you on the Moon—I hope."

But Oscar wasn't going to the Moon. Oscar was going to Akron, Ohio, to "Salvage." They were going to unscrew parts they could use and throw the rest of him on the junk pile.

My mouth felt dry.

("It's okay, pal," Oscar answered.)

See that? Out of my silly head! Oscar didn't really speak; I had let my imagination run wild too long. So I quit patting him, hauled the crate out and took a wrench from his belt to remove the gas bottles.

I stopped.

Both bottles were charged, one with oxygen, one with oxy-helium. I had wasted money to do so because I wanted, just once, to try a spaceman's mix.

The batteries were fresh and power packs were charged.

"Oscar," I said softly, "we're going to take a last walk together. Okay?"

("Swell!")

I made it a dress rehearsal—water in the drinking tank, pill dispensers loaded, first-aid kit inside, vacuum-proof duplicate (I hoped it was vacuum-proof) in an outside pocket. All tools on belt, all lanyards tied so that tools wouldn't float away in free fall. Everything.

Then I heated up a circuit that the F.C.C. would have squelched had they noticed, a radio link I had salvaged out of my effort to build a radio for Oscar, and had modified as a test rig for Oscar's ears and to let me check the aiming of the directional antenna. It was hooked in with an echo circuit that would answer back if I called it—a thing I had breadboarded out of an old Webcor wire recorder, vintage 1950.

Then I climbed into Oscar and buttoned up. "Tight?"

("Tight!")

I glanced at the reflected dials, noticed the blood-color reading, reduced pressure until Oscar almost collapsed. At nearly sea-level pressure I was in no danger from hypoxia; the trick was to avoid too much oxygen.

We started to leave when I remembered something. "Just a second, Oscar." I wrote a note to my folks, telling them that I was going to get up early and catch the first bus to the lake. I could write while suited up now, I could even thread a needle. I stuck the note under the kitchen door.

Then we crossed the creek into the pasture. I didn't stumble in wading; I was used to Oscar now, sure-footed as a goat.

Out in the field I keyed my talkie and said, "Junebug, calling Peewee. Come in, Peewee."

Seconds later my recorded voice came back: " 'Junebug, calling Peewee. Come in, Peewee.' "

I shifted to the horn antenna and tried again. It wasn't easy to aim in the dark but it was okay. Then I shifted back to spike antenna and went on calling Peewee while moving across the pasture and pretending that I was on Venus and had to stay in touch with base because it was unknown terrain and unbreathable atmosphere. Everything worked perfectly and if it had been Venus, I would have been all right.

Two lights moved across the southern sky, planes I thought, or maybe helis. Just the sort of thing yokels like to report as "flying saucers." I watched them, then moved behind a little rise that would tend to spoil reception and called Peewee. Peewee answered and I shut up; it gets dull talking to an idiot circuit which can only echo what you say to it.

Then I heard: "Peewee to Junebug! Answer!"

I thought I had been monitored and was in trouble—then decided that some ham had picked me up. "Junebug here. I read you. Who are you?"

The test rig echoed my words.

Then the new voice shrilled, "Peewee here! Home me in!"

This was silly. But I found myself saying, "Junebug to Peewee, shift to directional frequency at one centimeter—and keep talking, keep talking!" I shifted to the horn antenna.

"Junebug, I read you. Fix me. One, two, three, four, five, six, seven—"

"You're due south of me, about forty degrees. Who are you?"

It must be one of those lights. It had to be.

But I didn't have time to figure it out. A space ship almost landed on me.

Chapter 4

I said "space ship," not "rocket ship." It made no noise but a whoosh and there weren't any flaming jets—it seemed to move by clean living and righteous thoughts.

I was too busy keeping from being squashed to worry about details. A space suit in one gravity is no track suit; it's a good thing I had practiced. The ship sat down where I had just been, occupying more than its share of pasture, a big black shape.

The other one whooshed down, too, just as a door opened in the first. Light poured through the door; two figures spilled out and started to run. One moved like a cat; the other moved clumsily and slowly—handicapped by a space suit. S'help me, a person in a space suit does look silly. This one was less than five feet tall and looked like the Gingerbread Man.

A big trouble with a suit is your limited angle of vision. I was trying to watch both of them and did not see the second ship open. The first figure stopped, waiting for the one in the space suit to catch up, then suddenly collapsed—just a gasping sound, "Eee*ah!*"—and clunk.

You can tell the sound of pain. I ran to the spot at a lumbering dogtrot, leaned over and tried to see what was wrong, tilting my helmet to bring the beam of my headlight onto the ground.

A bug-eyed monster—

That's not fair but it was my first thought. I couldn't believe it and would have pinched myself except that it isn't practical when suited up.

An unprejudiced mind (which mine wasn't) would have said that this monster was rather pretty. It was small, not more than half my size, and its curves were graceful, not as a girl is but more like a leopard, although it wasn't shaped like either one. I couldn't grasp its shape—I didn't have any pattern to fit it to; it wouldn't add up.

But I could see that it was hurt. Its body was quivering like a frightened rabbit. It had enormous eyes, open but milky and featureless, as if nictitating membranes were across them. What appeared to be its mouth—

That's as far as I got. Something hit me in the spine, right between the gas bottles.

I woke up on a bare floor, staring at a ceiling. It took several moments to recall what had happened and then I shied away because it was so darn silly. I had been out for a walk in Oscar . . . and then a space ship had landed . . . and a bug-eyed—

I sat up suddenly as I realized that Oscar was gone. A light cheerful voice said, "Hi, there!"

I snapped my head around. A kid about ten years old was seated on the floor, leaning against a wall. He—I corrected myself. Boys don't usually clutch rag dolls. This kid was the age when the difference doesn't show much and was dressed in shirt, shorts and dirty tennis shoes, and had short hair, so I didn't have much to go on but the rag dolly.

"Hi, yourself," I answered. "What are we doing here?"

"I'm surviving. I don't know about you."

"Huh?"

"Surviving. Pushing my breath in and out. Conserving my strength. There's nothing else to do at the moment; they've got us locked in."

I looked around. The room was about ten feet across, four-sided but wedge-shaped, and nothing in it but us. I couldn't see a door; if we weren't locked, we might as well be. "Who locked us in?"

"Them. Space pirates. And *him*."

"Space pirates? Don't be silly!"

The kid shrugged. "Just my name for them. But better not think they're silly if you want to keep on surviving. Are you 'Junebug'?"

"Huh? You sound like a junebug yourself. Space pirates, my aunt!" I was worried and very confused and this nonsense didn't help. Where was Oscar? And where was *I?*

"No, no, not a junebug but 'Junebug'—a radio call. You see, I'm Peewee."

I said to myself, Kip old pal, walk slowly to the nearest hospital and give yourself up. When a radio rig you wired yourself starts looking like a skinny little girl with a rag doll, you've flipped. It's going to be wet packs and tranquilizers and no excitement for you—you've blown every fuse. "You're 'Peewee'?"

"That's what I'm called—I'm relaxed about it. You see, I heard, 'Junebug, calling Peewee,' and decided that Daddy had found out about the spot I was in and had alerted people to help me land. But if you aren't 'Junebug,' you wouldn't know about that. Who are you?"

"Wait a minute, I *am* 'Junebug.' I mean I was using that call. But I'm Clifford Russell—'Kip' they call me."

"How do you do, Kip?" she said politely.

"And howdy to you, Peewee. Uh, are you a boy or a girl?"

Peewee looked disgusted. "I'll make you regret that remark. I realize I am undersized for my age but I'm actually eleven, going on twelve. There's no need to be rude. In another five years I expect to be quite a dish—you'll probably beg me for every dance."

At the moment I would as soon have danced with a kitchen stool, but I had things on my mind and didn't want a useless argument. "Sorry, Peewee. I'm still groggy. You mean you were in that first ship?"

Again she looked miffed. "I was piloting it."

Sedation every night and a long course of psychoanalysis. At *my* age. "You were—piloting?"

"You surely don't think the Mother Thing could? She wouldn't fit their controls. She curled up beside me and coached. But if you think it's easy, when you've never piloted anything but a Cessna with your Daddy at your elbow and never made *any* kind of landing, then think again. I did very well!—and your landing instructions weren't too specific. What have they done with the Mother Thing?"

"The what?"

"You don't know? Oh, dear!"

"Wait a minute, Peewee. Let's get on the same frequency. I'm 'Junebug' all right and I homed you in—and if you think *that's* easy, to have a voice out of nowhere demand emergency landing instructions, you better think again, too. Anyhow, a ship landed and another ship landed right after it and a door opened in the first ship and a guy in a space suit jumped out—"

"That was I."

"—and something else jumped out—"

"The Mother Thing."

"Only she didn't get far. She gave a screech and flopped. I went to see what the trouble was and something hit me. The next thing I know you're saying, 'Hi, there.' " I wondered if I ought to tell her that the rest, including her, was likely a morphine dream because I was probably lying in a hospital with my spine in a cast.

Peewee nodded thoughtfully. "They must have blasted you at low power, or you wouldn't be here. Well, they caught you and they caught me, so they almost certainly caught her. Oh, dear! I do hope they didn't hurt her."

"She looked like she was dying."

"As if she were dying," Peewee corrected me. "Subjunctive. I rather doubt it; she's awfully hard to kill—and they wouldn't kill her except to keep her from escaping; they need her alive."

"Why? And why do you call her 'the Mother Thing'?"

"One at a time, Kip. She's the Mother Thing because . . . well, because she is, that's all. You'll know, when you meet her. As to why they wouldn't kill her, it's because she's worth more as a hostage than as a corpse—the same reason the kept me alive. Although she's worth incredibly more than I am—they'd write me off without a blink if I became inconvenient. Or you. But since she was alive when you saw her, then it's logical that she's a prisoner again. Maybe right next door. That makes me feel *much* better."

It didn't make me feel better. "Yes, but where's *here?*"

Peewee glanced at a Mickey Mouse watch, frowned and said, "Almost halfway to the Moon, I'd say."

"What?!"

"Of course I don't *know*. But it makes sense that they would go back to their nearest base; that's where the Mother Thing and I scrammed from."

"You're telling me we're in that ship?"

"Either the one I swiped or the other one. Where did you think you were, Kip? Where else *could* you be?"

"A mental hospital."

She looked big-eyed and then grinned. "Why, Kip, surely your grip on reality is not that weak?"

"I'm not sure about anything. Space pirates—Mother Things."

She frowned and bit her thumb. "I suppose it must be confusing. But trust your ears and eyes. My grip on reality is quite strong, I assure you—you see, I'm a genius." She made it a statement, not a boast, and somehow I was not inclined to doubt the claim, even though it came from a skinny-shanked kid with a rag doll in her arms.

But I didn't see how it was going to help.

Peewee went on: " 'Space pirates' . . . mmm. Call them what you wish. Their actions are piratical and they operate in space— you name them. As for the Mother Thing . . . wait until you meet her."

"What's she doing in this hullabaloo?"

"Well, it's complicated. She had better explain it. She's a cop and she was after them—"

"A cop?"

"I'm afraid that is another semantic inadequacy. The Mother Thing knows what we mean by 'cop' and I think she finds the idea bewildering if not impossible. But what would you call a person who hunts down miscreants? A cop, no?"

"A cop, yes, I guess."

"So would I." She looked again at her watch. "But right now I think we had better hang on. We ought to be at halfway point in a few minutes—and a skew-flip is disconcerting even if you are strapped down."

I had read about skew-flip turn-overs, but only as a theoretical maneuver; I had never heard of a ship that could do one. If this was a ship. The floor felt as solid as concrete and as motionless. "I don't see anything to hang on to."

"Not much, I'm afraid. But if we sit down in the narrowest part and push against each other, I think we can brace enough not to slide around. But let's hurry; my watch might be slow."

We sat on the floor in the narrow part where the angled walls were about five feet apart. We faced each other and pushed our shoes against each other, each of us bracing like an Alpinist inching his way up a rock chimney—my socks against her tennis shoes, rather, for my shoes were still on my workbench, so far as I knew. I wondered if they had simply dumped Oscar in the pasture and if Dad would find him.

"Push hard, Kip, and brace your hands against the deck."

I did so. "How do you know when they'll turn over, Peewee?"

"I haven't been unconscious—they just tripped me and carried me inside—so I know when we took off. If we assume that the Moon is their destination, as it probably is, and if we assume one gravity the whole jump—which can't be far off; my weight feels normal. Doesn't yours?"

I considered it. "I think so."

"Then it probably is, even though my own sense of weight may be distorted from being on the Moon. If those assumptions are correct, then it is almost exactly a three-and-a-half-hour trip and—" Peewee looked at her watch. "—E.T.A. should be nine-thirty in the morning and turn-over at seven-forty-five. Any moment now."

"Is it that late?" I looked at my watch. "Why, I've got a quarter of two."

"You're on your zone time. I'm on Moon time—Greenwich time, that is. Oh, oh! Here we go!"

The floor tilted, swerved, and swooped like a roller coaster, and my semicircular canals did a samba. Things steadied down as I pulled out of acute dizziness.

"You all right?" asked Peewee.

I managed to focus my eyes. "Uh, I think so. It felt like a one-and-a-half gainer into a dry pool."

"This pilot does it faster than I dared to. It doesn't really hurt, after your eyes uncross. But that settles it. We're headed for the Moon. We'll be there in an hour and three quarters."

I still couldn't believe it. "Peewee? What kind of a ship can gun at one gee all the way to the Moon? They been keeping it secret? And what were *you* doing on the Moon anyhow? And why were you stealing a ship?"

She sighed and spoke to her doll. "He's a quiz kid, Madame Pompadour. Kip, how can I answer three questions at once? This is a flying saucer, and—"

"Flying saucer! Now I've heard everything."

"It's rude to interrupt. Call it anything you like; there's nothing official about the term. Actually it's shaped more like a loaf of pumpernickel, an oblate spheroid. That's a shape defined—"

"I know what an oblate spheroid is," I snapped. I was tired and upset from too many things, from a cranky air conditioner that had ruined a good pair of pants to being knocked out while on an errand of mercy. Not to mention Ace Quiggle. I was beginning to think that little girls who were geniuses ought to have the grace not to show it.

"No need to be brisk," she said reprovingly. "I am aware that people have called everything from weather balloons to street lights 'flying saucers.' But it is my considered opinion—by Occam's Razor—that—"

"Whose razor?"

"Occam's. Least hypothesis. Don't you know anything about logic?"

"Not much."

"Well . . . I suspected that about every five-hundredth 'saucer sighting' was a ship like this. It adds up. As for what I was doing on the Moon—" She stopped and grinned. "I'm a pest."

I didn't argue it.

"A long time ago when my Daddy was a boy, the Hayden Planetarium took reservations for trips to the Moon. It was just a publicity gag, like that silly soap contest recently, but Daddy got his name on the list. Now, years and years later, they are letting people go to the Moon—and sure enough, the Hayden people turned the list over to American Express—and American Express notified the applicants they could locate that they would be given preference."

"So your father took you to the Moon?"

"Oh, heavens, no! Daddy filled out that form when he was only a boy. Now he is just about the biggest man at the Institute for Advanced Study and hasn't time for such pleasures. And Mama wouldn't go if you paid her. So I said *I* would. Daddy said *'No!'* and Mama said *'Good gracious, no!'* . . . and so I went. I can be an awful nuisance when I put my mind on it," she said proudly. "I have talent for it. Daddy says I'm an amoral little wretch."

"Uh, do you suppose he might be right?"

"Oh, I'm sure he is. He understands me, whereas Mama throws up her hands and says she can't cope. I was perfectly beastly and unbearable for two whole weeks and at last Daddy said 'For Blank's sake let her go!—maybe we'll collect her insurance!' So I did."

"Mmmmm . . . that still doesn't explain why you are here."

"Oh, that. I was poking around where I shouldn't, doing things they told us not to. I always get around; it's very educational. So they grabbed me. They would rather have Daddy but they hope to swap me for him. I couldn't let that happen, so I had to escape."

I muttered, " 'The butler did it.' "

"What?"

"Your story has as many holes as the last chapter of most whodunits."

"Oh. But I assure you it is the simple—oh, oh! here we go again!"

All that happened was that the lighting changed from white to blue. There weren't any light fixtures; the whole ceiling glowed.

We were still sprawled on the floor. I started to get up—and found I couldn't.

I felt as if I had just finished a cross-country race, too weak to do anything but breathe. Blue light can't do that; it's merely wavelengths 4300 to 5100 angstroms and sunlight is loaded with it. But whatever they used with the blue light made us as limp as wet string.

Peewee was struggling to tell me something. "If . . . they're coming for us . . . don't resist . . . and . . . above all—"

The blue light changed to white. The narrow wall started to slide aside.

Peewee looked scared and made a great effort. "—above all . . . don't antagonize . . . *him.*"

Two men came in, shoved Peewee aside, strapped my wrists and ankles and ran another strap around my middle, binding my arms. I started to come out of it—not like flipping a switch, as I still didn't have energy enough to lick a stamp. I wanted to bash their heads but I stood as much chance as a butterfly has of hefting a bar bell.

They carried me out. I started to protest. "Say, where are you guys taking me? What do you think you're doing? I'll have you arrested. I'll—"

"Shaddap," said one. He was a skinny runt, fifty or older, and looked as if he never smiled. The other was fat and younger, with a petulant babyish mouth and a dimple in his chin; he looked as if he could laugh if he weren't worried. He was worrying now.

"Tim, this can get us in trouble. We ought to space him—we ought to space both of 'em—and tell *him* it was an accident. We can say they got out and tried to escape through the lock. *He* won't know the dif—"

"Shaddap," answered Tim with no inflection. He added, "You want trouble with *him?* You want to chew space?"

"But—"

"Shaddap."

They carried me around a curved corridor, into an inner room and dumped me on the floor.

I was face up but it took time to realize this must be the control room. It didn't look like anything any human would design as a control room, which wasn't surprising as no human had. Then I saw *him.*

Peewee needn't have warned me; I didn't want to antagonize *him.*

The little guy was tough and dangerous, the fat guy was mean and murderous; they were cherubs compared with *him*. If I had had my strength I would have fought those two any way they liked; I don't think I'm too afraid of any human as long as the odds aren't impossible.

But not *him*.

He wasn't human but that wasn't what hurt. Elephants aren't human but they are very nice people. *He* was built more like a human than an elephant is but that was no help—I mean he stood erect and had feet at one end and a head at the other. He was no more than five feet tall but that didn't help either; he dominated us the way a man dominates a horse. The torso part was as long as mine; his shortness came from very squat legs, with feet (I guess you would call them feet) which bulged out, almost disc-like. They made squashy, sucking sounds when he moved. When he stood still a tail, or third leg, extruded and turned him into a tripod—he didn't need to sit down and I doubt if he could.

Short legs did not make him slow. His movements were blurringly fast, like a striking snake. Does this mean a better nervous system and more efficient muscles? Or a native planet with higher gravity?

His arms looked like snakes—they had more joints than ours. He had two sets, one pair where his waist should have been and another set under his head. No shoulders. I couldn't count his fingers, or digit tendrils; they never held still. He wasn't dressed except for a belt below and above the middle arms which carried whatever such a thing carries in place of money and keys. His skin was purplish brown and looked oily.

Whatever *he* was, he was *not* the same race as the Mother Thing.

He had a faint sweetish musky odor. Any crowded room smells worse on a hot day, but if I ever whiff that odor again, my skin will crawl and I'll be tongue-tied with fright.

I didn't take in these details instantly; at first all I could see was his face. A "face" is all I can call it. I haven't described it yet because I'm afraid I'll get the shakes. But I will, so that if you ever see one, you'll shoot first, before your bones turn to jelly.

No nose. He was an oxygen breather but where the air went in and out I couldn't say—some of it through the mouth, for he could talk. The mouth was the second worst part of him; in place of jawbone and chin he had mandibles that opened sideways as well as down, gaping in three irregular sides. There were rows of tiny teeth but no tongue that I could see; instead the mouth was rimmed with cilia as long as angleworms. They never stopped squirming.

I said the mouth was "second worst"; he had eyes. They were big and bulging and protected by horny ridges, two on the front of his head, set wide apart.

They scanned. They scanned like radar, swinging up and down and back and forth. He never looked at you and yet was *always* looking at you.

When he turned around, I saw a third eye in back. I think he scanned his whole surroundings at all times, like a radar warning system.

What kind of brain can put together everything in all directions at once? I doubt if a human brain could, even if there were any way to feed in the data. He didn't seem to have room in his head to stack much of a brain, but maybe he didn't keep it there. Come to think of it, humans wear their brains in an exposed position; there may be better ways.

But he certainly had a brain. He pinned me down like a beetle and squeezed out what he wanted. He didn't have to stop to brainwash me; he questioned and I gave, for an endless time—it seemed more like days than hours. He spoke English badly but understandably. His labials were all alike—"buy" and "pie" and "vie" sounded the same. His gutturals were harsh and his dentals had a clucking quality. But I could usually understand and when I didn't, he didn't threaten or punish; he just tried again. He had no expression in his speech.

He kept at it until he had found out who I was and what I did and as much of what I knew as interested him. He asked questions about how I happened to be where I was and dressed the way I was when I was picked up. I couldn't tell whether he liked the answers or not.

He had trouble understanding what a "soda jerk" was and, while he learned about the Skyway Soap contest, he never seemed to understand why it took place. But I found that there were a lot of things I didn't know either—such as how many people there are on Earth and how many tons of protein we produce each year.

After endless time he had all he wanted and said, "Take it out." The stooges had been waiting. The fat boy gulped and said, "Space him?"

He acted as if killing me or not were like saving a piece of string. "No. It is ignorant and untrained, but I may have use for it later. Put it back in the pen."

"Yes, boss."

They dragged me out. In the corridor Fatty said, "Let's untie his feet and make him walk."

Skinny said, "Shaddap."

Peewee was just inside the entrance panel but didn't move, so I guess she had had another dose of that blue-light effect. They stepped over her and dumped me. Skinny chopped me on the side of the neck to stun me. When I came to, they were gone, I was un-strapped, and Peewee was sitting by me. She said anxiously, "Pretty bad?"

"Uh, yeah," I agreed, and shivered. "I feel ninety years old."

"It helps if you don't look *at him*—especially his eyes. Rest a while and you'll feel better." She glanced at her watch. "It's only forty-five minutes till we land. You probably won't be disturbed before then."

"Huh?" I sat up. "I was in there only an *hour?*"

"A little less. But it seems forever. I know."

"I feel like a squeezed orange." I frowned, remembering something. "Peewee, I wasn't too scared when they came for me. I was going to demand to be turned loose and insist on explana-tions. But I never asked *him* a question, not one."

"You never will. I tried. But your will just drains out. Like a rabbit in front of a snake."

"Yes."

"Kip, do you see why I had to take just any chance to get away? You didn't seem to believe my story—do you believe it now?"

"Uh, yes. I believe it."

"Thanks. I always say I'm too proud to care what people think, but I'm not, really. I had to get back to Daddy and tell him . . . because he's the only one in the entire world who would simply believe me, no matter how crazy it sounded."

"I see. I guess I see. But how did you happen to wind up in Centerville?"

"Centerville?"

"Where I live. Where 'Junebug' called 'Peewee.' "

"Oh. I never meant to go there. I meant to land in New Jersey, in Princeton if possible, because I had to find Daddy."

"Well, you sure missed your aim."

"Can you do better? I would have done all right but I had my elbow joggled. Those things aren't hard to fly; you just aim and push for where you want to go, not like the complicated things they do about rocket ships. And I had the Mother Thing to coach me. But I had to slow down going into the atmosphere and compensate for Earth's spin and I didn't know quite how. I found myself too far west and they were chasing me and I didn't know *what* to do . . . and then I heard you on the space-operations band and thought everything was all right—and there I was." She spread her hands. "I'm sorry, Kip."

"Well, you landed it. They say any landing you walk away from is a good one."

"But I'm sorry I got you mixed up in it."

"Uh . . . don't worry about that. It looks like somebody has to get mixed up in it. Peewee . . . what's *he* up to?"

"*They,* you mean."

"Huh? I don't think the other two amount to anything. *He* is the one."

"I didn't mean Tim and Jock—they're just people gone bad. I meant *them—him* and others like him."

I wasn't at my sharpest—I had been knocked out three times and was shy a night's sleep and more confusing things had happened than in all my life. But until Peewee pointed it out I hadn't considered that there could be more than one like *him*—one seemed more than enough.

But if there was one, then there were thousands—maybe millions or billions. I felt my stomach twist and wanted to hide. "You've seen others?"

"No. Just *him.* But the Mother Thing told me."

"Ugh! Peewee . . . what are they up to?"

"Haven't you guessed? They're moving in on us."

My collar felt tight, even though it was open. "How?"

"I don't know."

"You mean they're going to kill us off and take over Earth?"
She hesitated. "It might not be anything that nice."

"Uh . . . make slaves of us?"

"You're getting warmer. Kip—I think they eat meat."

I swallowed. "You have the jolliest ideas, for a little girl."

"You think I like it? That's why I had to tell Daddy."

There didn't seem to be anything to say. It was an old, old fear for human beings. Dad had told me about an invasion-from-Mars radio broadcast when he was a kid—pure fiction but it had scared people silly. But people didn't believe in it now; ever since we got to the Moon and circled Mars and Venus everybody seemed to agree that we weren't going to find life anywhere.

Now here it was, in our laps. "Peewee? Are these things Martians? Or from Venus?"

She shook her head. "They're not from anywhere close. The Mother Thing tried to tell me, but we ran into a difficulty of understanding."

"Inside the Solar System?"

"That was part of the difficulty. Both yes and no."

"It can't be both."

"*You* ask her."

"I'd like to." I hesitated, then blurted, "I don't care where they're from—we can shoot them down . . . if we don't have to look at them!"

"Oh, I hope so!"

"It figures. You say these are flying saucers . . . real saucer sightings, I mean; not weather balloons. If so, they have been scouting us for years. Therefore they aren't sure of themselves, even if they do look horrible enough to curdle milk. Otherwise they would have moved in at once the way we would on a bunch of animals. But they haven't. That means we can kill them—if we go about it right."

She nodded eagerly. "I hope so. I hoped Daddy would see a way. But—" She frowned. "—we don't know much about them . . . and Daddy always warned me not to be cocksure when data was incomplete. 'Don't make so much stew from one oyster, Peewee,' he always says."

"But I'll bet we're right. Say, who is your Daddy? And what's your full name?"

"Why, Daddy is Professor Reisfeld. And my name is Patricia Wynant Reisfeld. Isn't that awful? Better call me Peewee."

"Professor Reisfeld—What does he teach?"

"Huh? You don't *know?* You don't know about Daddy's Nobel Prize? Or anything?"

"I'm just a country boy, Peewee. Sorry."

"You must be. Daddy doesn't *teach* anything. He *thinks*. He thinks better than anybody . . . except me, possibly. He's the synthesist. Everybody else specializes. Daddy knows everything and puts the pieces together."

Maybe so, but I hadn't heard of him. It sounded like a good idea . . . but it would take an awfully smart man—if I had found out anything, it was that they could print it faster than I could study it. Professor Reisfeld must have three heads. Five.

"Wait till you meet him," she added, glancing at her watch. "Kip, I think we had better get braced. We'll be landing in a few minutes . . . and *he* won't care how he shakes up passengers."

So we crowded into the narrow end and braced each other. We waited. After a bit the ship shook itself and the floor tilted. There was a slight bump and things got steady and suddenly I felt very light. Peewee pulled her feet under her and stood up. "Well, we're on the Moon."

Chapter 5

When I was a kid, we used to pretend we were making the first landing on the Moon. Then I gave up romantic notions and realized that I would have to go about it another way. But I never thought I would get there penned up, unable to see out, like a mouse in a shoe box.

The only thing that proved I was on the Moon was my weight. High gravity can be managed anywhere, with centrifuges. Low gravity is another matter; on Earth the most you can squeeze out is a few seconds going off a high board, or by parachute delay, or stunts in a plane.

If low gravity goes on and on, then wherever you are, you are *not* on Earth. Well, I wasn't on Mars; it had to be the Moon.

On the Moon I should weigh a little over twenty-five pounds. It felt about so—I felt light enough to walk on a lawn and not bend the grass.

For a few minutes I simply exulted in it, forgetting *him* and the trouble we were in, just heel-and-toe around the room, getting the wonderful feel of it, bouncing a little and bumping my head against the ceiling and feeling how slowly, slowly, slowly I settled back to the floor. Peewee sat down, shrugged her shoulders and gave a little smile, an annoyingly patronizing one. The "Old Moon-Hand"—all of two weeks more of it than I had had.

Low gravity has its disconcerting tricks. Your feet have hardly any traction and they fly out from under you. I had to learn with muscles and reflexes what I had known only intellectually: that when weight goes down, mass and inertia do not. To change direction, even in walking, you have to lean the way you would to round a turn on a board track—and even then if you don't have traction (which I didn't in socks on a smooth floor) your feet go out from under you.

A fall doesn't hurt much in one-sixth gravity but Peewee giggled. I sat up and said, "Go and laugh, smartie. You can afford to—you've got tennis shoes."

"I'm sorry. But you looked silly, hanging there like a slow-motion picture and grabbing air."

"No doubt. Very funny."

"I said I was sorry. Look, you can borrow my shoes."

I looked at her feet, then at mine, and snorted. "Gee, thanks!"

"Well . . . you could cut the heels out, or something. It wouldn't bother me. Nothing ever does. Where are your shoes, Kip?"

"Uh, about a quarter-million miles away—unless we got off at the wrong stop."

"Oh. Well, you won't need them much, here."

"Yeah." I chewed my lip, thinking about "here" and no longer interested in games with gravity. "Peewee? What do we do now?"

"About what?"

"About *him*."

"Nothing. What *can* we do?"

"Then what do we do?"

"Sleep."

"Huh?"

"Sleep. 'Sleep, that knits up the ravell'd sleave of care.' 'Tired Nature's sweet restorer, balmy sleep.' 'Blessings on him who invented sleep, the mantle that covers all human thoughts.' "

"Quit showing off and talk sense!"

"I *am* talking sense. At the moment we're as helpless as goldfish. We're simply trying to survive—and the first principle of survival is not to worry about the impossible and concentrate on what's possible. I'm hungry and thirsty and uncomfortable and very, very tired . . . and all I can do about it is sleep. So if you will kindly keep quiet, that's what I'll do."

"I can take a hint. No need to snap at me."

"I'm sorry. But I get cross as two sticks when I'm tired and Daddy says I'm simply frightful before breakfast." She curled up in a little ball and tucked that filthy rag doll under her chin. "G'night, Kip."

"Good night, Peewee."

I thought of something and started to speak . . . and saw that she was asleep. She was breathing softly and her face had smoothed out and no longer looked alert and smart-alecky. Her upper lip pooched out in a baby pout and she looked like a dirty-faced cherub. There were streaks where she had apparently cried and not wiped it away. But she had never let me see her crying.

Kip, I said to myself, you get yourself into the darndest things; this is much worse than bringing home a stray pup or a kitten.

But I had to take care of her . . . or die trying.

Well, maybe I would. Die trying, I mean. It didn't look as if I were any great shakes even taking care of myself.

I yawned, then yawned again. Maybe the shrimp had more sense than I had, at that. I was more tired than I had ever been, and hungry and thirsty and not comfortable other ways. I thought about banging on the door panel and trying to attract the fat one or his skinny partner. But that would wake Peewee—and it might antagonize *him*.

So I sprawled on my back the way I nap on the living-room rug at home. I found that a hard floor does not require any one sleeping position on the Moon; one-sixth gravity is a better mattress than all the foam rubber ever made—that fussy princess in Hans Christian Andersen's story would have had no complaints.

I want to sleep at once.

It was the wildest space opera I had ever seen, loaded with dragons and Arcturian maidens and knights in shining space armor and shuttling between King Arthur's Court and the Dead Sea Bottoms of Barsoom. I didn't mind that but I did mind the announcer. He had the voice of Ace Quiggle and the face of *him*. He leaned out of the screen and leered, those wormy cilia writhing. "Will Beowulf conquer the Dragon? Will Tristan return to Iseult? Will Peewee find her dolly? Tune in this channel tomorrow night and in the meantime, wake up and hurry to your neighborhood druggist for a cake of Skyway's Kwikbrite Armor Polish, the better polish used by the better knights *sans peur et sans reproche*. Wake up!" He shoved a snaky arm out of the screen and grabbed my shoulder.

I woke up.

"Wake up," Peewee was saying, shaking my shoulder. "Please wake up, Kip."

"Lea' me alone!"

"You were having a nightmare."

The Arcturian princess had been in a bad spot. "Now I'll never know how it came out. Wha' did y' want to wake me for? I thought the idea was to sleep?"

"You've slept for hours—and now perhaps there is something we can do."

"Breakfast, maybe?"

She ignored that. "I think we should try to escape."

I sat up suddenly, bounced off the floor, settled back. "Wups! How?"

"I don't know exactly. But I think they have gone away and left us. If so, we'll never have a better chance."

"They have? What makes you think so?"

"Listen. Listen hard."

I listened. I could hear my heart beat, I could hear Peewee breathing, and presently I could hear her heart beating. I've never heard deeper silence in a cave.

I took my knife, held it in my teeth for bone conduction and pushed it against a wall. Nothing. I tried the floor and the other walls. Still nothing. The ship ached with silence—no throb, no thump, not even those vibrations you can sense but not hear. "You're right, Peewee."

"I noticed it when the air circulation stopped."

I sniffed. "Are we running out of air?"

"Not right away. But the air stopped—it comes out of those tiny holes up there. You don't notice it but I missed something when it stopped."

I thought hard. "I don't see where this gets us. We're still locked up."

"I'm not sure."

I tried the blade of my knife on a wall. It wasn't metal or anything I knew as plastic, but it didn't mind a knife. Maybe the Comte de Monte Cristo could have dug a hole in it—but he had more time. "How do you figure?"

"Every time they've opened or closed that door panel, I've heard a click. So after they took you out I stuck a wad of bubble gum where the panel meets the wall, high up where they might not notice."

"You've got some gum?"

"Yes. It helps, when you can't get a drink of water. I—"

"Got any more?" I asked eagerly. I wasn't fresh in any way but thirst was the worst—I'd never been so thirsty.

Peewee looked upset. "Oh, poor Kip! I haven't any more . . . just an old wad I kept parked on my belt buckle and chewed when I felt driest." She frowned. "But you can have it. You're welcome."

"Uh, thanks, Peewee. Thanks a lot. But I guess not."

She looked insulted. "I assure you, Mr. Russell, that I do not have anything contagious. I was merely trying to—"

"Yes, yes," I said hastily. "I'm sure you were. But—"

"I assumed that these were emergency conditions. It is surely no more unsanitary than kissing a girl—but then I don't suppose you've ever kissed a girl!"

"Not lately," I evaded. "But what I want is a drink of clear cold water—or murky warm water. Besides, you used up your gum on the door panel. What did you expect to accomplish?"

"Oh. I told you about that click. Daddy says that, in a dilemma, it is helpful to change any variable, then reexamine the problem. I tried to introduce a change with my bubble gum."

"Well?"

"When they brought you back, then closed the door, I didn't hear a click."

"*What?* Then you thought you had bamboozled their lock hours and hour ago—and you didn't tell *me?*"

"That is correct."

"Why, I ought to spank you!"

"I don't advise it," she said frostily. "I bite."

I believed her. And scratch. And other things. None of them pleasant. I changed the subject. "Why didn't you tell me, Peewee?"

"I was afraid you might try to get out."

"Huh? I certainly would have!"

"Precisely. But I *wanted* that panel closed . . . as long as *he* was out there."

Maybe she was a genius. Compared with me. "I see your point. All right, let's see if we can get it open." I examined the panel. The wad of gum was there, up high as she could reach, and from the way it was mashed it did seem possible that it had fouled the groove the panel slid into, but I couldn't see any crack down the edge.

I tried the point of my big blade on it. The panel seemed to creep to the right an eighth of an inch—then the blade broke.

I closed the stub and put the knife away. "Any ideas?"

"Maybe if we put our hands flat against it and tried to drag it?"

"Okay." I wiped sweat from my hands on my shirt. "Now . . . easy does it. Just enough pressure for friction."

The panel slid to the right almost an inch—and stopped firmly. But there was a hairline crack from floor to ceiling.

I broke off the stub of the big blade this time. The crack was no wider. Peewee said, "Oh, dear!"

"We aren't licked." I backed off and ran toward the door.

"Toward," not "to"—my feet skidded, I leveled off and did a leisurely bellywhopper. Peewee didn't laugh.

I picked myself up, got against the far wall, braced one foot against it and tried a swimming racing start.

I got as far as the door panel before losing my footing. I didn't hit it very hard, but I felt it spring. It bulged a little, then sprang back.

"Wait a sec, Kip," said Peewee. "Take your socks off. I'll get behind you and push—my tennis shoes don't slip."

She was right. On the Moon, if you can't get rubber-soled shoes, you're better off barefooted. We backed against the far wall, Peewee behind me with her hands on my hips. "One . . . two . . . three . . . Go!" We advanced with the grace of a hippopotamus.

I hurt my shoulder. But the panel sprung out of its track, leaving a space four inches wide at the bottom and tapering to the top.

I left skin on the door frame and tore my shirt and was hampered in language by the presence of a girl. But the opening widened. When it was wide enough for my head, I got down flat and peered out. There was nobody in sight—a foregone conclusion, with the noise I had made, unless they were playing cat-and-mouse. Which I wouldn't put past them. Especially *him*.

Peewee started to wiggle through; I dragged her back. "Naughty, naughty! I go first." Two more heaves and it was wide enough for me. I opened the small blade of my knife and handed it to Peewee. "With your shield or on it, soldier."

"You take it."

"I won't need it. 'Two-Fisted Death,' they call me around dark alleys." This was propaganda, but why worry her? *Sans peur et sans reproche*—maiden-rescuing done cheaply, special rates for parties.

I eased out on elbows and knees, stood up and looked around. "Come on out," I said quietly.

She started to, then backed up suddenly. She reappeared clutching that bedraggled dolly. "I almost forgot Madame Pompadour," she said breathlessly.

I didn't even smile.

"Well," she said defensively, "I have to have her to get to sleep at night. It's my one neurotic quirk—but Daddy says I'll outgrow it."

"Sure, sure."

"Well, don't look so smug! It's not fetishism, not even primitive animism; it's merely a conditioned reflex. I'm aware that it's just a doll—I've understood the pathetic fallacy for . . . oh, years and years!"

"Look, Peewee," I said earnestly, "I don't care how you get to sleep. Personally I hit myself over the head with a hammer. But quit yakking. Do you know the layout of these ships?"

She looked around. "I think this is the ship that chased me. But it looks the same as the one I piloted."

"All right. Should we head for the control room?"

"Huh?"

"You flew the other heap. Can you fly this one?"

"Unh . . . I guess so. Yes, I can."

"Then let's go." I started in the direction they had lugged me.

"But the other time I had the Mother Thing to tell me what to do! Let's find her."

I stopped. "Can you get it off the ground?"

"Well . . . yes."

"We'll look for her after we're in the air—'in space,' I mean. If she's aboard we'll find her. If she's not, there's not a thing we can do."

"Well . . . all right. I see your logic; I don't have to like it." She tagged along. "Kip? How many gravities can you stand?"

"Huh? I haven't the slightest idea. Why?"

"Because these things can go lots faster than I dared try when I escaped before. That was my mistake."

"Your mistake was in heading for New Jersey."

"But I had to find Daddy!"

"Sure, sure, eventually. But you should have ducked over to Lunar Base and yelled for the Federation Space Corps. This is no job for a popgun; we need help. Any idea where we are?"

"Mmm . . . I think so. If *he* took us back to their base. I'll know when I look at the sky."

"All right. If you can figure out where Lunar Base is from here, that's where we'll go. If not—Well, we'll head for New Jersey at all the push it has."

The control-room door latched and I could not figure out how to open it. Peewee did what she said should work—which was to tuck her little finger into a hole mine would not enter—and told me it must be locked. So I looked around.

I found a metal bar racked in the corridor, a thing about five feet long, pointed on one end and with four handles like brass knucks on the other. I didn't know what it was—the hobgoblin equivalent of a fire ax, possibly—but it was a fine wrecking bar.

I made a shambles of that door in three minutes. We went in.

My first feeling was gooseflesh because here was where I had been grilled by *him*. I tried not to show it. If *he* turned up, I was going to let him have his wrecking bar right between his grisly eyes. I looked around, really seeing the place for the first time. There was sort of a nest in the middle surrounded by what could have been a very fancy coffee maker or a velocipede for an octopus; I was glad Peewee knew which button to push. "How do you see out?"

"Like this." Peewee squeezed past and put a finger into a hole I hadn't noticed.

The ceiling was hemispherical like a planetarium. Which was what it was, for it lighted up. I gasped.

It was suddenly not a floor we were on, but a platform, apparently out in the open and maybe thirty feet in the air. Over me were star images, thousands of them, in a black "sky"—and facing toward me, big as a dozen full moons and green and lovely and beautiful, was Earth!

Peewee touched my elbow. "Snap out of it, Kip."

I said in a choked voice, "Peewee, don't you have any poetry in your soul?"

"Surely I have. Oodles. But we haven't time. I know where we are, Kip—back where I started from. Their base. See those rocks with long jagged shadows? Some of them are ships, camouflaged. And over to the left—that high peak, with the saddle?—a little farther left, almost due west, is Tombaugh Station, forty miles away. About two hundred miles farther is Lunar Base and beyond is Luna City."

"How long will it take?"

"Two hundred, nearly two hundred and fifty miles? Uh, I've never tried a point-to-point on the Moon—but it shouldn't take more than a few minutes."

"Let's go! They might come back any minute."

"Yes, Kip." She crawled into that jackdaw's nest and bent over a sector.

Presently she looked up. Her face was white and thin and very little-girlish. "Kip . . . we aren't going anywhere. I'm sorry."

I let out a yelp. "What! What's the matter? Have you forgotten how to run it?"

"No. The 'brain' is gone."

"The which?"

"The 'brain.' Little black dingus about the size of a walnut that fits in this cavity." She showed me. "We got away before because the Mother Thing managed to steal one. We were locked in an empty ship, just as you and I are now. But she had one and we got away." Peewee looked bleak and very lost. "I should have known that *he* wouldn't leave one in the control room—I guess I did and didn't want to admit it. I'm sorry."

"Uh . . . look, Peewee, we won't give up that easily. Maybe I can make something to fit that socket."

"Like jumping wires in a car?" She shook her head. "It's not that simple, Kip. If you put a wooden model in place of the generator in a car, would it run? I don't know quite what it does, but I called it the 'brain' because it's very complex."

"But—" I shut up. If a Borneo savage had a brand-new car, complete except for spark plugs, would he get it running? Echo answers mournfully. "Peewee, what's the next best thing? Any ideas? Because if you haven't, I want you to show me the air lock. I'll take this—" I shook my wrecking bar "—and bash anything that comes through."

"I'm stumped," she admitted. "I want to look for the Mother Thing. If she's shut up in this ship, she may know what to do."

"All right. But first show me the air lock. You can look for her while I stand guard." I felt the reckless anger of desperation. I didn't see how we were ever going to get out and I was beginning to believe that we weren't—but there was still a reckoning due. *He* was going to learn that it wasn't safe to push people around. I was sure—I was fairly sure—that I could sock him before my spine turned to jelly. Splash that repulsive head.

If I didn't look at his eyes.

Peewee said slowly, "There's one other thing—"

"What?"

"I hate to suggest it. You might think I was running out on you."

"Don't be silly. If you've got an idea, spill it."

"Well . . . there's Tombaugh Station, over that way about forty miles. If my space suit is in the ship—"

I suddenly quit feeling like Bowie at the Alamo. Maybe the game would go an extra period—"We can walk it!"

She shook her head. "No, Kip. That's why I hesitated to mention it. *I* can walk it . . . if we find my suit. But you couldn't wear my suit even if you squatted."

"I don't need your suit," I said impatiently.

"Kip, Kip! This is the Moon, remember? No air."

"Yes, yes, sure! Think I'm an idiot? But if they locked up your suit, they probably put mine right beside it and—"

"*You've* got a space suit?" she said incredulously.

Our next remarks were too confused to repeat but finally Pee-wee was convinced that I really did own a space suit, that in fact the only reason I was sending on the space-operations band twelve hours and a quarter of a million miles back was that I was wearing it when they grabbed me.

"Let's tear the joint apart!" I said. "No—show me that air lock, then *you* take it apart."

"All right."

She showed me the lock, a room much like the one we had been cooped in, but smaller and with an inner door built to take a pressure load. It was not locked. We opened it cautiously. It was empty, and its outer door was closed or we would never been able to open the inner. I said, "If Wormface had been a suspenders-and-belt man, he would have left the outer door open, even though he had us locked up. Then—Wait a second! Is there a way to latch the inner door open?"

"I don't know."

"We'll see." There was, a simple hook. But to make sure that it couldn't be unlatched by button-pushing from outside I wedged it with my knife. "You're sure this is the only air lock?"

"The other ship had only one and I'm pretty certain they are alike."

"We'll keep our eyes open. Nobody can get at us through this one. Even old Wormface has to use an air lock."

"But suppose he opens the outer door anyhow?" Peewee said nervously. "We'd pop like balloons."

I looked at her and grinned. "*Who* is a genius? Sure we would . . . if he did. But he won't. Not with twenty, twenty-five tons of pressure holding it closed. As you reminded me, this is the Moon. No air outside, remember?"

"Oh." Peewee looked sheepish.

So we searched. I enjoyed wrecking doors; Wormface wasn't going to like me. One of the first things we found was a smelly little hole that Fatty and Skinny lived in. The door was not locked, which was a shame. That room told me a lot about that pair. It showed that they were pigs, with habits as unattractive as their morals. The room also told me that they were not casual prisoners; it had been refitted for humans. Their relationship with Wormface, whatever it was, had gone on for some time and was continuing. There were two empty racks for space suits, several dozen canned rations of the sort sold in military-surplus stores, and best of all, there was drinking water and a washroom of sorts—and something more precious than fine gold or frankincense if we found our suits: two charged bottles of oxy-helium.

I took a drink, opened a can of food for Peewee—it opened with a key; we weren't in the predicament of the *Three Men in a Boat* with their tin of pineapple—told her to grab a bite, then search that room. I went on with my giant toad sticker; those charged air bottles had given me an unbearable itch to find our suits—and get out!—before Wormface returned.

I smashed a dozen doors as fast as the Walrus and the Carpenter opened oysters and found all sorts of things, including what must have been living quarters for wormfaces. But I didn't stop to look—the Space Corps could do that, if and when—I simply made sure that there was not a space suit in any of them.

And found them!—in a compartment next to the one we had been prisoners in.

I was so glad to see Oscar that I could have kissed him. I shouted, "Hi. Pal! *Mirabile visu!*" and ran to get Peewee. My feet went out from under me again but I didn't care.

Peewee looked up as I rushed in. "I was just going to look for you."

"Got it! Got it!"

"You found the Mother Thing?" she said eagerly.

"Huh? No, no! The space suits—yours and mine! Let's go!"

"Oh." She looked disappointed and I felt hurt. "That's good . . . but we have to find the Mother Thing first."

I felt tried beyond endurance. Here we had a chance, slim but real, to escape a fate-worse-than-death (I'm not using a figure of speech) and *she* wanted to hang around to search for a bug-eyed monster. For any human being, even a stranger with halitosis, I would have done it. For a dog or cat I would, although reluctantly.

But what was a bug-eyed monster to me? All this one had done was to get me into the worst jam I had ever been in.

I considered socking Peewee and stuffing her into her suit. But I said, "Are you crazy? We're leaving—right now!"

"We can't go till we find her."

"Now I know you're crazy. We don't even know she's here . . . and if we do find her, we can't take her with us."

"Oh, but we will!"

"How? This is the Moon, remember? No air. Got a space suit for her?"

"But—" That stonkered her. But not for long. She had been

sitting on the floor, holding the ration can between her knees. She stood up suddenly, bouncing a little, and said, "Do as you like; I'm going to find her. Here." She shoved the can at me.

I should have used force. But I am handicapped by training from early childhood never to strike a female, no matter how richly she deserves it. So the opportunity and Peewee both slid past while I was torn between common sense and upbringing. I simply groaned helplessly.

Then I became aware of an unbearably attractive odor. I was holding that can. It contained boiled shoe leather and gray gravy and smelled ambrosial.

Peewee had eaten half; I ate the rest while looking at what she had found. There was a coil of nylon rope which I happily put with the air bottles; Oscar had fifty feet of clothesline clipped to his belt but that had been a penny-saving expedient. There was a prospector's hammer which I salvaged, and two batteries which would do for headlamps and things.

The only other items of interest were a Government Printing Office publication titled *Preliminary Report on Selenology*, a pamphlet on uranium prospecting, and an expired Utah driver's license for "Timothy Johnson"—I recognized the older man's mean face. The pamphlets interested me but this was no time for excess baggage.

The main furniture was two beds, curved like contour chairs and deeply padded; they told me that Skinny and Fatty had ridden this ship at high acceleration.

When I had mopped the last of the gravy with a finger, I took a big drink, washed my hands—using water lavishly because I didn't care if that pair died of thirst—grabbed my plunder and headed for the room where the space suits were.

As I got there I ran into Peewee. She was carrying the crowbar and looking overjoyed. "I found her!"

"Where?"

"Come on! I can't get it open, I'm not strong enough."

I put the stuff with our suits and followed her. She stopped at a door panel farther along the corridor than my vandalism had taken me. "In there!"

I looked and I listened. "What makes you think so?"

"I know! Open it!"

I shrugged and got to work with the nutpick. The panel went *sprung!* and that was that.

Curled up in the middle of the floor was a creature.

So far as I could tell, it might or might not have been the one I had seen in the pasture the night before. The light had been poor, the conditions very different, and my examination had ended abruptly. But Peewee was in no doubt. She launched herself through the air with a squeal of joy and the two rolled over and over like kittens play-fighting.

Peewee was making sounds of joy, more or less in English. So was the Mother Thing, but not in English. I would not have been surprised if she had spoken English, since Wormface did and since Peewee had mentioned things the Mother Thing had told her. But she didn't.

Did you ever listen to a mockingbird? Sometimes singing melodies, sometimes just sending up a joyous noise unto the Lord? The endlessly varied songs of a mockingbird are nearest to the speech of the Mother Thing.

At last they held still, more or less, and Peewee said, "Oh, Mother Thing, I'm so happy!"

The creature sang to her. Peewee answered, "Oh. I'm forgetting my manners. Mother Thing, this is my dear friend Kip."

The Mother Thing sang to me:

—and I understood.

What she said was: "I am very happy to know you, Kip."

It didn't come out in words. But it might as well have been English. Nor was this half-kidding self-deception, such as my conversations with Oscar or Peewee's with Madame Pompadour—when I talk with Oscar I am both sides of the conversation; it's just my conscious talking to my subconscious, or some such. This was not that.

The Mother Thing sang to me and I understood.

I was startled but not unbelieving. When you see a rainbow you don't stop to argue the laws of optics. There it is, in the sky.

I would have been an idiot not to know that the Mother Thing was speaking to me because I *did* understand and understood her every time. If she directed a remark at Peewee alone, it was usually just birdsongs to me—but if it was meant for me, I got it.

Call it telepathy if you like, although it doesn't seem to be what they do at Duke University. I never read her mind and I don't think she read mine. We just talked.

But while I was startled, I minded my manners. I felt the way I do when Mother introduces me to one of her older grande-dame friends. So I bowed and said, "We're very happy that we've found you, Mother Thing."

It was simple, humble truth. I knew, without explanation, what it was that had made Peewee stubbornly determined to risk recapture rather than give up looking for her—the quality that made her "the Mother Thing."

Peewee has this habit of slapping names on things and her choices aren't always apt, for my taste. But I'll never question this one. The Mother Thing was the Mother Thing because she *was*. Around her you felt happy and safe and warm. You knew that if you skinned your knee and came bawling into the house, she would kiss it well and paint it with merthiolate and everything would be all right. Some nurses have it and some teachers . . . and, sadly, some mothers don't.

But the Mother Thing had it so strongly that I wasn't even worried by Wormface. We had her with us so everything was going to be all right. Logically I knew that she was as vulnerable as we were—I had seen them strike her down. She didn't have my size and strength, she couldn't pilot the ship as Peewee had been able to. It didn't matter.

I wanted to crawl into her lap. Since she was too small and didn't have a lap, I would gratefully hold her in mine, anytime.

I have talked more about my father but that doesn't mean that Mother is less important—just different. Dad is active, Mother is passive; Dad talks, Mother doesn't. But if she died, Dad would wither like an uprooted tree. She makes our world.

The Mother Thing had the effect on me that Mother has, only I'm used to it from Mother. Now I was getting it unexpectedly, far from home, when I *needed* it.

Peewee said excitedly, "Now we can go, Kip. Let's hurry!"
The Mother Thing sang:

("Where are we going, children?")
"To Tombaugh Station, Mother Thing. They'll help us."
The Mother Thing blinked her eyes and looked serenely sad.

She had great, soft, compassionate eyes—she looked more like a lemur than anything else but she was not a primate—she wasn't even in our sequence, unearthly. But she had these wonderful eyes and a soft, defenseless mouth out of which music poured. She wasn't as big as Peewee and her hands were tinier still—six fingers, any one of which could oppose the others the way our thumbs can. Her body—well, it never stayed the same shape so it's hard to describe, but it was right for her.

She didn't wear clothes but she wasn't naked; she had soft, creamy fur, sleek and fine as chinchilla. I thought at first she didn't wear anything, but presently I noticed a piece of jewelry, a shiny triangle with a double spiral in each corner. I don't know what made it stick on.

I didn't take all this in at once. At that instant the expression in the Mother Thing's eyes brought a crash of sorrow into the happiness I had been feeling.

Her answer made me realize that she didn't have a miracle ready:

("How are we to fly the ship? They have guarded me most carefully this time.")

Peewee explained eagerly about the space suits and I stood there like a fool, with a lump of ice in my stomach. What had been just a question of using my greater strength to force Peewee to behave was now an unsolvable dilemma. I could no more abandon the Mother Thing than I could have abandoned Peewee . . . and there were only two space suits.

Even if she could wear our sort, which looked as practical as roller skates on a snake.

The Mother Thing gently pointed out that her own vacuum gear had been destroyed. (I'm going to quit writing down *all* her songs; I don't remember them exactly anyhow.)

And so the fight began. It was an odd fight, with the Mother Thing gentle and loving and sensible and utterly firm, and Peewee throwing a tearful, bad-little-girl tantrum—and me standing miserably by, not even refereeing.

When the Mother Thing understood the situation, she analyzed it at once to the inevitable answer. Since she had no way to go (and probably couldn't have walked that far anyhow, even if she had had her sort of space suit) the only answer was for us two to leave at once. If we reached safety, then we would, if possible, convince our people of the danger from Wormface & Co.—in which case she might be saved as well . . . which would be nice but was not indispensable.

Peewee utterly, flatly, and absolutely refused to listen to any plan which called for leaving the Mother Thing behind. If the Mother Thing couldn't go, she wouldn't budge. "Kip! You go get help! Hurry! I'll stay here."

I stared at her. "Peewee, you know I can't do that."

"You must. You will so! You've *got* to. If you don't, I'll . . . I'll never speak to you again!"

"If I did, I'd never speak to myself again. Look, Peewee, it won't wash. You'll have to go—"

"No!"

"Oh, shut up for a change. You go and I stay and guard the door with the shillelagh. I'll hold 'em off while you round up the troops. But tell them to hurry!"

"I—" She stopped and looked very sober and utterly baffled. Then she threw herself on the Mother Thing, sobbing: "Oh, you don't *love* me any more!"

Which shows how far her logic had gone to pot. The Mother Thing sang softly to her while I worried the thought that our last chance was trickling away while we argued. Wormface might come back any second—and while I hoped to slug him a final one if he got in, more likely he had resources to outmaneuver me. Either way, we would not escape.

At last I said, "Look we'll *all* go."

Peewee stopped sobbing and looked startled. "You know we can't."

The Mother Thing sang: ("How, Kip?")

"Uh, I'll have to show you. Up on your feet, Peewee." We went where the suits were, while Peewee carried Madame Pompadour and half carried the Mother Thing. Lars Eklund, the rigger who had first worn Oscar according to his log, must have weighed about two hundred pounds; in order to wear Oscar I had to strap him tight to keep from bulging. I hadn't considered retailoring him to my size as I was afraid I would never get him gas-tight again. Arm and leg lengths were okay; it was girth that was too big.

There was room inside for both the Mother Thing and me.

I explained, while Peewee looked big-eyed and the Mother

Thing sang queries and approvals. Yes, she could hang on piggy-back—and she couldn't fall off, once we were sealed up and the straps cinched.

"All right. Peewee, get into your suit." I went to get my socks while she started to suit up. When I came back I checked her helmet gauges, reading them backwards through her lens. "We had better give you some air. You're only about half full."

I ran into a snag. The spare bottles I had filched from those ghouls had screw-thread fittings like mine—but Peewee's bottles had bayonet-and-snap joints. Okay, I guess, for tourists, chaperoned and nursed and who might get panicky while bottles were changed unless it was done fast—but not so good for serious work. In my workshop I would have rigged an adapter in twenty minutes. Here, with no real tools—well, that spare air might as well be on Earth for all the good it did Peewee.

For the first time, I thought seriously of leaving them behind while I made a fast forced march for help. But I didn't mention it. I thought that Peewee would rather die on the way than fall back into *his* hands—and I was inclined to agree.

"Kid," I said slowly, "that isn't much air. Not for forty miles." Her gauge was scaled in time as well as pressure; it read just under five hours. Could Peewee move as fast as a trotting horse? Even at lunar gravity? Not likely.

She looked at me soberly. "That's calibrated for full-size people. I'm little—I don't use much air."

"Uh . . . don't use it faster than you have to."

"I won't. Let's go."

I started to close her gaskets. "Hey!" she objected.

"What's the matter?"

"Madame Pompadour! Hand her to me—please. On the floor by my feet."

I picked up that ridiculous dolly and gave it to her. "How much air does *she* take?"

Peewee suddenly dimpled. "I'll caution her not to inhale." She stuffed it inside her shirt, I sealed her up. I sat down in my open suit, the Mother Thing crept up my back, singing reassuringly, and cuddled close. She felt good and I felt that I could hike a hundred miles, to get them both safe.

Getting me sealed in was cumbersome, as the straps had to be let out and then tightened to allow for the Mother Thing, and neither Peewee nor I had bare hands. We managed.

I made a sling from my clothesline for the spare bottles. With them around my neck, with Oscar's weight and the Mother Thing as well, I scaled perhaps fifty pounds at the Moon's one-sixth gee. It just made me fairly sure-footed for the first time.

I retrieved my knife from the air-lock latch and snapped it to Oscar's belt beside the nylon rope and the prospector's hammer. Then we went inside the air lock and closed its inner door. I didn't know how to waste its air to the outside but Peewee did. It started to hiss out.

"You all right, Mother Thing?"

("Yes, Kip.") She hugged me reassuringly.

"Peewee to Junebug," I heard in my phones: "radio check. Alfa, Bravo, Coca, Delta, Echo, Foxtrot—"

"Junebug to Peewee: I read you. Golf, Hotel, India, Juliette, Kilo—"

"I read you, Kip."

"Roger."

"Mind your pressure, Kip. You're swelling up too fast." I kicked the chin valve while watching the gauge—and kicking myself for letting a little girl catch me in a greenhorn trick. But she had used a space suit before, while I had merely pretended to.

I decided this was no time to be proud. "Peewee? Give me all the tips you can. I'm new to his."

"I will, Kip."

The outer door popped silently and swung inward—and I looked out over the bleak bright surface of a lunar plain. For a homesick moment I remembered the trip-to-the-Moon games I had played as a kid and wished I were back in Centerville. Then Peewee touched her helmet to mine. "See anyone?"

"No."

"We're lucky, the door faces away from the other ships. Listen carefully. We won't use radio until we are over the horizon— unless it's a desperate emergency. They listen on our frequencies. I know that for sure. Now see that mountain with the saddle in it? Kip, pay attention!"

"Yes." I had been staring at Earth. She was beautiful even in that shadow show in the control room—but I just hadn't realized. There she was, so close I could almost touch her . . . and so far away that we might never get home. You can't believe what a lovely planet we have, until you see her from outside . . . with clouds girdling her waist and polar cap set jauntily, like a spring hat. "Yes. I see the saddle."

"We head left of there, where you see a pass. Tim and Jock

brought me through it in a crawler. Once we pick up its tracks it will be easy. But first we head for those near hills just left of that—that ought to keep this ship between us and the other ships while we get out of sight. I hope."

It was twelve feet or so to the ground and I was prepared to jump, since it would be nothing much in that gravity. Peewee insisted on lowering me by rope. "You'll fall over your feet. Look, Kip, listen to old Aunt Peewee. You don't have Moon legs yet. It's going to be like your first time on a bicycle."

So I let her lower me and the Mother Thing while she snubbed the nylon rope around the side of the lock. Then she jumped with no trouble. I started to loop up the line but she stopped me and snapped the other end to her belt, then touched helmets. "I'll lead. If I go too fast or you need me, tug on the rope. I won't be able to see you."

"Aye aye, Cap'n!"

"Don't make fun of me, Kip. This is serious."

"I wasn't making fun, Peewee. You're boss."

"Let's go. Don't look back, it won't do any good and you might fall. I'm heading for those hills."

Chapter 6

I should have relished the weird, romantic experience, but I was as busy as Eliza crossing the ice and the things snapping at my heels were worse than bloodhounds. I wanted to look back but I was too busy trying to stay on my feet. I couldn't see my feet; I had to watch ahead and try to pick my footing—it kept me as busy as a lumberjack in a logrolling contest. I didn't skid as the ground was rough—dust or fine sand over raw rock—and fifty pounds weight was enough for footing. But I had three hundred pounds mass not a whit reduced by lowered weight; this does things to lifelong reflex habits. I had to lean heavily for the slightest turn, lean back and dig in to slow down, lean far forward to speed up.

I could have drawn a force diagram, but doing it is another matter. How long does it take a baby to learn to walk? This newborn Moon-baby was having to learn while making a forced march, half blind, at the greatest speed he could manage.

So I didn't have time to dwell on the wonder of it all.

Peewee moved into a brisk pace and kept stepping it up. Every little while my leash tightened and I tried still harder to speed up and not fall down.

The Mother Thing warbled at my spine: ("Are you all right, Kip? You seem worried.")

"I'm . . . all right! How . . . about . . . *you?*"

("I'm very comfortable. Don't wear yourself out, dear.")

"Okay!"

Oscar was doing his job. I began to sweat from exertion and naked Sun, but I didn't kick the chin valve until I saw from my blood-color gauge that I was short on air. The system worked perfectly and the joints, under a four-pound pressure, gave no trouble; hours of practice in the pasture was paying off. Presently my one worry was to keep a sharp eye for rocks and ruts. We were into those low hills maybe twenty minutes after H-hour. Peewee's first swerve as we reached rougher ground took me by surprise; I almost fell.

She slowed down and crept forward into a gulch. A few moments later she stopped; I joined her and she touched helmets with me. "How are you doing?"

"Okay."

"Mother Thing, can you hear me?"

("Yes, dear.")

"Are you comfortable? Can you breathe all right?"

("Yes, indeed. Our Kip is taking good care of me.")

"Good. You behave yourself, Mother Thing. Hear me?"

("I will, dear.") Somehow she put an indulgent chuckle into a birdsong.

"Speaking of breathing," I said to Peewee, "let's check your air." I tried to look into her helmet.

She pulled away, then touched again. "I'm all right!"

"So you say." I held her helmet with both hands, found I couldn't see the dials—with sunlight around us, trying to see in was like peering into a well. "What does it read—and don't fib."

"Don't be nosy!"

I turned her around and read her bottle gauges. One read zero; the other was almost full.

I touched helmets. "Peewee," I said slowly, "how many miles have we come?"

"About three, I think. Why?"

"Then we've got more than thirty to go?"

"At least thirty-five. Kip, quit fretting. I know I've got one empty bottle; I shifted to the full one before we stopped."

"One bottle won't take you thirty-five miles."

"Yes, it will . . . because it's *got* to."

"Look, we've got plenty of air. I'll figure a way to get it to you." My mind was trotting in circles, thinking what tools were on my belt, what else I had.

"Kip, you know you can't hook those spare bottles to my suit—so shut up!"

("What's the trouble, darlings? Why are you quarreling?")

"We aren't fighting, Mother Thing. Kip is a worry wart."

("Now, children—")

I said, "Peewee, I admit I can't hook the spares into your suit . . . but I'll jigger a way to recharge your bottle."

"But— How, Kip?"

"Leave it to me. I'll touch only the empty; if it doesn't work, we're no worse off. If it does, we've got it made."

"How long will it take?"

"Ten minutes with luck. Thirty without."

"No," she decided.

"Now, Peewee, don't be sil—"

"I'm not being silly! We aren't safe until we get into the mountains. I can get that far. Then, when we no longer show up like a bug on a plate, we can rest and recharge my empty bottle."

It made sense. "All right."

"Can you go faster? If we reach the mountains before they miss us, I don't think they'll ever find us. If we don't—"

"I can go faster. Except for these pesky bottles."

"Oh." She hesitated. "Do you want to throw one away?"

"Huh? Oh, no, no! But they throw me off balance. I've just missed a tumble a dozen times. Peewee, can you retie them so they don't swing?"

"Oh. Sure."

I had them hung around my neck and down my front—not smart but I had been hurried. Now Peewee lashed them firmly, still in front as my own bottles and the Mother Thing were on my back—no doubt she was finding it as crowded as Dollar Day. Peewee passed clothesline under my belt and around the yoke. She touched helmets. "I hope that's okay."

"Did you tie a square knot?"

She pulled her helmet away. A minute later she touched helmets again. "It was a granny," she admitted in a small voice, "but it's a square knot now."

"Good. Tuck the ends in my belt so that I can't trip, then we'll mush. Are you all right?"

"Yes," she said slowly. "I just wish I had salvaged my gum, old and tired as it was. My throat's awful dry."

"Drink some water. Not too much."

"Kip! It's not a nice joke."

I stared. "Peewee—your suit hasn't any *water?*"

"What? Don't be silly."

My jaw dropped. "But, baby," I said helplessly, "why didn't you fill your tank before we left?"

"What are you talking about? Does your suit have a water tank?"

I couldn't answer. Peewee's suit was for tourists—for those "scenic walks amidst incomparable grandeur on the ancient face of the Moon" that the ads promised. Guided walks, of course, not over a half-hour at a time—they wouldn't put in a water tank; some tourist might choke, or bite the nipple off and half drown in his helmet, or some silly thing. Besides, it was cheaper.

I began to worry about other shortcomings that cheap-jack equipment might have—with Peewee's life depending on it. "I'm sorry," I said humbly. "Look, I'll try to figure out some way to get water to you."

"I doubt if you can. I can't die of thirst in the time it'll take us to get there, so quit worrying. I'm all right. I just wish I had my bubble gum. Ready?"

"Uh . . . ready."

The hills were hardly more than giant folds in lava; we were soon through them, even though we had to take it cautiously over the very rough ground. Beyond them the ground looked flatter than western Kansas, stretching out to a close horizon, with mountains sticking up beyond, glaring in the Sun and silhouetted against a black sky like cardboard cutouts. I tried to figure how far the horizon was, on a thousand-mile radius and a height of eye of six feet—and couldn't do it in my head and wished for my slipstick. But it was awfully close, less than a mile.

Peewee let me overtake her, touched helmets. "Okay, Kip? All right, Mother Thing?"

"Sure."

("All right, dear.")

"Kip, the course from the pass when they fetched me here was east eight degrees north. I heard them arguing and sneaked a peek at their map. So we go back west eight degrees south—that doesn't count the jog to these hills but it's close enough to find the pass. Okay?"

"Sounds swell." I was impressed. "Peewee, were you an Indian scout once? Or Davy Crockett?"

"Pooh! Anybody can read a map"—she sounded pleased. "I want to check compasses. What bearing do you have on Earth?"

I said silently: Oscar, you've let me down. I've been cussing her suit for not having water—and *you* don't have a compass.

(Oscar protested: "Hey, pal, that's unfair! Why would I need a compass at Space Station Two? Nobody told *me* I was going to the Moon.") I said, "Peewee, this suit is for space station work. What use is a compass in space? Nobody told *me* I was going to the Moon."

"But—Well, don't stop to cry about it. You can get your directions by Earth."

"Why can't I use your compass?"

"Don't be silly; it's built into my helmet. Now just a moment—" She faced Earth, moved her helmet back and forth. Then she touched helmets again. "Earth is smacko on northwest . . . that makes the course fifty-three degrees left of there. Try to pick it out. Earth is two degrees wide, you know."

"I knew that before you were born."

"No doubt. Some people require a head start."

"Smart aleck!"

"You were rude first!"

"But—Sorry, Peewee. Let's save the fights for later. I'll spot you the first two bites."

"I won't need them! You don't know how nasty I can—"

"I have some idea."

("Children! Children!")

"I'm sorry, Peewee."

"So am I. I'm edgy. I wish we were *there*."

"So do I. Let me figure the course." I counted degrees using Earth as a yardstick. I marked a place by eye, then tried again judging fifty-three degrees as a proportion of ninety. The results didn't agree, so I tried to spot some stars to help me. They say you can see stars from the Moon even when the Sun is in the sky. Well, you can—but not easily. I had the Sun over my shoulder but was facing Earth, almost three-quarters full, and had the dazzling ground glare as well. The polarizer cut down the glare—and cut out the stars, too.

So I split my guesses and marked the spot. "Peewee? See that sharp peak with sort of a chin on its left profile? That ought to be the course, pretty near."

"Let me check." She tried it by compass, then touched helmets. "Nice going, Kip. Three degrees to the right and you've got it."

I felt smug. "Shall we get moving?"

"Right. We go through the pass, then Tombaugh Station is due west."

It was about ten miles to the mountains; we made short work

of it. You can make time on the Moon—*if* it is flat and *if* you can keep your balance. Peewee kept stepping it up until we were almost flying, long low strides that covered ground like an ostrich—and, do you know, it's easier fast than slow. The only hazard, after I got the hang of it, was landing on a rock or hole or something and tripping. But that was hazard enough because I couldn't pick my footing at that speed. I wasn't afraid of falling; I felt certain that Oscar could take the punishment. But suppose I landed on my back? Probably smash the Mother Thing to jelly.

I was worried about Peewee, too. That cut-rate tourist suit wasn't as rugged as Oscar. I've read about explosive decompression—I never want to see it. Especially not a little girl. But I didn't dare use radio to warn her even though we were probably shielded from Wormface—and if I tugged on my leash I might make her fall.

The plain started to rise and Peewee let it slow us down. Presently we were walking, then we were climbing a scree slope. I stumbled but landed on my hands and got up—one-sixth gravity has advantages as well as hazards. We reached the top and Peewee led us into a pocket in the rocks. She stopped and touched helmets. "Anybody home? You two all right?"

("All right, dear.")

"Sure," I agreed. "A little winded, maybe." That was an understatement but if Peewee could take it, I could.

"We can rest," she answered, "and take it easy from here on. I wanted to get us out of the open as fast as possible. They'll never find us here."

I thought she was right. A wormface ship flying over might spot us, if they could see down as well as up—probably just a matter of touching a control. But our chances were better now. "This is the time to recharge your empty bottle."

"Okay."

None too soon—the bottle which had been almost full had dropped by a third, more like half. She couldn't make it to Tombaugh Station on that—simple arithmetic. So I crossed my fingers and got to work. "Partner, will you untie this cat's cradle?"

While Peewee fumbled at knots, I started to take a drink—then stopped, ashamed of myself. Peewee must be chewing her tongue to work up saliva by now—and I hadn't been able to think of *any* way to get water to her. The tank was inside my helmet and there was no way to reach it without making me—and Mother Thing—dead in the process.

If I ever lived to be an engineer I'd correct that!

I decided that it was idiotic not to drink because she couldn't; the lives of all of us might depend on my staying in the best condition I could manage. So I drank and ate three malted milk tablets and a salt tablet, then had another drink. It helped a lot but I hoped Peewee hadn't noticed. She was busy unwinding clothesline—anyhow it was hard to see into a helmet.

I took Peewee's empty bottle off her back, making darn sure to close her outside stop valve first—there's supposed to be a one-way valve where an air hose enters a helmet but I no longer trusted her suit; it might have more cost-saving shortcomings. I laid the empty on the ground by a full one, looked at it, straightened up and touched helmets. "Peewee, disconnect the bottle on the left side of my back."

"Why, Kip?"

"Who's doing this job?" I had a reason but was afraid she might argue. My lefthand bottle held pure oxygen; the others were oxy-helium. It was full, except for a few minutes of fiddling last night in Centerville. Since I couldn't possibly give her bottle a full charge, the next best thing was to give her a half-charge of straight oxygen.

She shut up and removed it.

I set about trying to transfer pressure between bottles whose connections didn't match. There was no way to do it properly, short of tools a quarter of a million miles away—or over in Tombaugh Station which was just as bad. But I did have adhesive tape.

Oscar's manual called for two first-aid kits. I didn't know what was supposed to be in them; the manual had simply given USAF stock numbers. I hadn't been able to guess what would be useful in an outside kit—a hypodermic needle, maybe, sharp enough to stab through and give a man morphine when he needed it terribly. But since I didn't know, I had stocked inside and outside with bandage, dressings, and a spool of surgical tape.

I was betting on the tape.

I butted the mismatched hose connections together, tore off a scrap of bandage and wrapped it around the junction—I didn't want sticky stuff on the joint; it could foul the operation on a suit. Then I taped the junction, wrapping tightly, working very painstakingly and taping three inches on each side as well as around the joint—if tape could restrain that pressure a few moments, there would still be one deuce of a force trying to drag that joint apart. I didn't want it to pull apart at the first jolt. I used the entire roll.

I motioned Peewee to touch helmets. "I'm about to open the full bottle. The valve on the empty is already open. When you see me start to close the valve on the full one, you close the other one—*fast!* Got it?"

"Close the valve when you do, quickly. Roger."

"Stand by. Get your hand on the valve." I grabbed that lump of bandaged joint in one fist, squeezed as hard as I could, and put my other hand on the valve. If that joint let go, maybe my hand would go with it—but if the stunt failed, little Peewee didn't have long to live. So I really gripped.

Watching both gauges, I barely cracked the valve. The hose quivered; the needle gauge that read "empty" twitched. I opened the valve wide.

One needle swung left, the other right. Quickly they approached half-charge. "Now!" I yelled uselessly and started closing the valve.

And felt that patchwork joint start to give.

The hoses squeezed out of my fist but we lost only a fraction of gas. I found that I was trying to close a valve that was closed tight. Peewee had hers closed. The gauges each showed just short of half full—there was air for Peewee.

I sighed and found I had been holding my breath.

Peewee put her helmet against mine and said very soberly, "Thanks, Kip."

"Charton Drugs service, ma'am—no tip necessary. Let me tidy this mess, you can tie me and we'll go."

"You won't have to carry but one extra bottle now."

"Wrong, Peewee. We may do this stunt five or six times until there's only a whisper left"—or until the tape wears out, I added to myself. The first thing I did was to rewrap the tape on its spool—and if you think that is easy, wearing gloves and with the adhesive drying out as fast as you wind it, try it.

In spite of the bandage, sticky stuff had smeared the connections when the hoses parted. But it dried so hard that it chipped off the bayonet-and-snap joint easily. I didn't worry about the screw-thread joint; I didn't expect to use it on a suit. We mounted Peewee's recharged bottle and I warned her that it was straight oxygen. "Cut your pressure and feed from both bottles. What's your blood color reading?"

"I've been carrying it low on purpose."

"Idiot! You want to keel over? Kick your chin valve! Get into normal range!"

We mounted one bottle I had swiped on my back, tied the other and the oxy bottle on my front, and were on our way.

Earth mountains are predictable; lunar mountains aren't, they've never been shaped by water. We came to a hole too steep to go down other than by rope and a wall beyond I wasn't sure we could climb. With pitons and snap rings and no space suits it wouldn't have been hard in the Rockies—but not the way we were. Peewee reluctantly led us back. The scree slope was worse going down—I backed down on hands and knees, with Peewee belaying the line above me. I wanted to be a hero and belay for her—we had a brisk argument. "Oh, quit being big and male and gallantly stupid, Kip! You've got four big bottles and the Mother Thing and you're top-heavy and I climb like a goat."

I shut up.

At the bottom she touched helmets. "Kip," she said worriedly, "I don't know what to do."

"What's the trouble?"

"I kept a little south of where the crawler came through. I wanted to avoid crossing right where the crawler crossed. But I'm beginning to think there isn't any other way."

"I wish you had told me before."

"But I didn't want them to find us! The way the crawler came is the first place they'll look."

"Mmm . . . yes." I looked up at the range that blocked us. In pictures, the mountains of the Moon look high and sharp and rugged; framed by the lens of a space suit they look simply impossible.

I touched helmets again. "We might find another way—if we had time and air and the resources of a major expedition. We've got to take the route the crawler did. Which way?"

"A little way north . . . I think."

We tried to work north along the foothills but it was slow and difficult. Finally we backed off to the edge of the plain. It made us jumpy but it was a chance we had to take. We walked, briskly but not running, for we didn't dare miss the crawler's tracks. I counted paces and when I reached a thousand I tugged the line; Peewee stopped and we touched helmets. "We've come half a mile. How much farther do you think it is? Or could it possibly be behind us?"

Peewee looked up at the mountains. "I don't know," she admitted. "Everything looks different."

"We're lost?"

"Uh . . . it *ought* to be ahead somewhere. But we've come pretty far. Do you want to turn around?"

"Peewee, I don't even know the way to the post office."

"But what should we *do*?"

"I think we ought to keep going until you are absolutely certain the pass can't be any farther. You watch for the pass and I'll watch for crawler tracks. Then, when you're *certain* that we've come too far, we'll turn back. We can't afford to make short casts like a dog trying to pick up a rabbit's scent."

"All right."

I had counted two thousand more paces, another mile, when Peewee stopped. "Kip? It can't be ahead of us. The mountains are higher and solider than ever."

"You're sure? Think hard. Better to go another five miles than to stop too short."

She hesitated. She had her face pushed up close to her lens while we touched helmets and I could see her frown. Finally she said, "It's not up ahead, Kip."

"That settles it. To the rear, march! 'Lay on, Macduff, and curs'd be him who first cries, "Hold, enough!"' "

"King Lear."

"Macbeth. Want to bet?"

Those tracks were only half a mile behind us—I had missed them. They were on bare rock with only the lightest covering of dust; the Sun had been over my shoulder when we first crossed them, and the caterpillar-tread marks hardly showed—I almost missed them going back.

They led off the plain and straight up into the mountains.

We couldn't possibly have crossed those mountains without following the crawler's trail; Peewee had had the optimism of a child. It wasn't a road; it was just something a crawler on caterpillar treads could travel. We saw places that even a crawler hadn't been able to go until whoever pioneered it set a whopping big blast, backed off and waited for a chunk of mountain to get out of the way. I doubt if Skinny and Fatty carved that goat's path; they didn't look fond of hard work. Probably one of the exploration parties. If Peewee and I had attempted to break a new trail, we'd be there yet, relics for tourists of future generations.

But where a tread vehicle can go, a man can climb. It was no picnic; it was trudge, trudge, trudge, up and up and up—watch for loose rock and mind where you put your feet. Sometimes we belayed with the line. Nevertheless it was mostly just tedious.

When Peewee had used that half-charge of oxygen, we stopped and I equalized pressure again, this time being able to give her only a quarter-charge—like Achilles and the tortoise. I could go on indefinitely giving her half of what was left—if the tape held out. It was in bad shape but the pressure was only half as great and I managed to keep the hoses together until we closed valves.

I should say that *I* had it fairly easy. I had water, food, pills, dexedrine. The last was enormous help; any time I felt fagged I borrowed energy with a pep-pill. Poor Peewee had nothing but air and courage.

She didn't even have the cooling I had. Since she was on a richer mix, one bottle being pure oxygen, it did not take as much flow to keep up her blood-color index—and I warned her not to use a bit more than necessary; she could not afford air for cooling, she had to save it to breathe.

"I know, Kip," she answered pettishly. "I've got the needle jiggling the red light right now. Think I'm a fool?"

"I just want to keep you alive."

"All right, but quit treating me as a child. You put one foot in front of the other. I'll make it."

"Sure you will!"

As for the Mother Thing she always *said* she was all right and she was breathing the air I had (a trifle used), but I didn't know what was hardship to her. Hanging by his heels all day would kill a man; to a bat it is a nice rest—yet bats are our cousins.

I talked with her as we climbed. It didn't matter what; her songs had the effect on me that it has to have your own gang cheering. Poor Peewee didn't even have that comfort, except when we stopped and touched helmets—we still weren't using radio; even in the mountains we were fearful of attracting attention.

We stopped again and I gave Peewee one-eighth of a charge. The tape was in very poor shape afterwards; I doubted if it would serve again. I said, "Peewee, why don't you run your oxy-helium bottle dry while I carry this one? It'll save your strength."

"I'm all right."

"Well, you won't use air so fast with a lighter load."

"You have to have your arms free. Suppose you slip?"

"Peewee, I won't carry it in my arms, My righthand backpack bottle is empty; I'll chuck it. Help me make the change and I'll still be carrying only four—just balanced evenly."

"Sure, I'll help. But I'll carry two bottles. Honest, Kip, the weight isn't anything. But if I run the oxy-helium bottle dry, what would I breathe while you're giving me my next charge?"

I didn't want to tell her that I had doubts about another charge, even in those ever smaller amounts. "Okay, Peewee."

She changed bottles for me; we threw the dead one down a black hole and went on. I don't know how far we climbed nor how long; I know that it seemed like days—though it couldn't have been, not on that much air. During mile after mile of trail we climbed at least eight thousand feet. Heights are hard to guess— but I've seen mountains I knew the heights of. Look it up yourself—the first range east of Tombaugh Station.

There's a lot of climbing, even at one-sixth gee.

It seemed endless because I didn't know how far it was nor how long it had been. We both had watches—under our suits. A helmet ought to have a built-in watch. I should have read Greenwich time from the face of Earth. But I had no experience and most of the time I couldn't see Earth because we were deep in mountains—anyhow I didn't know what time it had been when we left the ship.

Another thing space suits should have is rear-view mirrors. While you are at it, add a window at the chin so that you can see where you step. But of the two, I would take a rear-view mirror. You can't glance behind you; you have to turn your entire body. Every few seconds I wanted to see if they were following us— and I couldn't spare the effort. All that nightmare trek I kept imagining them on my heels, expecting a wormy hand on my shoulder. I listened for footsteps which couldn't be heard in vacuum anyhow.

When you buy a space suit, make them equip it with a rear-view mirror. You won't have Wormface on your trail but it's upsetting to have even your best friend sneak up behind you. Yes, and if you are coming to the Moon, bring a sunshade. Oscar was doing his best and York had done an honest job on the air conditioning—but the untempered Sun is hotter than you would believe and I didn't dare use air just for cooling, any more than Peewee could.

It got hot and stayed hot and sweat ran down and I itched all over and couldn't scratch and sweat got into my eyes and burned. Peewee must have been parboiled. Even when the trail wound through deep gorges lighted only by reflection off the far wall, so dark that we turned on headlamps, I still was hot—and when we curved back into naked sunshine, it was almost unbearable. The temptation to kick the chin valve, let air pour in and cool me, was almost too much. The desire to be cool seemed more important than the need to breathe an hour hence.

If I had been alone, I might have done it and died. But Peewee was worse off than I was. If she could stand it, I *had* to.

I had wondered how we could be so lost so close to human habitation—and how crawly monsters could hide a base only forty miles from Tombaugh Station. Well, I had time to think and could figure it out because I could see the Moon around me.

Compared with the Moon the Arctic is swarming with people. The Moon's area is about equal to Asia—with fewer people than Centerville. It might be a century before anyone explored that plain where Wormface was based. A rocket ship passing over wouldn't notice anything even if camouflage hadn't been used; a man in a space suit would never go there; a man in a crawler would find their base only by accident even if he took the pass we were in and ranged around that plain. The lunar mapping satellite could photograph it and rephotograph, then a technician in London might note a tiny difference on two films. Maybe. Years later somebody might check up—if there wasn't something more urgent to do in a pioneer outpost where *everything* is new and urgent.

As for radar sightings—there were unexplained radar sightings before I was born.

Wormface could sit there, as close to Tombaugh Station as Dallas is to Fort Worth, and not fret, snug as a snake under a house. Too many square miles, not enough people.

Too incredibly many square miles. . . . Our whole world was harsh bright cliffs and dark shadows and black sky, and endless putting one foot in front of the other.

But eventually we were going downhill oftener than up and at weary last we came to a turn where we could see out over a hot bright plain. There were mountains awfully far away; even from our height, up a thousand feet or so, they were beyond the horizon. I looked out over that plain, too dead beat to feel triumphant, then glanced at Earth and tried to estimate due west.

Peewee touched her helmet to mine. "There it is, Kip."

"Where?" She pointed and I caught a glint on a silvery dome.

The Mother Thing trilled at my spine. ("What is it, children?")

"Tombaugh Station, Mother Thing."

Her answer was wordless assurance that we were good children and that she had known that we could do it.

The station may have been ten miles away. Distances were hard to judge, what with that funny horizon and never anything for comparison—I didn't even know how big the dome was. "Peewee, do we dare use radio?"

She turned and looked back. I did also; we were about as alone as could be. "Let's risk it."

"What frequency?"

"Same as before. Space operations. I think."

So I tried. "Tombaugh Station. Come in, Tombaugh Station. Do you read me?" Then Peewee tried. I listened up and down the band I was equipped for. No luck.

I shifted to horn antenna, aiming at the glint of light. No answer.

"We're wasting time, Peewee. Let's start slogging."

She turned slowly away. I could feel her disappointment—I had trembled with eagerness myself. I caught up with her and touched helmets. "Don't let it throw you, Peewee. They can't listen all day for us to call. We see it, now we'll walk it."

"I know," she said dully.

As we started down we lost sight of Tombaugh Station, not only from twists and turns but because we dropped it below the horizon. I kept calling as long as there seemed any hope, then shut it off to save breath and battery.

We were about halfway down the outer slope when Peewee slowed and stopped—sank to the ground and sat still.

I hurried to her. "Peewee!"

"Kip," she said faintly, "could you go get somebody? Please? You know the way now. I'll wait here. Please, Kip?"

"Peewee!" I said sharply. "Get up! You've got to keep moving."

"I c- c- can't!" She began to cry. "I'm so thirsty . . . and my legs—" She passed out.

"Peewee!" I shook her shoulder. "You *can't* quit now! Mother Thing!—you tell her!"

Her eyelids fluttered. "Keep telling her, Mother Thing!" I flopped Peewee over and got to work. Hypoxia hits as fast as a jab on the button. I didn't need to see her blood-color index to know it read DANGER; the gauges on her bottles told me. The oxygen bottles showed empty, the oxy-helium tank was practically so. I closed her exhaust valves, overrode her chin valve with the outside valve and let what was left in the oxy-helium bottle flow into her suit. When it started to swell I cut back the flow and barely cracked one exhaust valve. Not until then did I close stop valves and remove the empty bottle.

I found myself balked by a ridiculous thing.

Peewee had tied me too well; I couldn't reach the knot! I could feel it with my left hand but couldn't get my right hand around; the bottle on my front was in the way—and I couldn't work the knot loose with one hand.

I made myself stop panicking. My knife—of course, my knife! It was an old scout knife with a loop to hang it from a belt, which was where it was. But the map hooks on Oscar's belt were large for it and I had had to force it on. I twisted it until the loop broke.

Then I couldn't get the little blade open. Space-suit gauntlets don't have thumb nails.

I said to myself: Kip, quit running in circles. This is easy. All you have to do is open a knife—and you've *got* to . . . because Peewee is suffocating. I looked around for a sliver of rock, anything that could pinch-hit for a thumb nail. Then I checked my belt.

The prospector's hammer did it, the chisel end of the head was sharp enough to open the blade. I cut the clothesline away.

I was still blocked. I wanted very badly to get at a bottle on my back. When I had thrown away that empty and put the last fresh one on my back, I had started feeding from it and saved the almost-half-charge in the other one. I meant to save it for a rainy day and split it with Peewee. Now was the time—she was out of air, I was practically so in one bottle but still had that half-charge in the other—plus an eighth of a charge or less in the bottle that contained straight oxygen (the best I could hope for in equalizing pressures), I had planned to surprise her with a one-quarter charge of oxy-helium, which would last longer and give more cooling.

A real knight-errant plan, I thought. I didn't waste two seconds discarding it.

I *couldn't* get that bottle off my back!

Maybe if I hadn't modified the backpack for nonregulation bottles I could have done it. The manual says: "Reach over your shoulder with the opposite arm, close stop valves at bottle and helmet, disconnect the shackle—" My pack didn't have shackles; I had substituted straps. But I still don't think you can reach over your shoulder in a pressurized suit and do anything effective. I think that was written by a man at a desk. Maybe he had seen it done under favorable conditions. Maybe he had done it, but was one of those freaks who can dislocate both shoulders. But I'll bet a full charge of oxygen that the riggers around Space Station Two did it for each other as Peewee and I had, or went inside and deflated.

If I ever get a chance, I'll change that. *Everything* you have to do in a space suit should be arranged to do in *front*—valves, shackles, everything, even if it is to affect something in back. We aren't like Wormface, with eyes all around and arms that bend in a dozen places; we're built to work in *front* of us—that goes triple in a space suit.

You need a chin window to let you see what you're doing, too! A thing can look fine on paper and be utterly crumby in the field.

But I didn't waste time moaning; I had a one-eighth charge of oxygen I could reach. I grabbed it.

That poor, overworked adhesive tape was a sorry mess. I didn't bother with bandage; if I could get the tape to stick at all I'd be happy. I handled it as carefully as gold leaf, trying to get it tight, and stopped in the middle to close Peewee's exhaust entirely when it looked as if her suit was collapsing. I finished with trembling fingers.

I didn't have Peewee to close a valve. I simply gripped that haywired joint in one hand, opened Peewee's empty bottle with the other, swung over fast and opened the oxygen bottle wide— jerked my hand across and grabbed the valve of Peewee's bottle and watched those gauges.

The two needles moved toward each other. When they slowed down I started closing her bottle—and the taped joint blew out.

I got that valve closed in a hurry; I didn't lose much gas from Peewee's bottle. But what was left on the supply side leaked away.

I didn't stop to worry; I peeled away a scrap of adhesive, made sure the bayonet-and-snap joint was clean, got that slightly recharged bottle back on Peewee's suit, opened stop valves.

Her suit started to distend. I opened one exhaust valve a crack and touched helmets. "Peewee! Peewee! Can you hear me? Wake up, baby! Mother Thing!—make her wake up!"

"Peewee!"

"Yes, Kip?"

"Wake up! On your feet, Champ! Get up! Honey, *please* get up."

"Huh? Help me get my helmet off . . . I can't *breathe.*"

"Yes, you can. Kick your chin valve—feel it, taste it. Fresh air!"

She tried, feebly; I gave her a quick strong shot, overriding her chin valve from outside. *"Oh!"*

"See? You've got air. You've got lots of air. Now get up."

"Oh, *please,* just let me lie here."

"No, you don't! You're a nasty, mean, spoiled little brat—and if you don't get up, nobody will love you. The Mother Thing won't love you. Mother Thing!—tell her!"

("Stand up, daughter!")

Peewee tried. I helped her, once she was trying. She trembled and clung to me and I kept her from falling. "Mother Thing?" she said faintly. "I did it. You . . . still love me?"

("Yes, darling!")

"I'm dizzy . . . and I don't think I . . . can walk."

"You don't have to, honey," I said gently and picked her up in my arms. "You don't have to walk any farther."

She didn't weigh anything.

The trail disappeared when we were down out of the foothills but the crawler's tracks were sharp in the dust and led due west. I had my air trimmed down until the needle of the blood-color indicator hung at the edge of the danger sector. I held it there, kicking my chin valve only when it swung past into DANGER. I figured that the designer must have left some leeway, the way they do with gasoline gauges. I had long since warned Peewee never to take her eyes off her own indicator and hold it at the danger limit. She promised and I kept reminding her. I pressed her helmet against the yoke of mine, so that we could talk.

I counted paces and every half-mile I told Peewee to call Tombaugh Station. It was over the horizon but they might have a high mast that could "see" a long way.

The Mother Thing talked to her, too—anything to keep her from slipping away again. It saved my strength to have the Mother Thing talk and was good for all of us.

After a while I noticed that my needle had drifted into the red again. I kicked the valve and waited. Nothing happened. I kicked it again and the needle drifted slowly toward the white. "How you fixed for air, Peewee?"

"Just fine, Kip, just fine."

Oscar was yelling at me. I blinked and noticed that my shadow had disappeared. It had been stretched out ahead at an angle to the tracks. The tracks were there but my shadow was not. That made me sore, so I turned around and looked for it. It was behind me.

The darn thing had been hiding. Games!

("That better!" said Oscar.)

"It's hot in here, Oscar."

("You think it's cool out here? Keep your eye on that shadow, bud—and on those tracks.")

"All right, all right! Quit pestering me." I made up my mind that I wouldn't let that shadow get away again. Games it wanted to play, huh?

"There's darn little air in here, Oscar."

("Breathe shallow, chum. We can make it.")

"I'm breathing my socks, now."

("So breathe your shirt.")

"Did I see a ship pass over?"

("How should I know? You're the one with the blinkers.")

"Don't get smart. I'm in no mood to joke."

I was sitting on the ground with Peewee across my knees and Oscar was really shouting—and so was the Mother Thing. ("Get up, you big ape! Get up and *try*.") ("Get up, Kip dear! Only a little way now.")

"I just want to get my wind."

("All right, you've got it. Call Tombaugh Station.")

I said, "Peewee, call Tombaugh Station."

She didn't answer. That scared me and I snapped out of it. "Tombaugh Station, come in! Come in!" I got to my knees and then to my feet. "Tombaugh Station, do you read me? Help! Help!"

A voice answered, "I read you."

"Help! *M'aidez!* I've got a little girl dying! Help!"

Suddenly it sprang up in front of my eyes—great shiny domes, tall towers, radio telescopes, a giant Schmidt camera. I staggered toward it. *"May Day!"*

An enormous lock opened and a crawler came toward me. A voice in my phones said, "We're coming. Stay where you are. Over and out."

A crawler stopped near me. A man got out, came over and touched helmets. I gasped: "Help me get her inside."

I got back: "You've given me trouble, bub. I don't like people who give me trouble." A bigger, fatter man got out behind him.

The smaller man raised a thing like a camera and aimed it at me. That was the last I knew.

Chapter 7

I don't know if they took us all that weary way back in the crawler, or if Wormface sent a ship. I woke up being slapped and was inside, lying down. The skinny one was slapping me—the man the fat one called "Tim." I tried to fight back and found that I couldn't. I was in a straitjacket thing that held me as snugly as a wrapped mummy. I let out a yelp.

Skinny grabbed my hair, jerked my head up, tried to put a big capsule into my mouth.

I tried to bite him.

He slapped me harder and offered me the capsule again. His expression didn't change—it stayed mean.

I heard: "Take it, boy," and turned my eyes. The fat one was on the other side. "Better swallow it," he said. "You got five bad days ahead."

I took it. Not because of the advice but because a hand held my nose and another popped the pill into my mouth when I gasped. Fatty held a cup of water for me to wash it down; I didn't resist that, I needed it.

Skinny stuck a hypodermic needle big enough for a horse into my shoulder. I told him what I thought of him, using words I hardly ever use. The skinny one could have been deaf; the fat one chuckled. I rolled my eyes at him. "You, too," I added weakly. "Squared."

Fatty clucked reprovingly. "You ought to be glad we saved your life." He added, "Though it wasn't my idea, you strike me as a sorry team. *He* wanted you alive."

"Shaddap," Skinny said. "Strap his head."

"Let him break his neck. We better fix our ownselves. *He* won't wait." But he started to obey.

Skinny glanced at his watch. "Four minutes."

The fat one hastily tightened a strap across my forehead, then both moved very fast, swallowing capsules, giving each other hypos. I watched as best I could.

I was back in the ship. The ceiling glowed the same way, the walls looked the same. It was the room the two men used; their beds were on each side and I was strapped to a soft couch between them.

Each hurriedly got on his bed, began zipping up a tight wrapping like a sleeping bag. Each strapped his head in place before completing the process. I was not interested in them. "Hey! What did you do with Peewee?"

The fat man chuckled. "Hear that, Tim? That's a good one."

"Shaddap."

"You—" I was about to sum up Fatty's character but my thoughts got fuzzy and my tongue was thick. Besides, I wanted to ask about the Mother Thing, too.

I did not get out another word. Suddenly I was incredibly heavy and the couch was rock hard.

For a long, long time I wasn't awake or truly asleep. At first I couldn't feel anything but that terrible weight, then I hurt all over and wanted to scream. I didn't have the strength for it.

Slowly the pain went away and I stopped feeling anything. I wasn't a body—just me, no attachments. I dreamed a lot and none of it made sense; I seemed to be stuck in a comic book, the sort P.T.A. meetings pass resolutions against, and the baddies were way ahead no matter what I did.

Once the couch gave a twisting lurch and suddenly I had a body, one that was dizzy. After a few ages I realized vaguely that I had gone through a skew-flip turn-over. I had known, during lucid moments, that I was going somewhere, very fast, at terribly high acceleration. I decided solemnly that we must be halfway and tried to figure out how long two times eternity was. It kept coming out eighty-five cents plus sales tax; the cash register rang "NO SALE" and I would start over.

Fats was undoing my head strap. It stuck and skin came away. "Rise and shine, bub. Time's awastin'."

A croak was all I managed. The skinny one was unwrapping me. My legs sagged apart and hurt. "Get up!"

I tried and didn't make it. Skinny grabbed one of my legs and started to knead it.

I screamed.

"Here, lemme do that," said Fatty. "I used to be a trainer."

Fats did know something about it. I gasped when his thumbs dug into my calves and he stopped. "Too rough?" I couldn't answer. He went on massaging me and said almost jovially, "Five days at eight gravities ain't no joy ride. But you'll be okay. Got the needle, Tim?"

The skinny one jabbed me in my left thigh. I hardly felt it. Fats pulled me to a sitting position and handed me a cup. I thought it was water; it wasn't and I choked and sprayed. Fats waited, then gave it to me again. "Drink some, this time." I did.

"Okay, up on your feet. Vacation is over."

The floor swayed and I had to grab him until it stopped. "Where are we?" I said hoarsely.

Fats grinned, as if he knew an enormously funny joke. "Pluto, of course. Lovely place, Pluto. A summer resort."

"Shaddap. Get him moving."

"Shake it up, kid. You don't want to keep *him* waiting."

Pluto! It couldn't be; nobody could get that far. Why, they hadn't even attempted Jupiter's moons yet. Pluto was so much farther that—

My brain wasn't working. The experience just past had shaken me so badly that I couldn't accept the fact that the experience itself proved that I was wrong.

But Pluto!

I wasn't given time to wonder; we got into space suits. Although I hadn't known, Oscar was there, and I was so glad to see him that I forgot everything else. He hadn't been racked, just tossed on the floor. I bent down (discovering charley horses in every muscle) and checked him. He didn't seem hurt.

"Get in it," Fats ordered. "Quit fiddlin'."

"All right," I answered almost cheerfully. Then I hesitated. "Say—I haven't any air."

"Take another look," said Fats. I looked. Charged oxy-helium bottles were on the backpack. "Although," he continued, "if we didn't have orders from *him*, I wouldn't give you a whiff of Limburger. You made us for two bottles—*and* a rock hammer—*and* a line that cost four ninety-five, earthside. Sometime," he stated without rancor, "I'm gonna take it out of your hide."

"Shaddap," said Skinny. "Get going."

I spread Oscar open, wriggled in, clipped on the blood-color reader, and zipped the gaskets. Then I stood up, clamped my helmet, and felt better just to be inside. "Tight?"

("Tight!" Oscar agreed.)

"We're a long way from home."

("But we got air! Chin up, pal.")

Which reminded me to check the chin valve. Everything was working. My knife was gone and so were the hammer and line, but those were incidentals. We were tight.

I followed Skinny out with Fats behind me. We passed Wormface in the corridor—or a wormface—but while I shuddered, I had Oscar around me and felt that he couldn't get at me. Another creature joined us in the air lock and I had to look twice to realize that it was a wormface in a space suit. The material was smooth and did not bulge the way ours did. It looked like a dead tree trunk with bare branches and heavy roots, but the supreme improvement was its "helmet"—a glassy smooth dome. One-way glass, I suppose; I couldn't see in. Cased that way, a wormface was grotesquely ridiculous rather than terrifying. But I stood no closer than I had to.

Pressure was dropping and I was busy wasting air to keep from swelling up. It reminded me of what I wanted most to know: what had happened to Peewee and the Mother Thing. So I keyed my radio and announced: "Radio check. Alfa, Bravo, Coca—"

"Shaddap that nonsense. We want you, we'll tell you."

The outer door opened and I had my first view of Pluto.

I don't know what I expected. Pluto is so far out that they can't get decent photographs even at Luna Observatory. I had read articles in the *Scientific American* and seen pictures in *LIFE*, bone-stelled to look like photographs, and remembered that it was approaching its summer—if "summer" is the word for warm enough to melt air. I recalled that because they had announced that Pluto was showing an atmosphere as it got closer to the Sun.

But I had never been much interested in Pluto—too few facts and too much speculation, too far away and not desirable real estate. By comparison the Moon was a choice residential suburb. Professor Tombaugh (the one the station was named for) was working on a giant electronic telescope to photograph it, under a Guggenheim grant, but he had a special interest; he discovered Pluto years before I was born.

The first thing I noticed as the door was opening was *click . . .*

click . . . click—and a fourth click, in my helmet, as Oscar's heating units all cut in.

The Sun was in front of me—I didn't realize what it was at first; it looked no bigger than Venus or Jupiter does from Earth (although much brighter). With no disc you could be sure of, it looked like an electric arc.

Fats jabbed me in the ribs. "Snap out of your hop."

A drawbridge joined the door to an elevated roadway that led into the side of a mountain about two hundred yards away. The road was supported on spidery legs two or three feet high up to ten or twelve, depending on the lay of the land. The ground was covered with snow, glaringly white even under that pinpoint Sun. Where the stilts were longest, about halfway, the viaduct crossed a brook.

What sort of "water" was that? Methane? What was the "snow"? Solid ammonia? I didn't have tables to tell me what was solid, what was liquid, and what was gas at whatever hellish cold Pluto enjoyed in the "summer." All I knew was that it got so cold in its winter that it didn't have any gas or liquid—just vacuum, like the Moon.

I was glad to hurry. A wind blew from our left and was not only freezing that side of me in spite of Oscar's best efforts, it made the footing hazardous—I decided it would be far safer to do that forced march on the Moon again than to fall into that "snow." Would a man struggle before he shattered himself and his suit, or would he die as he hit?

Adding to hazard of wind and no guard rail was traffic, spacesuited wormfaces. They moved at twice our speed and shared the road the way a dog does a bone. Even Skinny resorted to fancy footwork and I had three narrow squeaks.

The way continued into a tunnel; ten feet inside a panel snapped out of the way as we got near it. Twenty feet beyond was another; it did the same and closed behind us. There were about two dozen panels, each behaving like fast-acting gate valves, and the pressure was a little higher after each. I couldn't see what operated them although it was light in the tunnel from glowing ceilings. Finally we passed through a heavy-duty air lock, but the pressure was already taken care of and its doors stood open. It led into a large room.

Wormface was inside. *The* Wormface, I think, because he spoke in English: "Come!" I heard it through my helmet. But I couldn't be sure it was he as there were others around and I would have less trouble telling wart hogs apart.

Wormface hurried away. He was not wearing a space suit and

I was relieved when he turned because I could no longer see his squirming mouth; but it was only a slight improvement as it brought into sight his rearview eye.

We were hard put to keep up. He led us down a corridor, to the right through another open double set of doors, and finally stopped suddenly just short of a hole in the floor about like a sewer manhole. "Undress it!" he commanded.

Fats and Skinny had their helmets open, so I knew it was safe, in one way. But in every other way I wanted to stay inside Oscar— as long as Wormface was around.

Fats unclamped my helmet. "Out of that skin, bub. Snap it up!" Skinny loosened my belt and they quickly had the suit off even though I hindered.

Wormface waited. As soon as I was out of Oscar he pointed at the hole. "Down!"

I gulped. That hole looked as deep as a well and less inviting.

"Down," he repeated. "Now."

"Do it, bub," Fats advised. "Jump or be pushed. Get down that hole before he gets annoyed."

I tried to run.

Wormface was around me and chivvying me back before I was well started. I slammed on the brakes and backed up—glanced behind just in time to turn a fall into a clumsy jump.

It was a long way to the bottom. Landing did not hurt the way it would have on Earth, but I turned an ankle. That didn't matter; I wasn't going anywhere; the hole in the ceiling was the only exit.

My cell was about twenty feet square. It was, I suppose, carved out of solid rock, although there was no way to tell as the walls and floor and ceiling were the same elephant hide used in the ship. A lighting panel covered half the ceiling and I could have read if I'd had anything to read. The only other detail was a jet of water that splashed out of a hole in the wall, landed in a depression the size of a washtub, and departed for parts unknown.

The place was warm, which was well as there was nothing resembling bed or bedclothes. I had already concluded that I might be here quite a while and was wondering about eating and sleeping.

I decided I was tired of this nonsense. I had been minding my own business, out back of my own house. Everything else was Wormface's fault! I sat down on the floor and thought about slow ways to kill him.

I finally gave up that foolishness and wondered about Peewee and the Mother Thing. Were they here? Or were they dead somewhere between the mountains and Tombaugh Station? Thinking it over glumly, I decided that poor little Peewee was best off if she had never wakened from that second coma. I wasn't sure about the Mother Thing because I didn't know enough about her—but in Peewee's case I was sure.

Well, there was a certain appropriateness to the fix I was in; a knight-errant usually lands in a dungeon at some point. But by rights, the maiden fair ought to be imprisoned in a tower in the same castle. Sorry, Peewee; as a knight-errant, I'm a good soda jerk. Or jerk. "His strength is as the strength of ten because his heart is pure."

It wasn't funny.

I got tired of punishing myself and looked to see what time it was—not that it mattered. But a prisoner is traditionally expected to scratch marks on the wall, tallying the days he's been in, so I thought I might as well start. My watch was on my wrist but not running and I couldn't start it. Maybe eight gees was too much for it, even though it was supposed to be shockproof, waterproof, magnetism-proof, and immune to un-American influences.

After a while I lay down and went to sleep.

I was awakened by a clatter.

It was a ration can hitting the floor and the fall hadn't helped it, but the key was on it and I got it open—corned beef hash and very good, too. I used the empty can to drink from—the water might be poisoned, but did I have a choice?—and then washed the can so that it wouldn't smell.

The water was warm. I took a bath.

I doubt if many American citizens during the past twenty years have ever needed a bath as much as I did. Then I washed my clothes. My shirt, shorts, and socks were wash-and-wear synthetics; my slacks were denim and took longer to dry, but I didn't mind: I just wished that I had one of the two hundred bars of Skyway Soap that were home on the floor of my closet. If I had known I was coming to Pluto, I would have brought one.

Washing clothes caused me to take inventory. I had a handkerchief, sixty-seven cents in change, a dollar bill so sweat-soaked and worn that it was hard to make out Washington's picture, a mechanical pencil stamped "Jay's Drive-In—the thickest malts in town!"—a canard; *I* make the thickest—and a grocery list I should have taken care of for Mother but hadn't because of that silly air conditioner in Charton's Drugstore. It wasn't as bedraggled as the dollar bill because it had been in my shirt pocket.

I lined up my assets and looked at them. They did not look like a collection that could be reworked into a miracle weapon with which I would blast my way out, steal a ship, teach myself to pilot it, and return triumphantly to warn the President and save the country. I rearranged them and they still didn't.

I was correct. They weren't.

I woke up from a terrible nightmare, remembered where I was, and wished I were back in the nightmare. I lay there feeling sorry for myself and presently tears started welling out of my eyes while my chin trembled. I had never been badgered "not to be a crybaby"; Dad says there is nothing wrong with tears; it's just that they are socially not acceptable—he says that in some cultures weeping is a social grace. But in Horace Mann Grammar School being a crybaby was no asset; I gave it up years ago. Besides, it's exhausting and gets you nowhere. I shut off the rain and took stock.

My action list ran like this:

1. Escape from this cell.

2. Find Oscar, suit up.

3. Go outdoors, steal a ship, head home—if I could figure out how to gun it.

4. Figure out a weapon or stratagem to fight off the worm-faces or keep them busy while I sneaked out and grabbed a ship. Nothing to it. Any superman capable of teleportation and other assorted psionic tricks could do it. Just be sure the plan is foolproof and that your insurance is paid up.

5. Crash priority: make sure, before bidding farewell to the romantic shores of exotic Pluto and its friendly colorful natives, that neither Peewee nor the Mother Thing is here—if they are, take them along—because, contrary to some opinions, it is better to be a dead hero than a live louse. Dying is messy and inconvenient but even a louse dies someday no matter what he will do to stay alive and he is forever having to explain his choice. The gummed-up spell that I had had at the hero business had shown that it was undesirable work but the alternative was still less attractive.

The fact that Peewee knew how to gun those ships, or that the Mother Thing could coach me, did not figure. I can't prove that, but I know.

Footnote: after I learned to run one of their ships, could I do so at eight gravities? That may simply call for arch supports for a wormface but I knew what eight gees did to me. Automatic pilot? If so, would it have directions on it, in English? (Don't be silly, Clifford!)

Subordinate footnote: how long would it take to get home at one gravity? The rest of the century? Or just long enough to starve to death?

6. Occupational therapy for the lulls when I went stale on the problems. This was important in order to avoid coming apart at the seams. O. Henry wrote stories in prison, St. Paul turned out his strongest epistles incarcerated in Rome, Hitler wrote Mein Kampf in jail—next time I would bring a typewriter and paper. This time I could work out magic squares and invent chess problems. Anything was better than feeling sorry for myself. Lions put up with zoos and wasn't I smarter than a lion? Some, anyhow?

And so to work—One: how to get out of this hole?

I came up with a straight-forward answer: there wasn't any way. The cell was twenty feet on a side with a ceiling twelve feet high; the walls were as smooth as a baby's cheek and as impervious as a bill collector. The other features were the hole in the ceiling, which ran about six feet still higher, the stream of water and its catch basin, and a glowing area in the ceiling. For tools I had the stuff previously listed (a few ounces of nothing much, nothing sharp, nor explosive, nor corrosive), my clothes, and an empty tin can.

I tested how high I could jump. Even a substitute guard needs springs in his legs—I touched the ceiling. That meant a gravity around one-half gee I hadn't been able to guess, as I had spent an endless time under one-sixth gravity followed by a few eons at eight gees; my reflexes had been mistreated.

But, although I could touch the ceiling, I could neither walk on it nor levitate. I could get that high, but there was nothing a mouse could cling to.

Well, I could rip my clothes and braid a rope. Was there anything near the hole on which to catch it? All I could recall was smooth floor. But suppose it did catch? What next? Paddle around in my skin until Wormface spotted me and herded me back down, this time with no clothes? I decided to postpone the rope trick until I worked out that next step which would confound Wormface and his tribe.

I sighed and looked around. All that was left was that jet of water and the floor basin that caught it.

There is a story about two frogs trapped in a crock of cream. One sees how hopeless it is, gives up and downs. The other is too stupid to know he's licked; he keeps on paddling. In a few hours he has churned so much butter that it forms an island, on which he floats, cool and comfortable, until the milkmaid comes and chucks him out.

That water spilled in and ran out. Suppose it didn't run out?

I explored the bottom of the catch basin. The drain was large by our standards, but I thought I could plug it. Could I stay afloat while the room filled up, filled the hole above, and pushed me out the spout? Well, I could find out, I had a can.

The can looked like a pint and a "pint's a pound the world 'round" and a cubic foot of water weighs (on Earth) a little over sixty pounds. But I had to be sure. My feet are eleven inches long; they've been that size since I was ten—I took a lot of ribbing until I grew up to them. I marked eleven inches on the floor with two pennies. It turns out that a dollar bill is two and a half inches wide and quarter is a smidgeon under an inch. Shortly I knew the dimensions of room and can pretty accurately.

I held the can under the stream, letting it fill and dumping it fast, while I ticked off cans of water on my left hand and counted seconds. Eventually I calculated how long it would take to fill the room. I didn't like the answer, so I did it over.

It would take fourteen hours to fill the room and the hole above, plus an hour to allow for crude methods. Could I stay afloat that long?

You're darn tootin' I could!—if I had to. And I had to. There isn't any limit to how long a man can float if he doesn't panic.

I balled my slacks and stuffed them in the drain. I almost lost them, so I wrapped them around the can and used the bundle as a cork. It stayed put and I used the rest of my clothes to caulk it. Then I waited, feeling cocky. Maybe the flood would create the diversion I needed for the rest of the caper. Slowly the basin filled.

The water got about an inch below floor level and stopped.

A pressure switch, I suppose. I should have known that creatures who could build eight-gee, constant-boost ships would design plumbing to "fail-safe." I wish we could.

I recovered my clothes, all but one sock, and spread them to dry. I hoped the sock would foul a pump or something but I doubted it; they were good engineers.

I never really believed that story about the frogs.

Another can was tossed down—roast beef and soggy potatoes. It was filling but I began to long for peaches. The can was stenciled "Available for subsidized resale on Luna" which made it possible that Skinny and Fatty had come by this food honestly. I wondered how they liked sharing their supplies? No doubt they did so only because Wormface had twisted their arms. Which made me wonder why Wormface wanted me alive? I was in favor of it but couldn't see why he was. I decided to call each can a "day" and let the emptics be my calendar.

Which reminded me that I had not worked out how long it would take to get home on a one-gee boost, if it turned out that I could not arrange automatic piloting at eight gees. I was stymied on getting out of the cell, I hadn't even nibbled at what I would do if I did get out (correction: *when* I got out), but I could work ballistics.

I didn't need books. I've met people, even in this day and age, who can't tell a star from a planet and who think of astronomical distances simply as "big." They remind me of those primitives who have just four numbers: one, two, three, and "many." But any tenderfoot Scout knows the basic facts and a fellow bitten by the space bug (such as myself) usually knows a number of figures.

"Mother very thoughtfully made a jelly sandwich under no protest." Could you forget that after saying it a few times? Okay, lay it out so:

Mother	MERCURY	$.39
Very	VENUS	$.72
Thoughtfully	TERRA	$1.00
Made	MARS	$1.50
A	ASTEROIDS	(assorted prices, unimportant)
Jelly	JUPITER	$5.20
Sandwich	SATURN	$9.50
Under	URANUS	$19.00
No	NEPTUNE	$30.00
Protest	PLUTO	$39.50

The "prices" are distances from the Sun in astronomical units. An A.U. is the mean distance of Earth from Sun, 93,000,000 miles. It is easier to remember one figure that everybody knows and some little figures than it is to remember figures in millions and billions. I use dollar signs because a figure has more flavor if

I think of it as money—which Dad considers deplorable. Some way you must remember them, or you don't know your own neighborhood.

Now we come to a joker. The list says that Pluto's distance is thirty-nine and a half times Earth's distance. But Pluto and Mercury have very eccentric orbits and Pluto's is a dilly; its distance varies almost *two billion* miles, more than the distance from the Sun to Uranus. Pluto creeps to the orbit of Neptune and a hair inside, then swings way out and stays there a couple of centuries—it makes only four round trips in a thousand years.

But I had seen that article about how Pluto was coming into its "summer." So I knew it was close to the orbit of Neptune now, and would be for the rest of my life—my life expectancy in Centerville; I didn't look like a preferred risk here. That gave an easy figure—30 astronomical units.

Acceleration problems are simple $s=\frac{1}{2}\ at^2$; distance equals half the acceleration times the square of elapsed time. If astrogation were that simple any sophomore could pilot a rocket ship— the complications come from gravitational fields and the fact that everything moves fourteen directions at once. But I could disregard gravitational fields and planetary motions; at the speeds a wormface ship makes neither factor matters until you are very close. I wanted a rough answer.

I missed my slipstick. Dad says that anyone who can't use a slide rule is a cultural illiterate and should not be allowed to vote. Mine is a beauty—a K&E 20" Log-log Duplex Decitrig. Dad surprised me with it after I mastered a ten-inch polyphase. We ate potato soup that week—but Dad says you should always budget luxuries first. I knew where it was. Home on my desk.

No matter. I had figures, formula, pencil and paper.

First a check problem. Fats had said "Pluto," "five days," and "eight gravities."

It's a two-piece problem; accelerate for half time (and half distance); do a skew-flip and decelerate the other half time (and distance). You can't use the whole distance in the equation, as "time" appears as a square—it's a parabolic.

Was Pluto in opposition? Or quadrature? Or conjunction? Nobody looks at Pluto—so why remember where it is on the ecliptic? Oh, well, the average distance was 30 A.U.s—that would give a close-enough answer.

Half that distance, in feet, is: $\frac{1}{2} \times 30 \times 93{,}000{,}000 \times 5280$.

Eight gravities is: 8×32.2 ft./sec./sec.—speed increases by 258 feet per second every second up to skew-flip and decreases just as fast thereafter. So—

$$\frac{1}{2} \times 30 \times 93{,}000{,}000 \times 5280 = \frac{1}{2} \times 8 \times 32.2 \times t^2$$

—and you wind up with the time for half the trip, in seconds. Double that for full trip. Divide by 3600 to get hours; divide by 24 and you have days. On a slide rule such a problem takes forty seconds, most of it to get your decimal point correct. It's as easy as computing sales tax.

It took me at least an hour and almost as long to prove it, using a different sequence— and a third time, because the answers didn't match (I had forgotten to multiply by 5280, and had "miles" on one side and "feet" on the other—a no-good way to do arithmetic)—then a fourth time because my confidence was shaken. I tell you, the slide rule is the greatest invention since girls.

But I got a proved answer. Five and a half days. I was on Pluto.

Or maybe Neptune—

No, on Neptune I would not be able to jump to a twelve-foot ceiling; Pluto alone matched all facts. So I erased and computed the trip at one gravity, with turnover.

Fifteen days.

It seemed to me that it ought to take at least eight times as long at one gee as at eight—more likely sixty-four. Then I was glad I had bulled my way through analytical geometry, for I made a rough plot and saw the trouble. Squared time *cut down* the advantage—because the more boost, the shorter the trip, and the shorter the trip the less time in which to use the built-up speed. To cut time in half, you need four times as much boost; to cut it to a quarter, you need *sixteen* times the boost, and so on. This way lies bankruptcy.

To learn that I could get home in about two weeks at one gravity cheered me. I couldn't starve in two weeks. If I could steal a ship. If I could run it. If I could climb out of this hole. If—

Not "if," but "when!" I was too late for college this year; fifteen more days wouldn't matter.

I had noticed, in the first problem, the speed we had been making at skew-flip. More than eleven thousand miles per second.

That's a nice speed, even in space. It made me think. Consider the nearest star, Proxima Centauri, four and three-tenths light-years away, the distance you hear so often on quiz shows. How long at eight gees?

The problem was the same sort but I had to be careful about decimal points; the figures mount up. A lightyear is—I had forgotten. So multiply 186,000 miles per second (the speed of light) by the seconds in a year (365.25 × 24 × 3600) and get—5,880,000,000,000 miles

—multiply that by 4.3 and get—

25,284,000,000,000

Call it twenty-five trillion miles. Whew!

It works out to a year and five months—not as long as a trip around the Horn only last century.

Why, these monsters had star travel!

I don't know why I was surprised; it had been staring me in the face. I had assumed that Wormface had taken me to his home planet, that he was a Plutonian, or Plutocrat, or whatever the word is. But he *couldn't* be.

He breathed air. He kept his ship warm enough for me. When he wasn't in a hurry, he cruised at one gee, near enough. He used lighting that suited my eyes. Therefore he came from the sort of planet I came from.

Proxima Centauri is a double star, as you know if you do crossword puzzles, and one is a twin for our own Sun—size, temperature, special pattern. Is it a fair guess that it has a planet like Earth? I had a dirty hunch that I knew Wormface's home address.

I knew where he *didn't* come from. Not from a planet that runs a couple of centuries in utter airlessness with temperatures pushing absolute zero, followed by a "summer" in which some gases melt but water is solid rock and even Wormface has to wear a space suit. Nor from anywhere in our system, for I was sure as taxes that Wormface felt at home only on a planet like ours. Never mind the way he looked; spiders don't look like us but they like the things we like—there must be a thousand spiders in our houses for every one of us.

Wormface and his kin would like Earth. My fear was that they liked it too much.

I looked at that Proxima Centauri problem and saw something else. The turn-over speed read 1,110,000 miles per second, six times the speed of light. Relativity theory says that's impossible.

I wanted to talk to Dad about it. Dad reads everything from

The Anatomy of Melancholy to Acta Mathematica and *Paris-Match* and will sit on a curbstone separating damp newspapers wrapped around garbage in order to see continued-on-page-eight. Dad would haul down a book and we'd look it up. Then he would try four or five more with other opinions. Dad doesn't hold with the idea that it-must-be-true-or-they-wouldn't-have-printed-it; he doesn't consider *any* opinion sacred—it shocked me the first time he took out a pen and changed something in one of my math books.

Still, even if speed-of-light was a limit, four or five years wasn't impossible, or even impractical. We've been told for so long that star trips, even to the nearest stars, would take generations that we may have a wrong slant. A mile of lunar mountains is a long way but a trillion miles in empty space may not be.

But what was Wormface doing on Pluto?

If you were invading another solar system, how would you start? I'm not joking; a dungeon on Pluto is no joke and I never laughed at Wormface. Would you just barge in, or toss your hat in first? They seemed far ahead of us in engineering but they couldn't have known that ahead of time. Wouldn't it be smart to build a supply base in that system in some spot nobody ever visited?

Then you could set up advance bases, say on an airless satellite of a likely-looking planet, from which you could scout the surface of the target planet. If you lost your scouting base, you would pull back to main base and work out a new attack.

Remember that while Pluto is a long way off to us, it was only five days from Luna for Wormface. Think about World War II, back when speeds were slow. Main Base is safely out of reach (U.S.A./Pluto) but only about five days from advance base (England/The Moon) which is three hours from theater-of-operations (France-Germany/Earth). That's a slow way to operate but it worked for the Allies in World War II.

I just hoped it would not work for Wormface's gang.

Though I didn't see anything to prevent it.

Somebody chucked down another can—spaghetti and meat balls. If it had been canned peaches, I might not have had the fortitude to do what I did next, which was to use it for a hammer before I opened it. I beat an empty can into a flat narrow shape and beat a point on it, which I sharpened on the edge of the catch basin. When I was through, I had a dagger—not a good one, but it made me feel less helpless.

Then I ate. I felt sleepy and went to sleep in a warm glow. I was still a prisoner but I had a weapon of sorts and I believed that I had figured out what I was up against. Getting a problem analyzed is two-thirds of solving it. I didn't have nightmares.

The next thing tossed down the hole was Fats.

Skinny landed on him seconds later. I backed off and held my dagger ready. Skinny ignored me, picked himself up, looked around, went to the water spout and got a drink. Fats was in no shape to do anything; his breath was knocked out.

I looked at him and thought what a nasty parcel he was. Then I thought, oh, what the deuce!—he had massaged me when I needed it. I heaved him onto his stomach and began artificial respiration. In four or five pushes his motor caught and he was able to breathe. He gasped, "That's enough!"

I backed off, got my knife out. Skinny was sitting against a wall, ignoring us. Fats looked at my feeble weapon and said, "Put that away, kid. We're bosom buddies now."

"We are?"

"Yeah. Us human types had better stick together." He sighed wretchedly. "After all we done for him! That's gratitude."

"What do you mean?" I demanded.

"Huh?" said Fats. "Just what I said. *He* decided he could do without us. So Annie doesn't live here any more."

"Shaddap," the skinny one said flatly.

Fats screwed his face into a pout. "*You* shaddap," he said peevishly. "I'm tired of that. It's shaddap here, shaddap there, all day long—and look where we are."

"Shaddap, I said."

Fats shut up. I never did find out what had happened, because Fats seldom gave the same explanation twice. The older man never spoke except for that tiresome order to shut up, or in monosyllables even less helpful. But one thing was clear: they had lost their jobs as assistant gangsters, or fifth columnists, or whatever you call a human being who would stooge against his own race. Once Fats said, "Matter of fact, it's *your* fault."

"Mine?" I dropped my hand to my tin-can knife.

"Yours. If you hadn't butted in, *he* wouldn't have got sore."

"I didn't do anything."

"Says you. You swiped his two best prizes, that's all, and held *him* up when *he* planned to high-tail it back here."

"Oh. But that wasn't your fault."

"So I told him. *You* try telling him. Take your hand away from that silly nail file." Fats shrugged. "Like I always say, let bygones be bygones."

I finally learned the thing I wanted most to know. About the fifth time I brought up the matter of Peewee, Fats said, "What d'you want to know about the brat for?"

"I just want to know whether she's alive or dead."

"Oh, she's alive. Leastwise she was last time I seen her."

"When was that?"

"You ask too many questions. Right here."

"She's *here*?" I said eagerly.

"That's what I said, wasn't it? Around everywhere and always underfoot. Living like a princess, if you ask me." Fats picked his teeth and frowned. "Why *he* should make a pet out of her and treat us the way he did, beats me. It ain't right."

I didn't think so, either, but for another reason. The idea that gallant little Peewee was the spoiled darling of Wormface I found impossible to believe. There was some explanation—or Fats was lying. "You mean he doesn't have her locked up?"

"What's it get him? Where's she gonna go?"

I pondered that myself. Where *could* you go?—when to step outdoors was suicide. Even if Peewee had her space suit (and that, at least, was probably locked up), even if a ship was at hand and empty when she got outside, even if she could get into it, she still wouldn't have a "ship's brain," the little gadget that served as a lock. "What happened to the Mother Thing?"

"The what?"

"The —" I hesitated. "Uh, the non-human who was in my space suit with me. You must know, you were there. Is she alive? Is she here?"

But Fats was brooding. "Them bugs don't interest me none," he said sourly and I could get no more out of him.

But Peewee was alive (and a hard lump in me was suddenly gone). She was here! Her chances, even as a prisoner, had been enormously better on the Moon; nevertheless I felt almost ecstatic to know that she was near. I began thinking about ways to get a message to her.

As for Fats' insinuation that she was playing footy with Wormface, it bothered me not at all. Peewee was unpredictable and sometimes a brat and often exasperating, as well as conceited, supercilious, and downright childish. But she would be burned alive rather than turn traitor. Joan of Arc had not been made of sterner stuff.

* * *

We three kept uneasy truce. I avoided them, slept with one eye open, and tried not to sleep unless they were asleep first, and I always kept my dagger at hand. I did not bathe after they joined me; it would have put me at a disadvantage. The older one ignored me, Fats was almost friendly. He pretended not to be afraid of my puny weapon, but I think he was. The reason I think so comes from the first time we were fed. Three cans dropped from the ceiling; Skinny picked up one, Fats got one, but when I circled around to take the third, Fats snatched it.

I said, "Give me that, please."

Fats grinned. "What makes you think this is for you, sonny boy?"

"Uh, three cans, three people."

"So what? I'm feeling a mite hungry. I don't hardly think I can spare it."

"I'm hungry, too. Be reasonable."

"Mmmm—" He seemed to consider it. "Tell you what. I'll sell it to you."

I hesitated. It had a shifty logic; Wormface couldn't walk into Lunar Base commissary and buy these rations; probably Fats or his partner had bought them. I wouldn't mind signing I.O.U.s—a hundred dollars a meal, a thousand, or a million; money no longer meant anything. Why not humor him?

No! If I gave in, if I admitted I had to dicker with him for my prison rations, he would own me. I'd wait on him hand and foot, do anything he told me, just to eat.

I let him see my tin dagger. "I'll fight you for it."

Fats glanced at my hand and grinned broadly. "Can't you take a joke?" He tossed me the can. There was no trouble at feeding times after that.

We lived like that "Happy Family" you sometimes see in traveling zoos: a lion caged with a lamb. It is a startling exhibit but the lamb has to be replaced frequently. Fats liked to talk and I learned things from him, when I could sort out truth from lies. His name—so he said—was Jacques de Barre de Vigny ("Call me 'Jock.'") and the older man was Timothy Johnson—but I had a hunch that their real names could be learned only by inspecting post office bulletin boards. Despite Jock's pretense of knowing everything, I soon decided that he knew nothing about Wormface's origin and little about his plans and purposes. Wormface did not seem the sort to discuss things with "lower animals"; he would simply make use of them, as we use horses.

Jock admitted one thing readily. "Yeah, we put the snatch on the brat. There's no uranium on the Moon; those stories are just to get suckers. We were wasting our time—and a man's got to eat, don't he?"

I didn't make the obvious retort; I wanted information. Tim said, "Shaddap!"

"Aw, what of it, Tim? You worried about the F.B.I.? You think the Man can put the arm on you—*here*?"

"Shaddap, I said."

"Happens I feel like talking. So blow it." Jock went on, "It was easy. The brat's got more curiosity than seven cats. *He* knew she was coming and when." Jock looked thoughtful. "*He* always knows—he's got lots of people working for him, some high up. All I had to do was be in Luna City and get acquainted—I made the contact because Tim here ain't the fatherly type, the way I am. I get to talking with her, I buy her a coke, I tell her about the romance of hunting uranium on the Moon and similar hogwash. Then I sigh and say it's too bad I can't show her the mine of my partner and I. That's all it took. When the tourist party visited Tombaugh Station, she got away and sneaked out the lock—she worked that part out her ownself. She's sly, that one. All we had to do was wait where I told her—didn't even have to be rough with her until she got worried about taking longer for the crawler to get to our mine than I told her." Jock grinned. "She fights pretty well for her weight. Scratched me some."

Poor little Peewee! Too bad she hadn't drawn and quartered him! But the story sounded true, for it was the way Peewee would behave—sure of herself, afraid of no one, unable to resist any "educational" experience.

Jock went on, "It wasn't the brat *he* wanted. *He* wanted her old man. Had some swindle to get him to the Moon, didn't work." Jock grinned sourly. "That was a bad time, things ain't good when *he* don't have his own way. But he had to settle for the brat. Tim here pointed out to him he could trade."

Tim chucked in one word which I took as a general denial. Jock raised his eyebrows. "Listen to vinegar puss. Nice manners, ain't he?"

Maybe I should have kept quiet since I was digging for facts, not philosophy. But I've got Peewee's failing myself; when I don't understand, I have an unbearable itch to know why. I didn't (and don't) understand what made Jock tick. "Jock? Why did you do it?"

"Huh?"

"Look, you're a human being." (At least he looked like one.) "As you pointed out, we humans had better stick together. How could you bring yourself to kidnap a little girl—and turn her over to *him?*"

"Are you crazy, boy?"

"I don't think so."

"You talk crazy. Have you ever tried not doing something *he* wanted? Try it some time."

I saw his point. Refusing Wormface would be like a rabbit spitting in a snake's eye—as I knew too well. Jock went on, "You got to understand the other man's viewpoint. Live and let live, I always say. We got grabbed while we were messin' around, lookin' for carnotite—and after that, we never stood no chance. You can't fight City Hall, that gets you nowhere. So we made a dicker—we run his errands, he pays us in uranium."

My faint sympathy vanished. I wanted to throw up. "And you got paid?"

"Well . . . you might say we got time on the books."

I looked around our cell. "You made a bad deal."

Jock grimaced, looking like a sulky baby. "Maybe so. But be reasonable, kid. You got to cooperate with the inevitable. These boys are moving in—they got what it takes. You seen that yourself. Well, a man's got to look out for number one, don't he? It's a cinch nobody else will. Now I seen a case like this when I was no older than you and it taught me a lesson. Our town had run quietly for years, but the Big Fellow was getting old and losing his grip . . . whereupon some boys from St. Louis moved in. Things were confused for a while. A man had to know which way to jump—else he woke up wearing a wooden overcoat, like as not. Those that seen the handwriting made out; those that didn't . . . well, it don't do no good to buck the current, I always say. That makes sense, don't it?"

I could follow his "logic"—provided you accepted his "live louse" standard. But he had left out a key point. "Even so, Jock, I don't see how you could do that to a little girl."

"Huh? I just explained how we couldn't help it."

"But you *could.* Even allowing how hard it is to face up to *him* and refuse orders, you had a perfect chance to duck out."

"Wha' d'you mean?"

"He sent you to Luna City to find her, you said so. You've got a return-fare benefit—I know you have, I know the rules. All you had to do was sit tight, where *he* couldn't reach you—and take the next ship back to Earth. You didn't have to do his dirty work."

"But—"

I cut him off. "Maybe you couldn't help yourself, out in a lunar desert. Maybe you wouldn't feel safe even inside Tombaugh Station. But when he sent you into Luna City, you had your chance. You didn't have to steal a little girl and turn her over to a—a bug-eyed *monster!*"

He looked baffled, then answered quickly. "Kip, I like you. You're a good boy. But you ain't smart. You don't understand."

"I think I do!"

"No, you don't." He leaned toward me, started to put a hand on my knee; I drew back. He went on, "There's something I didn't tell you . . . for fear you'd think I was a—well, a zombie, or something. They operated on us."

"Huh?"

"They operated on us," he went on glibly. "They planted bombs in our heads. Remote control, like a missile. A man gets out of line . . . *he* punches a button—*blooie!* Brains all over the ceiling." He fumbled at the nape of his neck. "See the scar? My hair's getting kind o' long . . . but if you look close I'm sure you'll see it; it can't 'ave disappeared entirely. See it?"

I started to look. I might even have been sold on it—I had been forced to believe less probable things lately. Tim cut short my suspended judgment with one explosive word.

Jock flinched, then braced himself and said, "Don't pay any attention to *him!*"

I shrugged and moved away. Jock didn't talk the rest of that "day." That suited me.

The next "morning" I was roused by Jock's hand on my shoulder. "Wake up, Kip! Wake up!"

I groped for my toy weapon. "It's over there by the wall," Jock said, "but it ain't ever goin' to do you any good *now.*"

I grabbed it. "What do you mean? Where's Tim?"

"You didn't wake up?"

"Huh?"

"This is what I've been scared of. Cripes, boy! I just had to talk to somebody. You slept through it?"

"Through what? And where's Tim?"

Jock was shivering and sweating. "They blue-lighted us, that's what. They took Tim." He shuddered. "I'm glad it was him. I thought—well, maybe you've noticed I'm a little stout . . . they like fat."

"What do you mean? What have they done with him?"

"Poor old Tim. He had his faults, like anybody, but—He's soup, by now . . . that's what." He shuddered again. "They like soup—bones and all."

"I don't believe it. You're trying to scare me."

"So?" He looked me up and down. "They'll probably take you next. Son, if you're smart, you'll take that letter opener of yours over to that horse trough and open your veins. It's better that way."

I said, "Why don't you? Here, I'll lend it to you."

He shook his head and shivered. "I ain't smart."

I don't know what became of Tim. I don't know whether the wormfaces ate people, or not. (You can't say "cannibal." We may be mutton, to them.) I wasn't especially scared because I had long since blown all fuses in my "scare" circuits.

What happens to my body after I'm through with it doesn't matter to me. But it did to Jock; he had a phobia about it. I don't think Jock was a coward; cowards don't even try to become prospectors on the Moon. He believed his theory and it shook him. He halfway admitted that he had more reason to believe it than I had known. He had been to Pluto once before, so he said, and other men who had come along, or been dragged, on that trip hadn't come back.

When feeding time came—two cans—he said he wasn't hungry and offered me his rations. That "night" he sat up and kept himself awake. Finally I just had to go to sleep before he did.

I awoke from one of those dreams where you can't move. The dream was correct; sometime not long before, I had surely been blue-lighted.

Jock was gone.

I never saw either of them again.

Somehow I missed them . . . Jock at least. It was a relief not to have to watch all the time, it was luxurious to bathe. But it gets mighty boring, pacing your cage alone.

I have no illusions about them. There must be well over three billion people I would rather be locked up with. But they were *people*.

Tim didn't have anything else to recommend him; he was as coldly vicious as a guillotine. But Jock had some slight awareness of right and wrong, or he wouldn't have tried to justify himself. You might say he was just weak.

But I don't hold with the idea that to understand all is to forgive all; you follow that and first thing you know you're sentimental over murderers and rapists and kidnappers and forgetting their victims. That's wrong. I'll weep over the likes of Peewee, not over criminals whose victims they are. I missed Jock's talk but if there were some way to drown such creatures at birth, I'd take my turn as executioner. That goes double for Tim.

If they ended up as soup for hobgoblins, I couldn't honestly be sorry—even though it might be my turn tomorrow.

As soup, they probably had their finest hour.

Chapter 8

I was jarred out of useless brain-cudgeling by an explosion, a sharp *crack*—a bass rumble—then a *whoosh!* of reduced pressure. I bounced to my feet—anyone who has ever depended on a space suit is never again indifferent to a drop in pressure.

I gasped, "What the deuce!"

Then I added, "Whoever is on watch had better get on the ball—or we'll *all* be breathing thin cold stuff." No oxygen outside, I was sure—or rather the astronomers were and I didn't want to test it.

Then I said, "Somebody bombing us? I hope.

"Or was it an earthquake?"

This was not an idle remark. That *Scientific American* article concerning "summer" on Pluto had predicted "sharp isostatic readjustments" as the temperature rose—which is a polite way of saying, "Hold your hats! Here comes the chimney!"

I was in an earthquake once, in Santa Barbara; I didn't need a booster shot to remember what every Californian knows and others learn in one lesson: when the ground does a jig, *get outdoors!*

Only I couldn't.

I spent two minutes checking whether adrenalin had given me the strength to jump eighteen feet instead of twelve. It hadn't. That was all I did for a half-hour, if you don't count nail biting.

Then I heard my name! "Kip! Oh, Kip!"

"Peewee!" I screamed. "Here! *Peewee!*"

Silence for an eternity of three heartbeats—"Kip?"

"Down HERE!"

"Kip? Are you down this hole?"

"*Yes!* Can't you see me?" I saw her head against the light above.

"Uh, I can now. Oh, Kip, I'm so *glad!*"

"Then why are you crying? So am I!"

"I'm not crying," she blubbered. "Oh Kip . . . *Kip.*"

"Can you get me out?"

"Uh—" She surveyed that drop. "Stay where you are."

"Don't go 'way!" She already had.

She wasn't gone two minutes; it merely seemed like a week. Then she was back and the darling had a nylon rope!

"Grab on!" she shrilled.

"Wait a sec. How is it fastened?"

"I'll pull you up."

"No, you won't—or we'll *both* be down here. Find somewhere to belay it."

"I can lift you."

"Belay it! *Hurry!*"

She left again, leaving an end in my hands. Shortly I heard very faintly: *"On belay!"*

I shouted, "Testing!" and took up the slack. I put my weight on it—it held. *"Climbing!"* I yelled, and followed the final "g" up the hole and caught it.

She flung herself on me, an arm around my neck, one around Madame Pompadour, and both of mine around her. She was even smaller and skinnier than I remembered. "Oh, Kip, it's been *just awful.*"

I patted her bony shoulder blades. "Yeah, I know. What do we do now? Where's W—"

I started to say, "Where's Wormface?" but she burst into tears.

"Kip—I think she's *dead!*"

My mind skidded—I was a bit stir-crazy anyhow. "Huh? Who?"

She looked as amazed as I was confused. "Why, the Mother Thing."

"Oh." I felt a flood of sorrow. "But, honey, are you *sure?* She was talking to me all right up to the last—and *I* didn't die."

"What in the world are you talk—Oh. I don't mean *then,* Kip; I mean *now.*"

"Huh? She was *here?*"

"Of course. Where else?"

Now that's a silly question, it's a big universe. I had decided long ago that the Mother Thing couldn't be here—because Jock had brushed off the subject. I reasoned that Jock would either have said that she was here or have invented an elaborate lie, for the pleasure of lying. Therefore she wasn't on his list—perhaps he had never seen her save as a bulge under my suit.

I was so sure of my "logic" that it took a long moment to throw off prejudice and accept fact. "Peewee," I said, gulping, "I feel like I'd lost my own mother. Are you sure?"

" 'Feel as if,' " she said automatically. "I'm not *sure* sure . . . but she's outside—so she *must* be dead."

"Wait a minute. If she's outside, she's wearing a space suit? Isn't she?"

"No, no! She hasn't had one—not since they destroyed her ship."

I was getting more confused. "How did they bring her in here?"

"They just sacked her and sealed her and carried her in. Kip—*what do we do now?*"

I knew several answers, all of them wrong—I had already considered them during my stretch in jail. "Where is Wormface? Where are all the wormfaces?"

"Oh. All dead. I think."

"I hope you're right." I looked around for a weapon and never saw a hallway so bare. My toy dagger was only eighteen feet away but I didn't feel like going back down for it. "What makes you think so?"

Peewee had reason to think so. The Mother Thing didn't look strong enough to tear paper but what she lacked in beef she made up in brains. She had done what I had tried to do: reasoned out a way to take them all on. She had not been able to hurry because her plan had many factors all of which had to mesh at once and many of them she could not influence; she had to wait for the breaks.

First, she needed a time when there were few wormfaces around. The base was indeed a large supply dump and space port and transfer point, but it did not need a large staff. It had been un- usually crowded the few moments I had seen it, because our ship was in.

Second, it also had to be when no ships were in because she couldn't cope with a ship—she couldn't get at it.

Third, H-Hour had to be while the wormfaces were feeding. They all ate together when there were few enough not to have to use their mess hall in relays—crowded around one big tub and sopping it up, I gathered—a scene out of Dante. That would place all her enemies on one target, except possibly one or two on engineering or communication watches.

"Wait a minute!" I interrupted. "You said they were *all* dead?"

"Well . . . I don't know. I haven't seen any."

"Hold everything until I find something to fight with."

"But—"

"First things first, Peewee."

Saying that I was going to find a weapon wasn't finding one. That corridor had nothing but more holes like the one I had been down—which was why Peewee had looked for me there; it was one of the few places where she had not been allowed to wander at will. Jock had been correct on one point: Peewee—and the Mother Thing—had been star prisoners, allowed all privileges except freedom . . . whereas Jock and Tim and myself had been third-class prisoners and/or soup bones. It fitted the theory that Peewee and the Mother Thing were hostages rather than ordinary P.W.s.

I didn't explore those holes after I looked down one and saw a human skeleton—maybe they got tired of tossing food to him. When I straightened up Peewee said, "What are you shaking about?"

"Nothing. Come on."

"I want to see."

"Peewee, every second counts and we've done nothing but yak. Come on. Stay behind me."

I kept her from seeing the skeleton, a major triumph over that little curiosity box—although it probably would not have affected her much; Peewee was sentimental only when it suited her.

"Stay behind me" had the correct gallant sound but it was not based on reason. I forgot that attack could come from the rear—I should have said: "Follow me and watch behind us."

She did anyway. I heard a squeal and whirled around to see a wormface with one of those camera-like things aimed at me. Even though Tim had used one on me I didn't realize what it was; for a moment I froze.

But not Peewee. She launched herself through the air, attacking with both hands and both feet in the gallant audacity and utter recklessness of a kitten.

That saved me. Her attack would not have hurt anything but another kitten but it mixed him up so that he didn't finish what he was doing, namely paralyzing or killing me; he tripped over her and went down.

And I stomped him. With my bare feet I stomped him, landing on that lobster-horror head with both feet.

His head *crunched*. It felt awful.

It was like jumping on a strawberry box. It splintered and crunched and went to pieces. I cringed at the feel, even though I was in an agony to fight, to kill. I trampled worms and hopped away, feeling sick. I scooped up Peewee and pulled her back, as anxious to get clear as I had been to join battle seconds before.

I hadn't killed it. For an awful moment I thought I was going to have to wade back in. Then I saw that while it was alive, it did not seem aware of us. It flopped like a chicken freshly chopped, then quieted and began to move purposefully.

But it couldn't see. I had smashed its eyes and maybe its ears—but certainly those terrible eyes.

It felt around the floor carefully, then got to its feet, still undamaged except that its head was a crushed ruin. It stood still, braced tripod-style by that third appendage, and felt the air. I pulled us back farther.

It began to walk. Not toward us or I would have screamed. It moved away, ricocheted off a wall, straightened out, and went back the way we had come.

It reached one of those holes they used for prisoners, walked into it and dropped.

I sighed, and realized that I had been holding Peewee too tightly to breathe. I put her down.

"There's your weapon," she said.

"Huh?"

"On the floor. Just beyond where I dropped Madame Pompadour. The gadget." She went over, picked up her dolly, brushed away bits of ruined wormface, then took the camera-like thing and handed it to me. "Be careful. Don't point it toward you. Or me."

"Peewee," I said faintly, "don't you ever have an attack of nerves?"

"Sure I do. When I have leisure for it. Which isn't now. Do you know how to work it?"

"No. Do you?"

"I think so. I've seen them and the Mother Thing told me about them." She took it, handling it casually but not pointing it at either of us. "These holes on top—uncover one of them, it stuns. If you uncover them all, it kills. To make it work you push it *here*."

She did and a bright blue light shot out, splashed against the wall. "The light doesn't do anything," she added. "It's for aiming. I hope there wasn't anybody on the other side of that wall. No, I hope there was. You know what I mean."

It looked like a cockeyed 35 mm camera, with a lead lens— one built from an oral description. I took it, being very cautious where I pointed it, and looked at it. Then I tried it—full power, by mistake.

The blue light was a shaft in the air and the wall where it hit glowed and began to smoke. I shut it off.

"You wasted power," Peewee chided. "You may need it later."

"Well, I had to try it. Come on, let's go."

Peewee glanced at her Mickey Mouse watch—and I felt irked that it had apparently stood up when my fancy one had not. "There's very little time, Kip. Can't we assume that only this one escaped?"

"What? We certainly *cannot!* Until we're sure that all of them are dead, we can't do *anything* else. Come on."

"But—Well, I'll lead. I know my way around, you don't."

"No."

"Yes!"

So we did it her way; she led and carried the blue-light projector while I covered the rear and wished for a third eye, like a wormface. I couldn't argue that my reflexes were faster when they weren't, and she knew more than I did about our weapon.

But it's graveling, just the same.

The base was huge; half that mountain must have been honeycombed. We did it at a fast trot, ignoring things as complicated as museum exhibits and twice as interesting, simply making sure that no wormface was anywhere. Peewee ran with the weapon at the ready, talking twenty to the dozen and urging me on.

Besides an almost empty base, no ships in, and the wormfaces feeding, the Mother Thing's plan required that all this happen shortly before a particular hour of the Plutonian night.

"Why?" I panted.

"So she could signal her people, of course."

"But—" I shut up. I had wondered about the Mother Thing's people but didn't even know as much about her as I did about Wormface—except that she was everything that made her the Mother Thing. Now she was dead—Peewee said that she was outside without a space suit, so she was surely dead; that little soft warm thing wouldn't last two seconds in that ultra-arctic weather. Not to mention suffocation and lung hemorrhage. I choked up.

Of course, Peewee might be wrong. I had to admit that she rarely was—but this might be one of the times . . . in which case we would find her. But if we didn't find her, she was outside and— "Peewee, do you know where my space suit is?"

"Huh? Of course. Right next to where I got this." She patted the nylon rope, which she had coiled around her waist and tied with a bow.

"Then the second we are sure that we've cleaned out the wormfaces I'm going outside and look for her!"

"Yes, yes! But we've got to find *my* suit, too. I'm going with you."

No doubt she would. Maybe I could persuade her to wait in the tunnel out of that bone-freezing wind. "Peewee, why did she have to send her message at night? To a ship in a rotation-period orbit? Or is there—"

My words were chopped off by a rumble. The floor shook in that loose-bearing vibration that frightens people and animals alike. We stopped dead. "What was that?" Peewee whispered.

I swallowed. "Unless it's part of this rumpus the Mother Thing planned—"

"It isn't. I think."

"It's a quake."

"An earthquake?"

"A Pluto quake. Peewee, we've got to get out of here!"

I wasn't thinking about *where*—you don't in a quake. Peewee gulped. "We can't bother with earthquakes; we haven't time. Hurry, Kip, hurry!" She started to run and I followed, gritting my teeth. If Peewee could ignore a quake, so could I—though it's like ignoring a rattlesnake in bed.

"Peewee . . . Mother Thing's people . . . is their ship in orbit around Pluto?"

"What? Oh, no, no! They're not in a ship."

"Then why at night? Something about the Heaviside layers here? How far away is their base?" I was wondering how far a man could walk here. We had done almost forty miles on the Moon. Could we do forty blocks here? Or even forty yards? You could insulate your feet, probably. But that wind—"Peewee, they don't *live* here, do they?"

"What? Don't be silly! They have a nice planet of their own. Kip, if you keep asking foolish questions, we'll be too late. Shut up and listen."

I shut up. What follows I got in snatches as we ran, and some of it later. When the Mother Thing had been captured, she had lost ship, space clothing, communicator, everything; Wormface had destroyed it all. There had been treachery, capture through violation of truce while parleying. "He grabbed her when they were supposed to be under a King's 'X'" was Peewee's indignant description, "and that's not fair! He had promised."

Treachery would be as natural in Wormface as venom in a Gila monster; I was surprised that the Mother Thing had risked a palaver with him. It left her a prisoner of ruthless monsters equipped with ships that made ours look like horseless carriages, weapons which started with a "death ray" and ended heaven knows where, plus bases, organization, supplies.

She had only her brain and her tiny soft hands.

Before she could use the rare combination of circumstances necessary to have any chance at all she had to replace her communicator (I think of it as her "radio" but it was more than that) and she had to have weapons. The only way she could get them was to build them.

She had nothing, not a bobby pin—only that triangular ornament with spirals engraved on it. To build anything she had to gain access to a series of rooms which I would describe as electronics labs—not that they looked like the bench where I jiggered with electronics, but electron-pushing has its built-in logic. If electrons are to do what you want them to, components have to look pretty much a certain way, whether built by humans, wormfaces, or the Mother Thing. A wave guide gets its shape from the laws of nature, an inductance has its necessary geometry, no matter who the technician is.

So it looked like an electronics lab—a very good one. It had gear I did not recognize, but which I felt I could understand if I had time. I got only a glimpse.

The Mother Thing spent many, many hours there. She would not have been permitted there, even though she was a prisoner-at-large with freedom in most ways and anything she wanted, including private quarters with Peewee. I think that Wormface was afraid of her, even though she was a prisoner—he did not want to offend her unnecessarily.

She got the run of their shops by baiting their cupidity. Her people had many things that wormfaces had not—gadgets, inventions, conveniences. She began by inquiring why they did a thing this way rather than another way which was so much more efficient? A tradition? Or religious reasons?

When asked what she meant she looked helpless and protested that she couldn't *explain*—which was a shame because it was simple and so easy to build, too.

Under close chaperonage she built something. The gadget worked. Then something else. Presently she was in the labs daily, making things for her captors, things that delighted them. She always delivered; the privilege depended on it.

But each gadget involved parts she needed herself.

"She sneaked bits and pieces into her pouch," Peewee told me. "They never knew exactly what she was doing. She would use five of a thing and the sixth would go into her pouch."

"Her pouch?"

"Of course. That's where she hid the 'brain' the time she and I swiped the ship. Didn't you know?"

"I didn't know she had a pouch."

"Well, neither did they. They watched to see she didn't carry anything out of the shop—and she never did. Not where it showed."

"Uh, Peewee, is the Mother Thing a marsupial?"

"Huh? Like possums? You don't have to be a marsupial to have a pouch. Look at squirrels, they have pouches in their cheeks."

"Mmm, yes."

"She sneaked a bit now and a bit then, and I swiped things, too. During rest time she worked on them in our room."

The Mother Thing had not slept all the time we had been on Pluto. She worked long hours publicly, making things for wormfaces—a stereo-telephone no bigger than a pack of cigarettes, a tiny beetle-like arrangement that crawled all over anything it was placed on and integrated the volume, many other things. But during hours set apart for rest she worked for herself, usually in darkness, those tiny fingers busy as a blind watchmaker's.

She made two bombs and a long-distance communicator-and-beacon.

I didn't get all this tossed over Peewee's shoulder while we raced through the base; she simply told me that the Mother Thing had managed to build a radio-beacon and had been responsible for the explosion I had felt. And that we must hurry, hurry, *hurry!*

"Peewee," I said, panting. "What's the rush? If the Mother Thing is outside, I want to bring her in—her body, I mean. But you act as if we had a deadline."

"We do!"

The communicator-beacon had to be placed outside at a particular local time (the Plutonian day is about a week—the astronomers were right again) so that the planet itself would not
blanket the beam. But the Mother Thing had no space suit. They
had discussed having Peewee suit up, go outside, and set the
beacon—it had been so designed that Peewee need only trigger it.
But that depended on locating Peewee's space suit, then breaking
in and getting it after the wormfaces were disposed of.

They had never located it. The Mother Thing had said
serenely, singing confident notes that I could almost hear ringing
in my head: ("Never mind, dear. I can go out and set it myself.")

"Mother Thing! You *can't!*" Peewee had protested. "It's *cold*
out there."

("I shan't be long.")

"You won't be able to *breathe*."

("It won't be necessary, for so short a time.")

That settled it. In her own way, the Mother Thing was as hard
to argue with as Wormface.

The bombs were built, the beacon was built, a time approached when all factors would match—no ship expected, few
wormfaces, Pluto faced the right way, feeding time for the staff—
and they still did not know where Peewee's suit was—if it had not
been destroyed. The Mother Thing resolved to go ahead.

"But she told me, just a few hours ago when she let me know
that today was the day, that if she did not come back in ten minutes or so, that she hoped I could find my suit and trigger the
beacon—if she hadn't been able to." Peewee started to cry. "That
was the f- f- first time she admitted that she wasn't sure she could
do it!"

"Peewee! Stop it! Then what?"

"I waited for the explosions—they came, right together—and
I started to search, places I hadn't been allowed to go. But I
couldn't find my suit! Then I found you and—oh, Kip, she's been
out there almost an hour!" She looked at her watch. "There's only
about twenty minutes left. If the beacon isn't triggered by then,
she's had all her trouble and died for n- n- nothing! She wouldn't
like that."

"Where's my suit!"

We found no more wormfaces—apparently there was only one on
duty while the others fed. Peewee showed me a door, air-lock
type, behind which was the feeding chamber—the bomb may

have cracked that section for gas-tight doors had closed themselves when the owners were blown to bits. We hurried past.

Logical as usual, Peewee ended our search at my space suit. It was one of more than a dozen human-type suits—I wondered how much soup those ghouls ate. Well, they wouldn't eat again! I wasted no time; I simply shouted, "Hi, Oscar!" and started to suit up.

("Where you been, chum?")

Oscar seemed in perfect shape. Fats' suit was next to mine and Tim's next to it; I glanced at them as I stretched Oscar out, wondering whether they had equipment I could use. Peewee was looking at Tim's suit. "Maybe I can wear this."

It was much smaller than Oscar, which made it only nine sizes too big for Peewee. "Don't be silly! It'd fit you like socks on a rooster. Help me. Take off that rope, coil it and clip it to my belt."

"You won't need it. The Mother Thing planned to take the beacon out the walkway about a hundred yards and sit it down. If she didn't manage it, that's all you do. Then twist the stud on top."

"Don't argue! How much time?"

"Yes, Kip. Eighteen minutes."

"Those winds are strong," I added. "I may need the line." The Mother Thing didn't weigh much. If she had been swept off, I might need a rope to recover her body. "Hand me that hammer off Fats' suit."

"Right away!"

I stood up. It felt good to have Oscar around me. Then I remembered how *cold* my feet got, walking in from the ship. "I wish I had asbestos boots."

Peewee looked startled. "Wait right here!" She was gone before I could stop her. I went on sealing up while I worried—she hadn't even stopped to pick up the projector weapon. Shortly I said, "Tight, Oscar?"

("Tight, boy!")

Chin valve okay, blood-color okay, radio—I wouldn't need it—water—The tank was dry. No matter, I wouldn't have time to grow thirsty. I worked the chin valve, making the pressure low because I knew that pressure outdoors was quite low.

Peewee returned with what looked like ballet slippers for a baby elephant. She leaned close to my face plate and shouted, "They wear these. Can you get them on?" It seemed unlikely, but I forced them over my feet like badly fitting socks. I stood up and found that they improved traction; they were clumsy but not hard to walk in.

A minute later we were standing at the exit of the big room I had first seen. Its air-lock doors were closed now as a result of the Mother Thing's other bomb, which she had placed to blow out the gate-valve panels in the tunnel beyond. The bomb in the feeding chamber had been planted by Peewee who had then ducked back to their room. I don't know whether the Mother Thing timed the two bombs to go off together, or triggered them by remote-control—nor did it matter; they had made a shambles of Worm-face's fancy base.

Peewee knew how to waste air through the air lock. When the inner door opened I shouted, "Time?"

"Fourteen minutes." She held up her watch.

"Remember what I said, just stay here. If anything moves, blue-light it first and ask questions afterwards."

"I remember."

I stepped in and closed the inner door, found the valve in the outer door, waited for pressure to equalize.

The two or three minutes it took that big lock to bleed off I spent in glum thought. I didn't like leaving Peewee alone. I *thought* all wormfaces were dead, but I wasn't sure. We had searched hastily; one could have zigged when we zagged—they were so fast.

Besides that, Peewee had said, "I remember," when she should have said, "Okay, Kip, I will." A slip of the tongue? That flea-hopping mind made "slips" only when it wanted to. There is a world of difference between "Roger" and "Wilco."

Besides I was doing this for foolish motives. Mostly I was going out to recover the Mother Thing's body—folly, because after I brought her in, she would spoil. It would be kinder to leave her in natural deep-freeze.

But I couldn't bear that—it was cold out there and I couldn't leave her out in the cold. She had been so little and warm . . . so alive. I had to bring her in where she could get warm.

You're in bad shape when your emotions force you into acts which you know are foolish.

Worse still, I was doing this in a reckless rush because the Mother Thing had wanted that beacon set before a certain second, now only twelve minutes away, maybe ten. Well, I'd do it, but what sense was it? Say her home star is close by—oh, say it's

Proxima Centauri and the wormfaces came from somewhere farther. Even if her beacon works—it still takes over four years for
her S.O.S. to reach her friends!

This might have been okay for the Mother Thing. I had an impression that she lived a very long time; waiting a few years for
rescue might not bother her. But Peewee and I were not creatures
of her sort. We'd be dead before that speed-of-light message
crawled to Proxima Centauri. I was glad that I had seen Peewee
again, but I knew what was in store for us. Death, in days, weeks,
or months at most, from running out of air, or water, or food—or a
wormface ship might land before we died—which meant one un-
holy sabbat of a fight in which, if we were lucky, we would die
quickly.

No matter how you figured, planting that beacon was merely
"carrying out the deceased's last wishes"—words you hear at fu-
nerals. Sentimental folly.

The outer door started to open. *Ave*, Mother Thing! *Nos
morituri—*

It was *cold* out there, biting cold, even though I was not yet in the
wind. The glow panels were still working and I could see that the
tunnel was a mess; the two dozen fractional-pressure stops had
ruptured like eardrums. I wondered what sort of bomb could be
haywired from stolen parts, kept small enough to conceal two in a
body pouch along with some sort of radio rig, and nevertheless
have force enough to blow out those panels. The blast had rattled
my teeth, several hundred feet away in solid rock.

The first dozen panels were blown inwards. Had she set it off
in the middle of the tunnel? A blast that big would fling her away
like a feather! She must have planted it there, then come inside
and triggered it—then gone back through the lock just as I had.
That was the only way I could see it.

It got colder every step. My feet weren't too cold yet, those
clumsy mukluks were okay; the wormfaces understood insulation.
"Oscar, you got the fires burning?"

("Roaring, chum. It's a cold night.")

"You're telling me!"

Just beyond the outermost burst panel, I found her.

She had sunk forward, as if too tired to go on. Her arms
stretched in front of her and, on the floor of the tunnel not quite
touched by her tiny fingers, was a small round box about the size
ladies keep powder in on dressing tables.

Her face was composed and her eyes were open except that nictitating membranes were drawn across as they had been when I had first seen her in the pasture back of our house, a few days or weeks or a thousand years ago. But she had been hurt then and looked it; now I half expected her to draw back those inner lids and sing a welcome.

I touched her.

She was hard as ice and much colder.

I blinked back tears and wasted not a moment. She wanted that little box placed a hundred yards out on the causeway and the bump on top twisted—and she wanted it done in the next six or seven minutes. I scooped it up. "Righto, Mother Thing! On my way!"

("Get cracking, chum!")

("Thank you, dear Kip. . . .")

I don't believe in ghosts. I had heard her sing thank-you so many times that the notes echoed in my head.

A few feet away at the mouth of the tunnel, I stopped. The wind hit me and was so cold that the deathly chill in the tunnel seemed summery. I closed my eyes and counted thirty seconds to give time to adjust to starlight while I fumbled on the windward side of the tunnel at a slanting strut that anchored the causeway to the mountain, tied my safety line by passing it around the strut and snapping it back on itself. I had known that it was night outside and I expected the causeway to stand out as a black ribbon against the white "snow" glittering under a skyful of stars. I thought I would be safer on that windswept way if I could see its edges—which I couldn't by headlamp unless I kept swinging my shoulders back and forth—clumsy and likely to throw me off balance or slow me down.

I had figured this carefully; I didn't regard this as a stroll in the garden—not at night, not on Pluto! So I counted thirty seconds and tied my line while waiting for eyes to adjust to starlight. I opened them.

And I couldn't see a darned thing!

Not a star. Not even the difference between sky and ground. My back was to the tunnel and the helmet shaded my face like a sunbonnet; I should have been able to see the walkway. Nothing.

I turned the helmet and saw something that accounted both for black sky and the quake we had felt—an active volcano. It may have been five miles away or fifty, but I could not doubt what it was—a jagged, angry red scar low in the sky.

But I didn't stop to stare. I switched on the headlamp, splashed it on the righthand windward edge, and started a clumsy trot, keeping close to that side, so that if I stumbled I would have the entire road to recover in before the wind could sweep me off. That wind scared me. I kept the line coiled in my left hand and paid it out as I went, keeping it fairly taut. The coil felt stiff in my fingers.

The wind not only frightened me, it *hurt*. It was a cold so intense that it felt like flame. It burned and blasted, then numbed. My right side, getting the brunt of it, began to go and then my left side hurt more than the right.

I could no longer feel the line. I stopped, leaned forward and got the coil in the light from the headlamp—that's another thing that needs fixing! the headlamp should swivel.

The coil was half gone, I had come a good fifty yards. I was depending on the rope to tell me; it was a hundred-meter climbing line, so when I neared its end I would be as far out as the Mother Thing had wanted. Hurry, Kip!

("Get cracking, boy! It's cold out here.")

I stopped again. *Did I have the box?*

I couldn't feel it. But the headlamp showed my right hand clutched around it. Stay there, fingers! I hurried on, counting steps. One! Two! Three! Four! . . .

When I reached forty I stopped and glanced over the edge, saw that I was at the highest part where the road crossed the brook and remembered that it was about midway. That brook—methane, was it?—was frozen solid, and I *knew* that the night was cold.

There were a few loops of line on my left arm—close enough. I dropped the line, moved cautiously to the middle of the way, eased to my knees and left hand, and started to put the box down.

My fingers wouldn't unbend.

I forced them with my left hand, got the box out of my fist. That diabolical wind caught it and I barely saved it from rolling away. With both hands I set it carefully upright.

("Work your fingers, bud. Pound your hands together!")

I did so. I could tighten the muscles of my forearms, though it was tearing agony to flex fingers. Clumsily steadying the box with my left hand, I groped for the little knob on top.

I couldn't feel it but it turned easily once I managed to close my fingers on it; I could see it turn.

It seemed to come to life, to purr. Perhaps I heard vibration, through gloves and up my suit; I certainly couldn't have felt it, not the shape my fingers were in. I hastily let go, got awkwardly to my feet and backed up, so that I could splash the headlamp on it without leaning over.

I was through, the Mother Thing's job was done, and (I hoped) before deadline. If I had had as much sense as the ordinary doorknob, I would have turned and hurried into the tunnel faster than I had come out.

But I was fascinated by what it was doing.

It seemed to shake itself and three spidery little legs grew out the bottom. It raised up until it was standing on its own little tripod, about a foot high. It shook itself again and I thought the wind would blow it over. But the spidery legs splayed out, seemed to bite into the road surface and it was rock firm.

Something lifted and unfolded out the top.

It opened like a flower, until it was about eight inches across. A finger lifted (an antenna?), swung as if hunting, steadied and pointed at the sky.

Then the beacon switched on. I'm sure that is what happened although all I saw was a flash of light—parasitic it must have been, for light alone would not have served even without that volcanic overcast. It was probably some harmless side effect of switching on an enormous pulse of power, something the Mother Thing hadn't had time, or perhaps equipment or materials, to eliminate or shield. It was about as bright as a peanut photoflash.

But I was looking at it. Polarizers can't work that fast. It blinded me.

I thought my headlamp had gone out, then I realized that I simply couldn't see through a big greenish-purple disc of dazzle.

("Take it easy, boy. It's just an after-image. Wait and it'll go away.")

"I can't wait! I'm freezing to death!"

("Hook the line with your forearm, where it's clipped to your belt. Pull on it.")

I did as Oscar told me, found the line, turned around, started to wind it on both forearms.

It shattered.

It did not break as you expect rope to break; it shattered like glass. I suppose that is what it was by then—glass, I mean. Nylon and glass are super-cooled liquids.

Now I know what "super-cooled" means.

But all I knew then was that my last link with life had gone. I couldn't see, I couldn't hear, I was all alone on a bare platform, billions of miles from home, and a wind out of the depths of a frozen hell was bleeding the last life out of a body I could barely feel—and where I *could* feel, it hurt like fire.

"Oscar!"

("I'm here, bud. You can make it. Now—can you see anything?")

"No!"

("Look for the mouth of the tunnel. It's got light in it. Switch off your headlamp. Sure, you can—it's just a toggle switch. Drag your hand back across the right side of our helmet.")

I did.

("See anything?")

"Not yet."

("Move your head. Try to catch it in the corner of your eye—the dazzle stays in front, you know. Well?")

"I caught something that time!"

("Reddish, wasn't it? Jagged, too. The volcano. Now we know which way we're facing. Turn slowly and catch the mouth of the tunnel as it goes by.")

Slowly was the only way I could turn. "There it is!"

("Okay, you're headed home. Get down on your hands and knees and crab slowly to your left. Don't turn—because you want to hang onto that edge and *crawl*. Crawl toward the tunnel.")

I got down. I couldn't feel the surface with my hands but I felt pressure on my limbs, as if all four were artificial. I found the edge when my left hand slipped over it and I almost fell off. But I recovered. "Am I headed right?"

("Sure you are. You haven't turned. You've just moved sideways. Can you lift your head to see the tunnel?")

"Uh, not without standing up."

("Don't do that! Try the headlamp again. Maybe your eyes are okay now.")

I dragged my hand forward against the right side of the helmet. I must have hit the switch, for suddenly I saw a circle of light, blurred and cloudy in the middle. The edge of the walkway sliced it on the left.

("Good boy! No, don't get up; you're weak and dizzy and likely to fall. Start crawling. Count 'em. Three hundred ought to do it.")

I started crawling, counting.

"It's a long way, Oscar. You think we can make it?"

("Of course we can! You think I want to be left out *here?*")

"I'd be with you."

("Knock off the chatter. You'll make me lose count. Thirty-six . . . thirty-seven . . . thirty-eight—")

We crawled.

("That's a hundred. Now we double it. Hundred one . . . hundred two . . . hundred three—")

"I'm feeling better, Oscar. I think it's getting warmer."

("WHAT!")

"I said I'm feeling a little warmer."

("You're not warmer, you blistering idiot! That's freeze-to-death you're feeling! Crawl faster! Work your chin valve. Get more air. Le' me hear that chin valve click!")

I was too tired to argue; I chinned the valve three or four times, felt a blast blistering my face.

("I'm stepping up the stroke. Warmer indeed! Hund'd *nine* . . . hund'd *ten* . . . hun'*leven* . . . hun'*twelve*—pick it up!")

At two hundred I said I would just have to rest.

("No, you don't!")

"But I've *got* to. Just a little while."

("Like that, uh? You know what happens. What's Peewee goin' to do? She's in there, waiting. She's already scared because you're late. What's she goin' to *do?* Answer me!")

"Uh . . . she's going to try to wear Tim's suit."

("Right! In case of duplicate answers the prize goes to the one postmarked first. How far will she get? *You* tell *me*.")

"Uh . . . to the mouth of the tunnel, I guess. Then the wind will get her."

("My opinion exactly. Then we'll have the whole family together. You, me, the Mother Thing, Peewee. Cozy. A family of stiffs.")

"But—"

("So start slugging, brother. Slug . . . slug . . . slug . . . slug . . . tw'und'd *five* . . . two'und'd *six* . . . tw'und'd *sev'n'*—")

I don't remember falling off. I don't even know what the "snow" felt like. I just remember being glad that the dreadful counting was over and I could rest.

But Oscar wouldn't let me. ("Kip! *Kip!* Get up! Climb back on the straight and narrow.")

"Go 'way."

("I *can't* go away. I wish I could. Right in front of you. Grab the edge and scramble up. It's only a little farther now.")

I managed to raise my head, saw the edge of the walkway in the light of my headlamp about two feet above my head. I sank back. "It's too high," I said listlessly. "Oscar, I think we've had it."

He snorted. ("So? Who was it, just the other day, cussed out a little bitty girl who was too tired to get up? 'Commander Comet,' wasn't it? Did I get the name right? The 'Scourge of the Space-ways' . . . the no-good lazy sky tramp. 'Have Space Suit—Will Travel.' Before you go to sleep, Commander, can I have your auto-graph! I've never met a real live space pirate before . . . one that goes around hijacking ships and kidnapping little girls.")

"That's not fair!"

("Okay, okay, I know when I'm not wanted. But just one thing before I leave: she's got more guts in her little finger than you have in your whole body—you lying, fat, lazy swine! Good-bye. Don't wait up.")

"Oscar! Don't leave me!"

("Eh? You want help?")

"Yes!"

("Well, if it's too high to reach, grab your hammer and hook it over the edge. Pull yourself up.")

I blinked. Maybe it would work. I reached down, decided I had the hammer even though I couldn't feel it, got it loose. Using both hands I hooked it over the edge above me. I pulled.

That silly hammer broke just like the line. Tool steel—and it went to pieces as if it had been cast out of type slugs.

That made me mad. I heaved myself to a sitting position, got both elbows on the edge, and struggled and groaned and burst into fiery sweat—and rolled over onto the road surface.

("That's my boy! Never mind counting, just crawl toward the light!")

The tunnel wavered in front of me. I couldn't get my breath, so I kicked the chin valve.

Nothing happened.

"Oscar! The chin valve is stuck!" I tried again.

Oscar was very slow in answering. ("No, pal, the valve isn't stuck. Your air hoses have frozen up. I guess that last batch wasn't as dry as it could have been.")

"I haven't any *air!*"

Again he was slow. But he answered firmly, ("Yes, you have. You've got a whole suit full. Plenty for the few feet left.")

"I'll never make it."

("A few feet, only. There's the Mother Thing, right ahead of you. Keep moving.")

I raised my head and, sure enough, there she was. I kept crawling, while she got bigger and bigger. Finally I said, "Oscar . . . this is as far as I go."

("I'm afraid it is. I've let you down . . . but thanks for not leaving me outside there.")

"You didn't let me down . . . you were *swell*. I just didn't quite make it."

("I guess we both didn't quite make it . . . but we sure let 'em know that we tried! So long, partner.")

"So long. *¡Hasta la vista, amigo!*" I managed to crawl two short steps and collapsed with my head near the Mother Thing's head.

She was smiling. ("Hello, Kip my son.")

"I didn't . . . quite make it, Mother Thing. I'm sorry."

("Oh, but you *did* make it!")

"Huh?"

("Between us, we've both made it.")

I thought about that for a long time. "And Oscar."

("And Oscar, of course.")

"And Peewee."

("And always Peewee. We've all made it. Now we can rest, dear.")

"G'night . . . Mother Thing."

It was a darn short rest. I was just closing my eyes, feeling warm and happy that the Mother Thing thought that I had done all right—when Peewee started shaking my shoulder. She touched helmets. "Kip! *Kip!* Get up. *Please* get up."

"Huh? Why?"

"Because I can't *carry* you! I tried, but I can't do it. You're just *too big!*"

I considered it. Of course she couldn't carry me—where did she get the silly notion that she could? I was twice her size. I'd carry her . . . just as soon as I caught my breath.

"*Kip! Please* get up." She was crying now, blubbering.

"Why, sure, honey," I said gently, "if that's what you want." I tried and had a clumsy bad time of it. She almost picked me up, she helped a lot. Once up, she steadied me.

"Turn around. Walk."

She almost did carry me. She got her shoulders under my right arm and kept pushing. Every time we came to one of those blown-out panels she either helped me step over, or simply pushed me through and helped me up again.

At last we were in the lock and she was bleeding air from inside to fill it. She had to let go of me and I sank down. She turned when the inner door opened, started to say something—then got my helmet off in a hurry.

I took a deep breath and got very dizzy and the lights dimmed. She was looking at me. "You all right now?"

"Me? Sure! Why shouldn't I be?"

"Let me help you inside."

I couldn't see why, but she did help and I needed it. She sat me on the floor near the door with my back to the wall—I didn't want to lie down. "Kip, I was so scared!"

"Why?" I couldn't see what she was worried about. Hadn't the Mother Thing said that we had all done all right?

"Well, I was. I shouldn't have let you go out."

"But the beacon had to be set."

"Oh, but—You set it?"

"Of course. The Mother Thing was pleased."

"I'm sure she would have been," she said gravely.

"She was."

"Can I do anything? Can I help you out of your suit?"

"Uh . . . no, not yet. Could you find me a drink of water?"

"Right away!"

She came back and held it for me—I wasn't as thirsty as I had thought; it made me a bit ill. She watched me for some time, then said, "Do you mind if I'm gone a little while? Will you be all right?"

"Me? Certainly." I didn't feel well, I was beginning to hurt, but there wasn't anything she could do.

"I won't be long." She began clamping her helmet and I noticed with detached interest that she was wearing her own suit—somehow I had had the impression that she had been wearing Tim's.

I saw her head for the lock and realized where she was going and why. I wanted to tell her that the Mother Thing would rather not be inside here, where she might . . . where she might—I didn't want to say "spoil" even to myself.

But Peewee was gone.

I don't think she was away more than five minutes. I had closed my eyes and I am not sure. I noticed the inner door open.

Through it stepped Peewee, carrying the Mother Thing in her arms like a long piece of firewood. She didn't bend at all.

Peewee put the Mother Thing on the floor in the same position I had last seen her, then unclamped her helmet and bawled.

I couldn't get up. My legs hurt too much. And my arms. "Peewee . . . please, honey. It doesn't do any good."

She raised her head. "I'm all through. I won't cry any more."

And she didn't.

We sat there a long time. Peewee again offered to help me out of my suit, but when we tried it, I hurt so terribly, especially my hands and my feet, that I had to ask her to stop. She looked worried. "Kip . . . I'm afraid you froze them."

"Maybe. But there's nothing to do about it now." I winced and changed the subject. "Where did you find your suit?"

"Oh!" She looked indignant, then almost gay. "You'd *never* guess. Inside Jock's suit."

"No, I guess I wouldn't. 'The Purloined Letter.' "

"The what?"

"Nothing. I hadn't realized that old Wormface had a sense of humor."

Shortly after that we had another quake, a bad one. Chandeliers would have jounced if the place had had any and the floor heaved. Peewee squealed. "Oh! That was almost as bad as the last one."

"A lot worse, I'd say. That first little one wasn't anything."

"No, I mean the one while you were outside."

"Was there one then?"

"Didn't you feel it?"

"No." I tried to remember. "Maybe that was when I fell off in the snow."

"You fell off? Kip!"

"It was all right. Oscar helped me."

There was another ground shock. I wouldn't have minded, only it shook me up and made me hurt worse. I finally came out of the fog enough to realize that I didn't have to hurt.

Let's see, medicine pills were on the right and the codeine dispenser was farthest back— "Peewee? Could I trouble you for some water again?"

"Of course!"

"I'm going to take codeine. It may make me sleep. Do you mind?"

"You ought to sleep if you can. You need it."

"I suppose so. What time is it?"

She told me and I couldn't believe it. "You mean it's been more than twelve hours?"

"Huh? Since what?"

"Since this started."

"I don't understand, Kip." She stared at her watch. "It has been exactly an hour and a half since I found you—not quite two hours since the Mother Thing set off the bombs."

I couldn't believe that, either. But Peewee insisted that she was right.

The codeine made me feel much better and I was beginning to be drowsy, when Peewee said, "Kip, do you smell anything?"

I sniffed. "Something like kitchen matches?"

"That's what I mean. I think the pressure is dropping, too. Kip . . . I think I had better close your helmet—if you're going to sleep."

"All right. You close yours, too?"

"Yes. Uh, I don't think this place is tight any longer."

"You may be right." Between explosions and quakes, I didn't see how it could be. But, while I knew what that meant, I was too weary and sick—and getting too dreamy from the drug—to worry. Now, or a month from now—what did it matter? The Mother Thing had said everything was okay.

Peewee clamped us in, we checked radios, and she sat down facing me and the Mother Thing. She didn't say anything for a long time. Then I heard: "Peewee to Junebug—"

"I read you, Peewee."

"Kip? It's been fun, mostly. Hasn't it?"

"Huh?" I glanced up, saw that the dial said I had about four hours of air left. I had had to reduce pressure twice, since we closed up, to match falling pressure in the room. "Yes, Peewee, it's been swell. I wouldn't have missed it for the world."

She sighed. "I just wanted to be sure you weren't blaming me. Now go to sleep."

I did almost go to sleep, when I saw Peewee jump up and my phones came to life. "Kip! Something's coming in the door!"

I came wide awake, realized what it meant. Why couldn't they have let us be? A few hours, anyhow? "Peewee. Don't panic. Move to the far side of the door. You've got your blue-light gadget?"

"Yes."

"Pick them off as they come in."

"You've got to move, Kip. You're right where they will come!"

"I can't get up." I hadn't been able to move, not even my arms, for quite a while. "Use low power, then if you brush me, it won't matter. Do what I say! *Fast!*"

"Yes, Kip." She got where she could snipe at them sideways, raised her projector and waited.

The inner door opened, a figure came in. I saw Peewee start to nail it—and I called into my radio: *"Don't shoot!"*

But she was dropping the projector and running forward even as I shouted.

They were "mother thing" people.

It took six of them to carry me, only two to carry the Mother Thing. They sang to me soothingly all the time they were rigging a litter. I swallowed another codeine tablet before they lifted me, as even with their gentleness any movement hurt. It didn't take long to get me into their ship, for they had landed almost at the tunnel mouth, no doubt crushing the walkway—I hoped so.

Once I was safely inside Peewee opened my helmet and un-zipped the front of my suit. "Kip! Aren't they wonderful?"

"Yes." I was getting dizzier from the drug but was feeling better. "When do we raise ship?"

"We've already started."

"They're taking us home?" I'd have to tell Mr. Charton what a big help the codeine was.

"Huh? Oh, my, no! We're headed for Vega."

I fainted.

Chapter 9

I had been dreaming that I was home; this awoke me with a jerk. "Mother Thing!"

("Good morning, my son. I am happy to see that you are feeling better.")

"Oh, I feel fine. I've had a good night's rest—" I stared, then blurted: "—you're *dead!*" I couldn't stop it.

Her answer sounded warmly, gently humorous, the way you correct a child who has made a natural mistake. ("No, dear, I was merely frozen. I am not as frail as you seem to think me.")

I blinked and looked again. "Then it wasn't a dream?"

("No, it was not a dream.")

"I thought I was home and—" I tried to sit up, managed only to raise my head. "I *am* home!" *My* room! Clothes closet on the left—hall door behind the Mother Thing—my desk on the right, piled with books and with a Centerville High pennant over it—window beyond it, with the old elm almost filling it—sun-speckled leaves stirring in a breeze.

My slipstick was where I had left it.

Things started to wobble, then I figured it out. I had dreamed only the silly part at the end. Vega—I had been groggy with codeine. "You brought me *home.*"

("We brought you home . . . to your other home. My home.")

The bed started to sway. I clutched at it but my arms didn't move. The Mother Thing was still singing. ("You needed your own nest. So we prepared it.")

"Mother Thing, I'm confused."

("We know that a bird grows well faster in its own nest. So we built yours.") "Bird" and "nest" weren't what she sang, but an Unabridged won't give anything closer.

I took a deep breath to steady down. I understood her—that's what she was best at, making you understand. This wasn't my room and I wasn't home; it simply looked like it. But I was still terribly confused.

I looked around and wondered how I could have been mistaken.

The light slanted in the window from a wrong direction. The ceiling didn't have the patch in it from the time I built a hide-out in the attic and knocked plaster down by hammering. It wasn't the right shade, either.

The books were too neat and clean; they had that candy-box look. I couldn't recognize the bindings. The over-all effect was mighty close, but details were not right.

("I like this room,") the Mother Thing was singing. ("It looks like you, Kip.")

"Mother Thing," I said weakly, "*how* did you do it?"

("We asked you. And Peewee helped.")

I thought, "But Peewee has never seen my room either," then decided that Peewee had seen enough American homes to be a consulting expert. "Peewee is here?"

("She'll be in shortly.")

With Peewee and the Mother Thing around things couldn't be too bad. Except—"Mother Thing, I can't move my arms and legs."

She put a tiny, warm hand on my forehead and leaned over me until her enormous, lemur-like eyes blanked out everything else. ("You have been damaged. Now you are growing well. Do not worry.")

When the Mother Thing tells you not to worry, you don't. I didn't want to do handstands anyhow; I was satisfied to look into her eyes. You could sink into them, you could have dived in and swum around. "All right, Mother Thing." I remembered something else. "Say . . . you *were* frozen? Weren't you?"

("Yes.")

"But—Look, when water freezes it ruptures living cells. Or so they say."

She answered primly, ("My body would never permit *that!*").

"Well—" I thought about it. "Just don't dunk *me* in liquid air! I'm not built for it."

Again her song held roguish, indulgent humor. ("We shall endeavor not to hurt you.") She straightened up and grew a little, swaying like a willow. ("I sense Peewee.")

There was a knock—another discrepancy; it didn't sound like a knock on a light-weight interior door—and Peewee called out, "May I come in?" She didn't wait (I wondered if she ever did) but came on in. The bit I could see past her looked like our upper hall; they'd done a thorough job.

("Come in, dear.")

"Sure, Peewee. You *are* in."

"Don't be captious."

"Look who's talking. Hi, kid!"

"Hi yourself."

The Mother Thing glided away. ("Don't stay long, Peewee. You are not to tire him.")

"I won't, Mother Thing."

("'Bye, dears.")

I said, "What are the visiting hours in this ward?"

"When *she* says, of course." Peewee stood facing me, fists on hips. She was really clean for the first time in our acquaintance—cheeks pink with scrubbing, hair fluffy—maybe she would be pretty, in about ten years. She was dressed as always but her clothes were fresh, all buttons present, and tears invisibly mended.

"Well," she said, letting out her breath, "I guess you're going to be worth keeping, after all."

"Me? I'm in the pink. How about yourself?"

She wrinkled her nose. "A little frost nip. Nothing. But you were a *mess*."

"I was?"

"I can't use adequate language without being what Mama calls 'unladylike.'"

"Oh, we wouldn't want you to be *that*."

"Don't be sarcastic. You don't do it well."

"You won't let me practice on you?"

She started to make a Peewee retort, stopped suddenly, smiled and came close. For a nervous second I thought she was going to kiss me. But she just patted the bedclothes and said solemnly, "You bet you can, Kip. You can be sarcastic, or nasty, or mean, or scold me, or anything, and I won't let out a peep. Why, I'll bet you could even talk back to the Mother Thing."

I couldn't imagine wanting to. I said, "Take it easy, Peewee. Your halo is showing."

"I'd have one if it weren't for you. Or flunked my test for it, more likely."

"So? I seem to remember somebody about your size lugging me indoors almost piggy-back. How about that?"

She wriggled. "That wasn't anything. *You* set the beacon. That was *everything*."

"Uh, each to his own opinion. It was cold out there." I changed the subject; it was embarrassing us. Mention of the beacon reminded me of something else. "Peewee? Where are we?"

"Huh? In the Mother Thing's home, of course." She looked around and said, "Oh, I forgot. Kip, this isn't really your—"

"I know," I said impatiently. "It's a fake. Anybody can see that."

"They can?" She looked crestfallen. "I thought we had done a perfect job."

"It's an incredibly good job. I don't see how you did it."

"Oh, your memory is most detailed. You must have a camera eye."

—and I must have spilled my guts, too! I added to myself. I wondered what else I had said—with Peewee listening. I was afraid to ask; a fellow ought to have privacy.

"But it's still a fake," I went on. "I know we're in the Mother Thing's home. But *where's that?*"

"Oh." She looked round-eyed. "I told you. Maybe you don't remember—you were sleepy."

"I remember," I said slowly, "something. But it didn't make sense. I thought you said we were going to *Vega*."

"Well, I suppose the catalogs will list it as Vega Five. But they call it—" She threw back her head and vocalized; it recalled to me the cockcrow theme in *Le Coq d'Or*. "—but I couldn't say *that*. So I told you Vega, which is close enough."

I tried again to sit up, failed. "You mean to stand there and tell me we're on *Vega?* I mean, a 'Vegan planet'?"

"Well, you haven't asked me to sit down."

I ignored the Peeweeism. I looked at "sunlight" pouring through the window. "That light is from *Vega?*"

"That stuff? That's artificial sunlight. If they had used real, bright, Vega light, it would look ghastly. Like a bare arc light. Vega is 'way up the Russell diagram, you know."

"It is?" I didn't know the spectrum of Vega; I had never expected to *need* to know it.

"Oh, yes! You be careful, Kip—when you're up, I mean. In ten seconds you can get more burn than all winter in Key West—and ten minutes would kill you."

I seemed to have a gift for winding up in difficult climates. What star class was Vega? "A," maybe? Probably "B." All I knew was that it was big and bright, bigger than the Sun, and looked pretty set in Lyra.

But *where* was it? How in the name of Einstein did we get here? "Peewee? How far is Vega? No, I mean, 'How far is the Sun?' You wouldn't happen to know?"

"Of course," she said scornfully. "Twenty-seven light-years."

Great Galloping Gorillas! "Peewee—get that slide rule. You know how to push one? I don't seem to have the use of my hands."

She looked uneasy. "Uh, what do you want it for?"

"I want to see what that comes to in miles."

"Oh. I'll figure it. No need for a slide rule."

"A slipstick is faster and more accurate. Look, if you don't know how to use one, don't be ashamed—I didn't, at your age. I'll show you."

"Of course I can use one!" she said indignantly. "You think I'm a stupe? But I'll work it out." Her lips moved silently. "One point five nine times ten to the fourteenth miles."

I had done that Proxima Centauri problem recently; I remembered the miles in a light-year and did a rough check in my head— uh, call it six times twenty-five makes a hundred and fifty—and where was the decimal point? "Your answer sounds about right." 159,000,000,000,000 weary miles! Too many zeroes for comfort.

"Of course I'm right!" she retorted. "I'm *always* right."

"Goodness me! The handy-dandy pocket encyclopedia."

She blushed. "I can't help being a genius."

Which left her wide open and I was about to rub her nose in it—when I saw how unhappy she looked.

I remembered hearing Dad say: "Some people insist that 'mediocre' is better than 'best.' They delight in clipping wings because they themselves can't fly. They despise brains because they have none. Pfah!"

"I'm sorry, Peewee," I said humbly. "I know you can't. And I can't help not being one . . . any more than you can help being little, or I can help being big."

She relaxed and looked solemn. "I guess I was being a show-off again." She twisted a button. "Or maybe I assumed that you understand me—like Daddy."

"I feel complimented. I doubt if I do—but from now on I'll try."

She went on worrying the button. "You're pretty smart yourself, Kip. You know that, don't you?"

I grinned. "If I were smart, would I be *here?* All thumbs and my ears rub together. Look, honey, would you mind if we checked you on the slide rule? I'm really interested." Twenty-seven light-years—why, you wouldn't be able to *see* the Sun. It isn't any great shakes as a star.

But I had made her uneasy again. "Uh, Kip, that isn't much of a slide rule."

"What? Why, that's the best that money can—"

"Kip, please! It's part of the desk. It's not a slide rule."

"Huh?" I looked sheepish. "I forgot. Uh, I suppose that hall out there doesn't go very far?"

"Just what you can see. Kip, the slide rule would have been real—if we had had time enough. They understand logarithms. Oh, indeed they do!"

That was bothering me—"time enough" I mean. "Peewee, how long did it take us to get here?" Twenty-seven light-years! Even at speed-of-light—well, maybe the Einstein business would make it seem like a quick trip to me—but not to Centerville. Dad could be dead! Dad was older than Mother, old enough to be my grandfather, really. Another twenty-seven years back—Why, that would make him well over a hundred. Even Mother might be dead.

"Time to get here? Why, it didn't take *any.*"

"No, no. I know it feels that way. You're not any older, I'm still laid up by frostbite. But it took at least twenty-seven years. Didn't it?"

"What are you talking about, Kip?"

"The relativity equations, of course. You've heard of them?"

"Oh, *those!* Certainly. But they don't apply. It didn't take *time.* Oh, fifteen minutes to get out of Pluto's atmosphere, about the same to cope with the atmosphere here. But otherwise, *pht!* Zero."

"At the speed of light you would think so."

"No, Kip." She frowned, then her face lighted up. "How long was it from the time you set the beacon till they rescued us?"

"Huh?" It hit me. Dad wasn't dead! Mother wouldn't even
have gray hair. "Maybe an hour."

"A little over. It would have been less if they had had a ship
ready . . . then they might have found you in the tunnel instead of
me. No time for the message to reach here. Half an hour frittered
away getting a ship ready—the Mother Thing was *vexed*. I hadn't
known she could be. You see, a ship is supposed to be *ready*."

"Any time she wants one?"

"Any and all the time—the Mother Thing is *important*. Another half-hour in atmosphere maneuvering—and that's all. *Real*
time. None of those funny contractions."

I tried to soak it up. They take an hour to go twenty-seven
light-years—and get bawled out for dallying. Dr. Einstein must be
known as "Whirligig Albert" among his cemetery neighbors.
"But *how?*"

"Kip, do you know any geometry? I don't mean Euclid—I
mean *geometry*."

"Mmm . . . I've fiddled with open and closed curved spaces—
and I've read Dr. Bell's popular books. But you couldn't say I
know any geometry."

"At least you won't boggle at the idea that a straight line is not
necessarily the shortest distance between two points." She made
motions as if squeezing a grapefruit in both hands. "Because it's
not. Kip—it all *touches*. You could put it in a bucket. In a thimble
if you folded it so that spins matched."

I had a dizzying picture of a universe compressed into a
teacup, nucleons and electrons packed solidly—really *solid* and
not the thin mathematical ghost that even the uranium nucleus is
said to be. Something like the "primal atom" that some cosmogo-
nists use to explain the expanding universe. Well, maybe it's
both—packed and expanding. Like the "wavicle" paradox. A particle isn't a wave and a wave can't be a particle—yet everything is
both. If you believe in wavicles, you can believe in anything—and
if you don't, then don't bother to believe at all. Not even in yourself, because that's what you are—wavicles. "How many dimensions?" I said weakly.

"How many would you like?"

"Me? Uh, twenty, maybe. Four more for each of the first four,
to give some looseness on the corners."

"Twenty isn't a starter. I don't know, Kip; I don't know geometry, either—I just thought I did. So I've pestered them."

"The Mother Thing?"

"Her? Oh, heavens, no! She doesn't know geometry. Just enough to pilot a ship in and out of the folds."

"Only that much?" I should have stuck to advanced finger-painting and never let Dad lure me into trying for an education. There isn't any end—the more you learn, the more you need to learn. "Peewee, you knew what that beacon was for, didn't you?"

"Me?" She looked innocent. "Well . . . yes."

"You knew we were going to Vega."

"Well . . . if the beacon worked. If it was set in time."

"Now the prize question. Why didn't you tell me?"

"Well—" Peewee was going to twist that button off. "I wasn't sure how much math you knew and—you might have gone all masculine and common-sensical and father-knows-best. Would you have believed me?"

("I told Orville and I told Wilbur and now I'm telling you—that contraption will never work!") "Maybe not, Peewee. But next time you're tempted not to tell me something 'for my own good,' will you take a chance that I'm not wedded to my own ignorance? I know I'm not a genius but I'll try to keep my mind open—and I might be able to help, if I knew what you were up to. Quit twisting that button."

She let go hastily. "Yes, Kip. I'll remember."

"Thanks. Another thing is fretting me. I was pretty sick?"

"Huh? You certainly were!"

"All right. They've got these, uh, 'fold ships' that go anywhere in no time. Why didn't you ask them to bounce me home and pop me into a hospital?"

She hesitated. "How do you feel?"

"Huh? I feel fine. Except that I seem to be under spinal anes-thesia, or something."

"Or something," she agreed. "But you feel as if you are getting well?"

"Shucks, I feel well."

"You aren't. But you're going to be." She looked at me closely. "Shall I put it bluntly, Kip?"

"Go ahead."

"If they had taken you to Earth to the best hospital we have, you'd be a 'basket case.' Understand me? No arms, no legs. As it is, you are getting completely well. No amputations, not even a toe."

I think the Mother Thing had prepared me. I simply said, "You're sure?"

"Sure. Sure both. You're going to be *all right*." Suddenly her face screwed up. "Oh, you were a mess! I *saw*."

"Pretty bad?"

"Awful. I have nightmares."

"They shouldn't have let you look."

"They couldn't stop me. I was next of kin."

"Huh? You told them you were my sister or something?"

"What? I *am* your next of kin."

I was about to say she was cockeyed when I tripped over my tongue. We were the only humans for a hundred and sixty trillion miles. As usual, Peewee was right.

"So I had to grant permission," she went on.

"For what? What did they do to me?"

"Uh, first they popped you into liquid helium. They left you there and the past month they have been using me as a guinea pig. Then, three days ago—three of ours—they thawed you out and got to work. You've been getting well ever since."

"What shape am I in now?"

"Uh . . . well, you're growing back. Kip, this isn't a bed. It just looks like it."

"What is it, then?"

"We don't have a name for it and the tune is pitched too high for me. But everything from here on down—" She patted the spread. "—on into the room below, does things for you. You're wired like a hi-fi nut's basement."

"I'd like to see it."

"I'm afraid you can't. You don't *know*, Kip. They had to cut your space suit off."

I felt more emotion at that than I had at hearing what a mess I had been. "Huh? Where is Oscar? Did they ruin him? My space suit, I mean."

"I know what you mean. Every time you're delirious you talk to 'Oscar'—and you answer back, too. Sometimes I think you're schizoid, Kip."

"You've mixed your terms, runt—that'ud make me a split personality. All right, but you're a paranoid yourself."

"Oh, I've known that for a long time. But I'm a very well adjusted one. You want to see Oscar? The Mother Thing said that you would want him near when you woke up." She opened the closet.

"Hey! You said he was all cut up!"

"Oh, they repaired him. Good as new. A little better than new." ("Time, dear! Remember what I said.")

"Coming, Mother Thing! 'Bye, Kip. I'll be back soon, and real often."

"Okay. Leave the closet open so I can see Oscar."

Peewee did come back, but not "real often." I wasn't offended, not much. She had a thousand interesting and "educational" things to poke her ubiquitous nose into, all new and fascinating—she was as busy as a pup chewing slippers. She ran our hosts ragged. But I wasn't bored. I was getting well, a full-time job and not boring if you are happy—which I was.

I didn't see the Mother Thing often. I began to realize that she had work of her own to do—even though she came to see me if I asked for her, with never more than an hour's delay, and never seemed in a hurry to leave.

She wasn't my doctor, nor my nurse. Instead I had a staff of veterinarians who were alert to supervise every heartbeat. They didn't come in unless I asked them to (a whisper was as good as a shout) but I soon realized that "my" room was bugged and telemetered like a ship in flight test—and my "bed" was a mass of machinery, gear that bore the relation to our own "mechanical hearts" and "mechanical lungs" and "mechanical kidneys" that a Lockheed ultrasonic courier does to a baby buggy.

I never saw that gear (they never lifted the spread, unless it was while I slept), but I know what they were doing. They were encouraging my body to repair itself—not scar tissue but the way it had been. Any lobster can do this and starfish do it so well that you can chop them to bits and wind up with a thousand brand-new starfish.

This is a trick any animal should do, since its gene pattern is in every cell. But a few million years ago we lost it. Everybody knows that science is trying to recapture it; you see articles—optimistic ones in *Reader's Digest*, discouraged ones in *The Scientific Monthly*, wildly wrong ones in magazines whose "science editors" seem to have received their training writing horror movies. But we're working on it. Someday, if anybody dies an accidental death, it will be because he bled to death on the way to the hospital.

Here I was with a perfect chance to find out about it—and I didn't.

I tried. Although I was unworried by what they were doing (the Mother Thing had told me not to worry and every time she

visited me she looked in my eyes and repeated the injunction),
nevertheless like Peewee, I like to *know*.

Pick a savage so far back in the jungle that they don't even
have installment-plan buying. Say he has an I.Q. of 190 and Peewee's yen to understand. Dump him into Brookhaven Atomic
Laboratories. How much will he learn? With all possible help?

He'll learn which corridors lead to what rooms and he'll learn
that a purple trefoil means: "Danger!"

That's all. Not because he *can't;* remember he's a
supergenius—but he needs twenty years schooling before he can
ask the right questions and understand the answers.

I asked questions and always got answers and formed notions.
But I'm not going to record them; they are as confused and con-
tradictory as the notions a savage would form about design and
operation of atomic equipment. As they say in radio, when noise
level reaches a certain value, no information is transmitted. All I
got was "noise."

Some of it was literally "noise." I'd ask a question and one of
the therapists would answer. I would understand part, then as it
reached the key point, I would hear nothing but birdsongs. Even
with the Mother Thing as an interpreter, the parts I had no background for would turn out to be a canary's cheerful prattle.

Hold onto your seats; I'm going to explain something I don't
understand: how Peewee and I could talk with the Mother Thing
even though her mouth could not shape English and we couldn't
sing the way she did and had not studied her language. The
Vegans—(I'll call them "Vegans" the way we might be called "So-
larians"; their real name sounds like a wind chime in a breeze. The
Mother Thing had a real name, too, but I'm not a coloratura so-
prano. Peewee used it when she wanted to wheedle her—fat lot of
good it did her.) The Vegans have a supreme talent to understand,
to put themselves in the other person's shoes. I don't think it was
telepathy, or I wouldn't have gotten so many wrong numbers. Call
it empathy.

But they have it in various degrees, just as all of us drive cars
but only a few are fit to be racing drivers. The Mother Thing had it
the way Novaës understands a piano. I once read about an actress
who could use Italian so effectively to a person who did not understand Italian that she always made herself understood. Her
name was "Duce." No, a "duce" is a dictator. Something like that.
She must have had what the Mother Thing had.

The first words I had with the Mother Thing were things like "hello" and "good-bye" and "thank you" and "where are we going?" She could project her meaning with those—shucks, you can talk to a strange dog that much. Later I began to understand her speech as *speech*. She picked up meanings of English words even faster; she had this great talent, and she and Peewee had talked for days while they were prisoners.

But while this is easy for "you're welcome" and "I'm hungry" and "let's hurry," it gets harder for ideas like "heterodyning" and "amino acid" even when both are familiar with the concept. When one party doesn't even have the concept, it breaks down. That's the trouble I had understanding those veterinarians. If we had all spoken English I still would not have understood.

An oscillating circuit sending out a radio signal produces dead silence unless there is another circuit capable of oscillating in the same way to receive it. I wasn't on the right frequency.

Nevertheless I understood them when the talk was not highbrow. They were nice people; they talked and laughed a lot and seemed to like each other. I had trouble telling them apart, except the Mother Thing. (I learned that the only marked difference to them between Peewee and myself was that I was ill and she wasn't.) They had no trouble telling each other apart; their conversations were interlarded with musical names, until you felt that you were caught in *Peter and the Wolf* or a Wagnerian opera. They even had a leit-motif for me. Their talk was cheerful and gay, like the sounds of a bright summer dawn.

The next time I meet a canary I'll know what he is saying even if he doesn't.

I picked up some of this from Peewee—a hospital bed is not a good place from which to study a planet. Vega Five has Earth-surface gravity, near enough, with an oxygen, carbon dioxide, and water life cycle. The planet would not suit humans, not only because the noonday "sun" would strike you dead with its jolt of ultraviolet but also the air has poisonous amounts of ozone—a trace of ozone is stimulating but a trifle more—well, you might as well sniff prussic acid. There was something else, too, nitrous oxide I think, which was ungood for humans if breathed too long. My quarters were air-conditioned; the Vegans could breathe what I used but they considered it tasteless.

I learned a bit as a by-product of something else; the Mother Thing asked me to dictate how I got mixed up in these things. When I finished, she asked me to dictate everything I knew about Earth, its history, and how we work and live together. This is a tall order—I'm not still dictating because I found out I don't know much. Take ancient Babylonia—how is it related to early Egyptian civilizations? I had only vague notions.

Maybe Peewee did better, since she remembers everything she has heard or read or seen the way Dad does. But they probably didn't get her to hold still long, whereas I had to. The Mother Thing wanted this for the reasons we study Australian aborigines and also as a record of our language. There was another reason, too.

The job wasn't easy but there was a Vegan to help me whenever I felt like it, willing to stop if I tired. Call him Professor Josephus Egghead; "Professor" is close enough and his name can't be spelled. I called him Joe and he called me the leitmotif that meant "Clifford Russell, the monster with the frostbite." Joe had almost as much gift for understanding as the Mother Thing. But how do you put over ideas like "tariffs" and "kings" to a person whose people have never had either? The English words were just noise.

But Joe knew histories of many peoples and planets and could call up scenes, in moving stereo and color, until we agreed on what I meant. We jogged along, with me dictating to a silvery ball floating near my mouth and with Joe curled up like a cat on a platform raised to my level, while he dictated to another microphone, making running notes on what I said. His mike had a gimmick that made it a hush-phone; I did not hear him unless he spoke to me.

Then we would stumble. Joe would stop and throw me a sample scene, his best guess of what I meant. The pictures appeared in the air, positioned for my comfort—if I turned my head, the picture moved to accommodate me. The pix were color-stereo-television with perfect life and sharpness—well, give us another twenty years and we'll have them as realistic. It was a good trick to have the projector concealed and to force images to appear as if they were hanging in air, but those are just gimmicks of stereo optics; we can do them anytime we really want to—after all, you can pack a lifelike view of the Grand Canyon into a viewer you hold in your hand.

The thing that did impress me was the organization behind it. I asked Joe about it. He sang to his microphone and we went on a galloping tour of their "Congressional Library."

Dad claims that library science is the foundation of all sciences just as math is the key—and that we will survive or founder, depending on how well the librarians do their jobs. Librarians didn't look glamorous to me but maybe Dad had hit on a not very obvious truth.

This "library" had hundreds, maybe thousands, of Vegans viewing pictures and listening to sound tracks, each with a silvery sphere in front of him. Joe said they were "telling the memory." This was equivalent to typing a card for a library's catalog, except that the result was more like a memory path in brain cells—nine-tenths of that building was an electronic brain.

I spotted a triangular sign like the costume jewelry worn by the Mother Thing, but the picture jumped quickly to something else. Joe also wore one (and others did not) but I did not get around to asking about it, as the sight of that incredible "library" brought up the word "cybernetics" and we went on a detour. I decided later that it might be a lodge pin, or like a Phi Beta Kappa key—the Mother Thing was smart even for a Vegan and Joe was not far behind.

Whenever Joe was sure that he understood some English word, he would wriggle with delight like a puppy being tickled. He was very dignified, but this is not undignified for a Vegan. Their bodies are so fluid and mobile that they smile and frown with the whole works. A Vegan holding perfectly still is either displeased or extremely worried.

The sessions with Joe let me tour places from my bed. The difference between "primary school" and "university" caused me to be shown examples. A "kindergarten" looked like an adult Vegan being overwhelmed by babies; it had the innocent rowdiness of a collie pup stepping on his brother's face to reach the milk dish. But the "university" was a place of quiet beauty, strange-looking trees and plants and flowers among buildings of surrealistic charm unlike any architecture I have ever seen—I suppose I would have been flabbergasted if they had looked familiar. Parabolas were used a lot and I think all the "straight" lines had that swelling the Greeks called "entasis"—delicate grace with strength.

Joe showed up one day simply undulating with pleasure. He had another silvery ball, larger than the other two. He placed it in front of me, then sang to his own. ("I want you to hear this, Kip!")

As soon as he ceased the larger sphere spoke in English: "I want you to hear this, Kip!"

Squirming with delight, Joe swapped spheres and told me to say something.

"What do you want me to say?" I asked.

("What do you want me to say?") the larger sphere sang in Vegan.

That was my last session with Prof Joe.

Despite unstinting help, despite the Mother Thing's ability to make herself understood, I was like the Army mule at West Point: an honorary member of the student body but not prepared for the curriculum. I never did understand their government. Oh, they *had* government, but it wasn't any system I've heard of. Joe knew about democracies and representation and voting and courts of law; he could fish up examples from many planets. He felt that democracy was "a very good system, for beginners." It would have sounded patronizing, except that is not one of their faults.

I never met one of their young. Joe explained that children should not see "strange creatures" until they had learned to feel understanding sympathy. That would have offended me if I hadn't been learning some "understanding sympathy" myself. Matter of fact, if a human ten-year-old saw a Vegan, he would either run, or poke it with a stick.

I tried to learn about their government from the Mother Thing, in particular how they kept the peace—laws, crimes, punishments, traffic regulations, etc.

It was as near to flat failure as I ever had with her. She pondered a long time, then answered: ("How could one possibly act against one's own nature?")

I guess their worst vice was that they didn't have any. This can be tiresome.

The medical staff were interested in the drugs in Oscar's helmet— like our interest in a witch doctor's herbs, but that is not idle interest; remember digitalis and curare.

I told them what each drug did and in most cases I knew the Geneva name as well as the commercial one. I knew that codeine was derived from opium, and opium from poppies. I knew that dexedrine was a sulphate but that was all. Organic chemistry and biochemistry are not easy even with no language trouble. We got together on what a benzene ring was, Peewee drawing it and sticking in her two dollars' worth, and we managed to agree on "element," "isotope," "half life," and the periodic table. I should have drawn structural formulas, using Peewee's hands—but neither of us had the slightest idea of the structural formula for codeine and couldn't do it even when supplied with kindergarten toys which stuck together only in the valences of the elements they represented.

Peewee had fun, though. They may not have learned much from her; she learned a lot from them.

I don't know when I became aware that the Mother Thing was not, or wasn't quite, a female. But it didn't matter; being a mother is an attitude, not a biological relation.

If Noah launched his ark on Vega Five, the animals would come in by twelves. That makes things complicated. But a "mother thing" is one who takes care of others. I am not sure that all mother things were the same gender; it may have been a matter of temperament.

I met one "father thing." You might call him "governor" or "mayor," but "parish priest" or "scoutmaster" is closer, except that his prestige dominated a continent. He breezed in during a session with Joe, stayed five minutes, urged Joe to do a good job, told me to be a good boy and get well, and left, all without hurrying. He filled me with the warm self-reliance that Dad does—I didn't need to be told that he was a "father thing." His visit had a flavor of "royalty visiting the wounded" without being condescending— no doubt it was hard to work me into a busy schedule.

Joe neither mothered nor fathered me; he taught me and studied me—"a professor thing."

Peewee showed up one day full of bubbles. She posed like a mannequin. "Do you like my new spring outfit?"

She was wearing silvery tights, plus a little hump like a knapsack. She looked cute but not glamorous, for she was built like two sticks and this get-up emphasized it.

"Very fancy," I said. "Are you learning to be an acrobat?"

"Don't be silly, Kip; it's my new space suit—a *real* one."

I glanced at Oscar, big and bulky and filling the closet and said privately, "Hear that, chum?"

("It takes all kinds to make a world.")

"Your helmet won't fit it, will it?"

She giggled. "I'm wearing it."

"You are? 'The Emperor's New Clothes'?"

"Pretty close. Kip, disconnect your prejudices and listen. This is like the Mother Thing's suit except that it's tailored for me. My old suit wasn't much good—and that *cold* cold about finished it. But you'll be amazed at this one. Take the helmet. It's there, only you can't see it. It's a field. Gas can't go in or out." She came close. "Slap me."

"With what?"

"Oh. I forgot. Kip, you've got to get well and up off that bed. I want to take you for a walk."

"I'm in favor. They tell me it won't be long now."

"It had better not be. Here, I'll show you." She hauled off and slapped herself. Her hand smacked into something inches from her face.

"Now watch," she went on. She moved her hand very slowly; it sank through the barrier, she thumbed her nose at me and giggled.

This impressed me—a space suit you could reach into! Why, I would have been able to give Peewee water and dexedrine and sugar pills when she needed them. "I'll be darned! What does it?"

"A power pack on my back, under the air tank. The tank is good for a week, too, and hoses can't give trouble because there aren't any."

"Uh, suppose you blow a fuse. There you are, with a lungful of vacuum."

"The Mother Thing says that can't happen."

Hmm—I had never known the Mother Thing to be wrong when she made a flat statement.

"That's not all," Peewee went on. "It feels like skin, the joints aren't clumsy, and you're never hot or cold. It's like street clothes."

"Uh, you risk a bad sunburn, don't you? Unhealthy, you tell me. Unhealthy even on the Moon."

"Oh, no! The field polarizes. That's what the field is, sort of. Kip, get them to make you one—we'll go places!"

I glanced at Oscar. ("Please yourself, pal," he said distantly. "I'm not the jealous type.")

"Uh, Peewee, I'll stick to one I understand. But I'd like to examine that monkey suit of yours."

"Monkey suit indeed!"

I woke up one morning, turned over, and realized that I was hungry.

Then I sat up with a jerk. I had *turned over in bed*.

I had been warned to expect it. The "bed" was a bed and my body was back under my control. Furthermore, I was hungry and I hadn't been hungry the whole time I had been on Vega Five. Whatever that machinery was, it included a way to nourish me without eating.

But I didn't stop to enjoy the luxury of hunger; it was too wonderful to be a body again, not just a head. I got out of bed, was suddenly dizzy, recovered and grinned. Hands! *Feet!*

I examined those wonderful things. They were unchanged and unhurt.

Then I looked more closely. No, not quite unchanged.

I had had a scar on my left shin where I had been spiked in a close play at second; it was gone. I once had "Mother" tattooed on my left forearm at a carnival. Mother had been distressed and Dad disgusted, but he had said to leave it as a reminder not to be a witling. It was gone.

There was not a callus on hand or foot.

I used to bite my nails. My nails were a bit long but perfect. I had lost the nail from my right little toe years ago through a slip with a hatchet. It was back.

I looked hastily for my appendectomy scar—found it and felt relieved. If it had been missing, I would have wondered if I was me.

There was a mirror over the chest of drawers. It showed me with enough hair to warrant a guitar (I wear a crew cut) but somebody had shaved me.

On the chest was a dollar and sixty-seven cents, a mechanical pencil, a sheet of paper, my watch, and a handkerchief. The watch was running. The dollar bill, the paper, and the handkerchief had been laundered.

My clothes, spandy clean and invisibly repaired, were on the desk. The socks weren't mine; the material was more like felt, if you will imagine felted material no thicker than Kleenex which stretches instead of tearing. On the floor were tennis shoes, like Peewee's even to a "U.S. Rubber" trademark, but in my size. The uppers were heavier felted material. I got dressed.

I was wearing the result when Peewee kicked the door. "Anybody home?" She came in, bearing a tray. "Want breakfast?"

"Peewee! Look at me!"

She did. "Not bad," she admitted, "for an ape. You need a haircut."

"Yes, but isn't it *wonderful!* I'm all together again!"

"You never were apart," she answered, "except in spots—I've had daily reports. Where do you want this?" She put the tray on the desk.

"Peewee," I asked, rather hurt, "don't you care that I'm well?"

"Of course I do. Why do you think I made 'em let me carry in

your breakfast? But I knew last night that they were going to uncork you. Who do you think cut your nails and shaved you? That'll
be a dollar, please. Shaves have gone up."

I got that tired dollar and handed it to her.

She didn't take it. "Aw, can't you take a joke?"

" 'Neither a borrower nor a lender be.' "

"Polonius. He was a stupid old bore. Honest, Kip, I wouldn't
take your last dollar."

"Now who can't take a joke?"

"Oh, eat your breakfast. That purple juice," she said, "tastes
like orange juice—it's very nice. The stuff that looks like scrambled eggs is a fair substitute and I had 'em color it yellow—the
eggs here are *dreadful*, which wouldn't surprise you if you knew
where they get them. The buttery stuff is vegetable fat and I had
them color it, too. The bread is bread, I toasted it myself. The salt
is salt and it surprises them that we eat it—they think it's poison.
Go ahead; I've guinea-pigged everything. No coffee."

"I won't miss it."

"I never touch the stuff—I'm trying to grow. Eat. Your sugar
count has been allowed to drop so that you will enjoy it."

The aroma was wonderful. "Where's your breakfast, Peewee?"

"I ate hours ago. I'll watch and swallow when you do."

The tastes were odd but it was just what the doctor ordered—
literally, I suppose. I've never enjoyed a meal so much.

Presently I slowed down to say, "Knife and fork? Spoons?"

"The only ones on—" She vocalized the planet's name. "I got
tired of fingers and I play hob using what they use. So I drew pictures. This set is mine but we'll order more."

There was even a napkin, more felted stuff. The water tasted
distilled and not aerated. I didn't mind. "Peewee, how did you
shave me? Not even a nick."

"Little gismo that beats a razor all hollow. I don't know what
they use it for, but if you could patent it, you'd make a fortune.
Aren't you going to finish that toast?"

"Uh—" I had thought that I could eat the tray. "No, I'm full."

"Then I will." She used it to mop up the "butter," then announced, "I'm off!"

"Where?"

"To suit up. I'm going to take you for a walk!" She was gone.

The hall outside did not imitate ours where it could not be
seen from the bed, but a door to the left was a bathroom, just

where it should have been. No attempt had been made to make it look like the one at home, and valving and lighting and such were typically Vegan. But everything worked.

Peewee returned while I was checking Oscar. If they had cut him off me, they had done a marvelous job of repairing; even the places I had patched no longer showed. He had been cleaned so thoroughly that there was no odor inside. He had three hours of air and seemed okay in every way. "You're in good shape, partner."

("In the pink! The service is excellent here.")

"So I've noticed." I looked up and saw Peewee; she was already in her "spring outfit."

"Peewee, do we need space suits just for a walk?"

"No. You could get by with a respirator, sun glasses, and a sun shade."

"You've convinced me. Say, where's Madame Pompadour? How do you get her inside that suit?"

"No trouble at all, she just bulges a little. But I left her in my room and told her to behave herself."

"Will she?"

"Probably not. She takes after me."

"Where is your room?"

"Next door. This is the only part of the house which is Earth-conditioned."

I started to suit up. "Say, has that fancy suit got a radio?"

"All that yours has and then some. Did you notice the change in Oscar?"

"Huh? What? I saw that he was repaired and cleaned up. What else have they done?"

"Just a little thing. One more click on the switch that changes antennas and you can talk to people around you who aren't wearing radios without shouting."

"I didn't see a speaker."

"They don't believe in making everything big and bulky."

As we passed Peewee's room I glanced in. It was not decorated Vegan style; I had seen Vegan interiors through stereo. Nor was it a copy of her own room—not if her parents were sensible. I don't know what to call it—"Moorish harem" style, perhaps, as conceived by Mad King Ludwig, with a dash of Disneyland.

I did not comment. I had a hunch that Peewee had been given a room "just like her own" because I had one; that fitted the Mother Thing's behavior—but Peewee had seen a golden chance to let her overfertile imagination run wild. I doubt if she fooled the Mother Thing one split second. She had probably let that indulgent overtone come into her song and had given Peewee what she wanted.

The Mother Thing's home was smaller than our state capitol but not much; her family seemed to run to dozens, or hundreds—"family" has a wide meaning under their complex interlinkage. We didn't see any young ones on our floor and I knew that they were being kept away from the "monsters." The adults all greeted me, inquired as to my health, and congratulated me on my recovery; I was kept busy saying "Fine, thank you! Couldn't be better."

They all knew Peewee and she could sing their names.

I thought I recognized one of my therapists, but the Mother Thing, Prof Joe and the boss veterinarian were the only Vegans I was sure of and we did not meet them.

We hurried on. The Mother Thing's home was typical—many soft round cushions about a foot thick and four in diameter, used as beds or chairs, floor bare, slick and springy, most furniture on the walls where it could be reached by climbing, convenient rods and poles and brackets a person could drape himself on while using the furniture, plants growing unexpectedly here and there as if the jungle were moving in—delightful, and as useful to me as a corset.

Through a series of parabolic arches we reached a balcony. It was not railed and the drop to a terrace below was about seventy-five feet; I stayed back and regretted again that Oscar had no chin window. Peewee went to the edge, put an arm around a slim pillar and leaned out. In the bright outdoor light her "helmet" became an opalescent sphere. "Come see!"

"And break my neck? Maybe you'd like to belay me?"

"Oh, pooh! Who's afraid of heights?"

"I am when I can't see what I'm doing."

"Well, for goodness' sakes, take my hand and grab a post."

I let her lead me to a pillar, then looked out.

It was a city in a jungle. Thick dark green, so tangled that I could not tell trees from vine and bush, spread out all around but was broken repeatedly by buildings as large and larger than the one we were in. There were no roads; their roads are underground in cities and sometimes outside the cities. But there was air traffic—individual fliers supported by contrivances even less substantial than our own one-man 'copter harnesses or flying carpets. Like birds they launched themselves from and landed in balconies such as the one we stood in.

There were real birds, too, long and slender and brilliantly colored, with two sets of wings in tandem—which looked aerodynamically unsound but seemed to suit them.

The sky was blue and fair but broken by three towering cumulous anvils, blinding white in the distance.

"Let's go on the roof," said Peewee.

"How?"

"Over here."

It was a scuttle hole reached by staggered slender brackets the Vegans use as stairs. "Isn't there a ramp?"

"Around on the far side, yes."

"I don't think those things will hold me. And that hole looks small for Oscar."

"Oh, don't be a sissy." Peewee went up like a monkey.

I followed like a tired bear. The brackets were sturdy despite their grace; the hole was a snug fit.

Vega was high in the sky. It appeared to be the angular size of our Sun, which fitted since we were much farther out than Terra is from the Sun, but it was too bright even with full polarization. I looked away and presently eyes and polarizers adjusted until I could see again. Peewee's head was concealed by what appeared to be a polished chrome basketball. I said, "Hey, are you still there?"

"Sure," she answered. "I can see out all right. It's a grand view. Doesn't it remind you of Paris from the top of the Arc de Triomphe?"

"I don't know, I've never done any traveling."

"Except no boulevards, of course. Somebody is about to land here."

I turned the way she was pointing—she could see in all directions while I was hampered by the built-in tunnel vision of my helmet. By the time I was turned around the Vegan was coming in beside us.

("Hello, children!")

"Hi, Mother Thing!" Peewee threw her arms around her, picking her up.

("Not so hasty, dear. Let me shed this.") The Mother Thing stepped out of her harness, shook herself in ripples, folded the flying gear like an umbrella and hung it over an arm. ("You're looking fit, Kip.")

"I feel fine, Mother Thing! Gee, it's nice to have you back."

("I wished to be back when you got out of bed. However, your therapists have kept me advised every minute.") She put a little hand against my chest, growing a bit to do so, and placed her eyes almost against my face plate. ("You are well?")

"I couldn't be better."

"He really is, Mother Thing!"

("Good. You agree that you are well, I sense that you are, Peewee is sure that you are and, most important, your leader therapist assures me that you are. We'll leave at once.")

"What?" I asked. "Where, Mother Thing?"

She turned to Peewee. ("Haven't you told him, dear?")

"Gee, Mother Thing, I haven't had a *chance*."

("Very well.") She turned to me. ("Dear Kip, we must now attend a gathering. Questions will be asked and answered, decisions will be made.") She spoke to us both. ("Are you ready to leave?")

"Now?" said Peewee. "Why, I guess so—except that I've got to get Madame Pompadour."

("Fetch her, then. And you, Kip?")

"Uh—" I couldn't remember whether I had put my watch back on after I washed and I couldn't tell because I can't feel it through Oscar's thick hide. I told her so.

("Very well. You children run to your rooms while I have a ship fetched. Meet me here and don't stop to admire flowers.")

We went down by ramp. I said, "Peewee, you've been holding out on me again."

"Why, I have not!"

"What do you call it?"

"Kip—please listen! I was *told* not to tell you while you were ill. The Mother Thing was very firm about it. You were not to be *disturbed*—that's what she said!—while you were growing well."

"Why should I feel disturbed? What is all this? What gathering? What questions?"

"Well . . . the gathering is sort of a court. A criminal court, you might say."

"Huh?" I took a quick look at my conscience. But I hadn't had any chance to do anything wrong—I had been helpless as a baby up to two hours ago. That left Peewee. "Runt," I said sternly, "what have you done now?"

"Me? Nothing."

"Think hard."

"No, Kip. Oh, I'm sorry I didn't tell you at breakfast! But Daddy says never to break any news until after his second cup of coffee and I thought how nice it would be to take a little walk before we had any worries and I was going to tell you—"

"Make it march."

"—as soon as we came down. *I* haven't done anything. But there's old Wormface."

"What? I thought he was dead."

"Maybe so, maybe not. But, as the Mother Thing says, there are still questions to be asked, decisions to be made. He's up for the limit, is my guess."

I thought about it as we wound our way through strange apartments toward the air lock that led to our Earth-conditioned rooms. High crimes and misdemeanors . . . skulduggery in the spaceways—yes, Wormface was probably in for it. If the Vegans could catch him. "Had caught him" apparently, since they were going to try him. "But where do we come in? As witnesses?"

"I suppose you could call it that."

What happened to Wormface was no skin off my nose—and it would be a chance to find out more about the Vegans. Especially if the court was some distance away, so that we would travel and see the country.

"But that isn't all," Peewee went on worriedly.

"What else?"

She sighed. "This is why I wanted us to have a nice sight-see first. Uh . . ."

"Don't chew on it. Spit it out."

"Well . . . *we* have to be tried, too."

"What?"

"Maybe 'examined' is the word. I don't know. But I know this: we can't go home until we've been judged."

"But what have we *done?*" I burst out.

"I don't know!"

My thoughts were boiling. "Are you sure they'll let us go home then?"

"The Mother Thing refuses to talk about it."

I stopped and took her arm. "What it amounts to," I said bitterly, "is that we are under arrest. Aren't we?"

"Yes—" She added almost in a sob, "But, Kip, I *told* you she was a cop!"

"Great stuff. We pull her chestnuts out of the fire—and now we're arrested—and going to be tried—and we don't even know why! Nice place, Vega Five. 'The natives are friendly.' " They had nursed me—as we nurse a gangster in order to hang him.

"But, Kip—" Peewee was crying openly now. "I'm *sure* it'll be all right. She may be a cop—but she's still the Mother Thing."

"Is she? I wonder." Peewee's manner contradicted her words. She was not one to worry over nothing. Quite the contrary.

My watch was on the washstand. I ungasketed to put it in an inside pocket. When I came out, Peewee was doing the same with Madame Pompadour. "Here," I said, "I'll take her with me. I've got more room."

"No, thank you," Peewee answered bleakly. "I need her with me. Especially now."

"Uh, Peewee, where is this court? This city? Or another one?"

"Didn't I tell you? No, I guess I didn't. It's not on this planet."

"I thought this was the only inhabited—"

"It's not a planet around Vega. Another star. Not even in the Galaxy."

"Say that again?"

"It's somewhere in the Lesser Magellanic Cloud."

Chapter 10

I didn't put up a fight—a hundred and sixty trillion miles from nowhere, I mean. But I didn't speak to the Mother Thing as I got into her ship.

It was shaped like an old-fashioned beehive and it looked barely big enough to jump us to the space port. Peewee and I crowded together on the floor, the Mother Thing curled up in front and twiddled a shiny rack like an abacus; we took off, straight up.

In a few minutes my anger grew from sullenness to a reckless need to settle it. "Mother Thing!"

("One moment, dear. Let me get us out of the atmosphere.") She pushed something, the ship quivered and steadied.

"Mother Thing," I repeated.

("Wait until I lower us, Kip.")

I had to wait. It's as silly to disturb a pilot as it is to snatch the wheel of a car. The little ship took a buffeting; the upper winds must have been dillies. But she could pilot.

Presently there was a gentle bump and I figured we must be at the space port. The Mother Thing turned her head. ("All right, Kip. I sense your fear and resentment. Will it help to say that you two are in no danger? That I would protect you with my body? As you protected mine?")

"Yes, but—"

("Then let be. It is easier to show than it is to explain. Don't clamp your helmet. This planet's air is like your own.")

"Huh? You mean we're *there?*"

"I told you," Peewee said at my elbow. "Just *poof!* and you're there."

I didn't answer. I was trying to guess how far we were from home.

("Come, children.")

It was midday when we left; it was night as we disembarked. The ship rested on a platform that stretched out of sight. Stars in front of me were in unfamiliar constellations; slaunchwise down the sky was a thin curdling which I spotted as the Milky Way. So Peewee had her wires crossed—we were far from home but still in the Galaxy—perhaps we had simply switched to the night side of Vega Five.

I heard Peewee gasp and turned around.

I didn't have strength to gasp.

Dominating that whole side of the sky was a great whirlpool of millions, maybe billions, of stars.

You've seen pictures of the Great Nebula in Andromeda?—a giant spiral of two curving arms, seen at an angle. Of all the lovely things in the sky it is the most beautiful. This was like that.

Only we weren't seeing a photograph nor even by telescope; we were so close (if "close" is the word) that it stretched across the sky twice as long as the Big Dipper as seen from home—so close that I saw the thickening at the center, two great branches coiling around and overtaking each other. We saw it from an angle so that it appeared elliptical, just as M31 in Andromeda does; you could feel its depth, you could see its shape.

Then I *knew* I was a long way from home. *That* was home, up there, lost in billions of crowded stars.

It was some time before I noticed another double spiral on my right, almost as wide-flung but rather lopsided and not nearly as brilliant—a pale ghost of our own gorgeous Galaxy. It slowly penetrated that this second one must be the Greater Magellanic Cloud—if we were in the Lesser and if that fiery whirlpool was our own Galaxy. What I had thought was "The Milky Way" was simply *a* milky way, the Lesser Cloud from inside.

I turned and looked at it again. It had the right shape, a roadway around the sky, but it was pale skim milk compared with our own, about as our Milky Way looks on a murky night. I don't know how it should look, since I'd never seen the Magellanic Clouds; I've never been south of the Rio Grande. But I did know that each cloud is a galaxy in its own right, but smaller than ours and grouped with us.

I looked again at our blazing spiral and was homesick in a way I hadn't been since I was six.

Peewee was huddling to the Mother Thing for comfort. She made herself taller and put an arm around Peewee. ("There, there, dear! I felt the same way when I was very young and saw it for the first time.")

"Mother Thing?" Peewee said timidly. "Where is *home?*"

("See the right half of it, dear, where the outer arm trails into nothingness? We came from a point two-thirds the way out from the center.")

"No, no! Not Vega. I want to know where the *Sun* is!"

("Oh, your star. But, dear, at this distance it is the same.")

We learned how far it is from the Sun to the planet Lanador—167,000 light-years. The Mother Thing couldn't tell us directly as she did not know how much time we meant by a "year"—how long it takes Terra to go around the Sun (a figure she might have used once or not at all and as worth remembering as the price of peanuts in Perth). But she did know the distance from Vega to the Sun and told us the distance from Lanador to Vega with that as a yardstick—six thousand one hundred and ninety times as great. 6190 times 27 light-years gives 167,000 light-years. She courteously gave it in powers of ten the way we figure, instead of using factorial five ($1 \times 2 \times 3 \times 4 \times 5$ equals 120) which is how Vegans figure. 167,000 light-years is 9.82×10^{17} miles. Round off 9.82 and call it ten. Then—

$$1,000,000,000,000,000,000 \text{ miles}$$

—is the distance from Vega to Lanador (or from the Sun to Lanador; Vega and the Sun are back-fence neighbors on this scale).

A thousand million billion miles.

I refuse to have anything to do with such a preposterous figure. It may be "short" as cosmic distances go, but there comes a time when the circuit breakers in your skull trip out from overload.

The platform we were on was the roof of an enormous triangular building, miles on a side. We saw that triangle repeated in many places and always with a two-armed spiral in each corner. It was the design the Mother Thing wore as jewelry.

It is the symbol for "Three Galaxies, One Law."

I'll lump here things I learned in driblets: The Three Galaxies are like our Federated Free Nations, or the United Nations before that, or the League of Nations still earlier; Lanador houses their

offices and courts and files—the League's capital, the way the
FFN is in New York and the League of Nations used to be in
Switzerland. The cause is historical; the people of Lanador are the
Old Race; that's where civilization began.

The Three Galaxies are an island group, like Hawaii State,
they haven't any other close neighbors. Civilization spread
through the Lesser Cloud, then through the Greater Cloud and is
seeping slowly through our own Galaxy—that is taking longer;
there are fifteen or twenty times as many stars in our Galaxy as in
the other two.

When I began to get these things straight I wasn't quite as
sore. The Mother Thing was a very important person at home but
here she was a minor official—all she could do was bring us in.
Still, I wasn't more than coolly polite for a while—she might have
looked the other way while we beat it for home.

They housed us in that enormous building in a part you could
call a "transients' hotel," although "detention barracks" or "jail" is
closer. I can't complain about accommodations but I was getting
confoundedly tired of being locked up every time I arrived in a
new place. A robot met us and took us down inside—there are ro-
bots wherever you turn on Lanador. I don't mean things looking
like the Tin Woodman; I mean machines that do things for you,
such as this one which led us to our rooms, then hung around like
a bellhop expecting a tip. It was a three-wheeled cart with a big
basket on top, for luggage if we had any. It met us, whistled to the
Mother Thing in Vegan and led us away, down a lift and through a
wide and endlessly long corridor.

I was given "my" room again—a fake of a fake, with all errors
left in and new ones added. The sight of it was not reassuring; it
shrieked that they planned to keep us there as long as—well, as
long as *they* chose.

But the room was complete even to a rack for Oscar and a
bathroom outside. Just beyond "my" room was a fake of another
kind—a copy of that Arabian Nights horror Peewee had occupied
on Vega Five. Peewee seemed delighted, so I didn't point out the
implications.

The Mother Thing hovered around while we got out of space
suits. ("Do you think you will be comfortable?")

"Oh, sure," I agreed unenthusiastically.

("If you want food or anything, just say so. It will come.")

"So? Is there a telephone somewhere?"

("Simply speak your wishes. You will be heard.")

I didn't doubt her—but I was almost as tired of rooms that were bugged as of being locked up; a person ought to have privacy.

"I'm hungry now," Peewee commented. "I had an early breakfast."

We were in her room. A purple drapery drew back, a light glowed in the wall. In about two minutes a section of wall disappeared; a slab at table height stuck out like a tongue. On it were dishes and silverware, cold cuts, fruit, bread, butter, and a mug of steaming cocoa. Peewee clapped and squealed. I looked at it with less enthusiasm.

("You see?") The Mother Thing went on with a smile in her voice. ("Ask for what you need. If you need me, I'll come. But I must go now.")

"Oh, please don't go, Mother Thing."

("I must, Peewee dear. But I will see you soon. By the bye, there are two more of your people here.")

"Huh?" I put in. "Who? Where?"

("Next door.") She was gone with gliding swiftness; the bell-hop speeded up to stay ahead of her.

I spun around. "Did you hear that?"

"I certainly did!"

"Well—you eat if you want to; I'm going to look for those other humans."

"Hey! Wait for me!"

"I thought you wanted to eat."

"Well . . ." Peewee looked at the food. "Just a sec." She hastily buttered two slices of bread and handed one to me. I was not in that much of a hurry; I ate it. Peewee gobbled hers, took a gulp from the mug and offered it to me. "Want some?"

It wasn't quite cocoa; there was a meaty flavor, too. But it was good. I handed it back and she finished it. "Now I can fight wild-cats. Let's go, Kip."

"Next door" was through the foyer of our three-room suite and fifteen yards down the corridor, where we came to a door arch. I kept Peewee back and glanced in cautiously.

It was a diorama, a fake scene.

This one was better than you see in museums. I was looking through a bush at a small clearing in wild country. It ended in a limestone bank. I could see overcast sky and a cave mouth in the rocks. The ground was wet, as if from rain.

A cave man hunkered down close to the cave. He was gnawing the carcass of a small animal, possibly a squirrel.

Peewee tried to shove past me; I stopped her. The cave man did not appear to notice us which struck me as a good idea. His legs looked short but I think he weighed twice what I do and he was muscled like a weight lifter, with short, hairy forearms and knotty biceps and calves. His head was huge, bigger than mine and longer, but his forehead and chin weren't much. His teeth were large and yellow and a front one was broken. I heard bones crunching.

In a museum I would have expected a card reading "Neanderthal Man—*circa* Last Ice Age." But wax dummies of extinct breeds don't crack bones.

Peewee protested, "Hey, let me look."

He heard. Peewee stared at him, he stared toward us. Peewee squealed; he whirled and ran into the cave, waddling but making time.

I grabbed Peewee. "Let's get out of here!"

"Wait a minute," she said calmly. "He won't come out in a hurry." She tried to push the bush aside.

"Peewee!"

"Try this," she suggested. Her hand was shoving air. "They've got him penned."

I tried it. Something transparent blocked the arch. I could push it a little but not more than an inch. "Plastic?" I suggested. "Like Lucite but springier?"

"Mmm . . ." said Peewee. "More like the helmet of my suit. Tougher, though—and I'll bet light passes only one way. I don't think he saw us."

"Okay, let's get back to our rooms. Maybe we can lock them."

She went on feeling that barrier. "Peewee!" I said sharply. "You're not listening."

"What were you doing talking," she answered reasonably, "when I wasn't listening?"

"Peewee! This is no time to be difficult."

"You sound like Daddy. He dropped that rat he was eating— he might come back."

"If he does, you won't be here, because I'm about to drag you—and if you bite, I'll bite back. I warn you."

She looked around with a trace of animosity. "I wouldn't bite you, Kip, no matter what you did. But if you're going to be stuffy—oh, well, I doubt if he'll come out for an hour or so. We'll come back."

"Okay." I pulled her away.

But we did not leave. I heard a loud whistle and a shout: "Hey, buster! Over here!"

The words were not English, but I understood—well enough. The yell came from an archway across the corridor and a little farther on. I hesitated, then moved toward it because Peewee did so.

A man about forty-five was loafing in this doorway. He was no Neanderthal; he was civilized—or somewhat so. He wore a long heavy woolen tunic, belted in at the waist, forming a sort of kilt. His legs below that were wrapped in wool and he was shod in heavy short boots, much worn. At the belt and supported by a shoulder sling was a short, heavy sword; there was a dagger on the other side of the belt. His hair was short and he was clean-shaven save for a few days' gray stubble. His expression was neither friendly nor unfriendly; it was sharply watchful.

"Thanks," he said gruffly. "Are you the jailer?"

Peewee gasped. "Why, that's Latin!"

What do you do when you meet a Legionary? Right after a cave man? I answered: "No, I am a prisoner myself." I said it in Spanish and repeated it in pretty fair classical Latin. I used Spanish because Peewee hadn't been quite correct. It was not Latin he spoke, not the Latin of Ovid and Gaius Julius Caesar. Nor was it Spanish. It was in between, with an atrocious accent and other differences. But I could worry out the meaning.

He sucked his lip and answered, "That's bad. I've been trying for three days to attract attention and all I get is another prisoner. But that's how the die rolls. Say, that's a funny accent you have."

"Sorry, amigo, but I have trouble understanding you, too." I repeated it in Latin, then split the difference. I added, in improvised lingua franca, "Speak slowly, will you?"

"I'll speak as I please. And don't call me 'amico'; I'm a Roman citizen—so don't get gay."

That's a free translation. His advice was more vulgar—I think. It was close to a Spanish phrase which certainly is vulgar.

"What's he saying?" demanded Peewee. "It *is* Latin, isn't it? Translate!"

I was glad she hadn't caught it. "Why, Peewee, don't you know 'the language of poetry and science'?"

"Oh, don't be a smartie! Tell me."

"Don't crowd me, hon. I'll tell you later. I'm having trouble following it."

"What is that barbarian grunting?" the Roman said pleasantly.

"Talk language, boy. Or will you have ten with the flat of the sword?"

He seemed to be leaning on nothing—so I felt the air. It was solid; I decided not to worry about his threat. "I'm talking as best I can. We spoke to each other in our own language."

"Pig grunts. Talk Latin. If you can." He looked at Peewee as if just noticing her. "Your daughter? Want to sell her? If she had meat on her bones, she might be worth a half denario."

Peewee clouded up. "I understood that!" she said fiercely. "Come out here and fight!"

"Try it in Latin," I advised her. "If he understands you, he'll probably spank you."

She looked uneasy. "You wouldn't let him?"

"You know I wouldn't."

"Let's go back."

"That's what I said earlier." I escorted her past the cave man's lair to our suite. "Peewee, I'm going back and see what our noble Roman has to say. Do you mind?"

"I certainly do!"

"Be reasonable, hon. If we could be hurt by them, the Mother Thing would know it. After all, she told us they were here."

"I'll go with you."

"What for? I'll tell you everything I learn. This may be a chance to find out what this silliness means. What's *he* doing here? Have they kept him in deep-freeze a couple of thousand years? How long has he been awake? What does he know that we don't? We're in a bad spot; all the data I can dig up we need. You can help by keeping out. If you're scared, send for the Mother Thing."

She pouted. "I'm not scared. All right—if that's the way you want it."

"I do. Eat your dinner."

Jo-Jo the dogface boy was not in sight; I gave his door a wide berth. If a ship can go anywhere in *no* time, could it skip a dimension and go anywhere to *any* time? How would the math work out? The soldier was still lounging at his door. He looked up. "Didn't you hear me say to stick around?"

"I heard you," I admitted, "but we're not going to get anywhere if you take that attitude. I'm not one of your privates."

"Lucky for you!"

"Do we talk peacefully? Or do I leave?"

He looked me over. "Peace. But don't get smart with me, barbarian."

He called himself "Iunio." He had served in Spain and Gaul, then transferred to the VIth Legion, the "Victrix"—which he felt that even a barbarian should know of. His legion's garrison was Eboracum, north of Londinium in Britain, but he had been on advance duty as a brevet centurion (he pronounced it "centurio")— his permanent rank was about like top sergeant. He was smaller than I am but I would not want to meet him in an alley. Nor at the palisades of a castra.

He had a low opinion of Britons and all barbarians including me ("nothing personal—some of my best friends are barbarians"), women, the British climate, high brass, and priests; he thought well of Caesar, Rome, the gods, and his own professional ability. The army wasn't what it used to be and the slump came from treating auxiliaries like Roman citizens.

He had been guarding the building of a wall to hold back barbarians—a nasty lot who would sneak up and slit your throat and eat you—which no doubt had happened to him, since he was now in the nether regions.

I thought he was talking about Hadrian's Wall, but it was three days' march north of there, where the seas were closest together. The climate there was terrible and the natives were bloodthirsty beasts who dyed their bodies and didn't appreciate civilization— you'd think the Eagles were trying to steal their dinky island. Provincial . . . like me. No offense meant.

Nevertheless he had bought a little barbarian to wife and had been looking forward to garrison duty at Eboracum—when this happened. Iunio shrugged. "Perhaps if I had been careful with lustrations and sacrifices, my luck wouldn't have run out. But I figure that if a man does his duty and keeps himself and his weapons clean, the rest is the C.O.'s worry. Careful of that doorway; it's witched."

The longer he talked the easier it was to understand him. The "-us" endings turned to "-o" and his vocabulary was not that of *De Bello Gallico*—"horse" wasn't "equus"; it was "caballo." His idioms bothered me, plus the fact that his Latin was diluted by a dozen barbarian tongues. But you can blank out every third word in a newspaper and still catch the gist.

I learned a lot about the daily life and petty politics of the Victrix and nothing that I wanted to know. Iunio did not know how he had gotten where he was nor why—except that he was dead and awaiting disposition in a receiving barracks somewhere in the nether world—a theory which I was not yet prepared to accept.

He knew the year of his "death"—Year Eight of the Emperor and Eight Hundred and Ninety-Nine of Rome. I wrote out the dates in Roman numerals to make sure. But I did not remember when Rome was founded nor could I identify the "Caesar" even by his full name—there have been so many Caesars. But Hadrian's Wall had been built and Britain was still occupied; that placed Iunio close to the third century.

He wasn't interested in the cave man across the way—it embodied to him the worst vice of a barbarian: cowardice. I didn't argue but I would be timid, too, if I had saber-toothed tigers yowling at my door. (Did they have saber-tooths then? Make it "cave bears.")

Iunio went back and returned with hard dark bread, cheese, and a cup. He did not offer me any and I don't think it was the barrier. He poured a little of his drink on the floor and started to chomp. It was a mud floor; the walls were rough stone and the ceiling was supported by wooden beams. It may have been a copy of dwellings during the occupation of Britain, but I'm no expert.

I didn't stay much longer. Not only did bread and cheese remind me that I was hungry, but I offended Iunio. I don't know what set him off, but he discussed me with cold thoroughness, my eating habits, ancestry, appearance, conduct, and method of earning a living. Iunio was pleasant—as long as you agreed with him, ignored insults, and deferred to him. Many older people demand this, even in buying a thirty-nine-cent can of talcum; you learn to give it without thinking—otherwise you get a reputation as a fresh kid and potential juvenile delinquent. The less respect an older person deserves the more certain he is to demand it from anyone younger. So I left, as Iunio didn't know anything helpful anyhow. As I went back I saw the cave man peering out his cave. I said, "Take it easy, Jo-Jo," and went on.

I bumped into another invisible barrier blocking our archway. I felt it, then said quietly, "I want to go in." The barrier melted away and I walked in—then found that it was back in place.

My rubber soles made no noise and I didn't call out because Peewee might be asleep. Her door was open and I peeped in. She was sitting tailor-fashion on that incredible Oriental divan, rocking Madame Pompadour and crying.

I backed away, then returned whistling, making a racket, and

calling to her. She popped out of her door, with smiling face and
no trace of tears. "Hi, Kip! It took you long enough."

"That guy talks too much. What's new?"

"Nothing. I ate and you didn't come back, so I took a nap. You
woke me. What did you find out?"

"Let me order dinner and I'll tell you while I eat."

I was chasing the last bit of gravy when a bellhop robot came for
us. It was like the other one except that it had in glowing gold on
its front that triangle with three spirals. "Follow me," it said in
English.

I looked at Peewee. "Didn't the Mother Thing say she was
coming back?"

"Why, I thought so."

The machine repeated, "Follow me. Your presence is required."

I laid my ears back. I have taken lots of orders, some of which
I shouldn't have, but I had never yet taken orders from a piece of
machinery. "Go climb a rope!" I said. "You'll have to drag me."

This is not what to say to a robot. It did.

Peewee yelled, "*Mother Thing!* Where are you? Help us!"

Her birdsong came out of the machine. ("It's all right, dears.
The servant will lead you to me.")

I quit struggling and started to walk. That refugee from an ap-
pliance dealer took us into another lift, then into a corridor whose
walls whizzed past as soon as we entered. It nudged us through an
enormous archway topped by the triangle and spirals and herded
us into a pen near one wall. The pen was not apparent until we
moved—more of that annoying solid air.

It was the biggest room I have ever been in, triangular, unbroken by post or pillar, with ceiling so high and walls so distant that
I half expected local thunderstorms. An enormous room makes
me feel like an ant; I was glad to be near a wall. The room was not
empty—hundreds in it—but it looked empty because they were all
near the walls; the giant floor was bare.

But there were three wormfaces out in the center—
Wormface's trial was in progress.

I don't know if our own Wormface was there. I would not have
known even if they had not been a long way off as the difference
between two wormfaces is the difference between having your
throat cut and being beheaded. But, as we learned, the presence or
absence of the individual offender was the least important part of
a trial. Wormface was being tried, present or not—alive or dead.

The Mother Thing was speaking. I could see her tiny figure, also far out on the floor but apart from the wormfaces. Her birdsong voice reached me faintly but I heard her words clearly—in English; from somewhere near us her translated words were piped to us. The feel of her was in the English translation just as it was in her bird tones.

She was telling what she knew of wormface conduct, as dispassionately as if describing something under a microscope, like a traffic officer testifying: "At 9:17 on the fifth, while on duty at—" etc. The facts. The Mother Thing was finishing her account of events on Pluto. She chopped it off at the point of explosion.

Another voice spoke, in English. It was flat with a nasal twang and reminded me of a Vermont grocer we had dealt with one summer when I was a kid. He was a man who never smiled nor frowned and what little he said was all in the same tone, whether it was, "She is a good woman," or, "That man would cheat his own son," or, "Eggs are fifty-nine cents," cold as a cash register. This voice was that sort.

It said to the Mother Thing: "Have you finished?"

"I have finished."

"The other witnesses will be heard. Clifford Russell—"

I jumped, as if that grocer had caught me in the candy jar.

The voice went on: "—listen carefully." Another voice started.

My *own*—it was the account I had dictated, flat on my back on Vega Five.

But it wasn't all of it; it was just that which concerned wormfaces. Adjectives and whole sentences had been cut—as if someone had taken scissors to a tape recording. The facts were there; what I thought about them was missing.

It started with ships landing in the pasture back of our house; it ended with that last wormface stumbling blindly down a hole. It wasn't long, as so much had been left out—our hike across the Moon, for example. My description of Wormface was left in but had been trimmed so much that I could have been talking about Venus de Milo instead of the ugliest thing in creation.

My recorded voice ended and the Yankee-grocer voice said, "Were those your words?"

"Huh? Yes."

"Is the account correct?"

"Yes, but—"

"Is it correct?"

"Yes."

"Is it complete?"

I wanted to say that it certainly was *not*—but I was beginning to understand the system. "Yes."

"Patricia Wynant Reisfeld—"

Peewee's story started earlier and covered all those days when she had been in contact with wormfaces while I was not. But it was not much longer, for, while Peewee has a sharp eye and a sharper memory, she is loaded with opinions. Opinions were left out.

When Peewee had agreed that her evidence was correct and complete the Yankee voice stated, "All witnesses have been heard, all known facts have been integrated. The three individuals may speak for themselves."

I think the wormfaces picked a spokesman, perhaps *the* Wormface, if he was alive and there. Their answer, as translated into English, did not have the guttural accent with which Wormface spoke English; nevertheless it was a wormface speaking. That bone-chilling yet highly intelligent viciousness, as unmistakable as a punch in the teeth, was in every syllable.

Their spokesman was so far away that I was not upset by his looks and after the first stomach-twisting shock of that voice I was able to listen more or less judicially. He started by denying that this court had jurisdiction over his sort. He was responsible only to his mother-queen and she only to their queen-groups—that's how the English came out.

That defense, he claimed, was sufficient. However, if the "Three Galaxies" confederation existed which he had no reason to believe other than that he was now being detained unlawfully before this hiveful of creatures met as a kangaroo court—if it existed, it still had no jurisdiction over the Only People, first, because the organization did not extend to his part of space; second, because even if it were there, the Only People had never joined and therefore its rules (if it had rules) could not apply; and third, it was inconceivable that their queen-group would associate itself with this improbable "Three Galaxies" because people do not contract with animals.

This defense was also sufficient.

But disregarding for the sake of argument these complete and sufficient defenses, this trial was a mockery because no offense existed even under the so-called rules of the alleged "Three Galaxies." They (the wormfaces) had been operating in their own part of space engaged in occupying a useful but empty planet, Earth. No possible crime could lie in colonizing land inhabited merely by animals. As for the agent of Three Galaxies, she had butted in; she had not been harmed; she had merely been kept from interfering and had been detained only for the purpose of returning her where she belonged.

He should have stopped. Any of these defenses might have stood up, especially the last one. I used to think of the human race as "lords of creation"—but things had happened to me since. I was not sure that this assemblage would think that humans had rights compared with wormfaces. Certainly the wormfaces were ahead of us in many ways. When we clear jungle to make farms, do we worry if baboons are there first?

But he discarded these defenses, explained that they were intellectual exercises to show how foolish the whole thing was under *any* rules, from *any* point of view. He would now make his defense.

It was an attack.

The viciousness in his voice rose to a crescendo of hatred that made every word slam like a blow. How *dared* they do this? They were mice voting to bell the cat! (I know—but that's how it came out in translation.) They were animals to be eaten, or merely vermin to be exterminated. Their mercy would be rejected if offered, no negotiation was possible, their crimes would never be forgotten, the Only People would destroy them!

I looked around to see how the jury was taking it. This almost-empty hall had hundreds of creatures around the three sides and many were close to us. I had been too busy with the trial to do more than glance at them. Now I looked, for the wormface's blast was so disturbing that I welcomed a distraction.

They were all sorts and I'm not sure that any two were alike. There was one twenty feet from me who was as horrible as Wormface and amazingly like him—except that this creature's grisly appearance did not inspire disgust. There were others almost human in appearance, although they were greatly in the minority. There was one really likely-looking chick as human as I am—except for iridescent skin and odd and skimpy notions of dress. She was so pretty that I would have sworn that the iridescence was just make-up—but I probably would have been wrong. I wondered in what language the diatribe was reaching her? Certainly not English.

Perhaps she felt my stare, for she looked around and unsmilingly examined me, as I might a chimpanzee in a cage. I guess the attraction wasn't mutual.

There was every gradation from pseudo-wormface to the iridescent girl—not only the range between, but also way out in left field; some had their own private aquaria.

I could not tell how the invective affected them. The girl creature was taking it quietly, but what can you say about a walrus thing with octopus arms? If he twitches, is he angry? Or laughing? Or itches where the twitch is?

The Yankee-voiced spokesman let the wormface rave on.

Peewee was holding my hand. Now she grabbed my ear, tilted her face and whispered, "He talks nasty." She sounded awed.

The wormface ended with a blast of hate that must have overtaxed the translator for instead of English we heard a wordless scream.

The Yankee voice said flatly, "But do you have anything to say in your defense?"

The scream was repeated, then the wormface became coherent. "I have made my defense—that no defense is necessary."

The emotionless voice went on, to the Mother Thing. "Do you speak for them?"

She answered reluctantly, "My lord peers . . . I am forced to say . . . that I found them to be quite naughty." She sounded grieved.

"You find against them?"

"I do."

"Then you may not be heard. Such is the Law."

" 'Three Galaxies, One Law.' I may not speak."

The flat voice went on, "Will any witness speak favorably?"

There was silence.

That was my chance to be noble. We humans were their victims; we were in a position to speak up, point out that from their standpoint they hadn't done anything wrong, and ask mercy—if they would promise to behave in the future.

Well, I didn't. I've heard all the usual Sweetness and Light that kids get pushed at them—how they should always forgive, how there's some good in the worst of us, etc. But when I see a black widow, I step on it; I don't plead with it to be a good little spider and please stop poisoning people. A black widow spider can't help it—but that's the point.

The voice said to the wormfaces: "Is there any race anywhere which might speak for you? If so, it will be summoned."

The spokesman wormface spat at the idea. That another race might be character witnesses for them disgusted him.

"So be it," answered the Yankee voice. "Are the facts sufficient to permit a decision?"

Almost immediately the voice answered itself: "Yes."

"What is the decision?"

Again it answered itself: "Their planet shall be rotated."

It didn't sound like much—shucks, all planets rotate—and the flat voice held no expression. But the verdict scared me. The whole room seemed to shudder.

The Mother Thing turned and came toward us. It was a long way but she reached us quickly. Peewee flung herself on her; the solid air that penned us solidified still more until we three were in a private room, a silvery hemisphere.

Peewee was trembling and gasping and the Mother Thing comforted her. When Peewee had control of herself, I said nervously, "Mother Thing? What did he mean? 'Their planet shall be rotated.'"

She looked at me without letting go of Peewee and her great soft eyes were sternly sad. ("It means that their planet is tilted ninety degrees out of the space-time of your senses and mine.")

Her voice sounded like a funeral dirge played softly on a flute. Yet the verdict did not seem tragic to me. I knew what she meant; her meaning was even clearer in Vegan than in English. If you rotate a plane figure about an axis in its plane—it disappears. It is no longer in a plane and Mr. A. Square of Flatland is permanently out of touch with it.

But it doesn't cease to exist; it just is no longer where it was. It struck me that the wormfaces were getting off easy. I had halfway expected their planet to be blown up (and I didn't doubt that Three Galaxies could do so), or something equally drastic. As it was, the wormfaces were to be run out of town and would never find their way back—there are so many, many dimensions—but they wouldn't be hurt; they were just being placed in Coventry.

But the Mother Thing sounded as if she had taken unwilling part in a hanging.

So I asked her.

("You do not understand, dear gentle Kip—*they do not take their star with them*.")

"Oh—" was all I could say.

Peewee turned white.

Stars are the source of life—planets are merely life's containers. Chop off the star . . . and the planet gets colder . . . and colder . . . and *colder*—then still colder.

How long until the very air freezes? How many hours or days

to absolute zero? I shivered and got goose pimples. Worse than Pluto—

"Mother Thing? How long before they do this?" I had a queasy misgiving that I should have spoken, that even wormfaces did not deserve *this*. Blow them up, shoot them down—but don't freeze them.

("It is done,") she sang in that same dirgelike way.

"What?"

("The agent charged with executing the decision waits for the word . . . the message goes out the instant we hear it. They were rotated out of our world even before I turned to join you. It is better so.")

I gulped and heard an echo in my mind: *"—'twere well it were done quickly."*

But the Mother Thing was saying rapidly. ("Think no more on 't, for now you must be brave!")

"Huh? What, Mother Thing? What happens now?"

("You'll be summoned any moment—for your own trial.")

I simply stared, I could not speak—I had thought it was all over. Peewee looked still thinner and whiter but did not cry. She wet her lips and said quietly, "You'll come with us, Mother Thing?"

("Oh, my children! I cannot. You must face this alone.")

I found my voice. "But what are *we* being tried for? We haven't hurt anybody. We haven't done a thing."

("Not you personally. Your race is on trial. Through you.")

Peewee turned away from her and looked at me—and I felt a thrill of tragic pride that in our moment of extremity she had turned, not to the Mother Thing, but to *me*, another human being.

I knew that she was thinking of the same thing I was: a ship, a ship hanging close to Earth, only an instant away and yet perhaps uncounted trillion miles in some pocket of folded space, where no DEW line gives warning, where no radar can reach.

The Earth, green and gold and lovely, turning lazily in the warm light of the Sun—

A flat voice— No more Sun.

No stars.

The orphaned Moon would bobble once, then continue around the Sun, a gravestone to the hopes of men. The few at Lunar Base and Luna City and Tombaugh Station would last weeks or even months, the only human beings left alive. Then they would go—if not of suffocation, then of grief and loneliness.

Peewee said shrilly, "Kip, she's not serious! Tell me she's not!"

I said hoarsely, "Mother Thing—are the executioners already waiting?"

She did not answer. She said to Peewee. ("It is very serious, my daughter. But do not be afraid. I exacted a promise before I surrendered you. If things go against your race, you two will return with me and be suffered to live out your little lives in my home. So stand up and tell the truth . . . and do not be afraid.")

The flat voice entered the closed space: "The human beings are summoned."

Chapter 11

We walked out onto that vast floor. The farther we went the more I felt like a fly on a plate. Having Peewee with me was a help; nevertheless it was that nightmare where you find yourself not decently dressed in a public place. Peewee clutched my hand and held Madame Pompadour pressed tightly to her. I wished that I had suited-up in Oscar—I wouldn't have felt quite so under a microscope with Oscar around me.

Just before we left, the Mother Thing placed her hand against my forehead and started to hold me with her eyes. I pushed her hand aside and looked away. "No," I told her. "No treatments! I'm not going to—oh, I know you mean well but I won't take an anesthetic. Thanks."

She did not insist; she simply turned to Peewee. Peewee looked uncertain, then shook her head. "We're ready," she piped.

The farther out we got on that great bare floor the more I regretted that I had not let the Mother Thing do whatever it was that kept one from worrying. At least I should have insisted that Peewee take it.

Coming at us from the other walls were two other flies; as they got closer I recognized them: the Neanderthal and the Legionary. The cave man was being dragged invisibly; the Roman covered ground in a long, slow, easy lope. We all arrived at the center at the same time and were stopped about twenty feet apart, Peewee and I at one point of a triangle, the Roman and the cave man each at another.

I called out, "Hail, Iunio!"

"Silence, barbarian." He looked around him, his eyes estimating the crowd at the walls.

He was no longer in casual dress. The untidy leggings were gone; strapped to his right shin was armor. Over the tunic he wore full cuirass and his head was brave with plumed helmet. All metal was burnished, all leather was clean.

He had approached with his shield on his back, route-march style. But even as we were stopped he unslung it and raised it on his left arm. He did not draw his sword as his right hand held his javelin at the ready—carried easily while his wary eyes assessed the foe.

To his left the cave man hunkered himself small, as an animal crouches who has no place to hide.

"Iunio!" I called out. "Listen!" The sight of those two had me still more worried. The cave man I could not talk to but perhaps I could reason with the Roman. "Do you know why we are here?"

"I know," he tossed over his shoulder. "Today the Gods try us in their arena. This is work for a soldier and a Roman citizen. You're no help so keep out. No—watch behind me and shout. Caesar will reward you."

I started to try to talk sense but was cut off by a giant voice from everywhere:

"YOU ARE NOW BEING JUDGED!"

Peewee shivered and got closer. I twisted my left hand out of her clutch, substituted my right, and put my left arm around her shoulders. "Head up, partner," I said softly. "Don't let them scare you."

"I'm not scared," she whispered as she trembled. "Kip? You do the talking."

"Is that the way you want it?"

"Yes. You don't get mad as fast as I do—and if I lost my temper . . . well, that'd be *awful*."

"Okay."

We were interrupted by that flat, nasal twang. As before, it seemed close by. "This case derives from the one preceding it. The three temporal samples are from a small Lanador-type planet around a star in an out-center part of the Third Galaxy. It is a very primitive area having no civilized races. This race, as you see from the samples, is barbaric. It has been examined twice before and would not yet be up for routine examination had not new facts about it come out in the case which preceded it."

The voice asked itself: "When was the last examination made?"

It answered itself: "Approximately one half-death of Thorium-230 ago." It added, apparently to us only: "About eighty thousand of your years."

Iunio jerked his head and looked around, as if trying to locate the voice. I concluded that he had heard the same figure in his corrupt Latin. Well, I was startled too—but I was numb to that sort of shock.

"Is it necessary again so soon?"

"It is. There has been a discontinuity. They are developing with unexpected speed." The flat voice went on, speaking to us: "I am your judge. Many of the civilized beings you see around you are part of me. Others are spectators, some are students, and a few are here because they hope to catch me in a mistake." The voice added, "This they have not managed to do in more than a million of your years."

I blurted out, "You are more than a million years old?" I did not add that I didn't believe it.

The voice answered, "I am older than that, but no part of me is that old. I am partly machine, which part can be repaired, replaced, recopied; I am partly alive, these parts die and are replaced. My living parts are more than a dozen dozens of dozens of civilized beings from throughout Three Galaxies, any dozen dozens of which may join with my non-living part to act. Today I am two hundred and nine qualified beings, who have at their instant disposal all knowledge accumulated in my non-living part and all its ability to analyze and integrate."

I said sharply, "Are your decisions made unanimously?" I thought I saw a loophole—I never had much luck mixing up Dad and Mother but there had been times as a kid when I had managed to confuse issues by getting one to answer one way and the other to answer another.

The voice added evenly, "Decisions are always unanimous. It may help you to think of me as one person." It addressed everyone: "Standard sampling has been followed. The contemporary sample is the double one; the intermediate sample for curve check is the clothed single sample and was taken by standard random at a spacing of approximately one half-death of Radium-226—" The voice supplemented: "—call it sixteen hundred of your years. The remote curve-check sample, by standard procedure, was taken at two dozen times that distance."

The voice asked itself: "Why is curve-check spacing so short? Why not at least a dozen times that?"

"Because this organism's generations are very short. It mutates rapidly."

The explanation appeared to satisfy for it went on, "The youngest sample will witness first."

I thought he meant Peewee and so did she; she cringed. But the voice barked and the cave man jerked. He did not answer; he simply crouched more deeply into himself.

The voice barked again.

It then said to itself, "I observe something."

"Speak."

"This creature is not ancestor to those others."

The voice of the machine almost seemed to betray emotion, as if my dour grocer had found salt in his sugar bin. "The sample was properly taken."

"Nevertheless," it answered, "it is not a correct sample. You must review all pertinent data."

For a long five seconds was silence. Then the voice spoke: "This poor creature is not ancestor to these others; he is cousin only. He has no future of his own. Let him be returned at once to the space-time whence he came."

The Neanderthal was dragged rapidly away. I watched him out of sight with a feeling of loss. I had been afraid of him at first. Then I had despised him and was ashamed of him. He was a coward, he was filthy, he stank. A dog was more civilized. But in the past five minutes I had decided that I had better love him, see his good points—for, unsavory as he was, he was *human*. Maybe he wasn't my remote grandfather, but I was in no mood to disown even my sorriest relation.

The voice argued with itself, deciding whether the trial could proceed. Finally it stated: "Examination will continue. If enough facts are not developed, another remote sample of correct lineage will be summoned. Iunio."

The Roman raised his javelin higher. "Who calls Iunio?"

"Stand forth and bear witness."

Just as I feared, Iunio told the voice where to go and what to do. There was no protecting Peewee from his language; it echoed back in English—not that it mattered now whether Peewee was protected from "unladylike" influences.

The flat voice went on imperturbably: "Is this your voice? Is this your witnessing?" Immediately another voice started up which I recognized as that of the Roman, answering questions, giving accounts of battle, speaking of treatment of prisoners. This we got only in English but the translation held the arrogant timbre of Iunio's voice.

Iunio shouted "Witchcraft!" and made horns at them.

The recording cut off. "The voice matches," the machine said dryly. "The recording will be integrated."

But it continued to peck at Iunio, asking him details about who he was, why he was in Britain, what he had done there, and why it was necessary to serve Caesar. Iunio gave short answers, then blew his top and gave none. He let out a rebel yell that bounced around that mammoth room, drew back and let fly his javelin.

It fell short. But I think he broke the Olympic record.

I found myself cheering.

Iunio drew his sword while the javelin was still rising. He flung it up in a gladiatorial challenge, shouting, "Hail, Caesar!" and dropped into guard.

He reviled them. He told them what he thought of vermin who were not citizens, not even *barbarians!*

I said to myself, "Oh, oh! There goes the game. Human race, you've had it."

Iunio went on and on, calling on his gods to help him, each way worse than the last, threatening them with Caesar's vengeance in gruesome detail. I hoped that, even though it was translated, Peewee would not understand much of it. But she probably did; she understood entirely too much.

I began to grow proud of him. That wormface, in diatribe, was evil; Iunio was not. Under bad grammar, worse language, and rough manner, that tough old sergeant had courage, human dignity, and a basic gallantry. He might be an old scoundrel—but he was *my* kind of scoundrel.

He finished by demanding that they come at him, one at a time—or let them form a turtle and he would take them all on at once. "I'll make a funeral pyre of you! I'll temper my blade in your guts! I, who am about to die, will show you a Roman's grave—piled high with Caesar's enemies!"

He had to catch his breath. I cheered again and Peewee joined in. He looked over his shoulder and grinned. "Slit their throats as I bring them down, boy! There's work to do!"

The cold voice said: "Let him now be returned to the space-time whence he came."

Iunio looked startled as invisible hands pulled him along. He called on Mars and Jove and laid about him. The sword clattered to the floor—picked itself up and returned itself to his scabbard. Iunio was moving rapidly away; I cupped my hands and yelled, "Good-bye, Iunio!"

"Farewell, boy! They're *cowards!*" He shook himself. "Nothing but filthy witchcraft!" Then he was gone.

"Clifford Russell—"

"Huh? I'm here." Peewee squeezed my hand.

"Is this your voice?"

I said, "Wait a minute—"

"Yes? Speak."

I took a breath. Peewee pushed closer and whispered, "Make it good, Kip. They mean it."

"I'll try, kid," I whispered, then went on, "What is this? I was told you intend to judge the human race."

"That is correct."

"But you *can't.* You haven't enough to go on. No better than witchcraft, just as Iunio said. You brought in a cave man—then decided he was a mistake. That isn't your only mistake. You had Iunio here. Whatever he was—and I'm not ashamed of him; I'm proud of him—he's got nothing to do with *now.* He's been dead two thousand years, pretty near—if you've sent him back, I mean—and all that he was is dead with him. Good or bad, he's not what the human race is *now.*"

"I know that. You two are the test sample of your race now."

"Yes—but you can't judge from *us.* Peewee and I are about as far from average as any specimens can be. We don't claim to be angels, either one of us. If you condemn our race on what *we* have done, you do a great injustice. Judge *us*—or judge *me*, at least—"

"Me, too!"

"—on whatever I've done. But don't hold my people responsible. That's not scientific. That's not valid mathematics."

"It is valid."

"It is *not.* Human beings aren't molecules; they're all different." I decided not to argue about jurisdiction; the wormfaces had ruined that approach.

"Agreed, human beings are not molecules. But they are not individuals, either."

"Yes, they are!"

"They are not independent individuals; they are parts of a single organism. Each cell in your body contains your whole pattern. From three samples of the organism you call the human race I can predict the future potentialities and limits of that race."

"We have no limits! There's no telling what our future will be."

"It may be that you have no limits," the voice agreed. "That is to be determined. But, if true, it is not a point in your favor. For *we* have limits."

"Huh?"

"You have misunderstood the purpose of this examination. You speak of 'justice.' I know what you think you mean. But no two races have ever agreed on the meaning of that term, no matter how they say it. It is not a concept I deal with here. This is not a court of justice."

"Then what is it?"

"You would call it a 'Security Council.' Or you might call it a committee of vigilantes. It does not matter what you call it; my sole purpose is to examine your race and see if you threaten our survival. If you do, I will now dispose of you. The only certain way to avert a grave danger is to remove it while it is small. Things that I have learned about you suggest a possibility that you may someday threaten the security of Three Galaxies. I will now determine the facts."

"But you said that you have to have at least three samples. The cave man was no good."

"We have three samples, you two and the Roman. But the facts could be determined from one sample. The use of three is a custom from earlier times, a cautious habit of checking and rechecking. I cannot dispense 'justice'; I can make sure not to produce error."

I was about to say that he was wrong, even if he was a million years old. But the voice went on, "I continue the examination. Clifford Russell, is this your voice?"

My voice sounded then—and again it was my own dictated account, but this time everything was left in—purple adjectives, personal opinions, comments about other matters, every word and stutter.

I listened to enough of it, held up my hand. "All right, all right, I said it."

The recording stopped. "Do you now confirm it?"

"Eh? Yes."

"Do you wish to add, subtract, or change?"

I thought hard. Aside from a few wisecracks that I had tucked in later it was a straight-forward account. "No. I stand on it."

"And is this also your voice?"

This one fooled me. It was that endless recording I had made for Prof Joe about—well, everything on Earth . . . history, customs, peoples, the works. Suddenly I knew why Prof Joe had worn the same badge the Mother Thing wore. What did they call that?—"Planting a stool pigeon." Good Old Prof Joe, the no-good, had been a stoolie.

I felt sick.

"Let me hear more of it."

They accommodated me. I didn't really listen; I was trying to remember, not what I was hearing, but what else I might have said—what I had admitted that could be used against the human race. The Crusades? Slavery? The gas chambers at Dachau? *How much had I said?*

The recording droned on. Why, that thing had taken *weeks* to record; we could stand here until our feet went flat.

"It's my voice."

"Do you stand on this, too? Or do you wish to correct, revise, or extend?"

I said cautiously, "Can I do the whole thing over?"

"If you so choose."

I started to say that I would, that they should wipe the tape and start over. But would they? Or would they keep both and compare them? I had no compunction about lying—"tell the truth and shame the devil" is no virtue when your family and friends and your whole race are at stake.

But could they tell if I lied?

"The Mother Thing said to tell the truth and not to be afraid."

"But she's not on our side!"

"Oh, yes, she is."

I had to answer. I was so confused that I couldn't think. I had tried to tell the truth to Prof Joe . . . oh, maybe I had shaded things, not included every horrid thing that makes a headline. But it was essentially true.

Could I do better under pressure? Would they let me start fresh and accept any propaganda I cooked up? Or would the fact that I changed stories be used to condemn our race?

"I stand on it!"

"Let it be integrated. Patricia Wynant Reisfeld—"

Peewee took only moments to identify and allow to be integrated her recordings; she simply followed my example.

The machine voice said: "The facts have been integrated. By their own testimony, these are a savage and brutal people, given to all manner of atrocities. They eat each other, they starve each other, they kill each other. They have no art and only the most primitive of science, yet such is their violent nature that even with so little knowledge they are now energetically using it to exterminate each other, tribe against tribe. Their driving will is such that they may succeed. But if by some unlucky chance they fail, they will inevitably, in time, reach other stars. It is this possibility which must be calculated: how soon they will reach us, if they live, and what their potentialities will be then."

The voice continued to us: "This is the indictment against you—your own savagery, combined with superior intelligence. What have you to say in your defense?"

I took a breath and tried to steady down. I knew that we had lost—yet I had to try.

I remembered how the Mother Thing had spoken. "My lord peers—"

"Correction. We are not your 'lords,' nor has it been established that you are our equals. If you wish to address someone, you may call me the 'Moderator.' "

"Yes, Mr. Moderator—" I tried to remember what Socrates had said to his judges. He knew ahead of time that he was condemned just as we knew—but somehow, though he had been forced to drink hemlock, he had won and they had lost.

No! I couldn't use his *Apologia*—all he had lost was his *own* life. This was *everybody*.

"—you say we have no art. Have you seen the Parthenon?"

"Blown up in one of your wars."

"Better see it before you rotate us—or you'll be missing something. Have you read our poetry? 'Our revels now are ended: these our actors, as I foretold you, were all spirits, and are melted into air, into thin air: And, like the baseless fabric of this vision, the cloud-capped towers, the gorgeous palaces, the solemn temples, the great globe itself . . . itself—yea—all which it . . . inherit— shall dissolve—"

I broke down. I heard Peewee sobbing beside me. I don't know why I picked that one—but they say the subconscious mind never does things "accidentally." I guess it had to be that one.

"As it well may," commented the merciless voice.

"I don't think it's any of your *business* what we do—as long as we leave you alone—" My stammer was back and I was almost sobbing.

"We have made it our business."

"We aren't under your government and—"

"Correction. Three Galaxies is not a government; conditions for government cannot obtain in so vast a space, such varied cultures. We have simply formed police districts for mutual protection."

"But—even so, we haven't troubled your cops. We were in our own backyards—I *was* in my own backyard!—when these wormface things came along and started troubling *us*. We haven't hurt *you*."

I stopped, wondering where to turn. I couldn't guarantee good behavior, not for the whole human race—the machine knew it and I knew it.

"Inquiry." It was talking to itself again. "These creatures appear to be identical with the Old Race, allowing for mutation. What part of the Third Galaxy are they from?"

It answered itself, naming co-ordinates that meant nothing to me. "But they are not of the Old Race; they are ephemerals. That is the danger; they change too fast."

"Didn't the Old Race lose a ship out that way a few half-deaths of Thorium-230 ago? Could that account for the fact that the youngest sample failed to match?"

It answered firmly, "It is immaterial whether or not they may be descended from the Old Race. An examination is in progress; a decision must be made."

"The decision must be sure."

"It will be." The bodyless voice went on, to us: "Have either of you anything to add in your defense?"

I had been thinking of what had been said about the miserable state of our science. I wanted to point out that we had gone from muscle power to atomic power in only two centuries—but I was afraid that fact would be used against us. "Peewee, can you think of *anything?*"

She suddenly stepped forward and shrilled to the air, "Doesn't it count that Kip saved the Mother Thing?"

"No," the cold voice answered. "It is irrelevant."

"Well, it ought to count!" She was crying again. "You ought to be *ashamed* of yourselves! Bullies! *Cowards!* Oh, you're worse than wormfaces!"

I pulled her back. She hid her head against my shoulder and shook. Then she whispered, "I'm sorry, Kip. I didn't mean to. I guess I've ruined it."

"It was ruined anyhow, honey."

"Have you anything more to say?" old no-face went on relentlessly.

I looked around at the hall. —*the cloud-capped towers . . . the great globe itself*— "Just this!" I said savagely. "It's not a defense, you don't *want* a defense. All right, take away our star— You will if you can and I guess you can. Go ahead! We'll *make* a star! Then, someday, we'll come back and hunt you down—*all of you!*"

"That's telling 'em, Kip! That's telling them!"

Nobody bawled me out. I suddenly felt like a kid who has made a horrible mistake at a party and doesn't know how to cover it up.

But I meant it. Oh, I didn't think we could *do* it. Not yet. But we'd *try*. "Die trying" is the proudest human thing.

"It is possible that you will," that infuriating voice went on. "Are you through?"

"I'm through." We all were through . . . every one of us.

"Does anyone speak for them? Humans, will any race speak for you?"

We didn't *know* any other races. Dogs— Maybe dogs would.

"I speak for them!"

Peewee raised her head with a jerk. "Mother Thing!"

Suddenly she was in front of us. Peewee tried to run to her, bounced off that invisible barrier. I grabbed her. "Easy, hon. She isn't there—it's some sort of television."

"My lord peers . . . you have the advantage of many minds and much knowledge—" It was odd to see her singing, hear her in English; the translation still held that singing quality.

"—but *I* know them. It is true that they are violent—especially the smaller one—but they are not more violent than is appropriate to their ages. Can we expect mature restraint in a race whose members all must die in early childhood? And are not we ourselves violent? Have we not this day killed our billions? Can any race survive without a willingness to fight? It is true that these creatures are often more violent than is necessary or wise. But, my peers, they all are so very young. Give them time to learn."

"That is exactly what there is to fear, that they may learn. Your race is overly sentimental; it distorts your judgment."

"Not true! We are compassionate, we are *not* foolish. I myself have been the proximate cause of how many, many adverse decisions? You know; it is in your records—I prefer not to remember. And I shall be again. When a branch is diseased beyond healing, it must be pruned. We are not sentimental; we are the best watchers you have ever found, for we do it without anger. Toward evil we have no mercy. But the mistakes of a child we treat with loving forbearance."

"Have you finished?"

"I say that this branch need not be pruned! I have finished."

The Mother Thing's image vanished. The voice went on, "Does any other race speak for them?"

"I do." Where she had been now stood a large green monkey. He stared at us and shook his head, then suddenly did a somersault and finished looking at us between his legs. "I'm no friend of theirs but I am a lover of 'justice'—in which I differ from my colleagues in this Council." He twirled rapidly several times. "As our sister has said, this race is young. The infants of my own noble race bite and scratch each other—some even die from it. Even *I* behaved so, at one time." He jumped into the air, landed on his hands, did a flip from that position. "Yet does anyone here deny that *I* am civilized?" He stopped, looked at us thoughtfully while scratching. "These are brutal savages and I don't see how anyone could ever *like* them—but *I* say: give them their chance!"

His image disappeared.

The voice said, "Have you anything to add before a decision is reached?"

I started to say: No, get it over with—when Peewee grabbed my ear and whispered. I listened, nodded, and spoke. "Mr. Moderator—if the verdict is against us—can you hold off your hangmen long enough to let us *go home?* We know that you can send us home in only a few minutes."

The voice did not answer quickly. "Why do you wish this? As I have explained, you are not personally on trial. It has been arranged to let you live."

"We know. We'd rather be home, that's all—with our people."

Again a tiny hesitation. "It shall be done."

"Are the facts sufficient to permit a decision?"

"Yes."

"What is the decision?"

"This race will be re-examined in a dozen half-deaths of radium. Meanwhile there is danger to it from itself. Against this mischance it will be given assistance. During the probationary period it will be watched closely by Guardian Mother—" the machine trilled the true Vegan name of the Mother Thing "—the cop on that beat, who will report at once any ominous change. In the meantime we wish this race good progress in its long journey upward.

"Let them now be returned forthwith to the space-time whence they came."

Chapter 12

I didn't think it was safe to make our atmosphere descent in New Jersey without filing a flight plan. Princeton is near important targets; we might be homed-on by everything up to A-missiles. The Mother Thing got that indulgent chuckle in her song: ("I fancy we can avoid that.")

She did. She put us down in a side street, sang good-bye and was gone. It's not illegal to be out at night in space suits, even carrying a rag dolly. But it's unusual—cops hauled us in. They phoned Peewee's father and in twenty minutes we were in his study, drinking cocoa and talking and eating shredded wheat.

Peewee's mother almost had a fit. While we told our story she kept gasping, "I can't believe it!" until Professor Reisfeld said, "Stop it, Janice. Or go to bed." I don't blame her. Her daughter disappears on the Moon and is given up for dead—then miraculously reappears on Earth. But Professor Reisfeld believed us. The way the Mother Thing had "understanding" he had "acceptance." When a fact came along, he junked theories that failed to match.

He examined Peewee's suit, had her switch on the helmet, shined a light to turn it opaque, all with a little smile. Then he reached for the phone. "Dario must see this."

"At midnight, Curt?"

"Please, Janice. Armageddon won't wait for office hours."

"Professor Reisfeld?"

"Yes, Kip?"

"Uh, you may want to see other things first."

"That's possible."

I took things from Oscar's pockets—two beacons, one for

each of us, some metal "paper" covered with equations, two "happy things," and two silvery spheres. We had stopped on Vega Five, spending most of the time under what I suppose was hypnosis while Prof Joe and another professor thing pumped us for what we knew of human mathematics. They hadn't been learning math from us—oh, no! They wanted the language we use in mathematics, from radicals and vectors to those weird symbols in higher physics, so that *they* could teach *us;* the results were on the metal paper.

First I showed Professor Reisfeld the beacons. "The Mother Thing's beat now includes us. She says to use these if we need her. She'll usually be close by—a thousand light-years at most. But even if she is far away, she'll come."

"Oh." He looked at mine. It was neater and smaller than the one she haywired on Pluto. "Do we dare take it apart?"

"Well, it's got a lot of power tucked in it. It might explode."

"Yes, it might." He handed it back, looking wistful.

A "happy thing" can't be explained. They look like those little abstract sculptures you feel as well as look at. Mine was like obsidian but warm and not hard; Peewee's was more like jade. The surprise comes when you touch one to your head. I had Professor Reisfeld do so and he looked awed—the Mother Thing is all around you and you feel warm and safe and *understood.*

He said, "She loves you. The message wasn't for me. Excuse me."

"Oh, she loves *you,* too."

"Eh?"

"She loves everything small and young and fuzzy and helpless. That's why she's a 'mother thing.' "

I didn't realize how it sounded. But he didn't mind. "You say she is a police officer?"

"Well, she's more of a juvenile welfare officer—this is a slum neighborhood we're in, backward and pretty tough. Sometimes she has to do things she doesn't like. But she's a good cop and somebody has to do nasty jobs. She doesn't shirk them."

"I'm sure she wouldn't."

"Would you like to try it again?"

"Do you mind?"

"Oh, no, it doesn't wear out."

He did and got that warm happy look. He glanced at Peewee, asleep with her face in her cereal. "I need not have worried about my daughter, between the Mother Thing—and you."

"It was a team," I explained. "We couldn't have made it without Peewee. The kid's got guts."

"Too much, sometimes."

"Other times you need that extra. These spheres are recorders. Do you have a tape recorder, Professor?"

"Certainly, sir." We set it up and let a sphere talk to it. I wanted a tape because the spheres are one-shot—the molecules go random again. Then I showed him the metal paper. I had tried to read it, got maybe two inches into it, then just recognized a sign here and there. Professor Reisfeld got halfway down the first page, stopped. "I had better make those phone calls."

At dawn a sliver of old Moon came up and I tried to judge where Tombaugh Station was. Peewee was asleep on her Daddy's couch, wrapped in his bathrobe and clutching Madame Pompadour. He had tried to carry her to bed but she had wakened and become very, very difficult, so he put her down. Professor Reisfeld chewed an empty pipe and listened to my sphere whispering softly to his recorder. Occasionally he darted a question at me and I'd snap out of it.

Professor Giomi and Dr. Bruck were at the other end of the study, filling a blackboard, erasing and filling it again, while they argued over that metal paper. Geniuses are common at the Institute for Advanced Study but these two wouldn't be noticed anywhere; Bruck looked like a truckdriver and Giomi like an excited Iunio. They both had that Okay-I-get-you that Professor Reisfeld had. They were excited but Dr. Bruck showed it only by a tic in his face—which Peewee's Daddy told me was a guarantee of nervous breakdowns—not for Bruck, for other physicists.

Two mornings later we were still there. Professor Reisfeld had shaved; the others hadn't. I napped and once I took a shower. Peewee's Daddy listened to recordings—he was now replaying Peewee's tape. Now and then Bruck and Giomi called him over, Giomi almost hysterical and Bruck stolid. Professor Reisfeld always asked a question or two, nodded and came back to his chair. I don't think he could work that math—but he could soak up results and fit them with other pieces.

I wanted to go home once they were through with me but Professor Reisfeld said please stay; the Secretary General of the Federated Free Nations was coming.

I stayed. I didn't call home because what was the use in upsetting them? I would rather have gone to New York City to meet the

Secretary General, but Professor Reisfeld had invited him here—I began to realize that anybody really important would come if Professor Reisfeld asked him.

Mr. van Duivendijk was slender and tall. He shook hands and said, "I understand that you are Dr. Samuel C. Russell's son."

"You know my father, sir?"

"I met him years ago, at the Hague."

Dr. Bruck turned—he had barely nodded at the Secretary General. "You're Sam Russell's boy?"

"Uh, you know him, too?"

"Of course. *On the Statistical Interpretation of Imperfect Data.* Brilliant." He turned back and got more chalk on his sleeve. I hadn't known that Dad had written such a thing, nor suspected that he knew the top man in the Federation. Sometimes I think Dad is eccentric.

Mr. van D. waited until the double domes came up for air, then said, "You have something, gentlemen?"

"Yeah," said Bruck.

"Superb!" agreed Giomi.

"Such as?"

"Well—" Dr. Bruck pointed at a line of chalk. "That says you can damp out a nuclear reaction at a distance."

"What distance?"

"How about ten thousand miles? Or must you do it from the Moon?"

"Oh, ten thousand miles is sufficient, I imagine."

"You could do it from the Moon," Giomi interrupted, "if you had enough power. Magnificent!"

"It is," agreed van Duivendijk. "Anything else?"

"What do you want?" demanded Bruck. "Egg in your suds?"

"Well?"

"See that seventeenth line? It may mean anti-gravity, I ain't promising. Or, if you rotate ninety degrees, this unstable Latin thinks it's time travel."

"It is!"

"If he's right, the power needed is a fair-sized star—so forget it." Bruck stared at hen's tracks. "A new approach to matter conversion—possibly. How about a power pack for your vest pocket that turns out more ergs than the Brisbane reactors?"

"This can be done?"

"Ask your grandson. It won't be soon." Bruck scowled.

"Dr. Bruck, why are you unhappy?" asked Mr. van D.

Bruck scowled harder. "Are you goin' to make this 'Top Secret'? I don't like classifying mathematics. It's shameful."

I batted my ears. I had explained to the Mother Thing about
"classified" and I think I shocked her. I said that the FFN *had* to
have secrets for survival, just like Three Galaxies. She couldn't
see it. Finally she had said that it wouldn't make any difference in
the long run. But I had worried because while I don't like science
being "secret," I don't want to be reckless, either.

Mr. van D. answered, "I don't like secrecy. But I have to put up
with it."

"I knew you would say that!"

"Please. Is this a U.S. government project?"

"Eh? Of course not."

"Nor a Federation one. Very well, you've shown me some
equations. I can't tell you not to publish them. They're yours."

Bruck shook his head. "Not ours." He pointed at me. "His."

"I see." The Secretary General looked at me. "I am a lawyer,
young man. If you wish to publish, I see no way to stop you."

"Me? It's not mine—I was just—well, a messenger."

"You seem to have the only claim. Do you wish this published? Perhaps with all your names?" I got the impression that he
wanted it published.

"Well, sure. But the third name shouldn't be mine; it should
be—" I hesitated. You can't put a birdsong down as author. "—uh,
make it 'Dr. M. Thing.' "

"Who is he?"

"She's a Vegan. But we could pretend it's a Chinese name."

The Secretary General stayed on, asking questions, listening
to tapes. Then he made a phone call—to the Moon. I knew it could
be done, I never expected to see it. "Van Duivendijk here . . . yes,
the Secretary General. Get the Commanding General . . . Jim? . . .
This connection is terrible . . . Jim, you sometimes order practice
maneuvers . . . My call is unofficial but you might check a
valley—" He turned to me; I answered quickly. "—a valley just
past the mountains east of Tombaugh Station. I haven't consulted
the Security Council; this is between friends. But if you go into
that valley I very strongly suggest that it be done in force, with all
weapons. It may have snakes in it. The snakes will be camouflaged. Call it a hunch. Yes, the kids are fine and so is Beatrix. I'll
phone Mary and tell her I talked with you."

The Secretary General wanted my address. I couldn't say
when I would be home because I didn't know how I would get

there—I meant to hitchhike but didn't say so. Mr. van D.'s eye-brows went up. "I think we owe you a ride home. Eh, Professor?"

"That would not be overdoing it."

"Russell, I heard on your tape that you plan to study engineering—with a view to space."

"Yes, sir. I mean, 'Yes, Mr. Secretary.' "

"Have you considered studying law? Many young engineers want to space—not many lawyers. But the Law goes everywhere. A man skilled in space law and meta-law would be in a strong position."

"Why not both?" suggested Peewee's Daddy. "I deplore this modern overspecialization."

"That's an idea," agreed Mr. van Duivendijk. "He could then write his own terms."

I was about to say I should stick to electronics—when suddenly I knew what I wanted to do. "Uh, I don't think I could handle both."

"Nonsense!" Professor Reisfeld said severely.

"Yes, sir. But I want to make space suits that work better. I've got some ideas."

"Mmm, that's mechanical engineering. And many other things, I imagine. But you'll need an M.E. degree." Professor Reisfeld frowned. "As I recall your tape, you passed College Boards but hadn't been accepted by a good school." He drummed his desk. "Isn't that silly, Mr. Secretary? The lad goes to the Magellanic Clouds but can't go to the school he wants."

"Well, Professor? You pull while I push?"

"Yes. But wait." Professor Reisfeld picked up his phone. "Susie, get me the President of M.I.T. I know it's a holiday; I don't care if he's in Bombay or in bed; get him. Good girl." He put down the phone. "She's been with the Institute five years and on the University switchboard before that. She'll get him."

I felt embarrassed and excited. M.I.T.—anybody would jump at the chance. But tuition alone would stun you. I tried to explain that I didn't have the money. "I'll work the rest of this school and next summer—I'll save it."

The phone rang. "Reisfeld here. Hi, Oppie. At the class reunion you made me promise to tell you if Bruck's tic started bothering him. Hold onto your chair; I timed it at twenty-one to the minute. That's a record. . . . Slow down; you won't send *anybody*, unless I get my pound of flesh. If you start your lecture on academic freedom and 'the right to know,' I'll hang up and call

Berkeley. I can do business there—and I know I can here, over on
the campus. . . . Not much, just a four-year scholarship, tuition
and fees. . . . Don't scream at me; use your discretionary fund—or
make it a wash deal in bookkeeping. You're over twenty-one; you
can do arithmetic. . . . Nope, no hints. Buy a pig in a poke or your
radiation lab won't be in on it. Did I say 'radiation lab'? I meant
the entire physical science department. You can flee to South
America, don't let me sway you. . . . What? I'm an embezzler,
too. Hold it." Professor Reisfeld said to me, "You applied for
M.I.T.?"

"Yes, sir, but—"

"He's in your application files, 'Clifford C. Russell.' Send the
letter to his home and have the head of your team fetch my
copy. . . . Oh, a broad team, headed by a mathematical physicist—
Farley, probably; he's got imagination. This is the biggest thing
since the apple konked Sir Isaac. . . . Sure, I'm a blackmailer, and
you are a chair warmer and a luncheon speaker. When are you returning to the academic life? . . . Best to Beulah. 'Bye."

He hung up. "That's settled. Kip, the one thing that confuses
me is why those worm-faced monsters wanted *me*."

I didn't know how to say it. He had told me only the day before that he had been correlating odd data—unidentified sightings,
unexpected opposition to space travel, many things that did not fit.
Such a man is likely to get answers—and be listened to. If he had
a weakness, it was modesty—which he hadn't passed on to Peewee. If I told him that invaders from outer space had grown nervous over his intellectual curiosity, he would have pooh-poohed it.
So I said, "They never told us, sir. But they thought you were important enough to grab."

Mr. van Duivendijk stood up. "Curt, I won't waste time listening to nonsense. Russell, I'm glad your schooling is arranged. If
you need me, call me."

When he was gone, I tried to thank Professor Reisfeld. "I
meant to pay my way, sir. I would have earned the money before
school opens again."

"In less than three weeks? Come now, Kip."

"I mean the rest of this year and—"

"Waste a year? No."

"But I already—" I looked past his head at green leaves in
their garden. "Professor . . . what date is it?"

"Why, Labor Day, of course."

(*"—forthwith to the space-time whence they came."*)

Professor Reisfeld flipped water in my face. "Feeling better?"

"I—I guess so. We were gone for *weeks*."

"Kip, you've been through too much to let this shake you. You can talk it over with the stratosphere twins—" He gestured at Giomi and Bruck. "—but you won't understand it. At least I didn't. Why not assume that a hundred and sixty-seven thousand light-years leaves room for Tennessee windage amounting to only a hair's breadth of a fraction of one per cent? Especially when the method doesn't properly use space-time at all?"

When I left, Mrs. Reisfeld kissed me and Peewee blubbered and had Madame Pompadour say good-bye to Oscar, who was in the back seat because the Professor was driving me to the airport.

On the way he remarked, "Peewee is fond of you."

"Uh, I hope so."

"And you? Or am I impertinent?"

"Am I fond of Peewee? I certainly am! She saved my life four or five times." Peewee could drive you nuts. But she was gallant and loyal and smart—and had guts.

"You won a life-saving medal or two yourself."

I thought about it. "Seems to me I fumbled everything I tried. But I had help and an awful lot of luck." I shivered at how luck alone had kept me out of the soup—real soup.

"'Luck' is a question-begging word," he answered. "You spoke of the 'amazing luck' that you were listening when my daughter called for help. That wasn't luck."

"Huh? I mean, 'Sir'?"

"Why were you on that frequency? Because you were wearing a space suit. Why were you wearing it? Because you were determined to space. When a space ship called, you answered, If that is luck, then it is luck every time a batter hits a ball. Kip, 'good luck' follows careful preparation; 'bad luck' comes from sloppiness. You convinced a court older than Man himself that you and your kind were worth saving. Was that mere chance?"

"Uh . . . fact is, I got mad and almost ruined things. I was tired of being shoved around."

"The best things in history are accomplished by people who get 'tired of being shoved around.'" He frowned. "I'm glad you like Peewee. She is about twenty years old intellectually and six emotionally; she usually antagonizes people. So I'm glad she has gained a friend who is smarter than she is."

My jaw dropped. "But, Professor, Peewee is much smarter than I am. She runs me ragged."

He glanced at me. "She's run me ragged for years—and I'm not stupid. Don't downgrade yourself, Kip."

"It's the truth."

"So? The greatest mathematical psychologist of our time, a man who always wrote his own ticket even to retiring when it suited him—very difficult, when a man is in demand—this man married his star pupil. I doubt if their offspring is less bright than my own child."

I had to untangle this to realize that he meant *me*. Then I didn't know what to say. How many kids really know their parents? Apparently I didn't.

He went on, "Peewee is a handful, even for me. Here's the airport. When you return for school, please plan on visiting us. Thanksgiving, too, if you will—no doubt you'll go home Christmas."

"Uh, thank you, sir. I'll be back."

"Good."

"Uh, about Peewee—if she gets too difficult, well, you've got the beacon. The Mother Thing can handle her."

"Mmm, that's a thought."

"Peewee tries to get around her but she never does. Oh—I almost forgot. Whom may I tell? Not about Peewee. About the whole thing."

"Isn't that obvious?"

"Sir?"

"Tell anybody anything. You won't very often. Almost no one will believe you."

I rode home in a courier jet—those things go *fast*. Professor Reisfeld had insisted on lending me ten dollars when he found out that I had only a dollar sixty-seven, so I got a haircut at the bus station and bought two tickets to Centerville to keep Oscar out of the luggage compartment; he might have been damaged. The best thing about that scholarship was that now I needn't ever sell him—not that I would.

Centerville looked mighty good, from elms overhead to the chuckholes under foot. The driver stopped near our house because of Oscar; he's clumsy to carry. I went to the barn and racked Oscar, told him I'd see him later, and went in the back door.

Mother wasn't around, Dad was in his study. He looked up from reading. "Hi, Kip."

"Hi, Dad."

"Nice trip?"

"Uh, I didn't go to the lake."

"I know. Dr. Reisfeld phoned—he briefed me thoroughly."

"Oh. It was a nice trip—on the whole." I saw that he was holding a volume of the Britannica, open to "Magellanic Clouds."

He followed my glance. "I've never seen them," he said regretfully. "I had a chance once, but I was busy except one cloudy night."

"When was that, Dad?"

"In South America, before you were born."

"I didn't know you had been there."

"It was a cloak-and-daggerish government job—not one to talk about. Are they beautiful?"

"Uh, not exactly." I got another volume, turned to "Nebulae" and found the Great Nebula of Andromeda. "*Here* is beauty. That's the way *we* look."

Dad sighed. "It must be lovely."

"It is. I'll tell you all about it. I've got a tape, too."

"No hurry. You've had quite a trip. Three hundred and thirty-three thousand light-years—is that right?"

"Oh, no, just half that."

"I meant the round trip."

"Oh. But we didn't come back the same way."

"Eh?"

"I don't know how to put it, but in these ships, if you make a jump, *any* jump, the short way back is the long way 'round. You go straight ahead until you're back where you started. Well, not 'straight' since space is curved—but straight as can be. That returns everything to zero."

"A cosmic great-circle?"

"That's the idea. All the way around in a straight line."

"Mmm—" He frowned thoughtfully. "Kip, how far is it, around the Universe? The red-shift limit?"

I hesitated. "Dad, I asked—but the answer didn't mean anything." (The Mother Thing had said, "How can there be 'distance' where there is *nothing?*") "It's not a distance; it's more of a condition. I didn't *travel* it; I just *went.* You don't go *through,* you slide past."

Dad looked pensive. "I should know not to ask a mathematical question in words."

I was about to suggest that Dr. Bruck could help when Mother sang out: "Hello, my darlings!"

For a split second I thought I was hearing the Mother Thing.
She kissed Dad, she kissed me. "I'm glad you're home, dear."

"Uh—" I turned to Dad.

"She knows."

"Yes," Mother agreed in a warm indulgent tone, "and I don't
mind where my big boy goes as long as he comes home safely. I
know you'll go as far as you want to." She patted my cheek. "And
I'll always be proud of you. Myself, I've just been down to the
corner for another chop."

Next morning was Tuesday, I went to work early. As I expected, the fountain was a mess. I put on my white jacket and got
cracking. Mr. Charton was on the phone; he hung up and came
over. "Nice trip, Kip?"

"Very nice, Mr. Charton."

"Kip, there's something I've been meaning to say. Are you
still anxious to go to the Moon?"

I was startled. Then I decided that he couldn't know.

Well, I hadn't seen the Moon, hardly, I was still eager—
though not as much in a hurry. "Yes, sir. But I'm going to college
first."

"That's what I mean. I— Well, I have no children. If you need
money, say so."

He had hinted at pharmacy school—but never this. And only
last night Dad had told me that he had bought an education policy for me the day I was born—he had been waiting to see what
I would do on my own. "Gee, Mr. Charton, that's mighty nice
of you!"

"I approve of your wanting an education."

"Uh, I've got things lined up, sir. But I might need a loan
someday."

"Or not a loan. Let me know." He bustled away, plainly fussed.

I worked in a warm glow, sometimes touching the happy
thing, tucked away in a pocket. Last night I had let Mother and
Dad put it to their foreheads. Mother had cried; Dad said
solemnly, "I begin to understand, Kip." I decided to let Mr. Charton try it when I could work around to it. I got the fountain shining
and checked the air conditioner. It was okay.

About midafternoon Ace Quiggle came in, plunked himself
down. "Hi, Space Pirate! What do you hear from the Galactic
Overlords? Yuk yuk yukkity yuk!"

What would he have said to a straight answer? I touched the
happy thing and said, "What'll it be, Ace?"

"My usual, of course, and snap it up!"

"A choc malt?"

"You know that. Look alive, Junior! Wake up and get hep to the world around you."

"Sure thing, Ace." There was no use fretting about Ace; his world was as narrow as the hole between his ears, no deeper than his own hog wallow. Two girls came in; I served them cokes while Ace's malt was in the mixer. He leered at them. "Ladies, do you know Commander Comet here?" One of them tittered; Ace smirked and went on: "I'm his manager. You want hero-ing done, see me. Commander, I've been thinking about that ad you're goin' to run."

"Huh?"

"Keep your ears open. 'Have Space Suit—Will Travel,' that doesn't say enough. To make money out of that silly clown suit, we got to have oomph. So we add: 'Bug-Eyed Monsters Exterminated—World Saving a Specialty—Rates on Request.' Right?"

I shook my head. "No, Ace."

"S'matter with you? No head for business?"

"Let's stick to the facts. I don't charge for world saving and don't do it to order; it just happens. I'm not sure I'd do it on purpose—with *you* in it."

Both girls tittered, Ace scowled. "Smart guy, eh? Don't you know that the customer is always right?"

"Always?"

"He certainly is. See that you remember it. Hurry up that malt!"

"Yes, Ace." I reached for it; he shoved thirty-five cents at me; I pushed it back. "This is on the house."

I threw it in his face.

STARSHIP
TROOPERS

ACKNOWLEDGMENTS

The stanza from "The Eathen" by Rudyard Kipling, at the head of Chapter VII, is used by permission of Mr. Kipling's estate. Quotations from the lyrics of the ballad "Rodger Young" are used by permission of the author, Frank Loesser.

To "SARGE" ARTHUR GEORGE SMITH

SOLDIER, CITIZEN, SCIENTIST, AND TO ALL SERGEANTS ANYWHERE WHO HAVE LEARNED TO MAKE MEN OUT OF BOYS.

R.A.H.

Chapter 1

Come on, you apes! You wanta live forever?

—Unknown platoon sergeant, 1918

I always get the shakes before a drop. I've had the injections, of course, and hypnotic preparation, and it stands to reason that I can't really be afraid. The ship's psychiatrist has checked my brain waves and asked me silly questions while I was asleep and he tells me that it isn't fear, it isn't anything important—it's just like the trembling of an eager race horse in the starting gate.

I couldn't say about that; I've never been a race horse. But the fact is: I'm scared silly, every time.

At D-minus-thirty, after we had mustered in the drop room of the *Rodger Young*, our platoon leader inspected us. He wasn't our regular platoon leader, because Lieutenant Rasczak had bought it on our last drop; he was really the platoon sergeant, Career Ship's Sergeant Jelal. Jelly was a Finno-Turk from Iskander around Proxima—a swarthy little man who looked like a clerk, but I've seen him tackle two berserk privates so big he had to reach up to grab them, crack their heads together like coconuts, step back out of the way while they fell.

Off duty he wasn't bad—for a sergeant. You could even call him "Jelly" to his face. Not recruits, of course, but anybody who had made at least one combat drop.

But right now he was on duty. We had all each inspected our combat equipment (look, it's your own neck—see?), the acting platoon sergeant had gone over us carefully after he mustered us, and now Jelly went over us again, his face mean, his eyes missing nothing. He stopped by the man in front of me, pressed the button on his belt that gave readings on his physicals. "Fall out!"

"But, Sarge, it's just a cold. The Surgeon said—"

Jelly interrupted. " 'But Sarge!' " he snapped. "The Surgeon ain't making no drop—and neither are you, with a degree and a half of fever. You think I got time to chat with you, just before a drop? *Fall out!*"

Jenkins left us, looking sad and mad—and I felt bad, too. Because of the Lieutenant buying it, last drop, and people moving up, I was assistant section leader, second section, this drop, and now I was going to have a hole in my section and no way to fill it. That's not good; it means a man can run into something sticky, call for help and have nobody to help him.

Jelly didn't downcheck anybody else. Presently he stepped out in front of us, looked us over and shook his head sadly. "What a gang of apes!" he growled. "Maybe if you'd all buy it this drop, they could start over and build the kind of outfit the Lieutenant expected you to be. But probably not—with the sort of recruits we get these days." He suddenly straightened up, shouted, "I just want to remind you apes that each and every one of you has cost the gov'ment, counting weapons, armor, ammo, instrumentation, and training, everything, including the way you overeat—has cost, on the hoof, better'n half a million. Add in the thirty cents you are actually worth and that runs to quite a sum." He glared at us. "So bring it back! We can spare you, but we can't spare that fancy suit you're wearing. I don't want any heroes in this outfit; the Lieutenant wouldn't like it. You got a job to do, you go down, you do it, you keep your ears open for recall, you show up for retrieval on the bounce and by the numbers. Get me?"

He glared again. "You're supposed to know the plan. But some of you ain't got any minds to hypnotize so I'll sketch it out. You'll be dropped in two skirmish lines, calculated two-thousand-yard intervals. Get your bearing on me as soon as you hit, get your bearing and distance on your squad mates, both sides, while you take cover. You've wasted ten seconds already, so you smash-and-destroy whatever's at hand until the flankers hit dirt." (He was talking about me—as assistant section leader I was going to be left flanker, with nobody at my elbow. I began to tremble.)

"Once they hit—straighten out those lines!—equalize those intervals! Drop what you're doing and do it! Twelve seconds.

Then advance by leapfrog, odd and even, assistant section leaders minding the count and guiding the envelopment." He looked at me. "If you've done this properly—which I doubt—the flanks will make contact as recall sounds . . . at which time, home you go. Any questions?"

There weren't any; there never were. He went on, "One more word—This is just a raid, not a battle. It's a demonstration of fire-power and frightfulness. Our mission is to let the enemy know that we could have destroyed their city—but didn't—but that they aren't safe even though we refrain from total bombing. You'll take no prisoners. You'll kill only when you can't help it. But the entire area we hit is to be smashed. I don't want to see any of you loafers back aboard here with unexpended bombs. Get me?" He glanced at the time. "Rasczak's Roughnecks have got a reputation to up-hold. The Lieutenant told me before he bought it to tell *you* that he will always have his eye on you every minute . . . and that he ex-pects your names to *shine!*"

Jelly glanced over at Sergeant Migliaccio, first section leader. "Five minutes for the Padre," he stated. Some of the boys dropped out of ranks, went over and knelt in front of Migliaccio, and not necessarily those of his creed, either—Moslems, Christians, Gnostics, Jews, whoever wanted a word with him before a drop, he was there. I've heard tell that there used to be military outfits whose chaplains did not fight alongside the others, but I've never been able to see how that could work. I mean, how can a chaplain bless anything he's not willing to do himself? In any case, in the Mobile Infantry, *everybody* drops and *everybody* fights—chaplain and cook and the Old Man's writer. Once we went down the tube there wouldn't be a Roughneck left aboard—except Jenkins, of course, and that not his fault.

I didn't go over. I was always afraid somebody would see me shake if I did, and, anyhow, the Padre could bless me just as hand-ily from where he was. But he came over to me as the last strag-glers stood up and pressed his helmet against mine to speak privately. "Johnnie," he said quietly, "this is your first drop as a non-com."

"Yeah." I wasn't really a non-com, any more than Jelly was re-ally an officer.

"Just this, Johnnie. Don't buy a farm. You know your job; do it. Just do it. Don't try to win a medal."

"Uh, thanks, Padre. I shan't."

He added something gently in a language I don't know, patted

me on the shoulder, and hurried back to his section. Jelly called
out, "Tenn . . . *shut!*" and we all snapped to.

"Pla*toon!*"

"Sec*tion!*" Migliaccio and Johnson echoed.

"By sections—port and starboard—prepare for drop!"

"Sec*tion!* Man your capsules! *Move!*"

"Squad!"—I had to wait while squads four and five manned
their capsules and moved on down the firing tube before my capsule showed up on the port track and I could climb into it. I wondered if those old-timers got the shakes as they climbed into the
Trojan Horse? Or was it just me? Jelly checked each man as he
was sealed in and he sealed me in himself. As he did so, he leaned
toward me and said, "Don't goof off, Johnnie. This is just like a
drill."

The top closed on me and I was alone. "Just like a drill," he
says! I began to shake uncontrollably.

Then, in my earphones. I heard Jelly from the center-line tube:
"Bridge! Rasczak's Roughnecks . . . ready for drop!"

"Seventeen seconds, Lieutenant!" I heard the ship captain's
cheerful contralto replying—and resented her calling Jelly "Lieutenant." To be sure, our lieutenant was dead and maybe Jelly
would get his commission . . . but we were still "Rasczak's
Roughnecks."

She added, "Good luck, boys!"

"Thanks, Captain."

"Brace yourselves! Five seconds."

I was strapped all over—belly, forehead, shins. But I shook
worse than ever.

It's better after you unload. Until you do, you sit there in total
darkness, wrapped like a mummy against the acceleration, barely
able to breathe—and knowing that there is just nitrogen around
you in the capsule even if you could get your helmet open, which
you can't—and knowing that the capsule is surrounded by the firing tube anyhow and if the ship gets hit before they fire you, you
haven't got a prayer, you'll just die there, unable to move, helpless. It's that endless wait in the dark that causes the shakes—
thinking that they've forgotten you . . . the ship has been hulled
and stayed in orbit, dead, and soon you'll buy it, too, unable to
move, choking. Or it's a crash orbit and you'll buy it that way, if
you don't roast on the way down.

Then the ship's braking program hit us and I stopped shaking.

Eight gees, I would say, or maybe ten. When a female pilot handles a ship there is nothing comfortable about it; you're going to have bruises every place you're strapped. Yes, yes, I know they make better pilots than men do; their reactions are faster, and they can tolerate more gee. They can get in faster, get out faster, and thereby improve everybody's chances, yours as well as theirs. But that still doesn't make it fun to be slammed against your spine at ten times your proper weight.

But I must admit that Captain Deladrier knows her trade. There was no fiddling around once the *Rodger Young* stopped braking. At once I heard her snap, "Center-line tube . . . *fire!*" and there were two recoil bumps as Jelly and his acting platoon sergeant unloaded—and immediately: "Port and starboard tubes— *automatic fire!*" and the rest of us started to unload.

Bump! and your capsule jerks ahead one place—*bump!* and it jerks again, precisely like cartridges feeding into the chamber of an old-style automatic weapon. Well, that's just what we were . . . only the barrels of the gun were twin launching tubes built into a spaceship troop carrier and each cartridge was a capsule big enough (just barely) to hold an infantryman with all field equipment.

Bump!—I was used to number three spot, out early; now I was Tail-End Charlie, last out after three squads. It makes a tedious wait, even with a capsule being fired every second; I tried to count the bumps—*bump!* (twelve) *bump!* (thirteen) *bump!* (fourteen— with an odd sound to it, the empty one Jenkins should have been in) *bump!*—

And *clang!*—it's my turn as my capsule slams into the firing chamber—then WHAMBO! the explosion hits with a force that makes the Captain's braking maneuver feel like a love tap.

Then suddenly nothing.

Nothing at all. No sound, no pressure, no weight. Floating in darkness . . . free fall, maybe thirty miles up, above the effective atmosphere, falling weightlessly toward the surface of a planet you've never seen. But I'm not shaking now; it's the wait beforehand that wears. Once you unload, you can't get hurt—because if anything goes wrong it will happen so fast that you'll buy it without noticing that you're dead, hardly.

Almost at once I felt the capsule twist and sway, then steady down so that my weight was on my back . . . weight that built up quickly until I was at my full weight (0.87 gee, we had been told) for that planet as the capsule reached terminal velocity for the thin upper atmosphere. A pilot who is a real artist (and the Captain was) will approach and brake so that your launching speed as you shoot out of the tube places you just dead in space relative to the rotational speed of the planet at that latitude. The loaded capsules are heavy; they punch through the high, thin winds of the upper atmosphere without being blown too far out of position—but just the same a platoon is bound to disperse on the way down, lose some of the perfect formation in which it unloads. A sloppy pilot can make this still worse, scatter a strike group over so much terrain that it can't make rendezvous for retrieval, much less carry out its mission. An infantryman can fight only if somebody else delivers him to his zone; in a way I suppose pilots are just as essential as we are.

I could tell from the gentle way my capsule entered the atmosphere that the Captain had laid us down with as near zero lateral vector as you could ask for. I felt happy—not only a tight formation when we hit and no time wasted, but also a pilot who puts you down properly is a pilot who is smart and precise on retrieval.

The outer shell burned away and sloughed off—unevenly, for I tumbled. Then the rest of it went and I straightened out. The turbulence brakes of the second shell bit in and the ride got rough . . . and still rougher as they burned off one at a time and the second shell began to go to pieces. One of the things that helps a capsule trooper to live long enough to draw a pension is that the skins peeling off his capsule not only slow him down, they also fill the sky over the target area with so much junk that radar picks up reflections from dozens of targets for each man in the drop, any one of which could be a man, or a bomb, or anything. It's enough to give a ballistic computer nervous breakdowns—and does.

To add to the fun your ship lays a series of dummy eggs in the seconds immediately following your drop, dummies that will fall faster because they don't slough. They get under you, explode, throw out "window," even operate as transponders, rocket sideways, and do other things to add to the confusion of your reception committee on the ground.

In the meantime your ship is locked firmly on the directional beacon of your platoon leader, ignoring the radar "noise" it has created and following you in, computing your impact for future use.

When the second shell was gone, the third shell automatically opened my first ribbon chute. It didn't last long but it wasn't expected to; one good, hard jerk at several gee and it went its way and I went mine. The second chute lasted a little bit longer and the third chute lasted quite a while; it began to be rather too warm inside the capsule and I started thinking about landing.

The third shell peeled off when its last chute was gone and now I had nothing around me but my suit armor and a plastic egg. I was still strapped inside it, unable to move; it was time to decide how and where I was going to ground. Without moving my arms (I couldn't) I thumbed the switch for a proximity reading and read it when it flashed on in the instrument reflector inside my helmet in front of my forehead.

A mile and eight-tenths—A little closer than I liked, especially without company. The inner egg had reached steady speed, no more help to be gained by staying inside it, and its skin temperature indicated that it would not open automatically for a while yet—so I flipped a switch with my other thumb and got rid of it.

The first charge cut all the straps; the second charge exploded the plastic egg away from me in eight separate pieces—and I was outdoors, sitting on air, and could *see!* Better still, the eight discarded pieces were metal-coated (except for the small bit I had taken proximity reading through) and would give back the same reflection as an armored man. Any radar viewer, alive or cybernetic, would now have a sad time sorting me out from the junk nearest me, not to mention the thousands of other bits and pieces for miles on each side, above, and below me. Part of a mobile infantryman's training is to let him see, from the ground and both by eye and by radar, just how confusing a drop is to the forces on the ground—because you feel awful naked up there. It is easy to panic and either open a chute too soon and become a sitting duck (do ducks really sit?—if so, why?) or fail to open it and break your ankles, likewise backbone and skull.

So I stretched, getting the kinks out, and looked around . . . then doubled up again and straightened out in a swan dive face down and took a good look. It was night down there, as planned, but infrared snoopers let you size up terrain quite well after you are used to them. The river that cut diagonally through the city was almost below me and coming up fast, shining out clearly with a higher temperature than the land. I didn't care which side of it I landed on but I didn't want to land in it; it would slow me down.

I noticed a flash off to the right at about my altitude; some unfriendly native down below had burned what was probably a piece of my egg. So I fired my first chute at once, intending if possible to jerk myself right off his screen as he followed the targets down in closing range. I braced for the shock, rode it, then floated down for about twenty seconds before unloading the chute—not wishing to call attention to myself in still another way by not falling at the speed of the other stuff around me.

It must have worked; I wasn't burned.

About six hundred feet up I shot the second chute . . . saw very quickly that I was being carried over into the river, found that I was going to pass about a hundred feet up over a flat-roofed warehouse or some such by the river. . . . blew the chute free and came in for a good enough if rather bouncy landing on the roof by means of the suit's jump jets. I was scanning for Sergeant Jelal's beacon as I hit.

And found that I was on the wrong side of the river; Jelly's star showed up on the compass ring inside my helmet far south of where it should have been—I was too far north. I trotted toward the river side of the roof as I took a range and bearing on the squad leader next to me, found that he was over a mile out of position, called, "Ace! dress your line," tossed a bomb behind me as I stepped off the building and across the river. Ace answered as I could have expected—Ace should have had my spot but he didn't want to give up his squad; nevertheless he didn't fancy taking orders from me.

The warehouse went up behind me and the blast hit me while I was still over the river, instead of being shielded by the buildings on the far side as I should have been. It darn near tumbled my gyros and I came close to tumbling myself. I had set that bomb for fifteen seconds . . . or had I? I suddenly realized that I had let myself get excited, the worst thing you can do once you're on the ground. "Just like a drill," that was the way, just as Jelly had warned me. Take your time and do it right, even if it takes another half second.

As I hit I took another reading on Ace and told him again to realign his squad. He didn't answer but he was already doing it. I let it ride. As long as Ace did his job, I could afford to swallow his surliness—for now. But back aboard ship (if Jelly kept me on as assistant section leader) we would eventually have to pick a quiet spot and find out who was boss. He was a career corporal and I was just a term lance acting as corporal, but he was under me and you can't afford to take any lip under those circumstances. Not permanently.

But I didn't have time then to think about it; while I was jumping the river I had spotted a juicy target and I wanted to get it before somebody else noticed it—a lovely big group of what looked like public buildings on a hill. Temples, maybe . . . or a palace. They were miles outside the area we were sweeping, but one rule of a smash & run is to expend at least half your ammo outside your sweep area; that way the enemy is kept confused as to where you actually are—that and keep moving, do everything fast. You're always heavily outnumbered; surprise and speed are what saves you.

I was already loading my rocket launcher while I was checking on Acc and telling him for the second time to straighten up. Jelly's voice reached me right on top of that on the all-hands circuit: "Pla*toon!* By leapfrog! *Forward!*"

My boss, Sergeant Johnson, echoed, "By leapfrog! Odd numbers! *Advance!*"

That left me with nothing to worry about for twenty seconds, so I jumped up on the building nearest me, raised the launcher to my shoulder, found the target and pulled the first trigger to let the rocket have a look at its target—pulled the second trigger and kissed it on its way, jumped back to the ground. "Second section, even numbers!" I called out . . . waited for the count in my mind and ordered, *"Advance!"*

And did so myself, hopping over the next row of buildings, and, while I was in the air, fanning the first row by the river front with a hand flamer. They seemed to be wood construction and it looked like time to start a good fire—with luck, some of those warehouses would house oil products, or even explosives. As I hit, the Y-rack on my shoulders launched two small H.E. bombs a couple of hundred yards each way to my right and left flanks but I never saw what they did as just then my first rocket hit— that unmistakable (if you've ever seen one) brilliance of an atomic explosion. It was just a peewee, of course, less than two kilotons nominal yield, with tamper and implosion squeeze to produce results from a less-than-critical mass—but then who wants to be bunk mates with a cosmic catastrophe? It was enough to clean off that hilltop and make everybody in the city take shelter against fallout. Better still, any of the local yokels who happened to be outdoors and looking that way wouldn't be seeing anything else for a couple of hours—meaning *me.* The flash hadn't dazzled me, nor would it dazzle any of us; our face bowls are heavily leaded, we wear snoopers over our eyes—and we're trained to duck and take it on the armor if we do happen to be looking the wrong way.

So I merely blinked hard—opened my eyes and stared straight

at a local citizen just coming out of an opening in the building
ahead of me. He looked at me, I looked at him, and he started to
raise something—a weapon, I suppose—as Jelly called out, "Odd
numbers! *Advance!*"

I didn't have time to fool with him: I was a good five hundred yards short of where I should have been by then. I still had
the hand flamer in my left hand; I toasted him and jumped over
the building he had been coming out of, as I started to count. A
hand flamer is primarily for incendiary work but it is a good defensive anti-personnel weapon in tight quarters; you don't have
to aim it much.

Between excitement and anxiety to catch up I jumped too high
and too wide. It's always a temptation to get the most out of your
jump gear—but *don't do it!* It leaves you hanging in the air for
seconds, a big fat target. The way to advance is to skim over each
building as you come to it, barely clearing it, and taking full advantage of cover while you're down—and never stay in one place
more than a second or two, never give them time to target in on
you. Be somewhere else, anywhere. Keep moving.

This one I goofed—too much for one row of buildings, too little for the row beyond it; I found myself coming down on a roof.
But not a nice flat one where I might have tarried three seconds to
launch another peewee A-rocket; this roof was a jungle of pipes
and stanchions and assorted ironmongery—a factory maybe, or
some sort of chemical works. No place to land. Worse still, half a
dozen natives were up there. These geezers are humanoid, eight or
nine feet tall, much skinnier than we are and with a higher body
temperature; they don't wear any clothes and they stand out in a
set of snoopers like a neon sign. They look still funnier in daylight
with your bare eyes but I would rather fight them than the
arachnids—those Bugs make me queasy.

If these laddies were up there thirty seconds earlier when my
rocket hit, then they couldn't see me, or anything. But I couldn't
be certain and didn't want to tangle with them in any case; it
wasn't that kind of a raid. So I jumped again while I was still in
the air, scattering a handful of ten-second fire pills to keep them
busy, grounded, jumped again at once, and called out, "Second
section! Even numbers! . . . Advance!" and kept right on going to
close the gap, while trying to spot, every time I jumped, something worth expending a rocket on. I had three more of the little
A-rockets and I certainly didn't intend to take any back with me.
But I had had pounded into me that you *must* get your money's

worth with atomic weapons—it was only the second time that I had been allowed to carry them.

Right now I was trying to spot their waterworks; a direct hit on it could make the whole city uninhabitable, force them to evacuate it without directly killing anyone—just the sort of nuisance we had been sent down to commit. It should—according to the map we had studied under hypnosis—be about three miles upstream from where I was.

But I couldn't see it; my jumps didn't take me high enough, maybe. I was tempted to go higher but I remembered what Migliaccio had said about not trying for a medal, and stuck to doctrine. I set the Y-rack launcher on automatic and let it lob a couple of little bombs every time I hit. I set fire to things more or less at random in between, and tried to find the waterworks, or some other worth-while target.

Well, there was *something* up there at the proper range—waterworks or whatever, it was big. So I hopped on top of the tallest building near me, took a bead on it, and let fly. As I bounced down I heard Jelly: "Johnnie! Red! Start bending in the flanks."

I acknowledged and heard Red acknowledge and switched my beacon to blinker so that Red could pick me out for certain, took a range and bearing on his blinker while I called out, "Second Section! Curve in and envelop! Squad leaders acknowledge!"

Fourth and fifth squads answered, "Wilco"; Ace said, "We're already doin' it—pick up your feet."

Red's beacon showed the right flank to be almost ahead of me and a good fifteen miles away. Golly! Ace was right; I would have to pick up my feet or I would never close the gap in time—and me with a couple of hundredweight of ammo and sundry nastiness still on me that I just had to find time to use up. We had landed in a V formation, with Jelly at the bottom of the V and Red and myself at the ends of the two arms; now we had to close it into a circle around the retrieval rendezvous . . . which meant that Red and I each had to cover more ground than the others and still do our full share of damage.

At least the leapfrog advance was over with once we started to encircle; I could quit counting and concentrate on speed. It was getting to be less healthy to be anywhere, even moving fast. We had started with the enormous advantage of surprise, reached the ground without being hit (at least I hoped nobody had been hit coming in), and had been rampaging in among them in a fashion that let us fire at will without fear of hitting each other while they stood a big chance of hitting their own people in shooting at us—if they could find us to shoot at, at all. (I'm no games-theory expert but I doubt if any computer could have analyzed what we were doing in time to predict where we would be next.)

Nevertheless the home defenses were beginning to fight back, coordinated or not. I took a couple of near misses with explosives, close enough to rattle my teeth even inside armor and once I was brushed by some sort of beam that made my hair stand on end and half paralyzed me for a moment—as if I had hit my funny bone, but all over. If the suit hadn't already been told to jump, I guess I wouldn't have got out of there.

Things like that make you pause to wonder why you ever took up soldiering—only I was too busy to pause for anything. Twice, jumping blind over buildings, I landed right in the middle of a group of them—jumped at once while fanning wildly around me with the hand flamer.

Spurred on this way, I closed about half of my share of the gap, maybe four miles, in minimum time but without doing much more than casual damage. My Y-rack had gone empty two jumps back; finding myself alone in sort of a courtyard I stopped to put my reserve H.E. bombs into it while I took a bearing on Ace—found that I was far enough out in front of the flank squad to think about expending my last two A-rockets. I jumped to the top of the tallest building in the neighborhood.

It was getting light enough to see; I flipped the snoopers up onto my forehead and made a fast scan with bare eyes, looking for anything behind us worth shooting at, anything at all; I had no time to be choosy.

There was something on the horizon in the direction of their spaceport—administration & control, maybe, or possibly even a starship. Almost in line and about half as far away was an enormous structure which I couldn't identify even that loosely. The range to the spaceport was extreme but I let the rocket see it, said, "Go find it, baby!" and twisted its tail—slapped the last one in, sent it toward the nearer target, and jumped.

That building took a direct hit just as I left it. Either a skinny had judged (correctly) that it was worth one of their buildings to try for one of us, or one of my own mates was getting mighty careless with fireworks. Either way, I didn't want to jump from that spot, even a skimmer; I decided to go through the next couple of buildings instead of over. So I grabbed the heavy flamer off my back as I hit and flipped the snoopers down over my eyes, tackled a wall in front of me with a knife beam at full power. A section of wall fell away and I charged in.

And backed out even faster.

I didn't know what it was I had cracked open. A congregation in church—a skinny flophouse—maybe even their defense headquarters. All I knew was that it was a very big room filled with more skinnies than I wanted to see in my whole life.

Probably not a church, for somebody took a shot at me as I popped back out—just a slug that bounced off my armor, made my ears ring, and staggered me without hurting me. But it reminded me that I wasn't supposed to leave without giving them a souvenir of my visit. I grabbed the first thing on my belt and lobbed it in—and heard it start to squawk. As they keep telling you in Basic, doing something constructive at once is better than figuring out the best thing to do hours later.

By sheer chance I had done the right thing. This was a special bomb, one each issued to us for this mission with instructions to use them if we found ways to make them effective. The squawking I heard as I threw it was the bomb shouting in skinny talk (free translation): "I'm a thirty-second bomb! I'm a thirty-second bomb! Twenty-nine! . . . twenty-eight! . . . twenty-seven!—"

It was supposed to frazzle their nerves. Maybe it did; it certainly frazzled mine. Kinder to shoot a man. I didn't wait for the countdown; I jumped, while I wondered whether they would find enough doors and windows to swarm out in time.

I got a bearing on Red's blinker at the top of the jump and one on Ace as I grounded. I was falling behind again—time to hurry.

But three minutes later we had closed the gap; I had Red on my left flank a half mile away. He reported it to Jelly. We heard Jelly's relaxed growl to the entire platoon: "Circle is closed, but the beacon is not down yet. Move forward slowly and mill around, make a little more trouble—but mind the lad on each side of you; don't make trouble for *him*. Good job, so far—don't spoil it. Platoon! By sections . . . *Muster!*"

It looked like a good job to me, too; much of the city was burning and, although it was almost full light now, it was hard to tell whether bare eyes were better than snoopers, the smoke was so thick.

Johnson, our section leader, sounded off: "Second section, call off!"

I echoed, "Squads four, five, and six—call off and report!"

The assortment of safe circuits we had available in the new model comm units certainly speeded things up; Jelly could talk to anybody or to his section leaders; a section leader could call his whole section, or his non-coms; and the platoon could muster twice as fast, when seconds matter. I listened to the fourth squad call off while I inventoried my remaining firepower and lobbed one bomb toward a skinny who poked his head around a corner. He left and so did I—"Mill around," the boss man had said.

The fourth squad bumbled the call off until the squad leader remembered to fill in with Jenkins' number; the fifth squad clicked off like an abacus and I began to feel good . . . when the call off stopped after number four in Ace's squad. I called out, "Ace, where's Dizzy?"

"Shut up," he said. "Number six! Call off!"

"Six!" Smith answered.

"Seven!"

"Sixth squad, Flores missing," Ace completed it. "Squad leader out for pickup."

"One man absent," I reported to Johnson. "Flores, squad six."

"Missing or dead?"

"I don't know. Squad leader and assistant section leader dropping out for pickup."

"Johnnie, you let Ace take it."

But I didn't hear him, so I didn't answer. I heard him report to Jelly and I heard Jelly cuss. Now look, I wasn't bucking for a medal—it's the assistant section leader's *business* to make pickup; he's the chaser, the last man in, expendable. The squad leaders have other work to do. As you've no doubt gathered by now the assistant section leader isn't necessary as long as the section leader is alive.

Right that moment I was feeling unusually expendable, almost expended, because I was hearing the sweetest sound in the universe, the beacon the retrieval boat would land on, sounding our recall. The beacon is a robot rocket, fired ahead of the retrieval boat, just a spike that buries itself in the ground and starts broadcasting that welcome, welcome music. The retrieval boat homes in on it automatically three minutes later and you had better be on hand, because the bus can't wait and there won't be another one along.

But you don't walk away on another cap trooper, not while there's a chance he's still alive—not in Rasczak's Roughnecks. Not in any outfit of the Mobile Infantry. You try to make pickup.

I heard Jelly order: "Heads up, lads! Close to retrieval circle and interdict! On the bounce!"

And I heard the beacon's sweet voice: "—*to the everlasting glory of the infantry, shines the name, shines the name of Rodger Young!*" and I wanted to head for it so bad I could taste it.

Instead I was headed the other way, closing on Ace's beacon and expending what I had left of bombs and fire pills and anything else that would weigh me down. "Ace! You got his beacon?"

"Yes. Go back, Useless!"

"I've got you by eye now. Where is he?"

"Right ahead of me, maybe quarter mile. Scram! He's *my* man."

I didn't answer; I simply cut left oblique to reach Ace about where he said Dizzy was.

And found Ace standing over him, a couple of skinnies flamed down and more running away. I lit beside him. "Let's get him out of his armor—the boat'll be down any second!"

"He's too bad hurt!"

I looked and saw that it was true—there was actually a *hole* in his armor and blood coming out. And I was stumped. To make a wounded pickup you get him out of his armor . . . then you simply pick him up in your arms—no trouble in a powered suit—and bounce away from there. A bare man weighs less than the ammo and stuff you've expended. "What'll we *do*?"

"We carry him," Ace said grimly. "Grab ahold the left side of his belt." He grabbed the right side, we manhandled Flores to his feet. "Lock on! Now . . . by the numbers, stand by to jump—one—*two!*"

We jumped. Not far, not well. One man alone couldn't have gotten him off the ground; an armored suit is too heavy. But split it between two men and it can be done.

We jumped—and we jumped—and again, and again, with Ace calling it and both of us steadying and catching Dizzy on each grounding. His gyros seemed to be out.

We heard the beacon cut off as the retrieval boat landed on it—I saw it land . . . and it was too far away. We heard the acting platoon sergeant call out: "In succession, prepare to embark!"

And Jelly called out, "Belay that order!"

We broke at last into the open and saw the boat standing on its tail, heard the ululation of its take-off warning—saw the platoon still on the ground around it, in interdiction circle, crouching behind the shield they had formed.

Heard Jelly shout, "In succession, man the boat—*move!*"

And we were *still* too far away! I could see them peel off from the first squad, swarm into the boat as the interdiction circle tightened.

And a single figure broke out of the circle, came toward us at a speed possible only to a command suit.

Jelly caught us while we were in the air, grabbed Flores by his Y-rack and helped us lift.

Three jumps got us to the boat. Everybody else was inside but the door was still open. We got him in and closed it while the boat pilot screamed that we had made her miss rendezvous and now we had *all* bought it! Jelly paid no attention to her; we laid Flores down and lay down beside him. As the blast hit us Jelly was saying to himself, "All present, Lieutenant. Three men hurt—but all present!"

I'll say this for Captain Deladrier: they don't make any better pilots. A rendezvous, boat to ship in orbit, is precisely calculated. I don't know how, but it is, and you don't change it. You *can't.*

Only she did. She saw in her scope that the boat had failed to blast on time; she braked back, picked up speed again—and matched and took us in, just by eye and touch, no time to compute it. If the Almighty ever needs an assistant to keep the stars in their courses, I know where he can look.

Flores died on the way up.

Chapter 2

It scared me so, I hooked it off,
Nor stopped as I remember,
Nor turned about till I got home,
Locked up in mother's chamber.
Yankee Doodle, keep it up,
Yankee Doodle dandy,
Mind the music and the step,
And with the girls be handy.

I never really intended to join up.

And certainly not the infantry! Why, I would rather have taken ten lashes in the public square and have my father tell me that I was a disgrace to a proud name.

Oh, I had mentioned to my father, late in my senior year in high school, that I was thinking over the idea of volunteering for Federal Service. I suppose every kid does, when his eighteenth birthday heaves into sight—and mine was due the week I graduated. Of course most of them just think about it, toy with the idea a little, then go do something else—go to college, or get a job, or something. I suppose it would have been that way with me . . . if my best chum had not, with dead seriousness, planned to join up.

Carl and I had done everything together in high school—eyed the girls together, double-dated together, been on the debate team together, pushed electrons together in his home lab. I wasn't much on electronic theory myself, but I'm a neat hand with a soldering gun; Carl supplied the skull sweat and I carried out his instructions. It was fun; anything we did together was fun. Carl's folks didn't have anything like the money that my father had, but it didn't matter between us. When my father bought me a Rolls copter for my fourteenth birthday, it was Carl's as much as it was mine; contrariwise, his basement lab was mine.

So when Carl told me that he was not going straight on with school, but serve a term first, it gave me to pause. He really meant it; he seemed to think that it was natural and right and obvious.

So I told him I was joining up, too.

He gave me an odd look. "Your old man won't let you."

"Huh? How can he stop me?" And of course he couldn't, not legally. It's the first completely free choice anybody gets (and maybe his last); when a boy, or a girl, reaches his or her eighteenth birthday, he or she can volunteer and nobody else has any say in the matter.

"You'll find out." Carl changed the subject.

So I took it up with my father, tentatively, edging into it sideways.

He put down his newspaper and cigar and stared at me. "Son, are you out of your mind?"

I muttered that I didn't think so.

"Well, it certainly sounds like it." He sighed. "Still . . . I should have been expecting it; it's a predictable stage in a boy's growing up. I remember when you learned to walk and weren't a baby any longer—frankly you were a little hellion for quite a while. You broke one of your mother's Ming vases—on purpose, I'm quite sure . . . but you were too young to know that it was valuable, so all you got was having your hand spatted. I recall the day you swiped one of my cigars, and how sick it made you. Your mother and I carefully avoided noticing that you couldn't eat dinner that night and I've never mentioned it to you until now—boys have to try such things and discover for themselves that men's vices are not for them. We watched when you turned the corner on adolescence and started noticing that girls were different—and wonderful."

He sighed again. "All normal stages. And the last one, right at the end of adolescence, is when a boy decides to join up and wear a pretty uniform. Or decides that he is in love, love such as no man ever experienced before, and that he just has to get married right away. Or both." He smiled grimly. "With me it was both. But I got over each of them in time not to make a fool of myself and ruin my life."

"But, Father, I wouldn't ruin my life. Just a term of service—not career."

"Let's table that, shall we? Listen, and let *me* tell *you* what you are going to do—because you *want* to. In the first place this family has stayed out of politics and cultivated its own garden for over a hundred years—I see no reason for you to break that fine record. I suppose it's the influence of that fellow at your high school—what's his name? You know the one I mean."

He meant our instructor in History and Moral Philosophy—a veteran, naturally. "Mr. Dubois."

"Hmmph, a silly name—it suits him. Foreigner, no doubt. It ought to be against the law to use the schools as undercover recruiting stations. I think I'm going to write a pretty sharp letter about it—a taxpayer has *some* rights!"

"But, Father, he doesn't do that at all! He—" I stopped, not knowing how to describe it. Mr. Dubois had a snotty, superior manner; he acted as if none of us was really *good* enough to volunteer for service. I didn't like him. "Uh, if anything, he discourages it."

"Hmmph! Do you know how to lead a pig? Never mind. When you graduate, you're going to study business at Harvard; you know that. After that, you will go on to the Sorbonne and you'll travel a bit along with it, meet some of our distributors, find out how business is done elsewhere. Then you'll come home and go to work. You'll start with the usual menial job, stock clerk or something, just for form's sake—but you'll be an executive before you can catch your breath, because I'm not getting any younger and the quicker you can pick up the load, the better. As soon as you're able and willing, you'll be boss. There! How does that strike you as a program? As compared with wasting two years of your life?"

I didn't say anything. None of it was news to me; I'd thought about it. Father stood up and put a hand on my shoulder. "Son, don't think I don't sympathize with you; I do. But look at the real facts. If there were a war, I'd be the first to cheer you on—and to put the business on a war footing. But there isn't, and praise God there never will be again. We've outgrown wars. This planet is now peaceful and happy and we enjoy good enough relations with other planets. So what is this so-called 'Federal Service'? Parasitism, pure and simple. A functionless organ, utterly obsolete, living on the taxpayers. A decidedly expensive way for inferior people who otherwise would be unemployed to live at public expense for a term of years, then give themselves airs for the rest of their lives. Is that what *you* want to do?"

"Carl isn't inferior!"

"Sorry. No, he's a fine boy . . . but misguided." He frowned, and then smiled. "Son, I had intended to keep something as a surprise for you—a graduation present. But I'm going to tell you now so that you can put this nonsense out of your mind more easily. Not that I am afraid of what you might do; I have confidence in your basic good sense, even at your tender years. But you are troubled, I know—and this will clear it away. Can you guess what it is?"

"Uh, no."

He grinned. "A vacation trip to Mars."

I must have looked stunned. "Golly Father, I had no idea—"

"I meant to surprise you and I see I did. I know how you kids feel about travel, though it beats me what anyone sees in it after the first time out. But this is a good time for you to do it—by yourself; did I mention that?—and get it out of your system . . . because you'll be hard-pressed to get in even a week on Luna once you take up your responsibilities." He picked up his paper. "No, don't thank me. Just run along and let me finish my paper—I've got some gentlemen coming in this evening, shortly. Business."

I ran along. I guess he thought that settled it . . . and I suppose I did, too. Mars! And on my own! But I didn't tell Carl about it; I had a sneaking suspicion that he would regard it as a bribe. Well, maybe it was. Instead I simply told him that my father and I seemed to have different ideas about it.

"Yeah," he answered, "so does mine. But it's *my* life."

I thought about it during the last session of our class in History and Moral Philosophy. H. & M. P. was different from other courses in that everybody had to take it but nobody had to pass it—and Mr. Dubois never seemed to care whether he got through to us or not. He would just point at you with the stump of his left arm (he never bothered with names) and snap a question. Then the argument would start.

But on the last day he seemed to be trying to find out what we had learned. One girl told him bluntly: "My mother says that violence never settles anything."

"So?" Mr. Dubois looked at her bleakly. "I'm sure the city fathers of Carthage would be glad to know that. Why doesn't your mother tell them so? Or why don't *you*?"

They had tangled before—since you couldn't flunk the course, it wasn't necessary to keep Mr. Dubois buttered up. She said shrilly, "You're making fun of me! Everybody knows that Carthage was destroyed!"

"You seemed to be unaware of it," he said grimly. "Since you do know it, wouldn't you say that violence had settled their destinies rather thoroughly? However, I was not making fun of you personally; I was heaping scorn on an inexcusably silly idea—a practice I shall always follow. Anyone who clings to the historically untrue—and thoroughly immoral—doctrine that 'violence never settles anything' I would advise to conjure up the ghosts of Napoleon Bonaparte and of the Duke of Wellington and let them debate it. The ghost of Hitler could referee, and the jury might well be the Dodo, the Great Auk, and the Passenger Pigeon. Violence, naked force, has settled more issues in history than has any other factor, and the contrary opinion is wishful thinking at its worst. Breeds that forget this basic truth have always paid for it with their lives and freedoms."

He sighed. "Another year, another class—and, for me, another failure. One can lead a child to knowledge but one *cannot* make him think." Suddenly he pointed his stump at me. "You. What is the moral difference, if any, between the soldier and the civilian?"

"The difference," I answered carefully, "lies in the field of civic virtue. A soldier accepts personal responsibility for the safety of the body politic of which he is a member, defending it, if need be, with his life. The civilian does not."

"The exact words of the book," he said scornfully. "But do you understand it? Do you *believe* it?"

"Uh, I don't know, sir."

"Of course you don't! I doubt if any of you here would recognize 'civic virtue' if it came up and barked in your face!" He glanced at his watch. "And that is all, a final all. Perhaps we shall meet again under happier circumstances. Dismissed."

Graduation right after that and three days later my birthday, followed in less than a week by Carl's birthday—and I still hadn't told Carl that I wasn't joining up. I'm sure he assumed that I would not, but we didn't discuss it out loud—embarrassing. I simply arranged to meet him the day after his birthday and we went down to the recruiting office together.

On the steps of the Federal Building we ran into Carmencita Ibañez, a classmate of ours and one of the nice things about being a member of a race with two sexes. Carmen wasn't my girl—she wasn't anybody's girl; she never made two dates in a row with the same boy and treated all of us with equal sweetness and rather impersonally. But I knew her pretty well, as she often came over and

used our swimming pool, because it was Olympic length—
sometimes with one boy, sometimes with another. Or alone, as
Mother urged her to—Mother considered her "a good influence."
For once she was right.

She saw us and waited, dimpling. "Hi, fellows!"

"Hello, *Ochee Chyornya,*" I answered. "What brings you
here?"

"Can't you guess? Today is my birthday."

"Huh? Happy returns!"

"So I'm joining up."

"Oh . . ." I think Carl was as surprised as I was. But Carmencita was like that. She never gossiped and she kept her own
affairs to herself. "No foolin'?" I added, brilliantly.

"Why should I be fooling? I'm going to be a spaceship pilot—
at least I'm going to try for it."

"No reason why you shouldn't make it," Carl said quickly. He
was right—I know now just how right he was. Carmen was small
and neat, perfect health and perfect reflexes—she could make
competitive diving routine look easy and she was quick at mathematics. Me, I tapered off with a "C" in algebra and a "B" in business arithmetic; she took all the math our school offered and a
tutored advance course on the side. But it had never occurred to
me to wonder why. Fact was, little Carmen was so ornamental that
you just never thought about her being useful.

"We—Uh, I," said Carl, "am here to join up, too."

"And me," I agreed. "Both of us." No, I hadn't made any decision; my mouth was leading its own life.

"Oh, wonderful!"

"And I'm going to buck for space pilot, too," I added firmly.

She didn't laugh. She answered very seriously, "Oh, how
grand! Perhaps in training we'll run into each other. I hope so."

"Collision courses?" asked Carl. "That's a no-good way to
pilot."

"Don't be silly, Carl. On the ground, of course. Are you going
to be a pilot, too?"

"*Me?*" Carl answered. "I'm no truck driver. You know me—
Starside R&D, if they'll have me. Electronics."

" 'Truck driver' indeed! I hope they stick you out on Pluto and
let you freeze. No, I don't—good luck! Let's go in, shall we?"

The recruiting station was inside a railing in the rotunda. A
fleet sergeant sat at a desk there, in dress uniform, gaudy as a cir-
cus. His chest was loaded with ribbons I couldn't read. But his

right arm was off so short that his tunic had been tailored without any sleeve at all . . . and, when you came up to the rail, you could see that he had no legs.

It didn't seem to bother him. Carl said, "Good morning. I want to join up."

"Me, too," I added.

He ignored us. He managed to bow while sitting down and said, "Good morning, young lady. What can I do for you?"

"I want to join up, too."

He smiled. "Good girl! If you'll just scoot up to room 201 and ask for Major Rojas, she'll take care of you." He looked her up and down. "Pilot?"

"If possible."

"You look like one. Well, see Miss Rojas."

She left, with thanks to him and a see-you-later to us; he turned his attention to us, sized us up with a total absence of the pleasure he had shown in little Carmen. "So?" he said. "For what? Labor battalions?"

"Oh, no!" I said. "I'm going to be a pilot."

He stared at me and simply turned his eyes away. "You?"

"I'm interested in the Research and Development Corps," Carl said soberly, "especially electronics. I understand the chances are pretty good."

"They are if you can cut it," the Fleet Sergeant said grimly, "and not if you don't have what it takes, both in preparation and ability. Look, boys, have you any idea why they have me out here in front?"

I didn't understand him. Carl said, "Why?"

"Because the government doesn't care one bucket of swill whether you join or not! Because it has become stylish, with some people—too many people—to serve a term and earn a franchise and be able to wear a ribbon in your lapel which says that you're a vet'ran . . . whether you've ever seen combat or not. But if you *want* to serve and I can't talk you out of it, then we have to take you, because that's your constitutional right. It says that everybody, male or female, shall have his born right to pay his service and assume full citizenship—but the facts are that we are getting hard pushed to find things for all the volunteers to do that aren't just glorified K.P. You can't all be real military men; we don't need that many and most of the volunteers aren't number-one soldier material anyhow. Got any idea what it takes to make a soldier?"

"No," I admitted.

"Most people think that all it takes is two hands and two feet and a stupid mind. Maybe so, for cannon fodder. Possibly that was all that Julius Caesar required. But a private soldier today is a specialist so highly skilled that he would rate 'master' in any other trade; we can't afford stupid ones. So for those who insist on serving their term—but haven't got what we want and must have—we've had to think up a whole list of dirty, nasty, dangerous jobs that will either run 'em home with their tails between their legs and their terms uncompleted . . . or at the very least make them remember for the rest of their lives that their citizenship is valuable to them because they've paid a high price for it. Take that young lady who was here—wants to be a pilot. I hope she makes it; we always need good pilots, not enough of 'em. Maybe she will. But if she misses, she may wind up in Antarctica, her pretty eyes red from never seeing anything but artificial light and her knuckles callused from hard, dirty work."

I wanted to tell him that the least Carmencita could get was computer programmer for the sky watch; she really was a whiz at math. But he was talking.

"So they put me out here to discourage you boys. Look at this." He shoved his chair around to make sure that we could see that he was legless. "Let's assume that you don't wind up digging tunnels on Luna or playing human guinea pig for new diseases through sheer lack of talent; suppose we do make a fighting man out of you. Take a look at *me*—this is what you may buy . . . if you don't buy the whole farm and cause your folks to receive a 'deeply regret' telegram. Which is more likely, because these days, in training or in combat, there aren't many wounded. If you buy at all, they likely throw in a coffin—I'm the rare exception; I was lucky . . . though maybe you wouldn't call it luck."

He paused, then added, "So why don't you boys go home, go to college, and then go be chemists or insurance brokers or whatever? A term of service isn't a kiddie camp; it's either real military service, rough and dangerous even in peacetime . . . or a most unreasonable facsimile thereof. Not a vacation. Not a romantic adventure. Well?"

Carl said, "I'm here to join up."

"Me, too."

"You realize that you aren't allowed to pick your service?"

Carl said, "I thought we could state our preferences?"

"Certainly. And that's the last choice you'll make until the end of your term. The placement officer pays attention to your choice, too. First thing he does is to check whether there's any demand for left-handed glass blowers this week—that being what you think would make you happy. Having reluctantly conceded that there is a need for your choice—probably at the bottom of the Pacific—he then tests you for innate ability and preparation. About once in twenty times he is forced to admit that everything matches and you get the job . . . until some practical joker gives you dispatch orders to do something very different. But the other nineteen times he turns you down and decides that you are just what they have been needing to field-test survival equipment on Titan." He added meditatively, "It's chilly on Titan. And it's amazing how often experimental equipment fails to work. Have to have real field tests, though—laboratories just never get all the answers."

"I can qualify for electronics," Carl said firmly, "if there are jobs open in it."

"So? And how about you, bub?"

I hesitated—and suddenly realized that, if I didn't take a swing at it, I would wonder all my life whether I was anything but the boss's son. "I'm going to chance it."

"Well, you can't say I didn't try. Got your birth certificates with you? And let's see your I.D.s."

Ten minutes later, still not sworn in, we were on the top floor being prodded and poked and fluoroscoped. I decided that the idea of a physical examination is that, if you *aren't* ill, then they do their darnedest to make you ill. If the attempt fails, you're in.

I asked one of the doctors what percentage of the victims flunked the physical. He looked startled. "Why, we *never* fail any-one. The law doesn't permit us to."

"Huh? I mean, excuse me, Doctor? Then what's the point of this goose-flesh parade?"

"Why, the purpose is," he answered, hauling off and hitting me in the knee with a hammer (I kicked him, but not hard), "to find out what duties you are physically able to perform. But if you came in here in a wheel chair and blind in both eyes and were silly enough to insist on enrolling, they would find something silly enough to match. Counting the fuzz on a caterpillar by touch, maybe. The only way you can fail is by having the psychiatrists decide that you are not able to understand the oath."

"Oh. Uh . . . Doctor, were you already a doctor when you

joined up? Or did they decide you ought to be a doctor and send you to school?"

"*Me?*" He seemed shocked. "Youngster, do I look that silly? I'm a civilian employee."

"Oh. Sorry, sir."

"No offense. But military service is for ants. Believe me. I see 'em go, I see 'em come back—when they do come back. I see what it's done to them. And for what? A purely nominal political privilege that pays not one centavo and that most of them aren't competent to use wisely anyhow. Now if they would let medical men run things—but never mind that; you might think I was talking treason, free speech or not. But, youngster, if you've got savvy enough to count ten, you'll back out while you still can. Here, take these papers back to the recruiting sergeant—and remember what I said."

I went back to the rotunda. Carl was already there. The Fleet Sergeant looked over my papers and said glumly, "Apparently you both are almost insufferably healthy—except for holes in the head. One moment, while I get some witnesses." He punched a button and two female clerks came out, one old battle-ax, one kind of cute.

He pointed to our physical examination forms, our birth certificates, and our I.D.'s, said formally: "I invite and require you, each and severally, to examine these exhibits, determine what they are and to determine, each independently, what relation, if any, each document bears to these two men standing here in your presence."

They treated it as a dull routine, which I'm sure it was; nevertheless they scrutinized every document, they took our fingerprints—again!—and the cute one put a jeweler's loupe in her eye and compared prints from birth to now. She did the same with signatures. I began to doubt if I was myself.

The Fleet Sergeant added, "Did you find exhibits relating to their present competence to take the oath of enrollment? If so, what?"

"We found," the older one said, "appended to each record of physical examination a duly certified conclusion by an authorized and delegated board of psychiatrists stating that each of them is mentally competent to take the oath and that neither one is under the influence of alcohol, narcotics, other disabling drugs, nor of hypnosis."

"Very good." He turned to us. "Repeat after me—

"I, being of legal age, of my own free will—"

" 'I,' " we each echoed, " 'being of legal age, of my own free will—' "

"—without coercion, promise, or inducement of any sort, after having been duly advised and warned of the meaning and consequences of this oath—

"—do now enroll in the Federal Service of the Terran Federation for a term of not less than two years and as much longer as may be required by the needs of the Service—"

(I gulped a little over that part. I had always thought of a "term" as two years, even though I knew better, because that's the way people talk about it. Why, we were signing up for *life*.)

"I swear to uphold and defend the Constitution of the Federation against all its enemies on or off Terra, to protect and defend the Constitutional liberties and privileges of all citizens and lawful residents of the Federation, its associated states and territories, to perform, on or off Terra, such duties of any lawful nature as may be assigned to me by lawful direct or delegated authority—

"—and to obey all lawful orders of the Commander-in-Chief of the Terran Service and of all officers or delegated persons placed over me—

"—and to require such obedience from all members of the Service or other persons or non-human beings lawfully placed under my orders—

"—and, on being honorably discharged at the completion of my full term of active service or upon being placed on inactive retired status after having completed such full term, to carry out all duties and obligations and to enjoy all privileges of Federation citizenship including but not limited to the duty, obligation and privilege of exercising sovereign franchise for the rest of my natural life unless stripped of honor by verdict, finally sustained, of court of my sovereign peers."

(*Whew!*) Mr. Dubois had analyzed the Service oath for us in History and Moral Philosophy and had made us study it phrase by phrase—but you don't really feel the *size* of the thing until it comes rolling over you, all in one ungainly piece, as heavy and unstoppable as Juggernaut's carriage.

At least it made me realize that I was no longer a civilian, with my shirttail out and nothing on my mind. I didn't know yet what I was, but I knew what I wasn't.

"So help me God!" we both ended and Carl crossed himself and so did the cute one.

After that there were more signatures and fingerprints, all five of us, and flat colorgraphs of Carl and me were snapped then and there and embossed into our papers. The Fleet Sergeant finally looked up. "Why, it's 'way past the break for lunch. Time for chow, lads."

I swallowed hard. "Uh . . . Sergeant?"

"Eh? Speak up."

"Could I flash my folks from here? Tell them what I—Tell them how it came out?"

"We can do better than that."

"Sir?"

"You go on forty-eight hours leave now." He grinned coldly. "Do you know what happens if you don't come back?"

"Uh . . . court-martial?"

"Not a thing. Not a blessed thing. Except that your papers get marked, *Term not completed satisfactorily,* and you never, never, never get a second chance. This is our cooling-off period, during which we shake out the overgrown babies who didn't really mean it and should never have taken the oath. It saves the government money and it saves a power of grief for such kids and their parents—the neighbors needn't guess. You don't even have to tell your parents." He shoved his chair away from his desk. "So I'll see you at noon day after tomorrow. If I see you. Fetch your personal effects."

It was a crumbly leave. Father stormed at me, then quit speaking to me; Mother took to her bed. When I finally left, an hour earlier than I had to, nobody saw me off but the morning cook and the houseboys.

I stopped in front of the recruiting sergeant's desk, thought about saluting and decided I didn't know how. He looked up. "Oh. Here are your papers. Take them up to room 201; they'll start you through the mill. Knock and walk in."

Two days later I knew I was not going to be a pilot. Some of the things the examiners wrote about me were:—*insufficient intuitive grasp of spatial relationships . . . insufficient mathematical talent . . . deficient mathematical preparation . . . reaction time adequate . . . eyesight good.* I'm glad they put in those last two; I was beginning to feel that counting on my fingers was my speed.

The placement officer let me list my lesser preferences, in order, and I caught four more days of the wildest aptitude tests I've ever heard of. I mean to say, what do they find out when a stenographer jumps on her chair and screams, "Snakes!" There was no snake, just a harmless piece of plastic hose.

The written and oral tests were mostly just as silly, but they seemed happy with them, so I took them. The thing I did most carefully was to list my preferences. Naturally I listed all of the Space Navy jobs (other than pilot) at the top; whether I went as power-room technician or as cook, I knew that I preferred any Navy job to any Army job—I wanted to travel.

Next I listed Intelligence—a spy gets around, too, and I figured that it couldn't possibly be dull. (I was wrong, but never mind.) After that came a long list; psychological warfare, chemical warfare, biological warfare, combat ecology (I didn't know what it was, but it sounded interesting), logistics corps (a simple mistake; I had studied logic for the debate team and "logistics" turns out to have two entirely separate meanings), and a dozen others. Clear at the bottom, with some hesitation, I put K-9 Corps, and Infantry.

I didn't bother to list the various non-combatant auxiliary corps because, if I wasn't picked for a combat corps, I didn't care whether they used me as an experimental animal or sent me as a laborer in the Terranizing of Venus—either one was a booby prize.

Mr. Weiss, the placement officer, sent for me a week after I was sworn in. He was actually a retired psychological-warfare major, on active duty for procurement, but he wore mufti and insisted on being called just "Mister" and you could relax and take it easy with him. He had my list of preferences and the reports on all my tests and I saw that he was holding my high school transcript—which pleased me, for I had done all right in school; I had stood high enough without standing so high as to be marked as a greasy grind, having never flunked any courses and dropped only one, and I had been rather a big man around school otherwise; swimming team, debate team, track squad, class treasurer, silver medal in the annual literary contest, chairman of the homecoming committee, stuff like that. A well-rounded record and it's all down in the transcript.

He looked up as I came in, said, "Sit down, Johnnie," and looked back at the transcript, then put it down. "You like dogs?"

"Huh? Yes, sir."

"How well do you like them? Did your dog sleep on your bed? By the way, where is your dog now?"

"Why, I don't happen to have a dog just at present. But when I did—well, no, he didn't sleep on my bed. You see, Mother didn't allow dogs in the house."

"But didn't you sneak him in?"

"Uh—" I thought of trying to explain Mother's not-angry-but-terribly-terribly-hurt routine when you tried to buck her on something she had her mind made up about. But I gave up. "No, sir."

"Mmm . . . have you ever seen a neodog?"

"Uh, once, sir. They exhibited one at the Macarthur Theater two years ago. But the S.P.C.A. made trouble for them."

"Let me tell you how it is with a K-9 team. A neodog is not just a dog that talks."

"I couldn't understand that neo at the Macarthur. Do they really talk?"

"They talk. You simply have to train your ear to their accent. Their mouths can't shape 'b,' 'm,' 'p,' or 'v' and you have to get used to their equivalents—something like the handicap of a split palate but with different letters. No matter, their speech is as clear as any human speech. But a neodog is not a talking dog; he is not a dog at all, he is an artificially mutated symbiote derived from dog stock. A neo, a trained Caleb, is about six times as bright as a dog, say about as intelligent as a human moron—except that the comparison is not fair to the neo; a moron is a defective, whereas a neo is a stable genius in his own line of work."

Mr. Weiss scowled. "Provided, that is, that he has his symbiote. That's the rub. Mmm . . . you're too young ever to have been married but you've seen marriage, your own parents at least. Can you imagine being married to a Caleb?"

"Huh? No. No, I can't."

"The emotional relationship between the dog-man and the man-dog in the K-9 team is a great deal closer and much more important than is the emotional relationship in most marriages. If the master is killed, we kill the neodog—at once! It is all that we can do for the poor thing. A mercy killing. If the neodog is killed . . . well, we can't kill the man even though it would be the simplest solution. Instead we restrain him and hospitalize him and slowly put him back together." He picked up a pen, made a mark. "I don't think we can risk assigning a boy to K-9 who didn't outwit his mother to have his dog sleep with him. So let's consider something else."

It was not until then that I realized that I must have already flunked every choice on my list above K-9 Corps—and now I had just flunked it, too. I was so startled that I almost missed his next remark. Major Weiss said meditatively, with no expression and as if he were talking about someone else, long dead and far away: "I was once half of a K-9 team. When my Caleb became a casualty, they kept me under sedation for six weeks, then rehabilitated me for other work. Johnnie, these courses you've taken—why didn't you study something useful?"

"Sir?"

"Too late now. Forget it. Mmm . . . your instructor in History and Moral Philosophy seems to think well of you."

"He does?" I was surprised. "What did he say?"

Weiss smiled. "He says that you are not stupid, merely ignorant and prejudiced by your environment. From him that is high praise—I know him."

It didn't sound like praise to me! That stuck-up stiff-necked old—

"And," Weiss went on, "a boy who gets a 'C-minus' in Appreciation of Television can't be all bad. I think we'll accept Mr. Dubois' recommendation. How would you like to be an infantryman?"

I came out of the Federal Building feeling subdued yet not really unhappy. At least I was a soldier; I had papers in my pocket to prove it. I hadn't been classed as too dumb and useless for anything but make-work.

It was a few minutes after the end of the working day and the building was empty save for a skeleton night staff and a few stragglers. I ran into a man in the rotunda who was just leaving; his face looked familiar but I couldn't place him.

But he caught my eye and recognized me. "Evening!" he said briskly. "You haven't shipped out yet?"

And then I recognized him—the Fleet Sergeant who had sworn us in. I guess my chin dropped; this man was in civilian clothes, was walking around on two legs and had two arms. "Uh, good evening, Sergeant," I mumbled.

He understood my expression perfectly, glanced down at himself and smiled easily. "Relax, lad. I don't have to put on my horror show after working hours—and I don't. You haven't been placed yet?"

"I just got my orders."

"For what?"

"Mobile Infantry."

His face broke in a big grin of delight and he shoved out his hand. "My outfit! Shake, son! We'll make a man of you—or kill you trying. Maybe both."

"It's a good choice?" I said doubtfully.

" 'A good choice'? Son, it's the *only* choice. The Mobile Infantry *is* the Army. All the others are either button pushers or professors, along merely to hand us the saw; *we* do the work." He shook hands again and added, "Drop me a card—'Fleet Sergeant Ho, Federal Building,' that'll reach me. Good luck!" And he was off, shoulders back, heels clicking, head up.

I looked at my hand. The hand he had offered me was the one that wasn't there—his right hand. Yet it had felt like flesh and had shaken mine firmly. I had read about these powered prosthetics, but it is startling when you first run across them.

I went back to the hotel where recruits were temporarily billeted during placement—we didn't even have uniforms yet, just plain coveralls we wore during the day and our own clothes after hours. I went to my room and started packing, as I was shipping out early in the morning—packing to send stuff home, I mean; Weiss had cautioned me not to take along anything but family photographs and possibly a musical instrument if I played one (which I didn't). Carl had shipped out three days earlier, having gotten the R&D assignment he wanted. I was just as glad, as he would have been just too confounded understanding about the billet I had drawn. Little Carmen had shipped out, too, with the rank of cadet midshipman (probationary)—she was going to be a pilot, all right, if she could cut it . . . and I suspected that she could.

My temporary roomie came in while I was packing. "Got your orders?" he asked.

"Yup."

"What?"

"Mobile Infantry."

"The *Infantry?* Oh, you poor stupid clown! I feel sorry for you, I really do."

I straightened up and said angrily, "Shut up! The Mobile Infantry is the best outfit in the Army—it *is* the Army! The rest of you jerks are just along to hand us the saw—*we* do the work."

He laughed. "You'll find out!"

"You want a mouthful of knuckles?"

Chapter 3

He shall rule them with a rod of iron.

—Revelations II:25

I did Basic at Camp Arthur Currie on the northern prairies, along with a couple of thousand other victims—and I do mean "Camp," as the only permanent buildings there were to shelter equipment. We slept and ate in tents; we lived outdoors—if you call that "living," which I didn't, at the time. I was used to a warm climate; it seemed to me that the North Pole was just five miles north of camp and getting closer. Ice Age returning, no doubt.

But exercise will keep you warm and they saw to it that we got plenty of that.

The first morning we were there they woke us up before daybreak. I had had trouble adjusting to the change in time zones and it seemed to me that I had just got to sleep; I couldn't believe that anyone seriously intended that I should get up in the middle of the night.

But they did mean it. A speaker somewhere was blaring out a military march, fit to wake the dead, and a hairy nuisance who had come charging down the company street yelling, *"Everybody out! Show a leg! On the bounce!"* came marauding back again just as I had pulled the covers over my head, tipped over my cot and dumped me on the cold hard ground.

It was an impersonal attention; he didn't even wait to see if I hit.

Ten minutes later, dressed in trousers, undershirt, and shoes, I was lined up with the others in ragged ranks for setting-up exercises just as the Sun looked over the eastern horizon. Facing us was a big broad-shouldered, mean-looking man, dressed just as we were—except that while I looked and felt like a poor job of embalming, his chin was shaved blue, his trousers were sharply creased, you could have used his shoes for mirrors, and his manner was alert, wide-awake, relaxed, and rested. You got the impression that he never needed to sleep—just ten-thousand-mile checkups and dust him off occasionally.

He bellowed, "C'p*nee! Atten . . . shut!* I am Career Ship's Sergeant Zim, your company commander. When you speak to me, you will salute and say, 'Sir'—you will salute and 'sir' anyone who carries an instructor's baton—" He was carrying a swagger cane and now made a quick reverse moulinet with it to show what he meant by an instructor's baton; I had noticed men carrying them when we had arrived the night before and had intended to get one myself—they looked smart. Now I changed my mind. "—because we don't have enough officers around here for you to practice on. You'll practice on us. Who sneezed?"

No answer—

"WHO SNEEZED?"

"I did," a voice answered.

" 'I did' *what?*"

"I sneezed."

" 'I sneezed,' SIR!"

"I sneezed, sir. I'm cold, sir."

"Oho!" Zim strode up to the man who had sneezed, shoved the ferrule of the swagger cane an inch under his nose and demanded, "Name?"

"Jenkins . . . sir."

"Jenkins . . ." Zim repeated as if the word were somehow distasteful, even shameful. "I suppose some night on patrol you're going to sneeze just because you've got a runny nose. Eh?"

"I hope not, sir."

"So do I. But you're cold. Hmm . . . we'll fix that." He pointed with his stick. "See that armory over there?" I looked and could see nothing but prairie except for one building that seemed to be almost on the skyline.

"Fall out. Run around it. *Run*, I said. Fast! Bronski! Pace him."

"Right, Sarge." One of the five or six other baton carriers took out after Jenkins, caught up with him easily, cracked him across the tight of his pants with the baton. Zim turned back to the rest of us, still shivering at attention. He walked up and down, looked us over, and seemed awfully unhappy. At last he stepped out in front of us, shook his head, and said, apparently to himself but he had a voice that carried: "To think that this had to happen to *me!*"

He looked at us. "You apes—No, not 'apes'; you don't rate that much. You pitiful mob of sickly monkeys . . . you sunken-chested, slack-bellied, drooling refugees from apron strings. In my whole life I never saw such a disgraceful huddle of momma's spoiled little darlings in—you, there! Suck up the gut! Eyes front! I'm talking to *you!*"

I pulled in my belly, even though I was not sure he had addressed me. He went on and on and I began to forget my goose flesh in hearing him storm. He never once repeated himself and he never used either profanity or obscenity. (I learned later that he saved those for *very* special occasions, which this wasn't.) But he described our shortcomings, physical, mental, moral, and genetic, in great and insulting detail.

But somehow I was not insulted; I became greatly interested in studying his command of language. I wished that we had had him on our debate team.

At last he stopped and seemed about to cry. "I can't *stand* it," he said bitterly. "I've just got to work some of it off—I had a better set of wooden soldiers when I was six. ALL RIGHT! Is there any one of you jungle lice who thinks he can whip me? Is there a *man* in the crowd? Speak up!"

There was a short silence to which I contributed. I didn't have any doubt at all that he could whip me; I was convinced.

I heard a voice far down the line, the tall end. "Ah reckon ah can . . . suh."

Zim looked happy. "Good! Step out here where I can see you." The recruit did so and he was impressive, at least three inches taller than Sergeant Zim and broader across the shoulders. "What's your name, soldier?"

"Breckinridge, suh—and ah weigh two hundred and ten pounds an' theah ain't *any* of it 'slack-bellied.' "

"Any particular way you'd like to fight?"

"Suh, you jus' pick youah own method of dyin'. Ah'm not fussy."

"Okay, no rules. Start when ever you like." Zim tossed his baton aside.

It started—and it was over. The big recruit was sitting on the ground, holding his left wrist in his right hand. He didn't say anything.

Zim bent over him. "Broken?"

"Reckon it might be . . . suh."

"I'm sorry. You hurried me a little. Do you know where the dispensary is? Never mind—Jones! Take Breckinridge over to the dispensary." As they left Zim slapped him on the right shoulder and said quietly, "Let's try it again in a month or so. I'll show you what happened." I think it was meant to be a private remark but they were standing about six feet in front of where I was slowly freezing solid.

Zim stepped back and called out, "Okay, we've got one man in this company, at least. I feel better. Do we have another one? Do we have two more? Any two of you scrofulous toads think you can stand up to me?" He looked back and forth along our ranks. "Chicken-livered, spineless—oh, oh! Yes? Step out."

Two men who had been side by side in ranks stepped out together; I suppose they had arranged it in whispers right there, but they also were far down the tall end, so I didn't hear. Zim smiled at them. "Names, for your next of kin, please."

"Heinrich."

"Heinrich *what?*"

"Heinrich, sir. Bitte." He spoke rapidly to the other recruit and added politely, "He doesn't speak much Standard English yet, sir."

"Meyer, mein Herr," the second man supplied.

"That's okay, lots of 'em don't speak much of it when they get here—I didn't myself. Tell Meyer not to worry, he'll pick it up. But he understands what we are going to do?"

"Jawohl," agreed Meyer.

"Certainly, sir. He understands Standard, he just can't speak it fluently."

"All right. Where did you two pick up those face scars? Heidelberg?"

"Nein—no, sir. Königsberg."

"Same thing." Zim had picked up his baton after fighting Breckinridge; he twirled it and asked, "Perhaps you would each like to borrow one of these?"

"It would not be fair to you, sir," Heinrich answered carefully. "Bare hands, if you please."

"Suit yourself. Though I might fool you. Königsberg, eh? Rules?"

"How can there be rules, sir, with three?"

"An interesting point. Well, let's agree that if eyes are gouged out they must be handed back when it's over. And tell your Korpsbruder that I'm ready now. Start when you like." Zim tossed his baton away; someone caught it.

"You joke, sir. We will not gouge eyes."

"No eye gouging, agreed. 'Fire when ready, Gridley.' "

"Please?"

"Come on and fight! Or get back into ranks!"

Now I am not sure that I saw it happen this way; I may have learned part of it later, in training. But here is what I think happened: The two moved out on each side of our company commander until they had him completely flanked but well out of contact. From this position there is a choice of four basic moves for the man working alone, moves that take advantage of his own mobility and of the superior coordination of one man as compared with two—Sergeant Zim says (correctly) that any group is weaker than a man alone unless they are perfectly trained to work together. For example, Zim could have feinted at one of them, bounced fast to the other with a disabler, such as a broken kneecap—then finished off the first at his leisure.

Instead he let them attack. Meyer came at him fast, intending to body check and knock him to the ground, I think, while Heinrich would follow through from above, maybe with his boots. That's the way it appeared to start.

And here's what I think I saw. Meyer never reached him with that body check. Sergeant Zim whirled to face him, while kicking out and getting Heinrich in the belly—and then Meyer was sailing through the air, his lunge helped along with a hearty assist from Zim.

But all I am sure of is that the fight started and then there were two German boys sleeping peacefully, almost end to end, one face down and one face up, and Zim was standing over them, not even breathing hard. "Jones," he said. "No, Jones left, didn't he? Mahmud! Let's have the water bucket, then stick them back into their sockets. Who's got my toothpick?"

A few moments later the two were conscious, wet, and back in ranks. Zim looked at us and inquired gently, "Anybody else? Or shall we get on with setting-up exercises?"

I didn't expect anybody else and I doubt if he did. But from down on the left flank, where the shorties hung out, a boy stepped out of ranks, came front and center. Zim looked down at him. "Just you? Or do you want to pick a partner?"

"Just myself, sir."

"As you say. Name?"

"Shujumi, sir."

Zim's eyes widened. "Any relation to Colonel Shujumi?"

"I have the honor to be his son, sir."

"Ah so! Well! Black Belt?"

"No, sir. Not yet."

"I'm glad you qualified that. Well, Shujumi, are we going to use contest rules, or shall I send for the ambulance?"

"As you wish, sir. But I think, if I may be permitted an opinion, that contest rules would be more prudent."

"I don't know just how you mean that, but I agree." Zim tossed his badge of authority aside, then, so help me, they backed off, faced each other, and bowed.

After that they circled around each other in a half crouch, making tentative passes with their hands, and looking like a couple of roosters.

Suddenly they touched—and the little chap was down on the ground and Sergeant Zim was flying through the air over his head. But he didn't land with the dull, breath-paralyzing thud that Meyer had; he lit rolling and was on his feet as fast as Shujumi was and facing him. "Banzai!" Zim yelled and grinned.

"Arigato," Shujumi answered and grinned back.

They touched again almost without a pause and I thought the Sergeant was going to fly again. He didn't; he slithered straight in, there was a confusion of arms and legs and when the motion slowed down you could see that Zim was tucking Shujumi's left foot in his right ear—a poor fit.

Shujumi slapped the ground with a free hand; Zim let him up at once. They again bowed to each other.

"Another fall, sir?"

"Sorry. We've got work to do. Some other time, eh? For fun . . . and honor. Perhaps I should have told you; your honorable father trained me."

"So I had already surmised, sir. Another time it is."

Zim slapped him hard on the shoulder. "Back in ranks, soldier. *C'pnee!*"

Then, for twenty minutes, we went through calisthenics that left me as dripping hot as I had been shivering cold. Zim led it himself, doing it all with us and shouting the count. He hadn't been mussed that I could see; he wasn't breathing hard as we finished. He never led the exercises after that morning (we never saw him again before breakfast; rank hath its privileges), but he did that morning, and when it was over and we were all bushed, he led us at a trot to the mess tent, shouting at us the whole way to "Step it up! On the bounce! You're dragging your tails!"

We *always* trotted *everywhere* at Camp Arthur Currie. I never did find out who Currie was, but he must have been a trackman.

Breckinridge was already in the mess tent, with a cast on his wrist but thumb and fingers showing. I heard him say, "Naw, just a green-stick fractchuh—ah've played a whole quahtuh with wuss. But you wait—ah'll fix him."

I had my doubts. Shujumi, maybe—but not that big ape. He simply didn't know when he was outclassed. I disliked Zim from the first moment I laid eyes on him. But he had style.

Breakfast was all right—all the meals were all right; there was none of that nonsense some boarding schools have of making your life miserable at the table. If you wanted to slump down and shovel it in with both hands, nobody bothered you—which was good, as meals were practically the only time somebody wasn't riding you. The menu for breakfast wasn't anything like what I had been used to at home and the civilians that waited on us slapped the food around in a fashion that would have made Mother grow pale and leave for her room—but it was hot and it was plentiful and the cooking was okay if plain. I ate about four times what I normally do and washed it down with mug after mug of coffee with cream and lots of sugar—I would have eaten a shark without stopping to skin him.

Jenkins showed up with Corporal Bronski behind him as I was starting on seconds. They stopped for a moment at a table where Zim was eating alone, then Jenkins slumped onto a vacant stool by mine. He looked mighty seedy—pale, exhausted, and his breath rasping. I said, "Here, let me pour you some coffee."

He shook his head.

"You better eat," I insisted. "Some scrambled eggs—they'll go down easily."

"Can't eat. Oh, that dirty, dirty so-and-so." He began cussing out Zim in a low, almost expressionless monotone. "All I asked him was to let me go lie down and skip breakfast. Bronski wouldn't let me—said I had to see the company commander. So I did and I *told* him I was sick, I *told* him. He just felt my cheek and counted my pulse and told me sick call was nine o'clock. Wouldn't let me go back to my tent. Oh, that rat! I'll catch him on a dark night, I will."

I spooned out some eggs for him anyway and poured coffee. Presently he began to eat. Sergeant Zim got up to leave while most of us were still eating, and stopped by our table. "Jenkins."

"Uh? Yes, sir."

"At oh-nine-hundred muster for sick call and see the doctor."

Jenkins' jaw muscles twitched. He answered slowly, "I don't need any pills—sir. I'll get by."

"Oh-nine-hundred. That's an order." He left.

Jenkins started his monotonous chant again. Finally he slowed down, took a bite of eggs and said somewhat more loudly, "I can't help wondering what kind of a mother produced *that*. I'd just like to have a look at her, that's all. Did he ever *have* a mother?"

It was a rhetorical question but it got answered. At the head of our table, several stools away, was one of the instructor-corporals. He had finished eating and was smoking and picking his teeth, simultaneously; he had evidently been listening. "Jenkins—"

"Uh—sir?"

"Don't you know about sergeants?"

"Well . . . I'm learning."

"They don't have mothers. Just ask any trained private." He blew smoke toward us. "They reproduce by fission . . . like all bacteria."

Chapter 4

And the LORD *said unto Gideon, The people that are with thee are too many ... Now therefore go to, proclaim in the ears of the people, saying, Whosoever is fearful and afraid, let him return ... And there returned of the people twenty and two thousand; and there remained ten thousand. And the* LORD *said unto Gideon, The people are yet too many; bring them down unto the water, and I will try them for thee there ... so he brought down the people unto the water: and the* LORD *said unto Gideon, Every one that lappeth of the water with his tongue, as a dog lappeth, him shalt thou set by himself; likewise everyone that boweth down upon his knees to drink. And the number of them that drank,* putting *their hand to their mouth, were three hundred men ...*

And the LORD *said unto Gideon, By the three hundred ... will I save you ... let all the* other *people go ...*

—Judges VII:2–7

Two weeks after we got there they took our cots away from us. That is to say that we had the dubious pleasure of folding them, carrying them four miles, and stowing them in a warehouse. By then it didn't matter; the ground seemed much warmer and quite soft—especially when the alert sounded in the middle of the night and we had to scramble out and play soldier. Which it did about three times a week. But I could get back to sleep after one of those mock exercises at once; I had learned to sleep any place, any time—sitting up, standing up, even marching in ranks. Why, I could even sleep through evening parade standing at attention, enjoy the music without being waked by it—and wake instantly at the command to pass in review.

I made a very important discovery at Camp Currie. Happiness consists in getting enough sleep. Just that, nothing more. All the wealthy, unhappy people you've ever met take sleeping pills; Mobile Infantrymen don't need them. Give a cap trooper a bunk and time to sack out in it and he's as happy as a worm in an apple—asleep.

Theoretically you were given eight full hours of sack time every night and about an hour and a half after evening chow for your own use. But in fact your night sack time was subject to alerts, to night duty, to field marches, and to acts of God and the whims of those over you, and your evenings, if not ruined by awkward squad or extra duty for minor offenses, were likely to be taken up by shining shoes, doing laundry, swapping haircuts (some of us got to be pretty fair barbers but a clean sweep like a billiard ball was acceptable and anybody can do that)—not to mention a thousand other chores having to do with equipment, person, and the demands of sergeants. For example we learned to answer morning roll call with: "Bathed!" meaning you had taken at least one bath since last reveille. A man might lie about it and get away with it (I did, a couple of times) but at least one in our company who pulled that dodge in the face of convincing evidence that he was not recently bathed got scrubbed with stiff brushes and floor soap by his squad mates while a corporal-instructor chaperoned and made helpful suggestions.

But if you didn't have more urgent things to do after supper, you could write a letter, loaf, gossip, discuss the myriad mental and moral shortcomings of sergeants and, dearest of all, talk about the female of the species (we became convinced that there were no such creatures, just mythology created by inflamed imaginations—one boy in our company claimed to have seen a girl, over at regimental headquarters; he was unanimously judged a liar and a braggart). Or you could play cards. I learned, the hard way, not to draw to an inside straight and I've never done it since. In fact I haven't played cards since.

Or, if you actually did have twenty minutes of your very own, you could sleep. This was a choice very highly thought of; we were always several weeks minus on sleep.

I may have given the impression that boot camp was made harder than necessary. This is not correct.

It was made *as hard as possible* and on purpose.

It was the firm opinion of every recruit that this was sheer meanness, calculated sadism, fiendish delight of witless morons in making other people suffer.

It was not. It was too scheduled, too intellectual, too efficiently and impersonally organized to be cruelty for the sick pleasure of cruelty; it was planned like surgery for purposes as unimpassioned as those of a surgeon. Oh, I admit that some of the instructors may have enjoyed it but I don't *know* that they did—and I *do* know (now) that the psych officers tried to weed out any bullies in selecting instructors. They looked for skilled and dedicated craftsmen to follow the art of making things as tough as possible for a recruit; a bully is too stupid, himself too emotionally involved and too likely to grow tired of his fun and slack off, to be efficient.

Still, there may have been bullies among them. But I've heard that some surgeons (and not necessarily bad ones) enjoy the cutting and the blood which accompanies the humane art of surgery.

That's what it was: surgery. Its immediate purpose was to get rid of, run right out of the outfit, those recruits who were too soft or too babyish ever to make Mobile Infantrymen. It accomplished that, in droves. (They darn near ran *me* out.) Our company shrank to platoon size in the first six weeks. Some of them were dropped without prejudice and allowed, if they wished, to sweat out their terms in the noncombatant services; others got Bad Conduct Discharges, or Unsatisfactory Performance Discharges, or Medical Discharges.

Usually you didn't know why a man left unless you saw him leave and he volunteered the information. But some of them got fed up, said so loudly, and resigned, forfeiting forever their chances of franchise. Some, especially the older men, simply couldn't stand the pace physically no matter how hard they tried. I remember one, a nice old geezer named Carruthers, must have been thirty-five; they carried him away in a stretcher while he was still shouting feebly that it wasn't fair!—and that he would be back.

It was sort of sad, because we liked Carruthers and he *did* try—so we looked the other way and figured we would never see him again, that he was a cinch for a medical discharge and civilian clothes. Only I *did* see him again, long after. He had refused discharge (you don't have to accept a medical) and wound up as third cook in a troop transport. He remembered me and wanted to talk old times, as proud of being an alumnus of Camp Currie as Father is of his Harvard accent—he felt that he was a little bit better than the ordinary Navy man. Well, maybe he was.

But, much more important than the purpose of carving away the fat quickly and saving the government the training costs of those who would never cut it, was the prime purpose of making as sure as was humanly possible that no cap trooper ever climbed into a capsule for a combat drop unless he was prepared for it—fit, resolute, disciplined and skilled. If he is not, it's not fair to the Federation, it's certainly not fair to his teammates, and worst of all it's not fair to *him*.

But was boot camp more cruelly hard than was necessary?

All I can say to that is this: The next time I have to make a combat drop, I want the men on my flanks to be graduates of Camp Currie or its Siberian equivalent. Otherwise I'll refuse to enter the capsule.

But I certainly thought it was a bunch of crumby, vicious nonsense at the time. Little things— When we were there a week, we were issued undress maroons for parade to supplement the fatigues we had been wearing. (Dress and full-dress uniforms came much later.) I took my tunic back to the issue shed and complained to the supply sergeant. Since he was only a supply sergeant and rather fatherly in manner I thought of him as a semi-civilian—I didn't know how, as of then, to read the ribbons on his chest or I wouldn't have dared speak to him. "Sergeant, this tunic is too large. My company commander says it fits like a tent."

He looked at the garment, didn't touch it. "Really?"

"Yeah. I want one that fits."

He still didn't stir. "Let me wise you up, sonny boy. There are just two sizes in this army—too large and too small."

"But my company commander—"

"No doubt."

"But what am I going to *do*?"

"Oh, it's *advice* you want! Well, I've got that in stock—new issue, just today. Mmm . . . tell you what I'll do. Here's a needle and I'll even give you a spool of thread. You won't need a pair of scissors; a razor blade is better. Now you tight 'em plenty across the hips but leave cloth to loose 'em again across the shoulders; you'll need it later."

Sergeant Zim's only comment on my tailoring was: "You can do better than that. Two hours extra duty."

So I did better than that by next parade.

Those first six weeks were all hardening up and hazing, with lots of parade drill and lots of route march. Eventually, as files dropped out and went home or elsewhere, we reached the point where we could do fifty miles in ten hours on the level—which is good mileage for a good horse in case you've never used your legs. We rested, not by stopping, but by changing pace, slow march, quick march, and trot. Sometimes we went out the full distance, bivouacked and ate field rations, slept in sleeping bags and marched back the next day.

One day we started out on an ordinary day's march, no bed bags on our shoulders, no rations. When we didn't stop for lunch, I wasn't surprised, as I had already learned to sneak sugar and hard bread and such out of the mess tent and conceal it about my person, but when we kept on marching away from camp in the afternoon I began to wonder. But I had learned not to ask silly questions.

We halted shortly before dark, three companies, now somewhat abbreviated. We formed a battalion parade and marched through it, without music, guards were mounted, and we were dismissed. I immediately looked up Corporal-Instructor Bronski because he was a little easier to deal with than the others . . . and because I felt a certain amount of responsibility; I happened to be, at the time, a recruit-corporal myself. These boot chevrons didn't mean much—mostly the privilege of being chewed out for whatever your squad did as well as for what you did yourself—and they could vanish as quickly as they appeared. Zim had tried out all of the older men as temporary noncoms first and I had inherited a brassard with chevrons on it a couple of days before when our squad leader had folded up and gone to hospital.

I said, "Corporal Bronski, what's the straight word? When is chow call?"

He grinned at me. "I've got a couple of crackers on me. Want me to split 'em with you?"

"Huh? Oh, no, sir. Thank you." (I had considerably more than a couple of crackers; I was learning.) "No chow call?"

"They didn't tell me either, sonny. But I don't see any copters approaching. Now if I was you, I'd round up my squad and figure things out. Maybe one of you can hit a jack rabbit with a rock."

"Yes, sir. But— Well, are we staying here all night? We don't have our bedrolls."

His eyebrows shot up. "No bedrolls? Well, I do declare!" He seemed to think it over. "Mmm . . . ever see sheep huddle together in a snowstorm?"

"Oh, no, sir."

"Try it. They don't freeze, maybe you won't. Or if you don't care for company, you might walk around all night. Nobody'll bother you, as long as you stay inside the posted guards. You won't freeze if you keep moving. Of course you may be a little tired tomorrow." He grinned again.

I saluted and went back to my squad. We divvied up, share and share alike—and I came out with less food than I had started; some of those idiots either hadn't sneaked out anything to eat, or had eaten all they had while we marched. But a few crackers and a couple of prunes will do a lot to quiet your stomach's sounding alert.

The sheep trick works, too; our whole section, three squads, did it together. I don't recommend it as a way to sleep; you are either in the outer layer, frozen on one side and trying to worm your way inside, or you are inside, fairly warm but with everybody else trying to shove his elbows, feet, and halitosis on you. You migrate from one condition to the other all night long in a sort of a Brownian movement, never quite waking up and never really sound asleep. All this makes a night about a hundred years long.

We turned out at dawn to the familiar shout of: "Up you come! On the bounce!" encouraged by instructors' batons applied smartly on fundaments sticking out of the piles . . . and then we did setting-up exercises. I felt like a corpse and didn't see how I could touch my toes. But I did, though it hurt, and twenty minutes later when we hit the trail I merely felt elderly. Sergeant Zim wasn't even mussed and somehow the scoundrel had managed to shave.

The Sun warmed our backs as we marched and Zim started us singing, oldies at first, like "*Le Regiment de Sambre et Meuse*" and "*Caissons*" and "*Halls of Montezuma*" and then our own "*Cap Trooper's Polka*" which moves you into quickstep and pulls you on into a trot. Sergeant Zim couldn't carry a tune in a sack; all he had was a loud voice. But Breckinridge had a sure, strong lead and could hold the rest of us in the teeth of Zim's terrible false notes. We all felt cocky and covered with spines.

But we didn't feel cocky fifty miles later. It had been a long night; it was an endless day—and Zim chewed us out for the way we looked on parade and several boots got gigged for failing to shave in the nine whole minutes between the time we fell out after the march and fell back in again for parade. Several recruits resigned that evening and I thought about it but didn't because I had those silly boot chevrons and hadn't been busted yet.

That night there was a two-hour alert.

But eventually I learned to appreciate the homey luxury of two or three dozen warm bodies to snuggle up to, because twelve weeks later they dumped me down raw naked in a primitive area of the Canadian Rockies and I had to make my way forty miles through mountains. I made it—and hated the Army every inch of the way.

I wasn't in too bad shape when I checked in, though. A couple of rabbits had failed to stay as alert as I was, so I didn't go entirely hungry . . . nor entirely naked; I had a nice warm thick coat of rabbit fat and dirt on my body and moccasins on my feet—the rabbits having no further use for their skins. It's amazing what you can do with a flake of rock if you have to—I guess our cave man ancestors weren't such dummies as we usually think.

The others made it, too, those who were still around to try and didn't resign rather than take the test—all except two boys who died trying. Then we all went back into the mountains and spent thirteen days finding them, working with copters overhead to direct us and all the best communication gear to help us and our instructors in powered command suits to supervise and to check rumors—because the Mobile Infantry doesn't abandon its own while there is any thin shred of hope.

Then we buried them with full honors to the strains of "This Land Is Ours" and with the posthumous rank of PFC, the first of our boot regiment to go that high—because a Cap trooper isn't necessarily expected to stay alive (dying is part of his trade) . . . but they care a lot about *how* you die. It has to be heads up, on the bounce, and still trying.

Breckinridge was one of them; the other was an Aussie boy I didn't know. They weren't the first to die in training; they weren't the last.

Chapter 5

But that was after we had left Camp Currie and a lot had happened
in between. Combat training, mostly—combat drill and combat
exercises and combat maneuvers, using everything from bare
hands to simulated nuclear weapons. I hadn't known there were so
many different ways to fight. Hands and feet to start with—and if
you think those aren't weapons you haven't seen Sergeant Zim
and Captain Frankel, our battalion commander, demonstrate *la savate*, or had little Shujumi work you over with just his hands and a
toothy grin—Zim made Shujumi an instructor for that purpose at
once and required us to take his orders, although we didn't have to
salute him and say "sir."

As our ranks thinned down Zim quit bothering with forma-
tions himself, except parade, and spent more and more time in
personal instruction, supplementing the corporal-instructors. He
was sudden death with anything but he loved knives, and made
and balanced his own, instead of using the perfectly good general-

issue ones. He mellowed quite a bit as a personal teacher, too, becoming merely unbearable instead of downright disgusting—he
could be quite patient with silly questions.

Once, during one of the two-minute rest periods that were
scattered sparsely through each day's work, one of the boys—a
kid named Ted Hendrick—asked, "Sergeant? I guess this knife
throwing is fun . . . but why do we have to learn it? What possible
use is it?"

"Well," answered Zim, "suppose all you have is a knife? Or
maybe not even a knife? What do you do? Just say your prayers
and die? Or wade in and make him buy it anyhow? Son, this is
real—it's not a checker game you can concede if you find yourself
too far behind."

"But that's just what I mean, sir. Suppose you aren't armed at
all? Or just one of these toadstickers, say? And the man you're up
against has all sorts of dangerous weapons? There's nothing you
can do about it; he's got you licked on showdown."

Zim said almost gently, "You've got it all wrong, son. There's
no such thing as a 'dangerous weapon.'"

"Huh? Sir?"

"There are no dangerous weapons; there are only dangerous
men. We're trying to teach you to be dangerous—to the enemy.
Dangerous even without a knife. Deadly as long as you still have
one hand or one foot and are still alive. If you don't know what I
mean, go read 'Horatius at the Bridge' or 'The Death of the Bon
Homme Richard'; they're both in the Camp library. But take the
case you first mentioned; I'm you and all you have is a knife. That
target behind me—the one you've been missing, number three—is
a sentry, armed with everything but an H-bomb. You've got to get
him . . . quietly, at once, and without letting him call for help." Zim
turned slightly—*thunk!*—a knife he hadn't even had in his hand
was quivering in the center of target number three. "You see? Best
to carry two knives—but get him you must, even barehanded."

"Uh—"

"Something still troubling you? Speak up. That's what I'm
here for, to answer your questions."

"Uh, yes, sir. You said the sentry didn't have any H-bomb. But
he *does* have an H-bomb; that's just the point. Well, at least we
have, if we're the sentry . . . and any sentry we're up against is
likely to have them, too. I don't mean the sentry, I mean the side
he's on."

"I understood you."

"Well . . . you see, sir? If we can use an H-bomb—and, as you said, it's no checker game; it's real, it's war and nobody is fooling around—isn't it sort of ridiculous to go crawling around in the weeds, throwing knives and maybe getting yourself killed . . . and even losing the war . . . when you've got a real weapon you can use to win? What's the point in a whole lot of men risking their lives with obsolete weapons when one professor type can do so much more just by pushing a button?"

Zim didn't answer at once, which wasn't like him at all. Then he said softly, "Are you happy in the Infantry, Hendrick? You can resign, you know."

Hendrick muttered something; Zim said, "Speak up!"

"I'm not itching to resign, sir. I'm going to sweat out my term."

"I see. Well, the question you asked is one that a sergeant isn't really qualified to answer . . . and one that you shouldn't ask me. You're supposed to *know* the answer before you join up. Or you should. Did your school have a course in History and Moral Philosophy?"

"What? Sure—yes, sir."

"Then you've heard the answer. But I'll give you my own—unofficial—views on it. If you wanted to teach a baby a lesson, would you cut its head off?"

"Why . . . no, sir!"

"Of course not. You'd paddle it. There can be circumstances when it's just as foolish to hit an enemy city with an H-bomb as it would be to spank a baby with an ax. War is not violence and killing, pure and simple; war is *controlled* violence, for a purpose. The purpose of war is to support your government's decisions by force. The purpose is never to kill the enemy just to be killing him . . . but to make him do what you want him to do. Not killing . . . but controlled and purposeful violence. But it's not your business or mine to decide the purpose of the control. It's never a soldier's business to decide when or where or how—or *why*—he fights; that belongs to the statesmen and the generals. The statesmen decide why and how much; the generals take it from there and tell us where and when and how. *We* supply the violence; other people—'older and wiser heads,' as they say—supply the control. Which is as it should be. That's the best answer I can give you. If it doesn't satisfy you, I'll get you a chit to go talk to the regimental commander. If *he* can't convince you—then go home and be a civilian! Because in that case you will certainly never make a soldier."

Zim bounced to his feet. "I think you've kept me talking just to goldbrick. Up you come, soldiers! On the bounce! Man stations, on target—Hendrick, you first. This time I want you to throw that knife south of you. *South*, get it? Not north. The target is due south of you and I want that knife to go in a general southerly direction, at least. I know you won't hit the target but see if you can't scare it a little. Don't slice your ear off, don't let go of it and cut somebody behind you—just keep what tiny mind you have fixed on the idea of 'south'! Ready—on target! *Let fly!*"

Hendrick missed it again.

We trained with sticks and we trained with wire (lots of nasty things you can improvise with a piece of wire) and we learned what can be done with really modern weapons and how to do it and how to service and maintain the equipment—simulated nuclear weapons and infantry rockets and various sorts of gas and poison and incendiary and demolition. As well as other things maybe best not discussed. But we learned a lot of "obsolete" weapons, too. Bayonets on dummy guns for example, and guns that weren't dummies, too, but were almost identical with the infantry rifle of the XXth century—much like the sporting rifles used in hunting game, except that we fired nothing but solid slugs, alloy-jacketed lead bullets, both at targets on measured ranges and at surprise targets on booby-trapped skirmish runs. This was supposed to prepare us to learn to use any armed weapon and to train us to be on the bounce, alert, ready for anything. Well, I suppose it did. I'm pretty sure it did.

We used these rifles in field exercises to simulate a lot of deadlier and nastier aimed weapons, too. We used a lot of simulation; we had to. An "explosive" bomb or grenade, against matériel or personnel, would explode just enough to put out a lot of black smoke; another sort of gave off a gas that would make you sneeze and weep—that told you that you were dead or paralyzed . . . and was nasty enough to make you careful about anti-gas precautions, to say nothing of the chewing out you got if you were caught by it.

We got still less sleep; more than half the exercises were held at night, with snoopers and radar and audio gear and such.

The rifles used to simulate aimed weapons were loaded with blanks except one in five hundred rounds at random, which was a real bullet. Dangerous? Yes and no. It's dangerous just to be alive . . . and a nonexplosive bullet probably won't kill you unless it hits you in the head or the heart and maybe not then. What that one-in-five-hundred "for real" did was to give us a deep interest in taking cover, especially as we knew that some of the rifles were being fired by instructors who were crack shots and actually trying their best to hit you—if the round happened not to be a blank. They assured us that they would not intentionally shoot a man in the head . . . but accidents do happen.

This friendly assurance wasn't very reassuring. That 500th bullet turned tedious exercises into large-scale Russian roulette; you stop being bored the very first time you hear a slug go *wheet!* past your ear before you hear the crack of the rifle.

But we did slack down anyhow and word came down from the top that if we didn't get on the bounce, the incidence of real ones would be changed to one in a hundred . . . and if that didn't work, to one in fifty. I don't know whether a change was made or not—no way to tell—but I do know we tightened up again, because a boy in the next company got creased across his buttocks with a live one, producing an amazing scar and a lot of half-witty comments and a renewed interest by all hands in taking cover. We laughed at this kid for getting shot where he did . . . but we all knew it could have been his head—or our *own* heads.

The instructors who were not firing rifles did not take cover. They put on white shirts and walked around upright with their silly canes, apparently calmly certain that even a recruit would not intentionally shoot an instructor—which may have been overconfidence on the part of some of them. Still, the chances were five hundred to one that even a shot aimed with murderous intent would not be live and the safety factor increased still higher because the recruit probably couldn't shoot that well anyhow. A rifle is not an easy weapon; it's got no target-seeking qualities at all—I understand that even back in the days when wars were fought and decided with just such rifles it used to take several thousand fired shots to average killing one man. This seems impossible but the military histories agree that it is true—apparently most shots weren't really aimed but simply acted to force the enemy to keep his head down and interfere with *his* shooting.

In any case we had no instructors wounded or killed by rifle fire. No trainees were killed, either, by rifle bullets; the deaths were all from other weapons or things—some of which could turn around and bite you if you didn't do things by the book. Well, one boy did manage to break his neck taking cover too enthusiastically when they first started shooting at him—but no bullet touched him.

However, by a chain reaction, this matter of rifle bullets and taking cover brought me to my lowest ebb at Camp Currie. In the first place I had been busted out of my boot chevrons, not over what I did but over something one of my squad did when I wasn't even around . . . which I pointed out. Bronski told me to button my lip. So I went to see Zim about it. He told me coldly that I was responsible for what my men did, regardless . . . and tacked on six hours of extra duty besides busting me for having spoken to him about it without Bronski's permission. Then I got a letter that upset me a lot; my mother finally wrote to me. Then I sprained a shoulder in my first drill with powered armor (they've got those practice suits rigged so that the instructor can cause casualties in the suit at will, by radio control; I got dumped and hurt my shoulder) and this put me on light duty with too much time to think at a time when I had many reasons, it seemed to me, to feel sorry for myself.

Because of "light duty" I was orderly that day in the battalion commander's office. I was eager at first, for I had never been there before and wanted to make a good impression. I discovered that Captain Frankel didn't want zeal; he wanted me to sit still, say nothing, and not bother him. This left me time to sympathize with myself, for I didn't dare go to sleep.

Then suddenly, shortly after lunch, I wasn't a bit sleepy; Sergeant Zim came in, followed by three men. Zim was smart and neat as usual but the expression on his face made him look like Death on a pale horse and he had a mark on his right eye that looked as if it might be shaping up into a shiner—which was impossible, of course. Of the other three, the one in the middle was Ted Hendrick. He was dirty—well, the company had been on a field exercise; they don't scrub those prairies and you spend a lot of your time snuggling up to the dirt. But his lip was split and there was blood on his chin and on his shirt and his cap was missing. He looked wild-eyed.

The men on each side of him were boots. They each had rifles; Hendrick did not. One of them was from my squad, a kid named Leivy. He seemed excited and pleased, and slipped me a wink when nobody was looking.

Captain Frankel looked surprised. "What is this, Sergeant?"

Zim stood frozen straight and spoke as if he were reciting something by rote. "Sir, H Company Commander reports to the

Battalion Commander. Discipline. Article nine-one-oh-seven. Disregard of tactical command and doctrine, the team being in simulated combat. Article nine-one-two-oh. Disobedience of orders, same conditions."

Captain Frankel looked puzzled. "You are bringing this to *me,* Sergeant? Officially?"

I don't see how a man can manage to look as embarrassed as Zim looked and still have no expression of any sort in his face or voice. "Sir. If the Captain pleases. The man refused administrative discipline. He insisted on seeing the Battalion Commander."

"I see. A bedroll lawyer. Well, I still don't understand it, Sergeant, but technically that's his privilege. What was the tactical command and doctrine?"

"A 'freeze,' sir." I glanced at Hendrick, thinking: Oh, oh, he's going to catch it. In a "freeze" you hit dirt, taking any cover you can, fast, and then *freeze*—don't move at all, not even twitch an eyebrow, until released. Or you can freeze when you're already in cover. They tell stories about men who had been hit while in freeze . . . and had died slowly but without ever making a sound or a move.

Frankel's brows shot up. "Second part?"

"Same thing, sir. After breaking freeze, failing to return to it on being so ordered."

Captain Frankel looked grim. "Name?"

Zim answered. "Hendrick, T.C., sir. Recruit Private R-P-seven-nine-six-oh-nine-two-four."

"Very well. Hendrick, you are deprived of all privileges for thirty days and restricted to your tent when not on duty or at meals, subject only to sanitary necessities. You will serve three hours extra duty each day under the Corporal of the Guard, one hour to be served just before taps, one hour just before reveille, one hour at the time of the noonday meal and in place of it. Your evening meal will be bread and water—as much bread as you can eat. You will serve ten hours extra duty each Sunday, the time to be adjusted to permit you to attend divine services if you so elect."

(I thought: Oh my! He threw the book.)

Captain Frankel went on: "Hendrick, the only reason you are getting off so lightly is that I am not permitted to give you any more than that without convening a court-martial . . . and I don't want to spoil your company's record. Dismissed." He dropped his eyes back to the papers on his desk, the incident already forgotten—

—and Hendrick yelled, "You didn't hear *my* side of it!"

The Captain looked up. "Oh. Sorry. You have a side?"

"You're darn right I do! Sergeant Zim's got it in for me! He's been riding me, riding me, riding me, all day long from the time I got here! He—"

"That's his job," the Captain said coldly. "Do you deny the two charges against you?"

"No, but— *He didn't tell you I was lying on an anthill.*"

Frankel looked disgusted. "Oh. So you would get yourself killed and perhaps your teammates as well because of a few little ants?"

"Not 'just a few'—there were hundreds of 'em. Stingers."

"So? Young man, let me put you straight. Had it been a nest of rattlesnakes you would still have been expected—and required—to freeze." Frankel paused. "Have you anything at all to say in your own defense?"

Hendrick's mouth was open. "I certainly do! He hit me! *He laid hands on me!* The whole bunch of 'em are always strutting around with those silly batons, whackin' you across the fanny, punchin' you between the shoulders and tellin' you to brace up—and I put up with it. But he hit me with his *hands*— he knocked me down to the ground and yelled, '*Freeze!* you stupid jackass!' How about *that?*"

Captain Frankel looked down at his hands, looked up again at Hendrick. "Young man, you are under a misapprehension very common among civilians. You think that your superior officers are not permitted to 'lay hands on you,' as you put it. Under purely social conditions, that is true—say if we happened to run across each other in a theater or a shop, I would have no more right, as long as you treated me with the respect due my rank, to slap your face than you have to slap mine. But in line of duty the rule is entirely different—"

The Captain swung around in his chair and pointed at some loose-leaf books. "There are the laws under which you live. You can search every article in those books, every court-martial case which has arisen under them, and you will not find *one word* which says, or implies, that your superior officer may not 'lay hands on you' or strike you in any other manner in line of duty. Hendrick, I could break your jaw . . . and I simply would be responsible to my own superior officers as to the appropriate necessity of the act. But I would not be responsible to *you*. I could do more than that. There are circumstances under which a superior officer, commissioned or not, is not only permitted but *required* to kill an officer or a man under him, without delay and perhaps without warning—and, far from being punished, be commended. To put a stop to pusillanimous conduct in the face of the enemy, for example."

The Captain tapped on his desk. "Now about those batons— They have two uses. First, they mark the men in authority. Second, we expect them to be used on you, to touch you up and keep you on the bounce. You can't possibly be hurt with one, not the way they are used; at most they sting a little. But they save thousands of words. Say you don't turn out on the bounce at reveille. No doubt the duty corporal could wheedle you, say 'pretty please with sugar on it,' inquire if you'd like breakfast in bed this morning—if we could spare one career corporal just to nursemaid you. We can't, so he gives your bedroll a whack and trots on down the line, applying the spur where needed. Of course he could simply kick you, which would be just as legal and nearly as effective. But the general in charge of training and discipline thinks that it is more dignified, both for the duty corporal and for you, to snap a late sleeper out of his fog with the impersonal rod of authority. And so do I. Not that it matters what you or I think about it; this is the way we do it."

Captain Frankel sighed. "Hendrick, I have explained these matters to you because it is useless to punish a man unless he knows why he is being punished. You've been a bad boy—I say 'boy' because you quite evidently aren't a man *yet*, although we'll keep trying—a surprisingly bad boy in view of the stage of your training. Nothing you have said is any defense, nor even any mitigation; you don't seem to know the score nor have any idea of your duty as a soldier. So tell me in your own words why you feel mistreated; I want to get you straightened out. There might even be something in your favor, though I confess that I cannot imagine what it could be."

I had sneaked a look or two at Hendrick's face while the Captain was chewing him out—somehow his quiet, mild words were a worse chewing-out than any Zim had ever given us. Hendrick's expression had gone from indignation to blank astonishment to sullenness.

"Speak up!" Frankel added sharply.

"Uh . . . well, we were ordered to freeze and I hit the dirt and I found I was on this anthill. So I got to my knees, to move over a couple of feet, and I was hit from behind and knocked flat and he yelled at me—and I bounced up and popped him one and he—"

"STOP!" Captain Frankel was out of his chair and standing ten feet tall, though he's hardly taller than I am. He stared at Hendrick. "You . . . *struck* . . . your . . . company commander?"

"Huh? I said so. But he hit me first. From behind, I didn't even see him. I don't take that off of anybody. I popped him and then he hit me again and then—"

"Silence!"

Hendrick stopped. Then he added, "I just want out of this lousy outfit."

"I think we can accommodate you," Frankel said icily. "And quickly, too."

"Just gimme a piece of paper, I'm resigning."

"One moment. Sergeant Zim."

"Yes, sir." Zim hadn't said a word for a long time. He just stood, eyes front and rigid as a statue, nothing moving but his twitching jaw muscles. I looked at him now and saw that it certainly was a shiner—a beaut. Hendrick must have caught him just right. But he hadn't said anything about it and Captain Frankel hadn't asked—maybe he had just assumed Zim had run into a door and would explain it if he felt like it, later.

"Have the pertinent articles been published to your company, as required?"

"Yes, sir. Published and logged, every Sunday morning."

"I know they have. I asked simply for the record."

Just before church call every Sunday they lined us up and read aloud the disciplinary articles out of the Laws and Regulations of the Military Forces. They were posted on the bulletin board, too, outside the orderly tent. Nobody paid them much mind—it was just another drill; you could stand still and sleep through it. About the only thing we noticed, if we noticed anything, was what we called "the thirty-one ways to crash land." After all, the instructors see to it that you soak up all the regulations you need to know, through your skin. The "crash landings" were a worn-out joke, like "reveille oil" and "tent jacks" . . . they were the thirty-one capital offenses. Now and then somebody boasted, or accused somebody else, of having found a thirty-second way—always something preposterous and usually obscene.

"Striking a superior officer—!"

It suddenly wasn't amusing any longer. Popping Zim? *Hang* a man for that? Why, almost everybody in the company had taken a swing at Sergeant Zim and some of us had even landed . . . when he was instructing us in hand-to-hand combat. He would take us

on after the other instructors had worked us over and we were beginning to feel cocky and pretty good at it—then he would put the
polish on. Why, shucks, I once saw Shujumi knock him unconscious. Bronski threw water on him and Zim got up and grinned
and shook hands—and threw Shujumi right over the horizon.

Captain Frankel looked around, motioned at me. "You. Flash
regimental headquarters."

I did it, all thumbs, stepped back when an officer's face came
on and let the Captain take the call. "Adjutant," the face said.

Frankel said crisply, "Second Battalion Commander's respects
to the Regimental Commander. I request and require an officer to
sit as a court."

The face said, "When do you need him, Ian?"

"As quickly as you can get him here."

"Right away. I'm pretty sure Jake is in his HQ. Article and
name?"

Captain Frankel identified Hendrick and quoted an article
number. The face in the screen whistled and looked grim. "On the
bounce, Ian. If I can't get Jake, I'll be over myself—just as soon
as I tell the Old Man."

Captain Frankel turned to Zim. "This escort—are they
witnesses?"

"Yes, sir."

"Did his section leader see it?"

Zim barely hesitated. "I think so, sir."

"Get him. Anybody out that way in a powered suit?"

"Yes, sir."

Zim used the phone while Frankel said to Hendrick, "What
witnesses do you wish to call in your defense?"

"Huh? I don't need any witnesses, he knows what he did! Just
hand me a piece of paper—I'm getting out of here."

"All in good time."

In very fast time, it seemed to me. Less than five minutes later
Corporal Jones came bouncing up in a command suit, carrying
Corporal Mahmud in his arms. He dropped Mahmud and bounced
away just as Lieutenant Spieksma came in. He said, "Afternoon,
Cap'n. Accused and witnesses here?"

"All set. Take it, Jake."

"Recorder on?"

"It is now."

"Very well. Hendrick, step forward." Hendrick did so, looking
puzzled and as if his nerve was beginning to crack. Lieutenant

Spieksma said briskly: "Field Court-Martial, convened by order of Major F. X. Malloy, commanding Third Training Regiment, Camp Arthur Currie, under General Order Number Four, issued by the Commanding General, Training and Discipline Command, pursuant to the Laws and Regulations of the Military Forces, Terran Federation. Remanding officer: Captain Ian Frankel, M.I., assigned to and commanding Second Battalion, Third Regiment. The Court: Lieutenant Jacques Spieksma, M.I., assigned to and commanding First Battalion, Third Regiment. Accused: Hendrick, Theodore C., Recruit Private RP7960924. Article 9080. Charge: Striking his superior officer, the Terran Federation then being in a state of emergency."

The thing that got me was how *fast* it went. I found myself suddenly appointed an "officer of the court" and directed to "remove" the witnesses and have them ready. I didn't know how I would "remove" Sergeant Zim if he didn't feel like it, but he gathered Mahmud and the two boots up by eye and they all went outside, out of earshot. Zim separated himself from the others and simply waited; Mahmud sat down on the ground and rolled a cigarette—which he had to put out; he was the first one called. In less than twenty minutes all three of them had testified, all telling much the same story Hendrick had. Zim wasn't called at all.

Lieutenant Spieksma said to Hendrick, "Do you wish to cross-examine the witnesses? The Court will assist you, if you so wish."

"No."

"Stand at attention and say 'sir' when you address the Court."

"No, sir." He added, "I want a lawyer."

"The Law does not permit counsel in field courts-martial. Do you wish to testify in your own defense? You are not required to do so and, in view of the evidence thus far, the Court will take no judicial notice if you choose not to do so. But you are warned that any testimony that you give may be used against you and that you will be subject to cross-examination."

Hendrick shrugged. "I haven't anything to say. What good would it do me?"

"The Court repeats: Will you testify in your own defense?"

"Uh, no, sir."

"The Court must demand of you one technical question. Was the article under which you are charged published to you *before* the time of the alleged offense of which you stand accused? You may answer yes, or no, or stand mute—but you are responsible for your answer under Article 9167 which relates to perjury."

The accused stood mute.

"Very well, the Court will reread the article of the charge aloud to you and again ask you that question. 'Article 9080: Any person in the Military Forces who strikes or assaults, or attempts to strike or assault—'"

"Oh, I suppose they did. They read a lot of stuff, every Sunday morning—a whole long list of things you couldn't do."

"Was or was not that particular article read to you?"

"Uh . . . yes, sir. It was."

"Very well. Having declined to testify, do you have any statement to make in mitigation or extenuation?"

"Sir?"

"Do you want to tell the Court anything about it? Any circumstance which you think might possibly affect the evidence already given? Or anything which might lessen the alleged offense? Such things as being ill, or under drugs or medication. You are not under oath at this point; you may say anything at all which you think may help you. What the Court is trying to find out is this: Does anything about this matter strike you as being unfair? If so, why?"

"Huh? Of course it is! Everything about it is unfair! He hit me first! You heard 'em!—*he hit me first!*"

"Anything more?"

"Huh? No, sir. Isn't that enough?"

"The trial is completed. Recruit Private Theodore C. Hendrick, stand forth!" Lieutenant Spieksma had been standing at attention the whole time; now Captain Frankel stood up. The place suddenly felt chilly.

"Private Hendrick, you are found guilty as charged."

My stomach did a flip-flop. They were going to do it to him . . . they were going to do the "Danny Deever" to Ted Hendrick. And I had eaten breakfast beside him just this morning.

"The Court sentences you," he went on, while I felt sick, "to ten lashes and Bad Conduct Discharge."

Hendrick gulped. "I want to resign!"

"The Court does not permit you to resign. The Court wishes to add that your punishment is light simply because this Court possesses no jurisdiction to assign greater punishment. The authority which remanded you specified a field court-martial—why it so chose, this Court will not speculate. But had you been remanded for general court-martial, it seems certain that the evidence before this Court would have caused a general court to sentence you to hang by the neck until dead. You are very lucky—and the remanding authority has been most merciful." Lieutenant Spieksma paused, then went on, "The sentence will be carried out at the earliest hour after the convening authority has reviewed and approved the record, if it does so approve. Court is adjourned. Remove and confine him."

The last was addressed to me, but I didn't actually have to do anything about it, other than phone the guard tent and then get a receipt for him when they took him away.

At afternoon sick call Captain Frankel took me off orderly and sent me to see the doctor, who sent me back to duty. I got back to my company just in time to dress and fall in for parade—and to get gigged by Zim for "spots on uniform." Well, he had a bigger spot over one eye but I didn't mention it.

Somebody had set up a big post in the parade ground just back of where the adjutant stood. When it came time to publish the orders, instead of "routine order of the day" or other trivia, they published Hendrick's court-martial.

Then they marched him out, between two armed guards, with his hands cuffed together in front of him.

I had never seen a flogging. Back home, while they do it in public of course, they do it back of the Federal Building—and Father had given me strict orders to stay away from there. I tried disobeying him on it once . . . but it was postponed and I never tried to see one again.

Once is too many.

The guards lifted his arms and hooked the manacles over a big hook high up on the post. Then they took his shirt off and it turned out that it was fixed so that it could come off and he didn't have an undershirt. The adjutant said crisply, "Carry out the sentence of the Court."

A corporal-instructor from some other battalion stepped forward with the whip. The Sergeant of the Guard made the count.

It's a slow count, five seconds between each one and it seems *much* longer. Ted didn't let out a peep until the third, then he sobbed.

The next thing I knew I was staring up at Corporal Bronski. He was slapping me and looking intently at me. He stopped and asked, "Okay now? All right, back in ranks. On the bounce; we're about to pass in review." We did so and marched back to our company areas. I didn't eat much dinner but neither did a lot of them.

Nobody said a word to me about fainting. I found out later that I wasn't the only one—a couple of dozen of us had passed out.

Chapter 6

> *What we obtain too cheap, we esteem too lightly ... it would be strange indeed if so celestial an article as* FREEDOM *should not be highly rated.*

> —Thomas Paine

It was the night after Hendrick was kicked out that I reached my lowest slump at Camp Currie. I couldn't sleep—and you have to have been through boot camp to understand just how far down a recruit has to sink before that can happen. But I hadn't had any real exercise all day so I wasn't physically tired, and my shoulder still hurt even though I had been marked "duty," and I had that letter from my mother preying on my mind, and every time I closed my eyes I would hear that *crack!* and see Ted slump against the whipping post.

I wasn't fretted about losing my boot chevrons. That no longer mattered at all because I was ready to resign, determined to. If it hadn't been the middle of the night and no pen and paper handy, I would have done so right then.

Ted had made a bad mistake, one that lasted all of half a second. And it really had been just a mistake, too, because, while he hated the outfit (who liked it?), he had been trying to sweat it out and win his franchise; he meant to go into politics—he talked a lot about how, when he got his citizenship, "There will be some changes made—you wait and see."

Well, he would never be in public office now; he had taken his finger off his number for a single instant and he was through.

If it could happen to him, it could happen to me. Suppose I slipped? Next day or next week? Not even allowed to resign . . . but drummed out with my back striped.

Time to admit that I was wrong and Father was right, time to put in that little piece of paper and slink home and tell Father that I was ready to go to Harvard and then go to work in the business—if he would still let me. Time to see Sergeant Zim, first thing in the morning, and tell him that I had had it. But not until morning, because you don't wake Sergeant Zim except for something you're certain that *he* will class as an emergency—believe me, you don't! Not Sergeant Zim.

Sergeant Zim—

He worried me as much as Ted's case did. After the court-martial was over and Ted had been taken away, he stayed behind and said to Captain Frankel, "May I speak with the Battalion Commander, sir?"

"Certainly. I was intending to ask you to stay behind for a word. Sit down."

Zim flicked his eyes my way and the Captain looked at me and I didn't have to be told to get out; I faded. There was nobody in the outer office, just a couple of civilian clerks. I didn't dare go outside because the Captain might want me; I found a chair back of a row of files and sat down.

I could hear them talking, through the partition I had my head against. BHQ was a building rather than a tent, since it housed permanent communication and recording equipment, but it was a "minimum field building," a shack; the inner partitions weren't much. I doubt if the civilians could hear as they each were wearing transcriber phones and were bent over typers—besides, they didn't matter. I didn't mean to eavesdrop. Uh, well, maybe I did.

Zim said: "Sir, I request transfer to a combat team."

Frankel answered: "I can't hear you, Charlie. My tin ear is bothering me again."

Zim: "I'm quite serious, sir. This isn't my sort of duty."

Frankel said testily, "Quit bellyaching your troubles to me, Sergeant. At least wait until we've disposed of duty matters. What in the world happened?"

Zim said stiffly, "Captain, that boy doesn't rate ten lashes."

Frankel answered, "Of course he doesn't. You know who goofed—and so do I."

"Yes, sir. I know."

"Well? You know even better than I do that these kids are wild animals at this stage. You know when it's safe to turn your back on them and when it isn't. You know the doctrine and the standing orders about article nine-oh-eight-oh—you must *never* give them a *chance* to violate it. Of course some of them are going to try it— if they weren't aggressive they wouldn't be material for the M.I. They're docile in ranks; it's safe enough to turn your back when they're eating, or sleeping, or sitting on their tails and being lectured. But get them out in the field in a combat exercise, or anything that gets them keyed up and full of adrenalin, and they're as explosive as a hatful of mercury fulminate. You know that, all you instructors know that; you're trained—trained to watch for it, trained to snuff it out before it happens. Explain to me how it was possible for an untrained recruit to hang a mouse on your eye? He should never have laid a hand on you; you should have knocked him cold when you saw what he was up to. So why weren't you on the bounce? Are you slowing down?"

"I don't know," Zim answered slowly. "I guess I must be."

"Hmm! If true, a combat team is the last place for you. But it's not true. Or wasn't true the last time you and I worked out together, three days ago. So what slipped?"

Zim was slow in answering. "I think I had him tagged in my mind as one of the safe ones."

"There are no such."

"Yes, sir. But he was so earnest, so doggedly determined to sweat it out—he didn't have any aptitude but he kept on trying— that I must have done that, subconsciously." Zim was silent, then added, "I guess it was because I liked him."

Frankel snorted. "An instructor can't afford to like a man."

"I know it, sir. But I do. They're a nice bunch of kids. We've dumped all the real twerps by now—Hendrick's only shortcoming, aside from being clumsy, was that he thought he knew all the answers. I didn't mind that; I knew it all at that age myself. The twerps have gone home and those that are left are eager, anxious to please, and on the bounce—as cute as a litter of collie pups. A lot of them will make soldiers."

"So *that* was the soft spot. You liked him . . . so you failed to clip him in time. So he winds up with a court and the whip and a B.C.D. Sweet."

Zim said earnestly, "I wish to heaven there were some way for me to take that flogging myself, sir."

"You'd have to take your turn, I outrank you. What do you think I've been wishing the past hour? What do you think I was afraid of from the moment I saw you come in here sporting a shiner? I did my best to brush it off with administrative punishment and the young fool wouldn't let well enough alone. But I never thought he would be crazy enough to blurt it out that he'd hung one on you—he's *stupid;* you should have eased him out of the outfit weeks ago . . . instead of nursing him along until he got into trouble. But blurt it out he did, to me, in front of witnesses, forcing me to take official notice of it—and that licked us. No way to get it off the record, no way to avoid a court . . . just go through the whole dreary mess and take our medicine, and wind up with one more civilian who'll be against us the rest of his days. Because he *has* to be flogged; neither you nor I can take it for him, even though the fault was ours. Because the regiment has to see what happens when nine-oh-eight-oh is violated. Our fault . . . but his lumps."

"*My* fault, Captain. That's why I want to be transferred. Uh, sir, I think it's best for the outfit."

"You do, eh? But I decide what's best for my battalion, not you, Sergeant. Charlie, who do you think pulled your name out of the hat? And why? Think back twelve years. You were a corporal, remember? Where were you?"

"Here, as you know quite well, Captain. Right here on this same godforsaken prairie—and I wish I had never come back to it!"

"Don't we all. But it happens to be the most important and the most delicate work in the Army—turning unspanked young cubs into soldiers. Who was the worst unspanked young cub in your section?"

"Mmm . . ." Zim answered slowly. "I wouldn't go so far as to say you were the worst, Captain."

"You wouldn't, eh? But you'd have to think hard to name another candidate. I hated your guts, 'Corporal' Zim."

Zim sounded surprised, and a little hurt. "You did, Captain? I didn't hate you—I rather liked you."

"So? Well, 'hate' is the other luxury an instructor can never afford. We must not hate them, we must not like them; we must teach them. But if you liked me then—mmm, it seemed to me that you had very strange ways of showing it. Do you still like me? Don't answer that; I don't care whether you do or not—or, rather, I don't want to know, whichever it is. Never mind; I despised you then and I used to dream about ways to get you. But you were always on the bounce and never gave me a chance to buy a nine-oh-eight-oh court of my own. So here I am, thanks to you. Now to handle your request: You used to have one order that you gave to me over and over again when I was a boot. I got so I loathed it almost more than anything else you did or said. Do you remember it? *I* do and now I'll give it back to you: 'Soldier, shut up and soldier!' "

"Yes, sir."

"Don't go yet. This weary mess isn't all loss; any regiment of boots needs a stern lesson in the meaning of nine-oh-eight-oh, as we both know. They haven't yet learned to think, they won't read, and they rarely listen—but they can *see* . . . and young Hendrick's misfortune may save one of his mates, some day, from swinging by the neck until he's dead, dead, dead. But I'm sorry the object lesson had to come from my battalion and I certainly don't intend to let this battalion supply another one. You get your instructors together and warn them. For about twenty-four hours those kids will be in a state of shock. Then they'll turn sullen and the tension will build. Along about Thursday or Friday some boy who is about to flunk out anyhow will start thinking over the fact that Hendrick didn't get so very much, not even the number of lashes for drunken driving . . . and he's going to start brooding that it might be worth it, to take a swing at the instructor he hates worst. Sergeant— *that blow must never land!* Understand me?"

"Yes, sir."

"I want them to be eight times as cautious as they have been. I want them to keep their distance, I want them to have eyes in the backs of their heads. I want them to be as alert as a mouse at a cat show. Bronski—you have a special word with Bronski; he has a tendency to fraternize."

"I'll straighten Bronski out, sir."

"See that you do. Because when the next kid starts swinging, it's *got* to be stop-punched—not muffed, like today. The boy has got to be knocked cold and the instructor must do so without ever being touched himself—or I'll damned well break him for incompetence. Let them know that. They've got to teach those kids that it's not merely expensive but *impossible* to violate nine-oh-eight-oh . . . that even trying it wins a short nap, a bucket of water in the face, and a very sore jaw—and nothing else."

"Yes, sir. It'll be done."

"It had better be done. I will not only break the instructor who slips, I will personally take him 'way out on the prairie and give him lumps . . . because *I will not have another one of my boys strung up to that whipping post* through sloppiness on the part of his teachers. Dismissed."

"Yes, sir. Good afternoon, Captain."

"What's good about it? Charlie—"

"Yes, sir."

"If you're not too busy this evening, why don't you bring your soft shoes and your pads over to officers' row and we'll go waltzing Matilda? Say about eight o'clock."

"Yes, sir."

"That's not an order, that's an invitation. If you really are slowing down, maybe I'll be able to kick your shoulder blades off."

"Uh, would the Captain care to put a small bet on it?"

"Huh? With me sitting here at this desk getting swivel-chair spread? I will not! Not unless you agree to fight with one foot in a bucket of cement. Seriously, Charlie, we've had a miserable day and it's going to be worse before it gets better. If you and I work up a good sweat and swap a few lumps, maybe we'll be able to sleep tonight despite all of mother's little darlings."

"I'll be there, Captain. Don't eat too much dinner—I need to work off a couple of matters myself."

"I'm not going to dinner; I'm going to sit right here and sweat out this quarterly report . . . which the Regimental Commander is graciously pleased to see right after *his* dinner . . . and which somebody whose name I won't mention has put me two hours behind on. So I may be a few minutes late for our waltz. Go 'way now, Charlie, and don't bother me. See you later."

Sergeant Zim left so abruptly that I barely had time to lean over and tie my shoe and thereby be out of sight behind the file case as he passed through the outer office. Captain Frankel was already shouting, "Orderly! *Orderly!* ORDERLY!—do I have to call you three times? What's your name? Put yourself down for an hour's extra duty, full kit. Find the company commanders of E, F, and G, my compliments and I'll be pleased to see them before parade. Then bounce over to my tent and fetch me a clean dress uniform, cap, side arms, shoes, ribbons—no medals. Lay it out for me here. Then make afternoon sick call—if you can scratch with that arm, as I've seen you doing, your shoulder can't be too sore. You've got thirteen minutes until sick call—on the bounce, soldier!"

I made it . . . by catching two of them in the senior instructors' shower (an orderly can go anywhere) and the third at his desk; the orders you get aren't impossible, they merely seem so because they nearly are. I was laying out Captain Frankel's uniform for parade as sick call sounded. Without looking up he growled, "Belay that extra duty. Dismissed." So I got home just in time to catch extra duty for "Uniform, Untidy in, Two Particulars" and see the sickening end of Ted Hendrick's time in the M.I.

So I had plenty to think about as I lay awake that night. I had known that Sergeant Zim worked hard, but it had never occurred to me that he could possibly be other than completely and smugly self-satisfied with what he did. He *looked* so smug, so self-assured, so at peace with the world and with himself.

The idea that this invincible robot could feel that he had failed, could feel so deeply and personally disgraced that he wanted to run away, hide his face among strangers, and offer the excuse that his leaving would be "best for the outfit," shook me up as much, and in a way even more, than seeing Ted flogged.

To have Captain Frankel agree with him—as to the seriousness of the failure, I mean—and then rub his nose in it, chew him out. Well! I mean really. Sergeants don't get chewed out; sergeants do the chewing. A law of nature.

But I had to admit that what Sergeant Zim had taken, and swallowed, was so completely humiliating and withering as to make the worst I had ever heard or overheard from a sergeant sound like a love song. And yet the Captain hadn't even raised his voice.

The whole incident was so preposterously unlikely that I was never even tempted to mention it to anyone else.

And Captain Frankel himself— Officers we didn't see very often. They showed up for evening parade, sauntering over at the last moment and doing nothing that would work up a sweat; they inspected once a week, making private comments to sergeants, comments that invariably meant grief for somebody else, not them; and they decided each week what company had won the honor of guarding the regimental colors. Aside from that, they popped up occasionally on surprise inspections, creased, immaculate, remote, and smelling faintly of cologne—and went away again.

Oh, one or more of them did always accompany us on route marches and twice Captain Frankel had demonstrated his virtuosity at *la savate*. But officers didn't work, not real work, and they had no worries because sergeants were *under* them, not *over* them.

But it appeared that Captain Frankel worked so hard that he skipped meals, was kept so busy with something or other that he complained of lack of exercise and would waste his own free time just to work up a sweat.

As for worries, he had honestly seemed to be even more upset at what had happened to Hendrick than Zim had been. And yet he hadn't even known Hendrick by sight; he had been forced to ask his name.

I had an unsettling feeling that I had been completely mistaken as to the very nature of the world I was in, as if every part of it was something wildly different from what it appeared to be—like discovering that your own mother isn't anyone you've ever seen before, but a stranger in a rubber mask.

But I was sure of one thing: I didn't even want to find out what the M.I. really was. If it was so tough that even the gods-that-be—sergeants and officers—were made unhappy by it, it was certainly too tough for Johnnie! How could you keep from making mistakes in an outfit you didn't understand? *I* didn't want to swing by my neck till I was dead, dead, dead! I didn't even want to risk being flogged . . . even though the doctor stands by to make certain that it doesn't do you any permanent injury. Nobody in our family had *ever* been flogged (except paddlings in school, of course, which isn't at all the same thing). There were no criminals in our family on either side, none who had even been accused of crime. We were a proud family; the only thing we lacked was citizenship and Father regarded that as no real honor, a vain and useless thing. But if I were flogged—Well, he'd probably have a stroke.

And yet Hendrick hadn't done anything that I hadn't thought about doing a thousand times. Why hadn't I? Timid, I guess. I *knew* that those instructors, any one of them, could beat the tar out of me, so I had buttoned my lip and hadn't tried it. No guts, Johnnie. At least Ted Hendrick had had guts. I didn't have . . . and a man with no guts has no business in the Army in the first place.

Besides that, Captain Frankel hadn't even considered it to be Ted's fault. Even if I didn't buy a 9080, through lack of guts, what day would I do something other than a 9080—something not my fault—and wind up slumped against the whipping post anyhow?

Time to get out, Johnnie, while you're still ahead.

My mother's letter simply confirmed my decision. I had been able to harden my heart to my parents as long as they were refusing me—but when they softened, I couldn't stand it. Or when Mother softened, at least. She had written:

—but I am afraid I must tell you that your father will still not permit your name to be mentioned. But, dearest, that is his way of grieving, since he cannot cry. You must understand, my darling baby, that he loves you more than life itself—more than he does me—and that you have hurt him very deeply. He tells the world that you are a grown man, capable of making your own decisions, and that he is proud of you. But that is his own pride speaking, the bitter hurt of a proud man who has been wounded deep in his heart by the one he loves best. You must understand, Juanito, that he does not speak of you and has not written to you because he cannot—not yet, not till his grief becomes bearable. When it has, I will know it, and then I will intercede for you—and we will all be together again.

Myself? How could anything her baby boy does anger his mother? You can hurt me, but you cannot make me love you the less. Wherever you are, whatever you choose to do, you are always my little boy who bangs his knee and comes running to my lap for comfort. My lap has shrunk, or perhaps you have grown (though I have never believed it), but nonetheless it will always be waiting, when you need it. Little boys never get over needing their mother's laps—do they, darling? I hope not. I hope that you will write and tell me so.

But I must add that, in view of the terribly long time that you have not written, it is probably best (until I let you know otherwise) for you to write to me care of your Aunt Eleanora. She will pass it on to me at once—and without causing any more upset. You understand?

A thousand kisses to my baby,
YOUR MOTHER

I understood, all right—and if Father could not cry, I could. I did.

And at last I got to sleep . . . and was awakened at once by an alert. We bounced out to the bombing range, the whole regiment, and ran through a simulated exercise, without ammo. We were wearing full unarmored kit otherwise, including ear-plug receivers, and we had no more than extended when the word came to freeze.

We held that freeze for at least an hour—and I mean we held

it, barely breathing. A mouse tiptoeing past would have sounded noisy. Something did go past and ran right over me, a coyote I think. I never twitched. We got awfully cold holding that freeze, but I didn't care; I knew it was my last.

I didn't even hear reveille the next morning; for the first time in weeks I had to be whacked out of my sack and barely made formation for morning jerks. There was no point in trying to resign before breakfast anyhow, since I had to see Zim as the first step. But he wasn't at breakfast. I did ask Bronski's permission to see the C.C. and he said, "Sure. Help yourself," and didn't ask me why.

But you can't see a man who isn't there. We started a route march after breakfast and I still hadn't laid eyes on him. It was an out-and-back, with lunch fetched out to us by copter—an unexpected luxury, since failure to issue field rations before marching usually meant practice starvation except for whatever you had cached . . . and I hadn't; too much on my mind.

Sergeant Zim came out with the rations and he held mail call in the field—which was not an unexpected luxury. I'll say this for the M.I.; they might chop off your food, water, sleep, or anything else, without warning, but they never held up a person's mail a minute longer than circumstances required. That was yours, and they got it to you by the first transportation available and you could read it at your earliest break, even on maneuvers. This hadn't been too important for me, as (aside from a couple of letters from Carl) I hadn't had anything but junk mail until Mother wrote to me.

I didn't even gather around when Zim handed it out; I figured now on not speaking to him until he got in—no point in giving him reason to notice me until we were actually in reach of headquarters. So I was surprised when he called my name and held up a letter. I bounced over and took it.

And was surprised again—it was from Mr. Dubois, my high school instructor in History and Moral Philosophy. I would sooner have expected a letter from Santa Claus.

Then, when I read it, it still seemed like a mistake. I had to check the address and the return address to convince myself that he had written it and had meant it for me.

MY DEAR BOY,

I would have written to you much sooner to express my delight and my pride in learning that you had not only volunteered to serve but also had chosen my own service. But not to express surprise; it is what I expected of you—except, possibly, the additional and very personal bonus that you chose the M.I. This is the sort of consummation, which does not happen too often, that nevertheless makes all of a teacher's efforts worth while. We necessarily sift a great many pebbles, much sand, for each nugget—but the nuggets are the reward.

By now the reason I did not write at once is obvious to you. Many young men, not necessarily through any reprehensible fault, are dropped during recruit training. I have waited (I have kept in touch through my own connections) until you had 'sweated it out' past the hump (how well we all know that hump!) and were certain, barring accidents or illness, of completing your training and your term.

You are now going through the hardest part of your service—not the hardest physically (though physical hardship will never trouble you again; you now have its measure), but the hardest spiritually . . . the deep, soul-turning readjustments and re-evaluations necessary to metamorphize a potential citizen into one in being. Or, rather I should say: you have already gone through the hardest part, despite all the tribulations you still have ahead of you and all the hurdles, each higher than the last, which you still must clear. But it is that "hump" that counts—and, knowing you, lad, I know that I have waited long enough to be sure that you are past your "hump"—or you would be home now.

When you reached that spiritual mountaintop you felt something, a new something. Perhaps you haven't words for it (I know I didn't, when I was a boot). So perhaps you will permit an older comrade to lend you the words, since it often helps to have discrete words. Simply this: The noblest fate that a man can endure is to place his own mortal body between his loved home and the war's desolation. The words are not mine, of course, as you will recognize. Basic truths cannot change and once a man of insight expresses one of them it is never necessary, no matter how much the world changes, to reformulate them. This is an immutable, true everywhere, throughout all time, for all men and all nations.

Let me hear from you, please, if you can spare an old man some of your precious sack time to write an occasional letter. And if you should happen to run across any of my former mates, give them my warmest greetings.

Good luck, trooper! You've made me proud.

JEAN V. DUBOIS
Lt.-Col., M.I., rtd.

The signature was as amazing as the letter itself. Old Sour Mouth was a short colonel? Why, our regional commander was only a major. Mr. Dubois had never used any sort of rank around school. We had supposed (if we thought about it at all) that he must have been a corporal or some such who had been let out when he lost his hand and had been fixed up with a soft job teaching a course that didn't have to be passed, or even taught—just audited. Of course we had known that he was a veteran since History and Moral Philosophy must be taught by a citizen. But an M.I.? He didn't look it. Prissy, faintly scornful, a dancing-master type— not one of us apes.

But that was the way he had signed himself.

I spent the whole long hike back to camp thinking about that amazing letter. It didn't sound in the least like anything he had ever said in class. Oh, I don't mean it contradicted anything he had told us in class; it was just entirely different in tone. Since when does a short colonel call a recruit private "comrade"?

When he was plain "Mr. Dubois" and I was one of the kids who had to take his course he hardly seemed to see me—except once when he got me sore by implying that I had too much money and not enough sense. (So my old man could have bought the school and given it to me for Christmas—is that a crime? It was none of his business.)

He had been droning along about "value," comparing the Marxist theory with the orthodox "use" theory. Mr. Dubois had said, "Of course, the Marxian definition of value is ridiculous. All the work one cares to add will not turn a mud pie into an apple tart; it remains a mud pie, value zero. By corollary, unskillful work can easily subtract value; an untalented cook can turn wholesome dough and fresh green apples, valuable already, into an inedible mess, value zero. Conversely, a great chef can fashion of those same materials a confection of greater value than a commonplace apple tart, with no more effort than an ordinary cook uses to prepare an ordinary sweet.

"These kitchen illustrations demolish the Marxian theory of value—the fallacy from which the entire magnificent fraud of communism derives—and illustrate the truth of the common-sense definition as measured in terms of use."

Dubois had waved his stump at us. "Nevertheless—wake up, back there!—nevertheless the disheveled old mystic of *Das Kapital*, turgid, tortured, confused, and neurotic, unscientific, illogical, this pompous fraud Karl Marx, *nevertheless* had a glimmering of a very important truth. If he had possessed an ana-

lytical mind, he might have formulated the first adequate definition of value . . . and this planet might have been saved endless
grief.

"Or might not," he added. "You!"

I had sat up with a jerk.

"If you can't listen, perhaps you can tell the class whether
'value' is a relative, or an absolute?"

I had been listening; I just didn't see any reason not to listen
with eyes closed and spine relaxed. But his question caught me
out; I hadn't read that day's assignment. "An absolute," I answered, guessing.

"Wrong," he said coldly. " 'Value' has no meaning other than
in relation to living beings. The value of a thing is always relative
to a particular person, is completely personal and different in
quantity for each living human—'market value' is a fiction,
merely a rough guess at the average of personal values, all of
which must be quantitatively different or trade would be impossible." (I had wondered what Father would have said if he had heard
"market value" called a "fiction"—snort in disgust, probably.)

"This very personal relationship, 'value,' has two factors for a
human being: first, what he can do with a thing, its *use* to him . . .
and second, what he must do to get it, its *cost* to him. There is an
old song which asserts 'the best things in life are free.' Not true!
Utterly false! This was the tragic fallacy which brought on the de-
cadence and collapse of the democracies of the twentieth century;
those noble experiments failed because the people had been led to
believe that they could simply vote for whatever they wanted . . .
and get it, without toil, without sweat, without tears.

"Nothing of value is free. Even the breath of life is purchased
at birth only through gasping effort and pain." He had been still
looking at me and added, "If you boys and girls had to sweat for
your toys the way a newly born baby has to struggle to live you
would be happier . . . and much richer. As it is, with some of you,
I pity the poverty of your wealth. You! I've just awarded you the
prize for the hundred-meter dash. Does it make you happy?"

"Uh, I suppose it would."

"No dodging, please. You have the prize—here, I'll write it
out: 'Grand prize for the championship, one hundred-meter
sprint.' " He had actually come back to my seat and pinned it on
my chest. "There! Are you happy? You value it—or don't you?"

I was sore. First that dirty crack about rich kids—a typical sneer of those who haven't got it—and now this farce. I ripped it off and chucked it at him.

Mr. Dubois had looked surprised. "It doesn't make you happy?"

"You know darn well I placed fourth!"

"*Exactly!* The prize for first place is worthless to you . . . because you haven't earned it. But you enjoy a modest satisfaction in placing fourth; you earned it. I trust that some of the somnambulists here understood this little morality play. I fancy that the poet who wrote that song meant to imply that the best things in life must be purchased other than with money—which is *true*—just as the literal meaning of his words is false. The best things in life are beyond money; their price is agony and sweat and devotion . . . and the price demanded for the most precious of all things in life is life itself—ultimate cost for perfect value."

I mulled over things I had heard Mr. Dubois—*Colonel* Dubois—say, as well as his extraordinary letter, while we went swinging back toward camp. Then I stopped thinking because the band dropped back near our position in column and we sang for a while, a French group—*"Marseillaise,"* of course, and *"Madelon"* and "Sons of Toil and Danger," and then *"Legion Étrangère"* and "Mademoiselle from Armentières."

It's nice to have the band play; it picks you right up when your tail is dragging the prairie. We hadn't had anything but canned music at first and that only for parade and calls. But the powers-that-be had found out early who could play and who couldn't; instruments were provided and a regimental band was organized, all our own—even the director and the drum major were boots.

It didn't mean they got out of anything. Oh no! It just meant they were allowed and encouraged to do it on their own time, practicing evenings and Sundays and such—and that they got to strut and countermarch and show off at parade instead of being in ranks with their platoons. A lot of things that we did were run that way. Our chaplain, for example, was a boot. He was older than most of us and had been ordained in some obscure little sect I had never heard of. But he put a lot of passion into his preaching whether his theology was orthodox or not (don't ask me) and he was certainly in a position to understand the problems of a recruit. And the singing was fun. Besides, there was nowhere else to go on Sunday morning between morning police and lunch.

The band suffered a lot of attrition but somehow they always kept it going. The camp owned four sets of pipes and some Scottish uniforms, donated by Lochiel of Cameron whose son had been killed there in training—and one of us boots turned out to be a piper; he had learned it in the Scottish Boy Scouts. Pretty soon we had four pipers, maybe not good but loud. Pipes seem very odd when you first hear them, and a tyro practicing can set your teeth on edge—it sounds and looks as if he had a cat under his arm, its tail in his mouth, and biting it.

But they grow on you. The first time our pipers kicked their heels out in front of the band, skirling away at "Alamein Dead," my hair stood up so straight it lifted my cap. It gets you—makes tears.

We couldn't take a parade band out on route march, of course, because no special allowances were made for the band. Tubas and bass drums had to stay behind because a boy in the band had to carry a full kit, same as everybody, and could only manage an instrument small enough to add to his load. But the M.I. has band instruments which I don't believe anybody else has, such as a little box hardly bigger than a harmonica, an electric gadget which does an amazing job of faking a big horn and is played the same way. Comes band call when you are headed for the horizon, each bandsman sheds his kit without stopping, his squadmates split it up, and he trots to the column position of the color company and starts blasting.

It helps.

The band drifted aft, almost out of earshot, and we stopped singing because your own singing drowns out the beat when it's too far away.

I suddenly realized I felt good.

I tried to think why I did. Because we would be in after a couple of hours and I could resign?

No. When I had decided to resign, it had indeed given me a measure of peace, quieted down my awful jitters and let me go to sleep. But this was something else—and no reason for it, that I could see.

Then I knew. *I had passed my hump!*

I was over the "hump" that Colonel Dubois had written about. I actually walked over it and started down, swinging easily. The prairie through there was flat as a griddle-cake, but just the same I had been plodding wearily uphill all the way out and about halfway back. Then, at some point—I think it was while we were singing—I had passed the hump and it was all downhill. My kit felt lighter and I was no longer worried.

When we got in, I didn't speak to Sergeant Zim; I no longer needed to. Instead he spoke to me, motioned me to him as we fell out.

"Yes, sir?"

"This is a personal question . . . so don't answer it unless you feel like it." He stopped, and I wondered if he suspected that I had overheard his chewing-out, and shivered.

"At mail call today," he said, "you got a letter. I noticed— purely by accident, none of my business—the name on the return address. It's a fairly common name, some places, but—this is the personal question you need not answer—by any chance does the person who wrote that letter have his left hand off at the wrist?"

I guess my chin dropped. "How did you know? Sir?"

"I was nearby when it happened. It *is* Colonel Dubois? Right?"

"Yes, sir." I added, "He was my high school instructor in History and Moral Philosophy."

I think that was the only time I ever impressed Sergeant Zim, even faintly. His eyebrows went up an eighth of an inch and his eyes widened slightly. "So? You were extraordinarily fortunate." He added, "When you answer his letter—if you don't mind—you might say that Ship's Sergeant Zim sends his respects."

"Yes, sir. Oh . . . I think maybe he sent you a message, sir."

"What?"

"Uh, I'm not certain." I took out the letter, read just: " '—if you should happen to run across any of my former mates, give them my warmest greetings.' Is that for you, sir?"

Zim pondered it, his eyes looking through me, somewhere else. "Eh? Yes, it is. For me among others. Thanks very much." Then suddenly it was over and he said briskly, "Nine minutes to parade. And you still have to shower and change. On the bounce, soldier."

Chapter 7

The young recruit is silly—'e thinks o'
   suicide.
'E's lost 'is gutter-devil; 'e 'asin't got 'is
   pride;
But day by day they kicks 'im, which
   'elps 'im on a bit,
Till 'e finds 'isself one mornin' with a
   full an' proper kit.
Gettin' clear o' dirtiness, gettin' done
   with mess,
Gettin' shut o' doin' things rather more-
   or-less.

—Rudyard Kipling

I'm not going to talk much more about my boot training. Mostly it was simply work, but I was squared away—enough said.

But I do want to mention a little about powered suits, partly because I was fascinated by them and also because that was what led me into trouble. No complaints—I rated what I got.

An M.I. lives by his suit the way a K-9 man lives by and with and on his doggie partner. Powered armor is one-half the reason we call ourselves "mobile infantry" instead of just "infantry." (The other half are the spaceships that drop us and the capsules we drop in.) Our suits give us better eyes, better ears, stronger backs (to carry heavier weapons and more ammo), better legs, more intelligence ("intelligence" in the military meaning; a man in a suit can be just as stupid as anybody else—only he had better not be), more firepower, greater endurance, less vulnerability.

A suit isn't a space suit—although it can serve as one. It is not primarily armor—although the Knights of the Round Table were not armored as well as we are. It isn't a tank—but a single M.I. private could take on a squadron of those things and knock them off unassisted if anybody was silly enough to put tanks against M.I. A suit is not a ship but it can fly, a little—on the other hand neither spaceships nor atmosphere craft can fight against a man in a suit except by saturation bombing of the area he is in (like burning down a house to get one flea!). Contrariwise we can do many things that no ship—air, submersible, or space—can do.

There are a dozen different ways of delivering destruction in impersonal wholesale, via ships and missiles of one sort or another, catastrophes so widespread, so unselective, that the war is over because that nation or planet has ceased to exist. What we do is entirely different. We make war as personal as a punch in the nose. We can be selective, applying precisely the required amount of pressure at the specified point at a designated time—we've never been told to go down and kill or capture all left-handed redheads in a particular area, but if they tell us to, we can. We will.

We are the boys who go to a particular place, at H-hour, occupy a designated terrain, stand on it, dig the enemy out of their holes, force them then and there to surrender or die. We're the bloody infantry, the doughboy, the duckfoot, the foot soldier who goes where the enemy is and takes him on in person. We've been doing it, with changes in weapons but very little change in our trade, at least since the time five thousand years ago when the foot sloggers of Sargon the Great forced the Sumerians to cry "Uncle!"

Maybe they'll be able to do without us someday. Maybe some mad genius with myopia, a bulging forehead, and a cybernetic mind will devise a weapon that can go down a hole, pick out the opposition, and force it to surrender or die—without killing that gang of your own people they've got imprisoned down there. I wouldn't know; I'm not a genius, I'm an M.I. In the meantime, until they build a machine to replace us, my mates can handle that job—and I might be some help on it, too.

Maybe someday they'll get everything nice and tidy and we'll have that thing we sing about, when "we ain't a-gonna study war no more." Maybe. Maybe the same day the leopard will take off his spots and get a job as a Jersey cow, too. But again, I wouldn't know; I am not a professor of cosmopolitics; I'm an M.I. When the government sends me, I go. In between, I catch a lot of sack time.

But, while they have not yet built a machine to replace us, they've surely thought up some honeys to help us. The suit, in particular.

No need to describe what it looks like, since it has been pictured so often. Suited up, you look like a big steel gorilla, armed with gorilla-sized weapons. (This may be why a sergeant generally opens his remarks with "You apes—" However, it seems more likely that Caesar's sergeants used the same honorific.)

But the suits are considerably stronger than a gorilla. If an M.I. in a suit swapped hugs with a gorilla, the gorilla would be dead, crushed; the M.I. and the suit wouldn't be mussed.

The "muscles," the pseudo-musculature, get all the publicity but it's the control of all that power which merits it. The real genius in the design is that you *don't* have to control the suit; you just wear it, like your clothes, like skin. Any sort of ship you have to learn to pilot; it takes a long time, a new full set of reflexes, a different and artificial way of thinking. Even riding a bicycle demands an acquired skill, very different from walking, whereas a spaceship—oh, brother! I won't live that long. Spaceships are for acrobats who are also mathematicians.

But a suit you just wear.

Two thousand pounds of it, maybe, in full kit—yet the very first time you are fitted into one you can immediately walk, run, jump, lie down, pick up an egg without breaking it (takes a trifle of practice, but anything improves with practice), dance a jig (if you can dance a jig, that is, *without* a suit)—and jump right over the house next door and come down to a feather landing.

The secret lies in negative feedback and amplification.

Don't ask me to sketch the circuitry of a suit; I can't. But I understand that some very good concert violinists can't build a violin, either. I can do field maintenance and field repairs and check off the three hundred and forty-seven items from "cold" to ready to wear, and that's all a dumb M.I. is expected to do. But if my suit gets really sick, I call the doctor—a doctor of science (electro-mechanical engineering) who is a staff Naval officer, usually a lieutenant (read "captain" for our ranks), and is part of the ship's company of the troop transport—or who is reluctantly assigned to a regimental headquarters at Camp Currie, a fate-worse-than-death to a Navy man.

But if you really are interested in the prints and stereos and schematics of a suit's physiology, you can find most of it, the un-classified part, in any fairly large public library. For the small amount that is classified, you must look up a reliable enemy agent—"reliable" I say, because spies are a tricky lot; he's likely to sell you the parts you could get free from the public library.

But here is how it works, minus the diagrams. The inside of the suit is a mass of pressure receptors, hundreds of them. You push with the heel of your hand; the suit feels it, amplifies it, pushes with you to take the pressure off the receptors that gave the order to push. That's confusing, but negative feedback is always a confusing idea the first time, even though your body has been do-ing it ever since you quit kicking helplessly as a baby. Young chil-dren are still learning it; that's why they are clumsy. Adolescents and adults do it without knowing they ever learned it—and a man with Parkinson's disease has damaged his circuits for it.

The suit has feedback which causes it to match *any* motion you make, exactly—but with great force.

Controlled force . . . force controlled without your having to think about it. You jump, that heavy suit jumps, but higher than you can jump in your skin. Jump really hard and the suit's jets cut in, amplifying what the suit's leg "muscles" did, giving you a three-jet shove, the axis of pressure of which passes through your center of mass. So you jump over that house next door. Which makes you come down as fast as you went up . . . which the suit notes through your proximity & closing gear (a sort of simple-minded radar resembling a proximity fuse) and therefore cuts in the jets again just the right amount to cushion your landing with-out your having to think about it.

And *that* is the beauty of a powered suit: you don't have to think about it. You don't have to drive it, fly it, conn it, operate it; you just wear it and it takes orders directly from your muscles and does for you what your muscles are trying to do. This leaves you with your whole mind free to handle your weapons and notice what is going on around you . . . which is *supremely* important to an infantryman who wants to die in bed. If you load a mud foot down with a lot of gadgets that he has to watch, somebody a lot more simply equipped—say with a stone ax—will sneak up and bash his head in while he is trying to read a vernier.

Your "eyes" and your "ears" are rigged to help you without cluttering up your attention, too. Say you have three audio cir-cuits, common in a marauder suit. The frequency control to maintain tactical security is very complex, at least two frequencies for each circuit both of which are necessary for any signal at all and each of which wobbles under the control of a cesium clock timed to a micromicrosecond with the other end—but all this is no problem of yours. You want circuit A to your squad leader, you bite down once—for circuit B, bite down twice—and so on. The mike is taped to your throat, the plugs are in your ears and can't be jarred out; just talk. Besides that, outside mikes on each side of your helmet give you binaural hearing for your immediate surroundings just as if your head were bare—or you can suppress any noisy neighbors and not miss what your platoon leader is saying simply by turning your head.

Since your head is the one part of your body not involved in the pressure receptors controlling the suit's muscles, you use your head—your jaw muscles, your chin, your neck—to switch things for you and thereby leave your hands free to fight. A chin plate handles all visual displays the way the jaw switch handles the audios. All displays are thrown on a mirror in front of your forehead from where the work is actually going on above and back of your head. All this helmet gear makes you look like a hydrocephalic gorilla but, with luck, the enemy won't live long enough to be offended by your appearance, and it is a very convenient arrangement; you can flip through your several types of radar displays quicker than you can change channels to avoid a commercial—catch a range & bearing, locate your boss, check your flank men, whatever.

If you toss your head like a horse bothered by a fly, your infrared snoopers go up on your forehead—toss it again, they come down. If you let go of your rocket launcher, the suit snaps it back until you need it again. No point in discussing water nipples, air supply, gyros, etc.—the point to *all* the arrangements is the same: to leave you free to follow your trade, slaughter.

Of course these things do require practice and you do practice until picking the right circuit is as automatic as brushing your teeth, and so on. But simply wearing the suit, moving in it, requires almost no practice. You practice jumping because, while you do it with a completely natural motion, you jump higher, faster, farther, and stay up longer. The last alone calls for a new orientation; those seconds in the air can be used—seconds are jewels beyond price in combat. While off the ground in a jump, you can get a range & bearing, pick a target, talk & receive, fire a weapon, reload, decide to jump again without landing and override your automatics to cut in the jets again. You can do *all* of these things in one bounce, with practice.

But, in general, powered armor doesn't require practice; it simply does it for you, just the way you were doing it, only better. All but one thing—you *can't* scratch where it itches. If I ever find a suit that will let me scratch between my shoulder blades, I'll marry it.

There are three main types of M.I. armor: marauder, command, and scout. Scout suits are very fast and very long-range, but lightly armed. Command suits are heavy on go juice and jump juice, are fast and can jump high; they have three times as much comm & radar gear as other suits, and a dead-reckoning tracker, inertial. Marauders are for those guys in ranks with the sleepy look—the executioners.

As I may have said, I fell in love with powered armor, even though my first crack at it gave me a strained shoulder. Any day thereafter that my section was allowed to practice in suits was a big day for me. The day I goofed I had simulated sergeant's chevrons as a simulated section leader and was armed with simulated A-bomb rockets to use in simulated darkness against a simulated enemy. That was the trouble; everything was simulated—but you are required to behave as if it is all real.

We were retreating—"advancing toward the rear," I mean— and one of the instructors cut the power on one of my men, by radio control, making him a helpless casualty. Per M.I. doctrine, I ordered the pickup, felt rather cocky that I had managed to get the order out before my number two cut out to do it anyhow, turned to do the next thing I had to do, which was to lay down a simulated atomic ruckus to discourage the simulated enemy overtaking us.

Our flank was swinging; I was supposed to fire it sort of diagonally but with the required spacing to protect my own men from blast while still putting it in close enough to trouble the bandits. On the bounce, of course. The movement over the terrain and the problem itself had been discussed ahead of time; we were still green—the only variations supposed to be left in were casualties.

Doctrine required me to locate *exactly*, by radar beacon, my own men who could be affected by the blast. But this all had to be done fast and I wasn't too sharp at reading those little radar displays anyhow. I cheated just a touch—flipped my snoopers up and looked, bare eyes in broad daylight. I left plenty of room. Shucks, I could *see* the only man affected, half a mile away, and all I had was just a little bitty H.E. rocket, intended to make a lot of smoke and not much else. So I picked a spot by eye, took the rocket launcher and let fly.

Then I bounced away, feeling smug—no seconds lost.

And had my power cut in the air. This doesn't hurt you; it's a delayed action, executed by your landing. I grounded and there I stuck, squatting, held upright by gyros but unable to move. You do not repeat *not* move when surrounded by a ton of metal with your power dead.

Instead I cussed to myself—I hadn't thought that they would make me a casualty when I was supposed to be leading the problem. Shucks and other comments.

I should have known that Sergeant Zim would be monitoring the section leader.

He bounced over to me, spoke to me privately on the face-to-face. He suggested that I might be able to get a job sweeping floors since I was too stupid, clumsy, and careless to handle dirty dishes. He discussed my past and probable future and several other things that I did not want to hear about. He ended by saying tonelessly, "How would you like to have Colonel Dubois see what you've done?"

Then he left me. I waited there, crouched over, for two hours until the drill was over. The suit, which had been feather-light, real seven-league boots, felt like an Iron Maiden. At last he returned for me, restored power, and we bounded together at top speed to BHQ.

Captain Frankel said less but it cut more.

Then he paused and added in that flat voice officers use when quoting regulations: "You may demand trial by court-martial if such be your choice. How say you?"

I gulped and said, "No, sir!" Until that moment I hadn't fully realized just how *much* trouble I was in.

Captain Frankel seemed to relax slightly. "Then we'll see what the Regimental Commander has to say. Sergeant, escort the prisoner." We walked rapidly over to RHQ and for the first time I met the Regimental Commander face to face—and by then I was sure that I was going to catch a court no matter what. But I remembered sharply how Ted Hendrick had talked himself into one; I said nothing.

Major Malloy said a total of five words to me. After hearing Sergeant Zim, he said three of them: "Is that correct?"

I said, "Yes, sir," which ended my part of it.

Major Malloy said, to Captain Frankel: "Is there any possibility of salvaging this man?"

Captain Frankel answered, "I believe so, sir."

Major Malloy said, "Then we'll try administrative punishment," turned to me and said:

"Five lashes."

Well, they certainly didn't keep me dangling. Fifteen minutes later the doctor had completed checking my heart and the Sergeant of the Guard was outfitting me with that special shirt which comes off without having to be pulled over the hands— zippered from the neck down the arms. Assembly for parade had just sounded. I was feeling detached, unreal . . . which I have learned is one way of being scared right out of your senses. The nightmare hallucination—

Zim came into the guard tent just as the call ended. He glanced at the Sergeant of the Guard—Corporal Jones—and Jones went out. Zim stepped up to me, slipped something into my hand. "Bite on that," he said quietly. "It helps. I know."

It was a rubber mouthpiece such as we used to avoid broken teeth in hand-to-hand combat drill. Zim left. I put it in my mouth. Then they handcuffed me and marched me out.

The order read: "—in simulated combat, gross negligence which would in action have caused the death of a teammate." Then they peeled off my shirt and strung me up.

Now here is a very odd thing: A flogging isn't as hard to *take* as it is to *watch*. I don't mean it's a picnic. It hurts worse than anything else I've ever had happen to me, and the waits between strokes are worse than the strokes themselves. But the mouthpiece did help and the only yelp I let out never got past it.

Here's the second odd thing: Nobody even mentioned it to me, not even other boots. So far as I could see, Zim and the instructors treated me exactly the same afterwards as they had before. From the instant the doctor painted the marks and told me to go back to duty it was all done with, completely. I even managed to eat a little at dinner that night and pretend to take part in the jawing at the table.

Another thing about administrative punishment: There is no permanent black mark. Those records are destroyed at the end of boot training and you start clean. The only record is one where it counts most.

You *don't* forget it.

Chapter 8

Train up a child in the way he should go; and when he is old he will not depart from it.

—Proverbs XXII:6

There were other floggings but darn few. Hendrick was the only man in our regiment to be flogged by sentence of court-martial; the others were administrative punishment, like mine, and for lashes it was necessary to go all the way up to the Regimental Commander—which a subordinate commander finds distasteful, to put it faintly. Even then, Major Malloy was much more likely to kick the man out, "Undesirable Discharge," than to have the whipping post erected. In a way, an administrative flogging is the mildest sort of a compliment; it means that your superiors think that there is a faint possibility that you just might have the character eventually to make a soldier and a citizen, unlikely as it seems at the moment.

I was the only one to get the maximum administrative punishment; none of the others got more than three lashes. Nobody else came as close as I did to putting on civilian clothes but still squeaked by. This is a social distinction of sorts. I don't recommend it.

But we had another case, much worse than mine or Ted Hendrick's—a really sick-making one. Once they erected gallows.

Now, look, get this straight. This case didn't really have anything to do with the Army. The crime didn't take place at Camp

Currie and the placement officer who accepted this boy for M.I. should turn in his suit.

He deserted, only two days after we arrived at Currie. Ridiculous, of course, but nothing about the case made sense—why didn't he resign? Desertion, naturally, is one of the "thirty-one crash landings" but the Army doesn't invoke the death penalty for it unless there are special circumstances, such as "in the face of the enemy" or something else that turns it from a highly informal way of resigning into something that can't be ignored.

The Army makes no effort to find deserters and bring them back. This makes the hardest kind of sense. We're all volunteers; we're M.I. because we want to be, we're proud to be M.I. and the M.I. is proud of us. If a man doesn't feel that way about it, from his callused feet to his hairy ears, I don't want him on my flank when trouble starts. If I buy a piece of it, I want men around me who will pick me up because they're M.I. and I'm M.I. and my skin means as much to them as their own. I don't want any ersatz soldiers, dragging their tails and ducking out when the party gets rough. It's a whole lot safer to have a blank file on your flank than to have an alleged soldier who is nursing the "conscript" syndrome. So if they run, let 'em run; it's a waste of time and money to fetch them back.

Of course most of them do come back, though it may take them years—in which case the Army tiredly lets them have their fifty lashes instead of hanging them, and turns them loose. I suppose it must wear on a man's nerves to be a fugitive when everybody else is either a citizen or a legal resident, even when the police aren't trying to find him. "The wicked flee when no man pursueth." The temptation to turn yourself in, take your lumps, and breathe easily again must get to be overpowering.

But this boy didn't turn himself in. He was gone four months and I doubt if his own company remembered him, since he had been with them only a couple of days; he was probably just a name without a face, the "Dillinger, N.L." who had to be reported, day after day, as absent without leave on the morning muster.

Then he killed a baby girl.

He was tried and convicted by a local tribunal but identity check showed that he was an undischarged soldier; the Department had to be notified and our commanding general at once intervened. He was returned to us, since military law and jurisdiction take precedence over civil code.

Why did the general bother? Why didn't he let the local sheriff do the job?

In order to "teach us a lesson"?

Not at all. I'm quite sure that our general did not think that any of his boys needed to be nauseated in order not to kill any baby girls. By now I believe that he would have spared us the sight—had it been possible.

We did learn a lesson, though nobody mentioned it at the time and it is one that takes a long time to sink in until it becomes second nature:

The M.I. take care of their own—no matter what.

Dillinger belonged to us, he was still on our rolls. Even though we didn't want him, even though we should never have had him, even though we would have been happy to disclaim him, he was a member of our regiment. We couldn't brush him off and let a sheriff a thousand miles away handle it. If it has to be done, a man—a real man—shoots his own dog himself; he doesn't hire a proxy who may bungle it.

The regimental records said that Dillinger was ours, so taking care of him was our duty.

That evening we marched to the parade grounds at slow march, sixty beats to the minute (hard to keep step, when you're used to a hundred and forty), while the band played "Dirge for the Unmourned." Then Dillinger was marched out, dressed in M.I. full dress just as we were, and the band played "Danny Deever" while they stripped off every trace of insignia, even buttons and cap, leaving him in a maroon and light blue suit that was no longer a uniform. The drums held a sustained roll and it was all over.

We passed in review and on home at a fast trot. I don't think anybody fainted and I don't think anybody quite got sick, even though most of us didn't eat much dinner that night and I've never heard the mess tent so quiet. But, grisly as it was (it was the first time I had seen death, first time for most of us), it was not the shock that Ted Hendrick's flogging was—I mean, you couldn't put yourself in Dillinger's place; you didn't have any feeling of: "It could have been *me*." Not counting the technical matter of desertion, Dillinger had committed at least four capital crimes; if his victim had lived, he still would have danced Danny Deever for any one of the other three—kidnaping, demand of ransom, criminal neglect, etc.

I had no sympathy for him and still haven't. That old saw

about "To understand all is to forgive all" is a lot of tripe. Some things, the more you understand the more you loathe them. My sympathy is reserved for Barbara Anne Enthwaite whom I had never seen, and for her parents, who would never again see their little girl.

As the band put away their instruments that night we started thirty days of mourning for Barbara and of disgrace for us, with our colors draped in black, no music at parade, no singing on route march. Only once did I hear anybody complain and another boot promptly asked him how he would like a full set of lumps? Certainly, it hadn't been our fault—but our business was to guard little girls, not kill them. Our regiment had been dishonored; we had to clean it. We were disgraced and we *felt* disgraced.

That night I tried to figure out how such things could be kept from happening. Of course, they hardly ever do nowadays—but even once is 'way too many. I never did reach an answer that satisfied me. This Dillinger—he looked like anybody else, and his behavior and record couldn't have been too odd or he would never have reached Camp Currie in the first place. I suppose he was one of those pathological personalities you read about—no way to spot them.

Well, if there was no way to keep it from happening once, there was only one sure way to keep it from happening twice. Which we had used.

If Dillinger had understood what he was doing (which seemed incredible) then he got what was coming to him . . . except that it seemed a shame that he hadn't suffered as much as had little Barbara Anne—he practically hadn't suffered at all.

But suppose, as seemed more likely, that he was so crazy that he had never been aware that he was doing anything wrong? What then?

Well, we shoot mad dogs, don't we?

Yes, but being crazy that way is a sickness—

I couldn't see but two possibilities. Either he couldn't be made well—in which case he was better dead for his own sake and for the safety of others—or he could be treated and made sane. In which case (it seemed to me) if he ever became sane enough for civilized society . . . and thought over what he had done while he was "sick"—what could be left for him but suicide? How could he *live* with himself?

And suppose he escaped *before* he was cured and did the same thing again? And maybe *again*? How do you explain *that* to bereaved parents? In view of his record?

I couldn't see but one answer.

I found myself mulling over a discussion in our class in History and Moral Philosophy. Mr. Dubois was talking about the disorders that preceded the breakup of the North American republic, back in the XXth century. According to him, there was a time just before they went down the drain when such crimes as Dillinger's were as common as dog-fights. The Terror had not been just in North America—Russia and the British Isles had it, too, as well as other places. But it reached its peak in North America shortly before things went to pieces.

"Law-abiding people," Dubois had told us, "hardly dared go into a public park at night. To do so was to risk attack by wolf packs of children, armed with chains, knives, homemade guns, bludgeons . . . to be hurt at least, robbed most certainly, injured for life probably—or even killed. This went on for years, right up to the war between the Russo-Anglo-American Alliance and the Chinese Hegemony. Murder, drug addiction, larceny, assault, and vandalism were commonplace. Nor were parks the only places— these things happened also on the streets in daylight, on school grounds, even inside school buildings. But parks were so notoriously unsafe that honest people stayed clear of them after dark."

I had tried to imagine such things happening in our schools. I simply couldn't. Nor in our parks. A park was a place for fun, not for getting hurt. As for getting killed in one—"Mr. Dubois, didn't they have police? Or courts?"

"They had many more police than we have. And more courts. All overworked."

"I guess I don't get it." If a boy in our city had done anything half that bad . . . well, he and his father would have been flogged side by side. But such things just didn't happen.

Mr. Dubois then demanded of me, "Define a 'juvenile delinquent.'"

"Uh, one of those kids—the ones who used to beat up people."

"Wrong."

"Huh? But the book said—"

"My apologies. Your textbook does so state. But calling a tail a leg does not make the name fit. 'Juvenile delinquent' is a contradiction in terms, one which gives a clue to their problem and their failure to solve it. Have you ever raised a puppy?"

"Yes, sir."

"Did you housebreak him?"

"Err . . . yes, sir. Eventually." It was my slowness in this that caused my mother to rule that dogs must stay out of the house.

"Ah, yes. When your puppy made mistakes, were you angry?"

"What? Why, he didn't know any better; he was just a puppy."

"What did you do?"

"Why, I scolded him and rubbed his nose in it and paddled him."

"Surely he could not understand your words?"

"No, but he could tell I was sore at him!"

"But you just said that you were not angry."

Mr. Dubois had an infuriating way of getting a person mixed up. "No, but I had to make him *think* I was. He had to learn, didn't he?"

"Conceded. But, having made it clear to him that you disapproved, how could you be so cruel as to spank him as well? You said the poor beastie didn't know that he was doing wrong. Yet you inflicted pain. Justify yourself! Or are you a sadist?"

I didn't then know what a sadist was—but I knew pups. "Mr. Dubois, you *have* to! You scold him so that he knows he's in trouble, you rub his nose in it so that he will know what trouble you mean, you paddle him so that he darn well won't do it again—and you have to do it right away! It doesn't do a bit of good to punish him later; you'll just confuse him. Even so, he won't learn from one lesson, so you watch and catch him again and paddle him still harder. Pretty soon he learns. But it's a waste of breath just to scold him." Then I added, "I guess you've never raised pups."

"Many. I'm raising a dachshund now—by your methods. Let's get back to those juvenile criminals. The most vicious averaged somewhat younger than you here in this class . . . and they often started their lawless careers much younger. Let us never forget that puppy. These children were often caught; police arrested batches each day. Were they scolded? Yes, often scathingly. Were their noses rubbed in it? Rarely. News organs and officials usually kept their names secret—in many places the law so required for criminals under eighteen. Were they spanked? Indeed not! Many had never been spanked even as small children; there was a widespread belief that spanking, or any punishment involving pain, did a child permanent psychic damage."

(I had reflected that my father must never have heard of that theory.)

"Corporal punishment in schools was forbidden by law," he had gone on. "Flogging was lawful as sentence of court only in

one small province, Delaware, and there only for a few crimes and
was rarely invoked; it was regarded as 'cruel and unusual punishment.' " Dubois had mused aloud, "I do not understand objections
to 'cruel and unusual' punishment. While a judge should be
benevolent in purpose, his awards should cause the criminal to
suffer, else there is no punishment—and pain is the basic mechanism built into us by millions of years of evolution which safe-
guards us by warning when something threatens our survival.
Why should society refuse to use such a highly perfected survival
mechanism? However, that period was loaded with pre-scientific
pseudo-psychological nonsense.

"As for 'unusual,' punishment *must* be unusual or it serves no
purpose." He then pointed his stump at another boy. "What would
happen if a puppy were spanked every hour?"

"Uh . . . probably drive him crazy!"

"Probably. It certainly will not teach him anything. How long
has it been since the principal of this school last had to switch a
pupil?"

"Uh, I'm not sure. About two years. The kid that swiped—"

"Never mind. Long enough. It means that such punishment is
so unusual as to be significant, to deter, to instruct. Back to these
young criminals—They probably were not spanked as babies;
they certainly were not flogged for their crimes. The usual sequence was: for a first offense, a warning—a scolding, often without trial. After several offenses a sentence of confinement but with
sentence suspended and the youngster placed on probation. A boy
might be arrested many times and convicted several times before
he was punished—and then it would be merely confinement, with
others like him from whom he learned still more criminal habits.
If he kept out of major trouble while confined, he could usually
evade most of even that mild punishment, be given probation—
'paroled' in the jargon of the times.

"This incredible sequence could go on for years while his
crimes increased in frequency and viciousness, with no punishment whatever save rare dull-but-comfortable confinements. Then
suddenly, usually by law on his eighteenth birthday, this so-called
'juvenile delinquent' becomes an adult criminal—and sometimes
wound up in only weeks or months in a death cell awaiting execu-
tion for murder. *You*—"

He had singled me out again. "Suppose you merely scolded
your puppy, never punished him, let him go on making messes in
the house . . . and occasionally locked him up in an outbuilding

but soon let him back into the house with a warning not to do it
again. Then one day you notice that he is now a grown dog and
still not housebroken—whereupon you whip out a gun and shoot
him dead. Comment, please?"

"Why . . . that's the craziest way to raise a dog I ever
heard of!"

"I agree. Or a child. Whose fault would it be?"

"Uh . . . why, mine, I guess."

"Again I agree. But I'm not guessing."

"Mr. Dubois," a girl blurted out, "but *why?* Why didn't they
spank little kids when they needed it and use a good dose of the
strap on any older ones who deserved it—the sort of lesson they
wouldn't forget! I mean ones who did things really *bad.* Why not?"

"I don't know," he had answered grimly, "except that the time-
tested method of instilling social virtue and respect for law in the
minds of the young did not appeal to a pre-scientific pseudo-
professional class who called themselves 'social workers' or
sometimes 'child psychologists.' It was too simple for them, apparently, since anybody could do it, using only the patience and
firmness needed in training a puppy. I have sometimes wondered
if they cherished a vested interest in disorder—but that is unlikely; adults almost always act from conscious 'highest motives'
no matter what their behavior."

"But—good heavens!" the girl answered. "I didn't like being
spanked any more than any kid does, but when I needed it, my
mama delivered. The only time I ever got a switching in school I
got another one when I got home—and that was years and years
ago. I don't ever expect to be hauled up in front of a judge and
sentenced to a flogging; you behave yourself and such things
don't happen. I don't see anything wrong with our system; it's a
lot better than not being able to walk outdoors for fear of your
life—why, that's *horrible!*"

"I agree. Young lady, the tragic wrongness of what those well-
meaning people did, contrasted with what they *thought* they were
doing, goes very deep. They had no scientific theory of morals.
They did have a theory of morals and they tried to live by it (I
should not have sneered at their motives), but their theory was
wrong—half of it fuzzy-headed wishful thinking, half of it ration-
alized charlatanry. The more earnest they were, the farther it led
them astray. You see, they assumed that Man has a moral instinct."

"Sir? I thought—But he does! *I* have."

"No, my dear, you have a cultivated conscience, a most carefully trained one. Man has *no moral instinct*. He is not born with moral sense. You were not born with it, I was not—and a puppy has none. We *acquire* moral sense, when we do, through training, experience, and hard sweat of the mind. These unfortunate juvenile criminals were born with none, even as you and I, and they had no chance to acquire any; their experiences did not permit it. What *is* 'moral sense'? It is an elaboration of the instinct to survive. The instinct to survive is human nature itself, and every aspect of our personalities derives from it. Anything that conflicts with the survival instinct acts sooner or later to eliminate the individual and thereby fails to show up in future generations. This truth is mathematically demonstrable, everywhere verifiable; it is the single eternal imperative controlling everything we do.

"But the instinct to survive," he had gone on, "can be cultivated into motivations more subtle and much more complex than the blind, brute urge of the individual to stay alive. Young lady, what you miscalled your 'moral instinct' was the instilling in you by your elders of the truth that survival can have stronger imperatives than that of your own personal survival. Survival of your family, for example. Of your children, when you have them. Of your nation, if you struggle that high up the scale. And so on up. A scientifically verifiable theory of morals must be rooted in the individual's instinct to survive—*and nowhere else!*—and must correctly describe the hierarchy of survival, note the motivations at each level, and resolve all conflicts.

"We have such a theory now; we can solve any moral problem, on any level. Self-interest, love of family, duty to country, responsibility toward the human race—we are even developing an exact ethic for extra-human relations. But all moral problems can be illustrated by one misquotation: 'Greater love hath no man than a mother cat dying to defend her kittens.' Once you understand the problem facing that cat and how she solved it, you will then be ready to examine yourself and learn how high up the moral ladder you are capable of climbing.

"These juvenile criminals hit a low level. Born with only the instinct for survival, the highest morality they achieved was a shaky loyalty to a peer group, a street gang. But the do-gooders attempted to 'appeal to their better natures,' to 'reach them,' to 'spark their moral sense.' *Tosh!* They *had* no 'better natures'; experience taught them that what they were doing was the way to survive. The puppy never got his spanking; therefore what he did with pleasure and success must be 'moral.'

"The basis of all morality is duty, a concept with the same relation to group that self-interest has to individual. Nobody preached duty to these kids in a way they could understand—that is, with a spanking. But the society they were in told them endlessly about their 'rights.'

"The results should have been predictable, since a human being has *no natural rights of any nature.*"

Mr. Dubois had paused. Somebody took the bait. "Sir? How about 'life, liberty, and the pursuit of happiness'?"

"Ah, yes, the 'unalienable rights.' Each year someone quotes that magnificent poetry. Life? What 'right' to life has a man who is drowning in the Pacific? The ocean will not hearken to his cries. What 'right' to life has a man who must die if he is to save his children? If he chooses to save his own life, does he do so as a matter of 'right'? If two men are starving and cannibalism is the only alternative to death, which man's right is 'unalienable'? And is it 'right'? As to liberty, the heroes who signed the great document pledged themselves to *buy* liberty with their lives. Liberty is *never* unalienable; it must be redeemed regularly with the blood of patriots or it *always* vanishes. Of all the so-called natural human rights that have ever been invented, liberty is least likely to be cheap and is *never* free of cost.

"The third 'right'?—the 'pursuit of happiness'? It is indeed unalienable but it is not a right; it is simply a universal condition which tyrants cannot take away nor patriots restore. Cast me into a dungeon, burn me at the stake, crown me king of kings, I can 'pursue happiness' as long as my brain lives—but neither gods nor saints, wise men nor subtle drugs, can insure that I will catch it."

Mr. Dubois then turned to me. "I told you that 'juvenile delinquent' is a contradiction in terms. 'Delinquent' means 'failing in duty.' But *duty* is an *adult* virtue—indeed a juvenile becomes an adult when, and only when, he acquires a knowledge of duty and embraces it as dearer than the self-love he was born with. There never was, there cannot *be*, a 'juvenile delinquent.' But for every juvenile criminal there are always one or more adult delinquents—people of mature years who either do not know their duty, or who, knowing it, fail.

"And *that* was the soft spot which destroyed what was in many ways an admirable culture. The junior hoodlums who roamed their streets were symptoms of a greater sickness; their citizens (all of them counted as such) glorified their mythology of 'rights' . . . and lost track of their duties. No nation, so constituted, can endure."

I wondered how Colonel Dubois would have classed Dillinger. Was he a juvenile criminal who merited pity even though you had to get rid of him? Or was he an adult delinquent who deserved nothing but contempt?

I didn't know, I would never know. The one thing I was sure of was that he would never again kill any little girls.

That suited me. I went to sleep.

Chapter 9

We've got no place in this outfit for good losers. We want tough hombres who will go in there and win!

—Admiral Jonas Ingram, 1926

When we had done all that a mud foot can do in flat country, we moved into some rough mountains to do still rougher things—the Canadian Rockies between Good Hope Mountain and Mount Waddington. Camp Sergeant Spooky Smith was much like Camp Currie (aside from its rugged setting) but it was much smaller. Well, the Third Regiment was much smaller now, too—less than four hundred whereas we had started out with more than two thousand. H Company was now organized as a single platoon and the battalion paraded as if it were a company. But we were still called "H Company" and Zim was "Company Commander," not platoon leader.

What the sweat-down meant, really, was much more personal instruction; we had more corporal-instructors than we had squads and Sergeant Zim, with only fifty men on his mind instead of the two hundred and sixty he had started with, kept his Argus eyes on each one of us all the time—even when he wasn't there. At least, if you goofed, it turned out he was standing right behind you.

However, the chewing-out you got had almost a friendly quality, in a horrid sort of way, because we had changed, too, as well as the regiment—the one-in-five who was left was almost a sol-

STARSHIP TROOPERS

dier and Zim seemed to be trying to make him into one, instead of running him over the hill.

We saw a lot more of Captain Frankel, too; he now spent most of his time teaching us, instead of behind a desk, and he knew all of us by name and face and seemed to have a card file in his mind of exactly what progress each man had made on every weapon, every piece of equipment—not to mention your extra-duty status, medical record, and whether you had had a letter from home lately.

He wasn't as severe with us as Zim was; his words were milder and it took a really stupid stunt to take that friendly grin off his face—but don't let that fool you; there was beryl armor under the grin. I never did figure out which one was the better soldier, Zim or Captain Frankel—I mean, if you took away the insignia and thought of them as privates. Unquestionably they were both better soldiers than any of the other instructors—but which was best? Zim did everything with precision and style, as if he were on parade; Captain Frankel did the same thing with dash and gusto, as if it were a game. The results were about the same—and it never turned out to be as easy as Captain Frankel made it look.

We needed the abundance of instructors. Jumping a suit (as I have said) was easy on flat ground. Well, the suit jumps just as high and just as easily in the mountains—but it makes a lot of difference when you have to jump up a vertical granite wall, between two close-set fir trees, and override your jet control at the last instant. We had three major casualties in suit practice in broken country, two dead and one medical retirement.

But that rock wall is even tougher without a suit, tackled with lines and pitons. I didn't really see what use alpine drill was to a cap trooper but I had learned to keep my mouth shut and try to learn what they shoved at us. I learned it and it wasn't too hard. If anybody had told me, a year earlier, that I could go up a solid chunk of rock, as flat and as perpendicular as a blank wall of a building, using only a hammer, some silly little steel pins, and a chunk of clothesline, I would have laughed in his face; I'm a sea-level type. Correction: I *was* a sea-level type. There had been some changes made.

Just how much I had changed I began to find out. At Camp Sergeant Spooky Smith we had liberty—to go to town, I mean. Oh, we had "liberty" after the first month at Camp Currie, too. This meant that, on a Sunday afternoon, if you weren't in the duty platoon, you could check out at the orderly tent and walk just as far away from camp as you wished, bearing in mind that you had to be back for evening muster. But there was nothing within walking distance, if you don't count jack rabbits—no girls, no theaters, no dance halls, et cetera.

Nevertheless, liberty, even at Camp Currie, was no mean privilege; sometimes it can be very important indeed to be able to go so far away that you can't see a tent, a sergeant, nor even the ugly faces of your best friends among the boots . . . not have to be on the bounce about anything, have time to take out your soul and look at it. You could lose that privilege in several degrees; you could be restricted to camp . . . or you could be restricted to your own company street, which meant that you couldn't go to the library nor to what was misleadingly called the "recreation" tent (mostly some parcheesi sets and similar wild excitements) . . . or you could be under close restriction, required to stay in your tent when your presence was not required elsewhere.

This last sort didn't mean much in itself since it was usually added to extra duty so demanding that you didn't have any time in your tent other than for sleep anyhow; it was a decoration added like a cherry on top of a dish of ice cream to notify you and the world that you had pulled not some everyday goof-off but something unbecoming of a member of the M.I. and were thereby unfit to associate with other troopers until you had washed away the stain.

But at Camp Spooky we could go into town—duty status, conduct status, etc., permitting. Shuttles ran to Vancouver every Sunday morning, right after divine services (which were moved up to thirty minutes after breakfast) and came back again just before supper and again just before taps. The instructors could even spend Saturday night in town, or cop a three-day pass, duty permitting.

I had no more than stepped out of the shuttle, my first pass, than I realized in part that I had changed. Johnnie didn't fit in any longer. Civilian life, I mean. It all seemed amazingly complex and unbelievably untidy.

I'm not running down Vancouver. It's a beautiful city in a lovely setting; the people are charming and they are used to having the M.I. in town and they make a trooper welcome. There is a social center for us downtown, where they have dances for us every week and see to it that junior hostesses are on hand to dance with, and senior hostesses to make sure that a shy boy (*me*, to my amazement—but you try a few months with nothing female around but lady jack rabbits) gets introduced and has a partner's feet to step on.

But I didn't go to the social center that first pass. Mostly I stood around and gawked—at beautiful buildings, at display windows filled with all manner of unnecessary things (and not a weapon among them), at all those people running around, or even strolling, doing exactly as they pleased and no two of them dressed alike—and at girls.

Especially at girls. I hadn't realized just how wonderful they were. Look, I've approved of girls from the time I first noticed that the difference was more than just that they dress differently. So far as I remember I never did go through that period boys are supposed to go through when they know that girls are different but dislike them; I've *always* liked girls.

But that day I realized that I had long been taking them for granted.

Girls are simply wonderful. Just to stand on a corner and watch them going past is delightful. They don't *walk*. At least not what we do when we talk. I don't know how to describe it, but it's much more complex and utterly delightful. They don't move just their feet; everything moves and in different directions . . . and all of it graceful.

I might have been standing there yet if a policeman hadn't come by. He sized us up and said, "Howdy, boys. Enjoying yourselves?"

I quickly read the ribbons on his chest and was impressed. "Yes, *sir!*"

"You don't have to say 'sir' to me. Not much to do here. Why don't you go to the hospitality center?" He gave us the address, pointed the direction and we started that way—Pat Leivy, "Kitten" Smith, and myself. He called after us, "Have a good time, boys . . . and stay out of trouble." Which was exactly what Sergeant Zim had said to us as we climbed into the shuttle.

But we didn't go there. Pat Leivy had lived in Seattle when he was a small boy and wanted to take a look at his old home town. He had money and offered to pay our shuttle fares if we would go with him. I didn't mind and it was all right; shuttles ran every twenty minutes and our passes were not restricted to Vancouver. Smith decided to go along, too.

Seattle wasn't so very different from Vancouver and the girls were just as plentiful; I enjoyed it. But Seattle wasn't quite as used to having M.I. around in droves and we picked a poor spot to eat dinner, one where we weren't quite so welcome—a bar-restaurant, down by the docks.

Now, look, we weren't drinking. Well, Kitten Smith had had one repeat *one* beer with his dinner but he was never anything but friendly and nice. That is how he got his name; the first time we had hand-to-hand combat drill Corporal Jones had said to him disgustedly: "A kitten would have hit me harder than *that!*" The nickname stuck.

We were the only uniforms in the place; most of the other customers were merchant marine sailors—Seattle handles an awful lot of surface tonnage. I hadn't known it at the time but merchant sailors don't like us. Part of it has to do with the fact that their guilds have tried and tried to get their trade classed as equivalent to Federal Service, without success—but I understand that some of it goes way back in history, centuries.

There were some young fellows there, too, about our age—the right age to serve a term, only they weren't—long-haired and sloppy and kind of dirty-looking. Well, say about the way I looked, I suppose, before I joined up.

Presently we started noticing that at the table behind us, two of these young twerps and two merchant sailors (to judge by clothes) were passing remarks that were intended for us to overhear. I won't try to repeat them.

We didn't say anything. Presently, when the remarks were even more personal and the laughs louder and everybody else in the place was keeping quiet and listening, Kitten whispered to me, "Let's get out of here."

I caught Pat Leivy's eye; he nodded. We had no score to settle; it was one of those pay-as-you-get-it places. We got up and left.

They followed us out.

Pat whispered to me, "Watch it." We kept on walking, didn't look back.

They charged us.

I gave my man a side-neck chop as I pivoted and let him fall past me, swung to help my mates. But it was over. Four in, four down. Kitten had handled two of them and Pat had sort of wrapped the other one around a lamppost from throwing him a little too hard.

Somebody, the proprietor I guess, must have called the police as soon as we stood up to leave, since they arrived almost at once while we were still standing around wondering what to do with the meat—two policemen; it was that sort of a neighborhood.

The senior of them wanted us to prefer charges, but none of us was willing—Zim had told us to "stay out of trouble." Kitten looked blank and about fifteen years old and said, "I guess they stumbled."

"So I see," agreed the police officer and toed a knife away from the outflung hand of my man, put it against the curb and broke the blade. "Well, you boys had better run along . . . farther uptown."

We left. I was glad that neither Pat nor Kitten wanted to make anything of it. It's a mighty serious thing, a civilian assaulting a member of the Armed Forces, but what the deuce?—the books balanced. They jumped us, they got their lumps. All even.

But it's a good thing we *never* go on pass armed . . . and have been trained to disable without killing. Because every bit of it happened by reflex. I didn't believe that they would jump us until they already had, and I didn't do any thinking at all until it was over.

But that's how I learned for the first time just how much I had changed.

We walked back to the station and caught a shuttle to Vancouver.

We started practice drops as soon as we moved to Camp Spooky—a platoon at a time, in rotation (a full platoon, that is—a company), would shuttle down to the field north of Walla Walla, go aboard, space, make a drop, go through an exercise, and home on a beacon. A day's work. With eight companies that gave us not quite a drop each week, and then it gave us a little more than a drop each week as attrition continued, whereupon the drops got tougher—over mountains, into the arctic ice, into the Australian desert, and, before we graduated, onto the face of the Moon, where your capsule is placed only a hundred feet up and explodes as it ejects—and you have to look sharp and land with only your suit (no air, no parachute) and a bad landing can spill your air and kill you.

Some of the attrition was from casualties, deaths or injuries, and some of it was just from refusing to enter the capsule—which some did, and that was that; they weren't even chewed out; they were just motioned aside and that night they were paid off. Even a man who had made several drops might get the panic and refuse . . . and the instructors were just gentle with him, treated him the way you do a friend who is ill and won't get well.

I never quite refused to enter the capsule—but I certainly

learned about the shakes. I always got them, I was scared silly every time. I still am.

But you're not a cap trooper unless you drop.

They tell a story, probably not true, about a cap trooper who was sight-seeing in Paris. He visited Les Invalides, looked down at Napoleon's coffin and said to a French guard there: "Who's he?"

The Frenchman was properly scandalized. "Monsieur does not *know?* This is the tomb of *Napoleon!* Napoleon Bonaparte—the greatest soldier who ever lived!"

The cap trooper thought about it. Then he asked, "So? Where were his drops?"

It is almost certainly not true, because there is a big sign outside there that tells you exactly who Napoleon was. But that is how cap troopers feel about it.

Eventually we graduated.

I can see that I've left out almost everything. Not a word about most of our weapons, nothing about the time we dropped everything and fought a forest fire for three days, no mention of the practice alert that was a real one, only we didn't know it until it was over, nor about the day the cook tent blew away—in fact not any mention of weather and, believe me, weather is important to a doughboy, rain and mud especially. But though weather is important while it happens it seems to me to be pretty dull to look back on. You can take descriptions of most any sort of weather out of an almanac and stick them in just anywhere; they'll probably fit.

The regiment had started with 2009 men; we graduated 187—of the others, fourteen were dead (one executed and his name struck) and the rest resigned, dropped, transferred, medical discharge, etc. Major Malloy made a short speech, we each got a certificate, we passed in review for the last time, and the regiment was disbanded, its colors to be cased until they would be needed (three weeks later) to tell another couple of thousand civilians that they were an outfit, not a mob.

I was a "trained soldier," entitled to put "TP" in front of my serial number instead of "RP." Big day.

The biggest I ever had.

Chapter 10

The tree of Liberty must be refreshed from time to time with the blood of patriots . . .

—Thomas Jefferson, 1787

That is, I thought I was a "trained soldier" until I reported to my ship. Any law against having a wrong opinion?

I see that I didn't make any mention of how the Terran Federation moved from "peace" to a "state of emergency" and then on into "war." I didn't notice it too closely myself. When I enrolled, it was "peace," the normal condition, at least so people think (who ever expects anything else?). Then, while I was at Currie, it became a "state of emergency" but I still didn't notice it, as what Corporal Bronski thought about my haircut, uniform, combat drill, and kit was much more important—and what Sergeant Zim thought about such matters was overwhelmingly important. In any case, "emergency" is still "peace."

"Peace" is a condition in which no civilian pays any attention to military casualties which do not achieve page-one, lead-story prominence—unless that civilian is a close relative of one of the casualties. But, if there ever was a time in history when "peace" meant that there was no fighting going on, I have been unable to find out about it. When I reported to my first outfit, "Willie's Wild-cats," sometimes known as Company K, Third Regiment, First M.I. Division, and shipped with them in the *Valley Forge* (with

that misleading certificate in my kit), the fighting had already
been going on for several years.

The historians can't seem to settle whether to call this one
"The Third Space War" (or the "Fourth"), or whether "The First
Interstellar War" fits it better. We just call it "The Bug War" if we
call it anything, which we usually don't, and in any case the historians date the beginning of "war" after the time I joined my first
outfit and ship. Everything up to then and still later were "incidents," "patrols," or "police actions." However, you are just as
dead if you buy a farm in an "incident" as you are if you buy it in
a declared war.

But, to tell the truth, a soldier doesn't notice a war much more
than a civilian does, except his own tiny piece of it and that just on
the days it is happening. The rest of the time he is much more concerned with sack time, the vagaries of sergeants, and the chances
of wheedling the cook between meals. However, when Kitten
Smith and Al Jenkins and I joined them at Luna Base, each of
Willies' Wildcats had made more than one combat drop; they
were soldiers and we were not. We weren't hazed for it—at least I
was not—and the sergeants and corporals were amazingly easy to
deal with after the calculated frightfulness of instructors.

It took a little while to discover that this comparatively gentle
treatment simply meant that we were nobody, hardly worth chewing out, until we had proved in a drop—a real drop—that we
might possibly replace real Wildcats who had fought and bought it
and whose bunks we now occupied.

Let me tell you how green I was. While the *Valley Forge* was
still at Luna Base, I happened to come across my section leader
just as he was about to hit dirt, all slicked up in dress uniform. He
was wearing in his left ear lobe a rather small earring, a tiny gold
skull beautifully made and under it, instead of the conventional
crossed bones of the ancient Jolly Roger design, was a whole bundle of little gold bones, almost too small to see.

Back home, I had always worn earrings and other jewelry
when I went out on a date—I had some beautiful ear clips, rubies
as big as the end of my little finger which had belonged to my
mother's grandfather. I like jewelry and had rather resented being
required to leave it all behind when I went to Basic . . . but here
was a type of jewelry which was apparently okay to wear with uniform. My ears weren't pierced—my mother didn't approve of it,
for boys—but I could have the jeweler mount it on a clip . . . and I
still had some money left from pay call at graduation and was anx-

ious to spend it before it mildewed. "Unh, Sergeant? Where do you get earrings like that one? Pretty neat."

He didn't look scornful, he didn't even smile. He just said, "You like it?"

"I certainly do!" The plain raw gold pointed up the gold braid and piping of the uniform even better than gems would have done. I was thinking that a pair would be still handsomer, with just crossbones instead of all that confusion at the bottom. "Does the base PX carry them?"

"No, the PX here never sells them." He added, "At least I don't think you'll ever be able to buy one here—I hope. But I tell you what—when we reach a place where you can buy one of your own, I'll see to it you know about it. That's a promise."

"Uh, thanks!"

"Don't mention it."

I saw several of the tiny skulls thereafter, some with more "bones," some with fewer; my guess had been correct, this was jewelry permitted with uniform, when on pass at least. Then I got my own chance to "buy" one almost immediately thereafter and discovered that the prices were unreasonably high, for such plain ornaments.

It was Operation Bughouse, the First Battle of Klendathu in the history books, soon after Buenos Aires was smeared. It took the loss of B.A. to make the groundhogs realize that anything was going on, because people who haven't been out don't really believe in other planets, not down deep where it counts. I know I hadn't and I had been space-happy since I was a pup.

But B.A. really stirred up the civilians and inspired loud screams to bring all our forces home, from everywhere—orbit them around the planet practically shoulder to shoulder and interdict the space Terra occupies. This is silly, of course; you don't win a war by defense but by attack—no "Department of Defense" ever won a war; see the histories. But it seems to be a standard civilian reaction to scream for defensive tactics as soon as they do notice a war. They then want to run the war—like a passenger trying to grab the controls away from the pilot in an emergency.

However, nobody asked my opinion at the time; I was told. Quite aside from the impossibility of dragging the troops home in view of our treaty obligations and what it would do to the colony planets in the Federation and to our allies, we were awfully busy doing something else, to wit: carrying the war to the Bugs. I sup-

pose I noticed the destruction of B.A. much less than most civilians did. We were already a couple of parsecs away under
Cherenkov drive and the news didn't reach us until we got it from
another ship after we came out of drive.

I remember thinking, "Gosh, that's terrible!" and feeling sorry
for the one Porteño in the ship. But B.A. wasn't my home and
Terra was a long way off and I was very busy, as the attack on
Klendathu, the Bugs' home planet, was mounted immediately after that and we spent the time to rendezvous strapped in our bunks,
doped and unconscious, with the internal-gravity field of the *Valley Forge* off, to save power and give greater speed.

The loss of Buenos Aires did mean a great deal to me; it
changed my life enormously, but this I did not know until many
months later.

When it came time to drop onto Klendathu, I was assigned to
PFC Dutch Bamburger as a supernumerary. He managed to conceal his pleasure at the news and as soon as the platoon sergeant
was out of earshot, he said, "Listen, boot, you stick close behind
me and stay out of my way. You go slowing me down, I break your
silly neck."

I just nodded. I was beginning to realize that this was not a
practice drop.

Then I had the shakes for a while and then we were down—

Operation Bughouse should have been called "Operation
Madhouse." Everything went wrong. It had been planned as an
all-out move to bring the enemy to their knees, occupy their capital and the key points of their home planet, and end the war. Instead it darn near lost the war.

I am not criticizing General Diennes. I don't know whether
it's true that he demanded more troops and more support and allowed himself to be overruled by the Sky Marshal-in-Chief—or
not. Nor was it any of my business. Furthermore I doubt if some
of the smart second-guessers know all the facts.

What I do know is that the General dropped with us and commanded us on the ground and, when the situation became impossible, he personally led the diversionary attack that allowed quite
a few of us (including me) to be retrieved—and, in so doing,
bought his farm. He's radioactive debris on Klendathu and it's
much too late to court-martial him, so why talk about it?

I do have one comment to make to any armchair strategist who
has never made a drop. Yes, I agree that the Bugs' planet possibly

could have been plastered with H-bombs until it was surfaced with radioactive glass. But would that have won the war? The Bugs are not like us. The Pseudo-Arachnids aren't even like spiders. They are arthropods who happen to look like a madman's conception of a giant, intelligent spider, but their organization, psychological and economic, is more like that of ants or termites; they are communal entities, the ultimate dictatorship of the hive. Blasting the surface of their planet would have killed soldiers and workers; it would not have killed the brain caste and the queens— I doubt if anybody can be certain that even a direct hit with a burrowing H-rocket would kill a queen; we don't know how far down they are. Nor am I anxious to find out; none of the boys who went down those holes came up again.

So suppose we did ruin the productive surface of Klendathu? They still would have ships and colonies and other planets, same as we have, and their HQ is still intact—so unless they surrender, the war isn't over. We didn't have nova bombs at that time; we couldn't crack Klendathu open. If they absorbed the punishment and didn't surrender, the war was still on.

If they *can* surrender—

Their soldiers can't. Their workers can't fight (and you can waste a lot of time and ammo shooting up workers who wouldn't say *boo!*) and their soldier caste can't surrender. But don't make the mistake of thinking that the Bugs are just stupid insects because they look the way they do and don't know how to surrender. Their warriors are smart, skilled, and aggressive—smarter than you are, by the only universal rule, if the Bug shoots first. You can burn off one leg, two legs, three legs, and he just keeps on coming; burn off four on one side and he topples over—but keeps on shooting. You have to spot the nerve case and get it . . . whereupon he will trot right on past you, shooting at nothing, until he crashes into a wall or something.

The drop was a shambles from the start. Fifty ships were in our piece of it and they were supposed to come out of Cherenkov drive and into reaction drive so perfectly coordinated that they could hit orbit and drop us, in formation and where we were supposed to hit, without even making one planet circuit to dress up their own formation. I suppose this is difficult. Shucks, I *know* it is. But when it slips, it leaves the M.I. holding the sack.

We were lucky at that, because the *Valley Forge* and every Navy file in her bought it before we ever hit the ground. In that tight, fast formation (4.7 miles/sec. orbital speed is not a stroll) she collided with the *Y pres* and both ships were destroyed. We were lucky to get out of her tubes—those of us who did get out, for she was still firing capsules as she was rammed. But I wasn't aware of it; I was inside my cocoon, headed for the ground. I suppose our company commander knew that the ship had been lost (and half his Wildcats with it) since he was out first and would know when he suddenly lost touch, over the command circuit, with the ship's captain.

But there is no way to ask him, because he wasn't retrieved. All I ever had was a gradually dawning realization that things were in a mess.

The next eighteen hours were nightmare. I shan't tell much about it because I don't remember much, just snatches, stop-motion scenes of horror. I have never liked spiders, poisonous or otherwise; a common house spider in my bed can give me the creeps. Tarantulas are simply unthinkable, and I can't eat lobster, crab, or anything of that sort. When I got my first sight of a Bug, my mind jumped right out of my skull and started to yammer. It was seconds later that I realized that I had killed it and could stop shooting. I suppose it was a worker; I doubt if I was in any shape to tackle a warrior and win.

But, at that, I was in better shape than was the K-9 Corps. They were to be dropped (if the drop had gone perfectly) on the periphery of our entire target and the neodogs were supposed to range outward and provide tactical intelligence to interdiction squads whose business it was to secure the periphery. Those Calebs aren't armed, of course, other than their teeth. A neodog is supposed to hear, see, and smell and tell his partner what he finds by radio; all he carries is a radio and a destruction bomb with which he (or his partner) can blow the dog up in case of bad wounds or capture.

Those poor dogs didn't wait to be captured; apparently most of them suicided as soon as they made contact. They felt the way I do about the Bugs, only worse. They have neodogs now that are indoctrinated from puppyhood to observe and evade without blowing their tops at the mere sight or smell of a Bug. But these weren't.

But that wasn't all that went wrong. Just name it, it was fouled up. I didn't know what was going on, of course; I just stuck close behind Dutch, trying to shoot or flame anything that moved, dropping a grenade down a hole whenever I saw one. Presently I got so that I could kill a Bug without wasting ammo or juice, although I did not learn to distinguish between those that were harmless and those that were not. Only about one in fifty is a warrior—but he makes up for the other forty-nine. Their personal weapons aren't as heavy as ours but they are lethal just the same—they've got a beam that will penetrate armor and slice flesh like cutting a hard-boiled egg, and they co-operate even better than we do . . . because the brain that is doing the heavy thinking for a "squad" isn't where you can reach it; it's down one of the holes.

Dutch and I stayed lucky for quite a long time, milling around over an area about a mile square, corking up holes with bombs, killing what we found above surface, saving our jets as much as possible for emergencies. The idea was to secure the entire target and allow the reinforcements and the heavy stuff to come down without important opposition; this was not a raid, this was a battle to establish a beachhead, stand on it, hold it, and enable fresh troops and heavies to capture or pacify the entire planet.

Only we didn't.

Our own section was doing all right. It was in the wrong pew and out of touch with the other section—the platoon leader and sergeant were dead and we never re-formed. But we had staked out a claim, our special-weapons squad had set up a strong point, and we were ready to turn our real estate over to fresh troops as soon as they showed up.

Only they didn't. They dropped in where we should have dropped, found unfriendly natives and had their own troubles. We never saw them. So we stayed where we were, soaking up casualties from time to time and passing them out ourselves as opportunity offered—while we ran low on ammo and jump juice and even power to keep the suits moving. This seemed to go on for a couple of thousand years.

Dutch and I were zipping along close to a wall, headed for our special-weapons squad in answer to a yell for help, when the ground suddenly opened in front of Dutch, a Bug popped out, and Dutch went down.

I flamed the Bug and tossed a grenade and the hole closed up, then turned to see what had happened to Dutch. He was down but he didn't look hurt. A platoon sergeant can monitor the physicals of every man in his platoon, sort out the dead from those who merely can't make it unassisted and must be picked up. But you can do the same thing manually from switches right on the belt of a man's suit.

Dutch didn't answer when I called to him. His body temperature read ninety-nine degrees, his respiration, heartbeat, and brain wave read zero—which looked bad but maybe his suit was dead rather than he himself. Or so I told myself, forgetting that the temperature indicator would give no reading if it were the suit rather than the man. Anyhow, I grabbed the can-opener wrench from my own belt and started to take him out of his suit while trying to watch all around me.

Then I heard an all-hands call in my helmet that I never want to hear again. "*Sauve qui peut!* Home! Home! Pickup and *home!* Any beacon you can hear. Six minutes! All hands, save yourselves, pick up your mates. Home on any beacon! *Sauve qui—*"

I hurried.

His head came off as I tried to drag him out of his suit, so I dropped him and got out of there. On a later drop I would have had sense enough to salvage his ammo, but I was far too sluggy to think; I simply bounced away from there and tried to rendezvous with the strong point we had been heading for.

It was already evacuated and I felt lost . . . lost and deserted. Then I heard recall, not the recall it should have been: "Yankee Doodle" (if it had been a boat from the *Valley Forge*)—but "Sugar Bush," a tune I didn't know. No matter, it was a beacon; I headed for it, using the last of my jump juice lavishly—got aboard just as they were about to button up and shortly thereafter was in the *Voortrek*, in such a state of shock that I couldn't remember my serial number.

I've heard it called a "strategic victory"—but I was there and I claim we took a terrible licking.

Six weeks later (and feeling about sixty years older) at Fleet Base on Sanctuary I boarded another ground boat and reported for duty to Ship's Sergeant Jelal in the *Rodger Young*. I was wearing, in my pierced left ear lobe, a broken skull with one bone. Al Jenkins was with me and was wearing one exactly like it (Kitten never made it out of the tube). The few surviving Wildcats were distributed elsewhere around the Fleet; we had lost half our strength, about, in the collision between the *Valley Forge* and the *Y pres*; that disastrous mess on the ground had run our casualties up over 80 per cent and the powers-that-be decided that it was impossible to put the outfit back together with the survivors—close it out, put the records in the archives, and wait until the scars had healed before reactivating Company K (Wildcats) with new faces but old traditions.

Besides, there were a lot of empty files to fill in other outfits.

Sergeant Jelal welcomed us warmly, told us that we were joining a smart outfit, "best in the Fleet," in a taut ship, and didn't seem to notice our ear skulls. Later that day he took us forward to meet the Lieutenant, who smiled rather shyly and gave us a fatherly little talk. I noticed that Al Jenkins wasn't wearing his gold skull. Neither was I—because I had already noticed that nobody in Rasczak's Roughnecks wore the skulls.

They didn't wear them because, in Rasczak's Roughnecks, it didn't matter in the least how many combat drops you had made, nor which ones; you were either a Roughneck or you weren't—and if you were not, they didn't care who you were. Since we had come to them not as recruits but as combat veterans, they gave us all possible benefit of doubt and made us welcome with no more than that unavoidable trace of formality anybody necessarily shows to a house guest who is not a member of the family.

But, less than a week later when we had made one combat drop with them, we were full-fledged Roughnecks, members of the family, called by our first names, chewed out on occasion without any feeling on either side that we were less than blood brothers thereby, borrowed from and lent to, included in bull sessions and privileged to express our own silly opinions with complete freedom—and have them slapped down just as freely. We even called non-coms by their first names on any but strictly duty occasions. Sergeant Jelal was always on duty, of course, unless you ran across him dirtside, in which case he was "Jelly" and went out of his way to behave as if his lordly rank meant nothing between Roughnecks.

But the Lieutenant was always "The Lieutenant"—never "Mr. Rasczak," nor even "Lieutenant Rasczak." Simply "The Lieutenant," spoken to and of in the third person. There was no god but the Lieutenant and Sergeant Jelal was his prophet. Jelly could say "No" in his own person and it might be subject to further argument, at least from junior sergeants, but if he said, "The Lieutenant wouldn't like it," he was speaking *ex cathedra* and the matter was dropped permanently. Nobody ever tried to check up on whether or not the Lieutenant would or would not like it; the Word had been spoken.

The Lieutenant was father to us and loved us and spoiled us and was nevertheless rather remote from us aboard ship—and even dirt-side . . . unless we reached dirt via a drop. But in a drop—well, you wouldn't think that an officer could worry about every man of a platoon spread over a hundred square miles of terrain. But he can. He can worry himself sick over each one of them. How he could keep track of us all I can't describe, but in the midst of a ruckus his voice would sing out over the command circuit: "Johnson! Check squad six! Smitty's in trouble," and it was better than even money that the Lieutenant had noticed it before Smith's squad leader.

Besides that, you knew with utter and absolute certainty that, as long as you were still alive, the Lieutenant would not get into the retrieval boat without you. There have been prisoners taken in the Bug War, but none from Rasczak's Roughnecks.

Jelly was mother to us and was close to us and took care of us and didn't spoil us at all. But he didn't report us to the Lieutenant—there was never a court-martial among the Roughnecks and no man was *ever* flogged. Jelly didn't even pass out extra duty very often; he had other ways of paddling us. He could look you up and down at daily inspection and simply say, "In the Navy you might look good. Why don't you transfer?"—and get results, it being an article of faith among us that the Navy crew members slept in their uniforms and never washed below their collar lines.

But Jelly didn't have to maintain discipline among privates because he maintained discipline among his non-coms and expected them to do likewise. My squad leader, when I first joined, was "Red" Greene. After a couple of drops, when I knew how *good* it was to be a Roughneck, I got to feeling gay and a bit too big for my clothes—and talked back to Red. He didn't report me to Jelly; he just took me back to the washroom and gave me a medium set of lumps, and we got to be pretty good friends. In fact, he recommended me for lance, later on.

Actually we didn't know whether the crew members slept in their clothes or not; we kept to our part of the ship and the Navy men kept to theirs, because they were made to feel unwelcome if they showed up in our country other than on duty—after all, one has social standards one must maintain, mustn't one? The Lieutenant had his stateroom in male officers' country, a Navy part of the ship, but we never went there, either, except on duty and rarely. We did go forward for guard duty, because the *Rodger Young* was a mixed ship, female captain and pilot officers, some female Navy ratings; forward of bulkhead thirty was ladies' country—and two armed M.I. day and night stood guard at the one door cutting it. (At battle stations that door, like all other gastight doors, was secured; nobody missed a drop.)

Officers were privileged to go forward of bulkhead thirty on duty and all officers, including the Lieutenant, ate in a mixed mess just beyond it. But they didn't tarry there; they ate and got out. Maybe other corvette transports were run differently, but that was the way the *Rodger Young* was run—both the Lieutenant and Captain Deladrier wanted a taut ship and got it.

Nevertheless guard duty was a privilege. It was a rest to stand beside that door, arms folded, feet spread, doping off and thinking about nothing . . . but always warmly aware that any moment you might see a feminine creature even though you were not privileged to speak to her other than on duty. Once I was called all the way into the Skipper's office and she spoke to me—she looked right at me and said, "Take this to the Chief Engineer, please."

My daily shipside job, aside from cleaning, was servicing electronic equipment under the close supervision of "Padre" Migliaccio, the section leader of the first section, exactly as I used to work under Carl's eye. Drops didn't happen too often and everybody worked every day. If a man didn't have any other talent he could always scrub bulkheads; nothing was ever quite clean enough to suit Sergeant Jelal. We followed the M.I. rule; everybody fights, everybody works. Our first cook was Johnson, the second section's sergeant, a big friendly boy from Georgia (the one in the western hemisphere, not the other one) and a very talented chef. He wheedled pretty well, too; he liked to eat between meals himself and saw no reason why other people shouldn't.

With the Padre leading one section and the cook leading the other, we were well taken care of, body and soul—but suppose one of them bought it? Which one would you pick? A nice point that we never tried to settle but could always discuss.

The *Rodger Young* kept busy and we made a number of drops, all different. Every drop has to be different so that they never can figure out a pattern on you. But no more pitched battles; we operated alone, patrolling, harrying, and raiding. The truth was that the Terran Federation was not then able to mount a large battle; the foul-up with Operation Bughouse had cost too many ships, 'way too many trained men. It was necessary to take time to heal up, train more men.

In the meantime, small fast ships, among them the *Rodger Young* and other corvette transports, tried to be everywhere at once, keeping the enemy off balance, hurting him and running. We suffered casualties and filled our holes when we returned to Sanctuary for more capsules. I still got the shakes every drop, but actual drops didn't happen too often nor were we ever down long—and between times there were days and days of shipboard life among the Roughnecks.

It was the happiest period of my life although I was never quite consciously aware of it—I did my full share of beefing just as everybody else did, and enjoyed that, too.

We weren't *really* hurt until the Lieutenant bought it.

I guess that was the worst time in all my life. I was already in bad shape for a personal reason: My mother had been in Buenos Aires when the Bugs smeared it.

I found out about it one time when we put in at Sanctuary for more capsules and some mail caught up with us—a note from my Aunt Eleanora, one that had not been coded and sent fast because she had failed to mark for that; the letter itself came. It was about three bitter lines. Somehow she seemed to blame me for my mother's death. Whether it was my fault because I was in the Armed Services and should have therefore prevented the raid, or whether she felt that my mother had made a trip to Buenos Aires because I wasn't home where I should have been, was not quite clear; she managed to imply both in the same sentence.

I tore it up and tried to walk away from it. I thought that both my parents were dead—since Father would never send Mother on a trip that long by herself. Aunt Eleanora had not said so, but she wouldn't have mentioned Father in any case; her devotion was entirely to her sister. I was almost correct—eventually I learned that Father had planned to go with her but something had come up and he stayed over to settle it, intending to come along the next day. But Aunt Eleanora did not tell me this.

A couple of hours later the Lieutenant sent for me and

asked me very gently if I would like to take leave at Sanctuary while the ship went out on her next patrol—he pointed out that I had plenty of accumulated R&R and might as well use some of it. I don't know how he knew that I had lost a member of my family, but he obviously did. I said no, thank you, sir; I preferred to wait until the outfit all took R&R together.

I'm glad I did it that way, because if I hadn't, I wouldn't have been along when the Lieutenant bought it ... and that would have been just too much to be borne. It happened very fast and just before retrieval. A man in the third squad was wounded, not badly but he was down; the assistant section leader moved in to pick up—and bought a small piece of it himself. The Lieutenant, as usual, was watching everything at once—no doubt he had checked physicals on each of them by remote, but we'll never know. What he did was to make sure that the assistant section leader was still alive; then made pickup on both of them himself, one in each arm of his suit.

He threw them the last twenty feet and they were passed into the retrieval boat—and with everybody else in, the shield gone and no interdiction, was hit and died instantly.

I haven't mentioned the names of the private and of the assistant section leader on purpose. The Lieutenant was making pickup on *all* of us, with his last breath. Maybe I was the private. It doesn't matter who he was. What did matter was that our family had had its head chopped off. The head of the family from which we took our name, the father who made us what we were.

After the Lieutenant had to leave us Captain Deladrier invited Sergeant Jelal to eat forward, with the other heads of departments. But he begged to be excused. Have you ever seen a widow with stern character keep her family together by behaving as if the head of the family had simply stepped out and would return at any moment? That's what Jelly did. He was just a touch more strict with us than ever and if he ever had to say: "The Lieutenant wouldn't like that," it was almost more than a man could take. Jelly didn't say it very often.

He left our combat team organization almost unchanged; instead of shifting everybody around, he moved the assistant section leader of the second section over into the (nominal) platoon sergeant spot, leaving his section leaders where they were needed—

with their sections—and he moved me from lance and assistant squad leader into acting corporal as a largely ornamental assistant section leader. Then he himself behaved as if the Lieutenant were merely out of sight and that he was just passing on the Lieutenant's orders, as usual.

It saved us.

Chapter 11

I have nothing to offer but blood, toil, tears, and sweat.

—W. Churchill, XXth century soldier-statesman

As we came back into the ship after the raid on the Skinnies—the raid in which Dizzy Flores bought it, Sergeant Jelal's first drop as platoon leader—a ship's gunner who was tending the boat lock spoke to me:

"How'd it go?"

"Routine," I answered briefly. I suppose his remark was friendly but I was feeling very mixed up and in no mood to talk—sad over Dizzy, glad that we had made pickup anyhow, mad that the pickup had been useless, and all of it tangled up with that washed-out but happy feeling of being back in the ship again, able to muster arms and legs and note that they are all present. Besides, how can you talk about a drop to a man who has never made one?

"So?" he answered. "You guys have got it soft. Loaf thirty days, work thirty minutes. Me, I stand a watch in three *and* turn to."

"Yeah, I guess so," I agreed and turned away. "Some of us are born lucky."

"Soldier, you ain't peddlin' vacuum," he said to my back.

And yet there was much truth in what the Navy gunner had said. We cap troopers are like aviators of the earlier mechanized wars; a long and busy military career could contain only a few hours of actual combat facing the enemy, the rest being: train, get ready, go out—then come back, clean up the mess, get ready for another one, and practice, practice, practice, in between. We didn't make another drop for almost three weeks and that on a different planet around another star—a Bug colony. Even with Cherenkov drive, stars are far apart.

In the meantime I got my corporal's stripes, nominated by Jelly and confirmed by Captain Deladrier in the absence of a commissioned officer of our own. Theoretically the rank would not be permanent until approved against vacancy by the Fleet M.I. repple-depple, but that meant nothing, as the casualty rate was such that there were always more vacancies in the T.O. than there were warm bodies to fill them. I was a corporal when Jelly said I was a corporal; the rest was red tape.

But the gunner was not quite correct about "loafing"; there were fifty-three suits of powered armor to check, service, and repair between each drop, not to mention weapons and special equipment. Sometimes Migliaccio would down-check a suit, Jelly would confirm it, and the ship's weapons engineer, Lieutenant Farley, would decide that he couldn't cure it short of base facilities—whereupon a new suit would have to be broken out of stores and brought from "cold" to "hot," an exacting process requiring twenty-six man-hours not counting the time of the man to whom it was being fitted.

We kept busy.

But we had fun, too. There were always several competitions going on, from acey-deucy to Honor Squad, and we had the best jazz band in several cubic light-years (well, the only one, maybe), with Sergeant Johnson on the trumpet leading them mellow and sweet for hymns or tearing the steel right off the bulkheads, as the occasion required. After that masterful (or should it be "mistressful"?) retrieval rendezvous without a programmed ballistic, the platoon's metalsmith, PFC Archie Campbell, made a model of the *Rodger Young* for the Skipper and we all signed and Archie engraved our signatures on a base plate: *To Hot Pilot Yvette Deladrier, with thanks from Rasczak's Roughnecks,* and we invited her aft to eat with us and the Roughneck Downbeat Combo played during dinner and then the junior private presented it to her. She got tears and kissed him—and kissed Jelly as well and he blushed purple.

After I got my chevrons I simply had to get things straight with Ace, because Jelly kept me on as assistant section leader. This is not good. A man ought to fill each spot on his way up; I should have had a turn as squad leader instead of being bumped from lance and assistant squad leader to corporal and assistant section leader. Jelly knew this, of course, but I know perfectly well that he was trying to keep the outfit as much as possible the way it had been when the Lieutenant was alive—which meant that he left his squad leaders and section leaders unchanged.

But it left me with a ticklish problem; all three of the corporals under me as squad leaders were actually senior to me—but if Sergeant Johnson bought it on the next drop, it would not only lose us a mighty fine cook, it would leave me leading the section. There mustn't be any shadow of doubt when you give an order, not in combat; I had to clear up any possible shadow before we dropped again.

Ace was the problem. He was not only senior of the three, he was a career corporal as well and older than I was. If Ace accepted me, I wouldn't have any trouble with the other two squads.

I hadn't really had any trouble with him aboard. After we made pickup on Flores together he had been civil enough. On the other hand we hadn't had anything to have trouble over; our ship-side jobs didn't put us together, except at daily muster and guard mount, which is all cut and dried. But you can feel it. He was not treating me as somebody he took orders from.

So I looked him up during off hours. He was lying in his bunk, reading a book, *Space Rangers against the Galaxy*—a pretty good yarn, except that I doubt if a military outfit ever had so many adventures and so few goof-offs. The ship had a good library.

"Ace. Got to see you."

He glanced up. "So? I just left the ship, I'm off duty."

"I've got to see you now. Put your book down."

"What's so aching urgent? I've got to finish this chapter."

"Oh, come off it, Ace. If you can't wait, I'll tell you how it comes out."

"You do and I'll clobber you." But he put the book down, sat up, and listened.

I said, "Ace, about this matter of the section organization— you're senior to me, you ought to be assistant section leader."

"Oh, so it's *that* again!"

"Yep. I think you and I ought to go see Johnson and get him to fix it up with Jelly."

"You do, eh?"

"Yes, I do. That's how it's got to be."

"So? Look, Shortie, let me put you straight. I got nothing

against you at all. Matter of fact, you were on the bounce that day we had to pick up Dizzy; I'll hand you that. But if you want a squad, you go dig up one of your own. Don't go eyeing mine. Why, my boys wouldn't even peel potatoes for you."

"That's your final word?"

"That's my first, last, and only word."

I sighed. "I thought it would be. But I had to make sure. Well, that settles that. But I've got one thing on my mind. I happened to notice that the washroom needs cleaning . . . and I think maybe you and I ought to attend to it. So put your book aside . . . as Jelly says, non-coms are always on duty."

He didn't stir at once. He said quietly, "You really think it's necessary, Shortie? As I said, I got nothing against you."

"Looks like."

"Think you can do it?"

"I can sure try."

"Okay. Let's take care of it."

We went aft to the washroom, chased out a private who was about to take a shower he didn't really need, and locked the door. Ace said, "You got any restrictions in mind, Shortie?"

"Well . . . I hadn't planned to kill you."

"Check. And no broken bones, nothing that would keep either one of us out of the next drop—except maybe by accident, of course. That suit you?"

"Suits," I agreed. "Uh, I think maybe I'll take my shirt off."

"Wouldn't want to get blood on your shirt." He relaxed. I started to peel it off and he let go a kick for my kneecap. No wind up. Flat-footed and not tense.

Only my kneecap wasn't there—I had learned.

A real fight ordinarily can last only a second or two, because that is all the time it takes to kill a man, or knock him out, or disable him to the point where he can't fight. But we had agreed to avoid inflicting permanent damage; this changes things. We were both young, in top condition, highly trained, and used to absorbing punishment. Ace was bigger, I was maybe a touch faster. Under such conditions the miserable business simply has to go on until one or the other is too beaten down to continue—unless a fluke settles it sooner. But neither one of us was allowing any flukes; we were professionals and wary.

So it did go on, for a long, tedious, painful time. Details would be trivial and pointless; besides, I had no time to take notes.

A long time later I was lying on my back and Ace was flipping water in my face. He looked at me, then hauled me to my feet, shoved me against a bulkhead, steadied me. "Hit me!"

"Huh?" I was dazed and seeing double.

"Johnnie . . . hit me."

His face was floating in the air in front of me; I zeroed in on it and slugged it with all the force in my body, hard enough to mash any mosquito in poor health. His eyes closed and he slumped to the deck and I had to grab at a stanchion to keep from following him.

He got slowly up. "Okay, Johnnie," he said, shaking his head, "I've had my lesson. You won't have any more lip out of me . . . nor out of anybody in the section. Okay?"

I nodded and my head hurt.

"Shake?" he asked.

We shook on it, and that hurt, too.

Almost anybody else knew more about how the war was going than we did, even though we were in it. This was the period, of course, after the Bugs had located our home planet, through the Skinnies, and had raided it, destroying Buenos Aires and turning "contact troubles" into all-out war, but *before* we had built up our forces and before the Skinnies had changed sides and become our co-belligerents and de facto allies. Partly effective interdiction for Terra had been set up from Luna (we didn't know it), but speaking broadly, the Terran Federation was losing the war.

We didn't know that, either. Nor did we know that strenuous efforts were being made to subvert the alliance against us and bring the Skinnies over to our side; the nearest we came to being told about that was when we got instructions, before the raid in which Flores was killed, to go easy on the Skinnies, destroy as much property as possible but to kill inhabitants only when unavoidable.

What a man doesn't know he can't spill if he is captured; neither drugs, nor torture, nor brainwash, nor endless lack of sleep can squeeze out a secret he doesn't possess. So we were told only what we had to know for tactical purposes. In the past, armies have been known to fold up and quit because the men didn't know what they were fighting for, or why, and therefore lacked the will to fight. But the M.I. does not have that weakness. Each one of us was a volunteer to begin with, each for some reason or other— some good, some bad. But now we fought because we were M.I. We were professionals, with *esprit de corps*. We were Rasczak's Roughnecks, the best unprintable outfit in the whole expurgated

M.I.; we climbed into our capsules because Jelly told us it was time to do so and we fought when we got down there because that is what Rasczak's Roughnecks do.

We certainly didn't know that we were losing.

Those Bugs lay eggs. They not only lay them, they hold them in reserve, hatch them as needed. If we killed a warrior—or a thousand, or ten thousand—his or their replacements were hatched and on duty almost before we could get back to base. You can imagine, if you like, some Bug supervisor of population flashing a phone to somewhere down inside and saying, "Joe, warm up ten thousand warriors and have 'em ready by Wednesday . . . and tell engineering to activate reserve incubators N, O, P, Q, and R; the demand is picking up."

I don't say they did exactly that, but those were the results. But don't make the mistake of thinking that they acted purely from instinct, like termites or ants; their actions were as intelligent as ours (stupid races don't build spaceships!) and were much better coordinated. It takes a minimum of a year to train a private to fight and to mesh his fighting in with his mates; a Bug warrior is *hatched* able to do this.

Every time we killed a thousand Bugs at a cost of one M.I. it was a net victory for the Bugs. We were learning, expensively, just how efficient a total communism can be when used by a people actually adapted to it by evolution; the Bug commissars didn't care any more about expending soldiers than we cared about expending ammo. Perhaps we could have figured this out about the Bugs by noting the grief the Chinese Hegemony gave the Russo-Anglo-American Alliance; however the trouble with "lessons from history" is that we usually read them best after falling flat on our chins.

But we were learning. Technical instructions and tactical doctrine orders resulted from every brush with them, spread through the Fleet. We learned to tell the workers from the warriors—if you had time, you could tell from the shape of the carapace, but the quick rule of thumb was: If he comes at you, he's a warrior; if he runs, you can turn your back on him. We learned not to waste ammo even on warriors except in self-protection; instead we went after their lairs. Find a hole, drop down it first a gas bomb which explodes gently a few seconds later, releasing an oily liquid which evaporates as a nerve gas tailored to Bugs (it is harmless to us) and which is heavier than air and keeps on going down—then you use a second grenade of H.E. to seal the hole.

We still didn't know whether we were getting deep enough to kill the queens—but we did know that the Bugs didn't like these tactics; our intelligence through the Skinnies and on back into the Bugs themselves was definite on this point. Besides, we cleaned their colony off Sheol completely this way. Maybe they managed to evacuate the queens and the brains . . . but at least we were learning to hurt them.

But so far as the Roughnecks were concerned, these gas bombings were simply another drill, to be done according to orders, by the numbers, and on the bounce.

Eventually we had to go back to Sanctuary for more capsules. Capsules are expendable (well, so were we) and when they are gone, you must return to base, even if the Cherenkov generators could still take you twice around the Galaxy. Shortly before this a dispatch came through breveting Jelly to lieutenant, vice Rasczak. Jelly tried to keep it quiet but Captain Deladrier published it and then required him to eat forward with the other officers. He still spent all the rest of his time aft.

But we had taken several drops by then with him as platoon leader and the outfit had gotten used to getting along without the Lieutenant—it still hurt but it was routine now. After Jelal was commissioned the word was slowly passed around among us and chewed over that it was time for us to name ourselves for our boss, as with other outfits.

Johnson was senior and took the word to Jelly; he picked me to go along with him as moral support. "Yeah?" growled Jelly.

"Uh, Sarge I mean Lieutenant, we've been thinking—"

"With what?"

"Well, the boys have sort of been talking it over and they think—well, they say the outfit ought to call itself: 'Jelly's Jaguars.' "

"They do, eh? How many of 'em favor that name?"

"It's unanimous," Johnson said simply.

"So? Fifty-two ayes . . . and one no. The noes have it." Nobody ever brought up the subject again.

Shortly after that we orbited at Sanctuary. I was glad to be there, as the ship's internal pseudo-gravity field had been off for most of two days before that, while the Chief Engineer tinkered with it, leaving us in free fall—which I hate. I'll never be a real spaceman. Dirt underfoot felt good. The entire platoon went on ten days' rest & recreation and transferred to accommodation barracks at the Base.

I never have learned the co-ordinates of Sanctuary, nor the name or catalogue number of the star it orbits—because what you don't know, you can't spill; the location is ultra-top-secret, known only to ships' captains, piloting officers, and such . . . and, I understand, with each of them under orders and hypnotic compulsion to suicide if necessary to avoid capture. So I don't want to know. With the possibility that Luna Base might be taken and Terra herself occupied, the Federation kept as much of its beef as possible at Sanctuary, so that a disaster back home would not necessarily mean capitulation.

But I can tell you what sort of a planet it is. Like Earth, but retarded.

Literally retarded, like a kid who takes ten years to learn to wave bye-bye and never does manage to master patty-cake. It is a planet as near like Earth as two planets can be, same age according to the planetologists and its star is the same age as the Sun and the same type, so say the astrophysicists. It has plenty of flora and fauna, the same atmosphere as Earth, near enough, and much the same weather; it even has a good-sized moon and Earth's exceptional tides.

With all these advantages it barely got away from the starting gate. You see, it's short on mutations; it does not enjoy Earth's high level of natural radiation.

Its typical and most highly developed plant life is a very primitive giant fern; its top animal life is a proto-insect which hasn't even developed colonies. I am not speaking of transplanted Terran flora and fauna—*our* stuff moves in and brushes the native stuff aside.

With its evolutionary progress held down almost to zero by lack of radiation and a consequent most unhealthily low mutation rate, native life forms on Sanctuary just haven't had a decent chance to evolve and aren't fit to compete. Their gene patterns remain fixed for a relatively long time; they aren't adaptable—like being forced to play the same bridge hand over and over again, for eons, with no hope of getting a better one.

As long as they just competed with each other, this didn't matter too much—morons among morons, so to speak. But when types that had evolved on a planet enjoying high radiation and fierce competition were introduced, the native stuff was outclassed.

Now all the above is perfectly obvious from high school biology . . . but the high forehead from the research station there who was telling me about this brought up a point I would never have thought of.

What about the human beings who have colonized Sanctuary?

Not transients like me, but the colonists who live there, many of whom were born there, and whose descendants will live there, even unto the umpteenth generation—what about those descendants? It doesn't do a person any harm not to be radiated; in fact it's a bit safer—leukemia and some types of cancer are almost unknown there. Besides that, the economic situation is at present all in their favor; when they plant a field of (Terran) wheat, they don't even have to clear out the weeds. Terran wheat displaces anything native.

But the descendants of those colonists won't evolve. Not much, anyhow. This chap told me that they could improve a little through mutation from other causes, from new blood added by immigration, and from natural selection among the gene patterns they already own—but that is all very minor compared with the evolutionary rate on Terra and on any usual planet. So what happens? Do they stay frozen at their present level while the rest of the human race moves on past them, until they are living fossils, as out of place as a pithecanthropus in a spaceship?

Or will they worry about the fate of their descendants and dose themselves regularly with X-rays or maybe set off lots of dirty-type nuclear explosions each year to build up a fallout reservoir in their atmosphere? (Accepting, of course, the immediate dangers of radiation to themselves in order to provide a proper genetic heritage of mutation for the benefit of their descendants.)

This bloke predicted that they would not do anything. He claims that the human race is too individualistic, too self-centered, to worry that much about future generations. He says that the genetic impoverishment of distant generations through lack of radiation is something most people are simply incapable of worrying about. And of course it is a far-distant threat; evolution works so slowly, even on Terra, that the development of a new species is a matter of many, many thousands of years.

I don't know. Shucks, I don't know what I myself will do more than half the time; how can I predict what a colony of strangers will do? But I'm sure of this: Sanctuary is going to be fully settled, either by us or by the Bugs. Or by somebody. It is a potential utopia, and, with desirable real estate so scarce in this end of the Galaxy, it will not be left in the possession of primitive life forms that failed to make the grade.

Already it is a delightful place, better in many ways for a few days R&R than is most of Terra. In the second place, while it has an awful lot of civilians, more than a million, as civilians go they aren't bad. They know there is a war on. Fully half of them are employed either at the Base or in war industry; the rest raise food and sell it to the Fleet. You might say they have a vested interest in war, but, whatever their reasons, they respect the uniform and don't resent the wearers thereof. Quite the contrary. If an M.I. walks into a shop there, the proprietor calls him "Sir," and really seems to mean it, even while he's trying to sell something worthless at too high a price.

But in the *first* place, half of those civilians are female.

You have to have been out on a long patrol to appreciate this properly. You need to have looked forward to your day of guard duty, for the privilege of standing two hours out of each six with your spine against bulkhead thirty and your ears cocked for just the *sound* of a female voice. I suppose it's actually easier in the all-stag ships . . . but I'll take the *Rodger Young*. It's good to know that the ultimate reason you are fighting actually exists and that they are not just a figment of the imagination.

Besides the civilian wonderful 50 per cent, about 40 per cent of the Federal Service people on Sanctuary are female. Add it all up and you've got the most beautiful scenery in the explored universe.

Besides these unsurpassed natural advantages, a great deal has been done artificially to keep R&R from being wasted. Most of the civilians seem to hold two jobs; they've got circles under their eyes from staying up all night to make a service man's leave pleasant. Churchill Road from the Base to the city is lined both sides with enterprises intended to separate painlessly a man from money he really hasn't any use for anyhow, to the pleasant accompaniment of refreshment, entertainment, and music.

If you are able to get past these traps, through having already been bled of all valuta, there are still other places in the city almost as satisfactory (I mean there are girls there, too) which are provided free by a grateful populace—much like the social center in Vancouver, these are, but even more welcome.

Sanctuary, and especially Espiritu Santo, the city, struck me as such an ideal place that I toyed with the notion of asking for my discharge there when my term was up—after all, I didn't really care whether my descendants (if any) twenty-five thousand years hence had long green tendrils like everybody else, or just the equipment I had been forced to get by with. That professor type from the Research Station couldn't frighten me with that no radiation scare talk; it seemed to me (from what I could see around me) that the human race had reached its ultimate peak anyhow.

No doubt a gentleman wart hog feels the same way about a lady wart hog—but, if so, both of us are very sincere.

There are other opportunities for recreation there, too. I remember with particular pleasure one evening when a table of Roughnecks got into a friendly discussion with a group of Navy men (not from the *Rodger Young*) seated at the next table. The debate was spirited, a bit noisy, and some Base police came in and broke it up with stun guns just as we were warming to our rebuttal. Nothing came of it, except that we had to pay for the furniture—the Base Commandant takes the position that a man on R&R should be allowed a little freedom as long as he doesn't pick one of the "thirty-one crash landings."

The accommodation barracks are all right, too—not fancy, but comfortable and the chow line works twenty-five hours a day with civilians doing all the work. No reveille, no taps, you're actually on leave and you don't have to go to the barracks at all. I did, however, as it seemed downright preposterous to spend money on hotels when there was a clean, soft sack free and so many better ways to spend accumulated pay. That extra hour in each day was nice, too, as it meant nine hours solid and the day still untouched—I caught up sack time clear back to Operation Bughouse.

It might as well have been a hotel; Ace and I had a room all to ourselves in visiting non-com quarters. One morning, when R&R was regrettably drawing to a close, I was just turning over about local noon when Ace shook my bed. "On the bounce, soldier! The Bugs are attacking."

I told him what to do with the Bugs.

"Let's hit dirt," he persisted.

"No dinero." I had had a date the night before with a chemist (female, of course, and charmingly so) from the Research Station. She had known Carl on Pluto and Carl had written to me to look her up if I ever got to Sanctuary. She was a slender redhead, with expensive tastes. Apparently Carl had intimated to her that I had more money than was good for me, for she decided that the night before was just the time for her to get acquainted with the local champagne. I didn't let Carl down by admitting that all I had was a trooper's honorarium; I bought it for her while I drank what they said was (but wasn't) fresh pineapple squash. The result was that I had to walk home, afterwards—the cabs aren't free. Still, it had been worth it. After all, what is money?—I'm speaking of Bug money, of course.

"No ache," Ace answered. "I can juice you—I got lucky last night. Ran into a Navy file who didn't know percentages."

So I got up and shaved and showered and we hit the chow line for half a dozen shell eggs and sundries such as potatoes and ham and hot cakes and so forth and then we hit dirt to get something to eat. The walk up Churchill Road was hot and Ace decided to stop in a cantina. I went along to see if their pineapple squash was real. It wasn't, but it was cold. You can't have everything.

We talked about this and that and Ace ordered another round. I tried their strawberry squash—same deal. Ace stared into his glass, then said, "Ever thought about greasing for officer?"

I said, "*Huh?* Are you crazy?"

"Nope. Look, Johnnie, this war may run on quite a piece. No matter what propaganda they put out for the folks at home, you and I know that the Bugs aren't ready to quit. So why don't you plan ahead? As the man says, if you've got to play in the band, it's better to wave the stick than to carry the big drum."

I was startled by the turn the talk had taken, especially from Ace. "How about you? Are you planning to buck for a commission?"

"Me?" he answered. "Check your circuits, son—you're getting wrong answers. I've got no education and I'm ten years older than you are. But you've got enough education to hit the selection exams for O.C.S. *and* you've got the I.Q. they like. I guarantee that if you go career, you'll make sergeant before I do . . . and get picked for O.C.S. the day after."

"Now I know you're crazy!"

"You listen to your pop. I hate to tell you this, but you are just stupid and eager and sincere enough to make the kind of officer that men love to follow into some silly predicament. But me—well, I'm a natural non-com, with the proper pessimistic attitude to offset the enthusiasm of the likes of you. Someday I'll make sergeant . . . and presently I'll have my twenty years in and retire and get one of the reserved jobs—cop, maybe—and marry a nice fat wife with the same low tastes I have, and I'll follow the sports and fish and go pleasantly to pieces."

Ace stopped to wet his whistle. "But *you*," he went on. "You'll stay in and probably make high rank and die gloriously and I'll read about it and say proudly, 'I knew him when. Why, I used to lend him money—we were corporals together.' Well?"

"I've never thought about it," I said slowly. "I just meant to serve my term."

He grinned sourly. "Do you see any term enrollees being paid off today? You expect to make it on two years?"

He had a point. As long as the war continued, a "term" didn't end—at least not for cap troopers. It was mostly a difference in attitude, at least for the present. Those of us on "term" could at least feel like short-timers; we could talk about: "When this flea-bitten war is over." A career man didn't say that; he wasn't going anywhere, short of retirement—or buying it.

On the other hand, neither were we. But if you went "career" and then didn't finish twenty . . . well, they could be pretty sticky about your franchise even though they wouldn't keep a man who didn't want to stay.

"Maybe not a two-year term," I admitted. "But the war won't last forever."

"It won't?"

"How can it?"

"Blessed if I know. They don't tell me these things. But I know that's not what is troubling you, Johnnie. You got a girl waiting?"

"No. Well, I had," I answered slowly, "but she 'Dear-Johnned' me." As a lie, this was no more than a mild decoration, which I tucked in because Ace seemed to expect it. Carmen wasn't my girl and she never waited for anybody—but she *did* address letters with "Dear Johnnie" on the infrequent occasions when she wrote to me.

Ace nodded wisely. "They'll do it every time. They'd rather marry civilians and have somebody around to chew out when they feel like it. Never you mind, son—you'll find plenty of them more than willing to marry when you're retired . . . and you'll be better able to handle one at that age. Marriage is a young man's disaster and an old man's comfort." He looked at my glass. "It nauseates me to see you drinking that slop."

"I feel the same way about the stuff you drink," I told him.

He shrugged. "As I say, it takes all kinds. You think it over."

"I will."

Ace got into a card game shortly after, and lent me some money and I went for a walk; I needed to think.

Go career? Quite aside from that noise about a commission, did I want to go career? Why, I had gone through all this to get my franchise, hadn't I?—and if I went career, I was just as far away from the privilege of voting as if I had never enrolled . . . because as long as you were still in uniform you weren't entitled to vote. Which was the way it should be, of course—why, if they let the Roughnecks vote the idiots might vote not to make a drop. Can't have that.

Nevertheless I had signed up in order to win a vote.

Or had I?

Had I ever cared about voting? No, it was the prestige, the pride, the status . . . of being a citizen.

Or was it?

I couldn't to save my life remember *why* I had signed up.

Anyhow, it wasn't the process of voting that made a citizen— the Lieutenant had been a citizen in the truest sense of the word, even though he had not lived long enough ever to cast a ballot. He had "voted" every time he made a drop.

And so had I!

I could hear Colonel Dubois in my mind: "Citizenship is an attitude, a state of mind, an emotional conviction that the whole is greater than the part . . . and that the part should be humbly proud to sacrifice itself that the whole may live."

I still didn't know whether I yearned to place my one-and-only body "between my loved home and the war's desolation"—I still got the shakes every drop and that "desolation" could be pretty desolate. But nevertheless I knew at last what Colonel Dubois had been talking about. The M.I. was mine and I was theirs. If that was what the M.I. did to break the monotony, then that was what I did. Patriotism was a bit esoteric for me, too large-scale to see. But the M.I. was my gang, I belonged. They were all the family I had left; they were the brothers I had never had, closer than Carl had ever been. If I left them, I'd be lost.

So why shouldn't I go career?

All right, all right—but how about this nonsense of greasing for a commission? That was something else again. I could see myself putting in twenty years and then taking it easy, the way Ace had described, with ribbons on my chest and carpet slippers on my feet . . . or evenings down at the Veterans Hall, rehashing old times with others who belonged. But O.C.S.? I could hear Al Jenkins, in one of the bull sessions we had about such things: "I'm a private! I'm going to stay a private! When you're a private they don't expect anything of you. Who wants to be an officer? Or even a sergeant? You're breathing the same air, aren't you? Eating the same food. Going the same places, making the same drops. But no worries."

Al had a point. What had chevrons ever gotten me?—aside from lumps.

Nevertheless I knew I would take sergeant if it was ever offered to me. You don't refuse, a cap trooper doesn't refuse anything; he steps up and takes a swing at it. Commission, too, I supposed.

Not that it would happen. Who was I to think that I could ever be what Lieutenant Rasczak had been?

My walk had taken me close to the candidates' school, though I don't believe I intended to come that way. A company of cadets were out on their parade ground, drilling at trot, looking for all the world like boots in Basic. The sun was hot and it looked not nearly as comfortable as a bull session in the drop room of the *Rodger Young*—why, I hadn't marched farther than bulkhead thirty since I had finished Basic; that breaking-in nonsense was past.

I watched them a bit, sweating through their uniforms; I heard them being chewed out—by sergeants, too. Old Home Week. I shook my head and walked away from there—

—went back to the accommodation barracks, over to the B.O.Q. wing, found Jelly's room.

He was in it, his feet up on a table and reading a magazine. I knocked on the frame of the door. He looked up and growled, "Yeah?"

"Sarge—I mean, Lieutenant—"

"Spit it out!"

"Sir, I want to go career."

He dropped his feet to the desk. "Put up your right hand."

He swore me, reached into the drawer of the table and pulled out papers.

He had my papers already made out, waiting for me ready to sign. And I hadn't even told Ace. How about that?

Chapter 12

The *Rodger Young* was again returning to Base for replacements, both capsules and men. Al Jenkins had bought his farm, covering a pickup—and that one had cost us the Padre, too. And besides that, I had to be replaced. I was wearing brand-new sergeant's chevrons (vice Migliaccio) but I had a hunch that Ace would be wearing them as soon as I was out of the ship—they were mostly honorary, I knew; the promotion was Jelly's way of giving me a good send-off as I was detached for O.C.S.

But it didn't keep me from being proud of them. At the Fleet landing field I went through the exit gate with my nose in the air and strode up to the quarantine desk to have my orders stamped. As this was being done I heard a polite, respectful voice behind me: "Excuse me, Sergeant, but that boat that just came down—is it from the *Rodger*—"

I turned to see the speaker, flicked my eyes over his sleeves, saw that it was a small, slightly stoop-shouldered corporal, no doubt one of our—

"Father!"

Then the corporal had his arms around me. "Juan! Juan! Oh, my little Johnnie!"

I kissed him and hugged him and started to cry. Maybe that civilian clerk at the quarantine desk had never seen two non-coms kiss each other before. Well, if I had noticed him so much as lifting an eyebrow, I would have pasted him. But I didn't notice him; I was busy. He had to remind me to take my orders with me.

By then we had blown our noses and quit making an open spectacle of ourselves. I said, "Father, let's find a corner somewhere and sit down and talk. I want to know . . . well, *everything!*" I took a deep breath. "I thought you were dead."

"No. Came close to buying it once or twice, maybe. But, Son . . . Sergeant—I really do have to find out about that landing boat. You see—"

"Oh, that. It's from the *Rodger Young*. I just—"

He looked terribly disappointed. "Then I've got to bounce, right now. I've got to report in." Then he added eagerly, "But you'll be back aboard soon, won't you, Juanito? Or are you going on R&R?"

"Uh, no." I thought fast. Of all the ways to have things roll! "Look, Father, I know the boat schedule. You can't go aboard for at least an hour and a bit. That boat is not on a fast retrieve; she'll make a minimum-fuel rendezvous when the *Rog* completes this pass—if the pilot doesn't have to wait over for the next pass after that; they've got to load first."

He said dubiously, "My orders read to report at once to the pilot of the first available ship's boat."

"Father, Father! Do you have to be so confounded regulation? The girl who's pushing that heap won't care whether you board the boat now, or just as they button up. Anyhow they'll play the ship's recall over the speakers in here ten minutes before boost and announce it. You *can't* miss it."

He let me lead him over to an empty corner. As we sat down he added, "Will you be going up in the same boat, Juan? Or later?"

"Uh—" I showed him my orders; it seemed the simplest way to break the news. Ships that pass in the night, like the Evangeline story—cripes, what a way for things to break!

He read them and got tears in his eyes and I said hastily, "Look, Father, I'm going to try to come back—I wouldn't want any other outfit than the Roughnecks. And with you in them . . . oh, I know it's disappointing but—"

"It's not disappointment, Juan."

"Huh?"

"It's pride. My boy is going to be an officer. My little Johnnie—Oh, it's disappointment, too; I had waited for this day. But I can wait a while longer." He smiled through his tears. "You've grown, lad. And filled out, too."

"Uh, I guess so. But, Father, I'm not an officer yet and I might only be out of the *Rog* a few days. I mean, they sometimes bust 'em out pretty fast and—"

"Enough of that, young man!"

"Huh?"

"You'll make it. Let's have no more talk of 'busting out.'" Suddenly he smiled. "That's the first time I've been able to tell a sergeant to shut up."

"Well . . . I'll certainly try, Father. And if I do make it, I'll certainly put in for the old *Rog*. But—" I trailed off.

"Yes, I know. Your request won't mean anything unless there's a billet for you. Never mind. If this hour is all we have, we'll make the most of it—and I'm so proud of you I'm splitting my seams. How have you been, Johnnie?"

"Oh, fine, just fine." I was thinking that it wasn't all bad. He would be better off in the Roughnecks than in any other outfit. All my friends . . . they'd take care of him, keep him alive. I'd have to send a gram to Ace—Father like as not wouldn't even let them know he was related. "Father, how long have you been in?"

"A little over a year."

"And corporal already!"

Father smiled grimly. "They're making them fast these days."

I didn't have to ask what he meant. Casualties. There were always vacancies in the T.O.; you couldn't get enough trained soldiers to fill them. Instead I said, "Uh . . . but, Father, you're—

Well, I mean, aren't you sort of old to be soldiering? I mean the Navy, or Logistics, or—"

"I wanted the M.I. and I got it!" he said emphatically. "And I'm no older than many sergeants—not as old, in fact. Son, the mere fact that I am twenty-two years older than you are doesn't put me in a wheel chair. And age has its advantages, too."

Well, there was something in that. I recalled how Sergeant Zim had always tried the older men first, when he was dealing out boot chevrons. And Father would never have goofed in Basic the way I had—no lashes for him. He was probably spotted as non-com material before he ever finished Basic. The Army needs a lot of really grown-up men in the middle grades; it's a paternalistic organization.

I didn't have to ask him why he had wanted M.I., nor why or how he had wound up in my ship—I just felt warm about it, more flattered by it than any praise he had ever given me in words. And I didn't want to ask him *why* he had joined up; I felt that I knew. Mother. Neither of us had mentioned her—too painful.

So I changed the subject abruptly. "Bring me up to date. Tell me where you've been and what you've done."

"Well, I trained at Camp San Martín—"

"Huh? Not Currie?"

"New one. But the same old lumps, I understand. Only they rush you through two months faster, you don't get Sundays off. Then I requested the *Rodger Young*—and didn't get it—and wound up in McSlattery's Volunteers. A good outfit."

"Yes, I know." They had had a reputation for being rough, tough, and nasty—almost as good as the Roughnecks.

"I should say that it *was* a good outfit. I made several drops with them and some of the boys bought it and after a while I got these." He glanced at his chevrons. "I was a corporal when we dropped on Sheol—"

"You were *there?* So was I!" With a sudden warm flood of emotion I felt closer to my father than I ever had before in my life.

"I know. At least I knew your outfit was there. I was about fifty miles north of you, near as I can guess. We soaked up that counter-attack when they came boiling up out of the ground like bats out of a cave." Father shrugged. "So when it was over I was a corporal without an outfit, not enough of us left to make a healthy cadre. So they sent me here. I could have gone with King's Kodiak Bears, but I had a word with the placement sergeant—and, sure as sunrise, the *Rodger Young* came back with a billet for a corporal. So here I am."

"And when did you join up?" I realized that it was the wrong remark as soon as I had made it—but I had to get the subject away from McSlattery's Volunteers; an orphan from a dead outfit wants to forget it.

Father said quietly, "Shortly after Buenos Aires."

"Oh. I see."

Father didn't say anything for several moments. Then he said softly, "I'm not sure that you do see, Son."

"Sir?"

"Mmm . . . it will not be easy to explain. Certainly, losing your mother had a great deal to do with it. But I didn't enroll to avenge her—even though I had that in mind, too. You had more to do with it—"

"Me?"

"Yes, you. Son, I always understood what you were doing better than your mother did—don't blame her; she never had a chance to know, any more than a bird can understand swimming. And perhaps I knew *why* you did it, even though I beg to doubt that you knew yourself, at the time. At least half of my anger at you was sheer resentment . . . that you had actually done something that I knew, buried deep in my heart, I should have done. But you weren't the cause of my joining up, either . . . you merely helped trigger it and you did control the service I chose."

He paused. "I wasn't in good shape at the time you enrolled. I was seeing my hypnotherapist pretty regularly—you never suspected that, did you?—but we had gotten no farther than a clear recognition that I was enormously dissatisfied. After you left, I took it out on you—but it was not you, and I knew it and my therapist knew it. I suppose I knew that there was real trouble brewing earlier than most; we were invited to bid on military components fully a month before the state of emergency was announced. We had converted almost entirely to war production while you were still in training.

"I felt better during that period, worked to death and too busy to see my therapist. Then I became more troubled than ever." He smiled. "Son, do you know about civilians?"

"Well . . . we don't talk the same language. I know that."

"Clearly enough put. Do you remember Madame Ruitman? I was on a few days leave after I finished Basic and I went home. I saw some of our friends, said good-by—she among them. She chattered away and said, 'So you're really going out? Well, if you reach Faraway, you really must look up my dear friends the Regatos.'

"I told her, as gently as I could, that it seemed unlikely, since the Arachnids had occupied Faraway.

"It didn't faze her in the least. She said, 'Oh, that's all right— they're civilians!' " Father smiled cynically.

"Yes, I know."

"But I'm getting ahead of my story. I told you that I was getting still more upset. Your mother's death released me for what I had to do . . . even though she and I were closer than most, nevertheless it set me free to do it. I turned the business over to Morales—"

"Old man Morales? Can *he* handle it?"

"Yes. Because he has to. A lot of us are doing things we didn't know we could. I gave him a nice chunk of stock—you know the old saying about the kine that tread the grain—and the rest I split two ways, in a trust: half to the Daughters of Charity, half to you whenever you want to go back and take it. If you do. Never mind. I had at last found out what was wrong with me." He stopped, then said very softly, "I had to perform an act of faith. I had to prove to myself that I was a man. Not just a producing-consuming economic animal . . . but a *man*."

At that moment, before I could answer anything, the wall speakers around us sang: *"—shines the name, shines the name of Rodger Young!"* and a girl's voice added, "Personnel for F.C.T. *Rodger Young*, stand to boat. Berth H. Nine minutes."

Father bounced to his feet, grabbed his kit roll. "That's mine! Take care of yourself, Son—and hit those exams. Or you'll find you're still not too big to paddle."

"I will, Father."

He embraced me hastily. "See you when we get back!" And he was gone, on the bounce.

In the Commandant's outer office I reported to a fleet sergeant who looked remarkably like Sergeant Ho, even to lacking an arm. However, he lacked Sergeant Ho's smile as well. I said, "Career Sergeant Juan Rico, to report to the Commandant pursuant to orders."

He glanced at the clock. "Your boat was down seventy-three minutes ago. Well?"

So I told him. He pulled his lip and looked at me meditatively. "I've heard every excuse in the book. But you've just added a new page. Your father, your own father, really was reporting to your old ship just as you were detached?"

"The bare truth, Sergeant. You can check it—Corporal Emilio Rico."

"We don't check the statements of the 'young gentlemen' around here. We simply cashier them if it ever turns out that they have not told the truth. Okay, a boy who wouldn't be late in order to see his old man off wouldn't be worth much in any case. Forget it."

"Thanks, Sergeant. Do I report to the Commandant now?"

"You've reported to him." He made a check mark on a list. "Maybe a month from now he'll send for you along with a couple of dozen others. Here's your room assignment, here's a checkoff list you start with—and you can start by cutting off those chevrons. But save them; you may need them later. But as of this moment you are 'Mister,' not 'Sergeant.' "

"Yes, sir."

"Don't call me 'sir.' *I* call *you* 'sir.' But you won't like it."

I am not going to describe Officer Candidates School. It's like Basic, but squared and cubed with books added. In the mornings we behaved like privates, doing the same old things we had done in Basic and in combat and being chewed out for the way we did them—by sergeants. In the afternoons we were cadets and "gentlemen," and recited on and were lectured concerning an endless list of subjects: math, science, galactography, xenology, hypnopedia, logistics, strategy and tactics, communications, military law, terrain reading, special weapons, psychology of leadership, anything from the care and feeding of privates to why Xerxes lost the big one. Most especially how to be a one-man catastrophe yourself while keeping track of fifty other men, nursing them, loving them, leading them, saving them—but *never* babying them.

We had beds, which we used all too little; we had rooms and showers and inside plumbing; and each four candidates had a civilian servant, to make our beds and clean our rooms and shine our shoes and lay out our uniforms and run errands. This service was not intended as a luxury and was not; its purpose was to give the student more time to accomplish the plainly impossible by relieving him of things any graduate of Basic can already do perfectly.

Six days shalt thou work and do all thou art able,
The seventh the same and pound on the cable.

Or the Army version ends:—*and clean out the stable*, which shows you how many centuries this sort of thing has been going on. I wish I could catch just one of those civilians who think we loaf and put them through one month of O.C.S.

In the evenings and all day Sundays we studied until our eyes burned and our ears ached—then slept (if we slept) with a hypnopedic speaker droning away under the pillow.

Our marching songs were appropriately downbeat: "No Army for mine, no Army for mine! I'd rather be behind the plow any old time!" and "Don't wanta study war no more," and "Don't make my boy a soldier, the weeping mother cried," and—favorite of all—the old classic "Gentlemen Rankers" with its chorus about the Little Lost Sheep: "—God ha' pity on such as we. Baa! Yah! Bah!"

Yet somehow I don't remember being unhappy. Too busy, I guess. There was never that psychological "hump" to get over, the one everybody hits in Basic; there was simply the ever-present fear of flunking out. My poor preparation in math bothered me especially. My roommate, a colonial from Hesperus with the oddly appropriate name of "Angel," sat up night after night, tutoring me.

Most of the instructors, especially the officers, were disabled. The only ones I can remember who had a full complement of arms, legs, eyesight, hearing, etc., were some of the non-commissioned combat instructors—and not all of those. Our coach in dirty fighting sat in a powered chair, wearing a plastic collar, and was completely paralyzed from the neck down. But his tongue wasn't paralyzed, his eye was photographic, and the savage way in which he could analyze and criticize what he had seen made up for his minor impediment.

At first I wondered why those obvious candidates for physical retirement and full-pay pension didn't take it and go home. Then I quit wondering.

I guess the high point in my whole cadet course was a visit from Ensign Ibañez, she of the dark eyes, junior watch officer and pilot-under-instruction of the Corvette Transport *Mannerheim*. Carmencita showed up, looking incredibly pert in Navy dress whites and about the size of a paperweight, while my class was lined up for evening meal muster—walked down the line and you could hear eyeballs click as she passed—walked straight up to the duty officer and asked for me by name in a clear, penetrating voice.

The duty officer, Captain Chandar, was widely believed never to have smiled at his own mother, but he smiled down at little Car-

men, straining his face out of shape, and admitted my existence . . . whereupon she waved her long black lashes at him, explained that her ship was about to boost and could she *please* take
me out to dinner?

And I found myself in possession of a highly irregular and totally unprecedented three-hour pass. It may be that the Navy has
developed hypnosis techniques that they have not yet gotten
around to passing on to the Army. Or her secret weapon may be
older than that and not usable by M.I. In any case I not only had a
wonderful time but my prestige with my classmates, none too high
until then, climbed to amazing heights.

It was a glorious evening and well worth flunking two classes
the next day. It was somewhat dimmed by the fact that we had
each heard about Carl—killed when the Bugs smashed our research station on Pluto—but only somewhat, as we had each
learned to live with such things.

One thing did startle me. Carmen relaxed and took off her hat
while we were eating, and her blue-black hair was all gone. I knew
that a lot of the Navy girls shaved their heads—after all, it's not
practical to take care of long hair in a war ship and, most especially, a pilot can't risk having her hair floating around, getting in
the way, in any free-fall maneuvers. Shucks, I shaved my own
scalp, just for convenience and cleanliness. But my mental picture
of little Carmen included this mane of thick, wavy hair.

But, do you know, once you get used to it, it's rather cute. I
mean, if a girl looks all right to start with, she still looks all right
with her head smooth. And it does serve to set a Navy girl apart
from civilian chicks—sort of a lodge pin, like the gold skulls for
combat drops. It made Carmen look distinguished, gave her dignity, and for the first time I fully realized that she really was an officer and a fighting man—as well as a very pretty girl.

I got back to barracks with stars in my eyes and whiffing
slightly of perfume. Carmen had kissed me good-by.

The only O.C.S. classroom course the content of which I'm even
going to mention was: History and Moral Philosophy.

I was surprised to find it in the curriculum. H. & M. P. has
nothing to do with combat and how to lead a platoon; its connection with war (where it is connected) is in *why* to fight—a matter
already settled for any candidate long before he reaches O.C.S. An
M.I. fights because he is M.I.

I decided that the course must be a repeat for the benefit of those of us (maybe a third) who had never had it in school. Over 20 per cent of my cadet class were not from Terra (a much higher percentage of colonials sign up to serve than do people born on Earth—sometimes it makes you wonder) and of the three-quarters or so from Terra, some were from associated territories and other places where H. & M.P. might not be taught. So I figured it for a cinch course which would give me a little rest from tough courses, the ones with decimal points.

Wrong again. Unlike my high school course, you had to pass it. Not by examination, however. The course included examinations and prepared papers and quizzes and such—but no marks. What you had to have was the instructor's opinion that you were worthy of commission.

If he gave you a downcheck, a board sat on you, questioning not merely whether you could be an officer but whether you belonged in the Army at *any* rank, no matter how fast you might be with weapons—deciding whether to give you extra instruction . . . or just kick you out and let you be a civilian.

History and Moral Philosophy works like a delayed-action bomb. You wake up in the middle of the night and think: Now what did he mean by *that?* That had been true even with my high school course; I simply hadn't known what Colonel Dubois was talking about. When I was a kid I thought it was silly for the course to be in the science department. It was nothing like physics or chemistry; why wasn't it over in the fuzzy studies where it belonged? The only reason I paid attention was because there were such lovely arguments.

I had no idea that "Mr." Dubois was trying to teach me *why* to fight until long after I had decided to fight anyhow.

Well, why *should* I fight? Wasn't it preposterous to expose my tender skin to the violence of unfriendly strangers? Especially as the pay at any rank was barely spending money, the hours terrible, and the working conditions worse? When I could be sitting at home while such matters were handled by thick-skulled characters who *enjoyed* such games? Particularly when the strangers against whom I fought never had done anything to me personally until I showed up and started kicking over their tea wagon—what sort of nonsense *is* this?

Fight because I'm an M.I.? Brother, you're drooling like Dr. Pavlov's dogs. Cut it out and start thinking.

Major Reid, our instructor, was a blind man with a disconcerting habit of looking straight at you and calling you by name. We were reviewing events after the war between the Russo-Anglo-American Alliance and the Chinese Hegemony, 1987 and following. But this was the day that we heard the news of the destruction of San Francisco and the San Joaquin Valley; I thought he would give us a pep talk. After all, even a civilian ought to be able to figure it out now—the Bugs or us. Fight or die.

Major Reid didn't mention San Francisco. He had one of us apes summarize the negotiated treaty of New Delhi, discuss how it ignored prisoners of war . . . and, by implication, dropped the subject forever; the armistice became a stalemate and prisoners stayed where they were—on one side; on the other side they were turned loose and, during the Disorders, made their way home—or not if they didn't want to.

Major Reid's victim summed up the unreleased prisoners: survivors of two divisions of British paratroopers, some thousands of civilians, captured mostly in Japan, the Philippines, and Russia and sentenced for "political" crimes.

"Besides that, there were many other military prisoners," Major Reid's victim went on, "captured during and before the war—there were rumors that some had been captured in an earlier war and never released. The total of unreleased prisoners was never known. The best estimates place the number around sixty-five thousand."

"Why the 'best'?"

"Uh, that's the estimate in the textbook, sir."

"Please be precise in your language. Was the number greater or less than one hundred thousand?"

"Uh, I don't know, sir."

"And nobody else knows. Was it greater than one thousand?"

"Probably, sir. Almost certainly."

"Utterly certain—because more than that eventually escaped, found their ways home, were tallied by name. I see you did not read your lesson carefully. *Mr. Rico!*"

Now I am the victim. "Yes, sir."

"Are a thousand unreleased prisoners sufficient reason to start or resume a war? Bear in mind that millions of innocent people may die, almost certainly *will* die, if war is started or resumed."

I didn't hesitate. "Yes, *sir!* More than enough reason."

" 'More than enough.' Very well, is *one* prisoner, unreleased by the enemy, enough reason to start or resume a war?"

I hesitated. I knew the M.I. answer—but I didn't think that was the one he wanted. He said sharply, "Come, come, Mister! We have an upper limit of one thousand; I invited you to consider a lower limit of one. But you can't pay a promissory note which reads 'somewhere between one and one thousand pounds'—and starting a war is *much* more serious than paying a trifle of money. Wouldn't it be criminal to endanger a country—two countries in fact—to save one man? Especially as he may not deserve it? Or may die in the meantime? Thousands of people get killed every day in accidents . . . so why hesitate over one man? Answer! Answer yes, or answer no—you're holding up the class."

He got my goat. I gave him the cap trooper's answer. "Yes, sir!"

" 'Yes' what?"

"It doesn't matter whether it's a thousand—or just one, sir. You fight."

"Aha! The number of prisoners is irrelevant. Good. Now prove your answer."

I was stuck. I *knew* it was the right answer. But I didn't know why. He kept hounding me. "Speak up, Mr. Rico. This is an exact science. You have made a mathematical statement; you must give proof. Someone may claim that you have asserted, by analogy, that one potato is worth the same price, no more, no less, as one thousand potatoes. No?"

"No, sir!"

"Why not? Prove it."

"Men are not potatoes."

"Good, good, Mr. Rico! I think we have strained your tired brain enough for one day. Bring to class tomorrow a written proof, in symbolic logic, of your answer to my original question. I'll give you a hint. See reference seven in today's chapter. Mr. Salomon! How did the present political organization evolve out of the Disorders? And what is its moral justification?"

Sally stumbled through the first part. However, nobody can describe accurately how the Federation came about; it just grew. With national governments in collapse at the end of the XXth century, something had to fill the vacuum, and in many cases it was returned veterans. They had lost a war, most of them had no jobs, many were sore as could be over the terms of the Treaty of New Delhi, especially the P.O.W. foul-up—and they knew how to fight. But it wasn't revolution; it was more like what happened in Russia in 1917—the system collapsed; somebody else moved in.

The first known case, in Aberdeen, Scotland, was typical. Some veterans got together as vigilantes to stop rioting and loot-

ing, hanged a few people (including two veterans) and decided not
to let anyone but veterans on their committee. Just arbitrary at
first—they trusted each other a bit, they didn't trust anyone else.
What started as an emergency measure became constitutional
practice . . . in a generation or two.

Probably those Scottish veterans, since they were finding it
necessary to hang some veterans, decided that, if they had to do
this, they weren't going to let any "bleedin', profiteering, black-
market, doubletime-for-overtime, army-dodging, unprintable"
civilians have any say about it. They'd do what they were told,
see?—while us apes straightened things out! That's my guess, because I might feel the same way . . . and historians agree that an-
tagonism between civilians and returned soldiers was more
intense than we can imagine today.

Sally didn't tell it by the book. Finally Major Reid cut him off.
"Bring a summary to class tomorrow, three thousand words. Mr.
Salomon, can you give me a reason—not historical nor theoretical
but practical—why the franchise is today limited to discharged
veterans?"

"Uh, because they are picked men, sir. Smarter."

"Preposterous!"

"Sir?"

"Is the word too long for you? I said it was a silly notion. Service men are not brighter than civilians. In many cases civilians
are much more intelligent. That was the sliver of justification un-
derlying the attempted *coup d'état* just before the Treaty of New
Delhi, the so-called 'Revolt of the Scientists': let the intelligent
elite run things and you'll have utopia. It fell flat on its foolish face
of course. Because the pursuit of science, despite its social bene-
fits, is itself not a social virtue; its practitioners can be men so
self-centered as to be lacking in social responsibility. I've given
you a hint, Mister; can you pick it up?"

Sally answered, "Uh, service men are disciplined, sir."

Major Reid was gentle with him. "Sorry. An appealing theory
not backed up by facts. You and I are not permitted to vote as long
as we remain in the Service, nor is it verifiable that military discipline makes a man self-disciplined once he is out; the crime rate
of veterans is much like that of civilians. And you have forgotten
that in peacetime most veterans come from non-combatant auxiliary services and have not been subjected to the full rigors of military discipline; they have merely been harried, overworked, and
endangered—yet their votes count."

Major Reid smiled. "Mr. Salomon, I handed you a trick question. The practical reason for continuing our system is the same as the practical reason for continuing anything: It works satisfactorily.

"Nevertheless, it is instructive to observe the details. Throughout history men have labored to place the sovereign franchise in hands that would guard it well and use it wisely, for the benefit of all. An early attempt was absolute monarchy, passionately defended as the 'divine right of kings.'

"Sometimes attempts were made to select a wise monarch, rather than leave it up to God, as when the Swedes picked a Frenchman, General Bernadotte, to rule them. The objection to this is that the supply of Bernadottes is limited.

"Historic examples ranged from absolute monarch to utter anarch; mankind has tried thousands of ways and many more have been proposed, some weird in the extreme such as the antlike communism urged by Plato under the misleading title *The Republic*. But the intent has always been moralistic: to provide stable and benevolent government.

"All systems seek to achieve this by limiting franchise to those who are *believed* to have the wisdom to use it justly. I repeat '*all* systems'; even the so-called 'unlimited democracies' excluded from franchise not less than one quarter of their populations by age, birth, poll tax, criminal record, or other."

Major Reid smiled cynically. "I have never been able to see how a thirty-year-old moron can vote more wisely than a fifteen-year-old genius . . . but that was the age of the 'divine right of the common man.' Never mind, they paid for their folly.

"The sovereign franchise has been bestowed by all sorts of rules—place of birth, family of birth, race, sex, property, education, age, religion, et cetera. All these systems worked and none of them well. All were regarded as tyrannical by many, all eventually collapsed or were overthrown.

"Now here are we with still another system . . . and our system works quite well. Many complain but none rebel; personal freedom for all is greatest in history, laws are few, taxes are low, living standards are as high as productivity permits, crime is at its lowest ebb. Why? Not because our voters are smarter than other people; we've disposed of that argument. Mr. Tammany—can you tell us why our system works better than any used by our ancestors?"

I don't know where Clyde Tammany got his name; I'd take

him for a Hindu. He answered, "Uh, I'd venture to guess that it's because the electors are a small group who know that the decisions are up to them . . . so they study the issues."

"No guessing, please; this is exact science. And your guess is wrong. The ruling nobles of many another system were a small group fully aware of their grave power. Furthermore, our franchised citizens are not everywhere a small fraction; you know or should know that the percentage of citizens among adults ranges from over eighty per cent on Iskander to less than three per cent in some Terran nations—yet government is much the same everywhere. Nor are the voters picked men; they bring no special wisdom, talent, or training to their sovereign tasks. So what difference is there between our voters and wielders of franchise in the past? We have had enough guesses; I'll state the obvious: Under our system every voter and officeholder is a man who has demonstrated through voluntary and difficult service that he places the welfare of the group ahead of personal advantage.

"And that is the one practical difference.

"He may fail in wisdom, he may lapse in civic virtue. But his average performance is enormously better than that of any other class of rulers in history."

Major Reid paused to touch the face of an old-fashioned watch, "reading" its hands. "The period is almost over and we have yet to determine the moral reason for our success in governing ourselves. Now continued success is *never* a matter of chance. Bear in mind that this is science, not wishful thinking; the universe is what it *is*, not what we want it to be. To vote is to wield authority; it is the supreme authority from which all other authority derives—such as mine to make your lives miserable once a day. *Force*, if you will!—the franchise is force, naked and raw, the Power of the Rods and the Ax. Whether it is exerted by ten men or by ten billion, political authority is *force*.

"But this universe consists of paired dualities. What is the converse of authority? Mr. Rico."

He had picked one I could answer. "Responsibility, sir."

"Applause. Both for practical reasons and for mathematically verifiable moral reasons, authority and responsibility must be equal—else a balancing takes place as surely as current flows between points of unequal potential. To permit irresponsible authority is to sow disaster; to hold a man responsible for anything he does not control is to behave with blind idiocy. The unlimited democracies were unstable because their citizens were not responsible for the fashion in which they exerted their sovereign authority . . . other than through the tragic logic of history. The unique 'poll tax' that we must pay was unheard of. No attempt was made to determine whether a voter was socially responsible to the extent of his literally unlimited authority. If he voted the impossible, the disastrous possible happened instead—and responsibility was then forced on him willy-nilly and destroyed both him and his foundationless temple.

"Superficially, our system is only slightly different; we have democracy unlimited by race, color, creed, birth, wealth, sex, or conviction, and anyone may win sovereign power by a usually short and not too arduous term of service—nothing more than a light workout to our cave-man ancestors. But that slight difference is one between a system that works, since it is constructed to match the facts, and one that is inherently unstable. Since sovereign franchise is the ultimate in human authority, we insure that all who wield it accept the ultimate in social responsibility—we require each person who wishes to exert control over the state to wager his own life—and lose it, if need be—to save the life of the state. The maximum responsibility a human can accept is thus equated to the ultimate authority a human can exert. Yin and yang, perfect and equal."

The Major added, "Can anyone define why there has never been revolution against our system? Despite the fact that every government in history has had such? Despite the notorious fact that complaints are loud and unceasing?"

One of the older cadets took a crack at it. "Sir, revolution is impossible."

"Yes. But why?"

"Because revolution—armed uprising—requires not only dissatisfaction but aggressiveness. A revolutionist has to be willing to fight and die—or he's just a parlor pink. If you separate out the aggressive ones and make them the sheep dogs, the sheep will never give you trouble."

"Nicely put! Analogy is always suspect, but that one is close to the facts. Bring me a mathematical proof tomorrow. Time for one more question—you ask it and I'll answer. Anyone?"

"Uh, sir, why not go—well, go the limit? Require everyone to serve and let everybody vote?"

"Young man, can you restore my eyesight?"

"Sir? Why, no, sir!"

"You would find it much easier than to instill moral virtue—social responsibility—into a person who doesn't have it, doesn't want it, and resents having the burden thrust on him. This is why we make it so hard to enroll, so easy to resign. Social responsibility above the level of family, or at most of tribe, requires imagination—devotion, loyalty, all the higher virtues—which a man must develop himself; if he has them forced down him, he will vomit them out. Conscript armies have been tried in the past. Look up in the library the psychiatric report on brainwashed prisoners in the so-called 'Korean War,' circa 1950—the Mayor Report. Bring an analysis to class." He touched his watch. "Dismissed."

Major Reid gave us a busy time.

But it was interesting. I caught one of those master's-thesis assignments he chucked around so casually; I had suggested that the Crusades were different from most wars. I got sawed off and handed this: *Required*: to prove that war and moral perfection derive from the same genetic inheritance. Briefly, thus: All wars arise from population pressure. (Yes, even the Crusades, though you have to dig into trade routes and birth rate and several other things to prove it.) Morals—*all* correct moral rules—derive from the instinct to survive; moral behavior is survival behavior above the individual level—as in a father who dies to save his children. But since population pressure results from the process of surviving through others, then war, because it results from population pressure, derives from the same inherited instinct which produces all moral rules suitable for human beings.

Check of proof: Is it possible to abolish war by relieving population pressure (and thus do away with the all-too-evident evils of war) through constructing a moral code under which population is limited to resources?

Without debating the usefulness or morality of planned parenthood, it may be verified by observation that any breed which stops its own increase gets crowded out by breeds which expand. Some human populations did so, in Terran history, and other breeds moved in and engulfed them.

Nevertheless, let's assume that the human race manages to balance birth and death, just right to fit its own planets, and thereby becomes peaceful. What happens?

Soon (about next Wednesday) the Bugs move in, kill off this breed which "ain'ta gonna study war no more" and the universe forgets us. Which still may happen. Either we spread and wipe out the Bugs, or they spread and wipe us out—because both races are tough and smart and want the same real estate.

Do you know how fast population pressure could cause us to fill the entire universe shoulder to shoulder? The answer will astound you, just the flicker of an eye in terms of the age of our race.

Try it—it's a compound-interest expansion.

But does Man have any "right" to spread through the universe?

Man is what he is, a wild animal with the will to survive, and (so far) the ability, against all competition. Unless one accepts that, anything one says about morals, war, politics—you name it—is nonsense. Correct morals arise from knowing what Man *is*—not what do-gooders and well-meaning old Aunt Nellies would like him to be.

The universe will let us know—later—whether or not Man has any "right" to expand through it.

In the meantime the M.I. will be in there, on the bounce and swinging, on the side of our own race.

Toward the end each of us was shipped out to serve under an experienced combat commander. This was a semifinal examination, your 'board-ship instructor could decide that you didn't have what it takes. You could demand a board but I never heard of anybody who did; they either came back with an upcheck—or we never saw them again.

Some hadn't failed; it was just that they were killed—because assignments were to ships about to go into action. We were required to keep kit bags packed—once at lunch, all the cadet officers of my company were tapped; they left without eating and I found myself cadet company commander.

Like boot chevrons, this is an uncomfortable honor, but in less than two days my own call came.

I bounced down to the Commandant's office, kit bag over my shoulder and feeling grand. I was sick of late hours and burning eyes and never catching up, of looking stupid in class; a few weeks in the cheerful company of a combat team was just what Johnnie needed!

I passed some new cadets, trotting to class in close formation, each with the grim look that every O.C.S. candidate gets when he realizes that possibly he made a mistake in bucking for officer, and I found myself singing. I shut up when I was within earshot of the office.

Two others were there, Cadets Hassan and Byrd. Hassan the Assassin was the oldest man in our class and looked like something a fisherman had let out of a bottle, while Birdie wasn't much bigger than a sparrow and about as intimidating.

We were ushered into the Holy of Holies. The Commandant was in his wheel chair—we never saw him out of it except Saturday inspection and parade, I guess walking hurt. But that didn't mean you didn't see him—you could be working a prob at the board, turn around and find that wheel chair behind you, and Colonel Nielssen reading your mistakes.

He never interrupted—there was a standing order not to shout "Attention!" But it's disconcerting. There seemed to be about six of him.

The Commandant had a permanent rank of fleet general (yes, *that* Nielssen); his rank as colonel was temporary, pending second retirement, to permit him to be Commandant. I once questioned a paymaster about this and confirmed what the regulations seemed to say: The Commandant got only the pay of a colonel—but would revert to the pay of a fleet general on the day he decided to retire again.

Well, as Ace says, it takes all sorts—I can't imagine choosing half pay for the privilege of riding herd on cadets.

Colonel Nielssen looked up and said, "Morning, gentlemen. Make yourselves comfortable." I sat down but wasn't comfortable. He glided over to a coffee machine, drew four cups, and Hassan helped him deal them out. I didn't want coffee but a cadet doesn't refuse the Commandant's hospitality.

He took a sip. "I have your orders, gentlemen," he announced, "and your temporary commissions." He went on, "But I want to be sure you understand your status.

We had already been lectured about this. We were going to be officers just enough for instruction and testing—"supernumerary, probationary, and temporary." Very junior, quite superfluous, on good behavior, and extremely temporary; we would revert to cadet when we got back and could be busted at any time by the officers examining us.

We would be "temporary third lieutenants"—a rank as necessary as feet on a fish, wedged into the hairline between fleet sergeants and real officers. It is as low as you can get and still be called an "officer." If anybody ever saluted a third lieutenant, the light must have been bad.

"Your commission reads 'third lieutenant,'" he went on, "but your pay stays the same, you continue to be addressed as 'Mister,' the only change in uniform is a shoulder pip even smaller than cadet insignia. You continue under instruction since it has not yet been settled that you are fit to be officers." The Colonel smiled. "So why call you a 'third lieutenant'?"

I had wondered about that. Why this whoopty-do of "commissions" that weren't real commissions?

Of course I knew the textbook answer.

"Mr. Byrd?" the Commandant said.

"Uh . . . to place us in the line of command, sir."

"Exactly!" Colonel glided to a T.O. on one wall. It was the usual pyramid, with chain of command defined all the way down. "Look at this—" He pointed to a box connected to his own by a horizontal line; it read: ASSISTANT TO COMMANDANT (Miss Kendrick).

"Gentlemen," he went on, "I would have trouble running this place without Miss Kendrick. Her head is a rapid-access file to everything that happens around here." He touched a control on his chair and spoke to the air. "Miss Kendrick, what mark did Cadet Byrd receive in military law last term?"

Her answer came back at once: "Ninety-three per cent, Commandant."

"Thank you." He continued, "You see? I sign anything if Miss Kendrick has initialed it. I would hate to have an investigating committee find out how often she signs my name and I don't even see it. Tell me, Mr. Byrd . . . if I drop dead, does Miss Kendrick carry on to keep things moving?"

"Why, uh—" Birdie looked puzzled. "I suppose, with routine matters, she would do what was necess—"

"She wouldn't do a blessed thing!" the Colonel thundered. "Until Colonel Chauncey *told* her what to do—*his* way. She is a very smart woman and understands what you apparently do not, namely, that she is *not* in the line of command and has no authority."

He went on, " 'Line of command' isn't just a phrase; it's as real as a slap in the face. If I ordered you to combat *as a cadet* the most you could do would be to pass along somebody else's orders. If your platoon leader bought out and you then gave an order to a private—a good order, sensible and wise—you would be wrong and he would be just as wrong if he obeyed it. Because a cadet cannot be in the line of command. A cadet has no military existence, no rank, and is not a soldier. He is a student who will become a soldier—either an officer, or at his former rank. While he is under Army discipline, he is not *in* the Army. That is why—"

A zero. A nought with no rim. If a cadet wasn't even in the Army—"Colonel!"

"Eh? Speak up, young man. Mr. Rico."

I had startled myself but I had to say it. "But . . . if we aren't in the Army . . . then we aren't M.I. Sir?"

He blinked at me. "This worries you?"

"I, uh, don't believe I like it much, sir." I didn't like it at all. I felt naked.

"I see." He didn't seem displeased. "You let me worry about the space-lawyer aspects of it, son."

"But—"

"That's an order. You are technically not an M.I. But the M.I. hasn't forgotten you; the M.I. *never* forgets its own no matter where they are. If you are struck dead this instant, you will be cremated as Second Lieutenant Juan Rico, Mobile Infantry, of—" Colonel Nielssen stopped. "Miss Kendrick, what was Mr. Rico's ship?"

"The *Rodger Young.*"

"Thank you." He added, "—in and of TFCT *Rodger Young,* assigned to mobile combat team Second Platoon of George Company, Third Regiment, First Division, M.I.—the 'Roughnecks,'" he recited with relish, not consulting anything once he had been reminded of my ship. "A good outfit, Mr. Rico—proud and nasty. Your Final Orders go back to them for Taps and that's the way your name would read in Memorial Hall. That's why we always commission a dead cadet, son—so we can send him home to his mates."

I felt a surge of relief and homesickness and missed a few words. ". . . lip buttoned while I talk, we'll have you back in the M.I. where you belong. You must be temporary officers for your 'prentice cruise because there is no room for deadheads in a combat drop. You'll fight—and take orders—and *give* orders. *Legal* orders, because you will hold rank and be ordered to serve in that team; that makes any order you give in carrying out your assigned duties as binding as one signed by the C-in-C.

"Even more," the Commandant went on, "once you are in line of command, you must be ready instantly to assume higher command. If you are in a one-platoon team—quite likely in the present state of the war—and you are assistant platoon leader when your platoon leader buys it . . . then . . . *you* . . . are. . . . *It!*"

He shook his head. "Not 'acting platoon leader.' Not a cadet leading a drill. Not a 'junior officer under instruction.' Suddenly

you are the Old Man, the Boss, Commanding Officer Present—
and you discover with a sickening shock that fellow human beings are depending on *you alone* to tell them what to do, how to
fight, how to complete the mission and get out alive. They wait
for the sure voice of command—while seconds trickle away—
and it's up to you to *be* that voice, make decisions, give the right
orders . . . and not only the right ones but in a calm, unworried
tone. Because it's a cinch, gentlemen, that your team is in
trouble—*bad* trouble!—and a strange voice with panic in it can
turn the best combat team in the Galaxy into a leaderless, lawless,
fear-crazed mob.

"The whole merciless load will land without warning. You
must act at once and you'll have only God over you. Don't expect
Him to fill in tactical details; that's *your* job. He'll be doing all
that a soldier has a right to expect if He helps you keep the panic
you are sure to feel out of your voice."

The Colonel paused. I was sobered and Birdie was looking
terribly serious and awfully young and Hassan was scowling. I
wished that I were back in the drop room of the *Rog*, with not too
many chevrons and an after-chow bull session in full swing.
There was a lot to be said for the job of assistant section leader—
when you come right to it, it's a lot easier to *die* than it is to use
your head.

The Commandant continued: "That's the Moment of Truth,
gentlemen. Regrettably there is no method known to military science to tell a real officer from a glib imitation with pips on his
shoulders, other than through ordeal by fire. Real ones come
through—or die gallantly; imitations crack up.

"Sometimes, in cracking up, the misfits die. But the tragedy
lies in the loss of others . . . good men, sergeants and corporals
and privates, whose only lack is fatal bad fortune in finding themselves under the command of an incompetent.

"We try to avoid this. First is our unbreakable rule that every
candidate must be a trained trooper, blooded under fire, a veteran
of combat drops. No other army in history has stuck to this rule,
although some came close. Most great military schools of the
past—Saint Cyr, West Point, Sandhurst, Colorado Springs—
didn't even pretend to follow it; they accepted civilian boys,
trained them, commissioned them, sent them out with no battle experience to command men . . . and sometimes discovered too late
that this smart young 'officer' was a fool, a poltroon, or a hysteric.

"At least we have no misfits of those sorts. We know you are good soldiers—brave and skilled, proved in battle—else you would not be here. We know that your intelligence and education meet acceptable minimums. With this to start on, we eliminate as many as possible of the not-quite-competent—get them quickly back in ranks before we spoil good cap troopers by forcing them beyond their abilities. The course is very hard—because what will be expected of you later is still harder.

"In time we have a small group whose chances look fairly good. The major criterion left untested is one we *cannot* test here; that undefinable something which is the difference between a leader in battle . . . and one who merely has the earmarks but not the vocation. So we field-test for it.

"Gentlemen!—you have reached that point. Are you ready to take the oath?"

There was an instant of silence, then Hassan the Assassin answered firmly, "Yes, Colonel," and Birdie and I echoed.

The Colonel frowned. "I have been telling you how wonderful you are—physically perfect, mentally alert, trained, disciplined, blooded. The very model of the smart young officer—" He snorted. "Nonsense! You *may* become officers someday. I hope so . . . we not only hate to waste money and time and effort, but also, and *much* more important, I shiver in my boots every time I send one of you half-baked not-quite-officers up to the Fleet, knowing what a Frankensteinian monster I may be turning loose on a good combat team. If you understood what you are up against, you wouldn't be so all-fired ready to take the oath the second the question is put to you. You may turn it down and force me to let you go back to your permanent ranks. But you *don't* know.

"So I'll try once more. Mr. Rico! Have you ever thought how it would feel to be court-martialed for losing a regiment?"

I was startled silly. "Why—No, sir, I never have." To be court-martialed—for *any* reason—is eight times as bad for an officer as for an enlisted man. Offenses which will get privates kicked out (maybe with lashes, possibly without) rate death in an officer. Better never to have been born!

"Think about it," he said grimly. "When I suggested that your platoon leader might be killed, I was by no means citing the ultimate in military disaster. Mr. Hassan! What is the largest number of command levels ever knocked out in a single battle?"

The Assassin scowled harder than ever. "I'm not sure, sir. Wasn't there a while during Operation Bughouse when a major commanded a brigade, before the Sove-ki-poo?"

"There was and his name was Fredericks. He got a decoration and a promotion. If you go back to the Second Global War, you can find a case in which a naval junior officer took command of a major ship and not only fought it but sent signals as if he were admiral. He was vindicated even though there were officers senior to him in line of command who were not even wounded. Special circumstances—a breakdown in communications. But I am thinking of a case in which four levels were wiped out in six minutes— as if a platoon leader were to blink his eyes and find himself commanding a brigade. Any of you heard of it?"

Dead silence.

"Very well. It was one of those bush wars that flared up on the edges of the Napoleonic wars. This young officer was the most junior in a naval vessel—wet navy, of course—wind-powered, in fact. This youngster was about the age of most of your class and was not commissioned. He carried the title of 'temporary third lieutenant'—note that this is the title you are about to carry. He had no combat experience; there were four officers in the chain of command above him. When the battle started his commanding officer was wounded. The kid picked him up and carried him out of the line of fire. That's all—make a pickup on a comrade. But he did it without being ordered to leave his post. The other officers all bought it while he was doing this and he was tried for 'deserting his post of duty as *commanding officer* in the presence of the enemy.' Convicted. Cashiered."

I gasped. "For *that?* Sir."

"Why not? True, we make pickup. But we do it under different circumstances from a wet-navy battle, and by orders to the man making pickup. But pickup is never an excuse for breaking off battle in the presence of the enemy. This boy's family tried for a century and a half to get his conviction reversed. No luck, of course. There was doubt about some circumstances but no doubt that he had left his post during battle without orders. True, he was green as grass—but he was lucky not to be hanged." Colonel Nielssen fixed me with a cold eye. "Mr. Rico—could this happen to *you?*"

I gulped. "I hope not, sir."

"Let me tell you how it could on this very 'prentice cruise. Suppose you are in a multiple-ship operation, with a full regiment in the drop. Officers drop first, of course. There are advantages to this and disadvantages, but we do it for reasons of morale; no trooper ever hits the ground on a hostile planet without an officer.

Assume the Bugs know this—and they may. Suppose they work up some trick to wipe out those who hit the ground first . . . but not good enough to wipe out the whole drop. Now suppose, since you are a supernumerary, you have to take any vacant capsule instead of being fired with the first wave. Where does that leave you?"

"Uh, I'm not sure, sir."

"You have just inherited command of a regiment. *What are you going to do with your command, Mister?* Talk fast—the Bugs won't wait!"

"Uh . . ." I caught an answer right out of the book and parroted it. "I'll take command and act as circumstances permit, sir, according to the tactical situation as I see it."

"You will, eh?" The Colonel grunted. "And you'll buy a farm too—that's all anybody can do with a foul-up like that. But I hope you'll go down swinging—and shouting orders to somebody, whether they make sense or not. We don't expect kittens to fight wildcats and win—we merely expect them to try. All right, stand up. Put up your right hands."

He struggled to his feet. Thirty seconds later we were officers—"temporary, probationary, and supernumerary."

I thought he would give us our shoulder pips and let us go. We aren't supposed to buy them—they're a loan, like the temporary commission they represent. Instead he lounged back and looked almost human.

"See here, lads—I gave you a talk on how rough it's going to be. I want you to worry about it, doing it in advance, planning what steps you might take against any combination of bad news that can come your way, keenly aware that your life belongs to your men and is not yours to throw away in a suicidal reach for glory . . . and that your life isn't yours to save, either, if the situation requires that you expend it. I want you to worry yourself sick *before* a drop, so that you can be unruffled when the trouble starts.

"Impossible, of course. Except for one thing. What is the *only* factor that can save you when the load is too heavy? Anyone?"

Nobody answered.

"Oh, come now!" Colonel Nielssen said scornfully. "You aren't recruits. Mr. Hassan!"

"Your leading sergeant, sir," the Assassin said slowly.

"Obviously. He's probably older than you are, more drops under his belt, and he certainly knows his team better than you do. Since he isn't carrying that dreadful, numbing load of top command, he may be thinking more clearly than you are. Ask his advice. You've got one circuit just for that.

"It won't decrease his confidence in you; he's used to being consulted. If you don't, he'll decide you are a fool, a cocksure know-it-all—and he'll be right.

"But you don't have to *take* his advice. Whether you use his ideas, or whether they spark some different plan—make your decision and snap out orders. The one thing—the *only* thing!—that can strike terror in the heart of a good platoon sergeant is to find that he's working for a boss who can't make up his mind.

"There never has been an outfit in which officers and men were more dependent on each other than they are in the M.I., and sergeants are the glue that holds us together. Never forget it."

The Commandant whipped his chair around to a cabinet near his desk. It contained row on row of pigeonholes, each with a little box. He pulled out one and opened it. "Mr. Hassan—"

"Sir?"

"These pips were worn by Captain Terrence O'Kelly on his 'prentice cruise. Does it suit you to wear them?"

"Sir?" The Assassin's voice squeaked and I thought the big lunk was going to break into tears. "Yes, sir!"

"Come here." Colonel Nielssen pinned them on, then said, "Wear them as gallantly as he did . . . but *bring them back*. Understand me?"

"Yes, sir. I'll do my best."

"I'm sure you will. There's an air car waiting on the roof and your boat boosts in twenty-eight minutes. Carry out your orders, sir!"

The Assassin saluted and left; the Commandant turned and picked out another box. "Mr. Byrd, are you superstitious?"

"No, sir."

"Really? I am, quite. I take it you would not object to wearing pips which have been worn by five officers, all of whom were killed in action?"

Birdie barely hesitated. "No, sir."

"Good. Because these five officers accumulated seventeen citations, from the Terran Medal to the Wounded Lion. Come here. The pip with the brown discoloration must always be worn on your left shoulder—and don't try to buff it off! Just try not to get the other one marked in the same fashion. Unless necessary, and you'll know when it is necessary. Here is a list of former wearers.

You have thirty minutes until your transportation leaves. Bounce up to Memorial Hall and look up the record of each."

"Yes, sir."

"Carry out your orders, sir!"

He turned to me, looked at my face and said sharply, "Something on your mind, son? Speak up!"

"Uh—" I blurted it out. "Sir, that temporary third lieutenant—the one that got cashiered. How could I find out what happened?"

"Oh. Young man, I didn't mean to scare the daylights out of you; I simply intended to wake you up. The battle was on one June 1813 old style between USF *Chesapeake* and HMF *Shannon*. Try the *Naval Encyclopedia*; your ship will have it." He turned back to the case of pips and frowned.

Then he said, "Mr. Rico, I have a letter from one of your high school teachers, a retired officer, requesting that you be issued the pips he wore as a third lieutenant. I am sorry to say that I must tell him 'No.' "

"Sir?" I was delighted to hear that Colonel Dubois was still keeping track of me—and very disappointed, too.

"Because I *can't*. I issued those pips two years ago—and they never came back. Real estate deal. Hmm—" He took a box, looked at me. "You could start a new pair. The metal isn't important; the importance of the request lies in the fact that your teacher wanted you to have them."

"Whatever you say, sir."

"Or"—he cradled the box in his hands—"you could wear these. They have been worn five times . . . and the last four candidates to wear them have all failed of commission—nothing dishonorable but pesky bad luck. Are you willing to take a swing at breaking the hoodoo? Turn them into good-luck pips instead?"

I would rather have petted a shark. But I answered, "All right, sir. I'll take a swing at it."

"Good." He pinned them on me. "Thank you, Mr. Rico. You see, these were mine, I wore them first . . . and it would please me mightily to have them brought back to me with that streak of bad luck broken, have you go on and graduate."

I felt ten feet tall. "I'll try, sir!"

"I know you will. You may now carry out your orders, sir. The same air car will take both you and Byrd. Just a moment—Are your mathematics textbooks in your bag?"

"Sir? No, sir."

"Get them. The Weightmaster of your ship has been advised of your extra baggage allowance."

I saluted and left, on the bounce. He had me shrunk down to size as soon as he mentioned math.

My math books were on my study desk, tied into a package with a daily assignment sheet tucked under the cord. I gathered the impression that Colonel Nielssen never left anything unplanned—but everybody knew that.

Birdie was waiting on the roof by the air car. He glanced at my books and grinned. "Too bad. Well, if we're in the same ship, I'll coach you. What ship?"

"Tours."

"Sorry, I'm for the *Moskva.*" We got in, I checked the pilot, saw that it had been pre-set for the field, closed the door and the car took off. Birdie added, "You could be worse off. The Assassin took not only his math books but two other subjects."

Birdie undoubtedly knew and he had not been showing off when he offered to coach me; he was a professor type except that his ribbons proved that he was a soldier too.

Instead of studying math Birdie taught it. One period each day he was a faculty member, the way little Shujumi taught judo at Camp Currie. The M.I. doesn't waste anything; we can't afford to. Birdie had a B.S. in math on his eighteenth birthday, so naturally he was assigned extra duty as instructor—which didn't keep him from being chewed out at other hours.

Not that he got chewed out much. Birdie had that rare combo of brilliant intellect, solid education, common sense, and guts, which gets a cadet marked as a potential general. We figured he was a cinch to command a brigade by the time he was thirty, what with the war.

But my ambitions didn't soar that high. "It would be a dirty, rotten shame," I said, "if the Assassin flunked out," while thinking that it would be a dirty, rotten shame if *I* flunked out.

"He won't," Birdie answered cheerfully. "They'll sweat him through the rest if they have to put him in a hypno booth and feed him through a tube. Anyhow," he added, "Hassan could flunk out and get promoted for it."

"Huh?"

"Didn't you know? The Assassin's permanent rank is first lieutenant—field commission, naturally. He reverts to it if he flunks out. See the regs."

I knew the regs. If I flunked math, I'd revert to buck sergeant, which is better than being slapped in the face with a wet fish any way you think about it . . . and I'd thought about it, lying awake nights after busting a quiz.

But this was different. "Hold it," I protested. "He gave up *first* lieutenant, permanent grade . . . and has just made temporary *third* lieutenant . . . in order to become a *second* lieutenant? Are you crazy? Or is he?"

Birdie grinned. "Just enough to make us both M.I."

"But—I don't get it."

"Sure you do. The Assassin has no education that he didn't pick up in the M.I. So how high can he go? I'm sure he could command a regiment in battle and do a real swingin' job—provided somebody else planned the operation. But commanding in battle is only a fraction of what an officer does, especially a senior officer. To direct a war, or even to plan a single battle and mount the operation, you have to have theory of games, operational analysis, symbolic logic, pessimistic synthesis, and a dozen other skull subjects. You can sweat them out on your own if you've got the grounding. But have them you must, or you'll never get past captain, or possibly major. The Assassin knows what he is doing."

"I suppose so," I said slowly. "Birdie, Colonel Nielssen must know that Hassan was an officer—is an officer, really."

"Huh? Of course."

"He didn't talk as if he knew. We all got the same lecture."

"Not quite. Did you notice that when the Commandant wanted a question answered a particular way he always asked the Assassin?"

I decided it was true. "Birdie, what is your permanent rank?"

The car was just landing; he paused with a hand on the latch and grinned. "PFC—I don't dare flunk out!"

I snorted. "You won't. You can't!" I was surprised that he wasn't even a corporal, but a kid as smart and well educated as Birdie would go to O.C.S. just as quickly as he proved himself in combat . . . which, with the war on, could be only months after his eighteenth birthday.

Birdie grinned still wider. "We'll see."

"You'll graduate. Hassan and I have to worry, but not you."

"So? Suppose Miss Kendrick takes a dislike to me." He opened the door and looked startled. "Hey! They're sounding my call. So long!"

"See you, Birdie."

But I did not see him and he did not graduate. He was commissioned two weeks later and his pips came back with their eighteenth decoration—the Wounded Lion, posthumous.

Chapter 13

The *Rodger Young* carries one platoon and is crowded; the *Tours* carries six—and is roomy. She has the tubes to drop them all at once and enough spare room to carry twice that number and make a second drop. This would make her very crowded, with eating in shifts, hammocks in passageways and drop rooms, rationed water, inhale when your mate exhales, and get your elbow out of my eye! I'm glad they didn't double up while I was in her.

But she has the speed and lift to deliver such crowded troops still in fighting condition to any point in Federation space and much of Bug space; under Cherenkov drive she cranks Mike 400 or better—say Sol to Capella, forty-six light-years, in under six weeks.

Of course, a six-platoon transport is not big compared with a battle wagon or passenger liner; these things are compromises. The M.I. prefers speedy little one-platoon corvettes which give flexibility for any operation, while if it was left up to the Navy we would have nothing but regimental transports. It takes almost as many Navy files to run a corvette as it does to run a monster big enough for a regiment—more maintenance and housekeeping, of course, but soldiers can do that. After all, those lazy troopers do nothing but sleep and eat and polish buttons—do 'em good to have a little regular work. So says the Navy.

The real Navy opinion is even more extreme: The Army is obsolete and should be abolished.

The Navy doesn't say this officially—but talk to a Naval officer who is on R&R and feeling his oats; you'll get an earful. They think they can fight any war, win it, send a few of their own people down to hold the conquered planet until the Diplomatic Corps takes charge.

I admit that their newest toys can blow any planet right out of the sky—I've never seen it but I believe it. Maybe I'm as obsolete as *Tyrannosaurus rex*. I don't feel obsolete and us apes can do things that the fanciest ship cannot. If the government doesn't want those things done, no doubt they'll tell us.

Maybe it's just as well that neither the Navy nor the M.I. has the final word. A man can't buck for Sky Marshal unless he has commanded both a regiment and a capital ship—go through M.I. and take his lumps and then become a Naval officer (I think little Birdie had that in mind), or first become an astrogator-pilot and follow it with Camp Currie, etc.

I'll listen respectfully to any man who has done both.

Like most transports, the *Tours* is a mixed ship; the most amazing change for me was to be allowed "North of Thirty." The bulkhead that separates ladies' country from the rough characters who shave is not necessarily No. 30 but, by tradition, it is called "bulkhead thirty" in any mixed ship. The wardroom is just beyond it and the rest of ladies' country is farther forward. In the *Tours* the wardroom also served as messroom for enlisted women, who ate just before we did, and it was partitioned between meals into a recreation room for them and a lounge for their officers. Male officers had a lounge called the cardroom just abaft thirty.

Besides the obvious fact that drop & retrieval require the best pilots (i.e., female), there is very strong reason why female Naval officers are assigned to transports: It is good for trooper morale.

Let's skip M.I. traditions for a moment. Can you think of anything sillier than letting yourself be fired out of a spaceship with nothing but mayhem and sudden death at the other end? However, if someone must do this idiotic stunt, do you know of a surer way to keep a man keyed up to the point where he is willing than by keeping him constantly reminded that the only good reason why men fight is a living, breathing reality?

In a mixed ship, the last thing a trooper hears before a drop (maybe the last word he ever hears) is a woman's voice, wishing him luck. If you don't think this is important, you've probably resigned from the human race.

The *Tours* had fifteen Naval officers, eight ladies and seven men; there were eight M.I. officers including (I am happy to say) myself. I won't say "bulkhead thirty" caused me to buck for O.C.S. but the privilege of eating with the ladies is more incentive than any increase in pay. The Skipper was president of the mess, my boss Captain Blackstone was vice-president—not because of rank; three Naval officers ranked him; but as C.O. of the strike force he was de facto senior to everybody but the Skipper.

Every meal was formal. We would wait in the cardroom until the hour struck, follow Captain Blackstone in and stand behind our chairs; the Skipper would come in followed by her ladies and, as she reached the head of the table, Captain Blackstone would bow and say, "Madam President . . . ladies," and she would answer, "Mr. Vice . . . gentlemen," and the man on each lady's right would seat her.

This ritual established that it was a social event, not an officer's conference; thereafter ranks or titles were used, except that junior Naval officers and myself alone among the M.I. were called "Mister" or "Miss"—with one exception which fooled me.

My first meal aboard I heard Captain Blackstone called "Major," although his shoulder pips plainly read "captain." I got straightened out later. There can't be two captains in a Naval vessel so an Army captain is bumped one rank socially rather than commit the unthinkable of calling him by the title reserved for the one and only monarch. If a Naval captain is aboard as anything but skipper, he or she is called "Commodore" even if the skipper is a lowly lieutenant.

The M.I. observes this by avoiding the necessity in the wardroom and paying no attention to the silly custom in our own part of the ship.

Seniority ran downhill from each end of the table, with the Skipper at the head and the strike force C.O. at the foot, the junior midshipmen at his right and myself at the Skipper's right. I would most happily have sat by the junior midshipman; she was awfully pretty—but the arrangement is planned chaperonage; I never even learned her first name.

I knew that I, as the lowliest male, sat on the Skipper's right—but I didn't know that I was supposed to seat her. At my first meal she waited and nobody sat down—until the third assistant engineer jogged my elbow. I haven't been so embarrassed since a very unfortunate incident in kindergarten, even though Captain Jorgenson acted as if nothing had happened.

When the Skipper stands up the meal is over. She was pretty good about this but once she stayed seated only a few minutes and Captain Blackstone got annoyed. He stood up but called out, "Captain—"

She stopped. "Yes, Major?"

"Will the Captain please give orders that my officers and myself be served in the cardroom?"

She answered coldly, "Certainly, sir." And we were. But no Naval officer joined us.

The following Saturday she exercised her privilege of inspecting the M.I. aboard—which transport skippers almost never do. However, she simply walked down the ranks without commenting. She was not really a martinet and she had a nice smile when she wasn't being stern. Captain Blackstone assigned Second Lieutenant "Rusty" Graham to crack the whip over me about math; she found out about it, somehow, and told Captain Blackstone to have me report to her office for one hour after lunch each day, whereupon she tutored me in math and bawled me out when my "homework" wasn't perfect.

Our six platoons were two companies as a rump battalion; Captain Blackstone commanded Company D, Blackie's Blackguards, and also commanded the rump battalion. Our battalion commander by the T.O., Major Xera, was with A and B companies in the *Tours'* sister ship *Normandy Beach*—maybe half a sky away; he commanded us only when the full battalion dropped together—except that Cap'n Blackie routed certain reports and letters through him. Other matters went directly to Fleet, Division, or Base, and Blackie had a truly wizard fleet sergeant to keep such things straight and to help him handle both a company and a rump battalion in combat.

Administrative details are not simple in an army spread through many light-years in hundreds of ships. In the old *Valley Forge*, in the *Rodger Young*, and now in the *Tours* I was in the same regiment, the Third ("Pampered Pets") Regiment of the First ("Polaris") M.I. Division. Two battalions formed from available units had been called the "Third Regiment" in Operation Bughouse but I did not see "my" regiment; all I saw was PFC Bamburger and a lot of Bugs.

I might be commissioned in the Pampered Pets, grow old and retire in it—and never even see my regimental commander. The Roughnecks had a company commander but he also commanded the first platoon ("Hornets") in another corvette; I didn't know his name until I saw it on my orders to O.C.S. There is a legend about a "lost platoon" that went on R&R as its corvette was decommissioned. Its company commander had just been promoted and the other platoons had been attached tactically elsewhere. I've forgotten what happened to the platoon's lieutenant but R&R is a routine time to detach an officer—theoretically after a relief has been sent to understudy him, but reliefs are always scarce.

They say this platoon enjoyed a local year of the fleshpots along Churchill Road before anybody missed them.

I don't believe it. But it could happen.

The chronic scarcity of officers strongly affected my duties in Blackie's Blackguards. The M.I. has the lowest percentage of officers in any army of record and this factor is just part of the M.I.'s unique "divisional wedge." "D.W." is military jargon but the idea is simple: If you have 10,000 soldiers, how many fight? And how many just peel potatoes, drive lorries, count graves, and shuffle papers?

In the M.I., 10,000 men fight.

In the mass wars of the XXth century it sometimes took 70,000 men (fact!) to enable 10,000 to fight.

I admit it takes the Navy to place us where we fight; however, an M.I. strike force, even in a corvette, is at least three times as large as the transport's Navy crew. It also takes civilians to supply and service us; about 10 per cent of us are on R&R at any time; and a few of the very best of us are rotated to instruct at boot camps.

While a few M.I. are on desk jobs you will always find that they are shy an arm or leg, or some such. These are the ones—the Sergeant Hos and the Colonel Nielssens—who refuse to retire, and they really ought to count twice since they release able-bodied M.I. by filling jobs which require fighting spirit but not physical perfection. They do work that civilians can't do—or we would hire civilians. Civilians are like beans; you buy 'em as needed for any job which merely requires skill and savvy.

But you can't buy fighting spirit.

It's scarce. We use all of it, waste none. The M.I. is the smallest army in history for the size of the population it guards. You can't buy an M.I., you can't conscript him, you can't coerce him—

you can't even keep him if he wants to leave. He can quit thirty seconds before a drop, lose his nerve and not get into his capsule and all that happens is that he is paid off and can never vote.

At O.C.S. we studied armies in history that were driven like galley slaves. But the M.I. is a free man; all that drives him comes from inside—that self-respect and need for the respect of his mates and his pride in being one of them called morale, or *esprit de corps*.

The root of our morale is: "Everybody works, everybody fights." An M.I. doesn't pull strings to get a soft, safe job; there aren't any. Oh, a trooper will get away with what he can; any private with enough savvy to mark time to music can think up reasons why he should not clean compartments or break out stores; this is a soldier's ancient right.

But *all* "soft, safe" jobs are filled by civilians; that goldbricking private climbs into his capsule certain that *everybody*, from general to private, is doing it with him. Light-years away and on a different day, or maybe an hour or so later—no matter. What does matter is that *everybody* drops. This is why he enters the capsule, even though he may not be conscious of it.

If we ever deviate from this, the M.I. will go to pieces. All that holds us together is an idea—one that binds more strongly than steel but its magic power depends on keeping it intact.

It is this "everybody fights" rule that lets the M.I. get by with so few officers.

I know more about this than I want to, because I asked a foolish question in Military History and got stuck with an assignment which forced me to dig up stuff ranging from *De Bello Gallico* to Tsing's classic *Collapse of the Golden Hegemony*. Consider an ideal M.I. division—on paper, because you won't find one elsewhere. How many officers does it require? Never mind units attached from other corps; they may not be present during a ruckus and they are not like M.I.—the special talents attached to Logistics & Communications are all ranked as officers. If it will make a memory man, a telepath, a senser, or a lucky man happy to have me salute him, I'm glad to oblige; he is more valuable than I am and I could not replace him if I lived to be two hundred. Or take the K-9 Corps, which is 50 per cent "officers" but whose other 50 per cent are neodogs.

None of these is in line of command, so let's consider only us apes and what it takes to lead us.

This imaginary division has 10,800 men in 216 platoons, each with a lieutenant. Three platoons to a company calls for 72 captains; four companies to a battalion calls for 18 majors or lieutenant colonels. Six regiments with six colonels can form two or three brigades, each with a short general, plus a medium-tall general as top boss.

You wind up with 317 officers out of a total, all ranks, of 11,117.

There are no blank files and every officer commands a team. Officers total 3 per cent—which is what the M.I. does have, but arranged somewhat differently. In fact a good many platoons are commanded by sergeants and many officers "wear more than one hat" in order to fill some utterly necessary staff jobs.

Even a platoon leader should have "staff"—his platoon sergeant.

But he can get by without one and his sergeant can get by without him. But a general *must* have staff; the job is too big to carry in his hat. He needs a big planning staff and a small combat staff. Since there are never enough officers, the team commanders in his flag transport double as his planning staff and are picked from the M.I.'s best mathematical logicians—then they drop with their own teams. The general drops with a small combat staff, plus a small team of the roughest, on-the-bounce troopers in the M.I. Their job is to keep the general from being bothered by rude strangers while he is managing the battle. Sometimes they succeed.

Besides necessary staff billets, any team larger than a platoon ought to have a deputy commander. But there are never enough officers so we make do with what we've got. To fill each necessary combat billet, one job to one officer, would call for a 5 per cent ratio of officers—but 3 per cent is all we've got.

In place of that optimax of 5 per cent that the M.I. never can reach, many armies in the past commissioned 10 per cent of their number, or even 15 per cent—and sometimes a preposterous 20 per cent! This sounds like a fairy tale but it was a fact, especially during the XXth century. What kind of an army has more "officers" than corporals? (And more noncoms than privates!)

An army organized to lose wars—if history means anything. An army that is mostly organization, red tape, and overhead, most of whose "soldiers" never fight.

But what do "officers" *do* who do not command fighting men?

Fiddlework, apparently—officers' club officer, morale officer, athletics officer, public information officer, recreation officer, PX officer, transportation officer, legal officer, chaplain, assistant

chaplain, junior assistant chaplain, officer-in-charge of anything
anybody can think of—even *nursery* officer!

In the M.I., such things are extra duty for combat officers or, if
they are *real* jobs, they are done better and cheaper and without de-
moralizing a fighting outfit by hiring civilians. But the situation got
so smelly in one of the XXth century major powers that *real* officers, ones who commanded fighting men, were given special insignia to distinguish them from the swarms of swivel-chair
hussars.

The scarcity of officers got steadily worse as the war wore on,
because the casualty rate is always highest among officers . . .
and the M.I. *never* commissions a man simply to fill vacancy. In
the long run, each boot regiment must supply its own share of
officers and the percentage can't be raised without lowering
the standards—The strike force in the *Tours* needed thirteen
officers—six platoon leaders, two company commanders and
two deputies, and a strike force commander staffed by a deputy
and an adjutant.

What it had was six . . . and me.

Table of Organization
"Rump Battalion" Strike Force—
Cpt. Blackstone
("first hat")
Fleet Sergeant

C Company—"Warren's Wolverines" 1st Lt. Warren	D Company—"Blackie's Blackguards" Cpt. Blackstone ("second hat")
1st plat.— 1st Lt. Bayonne	1st plat.— (1st Lt. Silva, Hosp.)
2nd plat.— 2nd Lt. Sukarno	2nd plat.— 2nd Lt. Khoroshen
3rd plat.— 2nd Lt. N'gam	3rd plat.— 2nd Lt. Graham

I would have been under Lieutenant Silva, but he left for hospital the day I reported, ill with some sort of twitching awfuls. But
this did not necessarily mean that I would get his platoon. A temporary third lieutenant is not considered an asset; Captain Black-

stone could place me under Lieutenant Bayonne and put a sergeant in charge of his own first platoon, or even "put on a third
hat" and take the platoon himself.

In fact, he did both and nevertheless assigned me as platoon
leader of the first platoon of the Blackguards. He did this by bor-
rowing the Wolverine's best buck sergeant to act as his battalion
staffer, then he placed his fleet sergeant as platoon sergeant of his
first platoon—a job two grades below his chevrons. Then Captain
Blackstone spelled it out for me in a head-shrinking lecture: I
would appear on the T.O. as platoon leader, but Blackie himself
and the fleet sergeant would run the platoon.

As long as I behaved myself, I could go through the motions. I
would even be allowed to drop as platoon leader—but one word
from my platoon sergeant to my company commander and the
jaws of the nutcracker would close.

It suited me. It was my platoon as long as I could swing it—
and if I couldn't, the sooner I was shoved aside the better for
everybody. Besides, it was a lot less nerve-racking to get a platoon
that way than by sudden catastrophe in battle.

I took my job very seriously, for it was *my* platoon—the T.O.
said so. But I had not yet learned to delegate authority and, for
about a week, I was around troopers' country much more than is
good for a team. Blackie called me into his stateroom. "Son, what
in Ned do you think you are doing?"

I answered stiffly that I was trying to get my platoon ready for
action.

"So? Well, that's not what you are accomplishing. You are stirring them like a nest of wild bees. Why the deuce do you think I
turned over to you the best sergeant in the Fleet? If you will go to
your stateroom, hang yourself on a hook, and *stay* there! . . . until
'Prepare for Action' is sounded, he'll hand that platoon over to
you tuned like a violin."

"As the Captain pleases, sir," I agreed glumly.

"And that's another thing—I can't stand an officer who acts
like a confounded *kay*det. Forget that silly third-person talk
around me—save it for generals and the Skipper. Quit bracing
your shoulders and clicking your heels. Officers are supposed to
look *relaxed*, son."

"Yes, sir."

"And let that be the last time you say 'sir' to me for one solid
week. Same for saluting. Get that grim *kay*det look off your face
and hang a smile on it."

"Yes, s— Okay."

"That's better. Lean against the bulkhead. Scratch yourself. Yawn. Anything but that tin-soldier act."

I tried. . . . and grinned sheepishly as I discovered that breaking a habit is not easy. Leaning was harder work than standing at attention. Captain Blackstone studied me. "Practice it," he said. "An officer can't look scared or tense; it's contagious. Now tell me, Johnnie, what your platoon needs. Never mind the piddlin' stuff; I'm not interested in whether a man has the regulation number of socks in his locker."

I thought rapidly. "Uh . . . do you happen to know if Lieutenant Silva intended to put Brumby up for sergeant?"

"I do happen to know. What's *your* opinion?"

"Well . . . the record shows that he has been acting section leader the past two months. His efficiency marks are good."

"I asked for your recommendation, Mister."

"Well, s—Sorry. I've never seen him work on the ground, so I can't have a real opinion; anybody can soldier in the drop room. But the way I see it, he's been acting sergeant too long to bust him back to chaser and promote a squad leader over him. He ought to get that third chevron before we drop—or he ought to be transferred when we get back. Sooner, if there's a chance for a spaceside transfer."

Blackie grunted. "You're pretty generous in giving away my Blackguards—for a third lieutenant."

I turned red. "Just the same, it's a soft spot in my platoon. Brumby ought to be promoted, or transferred. I don't want him back in his old job with somebody promoted over his head; he'd likely turn sour and I'd have an even worse soft spot. If he can't have another chevron, he ought to go to repple-depple for cadre. Then he won't be humiliated and he gets a fair shake to make sergeant in another team—instead of a dead end here."

"Really?" Blackie did not quite sneer. "After that masterly analysis, apply your powers of deduction and tell me why Lieutenant Silva failed to transfer him three weeks ago when we arrived around Sanctuary."

I had wondered about that. The time to transfer a man is the earliest possible instant after you decide to let him go—and without warning; it's better for the man and the team—so says the book. I said slowly, "Was Lieutenant Silva already ill at that time, Captain?"

"No."

The pieces matched. "Captain, I recommend Brumby for immediate promotion."

His eyebrows shot up. "A minute ago you were about to dump him as useless."

"Uh, not quite. I said it had to be one or the other—but I didn't know which. Now I know."

"Continue."

"Uh, this assumes that Lieutenant Silva is an efficient officer—"

"*Hummmph!* Mister, for your information, 'Quick' Silva has an unbroken string of 'Excellent—Recommended for Promotion' on his Form Thirty-One."

"But I knew that he was good," I plowed on, "because I inherited a good platoon. A good officer might not promote a man for—oh, for many reasons—and still not put his misgivings in writing. But in this case, if he could not recommend him for sergeant, then he wouldn't keep him with the team—so he would get him out of the ship at the first opportunity. But he didn't. Therefore I know he intended to promote Brumby." I added, "But I can't see why he didn't push it through three weeks ago, so that Brumby could have worn his third chevron on R&R."

Captain Blackstone grinned. "That's because you don't credit *me* with being efficient."

"S—I beg pardon?"

"Never mind. You've proved who killed Cock Robin and I don't expect a still-moist *kay*det to know all the tricks. But listen and learn, son. As long as this war goes on, don't *ever* promote a man just before you return to Base."

"Uh . . . why not, Captain?"

"You mentioned sending Brumby to Replacement Depot if he was not to be promoted. But that's just where he would have gone if we *had* promoted him three weeks ago. You don't know how hungry that non-com desk at repple-depple is. Paw through the dispatch file and you'll find a demand that we supply two sergeants for cadre. With a platoon sergeant being detached for O.C.S. and a buck sergeant spot vacant, I was under complement and able to refuse." He grinned savagely. "It's a rough war, son, and your own people will steal your best men if you don't watch 'em." He took two sheets of paper out of a drawer. "There—"

One was a letter from Silva to Cap'n Blackie, recommending Brumby for sergeant; it was dated over a month ago.

The other was Brumby's warrant for sergeant—dated the day *after* we left Sanctuary.

"That suit you?" he asked.

"Huh? Oh, yes indeed!"

"I've been waiting for you to spot the weak place in your team, and tell me what had to be done. I'm pleased that you figured it out—but only middlin' pleased because an experienced officer would have analyzed it at once from the T.O. and the service records. Never mind, that's how you gain experience. Now here's what you do. Write me a letter like Silva's; date it yesterday. Tell your platoon sergeant to tell Brumby that you have put him up for a third stripe—and don't mention that Silva did so. You didn't know that when you made the recommendation, so we'll keep it that way. When I swear Brumby in, I'll let him know that both his officers recommended him independently—which will make him feel good. Okay, anything more?"

"Uh . . . not in organization—unless Lieutenant Silva planned to promote Naidi, vice Brumby. In which case we could promote one PFC to lance . . . and that would allow us to promote four privates to PFC, including three vacancies now existing. I don't know whether it's your policy to keep the T.O. filled up tight or not?"

"Might as well," Blackie said gently, "as you and I know that some of those lads aren't going to have many days in which to enjoy it. Just remember that we don't make a man a PFC until after he has been in combat—not in Blackie's Blackguards we don't. Figure it out with your platoon sergeant and let me know. No hurry . . . any time before bedtime tonight. Now. . . . anything else?"

"Well— Captain, I'm worried about the suits."

"So am I. All platoons."

"I don't know all the other platoons, but with five recruits to fit, plus four suits damaged and exchanged, and two more downchecked this past week and replaced from stores—well, I don't see how Cunha and Navarre can warm up that many and run routine tests on forty-one others and get it all done by our calculated date. Even if no trouble develops—"

"Trouble always develops."

"Yes, Captain. But that's two hundred and eighty-six man-hours just for warm & fit, and plus a hundred and twenty-three hours of routine checks. And it always takes longer."

"Well, what do you think can be done? The other platoons will lend you help if they finish their suits ahead of time. Which I doubt. Don't ask to borrow help from the Wolverines; we're more likely to lend them help."

"Uh . . . Captain, I don't know what you'll think of this, since you told me to stay out of troopers' country. But when I was a corporal, I was assistant to the Ordnance & Armor sergeant."

"Keep talking."

"Well, right at the last I was the O&A sergeant. But I was just standing in another man's shoes—I'm not a finished O&A mechanic. But I'm a pretty darn good assistant and if I was allowed to, well, I can either warm new suits, or run routine checks—and give Cunha and Navarre that much more time for trouble."

Blackie leaned back and grinned. "Mister, I have searched the regs carefully . . . and I can't find the one that says an officer mustn't get his hands dirty." He added, "I mention that because some 'young gentlemen' who have been assigned to me apparently had read such a regulation. All right, draw some dungarees—no need to get your uniform dirty along with your hands. Go aft and find your platoon sergeant, tell him about Brumby and order him to prepare recommendations to close the gaps in the T.O. in case I should decide to confirm your recommendation for Brumby. Then tell him that you are going to put in all your time on ordnance and armor—and that you want him to handle everything else. Tell him that if he has any problems to look you up in the armory. Don't tell him you consulted me—just give him orders. Follow me?"

"Yes, s—Yes, I do."

"Okay, get on it. As you pass through the cardroom, please give my compliments to Rusty and tell him to drag his lazy carcass in here."

For the next two weeks I was never so busy—not even in boot camp. Working as an ordnance & armor mech about ten hours a day was not all that I did. Math, of course—and no way to duck it with the Skipper tutoring me. Meals—say an hour and a half a day. Plus the mechanics of staying alive—shaving, showering, putting buttons in uniforms and trying to chase down the Navy master-at-arms, get him to unlock the laundry to locate clean uniforms ten minutes before inspection. (It is an unwritten law of the Navy that facilities must *always* be locked when they are most needed.)

Guard mount, parade, inspections, a minimum of platoon routine, took another hour a day. But besides, I was "George." Every outfit has a "George." He's the most junior officer and has the extra jobs—athletics officer, mail censor, referee for competitions, school officer, correspondence courses officer, prosecutor courts-martial, treasurer of the welfare mutual loan fund, custodian of registered publications, stores officer, troopers' mess officer, et cetera ad endless nauseam.

Rusty Graham had been "George" until he happily turned it over to me. He wasn't so happy when I insisted on a sight inventory on everything for which I had to sign. He suggested that if I didn't have sense enough to accept a commissioned officer's signed inventory then perhaps a direct order would change my tune. So I got sullen and told him to put his orders in writing— with a certified copy so that I could keep the original and endorse the copy over to the team commander.

Rusty angrily backed down—even a second lieutenant isn't stupid enough to put such orders in writing. I wasn't happy either as Rusty was my roommate and was then still my tutor in math, but we held the sight inventory. I got chewed out by Lieutenant Warren for being stupidly officious but he opened his safe and let me check his registered publications. Captain Blackstone opened his with no comment and I couldn't tell whether he approved of my sight inventory or not.

Publications were okay but accountable property was not. Poor Rusty! He had accepted his predecessor's count and now the count was short—and the other officer was not merely gone, he was dead. Rusty spent a restless night (and so did I!), then went to Blackie and told him the truth.

Blackie chewed him out, then went over the missing items, found ways to expend most of them as "lost in combat." It reduced Rusty's shortages to a few days' pay—but Blackie had him keep the job, thereby postponing the cash reckoning indefinitely.

Not all "George" jobs caused that much headache. There were no courts-martial; good combat teams don't have them. There was no mail to censor as the ship was in Cherenkov drive. Same for welfare loans for similar reasons. Athletics I delegated to Brumby; referee was "if and when." The troopers' mess was excellent; I initialed menus and sometimes inspected the galley, i.e., I scrounged a sandwich without getting out of dungarees when working late in the armory. Correspondence courses meant a lot of paperwork since quite a few were continuing their educations, war or no war—but I delegated my platoon sergeant and the records were kept by the PFC who was his clerk.

Nevertheless "George" jobs soaked up about two hours every day—there were so many.

You see where this left me—ten hours O&A, three hours math, meals an hour and a half, personal one hour, military fiddle-work one hour, "George" two hours, sleep eight hours; total, twenty-six and a half hours. The ship wasn't even on the twenty-five hour Sanctuary day; once we left we went on Greenwich standard and the universal calendar.

The only slack was in my sleeping time.

I was sitting in the cardroom about one o'clock one morning, plugging away at math, when Captain Blackstone came in. I said, "Good evening, Captain."

"Morning, you mean. What the deuce ails you, son? Insomnia?"

"Uh, not exactly."

He picked up a stack of sheets, remarking, "Can't your sergeant handle your paperwork? Oh, I see. Go to bed."

"But, Captain—"

"Sit back down. Johnnie, I've been meaning to talk to you. I never see you here in the cardroom, evenings. I walk past your room, you're at your desk. When your bunkie goes to bed, you move out here. What's the trouble?"

"Well . . . I just never seem to get caught up."

"Nobody ever does. How's the work going in the armory?"

"Pretty well. I think we'll make it."

"I think so, too. Look, son, you've got to keep a sense of proportion. You have two prime duties. First is to see that your platoon's equipment is ready—you're doing that. You don't have to worry about the platoon itself, I told you that. The second—and just as important—you've got to be ready to fight. You're muffing that."

"I'll be ready, Captain."

"Nonsense and other comments. You're getting no exercise and losing sleep. Is that how to train for a drop? When you lead a platoon, son, you've got to be on the bounce. From here on you will exercise from sixteen-thirty to eighteen hundred each day. You will be in your sack with lights out at twenty-three hundred—and if you lie awake fifteen minutes two nights in a row, you will report to the Surgeon for treatment. Orders."

"Yes, sir." I felt the bulkheads closing in on me and added desperately, "Captain, I don't see *how* I can get to bed by twenty-three—and still get everything *done*."

"Then you won't. As I said, son, you must have a sense of proportion. Tell me how you spend your time."

So I did. He nodded. "Just as I thought." He picked up my math "homework," tossed it in front of me. "Take this. Sure, you want to work on it. But why work so hard before we go into action?"

"Well, I thought—"

" 'Think' is what you didn't do. There are four possibilities, and only one calls for finishing these assignments. First, you might buy a farm. Second, you might buy a small piece and be retired with an honorary commission. Third, you might come through all right . . . but get a downcheck on your Form Thirty-One from your examiner, namely me. Which is just what you're aching for at the present time—why, son, I won't even let you drop if you show up with eyes red from no sleep and muscles flabby from too much chair parade. The fourth possibility is that you take a grip on yourself . . . in which case I might let you take a swing at leading a platoon. So let's assume that you do and put on the finest show since Achilles slew Hector and I pass you. In that case only—you'll need to finish these math assignments. So do them on the trip back.

"That takes care of that—I'll tell the Skipper. The rest of those jobs you are relieved of, right now. On our way home you can spend your time on math. If we get home. But you'll never get anywhere if you don't learn to keep first things first. Go to bed!"

A week later we made rendezvous, coming out of drive and coasting short of the speed of light while the fleet exchanged signals. We were sent Briefing, Battle Plan, our Mission & Orders—a stack of words as long as a novel—and were told not to drop.

Oh, we were to be in the operation but we would ride down like gentlemen, cushioned in retrieval boats. This we could do because the Federation already held the surface; Second, Third, and Fifth M.I. Divisions had taken it—and paid cash.

The described real estate didn't seem worth the price. Planet P is smaller than Terra, with a surface gravity of 0.7, is mostly arctic-cold ocean and rock, with lichenous flora and no fauna of interest. Its air is not breathable for long, being contaminated with nitrous oxide and too much ozone. Its one continent is about half the size of Australia, plus many worthless islands; it would probably require as much terraforming as Venus before we could use it.

However, we were not buying real estate to live on; we went there because Bugs were there—and they were there on our account, so Staff thought. Staff told us that Planet P was an uncompleted advance base (prob. 87 ± 6 per cent) to be used against us.

Since the planet was no prize, the routine way to get rid of this

Bug base would be for the Navy to stand off at a safe distance and render this ugly spheroid uninhabitable by Man or Bug. But the C-in-C had other ideas.

The operation was a raid. It sounds incredible to call a battle involving hundreds of ships and thousands of casualties a "raid," especially as, in the meantime, the Navy and a lot of other cap troopers were keeping things stirred up many light-years into Bug space in order to divert them from reinforcing Planet P.

But the C-in-C was not wasting men; this giant raid could determine who won the war, whether next year or thirty years hence. We needed to learn more about Bug psychology. Must we wipe out every Bug in the Galaxy? Or was it possible to trounce them and impose a peace? We did not know; we understood them as little as we understand termites.

To learn their psychology we had to communicate with them, learn their motivations, find out why they fought and under what conditions they would stop; for these, the Psychological Warfare Corps needed prisoners.

Workers are easy to capture. But a Bug worker is hardly more than animate machinery. Warriors can be captured by burning off enough limbs to make them helpless—but they are almost as stupid without a director as workers. From such prisoners our own professor types had learned important matters—the development of that oily gas that killed them but not us came from analyzing the biochemistries of workers and warriors, and we had had other new weapons from such research even in the short time I had been a cap trooper. But to discover why Bugs fight we needed to study members of their brain caste. Also, we hoped to exchange prisoners.

So far, we had never taken a brain Bug alive. We had either cleaned out colonies from the surface, as on Sheol, or (as had too often been the case) raiders had gone down their holes and not come back. A lot of brave men had been lost this way.

Still more had been lost through retrieval failure. Sometimes a team on the ground had its ship or ships knocked out of the sky. What happens to such a team? Possibly it dies to the last man. More probably it fights until power and ammo are gone, then survivors are captured as easily as so many beetles on their backs.

From our co-belligerents the Skinnies we knew that many missing troopers were alive as prisoners—thousands we hoped, hundreds we were sure. Intelligence believed that prisoners were always taken to Klendathu; the Bugs are as curious about us as we are about them—a race of individuals able to build cities, starships, armies, may be even more mysterious to a hive entity than a hive entity is to us.

As may be, we wanted those prisoners back!

In the grim logic of the universe this may be a weakness. Perhaps some race that never bothers to rescue an individual may exploit this human trait to wipe us out. The Skinnies have such a trait only slightly and the Bugs don't seem to have it at all—nobody *ever* saw a Bug come to the aid of another because he was wounded; they co-operate perfectly in fighting but units are abandoned the instant they are no longer useful.

Our behavior is different. How often have you seen a headline like this?—TWO DIE ATTEMPTING RESCUE OF DROWNING CHILD. If a man gets lost in the mountains, hundreds will search and often two or three searchers are killed. But the next time somebody gets lost just as many volunteers turn out.

Poor arithmetic . . . but very human. It runs through all our folklore, all human religions, all our literature—a racial conviction that when one human needs rescue, others should not count the price.

Weakness? It might be the unique strength that wins us a Galaxy.

Weakness or strength, Bugs don't have it; there was no prospect of trading fighters for fighters.

But in a hive polyarchy, some castes are valuable—or so our Psych Warfare people hoped. If we could capture brain Bugs, alive and undamaged, we might be able to trade on good terms.

And suppose we captured a queen!

What is a queen's trading value? A regiment of troopers? Nobody knew, but Battle Plan ordered us to capture Bug "royalty," brains and queens, *at any cost*, on the gamble that we could trade them for human beings.

The third purpose of Operation Royalty was to develop methods: how to go down, how to dig them out, how to win with less than total weapons. Trooper for warrior, we could now defeat them above ground; ship for ship, our Navy was better; but, so far, we had had no luck when we tried to go down their holes.

If we failed to exchange prisoners on any terms, then we still had to: (a) win the war, (b) do so in a way that gave us a fighting chance to rescue our own people, or (c)—might as well admit it— die trying and lose. Planet P was a field test to determine whether we could learn how to root them out.

Briefing was read to every trooper and he heard it again in his sleep during hypno preparation. So, while we all knew that Operation Royalty was laying the groundwork toward eventual rescue of our mates, we also knew that Planet P held no human prisoners—it had never been raided. So there was no reason to buck for medals in a wild hope of being personally in on a rescue; it was just another Bug hunt, but conducted with massive force and new techniques. We were going to peel that planet like an onion, until we *knew* that every Bug had been dug out.

The Navy had plastered the islands and that unoccupied part of the continent until they were radioactive glaze; we could tackle Bugs with no worries about our rear. The Navy also maintained a ball-of-yarn patrol in tight orbits around the planet, guarding us, escorting transports, keeping a spy watch on the surface to make sure that Bugs did not break out behind us despite that plastering.

Under the Battle Plan, the orders for Blackie's Blackguards charged us with supporting the prime Mission when ordered or as opportunity presented, relieving another company in a captured area, protecting units of other corps in that area, maintaining contact with M.I. units around us—and smacking down any Bugs that showed their ugly heads.

So we rode down in comfort to an unopposed landing. I took my platoon out at a powered-armor trot. Blackie went ahead to meet the company commander he was relieving, get the situation and size up the terrain. He headed for the horizon like a scared jack rabbit.

I had Cunha send his first sections' scouts out to locate the forward corners of my patrol area and I sent my platoon sergeant off to my left to make contact with a patrol from the Fifth Regiment. We, the Third Regiment, had a grid three hundred miles wide and eighty miles deep to hold; my piece was a rectangle forty miles deep and seventeen wide in the extreme left flank forward corner. The Wolverines were behind us, Lieutenant Khoroshen's platoon on the right and Rusty beyond him.

Our First Regiment had already relieved a Vth Div. regiment ahead of us, with a "brick wall" overlap which placed them on my corner as well as ahead. "Ahead" and "rear," "right flank" and "left," referred to orientation set up in deadreckoning tracers in each command suit to match the grid of the Battle Plan. We had no true front, simply an area, and the only fighting at the moment was going on several hundred miles away, to our arbitrary right and rear.

Somewhere off that way, probably two hundred miles, should be 2nd platoon, G Co, 2nd Batt, 3rd Reg—commonly known as "The Roughnecks."

Or the Roughnecks might be forty light-years away. Tactical organization never matches the Table of Organization; all I knew from Plan was that something called the "2nd Batt" was on our right flank beyond the boys from the *Normandy Beach*. But that battalion could have been borrowed from another division. The Sky Marshal plays his chess without consulting the pieces.

Anyhow, I should not be thinking about the Roughnecks; I had all I could do as a Blackguard. My platoon was okay for the moment—safe as you can be on a hostile planet—but I had plenty to do before Cunha's first squad reached the far corner. I needed to:

1. Locate the platoon leader who had been holding my area.

2. Establish corners and identify them to section and squad leaders.

3. Make contact liaison with eight platoon leaders on my sides and corners, five of whom should already be in position (those from Fifth and First Regiments) and three (Khoroshen of the Blackguards and Bayonne and Sukarno of the Wolverines) who were now moving into position.

4. Get my own boys spread out to their initial points as fast as possible by shortest routes.

The last had to be set up first, as the open column in which we disembarked would not do it. Brumby's last squad needed to deploy to the left flank; Cunha's leading squad needed to spread from dead ahead to left oblique; the other four squads must fan out in between.

This is a standard square deployment and we had simulated how to reach it quickly in the drop room; I called out: "Cunha! Brumby! Time to spread 'em out," using the noncom circuit.

"Roger sec one!"—"Roger sec two!"

"Section leaders take charge . . . and caution each recruit. You'll be passing a lot of Cherubs. I don't want 'em shot at by mistake!" I bit down for my private circuit and said, "Sarge, you got contact on the left?"

"Yes, sir. They see me, they see you."

"Good. I don't see a beacon on our anchor corner—"

"Missing."

"—so you coach Cunha by D.R. Same for the lead scout—that's Hughes—and have Hughes set a new beacon." I wondered why the Third or Fifth hadn't replaced that anchor beacon—my forward left corner where three regiments came together.

No use talking. I went on: "D.R. check. You bear two seven five, miles twelve."

"Sir, reverse is nine six, miles twelve scant."

"Close enough. I haven't found my opposite number yet, so I'm cutting out forward at max. Mind the shop."

"Got 'em, Mr. Rico."

I advanced at max speed while clicking over to officers' circuit: "Square Black One, answer. Black One, Chang's Cherubs—do you read me? Answer." I wanted to talk with the leader of the platoon we were relieving—and not for any perfunctory I-relieve-you-sir: I wanted the ungarnished word.

I didn't like what I had seen.

Either the top brass had been optimistic in believing that we had mounted overwhelming force against a small, not fully developed Bug base—or the Blackguards had been awarded the spot where the roof fell in. In the few moments I had been out of the boat I had spotted half a dozen armored suits on the ground—empty I hoped, dead men possibly, but 'way too many any way you looked at it.

Besides that, my tactical radar display showed a full platoon (my own) moving into position but only a scattering moving back toward retrieval or still on station. Nor could I see any system to their movements.

I was responsible for 680 square miles of hostile terrain and I wanted very badly to find out all I could *before* my own squads were deep into it. Battle Plan had ordered a new tactical doctrine which I found dismaying: Do not close the Bugs' tunnels. Blackie had explained this as if it had been his own happy thought, but I doubt if he liked it.

The strategy was simple, and, I guess, logical . . . if we could afford the losses. Let the Bugs come up. Meet them and kill them on the surface. Let them keep on coming up. Don't bomb their holes, don't gas their holes—let them out. After a while—a day, two days, a week—if we really did have overwhelming force, they would stop coming up. Planning Staff estimated (don't ask me how!) that the Bugs would expend 70 per cent to 90 per cent of their warriors before they stopped trying to drive us off the surface.

Then we would start the unpeeling, killing surviving warriors as we went down and trying to capture "royalty" alive. We knew what the brain caste looked like; we had seen them dead (in photographs) and we knew they could not run—barely functional legs, bloated bodies that were mostly nervous system. Queens no human had ever seen, but Bio War Corps had prepared sketches of what they should look like—obscene monsters larger than a horse and utterly immobile.

Besides brains and queens there might be other "royalty" castes. As might be—encourage their warriors to come out and die, then capture alive anything but warriors and workers.

A necessary plan and very pretty, on paper. What it meant to me was that I had an area 17×40 miles which might be riddled with unstopped Bug holes. I wanted co-ordinates on each one.

If there were too many . . . well, I might accidentally plug a few and let my boys concentrate on watching the rest. A private in a marauder suit can cover a lot of terrain, but he can look at only one thing at a time; he is not superhuman.

I bounced several miles ahead of the first squad, still calling the Cherub platoon leader, varying it by calling *any* Cherub officer and describing the pattern of my transponder beacon (dah-di-dah-dah).

No answer—

At last I got a reply from my boss: "Johnnie! Knock off the noise. Answer me on conference circuit."

So I did, and Blackie told me crisply to quit trying to find the Cherub leader for Square Black One; there wasn't one. Oh, there might be a non-com alive somewhere but the chain of command had broken.

By the book, somebody always moves up. But it *does* happen if too many links are knocked out. As Colonel Nielssen had once warned me, in the dim past . . . almost a month ago.

Captain Chang had gone into action with three officers besides himself; there was one left now (my classmate, Abe Moise) and Blackie was trying to find out from him the situation. Abe wasn't much help. When I joined the conference and identified myself, Abe thought I was his battalion commander and made a report almost heart-breakingly precise, especially as it made no sense at all.

Blackie interrupted and told me to carry on. "Forget about a relief briefing. The situation is whatever you see that it is—so stir around and *see*."

"Right, Boss!" I slashed across my own area toward the far

corner, the anchor corner, as fast as I could move, switching circuits on my first bounce. "Sarge! How about that beacon?"

"No place on that corner to put it, sir. A fresh crater there, about scale six."

I whistled to myself. You could drop the *Tours* into a size six crater. One of the dodges the Bugs used on us when we were sparring, ourselves on the surface, Bugs underground, was land mines. (They never seemed to use missiles, except from ships in space.) If you were near the spot, the ground shock got you; if you were in the air when one went off, the concussion wave could tumble your gyros and throw your suit out of control.

I had never seen larger than a scale-four crater. The theory was that they didn't dare use too big an explosion because of damage to their troglodyte habitats, even if they cofferdammed around it.

"Place an offset beacon," I told him. "Tell section and squad leaders."

"I have, sir. Angle one one oh, miles one point three. Da-di-dit. You should be able to read it, bearing about three three five from where you are." He sounded as calm as a sergeant-instructor at drill and I wondered if I were letting my voice get shrill.

I found it in my display, above my left eyebrow—long and two shorts. "Okay. I see Cunha's first squad is nearly in position. Break off that squad, have it patrol the crater. Equalize the areas—Brumby will have to take four more miles of depth." I thought with annoyance that each man already had to patrol fourteen square miles; spreading the butter so thin meant seventeen square miles per man—and a Bug can come out of a hole less than five feet wide.

I added, "How 'hot' is that crater?"

"Amber-red at the edge. I haven't been in it, sir."

"Stay out of it. I'll check it later." Amber-red would kill an unprotected human but a trooper in armor can take it for quite a time. If there was that much radiation at the edge, the bottom would no doubt fry your eyeballs. "Tell Naidi to pull Malan and Bjork back to amber zone, and have them set up ground listeners." Two of my five recruits were in that first squad—and recruits are like puppies; they stick their noses into things.

"Tell Naidi that I am interested in two things: movement inside the crater . . . and noises in the ground around it." We wouldn't send troopers out through a hole so radioactive that mere exit would kill them. But Bugs would, if they could reach us that way. "Have Naidi report to me. To you and me, I mean."

"Yes, sir." My platoon sergeant added, "May I make a suggestion?"

"Of course. And don't stop to ask permission next time."

"Navarre can handle the rest of the first section. Sergeant Cunha could take the squad at the crater and leave Naidi free to supervise the ground-listening watch."

I knew what he was thinking. Naidi, so newly a corporal that he had never before had a squad on the ground, was hardly the man to cover what looked like the worst danger point in Square Black One; he wanted to pull Naidi back for the same reasons I had pulled the recruits back.

I wondered if he knew what I was thinking? That "nut-cracker"—he was using the suit he had worn as Blackie's battalion staffer, he had one more circuit than I had, a private one to Captain Blackstone.

Blackie was probably patched in and listening via that extra circuit. Obviously my platoon sergeant did not agree with my disposition of the platoon. If I didn't take his advice, the next thing I heard might be Blackie's voice cutting in: "Sergeant, take charge. Mr. Rico, you're relieved."

But— Confound it, a corporal who wasn't allowed to boss his squad wasn't a corporal . . . and a platoon leader who was just a ventriloquist's dummy for his platoon sergeant was an empty suit!

I didn't mull this. It flashed through my head and I answered at once. "I can't spare a corporal to baby-sit with two recruits. Nor a sergeant to boss four privates and a lance."

"But—"

"Hold it. I want the crater watch relieved every hour. I want our first patrol sweep made rapidly. Squad leaders will check any hole reported and get beacon bearings so that section leaders, platoon sergeant and platoon leader can check them as they reach them. If there aren't too many, we'll put a watch on each—I'll decide later."

"Yes, sir."

"Second time around, I want a slow patrol, as tight as possible, to catch holes we miss on the first sweep. Assistant squad leaders will use snoopers on that pass. Squad leaders will get bearings on any troopers—or suits—on the ground; the Cherubs may have left some live wounded. But no one is to stop even to check physicals until I order it. We've got to know the Bug situation first."

"Yes, sir."

"Suggestions?"

"Just one," he answered. "I think the squad chasers should use their snoopers on that first fast pass."

"Very well, do it that way." His suggestion made sense as the surface air temperature was much lower than the Bugs use in their tunnels; a camouflaged vent hole should show a plume like a geyser by infrared vision. I glanced at my display. "Cunha's boys are almost at limit. Start your parade."

"Very well, sir!"

"Off." I clicked over to the wide circuit and continued to make tracks for the crater while I listened to everybody at once as my platoon sergeant revised the pre-plan—cutting out one squad, heading it for the crater, starting the rest of the first section in a two-squad countermarch while keeping the second section in a rotational sweep as pre-planned but with four miles increased depth; got the sections moving, dropped them and caught the first squad as it converged on the anchor crater, gave it its instructions; cut back to the section leaders in plenty of time to give them new beacon bearings at which to make their turns.

He did it with the smart precision of a drum major on parade and he did it faster and in fewer words than I could have done it. Extended-order powered suit drill, with a platoon spread over many miles of countryside, is much more difficult than the strutting precision of parade—but it has to be exact, or you'll blow the head off your mate in action . . . or, as in this case, you sweep part of the terrain twice and miss another part.

But the drillmaster has only a radar display of his formation; he can see with his eyes only those near him. While I listened I watched it in my own display—glowworms crawling past my face in precise lines, "crawling" because even forty miles an hour is a slow crawl when you compress a formation twenty miles across into a display a man can see.

I listened to everybody at once because I wanted to hear the chatter inside the squads.

There wasn't any. Cunha and Brumby gave their secondary commands—and shut up. The corporals sang out only as squad changes were necessary; section and squad chasers called out occasional corrections of interval or alignment—and privates said nothing at all.

I heard the breathing of fifty men like muted sibilance of surf, broken only by necessary orders in the fewest possible words. Blackie had been right; the platoon had been handed over to me "tuned like a violin."

They didn't need *me!* I could go home and my platoon would get along just as well.

Maybe better—

I wasn't sure I had been right in refusing to cut Cunha out to guard the crater; if trouble broke there and those boys couldn't be reached in time, the excuse that I had done it "by the book" was worthless. If you get killed, or let someone else get killed, "by the book" it's just as permanent as any other way.

I wondered if the Roughnecks had a spot open for a buck sergeant.

Most of Square Black One was as flat as the prairie around Camp Currie and much more barren. For this I was thankful; it gave us our only chance of spotting a Bug coming up from below and getting him first. We were spread so widely that four-mile intervals between men and about six minutes between waves of a fast sweep was as tight a patrol as we could manage. This isn't tight enough; any one spot would remain free of observation for at least three or four minutes between patrol waves—and a lot of Bugs can come out of a very small hole in three to four minutes.

Radar can see farther than the eye, of course, but it cannot see as accurately.

In addition we did not dare use anything but short-range selective weapons—our own mates were spread around us in all directions. If a Bug popped up and you let fly with something lethal, it was certain that not too far beyond that Bug was a cap trooper; this sharply limits the range and force of the frightfulness you dare use. On this operation only officers and platoon sergeants were armed with rockets and, even so, we did not expect to use them. If a rocket fails to find its target, it has a nasty habit of continuing to search until it finds one . . . and it cannot tell a friend from foe; a brain that can be stuffed into a small rocket is fairly stupid.

I would happily have swapped that area patrol with thousands of M.I. around us, for a simple one-platoon strike in which you know where your own people are and anything else is an enemy target.

I didn't waste time moaning; I never stopped bouncing toward that anchor-corner crater while watching the ground and trying to watch the radar picture as well. I didn't find any Bug holes but I did jump over a dry wash, almost a canyon, which could conceal quite a few. I didn't stop to see; I simply gave its co-ordinates to my platoon sergeant and told him to have somebody check it.

That crater was even bigger than I had visualized; the *Tours* would have been lost in it. I shifted my radiation counter to directional cascade, took readings on floor and sides—red to multiple red right off the scale, very unhealthy for long exposure even to a man in armor; I estimated its width and depth by helmet range finder, then prowled around and tried to spot openings leading underground.

I did not find any but I did run into crater watches set out by adjacent platoons of the Fifth and First Regiments, so I arranged to split up the watch by sectors such that the combined watch could yell for help from all three platoons, the patch-in to do this being made through First Lieutenant Do Campo of the "Head Hunters" on our left. Then I pulled out Naidi's lance and half his squad (including the recruits) and sent them back to platoon, reporting all this to my boss, and to my platoon sergeant.

"Captain," I told Blackie, "we aren't getting any ground vibrations. I'm going down inside and check for holes. The readings show that I won't get too much dosage if I—"

"Youngster, stay out of that crater."

"But Captain, I just meant to—"

"Shut up. You can't learn anything useful. Stay out."

"Yes, sir."

The next nine hours were tedious. We had been preconditioned for forty hours of duty (two revolutions of Planet P) through forced sleep, elevated blood sugar count, and hypno indoctrination, and of course the suits are self-contained for personal needs. The suits can't last that long, but each man was carrying extra power units and super H.P. air cartridges for recharging. But a patrol with no action is dull, it is easy to goof off.

I did what I could think of, having Cunha and Brumby take turn as drill sergeant (thus leaving platoon sergeant and leader free to rove around): I gave orders that no sweeps were to repeat in pattern so that each man would always check terrain that was new to him. There are endless patterns to cover a given area, by combining the combinations. Besides that, I consulted my platoon sergeant and announced bonus points toward honor squad for first verified hole, first Bug destroyed, etc.—boot camp tricks, but staying alert means staying alive, so anything to avoid boredom.

Finally we had a visit from a special unit: three combat engineers in a utility air car, escorting a talent—a spatial senser. Blackie warned me to expect them. "Protect them and give them what they want."

"Yes, sir. What will they need?"

"How should I know? If Major Landry wants you to take off your skin and dance in your bones, do it!"

"Yes, sir. Major Landry."

I relayed the word and set up a bodyguard by sub-areas. Then I met them as they arrived because I was curious; I had never seen a special talent at work. They landed beside my right flank and got out. Major Landry and two officers were wearing armor and hand flamers but the talent had no armor and no weapons—just an oxygen mask. He was dressed in a fatigue uniform without insignia and he seemed terribly bored by everything. I was not introduced to him. He looked like a sixteen-year-old boy . . . until I got close and saw a network of wrinkles around his weary eyes.

As he got out he took off his breathing mask. I was horrified, so I spoke to Major Landry, helmet to helmet without radio. "Major—the air around here is 'hot.' Besides that, we've been warned that—"

"Pipe down," said the Major. "He knows it."

I shut up. The talent strolled a short distance, turned and pulled his lower lip. His eyes were closed and he seemed lost in thought.

He opened them and said fretfully, "How can one be expected to work with all those silly people jumping around?"

Major Landry said crisply, "Ground your platoon."

I gulped and started to argue—then cut in the all-hands circuit: "First Platoon Blackguards—*ground and freeze!*"

It speaks well for Lieutenant Silva that all I heard was a double echo of my order, as it was repeated down to squad. I said, "Major, can I let them move around on the ground?"

"No. And shut up."

Presently the senser got back in the car, put his mask on. There wasn't room for me, but I was allowed—ordered, really—to grab on and be towed; we shifted a couple of miles. Again the senser took off his mask and walked around. This time he spoke to one of the other combat engineers, who kept nodding and sketching on a pad.

The special-mission unit landed about a dozen times in my area, each time going through the same apparently pointless routine; then they moved on into the Fifth Regiment's grid. Just before they left, the officer who had been sketching pulled a sheet out of the bottom of his sketch box and handed it to me. "Here's your sub map. The wide red band is the only Bug boulevard in your area. It is nearly a thousand feet down where it enters but it climbs steadily toward your left rear and leaves at about minus four hundred fifty. The light blue network joining it is a big Bug colony the only places where it comes within a hundred feet of the surface I have marked. You might put some listeners there until we can get over there and handle it."

I stared at it. "Is this map reliable?"

The engineer officer glanced at the senser, then said very quietly to me, "Of course it is, you idiot! What are you trying to do? Upset him?"

They left while I was studying it. The artist-engineer had done double sketching and the box had combined them into a stereo picture of the first thousand feet under the surface. I was so bemused by it that I had to be reminded to take the platoon out of "freeze"—then I withdrew the ground listeners from the crater, pulled two men from each squad and gave them bearings from that infernal map to have them listen along the Bug highway and over the town.

I reported it to Blackie. He cut me off as I started to describe the Bug tunnels by co-ordinates. "Major Landry relayed a facsimile to me. Just give me co-ordinates of your listening posts."

I did so. He said, "Not bad, Johnnie. But not quite what I want, either. You've placed more listeners than you need over their mapped tunnels. String four of them along that Bug race track, place four more in a diamond around their town. That leaves you four. Place one in the triangle formed by your right rear corner and the main tunnel; the other three go in the larger area on the other side of the tunnel."

"Yes, sir." I added, "Captain, can we depend on this map?"

"What's troubling you?"

"Well . . . it seems like magic. Uh, black magic."

"Oh. Look, son, I've got a special message from the Sky Marshal to you. He says to tell you that map is official . . . and that he will worry about everything else so that you can give full time to your platoon. Follow me?"

"Uh, yes, Captain."

"But the Bugs can burrow mighty fast, so you give special attention to the listening posts *outside* the area of the tunnels. Any noise from those four outside posts louder than a butterfly's roar is to be reported at once, regardless of its nature."

"Yes, sir."

"When they burrow, it makes a noise like frying bacon—in

case you've never heard it. Stop your patrol sweeps. Leave one man on visual observation of the crater. Let half your platoon sleep for two hours, while the other half pairs off to take turns listening."

"Yes, sir."

"You may see some more combat engineers. Here's the revised plan. A sapper company will blast down and cork that main tunnel where it comes nearest the surface, either at your left flank, or beyond in 'Head Hunter' territory. At the same time another engineer company will do the same where that tunnel branches about thirty miles off to your right in the First Regiment's bailiwick. When the corks are in, a long chunk of their main street and a biggish settlement will be cut off. Meanwhile, the same sort of thing will be going on a lot of other places. Thereafter—we'll see. Either the Bugs break through to the surface and we have a pitched battle, or they sit tight and we go down after them, a sector at a time."

"I see." I wasn't sure that I did, but I understood my part: rearrange my listening posts; let half my platoon sleep. Then a Bug hunt—on the surface if we were lucky, underground if we had to.

"Have your flank make contact with that sapper company when it arrives. Help 'em if they want help."

"Right, Cap'n," I agreed heartily. Combat engineers are almost as good an outfit as the infantry; it's a pleasure to work with them. In a pinch they fight, maybe not expertly but bravely. Or they go ahead with their work, not even lifting their heads while a battle rages around them. They have an unofficial, very cynical and very ancient motto: "First we dig 'em, then we die in 'em," to supplement their official motto: "Can do!" Both mottoes are literal truth.

"Get on it, son."

Twelve listening posts meant that I could put a half squad at each post, either a corporal or his lance, plus three privates, then allow two of each group of four to sleep while the other two took turns listening. Navarre and the other section chaser could watch the crater and sleep, turn about, while section sergeants could take turns in charge of the platoon. The redisposition took no more than ten minutes once I had detailed the plan and given out bearings to the sergeants; nobody had to move very far. I warned everybody to keep eyes open for a company of engineers. As soon as each section reported its listening posts in operation I clicked to the wide circuit: "Odd numbers! Lie down, prepare to sleep . . . one . . . two . . . three . . . four . . . five—sleep!"

A suit is not a bed, but it will do. One good thing about hypno preparation for combat is that, in the unlikely event of a chance to rest, a man can be put to sleep instantly by post-hypnotic command triggered by someone who is not a hypnotist—and awakened just as instantly, alert and ready to fight. It is a life-saver, because a man can get so exhausted in battle that he shoots at things that aren't there and can't see what he should be fighting.

But I had no intention of sleeping. I had not been told to—and I had not asked. The very thought of sleeping when I knew that perhaps many thousands of Bugs were only a few hundred feet away made my stomach jump. Maybe that senser was infallible, perhaps the Bugs could not reach us without alerting our listening posts.

Maybe—But I didn't want to chance it.

I clicked to my private circuit. "Sarge—"

"Yes, sir."

"You might as well get a nap. I'll be on watch. Lie down and prepare to sleep . . . one . . . two—"

"Excuse me, sir. I have a suggestion."

"Yes?"

"If I understand the revised plan, no action is expected for the next four hours. You could take a nap now, and then—"

"Forget it, Sarge! I am not going to sleep. I am going to make the rounds of the listening posts and watch for that sapper company."

"Very well, sir."

"I'll check number three while I'm here. You stay here with Brumby and catch some rest while I—"

"*Johnnie!*"

I broke off. "Yes, captain?" Had the Old Man been listening?

"Are your posts all set?"

"Yes, Captain, and my odd numbers are sleeping. I am about to inspect each post. Then—"

"Let your sergeant do it. I want you to rest."

"But, Captain—"

"Lie down. That's a direct order. Prepare to sleep . . . one . . . two . . . three—*Johnnie!*"

"Captain, with your permission, I would like to inspect my posts first. Then I'll rest, if you say so, but I would rather remain awake. I—"

Blackie guffawed in my ear. "Look, son, you've slept for an hour and ten minutes."

"*Sir?*"

"Check the time." I did so—and felt foolish. "You wide awake, son?"

"Yes, sir. I think so."

"Things have speeded up. Call your odd numbers and put your even numbers to sleep. With luck, they may get an hour. So swap 'em around, inspect your posts, and call me back."

I did so and started my rounds without a word to my platoon sergeant. I was annoyed at both him and Blackie—at my company commander because I resented being put to sleep against my wishes; and as for my platoon sergeant, I had a dirty hunch that it wouldn't have been done if he weren't the real boss and myself just a figurehead.

But after I had checked posts number three and one (no sounds of any sort, both were forward of the Bug area), I cooled down. After all, blaming a sergeant, even a fleet sergeant, for something a captain did was silly. "Sarge—"

"Yes, Mr. Rico?"

"Do you want to catch a nap with the even numbers? I'll wake you a minute or two before I wake them."

He hesitated slightly. "Sir, I'd like to inspect the listening posts myself."

"Haven't you already?"

"No, sir. I've been asleep the past hour."

"*Huh?*"

He sounded embarrassed. "The Captain required me to do so. He placed Brumby temporarily in charge and put me to sleep immediately after he relieved you."

I started to answer, then laughed helplessly. "Sarge? Let's you and I go off somewhere and go back to sleep. We're wasting our time; Cap'n Blackie is running this platoon."

"I have found, sir," he answered stiffly, "that Captain Blackstone invariably has a reason for anything he does."

I nodded thoughtfully, forgetting that I was ten miles from my listener. "Yes. You're right, he always has a reason. Mmm . . . since he had us both sleep, he must want us both awake and alert now."

"I think that must be true."

"Mmm . . . any idea why?"

He was rather long in answering. "Mr. Rico," he said slowly, "if the Captain knew he would tell us; I've never known him to hold back information. But sometimes he does things a certain

way without being able to explain why. The Captain's hunches—
well, I've learned to respect them."

"So? Squad leaders are all even numbers; they're asleep."

"Yes, sir."

"Alert the lance of each squad. We won't wake anybody . . .
but when we do, seconds may be important."

"Right away."

I checked the remaining forward post, then covered the four
posts bracketing the Bug village, jacking my phones in parallel
with each listener. I had to force myself to listen, because you
could *hear* them, down there below, chittering to each other. I
wanted to run and it was all I could do not to let it show.

I wondered if that "special talent" was simply a man with incredibly acute hearing.

Well, no matter how he did it, the Bugs were where he said they
were. Back at O.C.S. we had received demonstrations of recorded
Bug noises; these four posts were picking up typical nest noises of
a large Bug town—that chittering which may be their speech
(though why should they need to talk if they are all remotely controlled by the brain caste?), a rustling like sticks and dry leaves, a
high background whine which is always heard at a settlement and
which had to be machinery—their air conditioning perhaps.

I did not hear the hissing, cracking noise they make in cutting
through rock.

The sounds along the Bug boulevard were unlike the settlement sounds—a low background rumble which increased to a roar
every few moments, as if heavy traffic were passing. I listened at
post number five, then got an idea—checked it by having the
stand by man at each of the four posts along the tunnel call out
"*Mark!*" to me each time the roaring got loudest.

Presently I reported. "Captain—"

"Yeah, Johnnie?"

"The traffic along this Bug race is all moving one way, from
me toward you. Speed is approximately a hundred and ten miles
per hour, a load goes past about once a minute."

"Close enough," he agreed. "I make it one-oh-eight with a
headway of fifty-eight seconds."

"Oh." I felt dashed, and changed the subject. "I haven't seen
that sapper company."

"You won't. They picked a spot in the middle rear of 'Head
Hunter' area: Sorry, I should have told you. Anything more?"

"No, sir." We clicked off and I felt better. Even Blackie could forget . . . and there hadn't been anything *wrong* with my idea. I left the tunnel zone to inspect the listening post to right and rear of the Bug area, post twelve.

As with the others, there were two men asleep, one listening, one stand-by, I said to the stand-by, "Getting anything?"

"No, sir."

The man listening, one of my five recruits, looked up and said, "Mr. Rico, I think this pickup has just gone sour."

"I'll check it," I said. He moved to let me jack in with him.

"Frying bacon" so loud you could smell it!

I hit the all-hands circuit. "First platoon *up!* Wake up, call off, and report!"

—And clicked over to officers' circuit. "Captain! Captain Blackstone! *Urgent!*"

"Slow down, Johnnie. Report."

" 'Frying bacon' sounds, sir," I answered, trying desperately to keep my voice steady. "Post twelve at co-ordinates Easter Nine, Square Black One."

"Easter Nine," he agreed. "Decibels?"

I looked hastily at the meter on the pickup. "I don't know, Captain. Off the scale at the max end. It sounds like they're right under my feet!"

"Good!" he applauded—and I wondered how he could feel that way. "Best news we've had today! Now listen, son. Get your lads awake—"

"They are, sir!"

"Very well. Pull back two listeners, have them spot-check around post twelve. Try to figure where the Bugs are going to break out. *And stay away from that spot!* Understand me?"

"I hear you, sir," I said carefully. "But I do not understand."

He sighed. "Johnnie, you'll turn my hair gray yet. Look, son, we *want* them to come out, the more the better. You don't have the firepower to handle them other than by blowing up their tunnel as they reach the surface—and that is the one thing *you must not do!* If they come out in force, a regiment can't handle them. But that's just what the General wants, and he's got a brigade of heavy weapons in orbit, waiting for it. So you spot that breakthrough, fall back and keep it under observation. If you are lucky enough to have a major breakthrough in your area, your reconnaissance will be patched through all the way to the top. So stay lucky and stay alive! Got it?"

"Yes, sir. Spot the breakthrough. Fall back and avoid contact. Observe and report."

"Get on it!"

I pulled back listeners nine and ten from the middle stretch of "Bug Boulevard" and had them close in on co-ordinates Easter Nine from right and left, stopping every half mile to listen for "frying bacon." At the same time I lifted post twelve and moved it toward our rear, while checking for a dying away of the sound.

In the meantime my platoon sergeant was regrouping the platoon in the forward area between the Bug settlement and the crater—all but twelve men who were ground-listening. Since we were under orders not to attack, we both worried over the prospect of having the platoon spread too widely for mutual support. So he rearranged them in a compact line five miles long, with Brumby's section on the left, nearer the Bug settlement. This placed the men less than three hundred yards apart (almost shoulder to shoulder for cap troopers), and put nine of the men still on listening stations within support distance of one flank or the other. Only the three listeners working with me were out of reach of ready help.

I told Bayonne of the Wolverines and Do Campo of the Head Hunters that I was no longer patrolling and why, and I reported our regrouping to Captain Blackstone.

He grunted. "Suit yourself. Got a prediction on that break-through?"

"It seems to center about Easter Ten, Captain, but it is hard to pin down. The sounds are very loud in an area about three miles across—and it seems to get wider. I'm trying to circle it at an intensity level just barely on scale." I added, "Could they be driving a new horizontal tunnel just under the surface?"

He seemed surprised. "That's possible. I hope not—we want them to come up." He added, "Let me know if the center of the noise moves. Check on it."

"Yes, sir. Captain—"

"Huh? Speak up."

"You told us not to attack when they break out. If they break out. What *are* we to do? Are we just spectators?"

There was a longish delay, fifteen or twenty seconds, and he may have consulted "upstairs." At last he said, "Mr. Rico, you are not to attack at or near Easter Ten. Anywhere else—the idea is to hunt Bugs."

"Yes, sir," I agreed happily. "We hunt Bugs."

"Johnnie!" he said sharply. "If you go hunting medals instead

of Bugs—and I find out—you're going to have a mighty sad-
looking Form Thirty-One!"

"Captain," I said earnestly. "I don't *ever* want to win a medal.
The idea is to hunt Bugs."

"Right. Now quit bothering me."

I called my platoon sergeant, explained the new limits under
which we would work, told him to pass the word along and to
make sure that each man's suit was freshly charged, air and power.

"We've just finished that, sir. I suggest that we relieve the men
with you." He named three reliefs.

That was reasonable, as my ground listeners had had no time
to recharge. But the reliefs he named were all scouts.

Silently I cussed myself for utter stupidity. A scout's suit is as
fast as a command suit, twice the speed of a marauder. I had been
having a nagging feeling of something left undone, and had
checked it off to the nervousness I always feel around Bugs.

Now I knew. Here I was, ten miles away from my platoon with
a party of three men—each in a marauder suit. When the Bugs
broke through, I was going to be faced with an impossible decision . . . unless the men with me could rejoin as fast as I could.
"That's good," I agreed, "but I no longer need three men. Send
Hughes, right away. Have him relieve Nyberg. Use the other three
scouts to relieve the listening posts farthest forward."

"Just Hughes?" he said doubtfully.

"Hughes is enough. I'm going to man one listener myself. Two
of us can straddle the area; we know where they are now." I added,
"Get Hughes down here on the bounce."

For the next thirty-seven minutes nothing happened. Hughes
and I swung back and forth along the forward and rear arcs of the
area around Easter Ten, listening five seconds at a time, then moving on. It was no longer necessary to seat the microphone in rock;
it was enough to touch it to the ground to get the sound of "frying
bacon" strong and clear. The noise area expanded but its center
did not change. Once I called Captain Blackstone to tell him the
sound had abruptly stopped, and again three minutes later to tell
him it had resumed; otherwise I used the scouts' circuit and let my
platoon sergeant take care of the platoon and the listening posts
near the platoon.

At the end of this time everything happened at once.

A voice called out on the scouts' circuit, " 'Bacon Fry'! Albert Two!"

I clicked over and called out, "Captain! 'Bacon Fry' at Albert Two, Black One!"—clicked over to liaison with the platoons surrounding me: "Liaison flash! 'Bacon frying' at Albert Two, Square Black One"—and immediately heard Do Campo reporting: " 'Frying bacon' sounds at Adolf Three, Green Twelve."

I relayed that to Blackie and cut back to my own scouts' circuit, heard: "Bugs! *Bugs! HELP!*"

"Where?"

No answer. I clicked over. "Sarge! Who reported Bugs?"

He rapped back, "Coming up out of their town—about Bangkok Six."

"*Hit 'em!*" I clicked over to Blackie. "Bugs at Bangkok Six, Black One—I am attacking!"

"I heard you order it," he answered calmly. "How about Easter Ten?"

"Easter Ten is—" The ground fell away under me and I was engulfed in Bugs.

I didn't know what had happened to me. I wasn't hurt; it was a bit like falling into the branches of a tree—but those branches were alive and kept jostling me while my gyros complained and tried to keep me upright. I fell ten or fifteen feet, deep enough to be out of the daylight.

Then a surge of living monsters carried me back up into the light—and training paid off; I landed on my feet, talking and fighting: "Breakthrough at Easter Ten—no, Easter Eleven, where I am now. Big hole and they're pouring up. Hundreds. More than that." I had a hand flamer in each hand and was burning them down as I reported.

"Get out of there, Johnnie!"

"Wilco!"—and I started to jump.

And stopped. Checked the jump in time, stopped flaming, and really looked—for I suddenly realized that I ought to be dead. "Correction," I said, looking and hardly believing. "Breakthrough at Easter Eleven is a feint. No warriors."

"Repeat."

"Easter Eleven, Black One. Breakthrough here is entirely by workers so far. No warriors. I am surrounded by Bugs and they are still pouring out, but not a one of them is armed and those nearest me all have typical worker features. I have not been attacked." I added, "Captain, do you think this could be just a diversion? With their real breakthrough to come somewhere else?"

"Could be," he admitted. "Your report is patched through right

to Division, so let them do the thinking. Stir around and check
what you've reported. Don't assume that they are all workers—
you may find out the hard way."

"Right, Captain." I jumped high and wide, intending to get
outside that mass of harmless but loathsome monsters.

That rocky plain was covered with crawly black shapes in all
directions. I overrode my jet controls and increased the jump, calling out, "Hughes! Report!"

"Bugs, Mr. Rico! Zillions of 'em! I'm a-burnin' 'em down!"

"Hughes, take a close look at those Bugs. Any of them fighting
back? Aren't they all workers?"

"Uh—" I hit the ground and bounced again. He went on,
"Hey! You're right, sir! How did you know?"

"Rejoin your squad, Hughes." I clicked over. "Captain, several
thousand Bugs have exited near here from an undetermined number of holes. I have not been attacked. Repeat, I have not been attacked at all. If there are any warriors among them, they must be
holding their fire and using workers as camouflage."

He did not answer.

There was an extremely brilliant flash far off to my left, followed at once by one just like it but farther away to my right front;
automatically I noted time and bearings. "Captain Blackstone—
answer!" At the top of my jump I tried to pick out his beacon, but
that horizon was cluttered by low hills in Square Black Two.

I clicked over and called out, "Sarge! Can you relay to the
Captain for me?"

At that very instant my platoon sergeant's beacon blinked out.

I headed on that bearing as fast as I could push my suit. I had
not been watching my display closely, my platoon sergeant had
the platoon and I had been busy, first with ground-listening and,
most lately, with a few hundred Bugs. I had suppressed all but the
non-com's beacons to allow me to see better.

I studied the skeleton display, picked out Brumby and Cunha,
their squad leaders and section chasers. "Cunha! Where's the platoon sergeant?" "He's reconnoitering a hole, sir."

"Tell him I'm on my way, rejoining." I shifted circuits without
waiting. "First Platoon Blackguards to second platoon—answer!"

"What do you want?" Lieutenant Khoroshen growled.

"I can't raise the Captain."

"You won't, he's out."

"Dead?"

"No. But he's lost power—so he's out."

"Oh. Then you're company commander?"

"All right, all right, so what? Do you want help?"

"Uh . . . no. No, sir."

"Then shut up," Khoroshen told me, "until you do need help. We've got more than we can handle here."

"Okay." I suddenly found that *I* had more than I could handle. While reporting to Khoroshen, I shifted to full display and short range, as I was almost closed with my platoon—and now I saw my first section disappear one by one, Brumby's beacon disappearing first.

"Cunha! What's happening to the first section?"

His voice sounded strained. "They are following the platoon sergeant down."

If there's anything in the book that covers this, I don't know what it is. Had Brumby acted without orders? Or had he been given orders I hadn't heard? Look, the man was already down a Bug hole, out of sight and hearing—is this a time to go legal? We would sort such things out tomorrow. If any of us had a tomorrow—

"Very well," I said. "I'm back now. Report." My last jump brought me among them; I saw a Bug off to my right and I got him before I hit. No worker, this—it had been firing as it moved.

"I've lost three men," Cunha answered, gasping. "I don't know what Brumby lost. They broke out three places at once—that's when we took the casualties. But we're mopping them—"

A tremendous shock wave slammed me just as I bounced again, slapped me sideways. Three minutes thirty-seven seconds— call it thirty miles. Was that our sappers "putting down their corks"? "First section! Brace yourselves for another shock wave!" I landed sloppily, almost on top of a group of three or four Bugs. They weren't dead but they weren't fighting; they just twitched. I donated them a grenade and bounced again. "Hit 'em *now!*" I called out. "They're groggy. And mind that next—"

The second blast hit as I was saying it. It wasn't as violent. "Cunha! Call off your section. And everybody stay on the bounce and mop up."

The call-off was ragged and slow—too many missing files as I could see from my physicals display. But the mop-up was precise and fast. I ranged around the edge and got half a dozen Bugs myself—the last of them suddenly became active just before I flamed it. Why did concussion daze them more than it did us? Because they were unarmored? Or was it their brain Bug, somewhere down below, that was dazed?

The call-off showed nineteen effectives, plus two dead, two hurt, and three out of action through suit failure—and two of these latter Navarre was repairing by vandalizing power units from suits of dead and wounded. The third suit failure was in radio & radar and could not be repaired, so Navarre assigned the man to guard the wounded, the nearest thing to pickup we could manage until we were relieved.

In the meantime I was inspecting, with Sergeant Cunha, the three places where the Bugs had broken through from their nest below. Comparison with the sub map showed, as one could have guessed, that they had cut exits at the places where their tunnels were closest to the surface.

One hole had closed; it was a heap of loose rock. The second one did not show Bug activity; I told Cunha to post a lance and a private there with orders to kill single Bugs, close the hole with a bomb if they started to pour out—it's all very well for the Sky Marshal to sit up there and decide that holes must not be closed, but I had a situation, not a theory.

Then I looked at the third hole, the one that had swallowed up my platoon sergeant and half my platoon.

Here a Bug corridor came within twenty feet of the surface and they had simply removed the roof for about fifty feet. Where the rock went, what caused that "frying bacon" noise while they did it, I could not say. The rocky roof was gone and the sides of the hole were sloped and grooved. The map showed what must have happened; the other two holes came up from small side tunnels, this tunnel was part of their main labyrinth—so the other two had been diversions and their main attack had come from here.

Can those Bugs see through solid rock?

Nothing was in sight down that hole, neither Bug nor human. Cunha pointed out the direction the second section had gone. It had been seven minutes and forty seconds since the platoon sergeant had gone down, slightly over seven since Brumby had gone after him. I peered into the darkness, gulped and swallowed my stomach. "Sergeant, take charge of your section," I said, trying to make it sound cheerful. "If you need help, call Lieutenant Khoroshen."

"Orders, sir?"

"None. Unless some come down from above. I'm going down and find the second section—so I may be out of touch for a while."

Then I jumped down in the hole at once, because my nerve was slipping.

Behind me I heard: "Se*ction!*"

"First squad!"—"Second squad!"—"Third squad!"

"By squads! *Follow me!*"—and Cunha jumped down, too.

It's not nearly so lonely that way.

I had Cunha leave two men at the hole to cover our rear, one on the floor of the tunnel, one at surface level. Then I led them down the tunnel the second section had followed, moving as fast as possible—which wasn't fast as the roof of the tunnel was right over our heads. A man can move in sort of a skating motion in a powered suit without lifting his feet, but it is neither easy nor natural; we could have trotted without armor faster.

Snoopers were needed at once—whereupon we confirmed something that had been theorized: Bugs see by infrared. That dark tunnel was well lighted when seen by snoopers. So far it had no special features, simply glazed rock walls arching over a smooth, level floor.

We came to a tunnel crossing the one we were in and I stopped short of it. There are doctrines for how you should dispose a strike force underground—but what good are they? The only certainty was that the man who had written the doctrines had never himself tried them . . . because, before Operation Royalty, nobody had come back up to tell what had worked and what had not.

One doctrine called for guarding every intersection such as this one. But I had already used two men to guard our escape hole; if I left 10 per cent of my force at each intersection, mighty soon I would be ten-percented to death.

I decided to keep us together . . . decided, too, that none of us would be captured. Not by Bugs. Far better a nice, clean real estate deal . . . and with that decision a load was lifted from my mind and I was no longer worried.

I peered cautiously into the intersection, looked both ways. No Bugs. So I called out over the non-coms' circuit: "Brumby!"

The result was startling. You hardly hear your own voice when using suit radio, as you are shielded from your output. But here, underground in a network of smooth corridors, my output came back to me as if the whole complex were one enormous wave guide:

"BRRRRUMMBY!"

My ears rang with it.

And then rang again: "MR. RRRICCCO!"

"Not so loud," I said, trying to talk very softly myself. "Where are you?"

Brumby answered, not quite so deafeningly, "Sir, I don't know. We're lost."

"Well, take it easy. We're coming to get you. You can't be far away. Is the platoon sergeant with you?"

"No, sir. We never—"

"Hold it." I clicked in my private circuit. "Sarge—"

"I read you, sir." His voice sounded calm and he was holding the volume down. "Brumby and I are in radio contact but we have not been able to make rendezvous."

"Where are you?"

He hesitated slightly. "Sir, my advice is to make rendezvous with Brumby's section—then return to the surface."

"Answer my question."

"Mr. Rico, you could spend a week down here and not find me . . . and I am not able to move. You must—"

"Cut it, Sarge! Are you wounded?"

"No, sir, but—"

"Then why can't you move? Bug trouble?"

"Lots of it. They can't reach me now . . . but I can't come out. So I think you had better—"

"Sarge, you're wasting time! I am certain you know exactly what turns you took. Now tell me, while I look at the map. And give me a vernier reading on your D.R. tracer. That's a direct order. Report."

He did so, precisely and concisely. I switched on my head lamp, flipped up the snoopers, and followed it on the map. "All right," I said presently. "You're almost directly under us and two levels down—and I know what turns to take. We'll be there as soon as we pick up the second section. Hang on." I clicked over. "Brumby—"

"Here, sir."

"When you came to the first tunnel intersection, did you go right, left, or straight ahead?"

"Straight ahead, sir."

"Okay. Cunha, bring 'em along. Brumby, have you got Bug trouble?"

"Not now, sir. But that's how we got lost. We tangled with a bunch of them . . . and when it was over, we were turned around."

I started to ask about casualties, then decided that bad news could wait; I wanted to get my platoon together and get out of there. A Bug town with no bugs in sight was somehow more upsetting than the Bugs we had expected to encounter. Brumby coached us through the next two choices and I tossed tanglefoot bombs down each corridor we did not use. "Tanglefoot" is a derivative of the nerve gas we had been using on Bugs in the past—instead of killing, it gives any Bug that trots through it a sort of shaking palsy. We had been equipped with it for this one operation, and I would have swapped a ton of it for a few pounds of the real stuff. Still, it might protect our flanks.

In one long stretch of tunnel I lost touch with Brumby—some oddity in reflection of radio waves, I guess, for I picked him up at the next intersection.

But there he could not tell me which way to turn. This was the place, or near the place, where the Bugs had hit them.

And here the Bugs hit us.

I don't know where they came from. One instant everything was quiet. Then I heard the cry of "Bugs! *Bugs!*" from back of me in the column, I turned—and suddenly Bugs were everywhere. I suspect that those smooth walls are not as solid as they look; that's the only way I can account for the way they were suddenly all around us and among us.

We couldn't use flamers, we couldn't use bombs; we were too likely to hit each other. But the Bugs didn't have any such compunctions among themselves if they could get one of us. But we had hands and we had feet—

It couldn't have lasted more than a minute, then there were no more Bugs, just broken pieces of them on the floor . . . and four cap troopers down.

One was Sergeant Brumby, dead. During the ruckus the second section had rejoined. They had been not far away, sticking together to keep from getting further lost in that maze, and had heard the fight. Hearing it, they had been able to trace it by sound, where they had not been able to locate us by radio.

Cunha and I made certain that our casualties were actually dead, then consolidated the two sections into one of four squads and down we went—and found the Bugs that had our platoon sergeant besieged.

That fight didn't last any time at all, because he had warned me what to expect. He had captured a brain Bug and was using its bloated body as a shield. He could not get out, but they could not attack him without (quite literally) committing suicide by hitting their own brain.

We were under no such handicap; we hit them from behind.

Then I was looking at the horrid thing he was holding and I was feeling exultant despite our losses, when suddenly I heard close up that "frying bacon" noise. A big piece of roof fell on me and Operation Royalty was over as far as I was concerned.

I woke up in bed and thought that I was back at O.C.S. and had just had a particularly long and complicated Bug nightmare. But I was not at O.C.S.; I was in a temporary sick bay of the transport *Argonne*, and I really had had a platoon of my own for nearly twelve hours.

But now I was just one more patient, suffering from nitrous oxide poisoning and overexposure to radiation through being out of armor for over an hour before being retrieved, plus broken ribs and a knock in the head which had put me out of action.

It was a long time before I got everything straight about Operation Royalty and some of it I'll never know. Why Brumby took his section underground, for example. Brumby is dead and Naidi bought the farm next to his and I'm simply glad that they both got their chevrons and were wearing them that day on Planet P when nothing went according to plan.

I did learn, eventually, why my platoon sergeant decided to go down into that Bug town. He had heard my report to Captain Blackstone that the "major breakthrough" was actually a feint, made with workers sent up to be slaughtered. When real warrior Bugs broke out where he was, he had concluded (correctly and minutes sooner than Staff reached the same conclusion) that the Bugs were making a desperation push, or they would not expend their workers simply to draw our fire.

He saw that their counterattack made from Bug town was not in sufficient force, and concluded that the enemy did not have many reserves—and decided that, at this one golden moment, one man acting alone might have a chance of raiding, finding "royalty" and capturing it. Remember, that was the whole purpose of the operation; we had plenty of force simply to sterilize Planet P, but our object was to capture royalty castes and to learn how to go down in. So he tried it, snatched that one moment—and succeeded on both counts.

It made it "mission accomplished" for the First Platoon of the Blackguards. Not very many platoons, out of many, many hundreds, could say that; no queens were captured (the Bugs killed them first) and only six brains. None of the six were ever exchanged, they didn't live long enough. But the Psych Warfare boys did get live specimens, so I suppose Operation Royalty was a success.

My platoon sergeant got a field commission. I was not offered one (and would not have accepted)—but I was not surprised when I learned that he had been commissioned. Cap'n Blackie had told me that I was getting "the best sergeant in the fleet" and I had never had any doubt that Blackie's opinion was correct. I had met my platoon sergeant before. I don't think any other Blackguard knew this—not from me and certainly not from him. I doubt if Blackie himself knew it. But I had known my platoon sergeant since my first day as a boot.

His name is Zim.

My part in Operation Royalty did not seem a success to me. I was in the *Argonne* more than a month, first as a patient, then as an unattached casual, before they got around to delivering me and a few dozen others to Sanctuary; it gave me too much time to think—mostly about casualties, and what a generally messed-up job I had made out of my one short time on the ground as platoon leader. I knew I hadn't kept everything juggled the way the Lieutenant used to—why, I hadn't even managed to get wounded still swinging; I had let a chunk of rock fall on me.

And casualties—I didn't know how many there were; I just knew that when I closed ranks there were only four squads where I had started with six. I didn't know how many more there might have been before Zim got them to the surface, before the Blackguards were relieved and retrieved.

I didn't even know whether Captain Blackstone was still alive (he was—in fact he was back in command about the time I went underground) and I had no idea what the procedure was if a candidate was alive and his examiner was dead. But I felt that my Form Thirty-One was sure to make me a buck sergeant again. It really didn't seem important that my math books were in another ship.

Nevertheless, when I was let out of bed the first week I was in the *Argonne*, after loafing and brooding a day I borrowed some books from one of the junior officers and got to work. Math is hard work and it occupies your mind—and it doesn't hurt to learn all you can of it, no matter what rank you are; everything of any importance is founded on mathematics.

When I finally checked in at O.C.S. and turned in my pips, I learned that I was a cadet again instead of a sergeant. I guess Blackie gave me the benefit of the doubt.

My roommate, Angel, was in our room with his feet on the desk—and in front of his feet was a package, my math books. He looked up and looked surprised. "Hi, Juan! We thought you had bought it!"

"Me? The Bugs don't like me that well. When do you go out?"

"Why, I've been out," Angel protested. "Left the day after you did, made three drops and been back a week. What took you so long?"

"Took the long way home. Spent a month as a passenger."

"Some people are lucky. What drops did you make?"

"Didn't make any," I admitted.

He stared. "Some people have *all* the luck!"

Perhaps Angel was right; eventually I graduated. But he supplied some of the luck himself, in patient tutoring. I guess my "luck" has usually been people—Angel and Jelly and the Lieutenant and Carl and Lieutenant Colonel Dubois, yes and my father, and Blackie . . . and Brumby . . . and Ace—and always Sergeant Zim. Brevet Captain Zim, now, with permanent rank of First Lieutenant. It wouldn't have been *right* for me to have wound up senior to him.

Bennie Montez, a classmate of mine, and I were at the Fleet landing field the day after graduation, waiting to go up to our ships. We were still such brand-new second lieutenants that being saluted made us nervous and I was covering it by reading the list of ships in orbit around Sanctuary—a list so long that it was clear that something big was stirring, even though they hadn't seen fit to mention it to me. I felt excited. I had my two dearest wishes, in one package—posted to my old outfit and while my father was still there, too. And now this, whatever it was, meant that I was about to have the polish put on me by "makee-learnee" under Lieutenant Jelal, with some important drop coming up.

I was so full of it all that I couldn't talk about it, so I studied the lists. Whew, what a lot of ships! They were posted by types, too many to locate otherwise. I started reading off the troop carriers, the only ones that matter to an M.I.

There was the *Mannerheim!* Any chance of seeing Carmen? Probably not, but I could send a dispatch and find out.

Big ships—the new *Valley Forge* and the new *Y pres, Marathon, El Alamein, Iwo, Gallipoli, Leyte, Marne, Tours, Gettysburg, Hastings, Alamo, Waterloo*—all places where mud feet had made their names to shine.

Little ships, the ones named for foot sloggers: *Horatius, Alvin York, Swamp Fox,* the *Rog* herself, bless her heart, *Colonel Bowie, Devereux, Vercingetorix, Sandino, Aubrey Cousens, Kamehameha, Audie Murphy, Xenophon, Aguinaldo*—

I said, "There ought to be one named Magsaysay."

Bennie said, "What?"

"Ramón Magsaysay," I explained. "Great man, great soldier— probably be chief of psychological warfare if he were alive today. Didn't you ever study any history?"

"Well," admitted Bennie, "I learned that Simón Bolívar built the Pyramids, licked the Armada, and made the first trip to the moon."

"You left out marrying Cleopatra."

"Oh, that. Yup. Well, I guess every country has its own version of history."

"I'm sure of it." I added something to myself and Bennie said, "What did you say?"

"Sorry, Bernardo. Just an old saying in my own language. I suppose you could translate it, more or less, as: 'Home is where the heart is.' "

"But what language was it?"

"Tagalog. My native language."

"Don't they talk Standard English where you come from?"

"Oh, certainly. For business and school and so forth. We just talk the old speech around home a little. Traditions. You know."

"Yeah, I know. My folks chatter in Español the same way. But where do you—" The speaker started playing "Meadowland"; Bennie broke into a grin. "Got a date with a ship! Watch yourself, fellow! See you."

"Mind the Bugs." I turned back and went on reading ships' names: *Pal Maleter, Montgomery, Tchaka, Geronimo*—

Then came the sweetest sound in the world: "—*shines the name, shines the name of Rodger Young!*"

I grabbed my kit and hurried. "Home is where the heart is"— I was going home.

Chapter 14

Am I my brother's keeper?
—Genesis IV:9

*How think ye? If a man have an hundred sheep, and
one of them be gone astray, doth he not leave the
ninety and nine, and goeth into the mountains, and
seeketh that which is gone astray?*
—Matthew XII:12

How much then is a man better than a sheep?
—Matthew XVIII:12

*In the Name of God, the Beneficent, the Merciful . . .
whoso saveth the life of one, it shall be as if he had
saved the life of all mankind.*
—The Koran, Sûrah V, 32

Each year we gain a little. You have to keep a sense of proportion.

"Time, sir." My j.o. under instruction, Candidate or "Third
Lieutenant" Bearpaw, stood just outside my door. He looked and
sounded awfully young, and was about as harmless as one of his
scalp-hunting ancestors.

"Right, Jimmie." I was already in armor. We walked aft
to the drop room. I said, as we went, "One word, Jimmie.
Stick with me and keep out of my way. Have fun and use
up your ammo. If by any chance I buy it, you're the boss—

but if you're smart, you'll let your platoon sergeant call the signals."

"Yes, sir."

As we came in, the platoon sergeant called them to attention and saluted. I returned it, said, "At ease," and started down the first section while Jimmie looked over the second.

Then I inspected the second section, too, checking everything on every man. My platoon sergeant is much more careful than I am, so I didn't find anything, I never do. But it makes the men feel better if their Old Man scrutinizes everything—besides, it's my job.

Then I stepped out in the middle. "Another Bug hunt, boys. This one is a little different, as you know. Since they still hold prisoners of ours, we can't use a nova bomb on Klendathu—so this time we go down, stand on it, hold it, take it away from them. The boat won't be down to retrieve us; instead it'll fetch more ammo and rations. If you're taken prisoner, keep your chin up and follow the rules—because you've got the whole outfit behind you, you've got the whole Federation behind you; we'll come and get you. That's what the boys from the *Swamp Fox* and the *Montgomery* have been depending on. Those who are still alive are waiting, knowing that we will show up. And here we are. Now we go get 'em.

"Don't forget that we'll have help all around us, lots of help above us. All we have to worry about is our one little piece, just the way we rehearsed it.

"One last thing. I had a letter from Captain Jelal just before we left. He says that his new legs work fine. But he also told me to tell *you* that he's got you in mind . . . and he expects your names to *shine!*

"And so do I. Five minutes for the Padre."

I felt myself beginning to shake. It was a relief when I could call them to attention again and add: "By sections . . . port and starboard . . . prepare for drop!"

I was all right then while I inspected each man into his cocoon down one side, with Jimmie and the platoon sergeant taking the other. Then we buttoned Jimmie into the No. 3 center-line capsule. Once his face was covered up, the shakes really hit me.

My platoon sergeant put his arm around my armored shoulders. "Just like a drill, Son."

"I know it, Father." I stopped shaking at once. "It's the waiting, that's all."

"I know. Four minutes. Shall we get buttoned up, sir?"

"Right away, Father." I gave him a quick hug, let the Navy drop crew seal us in. The shakes didn't start up again. Shortly I was able to report: "Bridge! Rico's Roughnecks . . . ready for drop!"

"Thirty-one seconds, Lieutenant." She added, "Good luck, boys! This time we take 'em!"

"Right, Captain."

"Check. Now some music while you wait?" She switched it on: "To the everlasting glory of the Infantry—"

HISTORICAL NOTE

Young, Rodger W., Private, 148th Infantry, 37th Infantry Division (the Ohio Buckeyes); born Tiffin, Ohio, 28 April 1918; died 31 July 1943, on the island New Georgia, Solomons, South Pacific, while singlehandedly attacking and destroying an enemy machine-gun pillbox. His platoon had been pinned down by intense fire from this pillbox; Private Young was wounded in the first burst. He crawled toward the pillbox, was wounded a second time but continued to advance, firing his rifle as he did so. He closed on the pillbox, attacked and destroyed it with hand grenades, but in so doing he was wounded a third time and killed.

His bold and gallant action in the face of overwhelming odds enabled his teammates to escape without loss; he was awarded posthumously the Medal of Honor.

PODKAYNE OF MARS

For Gale and Astrid

Chapter 1

All my life I've wanted to go to Earth. Not to live, of course—just to see it. As everybody knows, Terra is a wonderful place to visit but not to live. Not truly suited to human habitation.

Personally, I'm not convinced that the human race originated on Earth. I mean to say, how much reliance should you place on the evidence of a few pounds of old bones plus the opinions of anthropologists who usually contradict each other anyhow when what you are being asked to swallow so obviously flies in the face of all common sense?

Think it through—The surface acceleration of Terra is clearly too great for the human structure; it is known to result in flat feet and hernias and heart trouble. The incident solar radiation on Terra will knock down dead an unprotected human in an amazingly short time—and do you know of any other organism which has to be artificially protected from what is alleged to be its own natural environment in order to stay alive? As to Terran ecology—

Never mind. We humans just *couldn't* have originated on Earth. Nor (I admit) on Mars, for that matter—although Mars is certainly as near ideal as you can find in this planetary system today. Possibly the Missing Planet was our first home—even though I think of Mars as "home" and will always want to return to it no matter how far I travel in later years . . . and I intend to travel a long, *long* way.

But I do want to visit Earth as a starter, not only to see how in the world eight billion people manage to live almost sitting in each other's laps (less than half of the land area of Terra is even marginally habitable) but mostly to see oceans . . .

from a safe distance. Oceans are not only fantasically unlikely
but to me the very thought of them is terrifying. All that
unimaginable amount of water, unconfined. And so deep that if
you fell into it, it would be over your head. Incredible!

But now we are going there!

Perhaps I should introduce us. The Fries Family, I mean. Myself: Podkayne Fries—"Poddy" to my friends and we might as
well start off being friendly. Adolescent female: I'm eight plus a
few months, at a point in my development described by my Uncle
Tom as "frying size and just short of husband high"—a fair-
enough description since a female citizen of Mars may contract
plenary marriage without guardian's waiver on her ninth birthday,
and I stand 157 centimeters tall in my bare feet and mass 49 kilograms. "Five feet two and eyes of blue" my daddy calls me, but he
is a historian and romantic. But I am not romantic and would not
consider even a limited marriage on my ninth birthday; I have
other plans.

Not that I am opposed to marriage in due time, nor do I expect to have any trouble snagging the male of my choice. In these
memoirs I shall be frank rather than modest because they will not
be published until I am old and famous, and I will certainly revise
them before then. In the meantime I am taking the precaution of
writing English in Martian Oldscript—a combination which I'm
sure Daddy could puzzle out, only he wouldn't do such a thing
unless I invited him to. Daddy is a dear and does not snooper-
vise me. My brother Clark would pry, but he regards English as a
dead language and would never bother his head with Oldscript
anyhow.

Perhaps you have seen a book titled: *Eleven Years Old: The
Pre-Adolescent Adjustment Crisis in the Male*. I read it, hoping
that it would help me to cope with my brother. Clark is just six, but
the "Eleven Years" referred to in that title are Terran years because
it was written on Earth. If you will apply the conversion factor of
1.8808 to attain real years, you will see that my brother is exactly
eleven of those undersized Earth years old.

That book did not help me much. It talks about "cushioning
the transition into the social group"—but there is no present indi-
cation that Clark ever intends to join the human race. He is more
likely to devise a way to blow up the universe just to hear the
bang. Since I am responsible for him much of the time and since
he has an I.Q. of 160 while mine is only 145, you can readily see

that I need all the advantage that greater age and maturity can give me. At present my standing rule with him is: Keep your guard up and *never* offer hostages.

Back to me—I'm colonial mongrel in ancestry, but the Swedish part is dominant in my looks, with Polynesian and Asiatic fractions adding no more than a not-unpleasing exotic flavor. My legs are long for my height, my waist is 48 centimeters and my chest is 90—not all of which is rib cage, I assure you, even though we old colonial families all run to hypertrophied lung development; some of it is burgeoning secondary sex characteristic. Besides that, my hair is pale blond and wavy and I'm pretty. Not beautiful—Praxiteles would not have given me a second look— but real beauty is likely to scare a man off, or else make him quite unmanageable, whereas prettiness, properly handled, is an asset.

Up till a couple of years ago I used to regret not being male (in view of my ambitions), but I at last realized how silly I was being; one might as well wish for wings. As Mother says: "One works with available materials" . . . and I found that the materials available were adequate. In fact I found that I *like* being female; my hormone balance is okay and I'm quite well adjusted to the world and vice versa. I'm smart enough not unnecessarily to show that I am smart; I've got a long upper lip and a short nose, and when I wrinkle my nose and look baffled, a man is usually only too glad to help me, especially if he is about twice my age. There are more ways of computing a ballistic than by counting it on your fingers.

That's me: Poddy Fries, free citizen of Mars, female. Future pilot and someday commander of deep-space exploration parties. Watch for me in the news.

Mother is twice as good-looking as I am and much taller than I ever will be; she looks like a Valkyrie about to gallop off into the sky. She holds a system-wide license as a Master Engineer, Heavy Construction, Surface or Free Fall, and is entitled to wear both the Hoover Medal with cluster and the Christiana Order, Knight Commander, for bossing the rebuilding of Deimos and Phobos. But she's more than just the traditional hairy engineer; she has a social presence which she can switch from warmly charming to frostily intimidating at will, she holds honorary degrees galore, and she publishes popular little gems such as "Design Criteria with Respect to the Effects of Radiation on the Bonding of Pressure-Loaded Sandwich Structures."

It is because Mother is often away from home for professional reasons that I am, from time to time, the reluctant custodian of my younger brother. Still, I suppose it is good practice, for how can I ever expect to command my own ship if I can't tame a six-year-old savage? Mother says that a boss who is forced to part a man's hair with a wrench has failed at some point, so I try to control our junior nihilist without resorting to force. Besides, using force on Clark is very chancy; he masses as much as I do and he fights dirty.

It was the job Mother did on Deimos that accounts for Clark and myself. Mother was determined to meet her construction dates; and Daddy, on leave from Ares U. with a Guggenheim grant, was even more frantically determined to save every scrap of the ancient Martian artifacts no matter how much it delayed construction; this threw them into such intimate and bitter conflict that they got married and for a while Mother had babies.

Daddy and Mother are Jack Spratt and his wife; he is interested in everything that has already happened, she is interested only in what is going to happen, especially if she herself is making it happen. Daddy's title is Van Loon Professor of Terrestrial History but his real love is Martian history, especially if it happened fifty million years ago. But do not think that Daddy is a cloistered don given only to contemplation and study. When he was even younger than I am now, he lost an arm one chilly night in the attack on the Company Offices during the Revolution—and he can still shoot straight and fast with the hand he has left.

The rest of our family is Great-Uncle Tom, Daddy's father's brother. Uncle Tom is a parasite. So he says. It is true that you don't see him work much, but he was an old man before I was born. He is a Revolutionary veteran, same as Daddy, and is a Past Grand Commander of the Martian Legion and a Senator-at-Large of the Republic, but he doesn't seem to spend much time on either sort of politics, Legion or public; instead he hangs out at the Elks Club and plays pinochle with other relics of the past. Uncle Tom is really my closest relative, for he isn't as intense as my parents, nor as busy, and will always take time to talk with me. Furthermore he has a streak of Original Sin which makes him sympathetic to my problems. He says that I have such a streak, too, much wider than his. Concerning this, I reserve my opinion.

That's our family and we are all going to Earth. Wups! I left out three—the infants. But they hardly count now and it is easy to forget them. When Daddy and Mother got married, the PEG

Board—Population, Ecology, & Genetics—pegged them at five and would have allowed them seven had they requested it, for, as you may have gathered, my parents are rather high-grade citizens even among planetary colonials all of whom are descended from, or are themselves, highly selected and drastically screened stock.

But Mother told the Board that five was all that she had time for and then had us as fast as possible, while fidgeting at a desk job in the Bureau of Planetary Engineering. Then she popped her babies into deep-freeze as fast as she had them, all but me, since I was the first. Clark spent two years at constant entropy, else he would be almost as old as I am—deep-freeze time doesn't count, of course, and his official birthday is the day he was decanted. I remember how jealous I was—Mother was just back from conditioning Juno and it didn't seem fair to me that she would immediately start raising a baby.

Uncle Tom talked me out of that, with a lot of lap sitting, and I am no longer jealous of Clark—merely wary.

So we've got Gamma, Delta, and Epsilon in the sub-basement of the crèche at Marsopolis, and we'll uncork and name at least one of them as soon as we get back from Earth. Mother is thinking of revivifying Gamma and Epsilon together and raising them as twins (they're girls) and then launching Delta, who is a boy, as soon as the girls are housebroken. Daddy says that is not fair, because Delta is entitled to be older than Epsilon by natural priority of birth date. Mother says that is mere worship of precedent and that she does wish Daddy would learn to leave his reverence for the past on the campus when he comes home in the evening.

Daddy says that Mother has no sentimental feelings—and Mother says she certainly hopes not, at least with any problem requiring rational analysis—and Daddy says let's be rational, then . . . twin older sisters would either break a boy's spirit or else spoil him rotten.

Mother says that is unscientific and unfounded. Daddy says that Mother merely wants to get two chores out of the way at once—whereupon Mother heartily agrees and demands to know why proved production engineering principles should not be applied to domestic economy?

Daddy doesn't answer this. Instead he remarks thoughtfully that he must admit that two little girls dressed just alike would be kind of cute . . . name them "Margret" and "Marguerite" and call them "Peg" and "Meg"—

Clark muttered to me, "Why uncork them at all? Why not just sneak down some night and open the valves and call it an accident?"

I told him to go wash out his mouth with prussic acid and not let Daddy hear him talk that way. Daddy would have walloped him properly. Daddy, although a historian, is devoted to the latest, most progressive theories of child psychology and applies them by canalizing the cortex through pain association whenever he really wants to ensure that a lesson will not be forgotten. As he puts it so neatly: "Spare the rod and spoil the child."

I canalize most readily and learned very early indeed how to predict and avoid incidents which would result in Daddy's applying his theories and his hand. But in Clark's case it is almost necessary to use a club simply to gain his divided attention.

So it is now clearly evident that we are going to have twin baby sisters. But it is no headache of mine, I am happy to say, for Clark is quite enough maturing trauma for one girl's adolescence. By the time the twins are a current problem I expect to be long gone and far away.

Interlude

Hi, Pod.

So you think I can't read your worm tracks.

A lot you know about me! Poddy—oh, excuse me, "Captain" Podkayne Fries, I mean, the famous Space Explorer and Master of Men—Captain Poddy dear, you probably will never read this because it wouldn't occur to you that I not only would break your "code" but also write comments in the big, wide margins you leave.

Just for the record, Sister dear, I read Old Anglish just as readily as I do System Ortho. Anglish isn't all that hard and I learned it as soon as I found out that a lot of books I wanted to read had never been translated. But it doesn't pay to tell everything you know, or somebody comes along and tells you to stop doing whatever it is you are doing. Probably your older sister.

But imagine calling a straight substitution a "code"! Poddy, if you had actually been able to write Old Martian, it would have taken me quite a lot longer. But you can't. Shucks, even Dad can't write it without stewing over it and he probably knows more about Old Martian than anyone else in the System.

But you won't crack my code—because I haven't any.

Try looking at this page under ultraviolet light—a sun lamp, for example.

Chapter 2

Oh, *Unspeakables*!

Dirty ears! Hangnails! Snel-frockey! *Spit!* WE AREN'T *GOING*!

At first I thought that my brother Clark had managed one of his more charlatanous machinations of malevolent legerdemain. But fortunately (the only fortunate thing about the whole miserable mess) I soon perceived that it was impossible for him to be in fact guilty no matter what devious subversions roil his id. Unless he has managed to invent and build in secret a time machine, which I misdoubt he *would* do if he could . . . nor am I prepared to offer odds that he can't. Not since the time he rewired the delivery robot so that it would serve him midnight snacks and charge them to my code number without (so far as anyone could ever prove) disturbing the company's seal on the control box.

We'll never know how he did that one, because, despite the fact that the company offered to Forgive All and pay a cash bonus to boot if only he would *please* tell them how he managed to beat their unbeatable seal—despite this, Clark looked blank and would not talk. That left only circumstantial evidence, i.e., it was clearly evident to anyone who knew us both (Daddy and Mother, namely) that *I* would never order candy-stripe ice cream smothered in hollandaise sauce, or—no, I can't go on; I feel ill. Whereas Clark is widely known to eat anything which does not eat him first.

Even this clinching psychological evidence would never have convinced the company's adjuster had not their own records proved that two of these obscene feasts had taken place while I was a house guest of friends in Syrtis Major, a thousand kilometers away. Never mind, I simply want to warn all girls not to have a Mad Genius for a baby brother. Pick instead a stupid, stolid, slightly subnormal one who will sit quietly in front of the solly box, mouth agape at cowboy classics, and never wonder what makes the pretty images.

But I have wandered far from my tragic tale.

We aren't going to have twins.

We already have triplets.

Gamma, Delta, and Epsilon, throughout all my former life mere topics of conversation, are now Grace, Duncan, and Elspeth in all too solid flesh—unless Daddy again changes his mind before final registration; they've had three sets of names already. But what's in a name?—they are here, already in our home with a nursery room sealed on to shelter them . . . three helpless unfinished humans about canal-worm pink in color and no features worthy of the name. Their limbs squirm aimlessly, their eyes don't track, and a faint, queasy odor of sour milk permeates every room even when they are freshly bathed. Appalling sounds come from one end of each—in which they heterodyne each other—and even more appalling conditions prevail at the other ends. (I've yet to find all three of them dry at the same time.)

And yet there is something decidedly engaging about the little things; were it not that they are the proximate cause of my tragedy I could easily grow quite fond of them. I'm sure Duncan is beginning to recognize me already.

But, if I am beginning to be reconciled to their presence, Mother's state can only be described as atavistically maternal. Her professional journals pile up unread, she has that soft Madonna look in her eyes, and she seems somehow both shorter and wider than she did a week ago.

First consequence: she won't even discuss going to Earth, with or without the triplets.

Second consequence: Daddy won't go if she won't go—he spoke quite sharply to Clark for even suggesting it.

Third consequence: since they won't go, we can't go. Clark and me, I mean. It is conceivably possible that I might have been permitted to travel alone (since Daddy agrees that I am now a "young adult" in maturity and judgment even though my ninth birthday lies still some months in the future), but the question is formal and without content since I am not considered quite old

enough to accept full responsible control of my brother with both
my parents some millions of kilometers away (nor am I sure that I
would wish to, unless armed with something at least as convincing
as a morning star) and Daddy is so dismayingly fair that he would
not even discuss permitting one of us to go and not the other when
both of us had been promised the trip.

Fairness is a priceless virtue in a parent—but just at the moment I could stand being spoiled and favored instead.

But the above is why I am sure that Clark does not have a time
machine concealed in his wardrobe. This incredible contretemps,
this idiot's dream of interlocking mishaps, is as much to his disadvantage as it is to mine.

How did it happen? Gather ye round—Little did we dream
that, when the question of a family trip to Earth was being
planned in our household more than a month ago, this disaster was
already complete and simply waiting the most hideous moment to
unveil itself. The facts are these: the crèche at Marsopolis has
thousands of newborn babies marbleized at just short of absolute
zero, waiting in perfect safety until their respective parents are
ready for them. It is said, and I believe it, that a direct hit with a
nuclear bomb would not hurt the consigned infants; a thousand
years later a rescue squad could burrow down and find that automatic, self-maintaining machinery had not permitted the tank
temperatures to vary a hundredth of a degree.

In consequence, we Marsmen (not "Martians," please!—
Martians are a non-human race, now almost extinct)—Marsmen
tend to marry early, have a full quota of babies quickly, then rear
them later, as money and time permit. It reconciles that discrepancy, so increasingly and glaringly evident ever since the Terran
Industrial Revolution, between the best biological age for having
children and the best social age for supporting and rearing them.

A couple named Breeze did just that, some ten years ago—
married on her ninth birthday and just past his tenth, while he was
still a pilot cadet and she was attending Ares U. They applied for
three babies, were pegged accordingly, and got them all out of the
way while they were both finishing school. Very sensible.

The years roll past, he as a pilot and later as master, she as a fi-
nance clerk in his ship and later as purser—a happy life. The
spacelines like such an arrangement; married couples spacing together mean a taut, happy ship.

Captain and Mrs. Breeze serve their ten-and-a-half (twenty
Terran) years and put in for half-pay retirement, have it

confirmed—and immediately radio the crèche to uncork their babies, all three of them.

The radio order is received, relayed back for confirmation; the crèche accepts it. Five weeks later the happy couple pick up three babies, sign for them, and start the second half of a perfect life.

So they thought—

But what they had deposited was two boys and a girl; what they got was two girls and a boy. Ours.

Believe this you must—it took them the better part of a week to notice it. I will readily concede that the difference between a brand-new boy baby and a brand-new girl baby is, at the time, almost irrelevant. Nevertheless there is a slight difference. Apparently it was a case of too much help—between a mother, a mother-in-law, a temporary nurse, and a helpful neighbor, and much running in and out, it seems unlikely that any one person bathed all three babies as one continuous operation that first week. Certainly Mrs. Breeze had not done so—until the day she did . . . and noticed . . . and fainted—and dropped one of our babies in the bath water, where it would have drowned had not her scream fetched both her husband and the neighbor lady.

So we suddenly had month-old triplets.

The lawyer man from the crèche was very vague about how it happened; he obviously did not want to discuss how their "foolproof" identification system could result in such a mixup. So I don't know myself—but it seems logically certain that, for all their serial numbers, babies' footprints, record machines, et cetera, there is some point in the system where one clerk read aloud "Breeze" from the radioed order and another clerk checked a file, then punched "Fries" into a machine that did the rest.

But the fixer man did not say. He was simply achingly anxious to get Mother and Daddy to settle out of court—accept a check and sign a release under which they agreed not to publicize the error.

They settled for three years of Mother's established professional earning power while the little fixer man gulped and looked relieved.

But nobody offered to pay *me* for the mayhem that had been committed on my life, my hopes, and my ambitions.

Clark did offer a suggestion that was almost a sensible one, for him. He proposed that we swap even with the Breezes, let them keep the warm ones, we could keep the cold ones. Everybody happy—and we all go to Earth.

My brother is far too self-centered to realize it, but the Angel of Death brushed him with its wings at that point. Daddy is a truly noble soul . . . but he had had almost more than he could stand.

And so have I. I had expected today to be actually on my way to Earth, my first space trip farther than Phobos—which was merely a school field trip, our "Class Honeymoon." A nothing thing.

Instead, guess what I'm doing.

Do you have any idea how many times a day *three* babies have to be changed?

Chapter 3

Hold it! Stop the machines! Wipe the tapes! Cancel all bulletins—
WE ARE GOING TO EARTH *AFTER ALL*!!!!

Well, not *all* of us. Daddy and Mother aren't going, and of course, the triplets are not. But— Never mind; I had better tell it in order.

Yesterday things just got to be Too Much. I had changed them in rotation, only to find as I got the third one dry and fresh that number one again needed service. I had been thinking sadly that just about that moment I should have been entering the dining saloon of S.S. *Wanderlust* to the strains of soft music. Perhaps on the arm of one of the officers . . . perhaps even on the arm of the Captain himself had I the chance to arrange an accidental Happy Encounter, then make judicious use of my "puzzled kitten" expression.

And, as I reached that point in my melancholy daydream, it was then that I discovered that my chores had started all over again. I thought of the Augean Stables and suddenly it was just Too Much and my eyes got blurry with tears.

Mother came in at that point and I asked if I could *please* have a couple of hours of recess?

She answered, "Why, certainly dear," and didn't even glance at me. I'm sure that she didn't notice that I was crying; she was already doing over, quite unnecessarily, the one that I had just done. She had been tied up on the phone, telling someone firmly that, while it was true as reported that she was not leaving Mars, nevertheless she would not now accept another commission even as a consultant—and no doubt being away from the infants for all of ten minutes had made her uneasy, so she just had to get her hands on one of them.

Mother's behavior had been utterly unbelievable. Her cortex has tripped out of circuit and her primitive instincts are in full charge. She reminds me of a cat we had when I was a little girl—Miss Polka Dot Ma'am and her first litter of kittens. Miss Pokie loved and trusted all of us—except about kittens. If we touched one of them, she was uneasy about it. If a kitten was taken out of her box and placed on the floor to be admired, she herself would hop out, grab the kitten in her teeth and immediately return it to the box, with an indignant waggle to her seat that showed all too plainly what she thought of irresponsible people who didn't know how to handle babies.

Mother is just like that now. She accepts my help simply because there is too much for her to do alone. But she doesn't really believe that I can even pick up a baby without close supervision.

So I left and followed my own blind instincts, which told me to go look up Uncle Tom.

I found him at the Elks Club, which was reasonably certain at that time of day, but I had to wait in the ladies' lounge until he came out of the card room. Which he did in about ten minutes, counting a wad of money as he came. "Sorry to make you wait," he said, "but I was teaching a fellow citizen about the uncertainties in the laws of chance and I had to stay long enough to collect the tuition. How marches it, Podkayne mavourneen?"

I tried to tell him and got all choked up, so he walked me to the park under the city hall and sat me on a bench and bought us both packages of Choklatpops and I ate mine and most of his and watched the stars on the ceiling and told him all about it and felt better.

He patted my hand. "Cheer up, Flicka. Always remember that, when things seem darkest, they usually get considerably worse." He took his phone out of a pocket and made a call. Presently he said, "Never mind the protocol routine, miss. This is Senator Fries. I want the Director." Then he added in a moment, "Hymie? Tom Fries here. How's Judith? Good, good . . . Hymie, I just called to tell you that I'm coming over to stuff you into one of your own liquid helium tanks. Oh, say about fourteen or a few minutes after. That'll give you time to get out of town. Clearing." He pocketed his phone. "Let's get some lunch. Never commit suicide on an empty stomach, my dear; it's bad for the digestion."

Uncle Tom took me to the Pioneers Club where I have been

only once before and which is even more impressive than I had
recalled— It has *real waiters* . . . men so old that they might have
been pioneers themselves, unless they met the first ship. Everybody fussed over Uncle Tom and he called them all by their first
names and they all called him "Tom" but made it sound like "Your
Majesty" and the master of the hostel came over and prepared my
sweet himself with about six other people standing around to hand
him things, like a famous surgeon operating against the swift on-
rush of death.

Presently Uncle Tom belched behind his napkin and I thanked
everybody as we left while wishing that I had had the forethought
to wear my unsuitable gown that Mother won't let me wear until
I'm nine and almost made me take back—one doesn't get to the
Pioneers Club every day.

We took the James Joyce Fogarty Express Tunnel and Uncle
Tom sat down the whole way, so I had to sit, too, although it makes
me restless; I prefer to walk in the direction a tunnel is moving and
get there a bit sooner. But Uncle Tom says that he gets plenty of
exercise watching other people work themselves to death.

I didn't really realize that we were going to the Marsopolis
Crèche until we were there, so bemused had I been earlier with
my own tumultuous emotions. But when we were there and facing
a sign reading: OFFICE OF THE DIRECTOR—PLEASE USE OTHER
DOOR, Uncle Tom said, "Hang around somewhere; I'll need you
later," and went on in.

The waiting room was crowded and the only magazines not in
use were *Kiddie Kapers* and *Modern Homemaker*, so I wandered
around a bit and presently found a corridor that led to the Nursery.

The sign on the door said that visiting hours were from 16 to
18.30. Furthermore, it was locked, so I moved on and found another door which seemed much more promising. It was marked:
POSITIVELY NO ADMITTANCE—but it didn't say "This Means You"
and it wasn't locked, so I went in.

You never saw so many babies in your whole life!

Row upon row upon row, each in its own little transparent cubicle. I could really see only the row nearest me, all of which
seemed to be about the same age—and much more finished than
the three we had at home. Little brown dumplings they were, cute
as puppies. Most of them were asleep, some were awake and kicking and cooing and grabbing at dangle toys that were just in reach.
If there had not been a sheet of glass between me and them I
would have grabbed me a double armful of babies.

There were a lot of girls in the room, too—well, young women, really. Each of them seemed to be busy with a baby and they didn't notice me. But shortly one of the babies nearest me started to cry whereupon a light came on over its cubicle, and one of the nurse girls hurried over, slid back the cover, picked it up and started patting its bottom. It stopped crying.

"Wet?" I inquired.

She looked up, saw me. "Oh, no, the machines take care of that. Just lonely, so I'm loving it." Her voice came through clearly in spite of the glass—a hear and speak circuit, no doubt, although the pickups were not in evidence. She made soft noises to the baby, then added, "Are you a new employee? You seem to be lost."

"Oh, no," I said hastily, "I'm not an employee. I just—"

"Then you don't belong here, not at this hour. Unless"—she looked at me rather skeptically—"just possibly you are looking for the instruction class for young mothers?"

"Oh, no, no!" I said hastily. "Not yet." Then I added still more hastily, "I'm a guest of the Director."

Well, it wasn't a fib. Not quite. I was a guest of a guest of the Director, one who was with him by appointment. The relationship was certainly concatenative, if not equivalent.

It seemed to reassure her. She asked, "Just what did you want? Can I help you?"

"Uh, just information. I'm making a sort of a survey. What goes on in this room?"

"These are age six-month withdrawal contracts," she told me. "All these babies will be going home in a few days." She put the baby, quiet now, back into its private room, adjusted a nursing nipple for it, made some other sort of adjustments on the outside of the cubicle so that the padding inside sort of humped up and held the baby steady against the milk supply, then closed the top, moved on a few meters and picked up another baby. "Personally," she added, "I think the age six-month contract is the best one. A child twelve months old is old enough to notice the transition. But these aren't. They don't care who comes along and pets them when they cry . . . but nevertheless six months is long enough to get a baby well started and take the worst of the load off the mother. We know how, we're used to it, we stand our watches in rotation so that we are never exhausted from being 'up with the baby all night' . . . and in consequence we aren't short-tempered and we never yell at them—and don't think for a minute that a baby doesn't understand a cross tone of voice simply because he can't talk yet. He knows! And it can start him off so twisted that he may take it out on somebody else, years and years later. There, there, honey," she went on but not to me, "feel better now? Feeling sleepy, huh? Now you just hold still and Martha will keep her hand on you until you are fast asleep."

She watched the baby for a moment longer, then withdrew her hand, closed the box and hurried on to where another light was burning. "A baby has no sense of time," she added as she removed a squalling lump of fury from its crib. "When it needs love, it needs it right now. It can't know that—" An older woman had come up behind her. "Yes, Nurse?"

"Who is this you're chatting with? You know the rules."

"But . . . she's a guest of the Director."

The older woman looked at me with a stern no-nonsense look. "The Director sent you in here?"

I was making a split-second choice among three non-responsive answers when I was saved by Fate. A soft voice coming from everywhere at once announced: "Miss Podkayne Fries is requested to come to the office of the Director. Miss Podkayne Fries, please come to the office of the Director."

I tilted my nose in the air and said with dignity, "That is I. Nurse, will you be so kind as to phone the Director and tell him that Miss Fries is on her way?" I exited with deliberate haste.

The Director's office was four times as big and sixteen times as impressive as the principal's office at school. The Director was short and had a dark brown skin and a gray goatee and a harried expression. In addition to him and to Uncle Tom, of course, there was present the little lawyer man who had had a bad time with Daddy a week earlier—and my brother Clark. I couldn't figure out how he got there . . . except that Clark has an infallible homing instinct for trouble.

Clark looked at me with no expression; I nodded. The Director and his legal beagle stood up. Uncle Tom didn't but he said, "Dr. Hyman Schoenstein, Mr. Poon Kwai Yau—my niece Podkayne Fries. Sit down, honey; nobody is going to bite you. The Director has a proposition to offer you."

The lawyer man interrupted. "I don't think—"

"Correct," agreed Uncle Tom. "You don't think. Or it would have occurred to you that ripples spread out from a splash."

"But— Dr. Schoenstein, the release I obtained from Professor

Fries explicitly binds him to silence, for separate good and sufficient consideration, over and above damages conceded by us and
made good. This is tantamount to blackmail. I—"

Then Uncle Tom did stand up. He seemed twice as tall as
usual and was grinning like a fright mask. "What was that last
word you used?"

"I?" The lawyer looked startled. "Perhaps I spoke hastily. I
simply meant—"

"I heard you," Uncle Tom growled. "And so did three witnesses. Happens to be one of the words a man can be challenged
for on this still free planet. But, since I'm getting old and fat, I
may just sue you for your shirt instead. Come along, kids."

The Director spoke quickly. "Tom . . . sit down, please. Mr.
Poon . . . please keep quiet unless I ask for your advice. Now,
Tom, you know quite well that you can't challenge nor sue over a
privileged communication, counsel to client."

"I can do both or either. Question is: will a court sustain me?
But I can always find out."

"And thereby drag out into the open the very point you know
quite well I can't afford to have dragged out. Simply because my
lawyer spoke in an excess of zeal. Mr. Poon?"

"I tried to withdraw it. I do withdraw it."

"Senator?"

Uncle Tom bowed stiffly to Mr. Poon, who returned it. "Accepted, sir. No offense meant and none taken." Then Uncle Tom
grinned merrily, let his potbelly slide back down out of his chest,
and said in his normal voice, "Okay, Hymie, let's get on with the
crime. Your move."

Dr. Schoenstein said carefully, "Young lady, I have just
learned that the recent disruption of family planning in your
home—which we all deeply regret—caused an additional sharp
disappointment to you and your brother."

"It certainly did!" I answered, rather shrilly I'm afraid.

"Yes. As your uncle put it, the ripples spread out. Another of
those ripples could wreck this establishment, make it insolvent
as a private business. This is an odd sort of business we are in
here, Miss Fries. Superficially we perform a routine engineering
function, plus some not unusual boarding nursery services. But
in fact what we do touches the most primitive of human emotions. If confidence in our integrity, or in the perfection with
which we carry out the service entrusted to us, were to be
shaken—" He spread his hands helplessly. "We couldn't last out

the year. Now I can show you exactly how the mishap occurred which affected your family, show you how wildly unlikely it was to have it happen even under the methods we did use . . . prove to you how utterly impossible it now is and always will be in the future for such a mistake to take place again, under our new procedures. Nevertheless"— he looked helpless again—"if you were to talk, merely tell the simple truth about what did indeed happen once . . . you could ruin us."

I felt so sorry for him that I was about to blurt out that I wouldn't even *dream* of talking!—even though they had ruined my life—when Clark cut in. "Watch it, Pod! It's loaded."

So I just gave the Director my Sphinx expression and said nothing. Clark's instinctive self-interest is absolutely reliable.

Dr. Schoenstein motioned Mr. Poon to keep quiet. "But, my dear lady, I am not asking you not to talk. As your uncle the Senator says, you are not here to blackmail and I have nothing with which to bargain. The Marsopolis Crèche Foundation, Limited, always carries out its obligations even when they do not result from formal contract. I asked you to come in here in order to suggest a measure of relief for the damage we have unquestionably—though unwittingly—done you and your brother. Your uncle tells me that he had intended to travel with you and your family . . . but that now he intends to go via the next Triangle Line departure. The *Tricorn*, I believe it is, about ten days from now. Would you feel less mistreated if we were to pay first-class fares for your brother and you—round trip, of course—in the Triangle Line?"

Would I! The *Wanderlust* has, as her sole virtue, the fact that she is indeed a spaceship and she was shaping for Earth. But she is an old, slow freighter. Whereas the Triangle Liners, as everyone knows, are utter palaces! I could but nod.

"Good. It is our privilege and we hope you have a wonderful trip. But, uh, young lady . . . do you think it possible that you could give us some assurance, for no consideration and simply out of kindness, that you wouldn't talk about a certain regrettable mishap?"

"Oh? I thought that was part of the deal."

"There is no deal. As your uncle pointed out to me, we owe you this trip, no matter what."

"Why—why, Doctor, I'm going to be so busy, so utterly rushed, just to get ready in time, that I won't have *time* to talk to anyone about any mishaps that probably weren't your fault anyhow!"

"Thank you." He turned to Clark. "And you, son?"

Clark doesn't like to be called "son" at best. But don't think it affected his answer. He ignored the vocative and said coldly, "What about our expenses?"

Dr. Schoenstein flinched. Uncle Tom guffawed and said, "That's my boy! Doc, I told you he had the simple rapacity of a sand gator. He'll go far—if somebody doesn't poison him."

"Any suggestions?"

"No trouble. Clark. Look me in the eye. Either you stay behind and we weld you into a barrel and feed you through the bunghole so that you *can't* talk—while your sister goes anyhow—or you accept these terms. Say a thousand each—no, fifteen hundred—for travel expenses, and you keep your snapper shut forever about the baby mix-up . . . or I personally, with the aid of four stout, blackhearted accomplices, will cut your tongue out and feed it to the cat. A deal?"

"I ought to get ten percent commission on Sis's fifteen hundred. She didn't have sense enough to ask for it."

"No cumshaw. I ought to be charging *you* commission on the whole transaction. A deal?"

"A deal," Clark agreed.

Uncle Tom stood up. "That does it, Doc. In his own unappetizing way he is as utterly reliable as she is. So relax. You, too, Kwai Yau, you can breathe again. Doc, you can send a check around to me in the morning. Come on, kids."

"Thanks, Tom. If that is the word. I'll have the check over before you get there. Uh . . . just one thing . . ."

"What, Doc?"

"Senator, you were here long before I was born, so I don't know too much about your early life. Just the traditional stories and what it says about you in *Who's Who on Mars*. Just what were you transported for? You *were* transported? Weren't you?"

Mr. Poon looked horror-stricken, and I was. But Uncle Tom didn't seem offended. He laughed heartily and answered, "I was accused of freezing babies for profit. But it was a frameup—I never did no such thing nohow. Come on, kids. Let's get out of this ghouls' nest before they smuggle us down into the subbasement."

Later that night in bed I was dreamily thinking over the trip. There hadn't even been the least argument with Mother and Daddy; Uncle Tom had settled it all by phone before we got home. I heard a sound from the nursery, got up and paddled in. It was Duncan, the little darling, not even wet but lonely. So I picked him up and cuddled him and he cooed and then he was wet, so I changed him.

I decided that he was just as pretty or prettier than all those other babies, even though he was five months younger and his eyes didn't track. When I put him down again, he was sound asleep; I started back to bed.

And stopped— The Triangle Line gets its name from serving the three leading planets, of course, but which direction a ship makes the Mars-Venus-Earth route depends on just where we all are in our orbits.

But just where were we?

I hurried into the living room and searched for the *Daily War Whoop*—found it, thank goodness, and fed it into the viewer, flipped to the shipping news, found the predicted arrivals and departures.

Yes, yes, *yes*! I am going not only to Earth—but to Venus as well!

Venus! Do you suppose Mother would let me— No, best just say nothing now. Uncle Tom will be more tractable, after we get there.

I'm going to miss Duncan—he's such a little doll.

Chapter 4

I haven't had time to write in this journal for *days*. Just getting ready
to leave was almost impossible—and would have been truly impossible had it not been that most preparations—all the special Terra inoculations and photographs and passports and such—were mostly
done before Everything Came Unstuck. But Mother came out of her
atavistic daze and was very helpful. She would even let one of the
triplets cry for a few moments rather than leave me half pinned up.

I don't know how Clark got ready or whether he had any
preparations to make. He continued to creep around silently, answering in grunts if he answered at all. Nor did Uncle Tom seem
to find it difficult. I saw him only twice during those frantic ten
days (once to borrow baggage mass from his allowance, which he
let me have, the dear!) and both times I had to dig him out of the
card room at the Elks Club. I asked him how he managed to get
ready for so important a trip and still have time to play cards?

"Nothing to it," he answered. "I bought a new toothbrush. Is
there something else I should have done?"

So I hugged him and told him he was an utterly utter beast and
he chuckled and mussed my hair. Query: Will I ever become that
blasé about space travel? I suppose I must if I am to be an astro-
naut. But Daddy says that getting ready for a trip is half the
fun . . . so perhaps I don't want to become that sophisticated.

Somehow Mother delivered me, complete with baggage and
all the myriad pieces of paper—tickets and medical records and
passport and universal identification complex and guardians'
assignment-and-guarantee and three kinds of money and travel-

ers' cheques and birth record and police certification and security clearance and I don't remember—all checked off, to the city shuttle port. I was juggling one package of things that simply *wouldn't* go into my luggage, and I had one hat on my head and one in my hand; otherwise everything came out even.

(I don't know where that second hat went. Somehow it never got aboard with me. But I haven't missed it.)

Good-bye at the shuttle port was most teary and exciting. Not just with Mother and Daddy, which was to be expected (when Daddy put his arm around me tight, I threw both mine around him and for a dreadful second I didn't want to leave at all), but also because about thirty of my classmates showed up (which I hadn't in the least expected), complete with a banner that two of them were carrying reading:

BON VOYAGE—PODKAYNE

I got kissed enough times to start a fair-sized epidemic if any one of them had had anything, which apparently they didn't. I got kissed by boys who had never even *tried* to, in the past—and I assure you that it is not utterly impossible to kiss me, if the project is approached with confidence and finesse, as I believe that one's instincts should be allowed to develop as well as one's overt cortical behavior.

The corsage Daddy had given me for going away got crushed and I didn't even notice it until we were aboard the shuttle. I suppose it was somewhere about then that I lost that hat, but I'll never know—I would have lost the last-minute package, too, if Uncle Tom had not rescued it. There were photographers, too, but not for me—for Uncle Tom. Then suddenly we had to scoot aboard the shuttle *right now* because a shuttle can't wait; it has to boost on the split second even though Deimos moves so much more slowly than Phobos. A reporter from the *War Whoop* was still trying to get a statement out of Uncle Tom about the forthcoming Three-Planets conference but he just pointed at his throat and whispered, "Laryngitis"—then we were aboard just before they sealed the airlock.

It must have been the shortest case of laryngitis on record; Uncle Tom's voice had been all right until we got to the shuttle port and it was okay again once we were in the shuttle.

One shuttle trip is exactly like another, whether to Phobos or Deimos. Still, that first tremendous *whoosh!* of acceleration is exciting as it pins you down into your couch with so much weight that you can't breathe, much less move—and free fall is always strange and eerie and rather stomach fluttering even if one doesn't tend to be nauseated by it, which, thank you, I don't.

Being on Deimos is just like being in free fall, since neither Deimos nor Phobos has enough surface gravitation for one to feel it. They put suction sandals on us before they unstrapped us so that we could walk, just as they do on Phobos. Nevertheless Deimos is different from Phobos for reasons having nothing to do with natural phenomena. Phobos is, of course, legally a part of Mars; there are no formalities of any sort about visiting it. All that is required is the fare, a free day, and a yen for a picnic in space.

But Deimos is a free port, leased in perpetuity to Three-Planets Treaty Authority. A known criminal, with a price on his head in Marsopolis, could change ships there right under the eyes of our own police—and we couldn't touch him. Instead, we would have to start most complicated legal doings at the Interplanetary High Court on Luna, practically win the case ahead of time and, besides that, prove that the crime was a crime under Three-Planet rules and not just under our own laws . . . and then all that we could do would be to ask the Authority's proctors to arrest the man if he was still around—which doesn't seem likely.

I knew about this, theoretically, because there had been about a half page on it in our school course *Essentials of Martian Government* in the section on "Extraterritoriality." But now I had plenty of time to think about it because, as soon as we left the shuttle, we found ourselves locked up in a room misleadingly called the "Hospitality Room" while we waited until they were ready to "process" us. One wall of the room was glass and I could see lots and lots of people hurrying around in the concourse beyond, doing all manner of interesting and mysterious things. But all we had to do was to wait beside our baggage and grow bored.

I found that I was growing furious by the minute, not at all like my normally sweet and lovable nature. Why, this place had been built by my own mother!—and here I was, caged up in it like white mice in a bio lab.

(Well, I admit that Mother didn't exactly build Deimos; the Martians did that, starting with a spare asteroid that they happened to have handy. But some millions of years back they grew tired of space travel and devoted all their time to the whichness of what and how to unscrew the inscrutable—so when Mother took over the job, Deimos was pretty run down; she had to start in from the ground up and rebuild it completely.)

In any case, it was certain that everything that I could see through that transparent wall was a product of Mother's creative, imaginative and hardheaded engineering ability. I began to fume. Clark was off in a corner, talking privately to some stranger— "stranger" to me, at least; Clark, for all his antisocial disposition, always seems to know somebody, or to know somebody who knows somebody, anywhere we go. I sometimes wonder if he is a member of some vast underground secret society; he has such unsavory acquaintances and never brings any of them home.

Clark is, however, a very satisfactory person to fume with, because, if he isn't busy, he is always willing to help a person hate anything that needs hating; he can even dig up reasons why a situation is even more vilely unfair than you thought it was. But he was busy, so that left Uncle Tom. So I explained to him bitterly how outrageous I thought it was that we should be penned up like animals—free Mars citizens on one of Mars' own moons!— simply because a sign read: *Passengers must wait until called—by order of Three-Planets Treaty Authority.*

"*Politics!*" I said bitterly. "I could run it better myself."

"I'm sure you could," he agreed gravely, "but, Flicka, you don't understand."

"I understand all too well!"

"No, honey bun. You understand that there is no good reason why you should not walk straight through that door and enjoy yourself by shopping until it is time to go inboard the *Tricorn.* And you are right about that, for there is no need at all for you to be locked up in here when you could be out there making some freeport shopkeeper happy by paying him a high price which seems to you a low price. So you say 'Politics!' as if it were a nasty word—and you think that settles it."

He sighed. "But you *don't* understand. Politics is not evil; politics is the human race's most magnificent achievement. When politics is good, it's wonderful . . . and when politics is bad— well, it's still pretty good."

"I guess I don't understand," I said slowly.

"Think about it. Politics is just a name for the way we get things done . . . without fighting. We dicker and compromise and everybody thinks he has received a raw deal, but somehow after a tedious amount of talk we come up with some jury-rigged way to do it without getting anybody's head bashed in. That's politics. The only other way to settle a dispute is by bashing a few heads in . . . and that is what happens when one or both sides is no longer willing to dicker. That's why I say politics is good even when it is bad . . . because the only alternative is force—and somebody gets hurt."

"Uh . . . it seems to me that's a funny way for a revolutionary veteran to talk. From what I've heard, Uncle Tom, you were one of the bloodthirsty ones who started the shooting. Or so Daddy says."

He grinned. "Mostly I ducked. If dickering won't work, then you have to fight. But I think maybe it takes a man who has been shot at to appreciate how much better it is to fumble your way through a political compromise rather than have the top of your head blown off." He frowned and suddenly looked very old. "When to talk and when to fight— That is the most difficult decision to make wisely of all the decisions in life." Then suddenly he smiled and the years dropped away. "Mankind didn't invent fighting; it was here long before we were. But we invented politics. Just think of it, hon— Homo sapiens is the most cruel, the most vicious, the most predatory, and certainly the most deadly of all the animals in this solar system. Yet he invented politics! He figured out a way to let most of us, most of the time, get along well enough so that we usually don't kill each other. So don't let me hear you using 'politics' as a swear word again."

"I'm sorry, Uncle Tom," I said humbly.

"Like fun you are. But if you let that idea soak for twenty or thirty years, you may— Oh, oh! There's your villain, baby girl— the politically appointed bureaucrat who has most unjustly held you in durance vile. So scratch his eyes out. Show him how little you think of his silly rules."

I answered this with dignified silence. It is hard to tell when Uncle Tom is serious because he loves to pull my leg, always hoping that it will come off in his hand. The Three-Planets proctor of whom he was speaking had opened the door to our bullpen and was looking around exactly like a zookeeper inspecting a cage for cleanliness. "Passports!" he called out. "Diplomatic passports first." He looked us over, spotted Uncle Tom. "Senator?"

Uncle Tom shook his head. "I'm a tourist, thanks."

"As you say, sir. Line up, please—reverse alphabetical order"—which put us near the tail of the line instead of near the head. There followed maddening delays for fully two hours—

passports, health clearance, outgoing baggage inspection—Mars Republic does not levy duties on exports but just the same there is a whole long list of things you can't export without a license, such as ancient Martian artifacts (the first explorers did their best to gut the place and some of the most priceless are in the British Museum or the Kremlin; I've heard Daddy fume about it), some things you can't export under *any* circumstances, such as certain narcotics, and some things you can take aboard ship only by surrendering them for safekeeping by the purser, such as guns and other weapons.

Clark picked outgoing inspection for some typical abnormal behavior. They had passed down the line copies of a long list of things we must not have in our baggage—a fascinating list; I hadn't known that there were so many things either illegal, immoral, or deadly. When the Fries contingent wearily reached the inspection counter, the inspector said, all in one word: "Nything-t'-d'clare?" He was a Marsman and as he looked up he recognized Uncle Tom. "Oh. Howdy, Senator. Honored to have you with us. Well, I guess we needn't waste time on your baggage. These two young people with you?"

"Better search my kit," Uncle Tom advised. "I'm smuggling guns to an out-planet branch of the Legion. As for the kids, they're my niece and nephew. But I don't vouch for them; they're both subversive characters. Especially the girl. She was soapboxing revolution just now while we waited."

The inspector smiled and said, "I guess we can allow you a few guns, Senator—you know how to use them. Well, how about it, kids? Anything to declare?"

I said, "Nothing to declare," with icy dignity—when suddenly Clark spoke up.

"Sure!" he piped, his voice cracking. "Two kilos of happy dust! And whose business is it? I paid for it. I'm not going to let it be stolen by a bunch of clerks." His voice was surly as only he can manage and the expression on his face simply ached for a slap.

That did it. The inspector had been just about to glance into one of my bags, a purely formal inspection, I think—when my brattish brother deliberately stirred things up. At the very word "happy dust" four other inspectors closed in. Two were Venusmen, to judge by their accents, and the other two might have been from Earth.

Of course, happy dust doesn't matter to us Marsmen. The Martians use it, have always used it, and it is about as important to them as tobacco is to humans, but apparently without any ill effects. What they get out of it I don't know. Some of the old sand rats among us have picked up the habit from the Martians—but my entire botany class experimented with it under our teacher's supervision and nobody got any thrill out of it and all I got was blocked sinuses that wore off before the day was out. Strictly zero squared.

But with the native Venerians it is another matter—when they can get it. It turns them into murderous maniacs and they'll do anything to get it. The (black market) price on it there is very high indeed . . . and possession of it by a human on Venus is at least an automatic life sentence to Saturn's moons.

They buzzed around Clark like angry jetta wasps.

But they did not find what they were looking for. Shortly Uncle Tom spoke up and said, "Inspector? May I make a suggestion?"

"Eh? Certainly, Senator."

"My nephew, I am sorry to say, has caused a disturbance. Why don't you put him aside—chain him up, I would—and let all these other good people go through?"

The inspector blinked. "I think that is an excellent idea."

"And I would appreciate it if you would inspect myself and my niece now. Then we won't hold up the others."

"Oh, that's not necessary." The inspector slapped seals on all of Uncle's bags, closed the one of mine he had started to open, and said, "I don't need to paw through the young lady's pretties. But I think we'll take this smart boy and search him to the skin and X-ray him."

"Do that."

So Uncle and I went on and checked at four or five other desks—fiscal control and migration and reservations and other nonsense—and finally wound up with our baggage at the centrifuge for weighing in. I never did get a chance to shop.

To my chagrin, when I stepped off the merry-go-round the record showed that my baggage and myself were nearly three kilos over my allowance, which didn't seem possible. I hadn't eaten more breakfast than usual—less actually—and I hadn't drunk any water because, while I do not become ill in free fall, drinking in free fall is very tricky; you are likely to get water up your nose or something and set off an embarrassing chain reaction.

So I was about to protest bitterly that the weightmaster had spun the centrifuge too fast and produced a false mass reading. But it occurred to me that I did not know for surely certain that the scales Mother and I had used were perfectly accurate. So I kept quiet.

Uncle Tom just reached for his purse and said, "How much?"

The weightmaster said, "Mmm . . . let's spin you first, Senator."

Uncle Tom was almost two kilos under his allowance. The weightmaster shrugged and said, "Forget it, Senator. I'm minus on a couple of other things; I think I can swallow it. If not, I'll leave a memo with the purser. But I'm fairly sure I can."

"Thank you. What did you say your name was?"

"Milo. Miles M. Milo—Aasvogel Lodge number seventy-four. Maybe you saw our crack drill team at the Legion convention two years ago—I was left pivot."

"I certainly did, I certainly did!" They exchanged that secret grip that they think other people don't know and Uncle Tom said, "Well, thanks, Miles. Be seeing you."

"Not at all—Tom. No, don't bother with your baggage." Mr. Milo touched a button and called out, "In the *Tricorn*! Get somebody out here fast for the Senator's baggage."

It occurred to me, as we stopped at the passenger tube sealed to the transfer station to swap our suction sandals for little magnet pads that clipped to our shoes, that we need not have waited for anything at anytime—if only Uncle Tom had been willing to use the special favors he so plainly could demand.

But, even so, it pays to travel with an important person—even though it's just your Uncle Tom whose stomach you used to jump up and down on when you were small enough for such things. Our tickets simply read FIRST CLASS—I'm sure, for I saw all three of them—but where we were placed was in what they call the "Owner's Cabin," which is actually a suite with three bedrooms and a living room. I was dazzled!

But I didn't have time to admire it just then. First they strapped our baggage down, then they strapped us down—to seat couches which were against one wall of the living room. That wall plainly should have been the floor, but it slanted up almost vertically with respect to the tiny, not-quite-nothing weight that we had. The warning sirens were already sounding when someone dragged Clark in and strapped him to one of the couches. He was looking mussed up but cocky.

"Hi, smuggler," Uncle Tom greeted him amiably. "They find it on you?"

"Nothing to find."

"That's what I thought. I trust they gave you a rough time."

"Naah!"

I wasn't sure I believed Clark's answer; I've heard that a skin and person search can be made quite annoying indeed, without doing anything the least bit illegal, if the proctors are feeling unfriendly. A "rough time" would be good for Clark's soul, I am sure—but he certainly did not act as if the experience had caused him any discomfort. I said, "Clark, that was a very foolish remark you made to the inspector. And it was a lie, as well—a silly, useless lie."

"Sign off," he said curtly. "If I'm smuggling anything, it's up to them to find it; that's what they're paid for. 'Any-thing-t'-d'clare?' " he added in a mimicking voice. "What nonsense! As if anybody would declare something he was trying to smuggle."

"Just the same," I went on, "if Daddy had heard you say—"

"Podkayne."

"Yes, Uncle Tom?"

"Table it. We're about to start. Let's enjoy it."

"But— Yes, Uncle."

There was a slight drop in pressure, then a sudden surge that would have slid us out of our couches if we had not been strapped—but not a strong one, not at all like that giant *whoosh!* with which we had left the surface. It did not last long, then we were truly in free fall for a few moments . . . then there started a soft, gentle push in the same direction, which kept on.

Then the room started very slowly to turn around . . . almost unnoticeable except for a slight dizziness it gave one.

Gradually, gradually (it took almost twenty minutes) our weight increased, until at last we were back to our proper weight . . . at which time the floor, which had been all wrong when we came in, was where it belonged, under us, and almost level. But not quite—

Here is what had happened. The first short boost was made by the rocket tugs of Deimos Port picking up the *Tricorn* and hurling her out into a free orbit of her own. This doesn't take much, because the attraction between even a big ship like the *Tricorn* and a tiny, tiny satellite such as Deimos isn't enough to matter; all that matters is getting the very considerable mass of the ship shoved free.

The second gentle shove, the one that kept up and never went away, was the ship's own main drive—one-tenth of a standard gee. The *Tricorn* is a constant-boost ship; she doesn't dillydally around with economical orbits and weeks and months in free fall. She goes very fast indeed . . . because even 0.1 gee adds up awfully fast.

But one-tenth gee is not enough to make comfortable passengers who have been used to more. As soon as the Captain had set her on her course, he started to spin her and kept it up until the centrifugal force and the boost added up (in vector addition, of course) to exactly the surface gravitation of Mars (or 37 percent of a standard gee) at the locus of the first-class staterooms.

But the floors will not be quite level until we approach Earth, because the inside of the ship had been constructed so that the floors would feel perfectly level when the spin and the boost added up to exactly one standard gravity—or Earth-Normal.

Maybe this isn't too clear. Well, it wasn't too clear to me, in school; I didn't see exactly how it worked out until (later) I had a chance to see the controls used to put spin on the ship and how the centrifugal force was calculated. Just remember that the *Tricorn*—and her sisters, the *Trice* and the *Triad* and the *Triangulum* and the *Tricolor* are enormous cylinders. The thrust is straight along the main axis; it has to be. Centrifugal force pushes away from the main axis—how else? The two forces add up to make the ship's "artificial gravity" in passenger country—but, since one force (the boost) is kept constant and the other (the spin) can be varied, there can be only one rate of spin which will add in with the boost to make those floors perfectly level.

For the *Tricorn* the spin that will produce level floors and exactly one Earth gravity in passenger country is 5.42 revolutions per minute—I know because the Captain told me so . . . and I checked his arithmetic and he was right. The floor of our cabin is just over thirty meters from the main axis of the ship, so it all comes out even.

As soon as they had the floor back under us and had announced the "all clear" I unstrapped me and hurried out. I wanted a quick look at the ship; I didn't even wait to unpack.

There's a fortune awaiting the man who invents a really good deodorizer for a spaceship. That's the one thing you can't fail to notice.

Oh, they try, I grant them that. The air goes through precipitators each time it is cycled; it is washed, it is perfumed, a precise fraction of ozone is added, and the new oxygen that is put in after the carbon dioxide is distilled out is as pure as a baby's mind; it has to be, for it is newly released as a by-product of the photosynthesis of living plants. That air is so pure that it really ought to be voted a medal by the Society for the Suppression of Evil Thoughts.

Besides that, a simply amazing amount of the crew's time is put into cleaning, polishing, washing, sterilizing—oh, they *try*!

But nevertheless, even a new, extra-fare luxury liner like the *Tricorn* simply reeks of human sweat and ancient sin, with undefinable overtones of organic decay and unfortunate accidents and matters best forgotten. Once I was with Daddy when a Martian tomb was being unsealed—and I found out why xenoarchaeologists always have gas masks handy. But a spaceship smells even worse than that tomb.

It does no good to complain to the purser. He'll listen with professional sympathy and send a crewman around to spray your stateroom with something which (I suspect) merely deadens your nose for a while. But his sympathy is not real, because the poor man simply cannot smell anything wrong himself. He has lived in ships for years; it is literally impossible for him to smell the unmistakable reek of a ship that has been lived in—and, besides, he *knows* that the air is pure; the ship's instruments show it. None of the professional spacers can smell it.

But the purser and all of them are quite used to having passengers complain about the "unbearable stench"—so they pretend sympathy and go through the motions of correcting the matter.

Not that *I* complained. I was looking forward to having this ship eating out of my hand, and you don't accomplish that sort of coup by becoming known first thing as a complainer. But other first-timers did, and I certainly understood why—in fact I began to have a glimmer of a doubt about my ambitions to become skipper of an explorer ship.

But— Well, in about two days it seemed to me that they had managed to clean up the ship quite a bit, and shortly thereafter I stopped thinking about it. I began to understand why the ship's crew can't smell the things the passengers complain about. Their nervous systems simply cancel out the old familiar stinks—like a cybernetic skywatch canceling out and ignoring any object whose predicted orbit has previously been programmed into the machine.

But the odor is still there. I suspect that it sinks right into polished metal and can never be removed, short of scrapping the ship and melting it down. Thank goodness the human nervous system is endlessly adaptable.

* * *

But my own nervous system didn't seem too adaptable during that first hasty tour of the *Tricorn;* it is a good thing that I had not eaten much breakfast and had refrained from drinking anything. My stomach did give me a couple of bad moments, but I told it sternly that I was busy—I was very anxious to look over the ship; I simply didn't have time to cater to the weaknesses to which flesh is heir.

Well, the *Tricorn* is lovely all right—every bit as nice as the travel folders say that she is . . . except for that dreadful ship's odor. Her ballroom is gorgeous and so big that you can see that the floor curves to match the ship . . . only it is not curved when you walk across it. It is level, too—it is the only room in the ship where they jack up the floor to match perfectly with whatever spin is on the ship. There is a lounge with a simulated sky of outer space, or it can be switched to blue sky and fleecy clouds. Some old biddies were already in there, gabbling.

The dining saloon is every bit as fancy, but it seemed hardly big enough—which reminded me of the warning in the travel brochure about first and second tables, so I rushed back to our cabin to urge Uncle Tom to make reservations for us quickly before all the best tables were filled.

He wasn't there. I took a quick look in all the rooms and didn't find him—but I found Clark in *my* room, just closing one of my bags!

"What are you doing?" I demanded.

He jumped and then looked perfectly blank. "I was just looking to see if you had any nausea pills," he said woodenly.

"Well, don't dig into my things! You know better." I came up and felt his cheek; he wasn't feverish. "I don't have any. But I noticed where the surgeon's office is. If you are feeling ill, I'll take you straight there and let him dose you."

He pulled away. "Aw, I'm all right—now."

"Clark Fries, you listen to me. If you—" But he wasn't listening; he slid past me, ducked into his own room and closed the door; I heard the lock click.

I closed the bag he had opened—and noticed something. It was the bag the inspector had been just about to search when Clark had pulled that silly stunt about "happy dust."

My younger brother never does anything without a reason. Never.

His reasons may be, and often are, inscrutable to others. But if you just dig deeply enough, you will always find that his mind is never a random-choice machine, doing things pointlessly. It is as logical as a calculator—and about as cold.

I now knew why he had made what seemed to be entirely unnecessary trouble for himself at outgoing inspection.

I knew why I had been unexpectedly three kilos over my allowance on the centrifuge.

The only thing I didn't know was: *What* had he smuggled aboard in my baggage?

And *why*?

Interlude

Well, Pod, I am glad to see that you've resumed keeping your diary. Not only do I find your girlish viewpoints entertaining but also you sometimes (not often) provide me with useful bits of information.

If I can do anything for you in return, do let me know. Perhaps you would like help in straightening out your grammar? Those incomplete sentences you are so fond of indicate incomplete thinking. You know that, don't you?

For example, let us consider a purely hypothetical case: a delivery robot with an unbeatable seal. Since the seal is in fact unbeatable, thinking about the seal simply leads to frustration. But a complete analysis of the situation leads one to the obvious fact that any cubical or quasi-cubical object has six sides, and that the seal applies to only one of these six sides.

Pursuing this line of thought one may note that, while the quasi cube may not be moved without cutting its connections, the floor under it may be lowered as much as forty-eight centimeters—if one has all afternoon in which to work.

Were this not a hypothetical case I would now suggest the use of a mirror and light on an extension handle and some around-the-corner tools, plus plenty of patience.

That's what you lack, Pod—patience.

I hope this may shed some light on the matter of the hypothetical happy dust—and do feel free to come to me with your little problems.

Chapter 5

Clark kept his stateroom door locked all the time the first three days we were in the *Tricorn*—I know, because I tried it every time he left the suite.

Then on the fourth day he failed to lock it at a time when it was predictable that he would be gone at least an hour, as he had signed up for a tour of the ship—the parts passengers ordinarily are not allowed in, I mean. I didn't mind missing it myself, for by then I had worked out my own private "Poddy special" escort service. Nor did I have to worry about Uncle Tom; he wasn't making the tour, it would have violated his no-exercise rule, but he had acquired new pinochle cronies and he was safely in the smoking room.

Those stateroom door locks are not impossible to pick—not for a girl equipped with a nail file, some bits of this and that, and *free* run of the purser's office—me, I mean.

But I found I did not have to pick the lock; the catch had not quite caught. I breathed the conventional sigh of relief, as I figured that the happy accident put me at least twenty minutes ahead of schedule.

I shan't detail the search, but I flatter myself that the Criminal Investigation Bureau could not have done it more logically nor more quickly if limited, as I was, to bare hands and no equipment. It had to be something forbidden by that list they had given us on Deimos—and I had carefully kept and studied my copy. It had to mass slightly over three kilos. It had to bulk so large and be sufficiently fixed in its shape and dimensions that Clark was forced to hide it in baggage—otherwise I am sure he would have concealed it on his person and coldly depended on his youth and "innocence," plus the chaperonage of Uncle Tom, to breeze him through the outgoing inspection. Otherwise he would never have taken the calculated risk of hiding it in my baggage, since he couldn't be sure of recovering it without my knowing.

Could he have predicted that I would at once go sightseeing without waiting to unpack? Well, perhaps he could, even though I had done so on the spur of the moment. I must reluctantly admit that Clark can outguess me with maddening regularity. As an opponent, he is never to be underrated. But still it was for him a "calculated risk," albeit a small one.

Very well. Largish, rather massy, forbidden—but I didn't know what it looked like and I had to assume that *anything* which met the first two requirements might be disguised to appear innocent.

Ten minutes later I knew that it had to be in one of his three bags, which I had left to the last on purpose as the least likely spots. A stateroom aboard ship has many cover plates, access holes, removable fixtures, and the like, but I had done a careful practice run in my own room; I knew which ones were worth opening, which ones could not be opened without power tools, which ones could not be opened without leaving unmistakable signs of tampering. I checked these all in great haste, then congratulated Clark on having the good sense not to use such obvious hiding places.

Then I checked everything readily accessible—out in the open, in his wardrobe, etc.—using the classic "Purloined Letter" technique, i.e., I never assumed that a book was a book simply because it looked like a book, nor that a jacket on a hanger was simply that and nothing more.

Null, negative, nothing— Reluctantly, I tackled his three pieces of luggage, first noting carefully exactly how they were stacked and in what order.

The first was empty. Oh, the linings could have been tampered with, but the bag was no heavier than it should have been and any false pocket in the linings could not have held anything large enough to meet the specifications.

The second bag was the same—and the bag on the bottom seemed to be the same . . . until I found an envelope in a pocket of it. Oh, nothing nearly mass enough, nor gross enough; just an ordinary envelope for a letter—but nevertheless I glanced at it.

And was immediately indignant!

It had printed on it:

MISS PODKAYNE FRIES
PASSENGER, S.S. *Tricorn*
For delivery in ship

Why, the little wretch! He had been intercepting my mail! With fingers trembling with rage so badly that I could hardly do so I opened it—and discovered that it had already been opened and was angrier than ever. But, at least, the note was still inside. Shaking, I pulled it out and read it.

Just six words—

Hi, Pod. Snooping again, I see.

—in Clark's handwriting.

I stood there, frozen, for a long moment, while I blushed scarlet and chewed the bitter realization that I had been hoaxed to perfection—*again*.

There are only three people in the world who can make me feel stupid—and Clark is two of them.

I heard a throat-clearing sound behind me and whirled around. Lounging in the open doorway (I had left it closed) was my brother. He smiled at me and said, "Hello, Sis. Looking for something? Need any help?"

I didn't waste time pretending that I didn't have jam all over my face; I simply said, "Clark Fries, what did you smuggle into this ship in my baggage?"

He looked blank—a look of malignant idiocy which has been known to drive well-balanced teachers to their therapists. "What in the world are you talking about, Pod?"

"You know what I'm talking about! Smuggling!"

"Oh!" His face lit up in a sunny smile. "You mean those two kilograms of happy dust. Goodness, Sis, is that still worrying you? There never were any two kilos of happy dust; I was just having my little joke with that stuffy inspector. I thought you knew that."

"I do not mean any 'two kilos of happy dust'! I am talking about at least three kilos of something else that you hid in my baggage!"

He looked worried. "Pod, do you feel well?"

"Ooooooh!—*dandruff!* Clark Fries, you stop that! You know what I mean! When I was centrifuged, my bags and I weighed three kilos over my allowance. Well?"

He looked at me thoughtfully, sympathetically. "It *has* seemed to me that you were getting a bit fat—but I didn't want to mention it. I thought it was all this rich food you've been tucking away here in the ship. You really ought to watch that sort of thing, Pod. After all, if a girl lets her figure go to pieces— Well, she doesn't have much else. So I hear."

Had that envelope been a blunt instrument I would have blunted him. I heard a low growling sound, and realized that I was making it. So I stopped. "Where's the letter that was in this envelope?"

Clark looked surprised. "Why, it's right there, in your other hand."

"This? This is all there was? No letter from somebody else?"

"Why, just that note from me, Sis. Didn't you like it? I thought that it just suited the occasion . . . I knew you would find it your very first chance." He smiled. "Next time you want to paw through my things, let me know and I'll help. Sometimes I have experiments running—and you might get hurt. That can happen to people who aren't very bright and don't look before they leap. I wouldn't want that to happen to *you*, Sis."

I didn't bandy any more words; I brushed past him and went to my own room and locked the door and bawled.

Then I got up and did very careful things to my face. I know when I'm licked; I don't have to have a full set of working drawings. I resolved never to mention the matter to Clark again.

But what was I to do? Go to the Captain? I already knew the Captain pretty well; his imagination extended as far as the next ballistic prediction and no further. Tell him that my brother had been smuggling something, I didn't know what—and that he had better search the entire ship most carefully, because, whatever it was, it was not in my brother's room? Don't be triple silly, Poddy. In the first place, he would laugh at you; in the second place, you don't *want* Clark to be caught— Mother and Daddy wouldn't like it.

Tell Uncle Tom about it? He might be just as unbelieving . . . or, if he did believe me, he might go to the Captain himself—with just as disastrous results.

I decided not to go to Uncle Tom—at least not yet. Instead I would keep my eyes and ears open and try to find an answer myself.

In any case I did not waste much time on Clark's sins (if any, I had to admit in bare honesty); I was in my first real spaceship— halfway to my ambition thereby—and there was much to learn and do.

Those travel brochures are honest enough, I guess—but they do not give you the full picture.

For example, take this phrase right out of the text of the Triangle Line's fancy folder . . . *romantic days in ancient Marsopolis, the city older than time; exotic nights under the hurtling moons of Mars* . . .

Let's rephrase it into everyday language, shall we? Marsopolis is my hometown and I love it—but it is as romantic as bread and butter with no jam. The parts people live in are new and were designed for function, not romance. As for the ruins outside town (which the Martians *never* called "Marsopolis"), a lot of high foreheads including Daddy have seen to it that the best parts are locked off so that tourists will not carve their initials in something that was old when stone axes were the last thing in superweapons. Furthermore, Martian ruins are neither beautiful, nor picturesque, nor impressive, to human eyes. The way to appreciate them is to read a really good book with illustrations, diagrams, and simple explanations—such as Daddy's *Other Paths Than Ours*. (Adv.)

As for those exotic nights, anybody who is outdoors after sundown on Mars other than through sheer necessity needs to have his head examined. It's *chilly* out there. I've seen Deimos and Phobos at night exactly twice, each time through no fault of my own—and I was so busy keeping from freezing to death that I wasted no thought on "hurtling moons."

This advertising brochure is just as meticulously accurate and just as deceptive in effect—concerning the ships themselves. Oh, the *Tricorn* is a palace; I'll vouch for that. It really is a miracle of engineering that anything so huge, so luxurious, so fantastically adapted to the health and comfort of human beings, should be able to "hurtle" (pardon the word) through space.

But take those pictures—

You know the ones I mean: full color and depth, showing groups of handsome young people of both sexes chatting or playing games in the lounge, dancing gaily in the ballroom—or views of a "typical stateroom."

That "typical stateroom" is not a fake. No, it has simply been photographed from an angle and with a lens that makes it look at least twice as big as it is. As for those handsome, gay, young people—well, they aren't along on the trip I'm making. It's my guess that they are professional models.

In the *Tricorn* this trip the young and handsome passengers like those in the pictures can be counted on the thumb of one hand. The typical passenger we have with us is a great-grandmother, Terran citizenship, widowed, wealthy, making her first trip into space—and probably her last, for she is not sure she likes it.

Honest, I'm not exaggerating; our passengers look like refugees from a geriatrics clinic. I am not scoffing at old age. I understand that it is a condition I will one day attain myself, if I go on breathing in and out enough times—say about 900,000,000 more times, not counting heavy exercise. Old age can be a charming condition, as witness Uncle Tom. But old age is not an accomplishment; it is just something that happens to you despite yourself, like falling downstairs.

And I must say that I am getting a wee bit tired of having youth treated as a punishable offense.

Our typical male passenger is the same sort, only not nearly so numerous. He differs from his wife primarily in that, instead of looking down his nose at me, he is sometimes inclined to pat me in a "fatherly" way that I do not find fatherly, don't like, avoid if humanly possible—and which nevertheless gets me talked about.

I suppose I should not have been surprised to find the *Tricorn* a super-deluxe old folks' home, but (I may as well admit it) my experience is still limited and I was not aware of some of the economic facts of life.

The *Tricorn* is expensive. It is *very* expensive. Clark and I would not be in it at all if Uncle Tom had not twisted Dr. Schoenstein's arm in our behalf. Oh, I suppose Uncle Tom can afford it, but, by age group though not by temperament, he fits the defined category. But Daddy and Mother had intended to take us in the *Wanderlust*, a low-fare, economy-orbit freighter. Daddy and Mother are not poor, but they are not rich—and after they finish raising and educating five children it is unlikely that they will ever be rich.

Who can afford to travel in luxury liners? Ans.: Rich old widows, wealthy retired couples, high-priced executives whose time is so valuable that their corporations gladly send them by the fastest ships—and an occasional rare exception of some other sort.

Clark and I are such exceptions. We have one other exception in the ship, Miss—well, I'll call her Miss Girdle Fitz-Snugglie, because if I used her right name and perchance anybody ever sees this, it would be all too easily recognizable. I think Girdie is a good sort. I don't care what the gossips in this ship say. She doesn't act jealous of me even though it appears that the younger officers in the ship were all her personal property until I boarded—all the trip out from Earth, I mean. I've cut into her monopoly quite a bit, but she isn't catty to me; she treats me warmly woman-to-woman, and I've learned quite a lot about Life and Men from her . . . more than Mother ever taught me.

(It is just possible that Mother is slightly naïve on subjects that Girdie knows best. A woman who tackles engineering and undertakes to beat men at their own game might have had a fairly limited social life, wouldn't you think? I must study this seriously . . . because it seems possible that much the same might happen to a female space pilot and it is no part of my Master Plan to become a soured old maid.)

Girdie is about twice my age, which makes her awfully young in this company; nevertheless it may be that I cause her to look just a bit wrinkled around the eyes. Contrariwise, my somewhat unfinished look may make her more mature contours appear even more Helen-of-Troyish. As may be, it is certain that my presence has relieved the pressure on her by giving the gossips two targets instead of one.

And gossip they do. I heard one of them say about her: "She's been in more laps than a napkin!"

If so, I hope she had fun.

Those gay ship's dances in the mammoth ballroom! Like this: they happen every Tuesday and Saturday night, when the ship is spacing. The music starts at 20.30 and the Ladies' Society for Moral Rectitude is seated around the edge of the floor, as if for a wake. Uncle Tom is there, as a concession to me, and very proudsome and distinguished he looks in evening formal. I am there in a party dress which is not quite as girlish as it was when Mother helped me pick it out, in consequence of some *very* careful retailoring I have done with my door locked. Even Clark attends because there is nothing else going on and he's afraid he might miss something—and looking so nice I'm proud of him, because he has to climb into his own monkey suit or he can't come to the ball.

Over by the punch bowl are half a dozen of the ship's junior officers, dressed in mess jacket uniforms and looking faintly uncomfortable.

The Captain, by some process known only to him, selects one of the widows and asks her to dance. Two husbands dance with their wives. Uncle Tom offers me his arm and leads me to the floor. Two or three of the junior officers follow the Captain's example. Clark takes advantage of the breathless excitement to raid the punch bowl.

But *nobody* asks Girdie to dance.

This is no accident. The Captain has given the Word (I have this intelligence with utter certainty through My Spies) that no ship's officer shall dance with Miss Fitz-Snugglie until he has danced at least two dances with other partners—and I am not an "other partner," because the proscription, since leaving Mars, has been extended to me.

This should be proof to anyone that a captain of a ship is, in sober fact, the Last of the Absolute Monarchs.

There are now six or seven couples on the floor and the fun is at its riotous height. The floor will never again be so crowded. Nevertheless nine-tenths of the chairs are still occupied and you could ride a bicycle around the floor without endangering the dancers. The spectators look as if they were knitting at the tumbrels. The proper finishing touch would be a guillotine in the empty space in the middle of the floor.

The music stops; Uncle Tom takes me back to my chair, then asks Girdie to dance—since he is a Cash Customer, the Captain has not attempted to make him toe the mark. But I am still out of bounds, so I walk over to the punch bowl, take a cup out of Clark's hands, finish it, and say, "Come on, Clark. I'll let you practice on me."

"Aw, it's a waltz!" (Or a "flea hop," or a "chassé," or "five step"—but whatever it is, it is just too utterly impossible.)

"Do it—or I'll tell Madame Grew that you want to dance with her, only you're too shy to ask her."

"You do and I'll trip her! I'll stumble and trip her."

However, Clark is weakening, so I move in fast. "Look, Bub, you either take me out there and walk on my feet for a while—or I'll see to it that Girdie doesn't dance with you at all."

That does it. Clark is in the throes of his first case of puppy love, and Girdie is such a gent that she treats him as an equal and accepts his attentions with warm courtesy. So Clark dances with me. Actually he is quite a good dancer and I have to lead him only a tiny bit. He likes to dance—but he wouldn't want anyone, especially me, to think that he likes to dance with his sister. We don't look too badly matched, since I am short. In the meantime Girdie is looking very good indeed with Uncle Tom, which is quite an accomplishment, as Uncle Tom dances with great enthusiasm and no rhythm. But Girdie can follow anyone—if her partner broke his leg, she would follow, fracturing her own at the same spot. But the crowd is thinning out now; husbands that danced the first dance are too tired for the second and no one has replaced them.

Oh, we have gay times in the luxury liner *Tricorn*!

Truthfully we *do* have gay times. Starting with the third dance Girdie and I have our pick of the ship's officers, most of whom are good dancers, or at least have had plenty of practice. About twenty-two o'clock the Captain goes to bed and shortly after that the chaperones start putting away their whetstones and fading, one by one. By midnight there is just Girdie and myself and half a dozen of the younger officers—and the Purser, who has dutifully danced with every woman and now feels that he owes himself the rest of the night. He is quite a good dancer, for an old man.

Oh, and there is usually Mrs. Grew, too—but she isn't one of the chaperones and she is always nice to Girdie. She is a fat old woman, full of sin and chuckles. She doesn't expect anyone to dance with her but she likes to watch—and the officers who aren't dancing at the moment like to sit with her; she's fun.

About one o'clock Uncle Tom sends Clark to tell me to come to bed or he'll lock me out. He wouldn't but I do—my feet are tired.

Good old *Tricorn*!

Chapter 6

The Captain is slowly increasing the spin of the ship to make the
fake gravity match the surface gravitation of Venus, which is 84
percent of one standard gravity or more than twice as much as I
have been used to all my life. So, when I am not busy studying astrogation or ship handling, I spend much of my time in the ship's
gymnasium, hardening myself for what is coming, for I have no
intention of being at a disadvantage on Venus in either strength or
agility.

If I can adjust to an acceleration of 0.84 gee, the later transition to the full Earth-normal of one gee should be sugar pie with
chocolate frosting. So I think.

I usually have the gymnasium all to myself. Most of the passengers are Earthmen or Venusmen who feel no need to prepare
for the heavy gravitation of Venus. Of the dozen-odd Marsmen I
am the only one who seems to take seriously the coming burden—
and the handful of aliens in the ship we never see; each remains in
his specially conditioned stateroom. The ship's officers do use the
gym; some of them are quite fanatic about keeping fit. But they
use it mostly at hours when passengers are not likely to use it.

So, on this day (Ceres thirteenth actually but the *Tricorn* uses
Earth dates and time, which made it March ninth—I don't mind
the strange dates but the short Earth day is costing me a half-
hour's sleep each night)—on Ceres thirteenth I went charging into
the gym, so angry I could spit venom and intending to derive a
double benefit by working off my mad (at least to the point where
I would not be clapped in irons for assault), and by strengthening
my muscles, too.

And found Clark inside, dressed in shorts and with a massy barbell.

I stopped short and blurted out, "What are *you* doing here?"

He grunted, "Weakening my mind."

Well, I had asked for it; there is no ship's regulation forbidding Clark to use the gym. His answer made sense to one schooled in his devious logic, which I certainly should be. I changed the subject, tossed aside my robe, and started limbering exercises to warm up. "How massy?" I asked.

"Sixty kilos."

I glanced at a weight meter on the wall, a loaded spring scale marked to read in fractions of standard gee; it read 52 percent. I did a fast rough in my mind—fifty-two thirty-sevenths of sixty—or unit sum, plus nine hundred over thirty-seven, so add about a ninth, top and bottom for a thousand over forty, to yield twenty-five—or call it the same as lifting eighty-five kilos back home on Mars. "Then why are you sweating?"

"I am not sweating!" He put the barbell down. "Let's see *you* lift it."

"All right." As he moved I squatted down to raise the barbell—and changed my mind.

Now, believe me, I work out regularly with ninety kilos at home and I had been checking that weight meter on the wall each day and loading that same barbell to match the weight I use at home, plus a bit extra each day. My objective (hopeless, it is beginning to seem) is eventually to lift as much mass under Venus conditions as I had been accustomed to lifting at home.

So I was certain I could lift sixty kilos at 52 percent of standard gee.

But it is a mistake for a girl to beat a male at any test of physical strength . . . even when it's your brother. Most especially when it's your brother and he has a fiendish disposition and you've suddenly had a glimmering of a way to put his fiendish proclivities to work. As I have said, if you're in a mood to hate something or somebody, Clark is the perfect partner.

So I grunted and strained, making a good show, got it up to my chest, started it on up—and squeaked, "Help me!"

Clark gave a one-handed push at the center of the bar and we got it all the way up. Then I said, "Catch for me," through clenched teeth, and he eased it down. I sighed. "Gee, Clark, you must be getting awful strong."

"Doing all right."

It works; Clark was now as mellow as his nature permits. I suggested companion tumbling—if he didn't mind being the bottom half of the team?—because I wasn't sure I could hold him, not at point-five-two gee . . . did he mind?

He didn't mind at all; it gave him another chance to be muscular and masculine—and I was certain he could lift me; I massed eleven kilos less than the barbell he had just been lifting. When he was smaller, we used to do quite a bit of it, with me lifting him—it was a way to keep him quiet when I was in charge of him. Now that he is as big as I am (and stronger, I fear), we still tumble a little, but taking turns at the ground-and-air parts—back home, I mean.

But with my weight almost half again what it ought to be I didn't risk any fancy capers. Presently, when he had me in a simple handstand over his head, I broached the subject on my mind. "Clark, is Mrs. Royer any special friend of yours?"

"Her?" He snorted and added a rude noise. "Why?"

"I just wondered. She—Mmm, perhaps I shouldn't repeat it."

He said, "Look, Pod, you want me to leave you standing on the ceiling?"

"Don't you dare!"

"Then don't start to say something and not finish it."

"All right. But steady while I swing my feet down to your shoulders." He let me do so, then I hopped down to the floor. The worst part about high acceleration is not how much you weigh, though that is bad enough, but how *fast* you fall—and I suspected that Clark was quite capable of leaving me head downwards high in the air if I annoyed him.

"What's this about Mrs. Royer?" he asked.

"Oh, nothing much. She thinks Marsmen are trash, that's all."

"She does, huh? That makes it mutual."

"Yes. She thinks it's disgraceful that the Line allows us to travel first class—and the Captain certainly ought not to allow us to eat in the same mess with decent people."

"Tell me more."

"Nothing to tell. We're riffraff, that's all. Convicts. You know."

"Interesting. Very, very interesting."

"And her friend Mrs. Garcia agrees with her. But I suppose I shouldn't have repeated it. After all, they are entitled to their own opinions. Aren't they?"

Clark didn't answer, which is a very bad sign. Shortly thereafter he left without a word. In a sudden panic that I might have started more than I intended to, I called after him but he just kept going. Clark is not hard of hearing but he can be very hard of listening.

Well, it was too late now. So I put on a weight harness, then loaded myself down all over until I weighed as much as I would on Venus and started trotting on the treadmill until I was covered with sweat and ready for a bath and a change.

Actually I did not really care what bad luck overtook those two harpies; I simply hoped that Clark's sleight-of-hand would be up to its usual high standards so that it could not possibly be traced back to him. Nor even guessed at. For I had not told Clark half of what was said.

Believe you me, I had never guessed, until we were in the *Tricorn*, that anyone could despise other persons simply over their ancestry or where they lived. Oh, I had encountered tourists from Earth whose manners left something to be desired—but Daddy had told me that all tourists, everywhere, seem obnoxious simply because tourists are strangers who do not know local customs . . . and I believed it, because Daddy is never wrong. Certainly the occasional visiting professor that Daddy brought home for dinner was always charming, which proves that Earthmen do not have to have bad manners.

I had noticed that the passengers in the *Tricorn* seemed a little bit stand-offish when we first boarded, but I did not think anything of it. After all, strangers do not run up and kiss you, even on Mars—and we Marsmen are fairly informal, I suppose; we're still a frontier society. Besides that, most passengers had been in the ship at least from Earth; they had already formed their friendships and cliques. We were like new kids in a strange school.

But I said "Good morning!" to anyone I met in the passageway and if I was not answered I just checked it off to hard-of-hearing—so many of them obviously *could* be hard of hearing. Anyhow, I wasn't terribly interested in getting chummy with passengers; I wanted to get acquainted with the ship's officers, pilot officers especially, so that I could get some practical experience to chink in what I already knew from reading. It's not easy for a girl to get accepted for pilot training; she has to be about four times as good as a male candidate—and every little bit helps.

I got a wonderful break right away. We were seated at the Captain's table!

Uncle Tom, of course. I am not conceited enough to think that "Miss Podkayne Fries, Marsopolis" means anything on a ship's passenger list (but wait ten years!)—whereas Uncle Tom, even though he is just my pinochle-playing, easygoing oldest relative, is nevertheless senior Senator-at-Large of the Republic, and it is certain that the Marsopolis General Agent for the Triangle Line knows this and no doubt the agent would see to it that the Purser of the *Tricorn* would know it if he didn't already.

As may be—I am not one to scorn gifts from heaven, no matter how they arrive. At our very first meal I started working on Captain Darling. That really is his name, Barrington Babcock Darling—and does his wife call him "Baby Darling"?

But of course a captain does not have a name aboard ship; he is "the Captain," "the Master," "the Skipper," or even "the Old Man" if it is a member of the ship's company speaking not in his august presence. But never a name—simply a majestic figure of impersonal authority.

(I wonder if I will someday be called "the Old Woman" when I am not in earshot? Somehow it doesn't sound quite the same.)

But Captain Darling is not too majestic or impersonal with *me*. I set out to impress him with the idea that I was awfully sweet, even younger than I am, terribly impressed by him and over-awed . . . and not too bright. It does not do to let a male of any age know that one has brains, not on first acquaintance; intelligence in a woman is likely to make a man suspicious and uneasy, much like Caesar's fear of Cassius' "lean and hungry look." Get a man solidly on your side first; after that it is fairly safe to let him become gradually aware of your intellect. He may even feel unconsciously that it rubbed off from his own.

So I set out to make him feel that it was a shame that I was not his daughter. (Fortunately he only has sons.) Before that first meal was over I confided in him my great yearning to take pilot training . . . suppressing, of course, any higher ambition.

Both Uncle Tom and Clark could see what I was up to. But Uncle Tom would never give me away and Clark just looked bored and contemptuous and said nothing, because Clark would not bother to interfere with Armageddon unless there was 10 percent in it for him.

But I do not mind what my relatives think of my tactics; they work. Captain Darling was obviously amused at my grandiose and "impossible" ambition . . . but he offered to show me the control room.

Round one to Poddy, on points.

I am now the unofficial ship's mascot, with free run of the

control room—and I am almost as privileged in the engineering department. Of course the Captain does not really want to spend hours teaching me the practical side of astrogation. He did show me through the control room and gave me a kindergarten explanation of the work—which I followed with wide-eyed awe—but his interest in me is purely social. He wants to not-quite hold me in his lap (he is much too practical and too discreet to do anything of the sort!), so I not-quite let him and make it a point to keep up my social relations with him, listening with my best astonished-kitten look to his anecdotes while he feeds me liters of tea. I really am a good listener because you never can tell when you will pick up something useful—and all in the world any woman has to do to be considered "charming" by men is to listen while they talk.

But Captain Darling is not the only astrogator in the ship.

He gave me the run of the control room; I did the rest. The second officer, Mr. Savvonavong, thinks it is simply amazing how fast I pick up mathematics. You see, he thinks he taught me differential equations. Well, he did, when it comes to those awfully complicated ones used in correcting the vector of a constant-boost ship, but if I hadn't worked hard in the supplementary course I was allowed to take last semester, I wouldn't know what he was talking about. Now he is showing me how to program a ballistic computer.

The junior third, Mr. Clancy, is still studying for his unlimited license, so he has all the study tapes and reference books I need and is just as helpful. He is near enough my age to develop groping hands . . . but only a very stupid male will make even an indirect pass unless a girl manages to let him know that it won't be resented, and Mr. Clancy is not stupid and I am very careful to offer neither invitation nor opportunity.

I may kiss him—two minutes before I leave the ship for the last time. Not sooner.

They are all very helpful and they think it is cute of me to be so dead serious about it. But, in truth, practical astrogation is *much* harder than I had ever dreamed.

I had guessed that part of the resentment I sensed—resentment that I could not fail to notice despite my cheery "Good mornings!"—lay in the fact that we were at the Captain's table. To be sure, the *Welcome in the Tricorn!* booklet in each stateroom states plainly that new seating arrangements are made at each port and that it is the ship's custom to change the guests at the Captain's table each time, making the selections from the new passengers.

But I don't suppose that warning makes it any pleasanter to be bumped, because I don't expect to like it when I'm bumped off the Captain's table at Venus.

But that is only part—

Only three of the passengers were really friendly to me: Mrs. Grew, Girdie, and Mrs. Royer. Mrs. Royer I met first and at first I thought that I was going to like her, in a bored sort of way, as she was awfully friendly and I have great capacity for enduring boredom if it suits my purpose. I met her in the lounge the first day and she immediately caught my eye, smiled, invited me to sit by her, and quizzed me about myself.

I answered her questions, mostly. I told her that Daddy was a teacher and that Mother was raising babies and that my brother and I were traveling with our uncle. I didn't boast about our family; boasting is not polite and it often is not believed—far better to let people find out nice things on their own and hope they won't notice any unnice things. Not that there is anything unnice about Daddy and Mother.

I told her that my name was Poddy Fries.

" 'Poddy'?" she said. "I thought I saw something else on the passenger list."

"Oh. It's really 'Podkayne,' " I explained. "For the Martian saint, you know."

But she didn't know. She answered, "It seems very odd to give a girl a man's name."

Well, my name is odd, even among Marsmen. But not for that reason. "Possibly," I agreed. "But with Martians gender is rather a matter of opinion, wouldn't you say?"

She blinked. "You're jesting."

I started to explain—how a Martian doesn't select which of three sexes to be until just before it matures . . . and how, even so, the decision is operative only during a relatively short period of its life.

But I gave up, as I could see that I was talking to a blank wall. Mrs. Royer simply could not imagine any pattern other than her own. So I shifted quickly. "Saint Podkayne lived a very *long* time ago. Nobody actually knows whether the saint was male or female. There are just traditions."

Of course the traditions are pretty explicit and many living

Martians claim descent from Saint Podkayne. Daddy says that we
know Martian history of millions of years ago much more accurately than we know human history a mere two thousand years
ago. In any case, most Martians include "Podkayne" in their long
lists of names (practically genealogies in synopsis) because of the
tradition that anyone named for Saint Podkayne can call on him
(or "her"—or "it") in time of trouble.

As I have said, Daddy is romantic and he thought it would be
nice to give a baby the luck, if any, that is attached to the saint's
name. I am neither romantic nor superstitious, but it suits me just
fine to have a name that belongs to me and to no other human. I
like being Podkayne "Poddy" Fries— It's better than being one of
a multitude of Elizabeths, or Dorothys, or such.

But I could see that it simply puzzled Mrs. Royer, so we
passed to other matters. Speaking from her seniority as an "old
space hand," based on her one just-completed trip out from Earth,
she told me a great many things about ships and space travel, most
of which weren't so, but I indulged her. She introduced me to a
number of people and handed me a large quantity of gossip about
passengers, ship's officers, et cetera. Between times she filled me
in on her aches, pains, and symptoms, what an important executive her son was, what a very important person her late husband
had been, and how, when I reached Earth, she really must see to it
that I met the Right People. "Perhaps such things don't matter in
an outpost like Mars, my dear child, but it is Terribly Important to
get Started Right in New York."

I tabbed her as garrulous, stupid, and well intentioned.

But I soon found that I couldn't get rid of her. If I passed
through the lounge—which I had to do in order to reach the control room—she would snag me and I couldn't get away short of
abrupt rudeness or flat lies.

She quickly started using me for chores. "Podkayne darling,
would you mind just slipping around to my stateroom and fetch-
ing my mauve wrap? I feel a tiny chill. It's on the bed, I think—or
perhaps in the wardrobe—that's a dear." Or, "Poddy child, I've
rung and I've rung and the stewardess simply *won't* answer.
Would you get my book and my knitting? Oh, and while you're at
it, you might bring me a nice cup of tea from the pantry."

Those things aren't too bad; she is probably creaky in the
knees and I'm not. But it went on endlessly . . . and shortly, in addition to being her personal stewardess, I was her private nurse.

First she asked me to read her to sleep. "Such a blinding headache and your voice is so soothing, my sweet."

I read to her for an hour and then found myself rubbing her head and temples for almost as long. Oh well, a person ought to manage a little kindness now and then, just for practice—and Mother sometimes has dreadful headaches when she has been working too hard; I know that a rub does help.

That time she tried to tip me. I refused it. She insisted. "Now, now, child, don't argue with your Aunt Flossie."

I said, "No, really, Mrs. Royer. If you want to give it to the fund for disabled spacemen as a thank-you, that's all right. But I can't take it."

She said pish and tosh and tried to shove it into my pocket. So I slid out and went to bed.

I didn't see her at breakfast; she always has a tray in her room. But about midmorning a stewardess told me that Mrs. Royer wanted to see me in her room. I was hardly gruntled at the summons, as Mr. Savvonavong had told me that if I showed up just before ten during his watch, I could watch the whole process of a ballistic correction and he would explain the steps to me. If she wasted more than five minutes of my time, I would be late.

But I called on her. She was as cheery as ever. "Oh, there you are, darling! I've been waiting ever so long! That stupid stewardess— Poddy dear, you did such wonders for my head last night . . . and this morning I find that I'm positively *crippled* with my back. You can't imagine, dear; it's *ghastly*! Now if you'll just be an angel and give me a few minutes massage—oh, say a half hour—I'm sure it'll do wonders for me. You'll find the cream for it over there on the dressing table, I think . . . And now, if you'll just help me slide out of this robe . . ."

"Mrs. Royer—"

"Yes, dear? The cream is in that big pink tube. Use just—"

"Mrs. Royer, I can't do it. I have an appointment."

"What, dear? Oh, tosh, let them wait. No one is ever on time aboard ship. Perhaps you had better warm your hands before—"

"Mrs. Royer, I am not going to do it. If something is wrong with your back, I shouldn't touch it; I might injure you. But I'll take a message to the Surgeon if you like and ask him to come see you."

Suddenly she wasn't at all cheery. "You mean you *won't* do it!"

"Have it your way. Shall I tell the surgeon?"

"Why, you impertinent—*Get out of here!*"

I got.

I met her in a passageway on my way to lunch. She stared straight through me, so I didn't speak either. She was walking as nimbly as I was; I guess her back had taken a turn for the better. I saw her twice more that day and twice more she simply couldn't see me.

The following morning I was using the viewer in the lounge to scan one of Mr. Clancy's study tapes, one on radar approach and contact. The viewer is off in a corner, behind a screen of fake potted palms, and perhaps they didn't notice me. Or perhaps they didn't care.

I stopped the scan to give my eyes and ears a rest, and heard Mrs. Garcia talking to Mrs. Royer.

". . . that I simply can't stand about Mars is that it is so *commercialized*. Why couldn't they have left it primitive and beautiful?"

MRS. ROYER: "What can you expect? Those *dreadful* people!"

The ship's official language is Ortho but many passengers talk English among themselves—and often act as if no one else could possibly understand it. These two weren't keeping their voices down. I went on listening.

MRS. GARCIA: "Just what I was saying to Mrs. Rimski. After all, they're all *criminals*."

MRS. ROYER: "Or worse. Have you noticed that little Martian girl? The niece—or so they claim—of that big black savage?"

I counted ten backwards in Old Martian and reminded myself of the penalty for murder. I didn't mind being called a "Martian." They didn't know any better, and anyhow, it's no insult; the Martians were civilized before humans learned to walk. But "big black savage"!— Uncle Tom is as dark as I am blond; his Maori blood and desert tan make him the color of beautiful old leather . . . and I love the way he looks. As for the rest—he is learned and civilized and gentle . . . and highly honored wherever he goes.

MRS. GARCIA: "I've seen her. Common, I would say. Flashy but cheap. A type that attracts a certain sort of man."

MRS. ROYER: "My dear, you don't know the half of it. I've tried to help her—I really felt sorry for her, and I always believe in being gracious, especially to one's social inferiors."

MRS. GARCIA: "Of course, dear."

MRS. ROYER: "I tried to give her a few hints as to proper

conduct among gentle people. Why, I was even *paying* her for little trifles, so that she wouldn't be uneasy among her betters. But she's an utterly ungrateful little snip—she thought she could squeeze more money out of me. She was rude about it, so rude that I feared for my safety. I had to order her out of my room, actually."

MRS. GARCIA: "You were wise to drop her. Blood will tell—bad blood or good blood—blood will always tell. And mixed blood is the Very Worst Sort. Criminals to start with . . . and then that Shameless Mixing of Races. You can see it right in that family. The boy doesn't look a bit like his sister, and as for the uncle—*hmmm*— My dear, you halfway hinted at something. Do you suppose that she is not his niece but something, shall we say, a bit *closer*?"

MRS. ROYER: "I wouldn't put it past one of them!"

MRS. GARCIA: "Oh, come, 'fess up, Flossie. Tell me what you found out."

MRS. ROYER: "I didn't say a word. But I have eyes—and so have you."

MRS. GARCIA: "Right in front of everyone!"

MRS. ROYER: "What I *can't* understand is why the Line permits *them* to mix with *us*. Perhaps they have to sell them passage—treaties or some such nonsense—but we shouldn't be forced to associate with them . . . and certainly not to *eat* with them!"

MRS. GARCIA: "I know. I'm going to write a very strong letter about it as soon as I get home. There are limits. You know, I had thought that Captain Darling was a gentleman . . . but when I saw those *creatures* actually seated at the Captain's table . . . well, I didn't believe my eyes. I thought I would faint."

MRS. ROYER: "I know. But after all, the Captain does come from Venus."

MRS. GARCIA: "Yes, but Venus was never a *prison* colony. That boy . . . he sits in the very chair I used to sit in, right across from the Captain."

(I made a mental note to ask the Chief Steward for a different chair for Clark; I didn't want him contaminated.)

After that they dropped us "Martians" and started dissecting Girdie and complaining about the food and the service, and even stuck pins in some of their shipboard coven who weren't present. But I didn't listen: I simply kept quiet and prayed for strength to go on doing so, because if I had made my presence known I feel sure that I would have stabbed them both with their own knitting needles.

Eventually they left—to rest a while to fortify themselves for lunch—and I rushed out and changed into my gym suit and hurried to the gymnasium to work up a good sweat instead of engaging in violent crime.

It was there that I found Clark and told him just enough—or maybe too much.

Chapter 7

Mr. Savvonavong tells me that we are likely to have a radiation storm almost any time now and that we'll have an emergency drill today to practice for it. The solar weather station on Mercury reports that "flare" weather is shaping up and has warned all ships in space and all manned satellites to be ready for it. The flares are expected to continue for about—

Wups! The emergency alarm caught me in the middle of a sentence. We've had our drill and I think the Captain has all the passengers properly scared now. Some ignored the alarm, or tried to, whereupon crewmen in heavy armor fetched them. Clark got fetched. He was the very last they tracked down, and Captain Darling gave him a public scolding that was a work of art and finished by warning Clark that if he failed to be the first passenger to reach shelter the next time the alarm sounded, Clark could expect to spend the rest of the trip *in* the shelter, twenty-four hours of the day, instead of having free run of passenger country.

Clark took it with his usual wooden face, but I think it hit home, especially the threat to confine him. I'm sure the speech impressed the other passengers; it was the sort that raises blisters at twenty paces. Perhaps the Captain intended it mostly for their benefit.

Then the Captain changed his tone to that of a patient teacher and explained in simple words what we could expect, why it was necessary to reach shelter *at once* even if one were taking a bath, why we would be perfectly safe if we did.

The solar flares trigger radiation, he told us, quite ordinary radiation, much like X-rays ("and other sorts," I mentally added), the sort of radiation which is found in space at all times. But the intensity reaches levels from a thousand to ten thousand times as high as "normal" space radiation—and, since we are already inside the orbit of Earth, this is bad medicine indeed; it would kill an unprotected man about as quickly as shooting him through the head.

Then he explained why we would not require a thousand to ten thousand times as much shielding in order to be safe. It's the cascade principle. The outer hull stops over 90 percent of any radiation; then comes the "cofferdam" (cargo holds and water tanks) which absorbs some more; then comes the inner hull which is actually the floor of the cylinder which is first-class passenger country.

This much shielding is plenty for all normal conditions; the radiation level in our staterooms is lower than it is at home, quite a lot lower than it is most places on Earth, especially in the mountains. (I'm looking forward to seeing real mountains. Scary!)

Then one day comes a really *bad* storm on the Sun and the radiation level jumps suddenly to 10,000 times normal—and you could get a killing dose right in your own bed and wake up dying.

No trouble. The emergency shelter is at the center of the ship, four shells farther in, each of which stops more than 90 percent of what hits it. Like this:

    10,000
        1,000 (after the first inner shell, the ceiling of passenger
            country)
                100 (after the second inner shell)
                10 (third)
                    1 (fourth—and you're inside the shelter)

But actually the shielding is better than that and it is safer to be in the ship's shelter during a bad solar storm than it is to be in Marsopolis.

The only trouble is—and no small matter—the shelter space is the geometrical core of the ship, just abaft the control room and not a whole lot bigger; passengers and crew are stacked into it about as intimately as puppies in a basket. My billet is a shelf space half a meter wide, half a meter deep, and just a trifle longer than I am—with other females brushing my elbows on each side of me. I am not a claustrophobe, but a coffin would be roomier.

Rations are canned ones, kept there against emergencies; sanitary facilities can only be described as "dreadful." I hope this storm is only a solar squall and is followed by good weather on the Sun. To finish the trip to Venus in the shelter would turn a wonderful experience into a nightmare.

The Captain finished by saying, "We will probably have five to ten minutes' warning from Hermes Station. But don't take five minutes getting here. The instant the alarm sounds *head for the shelter at once* as fast as possible. If you are not dressed, be sure you have clothes ready to grab—and dress when you get here. If you stop to worry about *anything*, it may kill you.

"Crewmen will search all passenger spaces the moment the alarm sounds—and each one is *ordered* to use force to send to shelter any passenger who fails to move fast. He won't argue with you—he'll hit you, kick you, drag you—and I'll back him up.

"One last word. Some of you have not been wearing your personal radiation meters. The law permits me to levy a stiff fine for such failure. Ordinarily I overlook such technical offenses—it's your health, not mine. But during this emergency, this regulation will be enforced. Fresh personal meters are now being passed out to each of you; old ones will be turned over to the Surgeon, examined, and exposures entered in your records for future guidance."

He gave the "all clear" order then and we all went back down to passenger country, sweaty and mussed—at least I was. I was just washing my face when the alarm sounded *again*, and I swarmed up those four decks like a frightened cat.

But I was only a close second. Clark passed me on the way.

It was just another drill. This time all passengers were in the shelter within four minutes. The Captain seemed pleased.

I've been sleeping raw but I'm going to wear pajamas tonight and all nights until this is over, and leave a robe where I can grab it. Captain Darling is a darling but I think he means exactly what he says—and I won't play Lady Godiva; there isn't a horse in the whole ship.

Neither Mrs. Royer nor Mrs. Garcia were at dinner this evening, although they were both amazingly agile both times the alarm sounded. They weren't in the lounge after dinner; their doors are closed, and I saw the Surgeon coming out of Mrs. Garcia's room.

I wonder. Surely Clark wouldn't poison them? Or would he? I don't dare ask him because of the remote possibility that he might tell me.

I don't want to ask the Surgeon, either, because it might attract attention to the Fries family. But I surely would like to have ESP sight (if there truly is such a thing) long enough to find out what is behind those two closed doors.

I hope Clark hasn't let his talents run away with him. Oh, I'm as angry at those two as ever . . . because there is just enough truth in the nasty things they said to make it hurt. I *am* of mixed races and I know that some people think that is bad, even though there is no bias against it on Mars. I *do* have "convicts" among my ancestors—but I've never been ashamed of it. Or not much, although I suppose I'm inclined to dwell more on the highly selected ones. But a "convict" is not always a criminal. Admittedly there was that period in the early history of Mars when the commissars were running things on Earth, and Mars was used as a penal colony; everybody knows that and we don't try to hide it.

But the vast majority of the transportees were political prisoners—"counterrevolutionists," "enemies of the people." Is this bad?

In any case there was the much longer period, involving fifty times as many colonists, when every new Marsman was selected as carefully as a bride selects her wedding gown and much more scientifically. And finally, there is the current period, since our Revolution and Independence, when we dropped all bars to immigration and welcome anyone who is healthy and has normal intelligence.

No, I'm not ashamed of my ancestors or my people, whatever their skin shades or backgrounds; I'm proud of them. It makes me boiling mad to hear anyone sneer at them. Why, I'll bet those two couldn't qualify for permanent visa even under our present "open door" policy! Feeble-minded—

But I do hope Clark hasn't done anything too drastic. I wouldn't want Clark to have to spend the rest of his life on Titan; I love the little wretch.

Sort of.

Chapter 8

We've had that radiation storm. I prefer hives. I don't mean the storm itself; it wasn't too bad. Radiation jumped to about 1500 times normal for where we are now—about eight-tenths of an astronomical unit from the Sun, say 120,000,000 kilometers in units you can get your teeth in. Mr. Savvonavong says that we would have been all right if the first-class passengers had simply gone up one deck to second-class passenger country—which certainly would have been more comfortable than stuffing all the passengers and crew into that maximum-safety mausoleum at the center of the ship. Second-class accommodations are cramped and cheerless, and as for third class, I would rather be shipped as freight. But either one would be a picnic compared with spending eighteen hours in the radiation shelter.

For the first time I envied the half-dozen aliens aboard. They don't take shelter; they simply remain locked in their specially conditioned staterooms as usual. No, they aren't allowed to fry; those X-numbered rooms are almost at the center of the ship anyhow, in officers' and crew's country, and they have their own extra layer of shielding, because you can't expect a Martian, for example, to leave the pressure and humidity he requires and join us humans in the shelter; it would be equivalent to dunking him in a bathtub and holding his head under. If he had a head, I mean.

Still, I suppose eighteen hours of discomfort is better than being sealed into one small room for the whole trip. A Martian can simply contemplate the subtle difference between zero and nothing for that long or longer and a Venerian just estivates. But not me. I need unrest oftener than I need rest—or my circuits get tangled and smoke pours out of my ears.

But Captain Darling couldn't know ahead of time that the storm would be short and relatively mild; he had to assume the worst and protect his passengers and crew. Eleven minutes would have been long enough for us to be in the shelter, as shown later by instrument records. But that is hindsight . . . and a captain doesn't save his ship and the lives depending on him by hindsight.

I am beginning to realize that being a captain isn't all glorious adventure and being saluted and wearing four gold stripes on your shoulders. Captain Darling is younger than Daddy and yet he has worry lines that make him look years older.

QUERY: Poddy, are you *sure* you have what it takes to captain an explorer ship?
ANSWERS: What did Columbus have that you don't? Aside from Isabella, I mean. *Semper toujours*, girl!

I spent a lot of time before the storm in the control room. Hermes Solar Weather Station doesn't actually warn us when the storm is coming; what they do is *fail* to warn us that the storm is *not* coming. That sounds silly but here is how it works:

The weathermen at Hermes are perfectly safe, as they are underground on the dark side of Mercury. Their instruments peek cautiously over the horizon in the twilight zone, gather data about Solar weather including running telephotos at several wave lengths.

But the Sun takes about twenty-five days to turn around, so Hermes Station can't watch all of it all the time. Worse yet. Mercury is going around the Sun in the same direction that the Sun rotates, taking eighty-eight days for one lap, so when the Sun again faces where Mercury was, Mercury has moved on. What this adds up to is that Hermes Station faces exactly the same face of the Sun about every seven weeks.

Which is obviously not good enough for weather-predicting storms that can gather in a day or two, peak in a few minutes, and kill you dead in seconds or less.

So the Solar weather is watched from Earth's Luna and from Venus' satellite station as well, plus some help from Deimos. But there is speed-of-light lag in getting information from these more distant stations back to the main station on Mercury. Maybe fifteen minutes for Luna and as high as a thousand seconds for Deimos . . . not good when seconds count.

But the season of bad storms is only a small part of the Sun's cycle as a variable star—say about a year out of each six. (Real years, I mean—Martian years. The Sun's cycle is about eleven of those Earth years that astronomers still insist on using.)

That makes things a lot easier; five years out of six a ship stands very little chance of being hit by a radiation storm.

But during the stormy season a careful skipper (the only sort who lives to draw a pension) will plan his orbit so that he is in the worst danger zone, say inside the orbit of Earth, only during such time as Mercury lies between him and the Sun, so that Hermes Station can always warn him of coming trouble. That is exactly what Captain Darling had done; the *Tricorn* waited at Deimos nearly three weeks longer than the guaranteed sightseeing time on Mars called for by the Triangle Line's advertising, in order to place his approach to Venus so that Hermes Station could observe and warn—because we are right in the middle of the stormy season.

I suppose the Linc's business office hates these expensive delays. Maybe they lose money during the stormy season. But three weeks' delay is better than losing a whole shipload of passengers.

But when the storm does start, radio communication goes all to pieces at once—Hermes Station can't warn the ships in the sky.

Stalemate? Not quite. Hermes Station can see a storm shaping up; they can spot the conditions on the Sun which are almost certainly going to produce a radiation storm very shortly. So they send out a storm warning—and the *Tricorn* and other ships hold radiation-shelter drills. Then we wait. One day, two days, or a whole week, and the storm either fails to develop, or it builds up and starts shooting nasty stuff in great quantities.

All during this time the space guard radio station on the dark side of Mercury sends a continuous storm warning, never an instant's break, giving a running account of how the weather looks on the Sun.

. . . and suddenly it stops.

Maybe it's a power failure and the stand-by transmitter will cut in. Maybe it's just a "fade" and the storm hasn't broken yet and transmission will resume with reassuring words.

But it may be that the first blast of the storm has hit Mercury with the speed of light, no last-minute warning at all, and the sta-

tion's eyes are knocked out and its voice is swallowed up in enormously more powerful radiation.

The officer-of-the-watch in the control room can't be sure and
he dare not take a chance. The instant he loses Hermes Station he
slaps a switch that starts a big clock with just a second hand.
When that clock has ticked off a certain number of seconds—and
Hermes Station is *still* silent—the general alarm sounds. The exact number of seconds depends on where the ship is, how far from
the Sun, how much longer it will take the first blast to reach the
ship after it has already hit Hermes Station.

Now here is where a captain bites his nails and gets gray hair
and earns his high pay . . . because *he* has to decide how many
seconds to set that clock for. Actually, if the first and worst blast is
at the speed of light, he hasn't any warning time at *all* because the
break in the radio signal from Hermes and that first wave front
from the Sun will reach him at the same instant. Or, if the angle is
unfavorable, perhaps it is his own radio reception that has been
clobbered, and Hermes Station is still trying to reach him with a
last-moment warning. He doesn't know.

But he does know that if he sounds the alarm and chases
everybody to shelter every time the radio fades for a few seconds,
he will get people so worn out and disgusted from his crying
"Wolf!" that when the trouble really comes they may not move
fast enough.

He knows, too, that the outer hull of his ship will stop almost
anything in the electromagnetic spectrum. Among photons (and
nothing else travels at speed-of-light) only the hardest X-radiation
will get through to passenger country and not much of that. But
traveling along behind, falling just a little behind each second, is
the really dangerous stuff—big particles, little particles, middle-
sized particles, all the debris of nuclear explosion. This stuff is
moving very fast but not quite at speed-of-light. He has to get his
people safe before it hits.

Captain Darling picked a delay of twenty-five seconds, for
where we were and what he expected from the weather reports. I
asked him how he picked it and he just grinned without looking
happy and said, "I asked my grandfather's ghost."

Five times while I was in the control room the officer of the
watch started that clock . . . and five times contact with Hermes
Station was picked up again before time ran out and the switch
was opened.

The sixth time the seconds trickled away while all of us held our breaths . . . and contact with Hermes wasn't picked up again and the alarm sounded like the wakeful trump of doom.

The Captain looked stony-faced and turned to duck down the hatch into the radiation shelter. I didn't move, because I expected to be allowed to remain in the control room. Strictly speaking, the control room is part of the radiation shelter, since it is just above it and is enclosed by the same layers of cascade shielding.

(It's amazing how many people think that a captain controls his ship by peering out a port as if he were driving a sand wagon. But he doesn't, of course. The control room is inside, where he can watch things much more accurately and conveniently by displays and instruments. The only viewport in the *Tricorn* is one at the top end of the main axis, to allow passengers to look out at the stars. But we have never been headed so that the mass of the ship would protect that sightseeing room from solar radiation, so it has been locked off this whole trip.)

I knew I was safe where I was, so I hung back, intending to take advantage of being "teacher's pet"—for I certainly didn't want to spend hours or days stretched out on a shelf with gabbling and maybe hysterical women crowding me on both sides.

I should have known. The Captain hesitated a split second as he started down the hatch and snapped, "Come along, Miss Fries."

I came. He *always* calls me "Poddy"—and his voice had spank in it.

Third-class passengers were already pouring in, since they have the shortest distance to go, and crew members were mustering them into their billets. The crew has been on emergency routine ever since we first were warned by Hermes Station, with their usual one watch in three replaced by four hours on and four hours off. Part of the crew had been staying dressed in radiation armor (which must be *very* uncomfortable) and simply hanging around passenger country. They can't take that heavy armor off for any reason at all until their reliefs show up, dressed also in armor. These crewmen are the "chasers" who bet their lives that they can check every passenger space, root out stragglers, and still reach the shelter fast enough not to accumulate radiation poisoning. They are all volunteers and the chasers on duty when the alarm sounds get a big bonus and the other half of them who were lucky enough not to be on duty get a little bonus.

The Chief Officer is in charge of the first section of chasers and the Purser is in charge of the second—but they don't get any bonus even though the one on duty when the alarm sounds is by tradition and law the last man to enter the safety of the shelter. This hardly seems fair . . . but it is considered their honor as well as their duty.

Other crewmen take turns in the radiation shelter and are equipped with mustering lists and billeting diagrams.

Naturally, service has been pretty skimpy of late, with so many of the crew pulled off their regular duties in order to do just one thing and do it *fast* at the first jangle of the alarm. Most of these emergency-duty assignments have to be made from the stewards and clerks; engineers and communicators and such usually can't be spared. So staterooms may not be made up until late afternoon—unless you make your own bed and tidy your room yourself, as I had been doing—and serving meals takes about twice as long as usual, and lounge service is almost non-existent.

But of course the passengers realize the necessity for this temporary mild austerity and are grateful because it is all done for safety.

You think so? My dear, if you believe that, you will believe anything. You haven't Seen Life until you've seen a rich, elderly Earthman deprived of something he feels is his rightful due, because he figures he paid for it in the price of his ticket. I saw one man, perhaps as old as Uncle Tom and certainly old enough to know better, almost have a stroke. He turned purple, really purple and gibbered—all because the bar steward didn't show up on the bounce to fetch him a new deck of playing cards.

The bar steward was in armor at the time and couldn't leave his assigned area, and the lounge steward was trying to be three places at once and answer stateroom rings as well. This didn't mean anything to our jolly shipmate; he was threatening to sue the Line and all its directors, when his speech became incoherent.

Not everybody is that way, of course. Mrs. Grew, fat as she is, has been making her own bed and she is never impatient. Some others who are ordinarily inclined to demand lots of service have lately been making a cheerful best of things.

But some of them act like children with tantrums—which isn't pretty in children and is even uglier in grandparents.

The instant I followed the Captain into the radiation shelter I discovered just how efficient *Tricorn* service can be when it really matters. I was snatched—snatched like a ball, right out of the air—and passed from hand to hand. Of course I don't weigh much at one-tenth gravity, all there is at the main axis; but it is rather breath-taking. Some more hands shoved me into my billet, already stretched out, as casually and impersonally as a housewife stows clean laundry, and a voice called out, "Fries, Podkayne!" and another voice answered, "Check."

The spaces around me, and above and below and across from me, filled up awfully fast, with the crewmen working with the unhurried efficiency of automatic machinery sorting mail capsules. Somewhere a baby was crying and through it I heard the Captain saying, "Is that the last?"

"Last one, Captain," I heard the Purser answer. "How's the time?"

"Two minutes thirty-seven seconds—and your boys can start figuring their payoff, because this one is no drill."

"I didn't think it was, Skipper—and I've won a small bet from the Mate myself." Then the Purser walked past my billet carrying someone, and I tried to sit up and bumped my head and my eyes bugged out.

The passenger he was carrying had fainted; her head lolled loosely over the crook of his arm. At first I couldn't tell who it was, as the face was a bright, bright red. And then I recognized her and I almost fainted. Mrs. Royer—

Of course the first symptom of any bad radiation exposure is erythema. Even with a sunburn, or just carelessness with an ultraviolet lamp, the first thing you see is the skin turning pink or bright red.

But was it possible that Mrs. Royer had been hit with such extremely sharp radiation in so very little time that her skin had *already* turned red in the worst "sunburn" imaginable? Just from being last man in?

In that case she hadn't fainted; she was dead.

And if that was true, then it was equally true that the passengers who were last to reach the shelter must all have received several times the lethal dosage. They might not feel ill for hours yet; they might not die for days. But they were just as dead as if they were already stretched out still and cold.

How many? I had no way of guessing. Possibly—*probably* I corrected myself—all the first-class passengers; they had the farthest to go and were most exposed to start with.

Uncle Tom and Clark—

I felt sudden sick sorrow and wished that I had not been in the control room. If my brother and Uncle Tom were dying, I didn't want to be alive myself.

I don't think I wasted any sympathy on Mrs. Royer. I did feel a shock of horror when I saw that flaming red face, but truthfully, I didn't like her, I thought she was a parasite with contemptible opinions, and if she had died of heart failure instead, I can't honestly say that it would have affected my appetite. None of us goes around sobbing over the millions and billions of people who have died in the past . . . nor over those still living and yet to be born whose single certain heritage is death (including Podkayne Fries herself). So why should you cry foolish tears simply because you happen to be in the neighborhood when someone you don't like— despise, in fact—comes to the end of her string?

In any case, I did not have time to feel sorrow for Mrs. Royer; my heart was filled with grief over my brother and my uncle. I was sorry that I hadn't been sweeter to Uncle Tom, instead of imposing on him and expecting him always to drop whatever he was doing to help me with my silly problems. I regretted all the many times I had fought with my brother. After all, he was a child and I am a woman; I should have made allowances.

Tears were welling out of my eyes and I almost missed the Captain's first words:

"Shipmates," he said, in a voice firm and very soothing, "my crew and our guests aboard . . . this is not a drill; this is indeed a radiation storm.

"Do not be alarmed; we are all, each and every one of us, perfectly safe. The Surgeon has examined the personal radiation exposure meter of the very last one to reach the shelter. It is well within safe limits. Even if it were added to the accumulated exposure of the most exposed person aboard—who is not a passenger, by the way, but one of the ship's company—the total would still be inside the conservative maximum for personal health and genetic hygiene.

"Let me say it again. No one has been hurt, no one is going to be hurt. We are simply going to suffer a mild inconvenience. I wish I could tell you how long we will have to remain here in the safety of the shelter. But I do not know. It might be a few hours, it might be several days. The longest radiation storm of record lasted less than a week. We hope that Old Sol is not that bad-tempered this time. But until we receive word from Hermes Station that the storm is over, we will all have to stay inside here. Once we know a storm is over it usually does not take too long to check the ship and make sure that your usual comfortable quarters are safe. Until then, be patient and be patient with each other."

I started to feel better as soon as the Captain started to talk.

His voice was almost hypnotic; it had the soothing all-better-now effect of a mother reassuring a child. I relaxed and was simply weak with the aftereffects of my fears.

But presently I began to wonder. Would Captain Darling tell us that everything was all right when really everything was All Wrong simply because it was too late and nothing could be done about it?

I thought over everything I had ever learned about radiation poisoning, from the simple hygiene they teach in kindergarten to a tape belonging to Mr. Clancy that I had scanned only that week.

And I decided that the Captain had been telling the truth.

Why? Because, even if my very worst fears had been correct, and we had been hit as hard and unexpectedly as if a nuclear weapon had exploded by us, nevertheless something can *always* be done about it. There would be three groups of us—those who hadn't been hurt at all and were not going to die (certainly everybody who was in the control room or in the shelter when it happened, plus all or almost all the third-class passengers if they had moved fast), a second group so terribly exposed that they were certain to die, no matter what (let's say everybody in first class country), and a third group, no telling how large, which had been dangerously exposed but could be saved by quick and drastic treatment.

In which case that quick and drastic action would be going on.

They would be checking our exposure meters and reshuffling us—sorting out the ones in danger who required rapid treatment, giving morphine shots to the ones who were going to die anyhow and moving them off by themselves, stacking those of us who were safe by ourselves to keep us from getting in the way, or drafting us to help nurse the ones who could be helped.

That was certain. But there was nothing going on, nothing at all—just some babies crying and a murmur of voices. Why, they hadn't even looked at the exposure meters of most of us; it seemed likely that the Surgeon had checked only the last few stragglers to reach the shelter.

Therefore the Captain had told us the simple, heartwarming truth.

I felt so good that I forgot to wonder why Mrs. Royer had looked like a ripe tomato. I relaxed and soaked in the warm and happy fact that darling Uncle Tom wasn't going to die and that my kid brother would live to cause me lots more homey grief. I almost went to sleep . . .

. . . and was yanked out of it by the woman on my right starting to scream: "Let me out of here! *Let me out of here!*"

Then I did see some fast and drastic emergency action.

Two crewmen swarmed up to our shelf and grabbed her; a stewardess was right behind them. She slapped a gag over the woman's mouth and gave her a shot in the arm, all in one motion. Then they held her until she stopped struggling. When she was quiet, one of the crewmen picked her up and took her somewhere.

Shortly thereafter a stewardess showed up who was collecting exposure meters and passing out sleeping pills. Most people took them but I resisted—I don't like pills at best and I certainly won't take one to knock me out so that I won't know what is going on. The stewardess was insistent but I can be awfully stubborn, so she shrugged and went away. After that there were three or four more cases of galloping claustrophobia or maybe just plain screaming funk; I wouldn't know. Each was taken care of promptly with no fuss and shortly the shelter was quiet except for snores, a few voices, and fairly continuous sounds of babies crying.

There aren't any babies in first class and not many children of any age. Second class has quite a few kids, but third class is swarming with them and every family seems to have at least one young baby. It's why they are there, of course; almost all of third class are Earth people emigrating to Venus. With Earth so crowded, a man with a big family can easily reach the point where emigration to Venus looks like the best way out of an impossible situation, so he signs a labor contract and Venus Corporation pays for their tickets as an advance against his wages.

I suppose it's all right. They need to get away and Venus needs all the people they can get. But I'm glad Mars Republic doesn't subsidize immigration, or we would be swamped. We take immigrants but they have to pay their own way and have to deposit return tickets with the PEG board, tickets they can't cash in for two of our years.

A good thing, too. At least a third of the immigrants who come to Mars just can't adjust. They get homesick and despondent and use those return tickets to go back to Earth. I can't understand anyone's not *liking* Mars, but if they don't then it's better if they don't stay.

I lay there, thinking about such things, a little bit excited and a little bit bored, and mostly wondering why somebody didn't do something about those poor babies.

The lights had been dimmed and when somebody came up to

my shelf I didn't see who it was at first. "Poddy?" came Girdie's
voice, softly but clearly. "Are you in there?"

"I think so. What's up, Girdie?" I tried to keep my voice
down too.

"Do you know how to change a baby?"

"I certainly do!" Suddenly I wondered how Duncan was doing . . . and realized that I hadn't really thought about him in *days*.
Had he forgotten me? Would he know Grandmaw Poddy the next
time he saw her?

"Then come along, chum. There's work to be done."

There certainly was! The lowest part of the shelter, four catwalks below my billet and just over the engineering spaces, was
cut like a pie into four quarters—sanitary units, two sick bays, for
men and for women and both crowded— and jammed into a little
corner between the infirmaries was a sorry pretense for a nursery,
not more than two meters in any dimension. On three walls of it
babies were stacked high in canvas crib baskets snap-hooked to
the walls, and more overflowed into the women's sick bay. A
sweeping majority of those babies were crying.

In the crowded middle of this pandemonium two harassed
stewardesses were changing babies, working on a barely big
enough shelf let down out of one wall. Girdie tapped one of them
on the shoulder. "All right, girls, reinforcements have landed. So
get some rest and a bite to eat."

The older one protested feebly, but they were awfully glad to
take a break; they backed out and Girdie and I moved in and took
over. I don't know how long we worked, as we never had time to
think about it—there was always more than we could do and we
never quite got caught up. But it was better than lying on a shelf
and staring at another shelf just centimeters above your nose. The
worst of it was that there simply wasn't enough room. I worked
with both elbows held in close, to keep from bumping Girdie on
one side and a basket crib that was nudging me on the other side.

But I'm not complaining about that. The engineer who designed that shelter into the *Tricorn* had been forced to plan as
many people as possible into the smallest possible space; there
wasn't any other way to do it and still give us all enough levels of
shielding during a storm. I doubt if he worried much about getting
babies changed and dry; he had enough to do just worrying about
how to keep them alive.

But you can't tell that to a baby.

Girdie worked with an easy, no-lost-motions efficiency that

surprised me; I would never have guessed that she had ever had her hands on a baby. But she knew what she was doing and was faster than I was. "Where are their mothers?" I asked, meaning: "Why aren't those lazy slobs down here helping instead of leaving it to the stewardesses and some volunteers?"

Girdie understood me. "Most of them—all of them, maybe— have other small children to keep quiet; they have their hands full. A couple of them went to pieces themselves; they're in there sleeping it off." She jerked her head toward the sick bay.

I shut up, as it made sense. You couldn't possibly take care of an infant properly in one of those shallow niches the passengers were stacked in, and if each mother tried to bring her own baby down here each time, the traffic jam would be indescribable. No, this assembly-line system was necessary. I said, "We're running out of Disposies."

"Stacked in a cupboard behind you. Did you see what happened to Mrs. Garcia's face?"

"Huh?" I squatted and got out more supplies. "You mean Mrs. Royer, don't you?"

"I mean both of them. But I saw milady Garcia first and got a better look at her, while they were quieting her down. You didn't see her?"

"No."

"Sneak a look into the women's ward first chance you get. Her face is the brightest, most amazing chrome yellow I've ever seen in a paint pot, much less on a human face."

I gasped. "Gracious! I did see Mrs. Royer—bright red instead of yellow. Girdie—what in the world happened to them?"

"I'm fairly sure I know what happened," Girdie answered slowly, "but no one can figure out *how* it happened."

"I don't follow you."

"The colors tell the story. Those are the exact shades of two of the water-activated dyes used in photography. Know anything about photography, hon?"

"Not much," I answered. I wasn't going to admit what little I did know, because Clark is a very accomplished amateur photographer. And I wasn't going to mention *that*, either!

"Well, surely you've seen someone taking snapshots. You pull out the tab and there is your picture—only there's no picture as yet. Clear as glass. So you dip it in water and slosh it around for about thirty seconds. Still no picture. Then you lay it anywhere in the light and the picture starts to show . . . and when the colors are bright enough to suit you, you cover it up and let it finish drying in darkness, so that the colors won't get too garish." Girdie suppressed a chuckle. "From the results, I would say that they didn't cover their faces in time to stop the process. They probably tried to scrub it off and made it worse."

I said, in a puzzled tone—and I *was* puzzled, about part of it— "I still don't see how it could happen."

"Neither does anybody else. But the Surgeon has a theory. Somebody booby-trapped their washcloths."

"Huh?"

"Somebody in the ship must have a supply of the pure dyes. That somebody soaked two washcloths in the inactive dyes— colorless, I mean—and dried them carefully, all in total darkness. Then that same somebody sneaked those two prepared washcloths into those two staterooms and substituted them for washcloths they found there on the stateroom wash trays. That last part wouldn't be hard for anyone with cool nerves—service in the staterooms has been pretty haphazard the last day or two, what with this flap over the radiation storm. Maybe a fresh washcloth appears in your room, maybe it doesn't—and all the ship's washcloths and towels are the same pattern. You just wouldn't know."

I certainly hope not! I said to myself—and added aloud, "I suppose not."

"Certainly not. It could be one of the stewardesses—or any of the passengers. But the real mystery is: where did the dyes come from? The ship's shop doesn't carry them . . . just the rolls of prepared film . . . and the Surgeon says that he knows enough about chemistry to be willing to stake his life that no one but a master chemist, using a special laboratory, could possibly separate out pure dyes from a roll of film. He thinks, too, that since the dyes aren't even manufactured on Mars, this somebody must be somebody who came aboard at Earth." Girdie glanced at me and smiled. "So you're not a suspect, Poddy. But I am."

"Why are you a suspect?" (And if I'm not a suspect then my brother isn't a suspect!) "Why, that's silly!"

"Yes, it is . . . because I wouldn't have known how even if I'd had the dyes. But it isn't, inasmuch as I could have bought them before I left Earth, and I don't have reason to like either of those women."

"I've never heard you say a word against them."

"No, but they've said a few thousand words about me—and other people have ears. So I'm a hot suspect, Poddy. But don't fret about it. I didn't do it, so there is no possible way to show that I did." She chuckled. "And I hope they never catch the somebody who did!"

I didn't even answer, "Me, too!" I could think of one person who might figure out a way to get pure dyes out of a roll of film without a complete chemistry laboratory, and I was checking quickly through my mind every item I had seen when I searched Clark's room.

There hadn't been *anything* in Clark's room which could have been photographic dyes. No, not even film.

Which proves precisely nothing where Clark is concerned. I just hope that he was careful about fingerprints.

Two other stewardesses came in presently and we fed all the babies, and then Girdie and I managed a sort of a washup and had a snack standing up, and then I went back up to my assigned shelf and surprised myself by falling asleep.

I must have slept three or four hours, because I missed the happenings when Mrs. Dirkson had her baby. She is one of the Terran emigrants to Venus and she shouldn't have had her baby until long after we reach Venus—I suppose the excitement stirred things up. Anyhow, when she started to groan they carried her down to that dinky infirmary, and Dr. Torland took one look at her and ordered her carried up into the control room because the control room was the only place inside the radiation-safe space roomy enough to let him do what needed to be done.

So that's where the baby was born, on the deck of the control room, right between the chart tank and the computer. Dr. Torland and Captain Darling are godfathers and the senior stewardess is godmother and the baby's name is "Radiant," which is a poor pun but rather pretty.

They jury-rigged an incubator for Radiant right there in the control room before they moved Mrs. Dirkson back to the infirmary and gave her something to make her sleep. The baby was still there when I woke up and heard about it.

I decided to take a chance that the Captain was feeling more mellow now, and sneaked up to the control room and stuck my head in. "Could I please see the baby?"

The Captain looked annoyed, then he barely smiled and said, "All right, Poddy. Take a quick look and get out."

So I did. Radiant masses about a kilo and, frankly, she looks like cat meat, not worth saving. But Dr. Torland says that she is doing well and that she will grow up to be a fine, healthy girl—prettier than I am. I suppose he knows what he is talking about, but if she is ever going to be prettier than I am, she has lots of kilometers to go. She is almost the color of Mrs. Royer and she's mostly wrinkles.

But no doubt she'll outgrow it, because she looks like one of the pictures toward the end of the series in a rather goody-goody schoolbook called *The Miracle of Life*—and the earlier pictures in that series were even less appetizing. It is probably just as well that we can't possibly see babies until they are ready to make their debut, or the human race would lose interest and die out.

It would probably be still better to lay eggs. Human engineering isn't all that it might be, especially for us female types.

I went back down where the more mature babies were to see if they needed me. They didn't, not right then, as the babies had been fed again and a stewardess and a young woman I had never met were on duty and claimed that they had been working only a few minutes. I hung around anyhow, rather than go back up to my shelf. Soon I was pretending to be useful by reaching past the two who really were working and checking the babies, then handing down the ones who needed servicing as quickly as shelf space was cleared.

It speeded things up a little. Presently I pulled a little wiggler out of his basket and was cuddling him; the stewardess looked up and said, "I'm ready for him."

"Oh, he's not wet," I answered. "Or 'she' as the case may be. Just lonely and needs loving."

"We haven't time for that."

"I wonder." The worst thing about the midget nursery was the high noise level. The babies woke each other and egged each other on and the decibels were something fierce. No doubt they were all lonely and probably frightened—I'm sure I would be. "Most of the babies need loving more than they need anything else."

"They've all had their bottles."

"A bottle can't cuddle."

She didn't answer, just started checking the other infants. But I didn't think what I had said was silly. A baby can't understand your words and he doesn't know where he is if you put him in a strange place, nor what has happened. So he cries. Then he needs to be soothed.

Girdie showed up just then. "Can I help?"

"You certainly can. Here . . . hold this one."

In a few minutes I rounded up three girls about my age and I ran across Clark prowling around the catwalks instead of staying quietly in his assigned billet so I drafted him, too. He wasn't exactly eager to volunteer; but doing anything was slightly better than doing nothing; he came along.

I couldn't use any more help as standing room was almost nonexistent. We worked it only by having two baby-cuddlers sort of back into each of the infirmaries with the mistress of ceremonies (me) standing in the little space at the bottom of the ladder, ready to scrunch in any direction to let people get in and out of the washrooms and up and down the ladder—and with Girdie, because she was tallest, standing back of the two at the changing shelf and dealing out babies, the loudest back to me for further assignment and the wet ones down for service—and vice versa: dry ones back to their baskets unless they started to yell; ones that had fallen asleep from being held and cuddled.

At least seven babies could receive personal attention at once, and sometimes as high as ten or eleven, because at one-tenth gee your feet never get tired and a baby doesn't weigh anything at all worth mentioning; it was possible to hold one in each arm and sometimes we did.

In ten minutes we had that racket quieted down to an occasional whimper, quickly soothed. I didn't think Clark would stick it out, but he did—probably because Girdie was part of the team. With a look of grim nobility on his face, the like of which I have never before seen there, he cuddled babies and presently was saying "Kitchy-koo kitchy-koo!" and "There, there, honey bun," as if he had been doing it all his life. Furthermore, the babies seemed to like him; he could soothe one down and put it to sleep quickest of any of us. Hypnotism, maybe?

This went on for several hours, with volunteers moving in and tired ones moving out and positions rotating. I was relieved once and had another snatched meal and then stretched out on my shelf for about an hour before going back on duty.

I was back at the changing shelf when the Captain called us all by speaker: "Attention, please. In five minutes power will be cut and the ship will be in free fall while a repair is made outside the ship. All passengers strap down. All crew members observe precautions for free fall."

I went right on changing the baby under my hands; you can't walk off on a baby. In the meantime, babies that had been being cuddled were handed back and stowed, and the cuddling team was chased back to their shelves to strap down—and spin was being taken off the ship. One rotation every twelve seconds you simply don't notice at the center of the ship, but you do notice when the *un*spinning starts. The stewardess with me on the changing bench said, "Poddy, go up and strap down. Hurry."

I said, "Don't be silly, Bergitta, there's work to be done," and popped the baby I had just dried into its basket and fastened the zipper.

"You're a passenger. That's an order— *please!*"

"Who's going to check all these babies? You? And how about those four in on the floor of the women's sick bay?"

Bergitta looked startled and hurried to fetch them. All the other stewardesses were busy checking on strap-down; she didn't bother me any more with That's-an-order; she was too busy hooking up the changing shelf and fastening baby baskets to the space. I was checking all the others and almost all of them had been left unzipped—logical enough while we were working with them, but zipping the cover on a baby basket is the same as strapping down for a grown-up. It holds them firmly but comfortably with just their heads free.

I still hadn't finished when the siren sounded and the Captain cut the power.

Oh, brother! Pandemonium. The siren woke the babies who were asleep and scared any who were awake, and every single one of those squirmy little worms started to cry at the top of its lungs—and one I hadn't zipped yet popped right out of its basket and floated out into the middle of the space and I snagged it by one leg and was loose myself, and the baby and I bumped gently against the baskets on one wall—only it wasn't a wall any longer, it was just an obstacle to further progress. Free fall can be very confusing when you are not used to it, which I admit I am not. Or wasn't.

The stewardess grabbed us both and shoved the elusive little darling back into her straitjacket and zipped it while I hung onto a handhold. And by then two more were loose.

I did better this time—snagged one without letting go and just kept it captive while Bergitta took care of the other one. Bergitta really knew how to handle herself in zero gravity, with unabrupt graceful movements like a dancer in a slow-motion solly. I made a mental note that this was a skill I must acquire.

I thought the emergency was over; I was wrong. Babies don't

like free fall; it frightens them. It also makes their sphincters most erratic. Most of the latter we could ignore—but Disposies don't catch everything; regrettably some six or seven of them had been fed in the last hour.

I know now why stewardesses are all graduate nurses; we kept five babies from choking to death in the next few minutes. That is, Bergitta cleared the throat of the first one that upchucked its milk and, seeing what she had done, I worked on the second one in trouble while she grabbed the third. And so on.

Then we were very busy trying to clear the air with clean Disposies because— Listen, dear, if you think you've had it tough because your baby brother threw up all over your new party dress, then you should try somewhat-used baby formula in free fall, where it doesn't settle anywhere in particular but just floats around like smoke until you either get it or it gets you.

From six babies. In a small compartment.

By the time we had that mess cleaned up, or 95 percent or so anyway, we were both mostly sour milk from hair part to ankle and the Captain was warning us to stand by for acceleration, which came almost at once to my great relief. The Chief Stewardess showed up and was horrified that I had not strapped down and I told her in a ladylike way to go to hell, using a more polite idiom suitable to my age and sex—and asked her what Captain Darling would think about a baby passenger choking to death simply because I had strapped down all regulation-like and according to orders? And Bergitta backed me up and told her that I had cleared choke from at least two and maybe more—she had been too busy to count.

Mrs. Peal, the C.S., changed her tune in a hurry and was sorry and thanked me, and sighed and wiped her forehead and trembled and you could see that she was dead on her feet. But nevertheless, she checked all the babies herself and hurried out. Pretty quickly we were relieved and Bergitta and I crowded into the women's washroom and tried to clean up some. Not much good, as we didn't have any clean clothes to change into.

The "All Clear" felt like a reprieve from purgatory, and a hot bath was heaven itself with the Angels singing. "A" deck had already been checked for radiation level and pronounced safe while the repair outside the ship was being made. The repair itself, I learned, was routine. Some of the antennas and receptors and things outside the ship can't take a flare storm; they burn out—so immediately after a storm, men go outside in armored space suits and replace them. This is normal and unavoidable, like replacing lighting tubes at home. But the men who do it get the same radiation bonus that the passenger chasers get, because old Sol could burn them down with one tiny little afterthought.

I soaked in warm, clean water and thought how miserable an eighteen hours it had been. Then I decided that it hadn't been so bad after all.

It's lots better to be miserable than to be bored.

Chapter 9

I am now twenty-seven years old.

Venus years, of course, but it sounds so much better. All is relative.

Not that I would stay here on Venus even if guaranteed the Perfect Age for a thousand years. Venusberg is sort of an organized nervous breakdown and the country outside the city is even worse. What little I've seen of it. And I don't want to see much of it. Why they ever named this dreary, smog-ridden place for the Goddess of Love and Beauty I'll never know. This planet appears to have been put together from the scrap left over after the rest of the Solar System was finished.

I don't think I would go outside Venusberg at all except that I've just got to see fairies in flight. The only one I've seen so far is in the lobby of the hilton we are staying in and is stuffed.

Actually I'm just marking time until we shape for Earth, because Venus is a Grave Disappointment—and now I'm keeping my fingers crossed that Earth will not be a G.D., too. But I don't see how it can be; there is something deliciously *primitive* about the very thought of a planet where one can go outdoors without any special preparations. Why, Uncle Tom tells me that there are places along the Mediterranean (that's an ocean in La Belle, France) where the natives bathe in the ocean itself without any clothing of any sort, much less insulasuits or masks.

I wouldn't like that. Not that I'm body proud; I enjoy a good sauna sweat-out as well as the next Marsman. But it would scare me cross-eyed to bathe in an ocean; I don't ever intend to get wet all over in anything larger than a bathtub. I saw a man fished out of the Grand Canal once, in early spring. They had to thaw him before they could cremate him.

But it is alleged that, along the Mediterranean shore, the air in the summertime is often blood temperature and the water not much cooler. As may be. Podkayne is not going to take any silly chances.

Nevertheless I am terribly eager to see Earth, in all its fantastic unlikeliness. It occurs to me that my most vivid conceptions of Earth come from the Oz stories—and when you come right down to it, I suppose that isn't too reliable a source. I mean, Dorothy's conversations with the Wizard are instructive—but about *what*? When I was a child I believed every word of my Oz tapes; but now I am no longer a child and I do not truly suppose that a whirlwind is a reliable means of transportation, nor that one is likely to encounter a Tin Woodman on a road of yellow brick.

Tik-Tok, yes—because we have Tik-Toks in Marsopolis for the simpler and more tedious work. Not precisely like Tik-Tok of Oz, of course, and not called "Tik-Toks" by anyone but children, but near enough, near enough, quite sufficient to show that the Oz stories are founded on fact if *not* precisely historical.

And I believe in the Hungry Tiger, too, in the most practical way possible, because there was one in the municipal zoo when I was a child, a gift from the Calcutta Kiwanis Klub to Marsopolis Kiwanians. It always looked at me as if it were sizing me up as an appetizer. It died when I was about five and I didn't know whether to be sorry or glad. It was beautiful . . . and so *very* Hungry.

But Earth is still many weeks away and, in the meantime, Venus does have some points of interest for the newcomer, such as I.

In traveling I strongly recommend traveling with my Uncle Tom. On arriving here, there were no silly waits in "Hospitality" (!) rooms; we were given the "courtesy of the port" at once—to the *extreme* chagrin of Mrs. Royer. "Courtesy of the port" means that your baggage isn't examined and that nobody bothers to look at that bulky mass of documents—passport and health record and security clearance and solvency proof and birth certificate and I.D.s, and nineteen other silly forms. Instead we were whisked from satellite station to spaceport in the private yacht of the Chairman of the Board and were met there by the Chairman himself!—and popped into his Rolls and wafted royally to Hilton Tannhäuser.

We were invited to stay at his official residence (his "cottage," that being the Venus word for a palace) but I don't think he really expected us to accept, because Uncle Tom just cocked his left or satirical eyebrow and, "Mr. Chairman, I don't think you would want me to appear to be bribed even if you manage it."

And the Chairman didn't seem offended at all; he just chuckled till his belly shook like Saint Nicholas' (whom he strongly resembles even to the beard and the red cheeks, although his eyes are cold even when he laughs, which is frequently).

"Senator," he said, "you know me better than that. My attempt to bribe you will be much more subtle. Perhaps through this young lady. Miss Podkayne, are you fond of jewelry?"

I told him honestly that I wasn't, very, because I always lose it. So he blinked and said to Clark, "How about you, son?"

Clark said, "I prefer cash."

The Chairman blinked again and said nothing.

Nor had he said anything to his driver when Uncle Tom declined the offer of his roof; nevertheless we flew straight to our hilton—which is why I don't think he ever expected us to stay with him.

But I am beginning to realize that this is not entirely a pleasure trip for Uncle Tom . . . and to grasp emotionally a fact known only intellectually in the past, i.e., Uncle Tom is not merely the best pinochle player in Marsopolis, he sometimes plays other games for higher stakes. I must confess that the what or why lies outside my admittedly youthful horizon—save that everyone knows that the Three-Planets conference is coming up.

Query: Could U.T. conceivably be involved in this? As a consultant or something? I hope not, as it might keep him tied up for weeks on Luna and I have no wish to waste time on a dreary ball of slag while the Wonders of Terra await me—and Uncle Tom just *might* be difficult about letting me go down to Earth without him.

But I wish still more strongly that Clark had not answered the Chairman truthfully.

Still, Clark would not sell out his own uncle for mere money.

On the other hand, Clark does not regard money as "mere." I must think about this—

But it is some comfort to realize that anyone who handed Clark a bribe would find that Clark had not only taken the bribe but the hand as well.

Possibly our suite at the Tannhäuser is intended as a bribe, too. Are we paying for it? I'm almost afraid to ask Uncle Tom, but I do know this: the servants that come with it won't accept tips. Not any. Although I very carefully studied up on the subject of tipping, both for Venus and Earth, so that I would know what to do when the time came—and it had been my understanding that *anyone* on Venus *always* accepts tips, even ushers in churches and bank tellers.

But not the servants assigned to us. I have two tiny little amber dolls, identical twins, who shadow me and would bathe me if I let them. They speak Portuguese but not Ortho— and at present my Portuguese is limited to "gobble-gobble" (which means "Thank you") and I have trouble explaining to them that I can dress and undress myself and I'm not too sure about their names—they both answer to "Maria."

Or at least I don't *think* they speak Ortho. I must think about this, too.

Venus is officially bilingual, Ortho and Portuguese, but I'll bet I heard at least twenty other languages the first hour we were down. German sounds like a man being choked to death, French sounds like a cat fight, while Spanish sounds like molasses gurgling gently out of a jug. Cantonese— Well, think of a man trying to vocalize Bach who doesn't like Bach very much to start with.

Fortunately almost everybody understands Ortho as well. Except Maria and Maria. If true.

I could live a long time without the luxury of personal maids but I must admit that this hilton suite is quite a treat to a plain-living, wholesome Mars girl, namely me. Especially as I am in it quite a lot of the time and will be for a while yet. The ship's Surgeon, Dr. Torland, gave me many of the special inoculations needed for Venus on the trip here—an unpleasant subject I chose not to mention—but there still remain many more before it will be safe for me to go outside the city, or even very much into the city. As soon as we reached our suite a physician appeared and played chess on my back with scratches, red to move and mate in five moves—and three hours later I had several tens of welts, with something horrid that must be done about each of them.

Clark ducked out and didn't get his scratch tests until the next morning and I misdoubt he will die of Purple Itch or some such, were it not that his karma is so clearly reserving him for hanging. Uncle Tom refused the tests. He was through all this routine more than twenty years ago, and anyhow he claims that the too, too mortal flesh is merely a figment of the imagination.

So I am more or less limited for a few days to lavish living here in the Tannhäuser. If I got out, I must wear gloves and a mask even in the city. But one whole wall of the suite's salon becomes a stereo stage simply by voice request, either taped or piped live from any theater or club in Venusberg—and some of the "entertainment" has widened my sophistication unbelievably, especially when Uncle Tom is not around. I am beginning to realize that Mars is an essentially puritanical culture. Of course Venus doesn't actually have laws, just company regulations, none of which seems to be concerned with personal conduct. But I had been brought up to believe that Mars Republic is a free society—and I suppose it is. However, there is "freedom" and "freedom."

Here the Venus Corporation owns everything worth owning and runs everything that shows a profit, all in a fashion that would make Marsmen swoon. But I guess Venusmen would swoon at how straitlaced *we* are. I know this Mars girl blushed for the first time in I don't know when and switched off a show that I didn't really believe.

But the solly screen is far from being the only astonishing feature of this suite. It is so big that one should carry food and water when exploring it, and the salon is so huge that local storms appear distinctly possible. My private bath is a suite in itself, with so many gadgets in it that I ought to have an advanced degree in engineering before risking washing my hands. But I've learned how to use them all and purely love them! I had never dreamed that I had been limping along all my life without Utter Necessities.

Up to now my top ambition along these lines has been not to have to share a washstand with Clark, because it has never been safe to reach for my own Christmas-present cologne without checking to see that it is not nitric acid or worse! Clark regards a bathroom as an auxiliary chemistry lab; he's not much interested in staying clean.

But the most astonishing thing in our suite is the piano. No, no, dear, I don't mean a keyboard hooked into the sound system; I mean a *real* piano. Three legs. Made out of wood. Enormous. That odd awkward-graceful curved shape that doesn't fit anything else and can't be put in a corner. A top that opens up and lets you see that it really does have a harp inside and very complex machinery for making it work.

I think that there are just four real pianos on all of Mars, the one in the Museum that nobody plays and probably doesn't work, the one in Lowell Academy that no longer has a harp inside it, just wiring connections that make it really the same as any other piano, the one in the Rose House (as if any President ever had time to play a piano!), and the one in the Beaux Arts Hall that actually is played sometimes by visiting artists although I've never heard it. I don't think there can be another one, or it would have been banner-lined in the news, wouldn't you think?

This one was made by a man named Steinway and it must have taken him a lifetime. I played Chopsticks on it (that being the best opus in my limited repertoire) until Uncle asked me to stop. Then I closed it up, keyboard and top, because I had seen Clark eying the machinery inside, and warned him sweetly but firmly that if he touched one finger to it I would break all his fingers while he was asleep. He wasn't listening but he knows I mean it. That piano is Sacred to the Muses and is not to be taken apart by our Young Archimedes.

I don't care what the electronics engineers say; there is a vast difference between a "piano" and a *real* piano. No matter if their silly oscilloscopes "prove" that the sound is identical. It is like the difference between being warmly clothed—or climbing up in your Daddy's lap and getting *really* warm.

I haven't been under house arrest all the time; I've been to the casinos, with Girdie and with Dexter Cunha, Dexter being the son of Mr. Chairman of the Board Kurt Cunha. Girdie is leaving us here, going to stay on Venus, and it makes me sad.

I asked her, "Why?"

We were sitting alone in our palatial salon. Girdie is staying in this same hilton, in a room not very different nor much larger than her cabin in the *Tricorn,* and I guess I'm just mean enough that I wanted her to see the swank we were enjoying. But my excuse was to have her help me dress. For now I am wearing (Shudder!) *support* garments. Arch supports in my shoes and tight things here and there intended to keep me from spreading out like an amoeba—and I won't say what Clark calls them because Clark is rude, crude, unrefined, and barbaric.

I hate them. But at 84 percent of one standard gee, I need them despite all that exercise I took aboard ship. This alone is reason enough not to live on Venus, or on Earth, even if they were as delightful as Mars.

Girdie did help me—she had bought them for me in the first place—but she also made me change my makeup, one which I had most carefully copied out of the latest issue of *Aphrodite.* She looked at me and said, "Go wash your face, Poddy. Then we'll start over."

I pouted out my lip and said, "Won't!" The one thing I had noticed most and quickest was that *every* female on Venus wears paint like a Red Indian shooting at the Good Guys in the sollies—even Maria and Maria wear three times as much makeup just to work in as Mother wears to a formal reception—and Mother doesn't wear any when working.

"Poddy, Poddy! Be a good girl."

"I *am* being a good girl. I learned that when I was just a child. And look at yourself in the mirror!" Girdie was wearing as High-styled a Venusberg face-do as any in that magazine.

"I know what I look like. But I am more than twice your age and no one even suspects me of being young and sweet and innocent. Always be what you are, Poddy. Never pretend. Look at Mrs. Grew. She's a comfortable fat old woman. She isn't kittenish, she's just nice to be around."

"You want me to look like a hick tourist!"

"I want you to look like Poddy. Come, dear, we'll find a happy medium. I grant you that even the girls your age here wear more makeup than grown-up women do on Mars—so we'll compromise. Instead of painting you like a Venusberg trollop, we'll make you a young lady of good family and gentle breeding, one who is widely traveled and used to all sorts of customs and manners, and so calmly sure of herself that she knows what is best for her—totally uninfluenced by local fads."

Girdie is an artist, I must admit. She started with a blank canvas and worked on me for more than an hour—and when she got through, you couldn't see that I was wearing any makeup at all.

But here is what you could see: I was at least two years older (real years, Mars years, or about six Venus years); my face was thinner and my nose not pug at all and I looked ever so slightly world-weary in a sweet and tolerant way. My eyes were enormous.

"Satisfied?" she asked.

"I'm *beautiful!*"

"Yes, you are. Because you are still Poddy. All I've done is make a picture of Poddy the way she is going to be. Before long."

My eyes filled with tears and we had to blot them up very hastily and she repaired the damage. "Now," she said briskly, "all we need is a club. And your mask."

"What's the club for? And I won't wear a mask, not on top of this."

"The club is to beat off wealthy stockholders who will throw themselves at your feet. And you will wear your mask, or else we won't go."

We compromised. I wore the mask until we got there and Girdie promised to repair any damage to my face—and promised that she would coach me as many times as necessary until I could put on that lovely, lying face myself. The casinos are safe, or supposed to be—the air not merely filtered and conditioned but freshly regenerated, free of any trace of pollen, virus, colloidal suspension or whatever. This is because lots of tourists don't like to take all the long list of immunizations necessary actually to *live* on Venus; but the Corporation wouldn't think of letting a tourist get away unbled. So the hiltons are safe and the casinos are safe and a tourist can buy a health insurance policy from the Corporation for a very modest premium. Then he finds that he can cash his policy back in for gambling chips any time he wants to. I understand that the Corporation hasn't had to pay off on one of these policies very often.

Venusberg assaults the eye and ear even from inside a taxi. I believe in free enterprise; all Marsmen do, it's an article of faith and the main reason we *won't* federate with Earth (and be outvoted five hundred to one). But free enterprise is not enough excuse to blare in your ears and glare in your eyes every time you leave your own roof. The shops never close (I don't think anything ever closes in Venusberg) and full color and stereo ads climb right inside your taxi and sit in your lap and shout in your ear.

Don't ask me how this horrid illusion is produced. The engineer who invented it probably flew off on his own broom. This red devil about a meter high appeared between us and the partition separating us from the driver (there wasn't a sign of a solly receiver) and started jabbing at us with a pitchfork. "Get the Hi-Ho Habit!" it shrieked. "Everybody drinks Hi-Ho! Soothing, Habit-Forming. Dee*lishus!* Get High with Hi-Ho!"

I shrank back against the cushions.

Girdie phoned the driver. "Please shut that thing off."

It faded down to just a pink ghost and the commercial dropped to a whisper while the driver answered, "Can't, madam. They rent the concession." Devil and noise came back on full blast.

And I learned something about tipping. Girdie took money from her purse, displayed one note. Nothing happened and she added a second; noise and image faded down again. She passed them through a slot to the driver and we weren't bothered any more. Oh, the transparent ghost of the red devil remained and a nagging whisper of his voice, until both were replaced by another and just as faint—but we could talk. The giant ads in the street outside were noisier and more dazzling; I didn't see how the driver could see or hear to drive, especially as traffic was unbelievably thick and heart-stoppingly fast and frantic and he kept cutting in and out of lanes and up and down in levels as if he were trying utmostly to beat Death to a hospital.

By the time we slammed to a stop on the roof of Dom Pedro Casino I figure Death wasn't more than half a lap behind.

I learned later why they drive like that. The hackie is an employee of the Corporation, like most everybody—but he is an "enterprise-employee," not on wages. Each day he has to take in a certain amount in fares to "make his nut"—the Corporation gets all of this. After he has rolled up that fixed number of paid kilometers, he splits the take with the Corporation on all other fares the rest of the day. So he drives like mad to pay off the nut as fast as possible and start making some money himself—then keeps on driving fast because he's got to get his while the getting is good.

Uncle Tom says that most people on Earth have much the same deal, except it's done by the year and they call it income tax.

In Xanadu did Kubla Khan
A stately pleasure dome decree—

Dom Pedro Casino is like that. Lavish. Beautiful. Exotic. The arch over the entrance proclaims EVERY DIVERSION IN THE KNOWN UNIVERSE, and from what I hear this may well be true. However, all Girdie and I visited were the gaming rooms.

I never saw so much money in my whole life!

A sign outside the gambling sector read:

HELLO, SUCKER!
All Games Are Honest
All Games Have a House Percentage
YOU CAN'T WIN!
So Come On In and Have Fun—
(While We Prove It)
Checks Accepted. All Credit
Cards Honored. Free Breakfast
and a Ride to Your Hilton When
You Go Broke. Your Host,

DOM PEDRO

I said, "Girdie, there really is somebody named Dom Pedro?"
She shrugged. "He's an employee and that's not his real name.
But he does look like an emperor. I'll point him out. You can meet
him if you like and he'll kiss your hand. If you like that sort of
thing. Come on."

She headed for the roulette tables while I tried to see everything at once. It was like being on the inside of a kaleidoscope.
People beautifully dressed (employees mostly), people dressed
every sort of way, from formal evening wear to sports shorts
(tourists mostly), bright lights, staccato music, click and tinkle
and shuffle and snap, rich hangings, armed guards in comic-opera
uniforms, trays of drinks and food, nervous excitement, and
money everywhere—

I stopped suddenly, so Girdie stopped. My brother Clark.
Seated at a crescent-shaped table at which a beautiful lady was
dealing cards. In front of him several tall stacks of chips and an
imposing pile of paper money.

I should not have been startled. If you think that a six-year-old
boy (or eighteen-year-old boy if you use their years) wouldn't be
allowed to gamble in Venusberg, then you haven't been to Venus.
Never mind what we do in Marsopolis, here there are just two requirements to gamble: a) you have to be alive; b) you have to have
money. You don't have to be able to talk Portuguese or Ortho, nor
any known language; as long as you can nod, wink, grunt, or flip a
tendril, they'll take your bet. And your shirt.

No, I shouldn't have been surprised. Clark heads straight for
money the way ions head for an electrode. Now I knew where he
had ducked out to the first night and where he had been most of
the time since.

I went up and tapped him on the shoulder. He didn't look
around at once but a man popped up out of the rug like a genie from
a lamp and had me by the arm. Clark said to the dealer, "Hit me,"
and looked around. "Hi, Sis. It's all right, Joe, she's my sister."

"Okay?" the man said doubtfully, still holding my arm.

"Sure, sure. She's harmless. Sis, this is Josie Mendoza, company cop, on lease to me for tonight. Hi, Girdie!" Clark's voice
was suddenly enthusiastic. But he remembered to say, "Joe, slip
into my seat and watch the stuff. Girdie, this is swell! You gonna
play black jack? You can have my seat."

(It must be love, dears. Or a high fever.)

She explained that she was about to play roulette. "Want me to
come help?" he said eagerly. "I'm pretty good on the wheel, too."

She explained to him gently that she did not want help because she was working on a system, and promised to see him later in the evening. Girdie is unbelievably patient with Clark. I would have— Come to think of it, she's unbelievably patient with me.

If Girdie has a system for roulette, it didn't show. We found two stools together and she tried to give me a few chips. I didn't want to gamble and told her so, and she explained that I would have to stand up if I didn't. Considering what 84 percent gee does to my poor feet I bought a few chips of my own and did just what she did, which was to place minimum bets on the colors, or on odd or even. This way you don't win, you don't lose—except that once in a long while the little ball lands on zero and you lose a chip permanently (that "house percentage" the sign warned against).

The croupier could see what we were doing but we actually were gambling and inside the rules; he didn't object. I discovered almost at once that the trays of food circulating and the drinks were absolutely free—to anyone who was gambling. Girdie had a glass of wine. I don't touch alcoholic drinks even on birthdays—and I certainly wasn't going to drink Hi-Ho, after that obnoxious ad!— but I ate two or three sandwiches and asked for, and got—they had to go get it—a glass of milk. I tipped the amount I saw Girdie tip.

We had been there over an hour and I was maybe three or four chips ahead when I happened to sit up straight—and knocked a glass out of the hand of a man standing behind me, all over him, some over me.

"Oh, dear!" I said, jumping down from my stool and trying to dab off the wet spots on him with my kerchief. "I'm terribly sorry!"

He bowed. "No harm done to me. Merely soda water. But I fear my clumsiness has ruined milady's gown."

Out of one corner of her mouth Girdie said, "Watch it, kid!" but I answered, "This dress? Huh uh! If that was just water, there won't be a wrinkle or a spot in ten minutes. Travel clothes."

"You are a visitor to our city? Then permit me to introduce myself less informally than by soaking you to the skin." He whipped out a card. Girdie was looking grim but I rather liked his looks. Actually not impossibly older than I am (I guessed at twelve Mars years, or say thirty-six of his own—and it turned out he was only thirty-two). He was dressed in the very elegant Venus evening wear, with cape and stick and formal ruff . . . and the cutest little waxed mustaches.

The card read:

DEXTER KURT CUNHA, STK.

I read it, then reread it, then said, "Dexter *Kurt* Cunha— Are you any relation to—"

"My father."

"Why, I know your father!"—and put out my hand.

Ever had your hand kissed? It makes chill bumps that race up your arm, across your shoulders, and down the other arm—and of course nobody would ever do it on Mars. This is a distinct shortcoming in our planet and one I intend to correct, even if I have to bribe Clark to institute the custom.

By the time we had names straight, Dexter was urging us to share a bite of supper and some dancing with him in the roof garden. But Girdie was balky. "Mr. Cunha," she said, "that is a very handsome calling card. But I am responsible for Podkayne to her uncle—and I would rather see your I.D."

For a split second he looked chilly. Then he smiled warmly at her and said, "I can do better," and held up one hand.

The most imposing old gentleman I have ever seen hurried over. From the medals on his chest I would say that he had won every spelling contest from first grade on. His bearing was kingly and his costume unbelievable. "Yes, Stockholder?"

"Dom Pedro, will you please identify me to these ladies?"

"With pleasure, sir." So Dexter was really Dexter and I got my hand kissed again. Dom Pedro does it with great flourish but it didn't have quite the same effect— I don't think he puts his heart into it the way Dexter does.

Girdie insisted on stopping to collect Clark—and Clark suffered an awful moment of spontaneous schizophrenia, for he was still winning. But love won out and Girdie went up on Clark's arm, with Josie trailing us with the loot. I must say I admire my brother in some ways; spending cash money to protect his winnings must have caused even deeper conflict in his soul, if any, than leaving the game while he was winning.

The roof garden is the Brasilia Room and is even more magnificent than the casino proper, with a night-sky roof to match its name, stars and the Milky Way and the Southern Cross such as nobody ever in history actually saw from anywhere on Venus. Tourists were lined up behind a velvet rope waiting to get in—but not us. It was, "This way, if you please, Stockholder," to an elevated table right by the floor and across from the orchestra and a perfect view of the floor show.

We danced and we ate foods I've never heard of and I let a glass of champagne be poured for me but didn't try to drink it because the bubbles go up my nose—and wished for a glass of milk or at least a glass of water because some of the food was quite spicy, but didn't ask for it.

But Dexter leaned over me and said, "Poddy, my spies tell me that you like milk."

"I do!"

"So do I. But I'm too shy to order it unless I have somebody to back me up." He raised a finger and two glasses of milk appeared instantly.

But I noticed that he hardly touched his.

However, I did not realize I had been hoaxed until later. A singer, part of the floor show, a tall handsome dark girl dressed as a gypsy—if gypsies did ever dress that way, which I doubt, but she was billed as "Romany Rose"—toured the ringside tables singing topical verses to a popular song.

She stopped in front of us, looked right at me and smiled, struck a couple of chords and sang:

> *"Poddy Fries-uh came to town,*
> *Pretty, winsome Poddy—*
> *Silver shoes and sky blue gown,*
> *Lovely darling Podkayne—*
>
> *"She has sailed the starry sea,*
> *Pour another toddy!*
> *Lucky Dexter, lucky we!*
> *Drink a toast to Poddy!"*

And everybody clapped and Clark pounded on the table and Romany Rose curtsied to me and I started to cry and covered my face with my hands and suddenly remembered that I mustn't cry because of my makeup and dabbed at my eyes with my napkin and hoped I hadn't ruined it, and suddenly silver buckets with champagne appeared all over that big room and everybody *did* drink a toast to me, standing up when Dexter stood up in a sudden silence brought on by a roll of drums and a crashing chord from the orchestra.

I was speechless and just barely knew enough to stay seated myself and nod and try to smile when he looked at me—

—and he broke his glass, just like story tapes, and everybody imitated him and for a while there was crash and tinkle all over the room, and I felt like Ozma just after she stops being Tip and is Ozma again and I had to remember my makeup very hard indeed!

Later on, after I had gulped my stomach back into place and could stand up without trembling, I danced with Dexter again. He is a dreamy dancer—a firm, sure lead without ever turning it into a wrestling match. During a slow waltz I said, "Dexter? *You* spilled that glass of soda water. On purpose."

"Yes. How did you know?"

"Because it *is* a sky-blue dress—or the color that is called 'sky-blue,' for Earth, although I've never seen a sky this color. And my shoes *are* silvered. So it couldn't have been an accident. Any of it."

He just grinned, not a bit ashamed. "Only a little of it. I went first to your hilton—and it took almost half an hour to find out who had taken you where and I was furious, because Papa would have been most vexed. But I found you."

I chewed that over and didn't like the taste. "Then you did it because your daddy told you to. Told you to entertain me because I'm Uncle Tom's niece."

"No, Poddy."

"Huh? Better check through the circuits again. That's how the numbers read."

"No, Poddy. Papa would never order me to entertain a lady—other than formally, at our cottage—lady on my arm at dinner, that sort of thing. What he did do was show me a picture of you and ask me if I wanted to. And I decided I did want to. But it wasn't a very good picture of you, didn't do you justice—just one snapped by one of the servants of the Tannhäuser when you didn't know it."

(I decided I had to find some way to get rid of Maria and Maria, a girl needs privacy. Although this hadn't turned out too dry.)

But he was still talking. ". . . and when I did find you I almost didn't recognize you, you were so much more dazzling than the photograph. I almost shied off from introducing myself. Then I got the wonderful idea of turning it into an accident. I stood behind you with that glass of soda water almost against your elbow for so long the bubbles all went out of it—and when you did move, you bumped me so gently I had to slop it over myself to make it enough of an accident to let me be properly apologetic." He grinned most disarmingly.

"I see," I said. "But look, Dexter, the photograph was probably a very good one. This isn't my own face." I explained what Girdie had done.

He shrugged. "Then someday wash it for me and let me look

at the real Poddy. I'll bet I'll recognize her. Look, dear, the accident was only half fake, too. We're even."

"What do you mean?"

"They named me 'Dexter' for my maternal grandfather, before they found out I was left-handed. Then it was a case of either renaming me 'Sinister,' which doesn't sound too well—or changing me over to right-handed. But that didn't work out either; it just made me the clumsiest man on three planets." (This while twirling me through a figure eight!)

"I'm always spilling things, knocking things over. You can follow me by the sound of fractured frangibles. The problem was not to cause an accident, but to keep from spilling that water until the right instant." He grinned that impish grin. "I feel very triumphant about it. But forcing me out of left-handedness did something else to me too. It's made me a rebel—and I think you are one, too."

"Uh . . . maybe."

"I certainly am. I am expected to be Chairman of the Board someday, like my papa and my grandpapa. But I shan't. I'm going to space!"

"Oh! So am I!" We stopped dancing and chattered about spacing. Dexter intends to be an explorer captain, just like me—only I didn't quite admit that my plans for spacing included pilot and master; it is never well in dealing with a male to let him know that you think *you* can do whatever it is he can do best or wants to do most. But Dexter intends to go to Cambridge and study paramagnetics and Davis mechanics and be ready when the first true starships are ready. Goodness!

"Poddy, maybe we'll even do it together. Lots of billets for women in starships."

I agreed that that was so.

"But let's talk about you. Poddy, it wasn't that you looked so much better than your picture."

"No?" (I felt vaguely disappointed.)

"No. Look. I know your background, I know you've lived all your life in Marsopolis. Me, I've been everywhere. Sent to Earth for school, took the Grand Tour while I was there, been to Luna, of course, and all over Venus—and to Mars. When you were a little girl and I wish I had met you then."

"Thank you." (I was beginning to feel like a poor relation.)

"So I know exactly what a honky-tonk town Venusberg is . . . and what a shock it is to people the first time. Especially anyone reared in a gentle and civilized place like Marsopolis. Oh, I love

my hometown but I know what it is— I've been other places.
Poddy? Look at me, Poddy. The thing that impressed me about
you was your aplomb."

"Me?"

"Your amazing and perfect savoir-faire . . . under conditions I
knew were strange to you. Your uncle has been everywhere—and
Girdie, I take it, has been, too. But lots of strangers here, older
women, become quite giddy when first exposed to the fleshpots of
Venusberg and behave frightfully. But you carry yourself like a
queen. Savoir-faire."

(This man I liked! Definitely. After years and years of "Beat it,
runt!" it does something to a woman to be told she has savoir-
faire. I didn't even stop to wonder if he told all the girls that—I
didn't want to!)

We didn't stay much longer; Girdie made it plain that I had to
get my "beauty sleep." So Clark went back to his game (Josie appeared out of nowhere at the right time—and I thought of telling
Clark he had better git fer home too, but I decided that wasn't
"savoir-faire" and anyhow he wouldn't have listened) and Dexter
took us to the Tannhäuser in his papa's Rolls (or maybe his own,
I don't know) and bowed over our hands and kissed them as he
left us.

I was wondering if he would try to kiss me good night and had
made up my mind to be cooperative about it. But he didn't try.
Maybe it's not a Venusberg custom, I don't know.

Girdie went up with me because I wanted to chatter. I bounced
myself on a couch and said, "Oh, Girdie, it's been the most wonderful night of my life!"

"It hasn't been a bad night for me," she said quietly. "It certainly can't hurt me to have met the son of the Chairman of the
Board." It was then that she told me that she was staying on Venus.

"But, Girdie—*why?*"

"Because I'm broke, dear. I need a job."

"You? But you're *rich*. Everybody knows that."

She smiled. "I *was* rich, dear. But my last husband went
through it all. He was an optimistic man and excellent company.
But not nearly the businessman he thought he was. So now Girdie
must gird her loins and get to work. Venusberg is better than Earth
for that. Back home I could either be a parasite on my old friends
until they got sick of me—the chronic house guest—or get one of
them to give me a job that would really be charity, since I don't
know anything. Or disappear into the lower depths and change my

name. Here, nobody cares and there is always work for anyone who wants to work. I don't drink and I don't gamble—Venusberg is made to order for me."

"But what will you *do*?" It was hard to imagine her as anything but the rich society girl whose parties and pranks were known even on Mars.

"Croupier, I hope. They make the highest wages . . . and I've been studying it. But I've been practicing dealing, too—for black jack, or faro, or chemin de fer. But I'll probably have to start as a change girl."

"*Change girl?* Girdie—would you dress that way?"

She shrugged. "My figure is still good . . . and I'm quite quick at counting money. It's honest work, Poddy—it has to be. Those change girls often have as much as ten thousand on their trays."

I decided I had fubbed and shut up. I guess you can take the girl out of Marsopolis but you can't quite take Marsopolis out of the girl. Those change girls practically don't wear anything but the trays they carry money on—but it certainly was honest work and Girdie has a figure that had all the junior officers in the *Tricorn* running in circles and dropping one wing. I'm sure she could have married any of the bachelors and insured her old age thereby with no effort.

Isn't it more honest to work? And, if so, why shouldn't she capitalize her assets?

She kissed me good night soon after and ordered me to go right to bed and to sleep. Which I did—all but the sleep. Well, she wouldn't be a change girl long; she'd be a croupier in a beautiful evening gown . . . and saving her wages and her tips . . . and someday she would be a stockholder, one share anyway, which is all anybody needs for old age in the Venus Corporation. And I would come back and visit her when I was famous.

I wondered if I could ask Dexter to put in a word for her to Dom Pedro?

Then I thought about Dexter—

I know that can't be love; I was in love once and it feels entirely different. It hurts.

This just feels grand.

Chapter 10

I hear that Clark has been negotiating to sell me (black market, of course) to one of the concessionaires who ship wives out to contract colonists in the bush. Or so they say. I do not know the truth. But There Are Rumors.

What infuriates me is that he is said to be offering me at a ridiculously low price!

But in truth it is this very fact that convinces me that it is just a rumor, carefully planted by Clark himself, to annoy me—because, while I would not put it past Clark to sell me into what is tantamount to chattel slavery and a Life of Shame if he could get away with it, nevertheless he would wring out of the sordid transaction every penny the traffic would bear. This is certain.

It is much more likely that he is suffering a severe emotional reaction from having opened up and become almost human with me the other night—and therefore found it necessary to counteract it with this rumor in order to restore our relations to their normal, healthy, cold-war status.

Actually I don't think he could get away with it, even on the black market, because I don't have any contract with the Corporation and even if he forged one, I could always manage to get a message to Dexter, and Clark knows this. Girdie tells me that the black market in wives lies mostly in change girls or clerks or hilton chambermaids who haven't managed to snag husbands in Venusberg (where men are in short supply) and are willing to cooperate in being sold out back (where women are scarce) in order to jump their contracts. They don't squawk and the Corporation overlooks the matter.

Most of the bartered brides, of course, are single women among the immigrants, right off a ship. The concessionaires pay their fare and squeeze whatever cumshaw they can out of the women themselves and the miners or ranchers to whom their contracts are assigned. All Kosher.

Not that I understand it— I don't understand *anything* about how this planet really works. No laws, just Corporate regulations. Want to get married? Find somebody who claims to be a priest or a preacher and have any ceremony you like—but it hasn't any legal standing because it is not a contract with the Corporation. Want a divorce? Pack your clothes and get out, leaving a note or not as you see fit. Illegitimacy? They've never heard of it. A baby is a baby and the Corporation won't let one want, because that baby will grow up and be an employee and Venus has a chronic labor shortage. Polygamy? Polyandry? Who cares? The Corporation doesn't.

Bodily assault? Don't try it in Venusberg; it is the most thoroughly policed city in the system—violent crime is bad for business. I don't wander around alone in some parts of Marsopolis, couth as my hometown is, because some of the old sand rats are a bit sunstruck and not really responsible. But I'm perfectly safe alone anywhere in Venusberg; the only assault I risk is from super salesmanship.

(The bush is another matter. Not the people so much, but Venus itself is lethal—and there is always a chance of encountering a Venerian who has gotten hold of a grain of happy dust. Even the little wingety fairies are bloodthirsty if they sniff happy dust.)

Murder? This is a *very* serious violation of regulations. You'll have your pay checked for years and years and years to offset both that employee's earning power for what would have been his working life . . . and his putative value to the Corporation, all calculated by the company's actuaries who are widely known to have no hearts at all, just liquid helium pumps.

So if you are thinking of killing anybody on Venus, *don't do it!* Lure him to a planet where murder is a social matter and all they do is hang you or something. No future in it on Venus.

There are three classes of people on Venus: stockholders, employees, and a large middle ground. Stockholder-employees (Girdie's ambition), enterprise employees (taxi drivers, ranchers, prospectors, some retailers, etc.), and of course future employees, children still being educated. And there are tourists but tourists aren't people; they have more the status of steers in a cattle pen—valuable assets to be treated with great consideration but no pity.

A person from out-planet can be a tourist for an hour or a lifetime—just as long as his money holds out. No visa, no rules of any sort, everybody welcome. But you must have a return ticket and you can't cash it in until *after* you sign a contract with the Corporation. If you do. I wouldn't.

I still don't understand how the system works even though Uncle Tom has been very patient in explaining. But he says he doesn't understand it either. He calls it "corporate fascism"—which explains nothing—and says that he can't make up his mind whether it is the grimmest tyranny the human race has ever known . . . or the most perfect democracy in history.

He says that nothing here is as bad in many ways as the conditions over 90 percent of the people on Earth endure, and that it isn't even as bad in creature comforts and standard of living as lots of people on Mars, especially the sand rats, even though we never knowingly let anyone starve or lack medical attention.

I Just Don't Know. I can see now that all my life I have simply taken for granted the way we do things on Mars. Oh, sure, I learned about other systems in school—but it didn't soak in. Now I am beginning to grasp emotionally that There Are Other Ways Than Ours . . . and that people can be happy under them. Take Girdie. I can see why she didn't want to stay on Earth, not the way things had changed for her. But she could have stayed on Mars; she's just the sort of high-class immigrant we want. But Mars didn't tempt her at all.

This bothered me because (as you may have gathered) I think Mars is just about perfect. And I think Girdie is just about perfect.

Yet a horrible place like Venusberg is what she picked. She says it is a Challenge.

Furthermore Uncle Tom says that she is Dead Right; Girdie will have Venusberg eating out of her hand in two shakes and be a stockholder before you can say Extra Dividend.

I guess he's right. I felt awfully sorry for Girdie when I found out she was broke. "I wept that I had no shoes—till I met a man who had no feet." Like that, I mean. I've never been broke, never missed any meals, never worried about the future—yet I used to feel sorry for Poddy when money was a little tight around home and I couldn't have a new party dress. Then I found out that the rich and glamorous Miss Fitz-Snugglie (I still won't use her right name, it wouldn't be fair) had only her ticket back to Earth and had borrowed the money for that. I was so sorry I hurt.

But now I'm beginning to realize that Girdie has "feet" no matter what—and will always land on them.

She has indeed been a change girl, for two whole nights—and asked me please to see to it that Clark did not go to Dom Pedro Casino those nights. I don't think she cared at all whether or not I saw her . . . but she knows what a horrible case of puppy love Clark has on her and she's just so sweet and good all through that she did not want to risk making it worse and/or shocking him.

But she's a dealer now and taking lessons for croupier—and Clark goes there every night. But she won't let him play at her table. She told him point-blank that he could know her socially or professionally, but not both—and Clark never argues with the inevitable; he plays at some other table and tags her around whenever possible.

Do you suppose that my kid brother actually does possess psionic powers? I know he's not a telepath, else he would have cut my throat long since. But he is still winning.

Dexter assures me that a) the games are absolutely honest, and b) no one can possibly beat them, not in the long run, because the house collects its percentage no matter what. "Certainly you can win, Poddy," he assured me. "One tourist came here last year and took home over half a million. We paid it happily—and advertised it all over Earth—and still made money the very week he struck it rich. Don't you even suspect that we are giving your brother a break. If he keeps it up long enough, we will not only win it all back but take every buck he started with. If he's as smart as you say he is, he'll quit while he's ahead. But most people aren't that smart—and Venus Corporation never gambles on anything but a sure thing."

Again, I don't know. But it was both Girdie and winning that caused Clark to become almost human with me. For a while.

It was last week, the night I met Dexter—and Girdie told me to go to bed and I did but I couldn't sleep and I left my door open so that I could hear Clark come in—or if I didn't, phone somebody and have him chased home because, while Uncle Tom is responsible for both of us, I'm responsible for Clark and always have been. I wanted Clark to be home and in bed before Uncle Tom got up. Habit, I guess.

He did come sneaking in about two hours after I did and I *psst'd* to him and he came into my room.

You never saw a six-year-old boy with so much money!

Josie had seen him to our door, so he said. Don't ask me why he didn't put it in the Tannhäuser's vault—or do ask me: I think he wanted to fondle it.

He certainly wanted to boast. He laid it out in stacks on my bed, counting it and making sure that I knew how much it was. He even shoved a pile toward me. "Need some, Poddy? I won't even charge you interest—plenty more where this came from."

I was breathless. Not the money, I didn't need any money. But the offer. There have been times in the past when Clark has lent me money against my allowance—and charged me exactly 100 percent interest come allowance day. Till Daddy caught on and spanked us both.

So I thanked him most sincerely and hugged him. Then he said, "Sis, how old would you say Girdie is?"

I began to understand his off-the-curve behavior. "I really couldn't guess," I answered carefully. (Didn't need to guess, I knew.) "Why don't you ask her?"

"I did. She just smiled at me and said that women don't have birthdays."

"Probably an Earth custom," I told him and let it go at that. "Clark, how in the world did you win so much money?"

"Nothing to it," he said. "All those games, somebody wins, somebody loses. I just make sure I'm one who wins."

"But how?"

He just grinned his worst grin.

"How much money did you start with?"

He suddenly looked guarded. But he was still amazingly mellow, for Clark, so I pushed ahead. I said, "Look, if I know you, you can't get all your fun out of it unless *somebody* knows, and you're safer telling me than anyone else. Because I've never told on you yet. Now have I?"

He admitted that this was true by not answering—and it is true. When he was small enough, I used to clip him one occasionally. But I never tattled on him. Lately clipping him has become entirely too dangerous; he can give me a fat lip quicker than I can give him one. But I've never tattled on him. "Loosen up," I urged him. "I'm the only one you dare boast to. How much were you paid to sneak those three kilos into the *Tricorn* in my baggage?"

He looked very smug. "Enough."

"Okay. I won't pry any further about that. But what was it you smuggled? You've had me utterly baffled."

"You would have found it if you hadn't been so silly anxious to explore the ship. Poddy, you're stupid. You know that, don't you? You're as predictable as the law of gravity. I can *always* out-guess you."

I didn't get mad. If Clark gets you sore, he's got you.

"Guess maybe," I admitted. "Are you going to tell me what it was? Not happy dust, I hope?"

"Oh, no!" he said and looked shocked. "You know what they do to you for happy dust around here? They turn you over to na-tives who are hopped up with it, that's what they do—and then they don't even have to bother to cremate you."

I shuddered and returned to the subject. "Going to tell me?"

"*Mmm . . .*"

"I swear by Saint Podkayne Not to Tell." This is my own pri-vate oath, nobody else would or could use it.

"By Saint Podkayne!" (And I should have kept my lip zipped.)

"Okay," he said. "But you swore it. A bomb."

"A *what*?"

"Oh, not much of a bomb. Just a little squeezer job. Total de-struction not more than a kilometer. Nothing much."

I reswallowed my heart. "Why a bomb? And what did you do with it?"

He shrugged. "They were stupid. They paid me this silly amount, see? Just to sneak this little package aboard. Gave me a lot of north wind about how it was meant to be a surprise for the Captain—and that I should give it to him at the Captain's party, last night out. Gift wrapped and everything. 'Sonny,' this silly zero says to me, 'just keep it out of sight and let him be surprised—because last night out is not only the Captain's party, it's his birthday.'

"Now, Sis, you know I wouldn't swallow anything like that. If it had really been a birthday present they would just have given it to the Purser to hold—no need to bribe me. So I just played stupid and kept jacking up the price. And the idiots paid me. They got real jumpy when time came to shove us through pass-port clearance and paid all I asked. So I shoved it into your bag while you were yakking to Uncle Tom—then saw to it you didn't get inspected.

"Then the minute we were aboard I went to get it—and got held up by a stewardess spraying your cabin and had to do a fast job and go back to relock your bag because Uncle Tom came back in looking for his pipe. That first night I opened the thing in the dark—and opened it from the bottom; I already had a hunch what it might be."

"Why?"

"Sis, use your brain. Don't just sit there and let it rust out. First they offer me what they probably figured was big money to a kid. When I turn it down, they start to sweat and up the ante. I kept crowding it and the money got important. And more important. They don't even give me a tale about how a man with a flower in his lapel will come aboard at Venus and give me a password. It *has* to be that they don't care what happens to it as long as it gets into the ship. What does that add up to? Logic."

He added, "So I opened it and took it apart. Time bomb. Set for three days after we space. *Blooey!*"

I shivered, thinking about it.

"What a horrible thing to do!"

"It could have turned out pretty dry," he admitted, "if I had been as stupid as they thought I was."

"But why would anybody want to do such a thing?"

"Didn't want the ship to get to Venus."

"But *why?*"

"You figure it out. I have."

"Uh . . . what did you do with it?"

"Oh, I saved it. The essential pieces. Never know when you might need a bomb."

And that's all I got out of him—and here I am stuck with a Saint Podkayne oath. And nineteen questions left unanswered. Was there *really* a bomb? Or was I swindled by my brother's talent for improvising explanations that throw one off the obvious track? If there was *where is it?* Still in the *Tricorn?* Right here in this suite? In an innocent-looking package in the safe of the Tannhäuser? Or parked with his private bodyguard, Josie? Or a thousand other places in this big city? Or is it still more likely that I simply made a mistake of three kilograms in my excitement and that Clark was snooping just to be snooping? (Which he will always do if not busy otherwise.)

No way to tell. So I decided to squeeze what else I could from this Moment of Truth—if it was one. "I'm awful glad you found it," I said. "But the slickest thing you ever did was that dye job on Mrs. Garcia and Mrs. Royer. Girdie admires it, too."

"She does?" he said eagerly.

"She certainly does. But I never let on you did it. So you can still tell her yourself, if you want to."

"Mmm . . ." He looked quite happy. "I gave Old Lady Royer a little extra, just for luck. Put a mouse in her bed."

"Clark! Oh, wonderful! But where did you get a mouse?"

"Made a deal with the ship's cat."

I wish I had a nice, normal, slightly stupid family. It would be a lot more comfortable. Still, Clark has his points.

But I haven't had too much time to worry about my brother's High Crimes and Misdemeanors; Venusberg offers too much to divert the adolescent female with a hitherto unsuspected taste for high living. Especially Dexter—

I am no longer a leper; I can now go anywhere, even outside the city, without wearing a filter snout that makes me look like a blue-eyed pig—and dashing, darling Dexter has been most flatteringly eager to escort me everywhere. Even shopping. Using both hands a girl could spend a national debt there on clothes alone. But I am being (almost) sensible and spending only that portion of my cash assets earmarked for Venus. If I were not firm with him, Dexter would buy me anything I admire, just by lifting his finger. (He never carries any money, not even a credit card, and even his tipping is done by some unobvious credit system.) But I haven't let him buy me anything more important than a fancy ice cream sundae; I have no intention of jeopardizing my amateur status for some pretty clothes. But I don't feel too compromised over ice cream and fortunately I do not as yet have to worry about my waistline—I'm hollow clear to my ankles.

So, after a hard day of sweating over the latest Rio styles Dexter takes me to an ice cream parlor—one that bears the same relation to our Plaza Sweet Shoppe that the *Tricorn* does to a sand car—and he sits and toys with café au lait and watches in amazement while I eat. First some little trifle like an everlasting strawberry soda, then more serious work on a sundae composed by a master architect from creams and syrups and imported fruits and nuts of course, and perhaps a couple of tens of scoops of ice cream in various flavors and named "The Taj Mahal" or "The Big Rock Candy Mountain" or such.

(Poor Girdie! She diets like a Stylite every day of the year. Query: Will I ever make that sacrifice to remain svelte and glamorous? Or will I get comfortably fat like Mrs. Grew? Echo Answereth Not and I'm not afraid to listen.)

I've had to be firm with him in other ways, too, but much less obviously. Dexter turns out to be a master of seductive logic and is ever anxious to tell me a bedtime story. But I have no intention of being a Maid Betrayed, not at my age. The tragedy about Romeo and Juliet is not that they died so young but that the boy-meets-girl reflex should be so overpowering as to defeat all common sense.

My own reflexes are fine, thank you, and my hormonal balance is just dandy. Dexter's fruitless overtures give me a nice warm feeling at the pit of my stomach and hike up my metabolism. Perhaps I should feel insulted at his dastardly intentions toward me—and possibly I would, at home, but this is Venusberg, where the distinction between a shameful proposition and a formal proposal of honorable marriage lies only in the mind and would strain a semantician to define. For all I know, Dexter already has seven wives at home, numbered for the days of the week. I haven't asked him, as I have no intention of becoming number eight, on any basis.

I talked this over with Girdie and asked why I didn't feel "insulted." Had they left the moral circuits out of my cybernet, as they so obviously did with my brother Clark?

Girdie smiled her sweet and secret smile that always means she is thinking about something she doesn't intend to be fully frank about. Then she said, "Poddy, girls are taught to be 'insulted' at such offers for their own protection—and it is a good idea, quite as good an idea as keeping a fire extinguisher handy even though you don't expect a fire. But you are right; it is not an insult, it is never an insult—it is the one utterly honest tribute to a woman's charm and femininity that a man can offer her. The rest of what they tell us is mostly polite lies . . . but on this one subject a man is nakedly honest. I don't see any reason ever to be insulted if a man is polite and gallant about it."

I thought about it. "Maybe you're right, Girdie. I guess it is a compliment, in a way. But why is it that that is all a boy is ever after? Nine times out of ten anyhow."

"You've got it just backwards, Poddy. Why should he *ever* be after anything else? Millions of years of evolution is the logic behind every proposition. Just be glad that the dears have learned to approach the matter with handkissing instead of a club. Some of them, anyhow. It gives us more choice in the matter than we've ever had before in all history. It's a woman's world today, dear—enjoy it and be grateful."

I had never thought of it that way. When I've thought of it at all, I've mostly been groused because it is so hard for a girl to break into a "male" profession, such as piloting.

*   *   *

I've been doing some hard thinking about piloting—and have concluded that there are more ways of skinning a cat than buttering it
with parsnips. Do I *really* want to be a "famous explorer captain"?
Or would I be just as happy to be some member of his crew?

Oh, I want to space, let there be no doubt about that! My one
little trip from Mars to Venus makes me certain that travel is for
me. I'd rather be a junior stewardess in the *Tricorn* than President
of the Republic. Shipboard life is fun; you take your home and
your friends along with you while you go to romantic new
places—and with Davis-drive starships being built those places
are going to be newer and more romantic every year. And Poddy is
going to go, somehow. I was born to roam—

But let's not kid ourselves, shall we? Is anybody going to let
Poddy captain one of those multimegabuck ships?

Dexter's chances are a hundred times as good as mine. He's as
smart as I am, or almost; he'll have the best education for it that
money can buy (while I'm loyal to Ares U., I know it is a hick college compared with where he plans to go); and also it is quite possible that his daddy could *buy* him a Star Rover ship. But the
clincher is that Dexter is twice as big as I am and male. Even if
you leave his father's wealth out of the equation, which one of us
gets picked?

But all is not lost. Consider Theodora, consider Catherine the
Great. Let a man boss the job . . . then boss that man. I am not opposed to marriage. (But if Dexter wants to marry me—or
anything—he'll have to follow me to Marsopolis where we are
pretty old-fashioned about such things. None of this lighthearted
Venusberg stuff.) Marriage should be every woman's end—but
not her finish. I do not regard marriage as a sort of death.

Girdie says always to "be what you are." All right, let's look at
ourselves in a mirror, dear, and forget "Captain Podkayne Fries,
the famous Explorer" for the nonce. What do we see?

Getting just a touch broad-shouldered in the hips, aren't we,
dear? No longer any chance of being mistaken for a boy in a dim
light. One might say that we were designed for having babies. And
that doesn't seem too bad an idea, now does it? Especially if we
could have one as nice as Duncan. Fact is, all babies are pretty
nice even when they're not.

Those eighteen miserable hours during the storm in the *Tricorn*—weren't they just about the most fun you ever had in your
life? A baby is lots more fun than differential equations.

Every starship has a crèche. So which is better? To study crèche engineering and pediatrics—and be a department head in a starship? Or buck for pilot training and make it . . . and wind up as a female pilot nobody wants to hire?

Well, we don't have to decide now—

I'm getting pretty anxious for us to shape for Earth. Truth is, Venusberg's fleshpots can grow monotonous to one of my wholesome (or should I say "limited") tastes. I haven't any more money for shopping, not if I am to have any to shop in Paris; I don't think I could ever get addicted to gambling (and don't want to; I'm one of those who lose and thereby offset in part Clark's winning); and the incessant noise and lights are going to put wrinkles where I now have dimples. And I think Dexter is beginning to be just a bit bored with my naïve inability to understand what he is driving at.

If there is any one thing I have learned about males in my eight and a half years, it is that one should sign off before he gets bored. I look forward to just one last encounter with Dexter now: a tearful farewell just before I *must* enter the *Tricorn*'s loading tube, with a kiss so grown-up, so utterly passionate and all-out giving, that he will believe the rest of his life that Things Could Have Been Different if Only He Had Played His Cards Right.

I've been outside the city just once, in a sealed tourist bus. Once is more than enough; this ball of smog and swamp should be given back to the natives, only they wouldn't take it. Once a fairy in flight was pointed out, so they said, but I didn't see anything. Just smog.

I'll settle now for just one fairy, in flight or even perched Dexter says that he knows of a whole colony, a thousand or more, less than two hundred kilometers away, and wants to show it to me in his Rolls. But I'm not warm to that idea; he intends to drive it himself—and that dratted thing has automatic controls. If I can sneak Girdie, or even Clark, into the picnic—well, maybe.

But I have learned a lot on Venus and would not have missed it for anything. The Art of Tipping, especially, and now I feel like an Experienced Traveler. Tipping can be a nuisance but it is not quite the vice Marsmen think it is; it is a necessary lubricant for perfect service.

Let's admit it; service in Marsopolis varies from indifferent to terrible—and I simply had not realized it. A clerk waits on you when he feels like it and goes on gossiping with another clerk, not even able to see you until he does feel like it.

Not like that in Venusberg! However, it is not just the money—and here follows the Great Secret of Happy Travel. I haven't soaked up much Portuguese and not everybody speaks Ortho. But it isn't necessary to be a linguist if you will learn just one word—in as many languages as possible. Just "thank you."

I caught onto this first with Maria and Maria—I say "gobble-gobble" to them a hundred times a day, only the word is actually "obrigado" which sounds like "gobble-gobble" if you say it quickly. A *small* tip is much more savoir-fairish—and gets better, more willing service—when accompanied by "thank you" than a big tip while saying nothing.

So I've learned to say "thank you" in as many languages as possible and I always try to say it in the home language of the person I'm dealing with, if I can guess it, which I usually can. Doesn't matter much if you miss, though; porters and clerks and taxi drivers and such usually know that one word in several languages and can spot it even if you can't talk with them at all in any other way. I've written a lot of them down and memorized them:

> Obrigado
> Donkey shane
> Mare-see
> Key toss
> M'goy
> Graht-see-eh
> Arigato
> Spawseebaw
> Gathee-oss
> Tock

Or "money tock" and Clark says this one means "money talks." But Clark is wrong; he has to tip too high because he won't bother to say "thank you." Oh, yes, Clark tips. It hurts him, but he soon discovered that he couldn't get a taxi and that even automatic vending machines were rude to him if he tried to buck the local system. But it infuriates him so much that he won't be pleasant about it and that costs him.

If you say "tock" instead of "key toss" to a Finn, he still understands it. If you mistake a Japanese for a Cantonese and say "m'goy" instead of "arigato"—well, that is the one word of Cantonese he knows. And "obrigado" everybody understands.

However, if you do guess right and pick their home language, they roll out the red carpet and genuflect, all smiles. I've even had tips refused—and this in a city where Clark's greediness about money is considered only natural.

All those other long, long lists of hints on How to Get Along While Traveling that I studied so carefully before I left turn out not to be necessary; this one rule does it all.

Uncle Tom is dreadfully worried about something. He's absent-minded and, while he will smile at me if I manage to get his attention (not easy), the smile soon fades and the worry lines show again. Maybe it's something here and things will be all right once we leave. I wish we were back in the happy Three-Cornered Hat with next stop Luna City.

Chapter 11

Things are really grim. Clark hasn't been home for two nights, and Uncle Tom is almost out of his mind. Besides that, I've had a quarrel with Dexter—which isn't important compared with Brother being missing but I could surely use a shoulder to cry on.

And Uncle Tom has had a real quarrel with Mr. Chairman—which was what led to my quarrel with Dexter because I was on Uncle Tom's side even though I didn't know what was going on and I discovered that Dexter was just as blind in his loyalty to his father as I am to Uncle Tom. I saw only a bit of the quarrel with Mr. Chairman and it was one of those frightening, cold, bitter, formally polite, grown-men quarrels of the sort that used to lead inevitably to pistols at dawn.

I think it almost did. Mr. Chairman arrived at our suite, looking not at all like Santa Claus, and I heard Uncle say coldly, "I would rather your friends had called on me, sir."

But Mr. Chairman ignored that and about then Uncle noticed that I was there—back of the piano, keeping quiet and trying to look small—and he told me to go to my room. Which I did.

But I know what part of it is. I had thought that both Clark and I had been allowed to run around loose in Venusberg—although I have usually had either Girdie or Dexter with me. Not so. Both of us have been guarded night and day, every instant we have been out of the Tannhäuser, by Corporation police. I never suspected this and I'm sure Clark didn't or he would never have hired Josie to watch his boodle. But Uncle did know it and had accepted it as a courtesy from Mr. Chairman, one that left him free to do whatever these things are that have kept him so busy here, without riding herd on two kids, one of them nutty as Christmas cake. (And I don't mean me.)

As near as I can reconstruct it Uncle blames Mr. Chairman for Clark's absence—although this is hardly fair as Clark, if he knew he was being watched, could evade eighteen private eyes, the entire Space Corps, and a pack of slavering bloodhounds. Or is it "wolfhounds"?

But, on top of this, Dexter says that they disagree completely on how to locate Clark. Myself, I think that Clark is missing because Clark wants to be missing because he intends to miss the ship and stay here on Venus where a) Girdie is, and b) where all that lovely money is. Although perhaps I have put them in the wrong order.

I keep telling myself this, but Mr. Chairman says that it is a kidnapping, that it has to be a kidnapping, and that there is only one way to handle a kidnapping on Venus if one ever expects to see the kidnappee alive again.

On Venus, kidnapping is just about the only thing a stockholder is afraid of. In fact they are so afraid of it that they have brought the thing down almost to a ritual. If the kidnapper plays by the rules and doesn't hurt his victim, he not only won't be punished but he has the Corporation's assurance that he can keep any ransom agreed on.

But if he doesn't play by the rules and they do catch him, well, it's pretty grisly. Some of the things Dexter just hinted at. But I understand that the mildest punishment is something called a "four-hour death." He wouldn't give me any details on this, either—except that there is some drug that is just the opposite of anesthesia; it makes pain hurt worse.

Dexter says that Clark is absolutely safe as long as Uncle Tom doesn't insist on meddling with things he doesn't understand. "Old fool" is one term that he used and that was when I slapped him.

Long sigh and a wish for my happy girlhood in Marsopolis, where I understood how things worked. I don't here. All I really know is that I can no longer leave the suite save with Uncle Tom—and must leave it and stay with him when he does and wherever he goes.

Which is how I at last saw the Cunha "cottage"—and would have been much interested if Clark hadn't been missing. A modest little place only slightly smaller than the Tannhäuser but much more lavish. Our President's Rose House would fit into its ballroom. That is where I quarreled with Dexter while Uncle and Mr.

Chairman were continuing their worst quarrel elsewhere in that "cottage."

Presently Uncle Tom took me back to the Tannhäuser and I've never seen him look so old—fifty at least, or call it a hundred and fifty of the years they use here. We had dinner in the suite and neither of us ate anything and after dinner I went over and sat by the living window. The view was from Earth, I guess. The Grand Canyon of El Dorado, or El Colorado, or whatever it is. Grand, certainly. But all I got was acrophobia and tears.

Uncle was just sitting, looking like Prometheus enduring the eagles. I put my hand in his and said, "Uncle Tom? I wish you would spank me."

"Eh?" He shook his head and seemed to see me. "Flicka! Why?"

"Because it's my fault."

"What do you mean, dear?"

"Because I'm responsibu—bul for Clark. I always have been. He hasn't any sense. Why, when he was a baby I must have kept him from falling in the Canal at least a thousand times."

He shook his head, negatively this time. "No, Poddy. It is my responsibility and not yours at all. I am in loco parentis to both of you—which means that your parents were loco ever to trust me with it."

"But I *feel* responsible. He's my Chinese obligation."

He shook his head still again. "No. In sober truth no person can ever be truly responsible for another human being. Each one of us faces up to the universe alone, and the universe is what it is and it doesn't soften the rules for any of us—and eventually, in the long run, the universe always wins and takes all. But that doesn't make it any easier when we *try* to be responsible for another—as you have, as I have—and then look back and see how we could have done it better." He sighed. "I should not have blamed Mr. Cunha. He tried to take care of Clark, too. Of both of you. I knew it."

He paused and added, "It was just that I had a foul suspicion, an unworthy one, that he was using Clark to bring pressure on me. I was wrong. In his way and by his rules, Mr. Cunha is an honorable man—and his rules do not include using a boy for political purposes."

"Political purposes?"

Uncle looked around at me, as if surprised that I was still in the room. "Poddy, I should have told you more than I have. I keep forgetting that you are now a woman. I always think of you as the baby who used to climb on my knee and ask me to tell her 'The Poddy Story.' " He took a deep breath. "I still won't burden you with all of it. But I owe Mr. Cunha an abject apology—because *I* was using Clark for political purposes. And you, too."

"Huh?"

"As a cover-up, dear. Doddering great-uncle escorts beloved niece and nephew on pleasure tour. I'm sorry, Poddy, but it isn't that way at all. The truth is I am Ambassador Extraordinary and Minister Plenipotentiary for the Republic. To the Three-Planets Summit. But it seemed desirable to keep it a secret until I present my credentials."

I didn't answer because I was having a little trouble soaking this in. I mean, I *know* Uncle Tom is pretty special and has done some important things, but all my life he has been somebody who always had time to hold a skein of yarn for me while I wound it and would take serious interest in helping me name paper dolls.

But he was talking. "So I used you, Flicka. You and your brother. Because— Poddy, do you really want to know all the ins and outs and snarls of the politics behind this?"

I did, very much. But I tried to be grown up. "Just whatever you think best to tell me, Uncle Tom."

"All right. Because some of it is sordid and all of it is complex and would take hours to explain— and some of it really isn't mine to tell; some of it involves commitments Bozo— sorry, the President— Some of it has to do with promises he made. Do you know who our Ambassador is now, at Luna City?"

I tried to remember. "Mr. Suslov?"

"No, that was last administration. Artie Finnegan. Artie isn't too bad a boy . . . but he thinks he should have been President and he's certain he knows more about interplanetary affairs and what is good for Mars than the President does. Means well, no doubt."

I didn't comment because the name "Arthur Finnegan" I recognized at once— I had once heard Uncle Tom sound off about him to Daddy when I was supposed to be in bed and asleep. Some of the milder expressions were "a head like a sack of mud," "larceny in his heart," and a "size twelve ego in a size nine soul."

"But even though he means well," Uncle Tom went on, "he doesn't see eye to eye with the President—and myself—on matters that will come before this conference. But unless the President sends a special envoy—me, in this case—the Ambassador in residence automatically speaks for Mars. Poddy, what do you know about Switzerland?"

"Huh? William Tell. The apple."

"That's enough, I guess, although there probably never was an apple. Poddy, Mars is the Switzerland of the solar System—or it isn't anything at all. So the President thinks, and so I think. A small man (and a small country, like Mars or Switzerland) can stand up to bigger, powerful neighbors only by being willing to fight. We've never had a war and I pray we never do, because we would probably lose it. But if we are willing enough, we may never have to fight."

He sighed. "That's the way I see it. But Mr. Finnegan thinks that, because Mars is small and weak, Mars should join up with the Terran Federation. Perhaps he's right and this really is the wave of the future. But I don't think so; I think it would be the end of Mars as an independent country and a free society. Furthermore, I think it is logical that if Mars gives up its independence, it is only a matter of time until Venus goes the same way. I've been spending the time since we got here trying to convince Mr. Cunha of this, cause him to have his Resident Commissioner make a common cause with us against Terra. This could persuade Luna to come in with us too, since both Venus and Mars can sell to Luna cheaper than Terra can. But it wasn't at all easy; the Corporation has such a long-standing policy of never meddling in politics at all. 'Put not your faith in princes'—which means to them that they buy and they sell and they ask no questions.

"But I have been trying to make Mr. Cunha see that if Luna and Mars and Terra (the Jovian moons hardly count), if those three were all under the same rules, in short order Venus Corporation would be no more free than is General Motors or I.G. Farbenindustrie. He got the picture too, I'm sure—until I jumped to conclusions about Clark's disappearance and blew my top at him." He shook his head. "Poddy, I'm a poor excuse for a diplomat."

"You aren't the only one who got sore," I said, and told him about slapping Dexter.

He smiled for the first time. "Oh, Poddy, Poddy, we'll never make a lady out of you. You're as bad as I am."

So I grinned back at him and started picking my teeth with a fingernail. This is an even ruder gesture than you might think— and utterly private between Uncle Tom and myself. We Maori have a very bloodthirsty history and I won't even hint at what it is we are supposed to be picking out of our teeth. Uncle Tom used to use this vulgar pantomime on me when I was a little girl, to tell me I wasn't being lady-like.

Whereupon he really smiled and mussed my hair. "You're the blondest blue-eyed savage I ever saw. But you're a savage, all right. And me, too. Better tell him you're sorry, hon, because, much as I appreciate your gallant defense of me, Dexter was perfectly right. I was an 'old fool.' I'll apologize to his father, doing the last hundred meters on my belly if he wants it that way; a man should admit it in full when he's wrong, and make amends. And you kiss and make up with Dexter— Dexter is a fine boy."

"I'll say I'm sorry and make up—but I don't think I'll kiss him. I haven't yet."

He looked surprised. "So? Don't you like him? Or have we brought too much Norse blood into the family?"

"I like Dexter just fine and you're crazy with the smog if you think Svenska blood is any colder than Polynesian. I could go for Dexter in a big way—and that's why I haven't kissed him."

He considered this. "I think you're wise, hon. Better do your practice kisses on boys who don't tend to cause your gauges to swing over into the red. Anyhow, although he's a good lad, he's not nearly good enough for my savage niece."

"Maybe so, maybe not. Uncle . . . what are you going to do about Clark?"

His halfway happy mood vanished. "Nothing. Nothing at all."

"But we've got to do something!"

"But what, Podkayne?"

There he had me. I had already chased it through all the upper and lower segments of my brain. Tell the police? Mr. Chairman is the police—they all work for him. Hire a private detective? If Venus has any (I don't know), then they all are under contract to Mr. Cunha, or rather, the Venus Corporation.

Run ads in newspapers? Question all the taxi drivers? Put Clark's picture in the sollies and offer rewards? It didn't matter what you thought of, everything on Venus belongs to Mr. Chairman. Or, rather, to the corporation he heads. Same thing, really, although Uncle Tom tells me that the Cunhas actually own only a fraction of the stock.

"Poddy, I've been over everything I could think of with Mr. Cunha—and he is either already doing it, or he has convinced me that there, under conditions he knows much better than I do, it should not be done."

"Then what do we do?"

"We wait. But if you think of anything—anything—that you think might help, tell me and if it isn't already being done, we'll call Mr. Cunha and find out if it should be done. If I'm asleep, wake me."

"I will." I doubted if he would be asleep. Or me. But something else had been bothering me. "If time comes for the *Tricorn* to shape for Earth—and Clark isn't back—what do you do then?"

He didn't answer; the lines in his face just got deeper. I knew what the Awful Decision was—and I knew how he had decided it.

But I had a little Awful Decision of my own to make . . . and I had talked to Saint Podkayne about it for quite a while and had decided that Poddy had to break a Saint-Podkayne oath. Maybe this sounds silly but it isn't silly to me. Never in my life had I broken one . . . and never in my life will I be utterly sure about Poddy again.

So I told Uncle all about the smuggled bomb.

Somewhat to my surprise he took it seriously—when I had about persuaded myself that Clark had been pulling my leg just for exercise. Smuggling—oh, sure, I understand that every ship in space has smuggling. But not a bomb. Just something valuable enough that it was worthwhile to bribe a boy to get it aboard . . . and probably Clark had been paid off again when he passed it along to a steward, or a cargo hand, or somebody. If I know Clark—

But Uncle wanted me to describe exactly the person I had seen talking to Clark at Deimos Station.

"Uncle, I can't! I barely glanced at him. A man. Not short, not tall, not especially fat or skinny, not dressed in any way that made me remember—and I'm not sure I looked at his face at all. Uh, yes, I did but I can't call up any picture of it."

"Could it have been one of the passengers?"

I thought hard about that. "No. Or I would have noticed his face later when it was still fresh in my mind. *Mmm* . . . I'm almost certain he didn't queue up with us. I think he headed for the exit, the one that takes you back to the shuttle ship."

"That is likely," he agreed. "Certain—*if* it was a bomb. And not just a product of Clark's remarkable imagination."

"But, Uncle Tom, *why* would it be a bomb?"

And he didn't answer and I already knew why. Why would anybody blow up the *Tricorn* and kill everybody in her, babies and all? Not for insurance like you sometimes find in adventure stories; Lloyd's won't insure a ship for enough to show a profit on that sort of crazy stunt—or at least that's the way it was explained to me in my high school economics class.

Why, then?

To keep the ship from getting to Venus.

But the *Tricorn* had been to Venus tens and tens of times—

To keep somebody in the ship from getting to Venus (or perhaps to Luna) *that trip*.

Who? Not Podkayne Fries. I wasn't important to anybody but me.

For the next couple of hours Uncle Tom and I searched that hilton suite. We didn't find anything, nor did I expect us to. If there was a bomb (which I still didn't fully believe) and if Clark had indeed brought it off the ship and hidden it there (which seemed unlikely with all of the *Tricorn* at one end and all of the city at the other end to choose from), nevertheless he had had days and days in which to make it look like anything from a vase of flowers to a—a *anything*.

We searched Clark's room last on the theory that it was the least likely place. Or rather, we started to search it together and Uncle had to finish it. Pawing through Clark's things got to be too much for me and Uncle sent me back into the salon to lie down.

I was all cried out by the time he gave up; I even had a suggestion to make. "Maybe if we sent for a Geiger counter?"

Uncle shook his head and sat down. "We aren't looking for a bomb, honey."

"We aren't?"

"No. If we found it, it would simply confirm that Clark had told you the truth, and I'm already using that as least hypothesis. Because . . . well because I know more about this than the short outline I gave to you . . . and I know just how deadly serious this is to some people, how far they might go. Politics is neither a game nor a bad joke the way some people think it is. War itself is merely an extension of politics . . . so I don't find anything surprising about a bomb in politics; bombs have been used in politics hundreds and even thousands of times in the past. No, we aren't looking for a bomb, we are looking for a man—a man you saw for a few seconds once. And probably not even for that man but for somebody that man might lead us back to. Probably somebody inside the President's office, somebody he trusts."

"Oh, gosh, I wish I had really looked at him!"

"Don't fret about it, hon. You didn't know and there was no reason to look. But you can bet that Clark knows what he looks like. If Clark—I mean, *when* Clark comes back, in time we will have him search the I.D. files at Marsopolis. And all the visa photographs for the past ten years, if necessary. The man will be found. And through him the person the President has been trusting who should not to be trusted." Uncle Tom suddenly looked all Maori and very savage. "And when we do, I may take care of the matter personally. We'll see."

Then he smiled and added, "But right now Poddy is going to bed. You're up way past your bedtime, even with all the dancing and late-sleeping you've been doing lately."

"Uh . . . what time is it in Marsopolis?"

He looked at his other watch. "Twenty-seventeen. You weren't thinking of phoning your parents? I hope not."

"Oh, no! I won't say a word to them unless—until Clark is back. And maybe not then. But if it's only twenty-seventeen, it's not late at all, real time, and I don't want to go to bed. Not until you do."

"I may not go to bed."

"I don't care. I want to sit with you."

He blinked at me, then said very gently, "All right, Poddy. Nobody ever grows up without spending at least one night of years."

We just sat then for quite a while, with nothing to say that had not already been said and would just hurt to say over again.

At last I said, "Unka Tom? Tell me the Poddy story—"

"At your age?"

"Please." I crawled up on his knees. "I want to sit in your lap once more and hear it. I need to."

"All right," he said, and put his arm around me. "Once upon a time, long, long ago when the world was young, in a specially favored city there lived a little girl named Poddy. All day long she was busy like a ticking clock. *Tick tick tick* went her heels, *tick tick tick* went her knitting needles, and, most especially, *tick tick tick* went her busy little mind. Her hair was the color of butter blossoms in the spring when the ice leaves canals, her eyes were the changing blue of sunshine playing down through the spring floods, her nose had not yet made up its mind what it would be, and her mouth was shaped like a question mark. She greeted the world as an unopened present and there was no badness in her anywhere.

"One day Poddy—"

I stopped him. "But I'm *not* young any longer . . . and I don't think the world was ever young!"

"Here's my hanky," he said. "Blow your nose. I never did tell you the end of it, Poddy; you always fell asleep. It ends with a miracle."

"A truly miracle?"

"Yes. This is the end. Poddy grew up and had another Poddy. And then the world was young again."

"Is that all?"

"That's all there ever is. But it's enough."

Chapter 12

I guess Uncle Tom put me to bed, for I woke up with just my shoes off and very rumpled. He was gone but he had left a note saying that I could reach him, if I needed to, on Mr. Chairman's private code. I didn't have any excuse to bother him and didn't want to face anyone, so I chased Maria and Maria out and ate breakfast in bed. Ate quite a lot, too, I must admit—the body goes on ticking anyhow.

Then I dug out my journal for the first time since landing. I don't mean I haven't been keeping it; I mean I've been talking it instead of writing it. The library in our suite has a recorder built into its desk and I discovered how easy it was to keep a diary that way. Well, I had really found out before that, because Mr. Clancy let me use the recorder they use to keep the log on.

The only shortcoming of the recorder in the library was that Clark might drop in most any time. But the first day I went shopping I found the most darling little minirecorder at Venus Macy—only ten-fifty and it just fits in the palm of your hand and you can talk into it without even being noticed if you want to and I just couldn't resist it. I've been carrying it in my purse ever since.

But now I wanted to look way back in my journal, the early written part, and see if I had said *anything* that might remind me of what That Man had looked like or anything about him.

I hadn't. No clues. But I FOUND A NOTE FROM CLARK.
It read:

POD,

If you find this at all, it's time you read it. Because I'm using 24-hr. ink and I expect to lift this out of here and you'll never see it.

Girdie is in trouble and I'm going to rescue her. I haven't told anybody because this is one job that is all mine and I don't want you or anybody horning in on it.

However, a smart gambler hedges his bets, if he can. If I'm gone long enough for you to read this, it's time to get hold of Uncle Tom and have him get hold of Chairman Cunha. All I can tell you is that there is a newsstand right at South Gate. You buy a copy of the *Daily Merchandiser* and ask if they carry Everlites. Then say, "Better give me two—it's quite dark where I'm going."

But don't *you* do this, I don't want it muffed up.

If this turns out dry, you can have my rock collection.

Count your change. Better use
your fingers.
CLARK

I got all blurry. That last line—I know a holographic last will and testament when I see one, even though I had never seen one before. Then I straightened up and counted ten seconds backwards including the rude word at the end that discharges nervous tension, for I knew this was no time to be blurry and weak; there was work to be done.

So I called Uncle Tom right away, as I agreed perfectly with Clark on one point: I wasn't going to try to emulate Space Ranger Stalwart, Man of Steel, the way Clark evidently had; I was going to get all the help I could get! With both Clark and Girdie in some sort of pinch I would have welcomed two regiments of Patrol Marines and the entire Martian Legion.

So I called Mr. Chairman's private code—and it didn't answer; it simply referred me to another code. This one answered all right . . . but with a recording. Uncle Tom. And this time all he said was to repeat something he had said in the note, that he expected to be busy all day and that I was not to leave the suite under any circumstances whatever until he got back—only this time he added that I was not to let anyone into the suite, either, not even a repairman, not even a servant except those who were already there, like Maria and Maria.

When the recording started to play back for the third time, I switched off. Then I called Mr. Chairman the public way, through the Corporation offices. A dry deal that was! By pointing out that I was Miss Fries, niece of Senator Fries, Mars Republic, I did get as far as his secretary, or maybe his secretary's secretary.

"Mr. Cunha cannot be reached. I am veree sorree, Miss Fries." So I demanded that she locate Uncle Tom. "I do not have that information. I am veree sorree, Miss Fries."

Then I demanded to be patched in to Dexter. "Mr. Dexter is on an inspection trip for Mr. Cunha. I am veree sorree."

She either couldn't, or wouldn't, tell me when Dexter was expected back—and wouldn't, or couldn't, find some way for me to call him. Which I just plain didn't believe, because if I owned a planetwide corporation there would be some way to phone every mine, every ranch, every factory, every air boat the company owned. All the time. And I don't even suspect that Mr. Chairman is less smart about how to run such a lash-up than I am.

I told her so, using the colorful rhetoric of sand rats and canal men. I mean I really got mad and used idioms I hadn't known I even remembered. I guess Uncle is right; scratch my Nordic skin and a savage is just underneath. I wanted to pick my teeth at her, only she wouldn't have understood it.

But would you believe it? I might as well have been cussing out a sand gator; it had no effect on her at all. She just repeated, "I'm-veree-sorree-Miss-Fries," and I growled and switched off.

Do you suppose Mr. Chairman uses an androidal Tik-Tok as his phone monitor? I wouldn't put it past him—and any live woman should have shown *some* reaction at some of the implausibilities I showered on her, even if she didn't understand most of the words. (Well, I don't understand some of them myself. But they are not compliments.)

I thought about phoning Daddy; I knew he would accept the charges, even if he had to mortgage his salary. But Mars was eleven minutes away; it said so, right on a dial of the phone. And the relays via Hermes Station and Luna City were even worse. With twenty-two minutes between each remark it would take me most of the day just to tell him what was wrong, even though they don't charge you for the waiting time.

But I still might have called except—well, what could Daddy *do*, three hundred million kilometers away? All it would do would be to turn his last six hairs white.

It wasn't until then that I steadied down enough to realize that there had been something else amiss about that note written into my journal—besides Clark's childish swashbuckling. Girdie—

It was true that I had not seen Girdie for a couple of days; she was on a shift that caused her to zig while I zagged; newly hired dealers don't get the best shifts. But I had indeed talked to her at a time when Clark was probably already gone even though at the time I had simply assumed that he had gotten up early for some inscrutable reason of his own, rather than not coming home at all that night.

But Uncle Tom had talked to her just before we had gone to the Cunha cottage the day before, asked her specifically if she had seen Clark—and she hadn't. Not as recently as we had.

I didn't have any trouble reaching Dom Pedro—not the Dom Pedro I met the night I met Dexter but the Dom Pedro of that shift. However, by now all the Dom Pedros know who Poddy Fries is; she's the girl that is seen with Mr. Dexter. He told me at once that Girdie had gone off shift half an hour earlier and I should try her hilton. Unless—he stopped and made some inquiries; somebody seemed to think that Girdie had gone shopping.

As may be. I already knew that she was not at the little hilton she had moved to from the stylish (and expensive) Tannhäuser; a message I had already recorded there was guaranteed to fetch a call back in seconds, if and when.

That ended it. There was no one left for me to turn to, nothing at all left for me to do, save wait in the suite until Uncle returned, as he had ordered me to do.

So I grabbed my purse and a coat and left.

And got all of three meters outside the door of the suite. A tall, wide, muscular character got in my way. When I tried to duck around him, he said, "Now, now, Miss Fries. Your uncle left orders."

I scurried the other way and found that he was awfully quick on his feet, for such a big man. So there I was, arrested! Shoved back into our own suite and held in durance vile. You know, I don't think Uncle entirely trusts me.

I went back to my room and closed the door and thought about it. The room was still not made up and still cluttered with dirty dishes because, despite the language barrier, I have made clear to Maria and Maria that Miss Fries becomes quite vexed if *anybody* disturbs my room until I signal that I no longer want privacy by leaving the door open.

The clumsy, two-decker, roll-around table that had fetched my breakfast was still by my bed, looking like a plundered city.

I took everything off the lower shelf, stowed it here and there in my bath, covered the stuff on top of the table with the extra cloth used to shield the tender eyes of cash customers from the sight of dirty dishes.

Then I grabbed the house phone and told them I wanted my breakfast dishes cleared away immediately.

I'm not very big. I mean you can fit forty-nine mass kilos only one hundred fifty-seven centimeters long into a fairly small space if you scrunch a little. That lower shelf was hard but not too cramped. It had some ketchup on it I hadn't noticed.

Uncle's orders (or perhaps Mr. Cunha's) were being followed meticulously, however. Ordinarily a pantry boy comes to remove the food wagon; this time the two Marias took it out the service entrance and as far as the service lift—and in the course of it I learned something interesting but not really surprising. Maria said something in Portuguese; the other Maria answered her in Ortho as glib as mine: "She's probably soaking in the tub, the lazy brat."

I made a note not to remember her on birthdays and at Christmas.

Somebody wheeled me off the lift many levels down and shoved me into a corner. I waited a few moments, then crawled out. A man in a well-spotted apron was looking astonished. I said, "Obrigado!" handed him a deuce note and walked out the service entrance with my nose in the air. Two minutes later I was in a taxi.

I've been catching up on this account while the taxi scoots to South Gate in order not to chew my nails back to the elbows. I must admit that I feel good even though nervous. Action is better than waiting. No amount of bad can stonker me, but not knowing drives me nuts.

The spool is almost finished, so I think I'll change spools and mail this one back to Uncle at South Gate. I should have left a note, I know—but this is better than a note. I hope.

Chapter 13

Well, I can't complain about not having seen fairies. They are every bit as cute as they are supposed to be—but I don't care greatly if I never see another one.

Throwing myself bravely into the fray against fearful odds, by sheer audacity I overcame—

It wasn't that way at all. I fubbed. Completely. So here I am, some nowhere place out in the bush, in a room with no windows, and only one door. That door isn't much use to me as there is a fairy perched over it. She's a cute little thing and the green part of her fur looks exactly like a ballet tutu. She doesn't look quite like a miniature human with wings—but they do say that the longer you stay here the more human they look. Her eyes slant up, like a cat's, and she has a very pretty built-in smile.

I call her "Titania" because I can't pronounce her real name. She speaks a few words of Ortho, not much because those little skulls are only about twice the brain capacity of a cat's skull—actually, she's an idiot studying to be a moron and not studying very hard.

Most of the time she just stays perched and nurses her baby—the size of a kitten and twice as cute. I call it "Ariel" although I'm not sure of its sex. I'm not dead sure of Titania's sex; they say that both males and females do this nursing thing, which is not quite nursing but serves the same purpose; they are not mammalians. Ariel hasn't learned to fly yet, but Titania is teaching it—tosses it into the air and it sort of flops and glides to the floor and then stays there, mewing piteously until she comes to get it and flies back to her perch.

I'm spending most of my time a) thinking, b) bringing this journal up to date, c) trying to persuade Titania to let me hold Ariel (making some progress; she now lets me pick it up and hand it to her—the baby isn't a bit afraid of me), and d) thinking, which seems to be a futile occupation.

Because I can go anywhere in the room and do anything as long as I stay a couple of meters away from that door. Guess why? Give up? Because fairies have very sharp teeth and claws; they're carnivorous. I have a nasty bite and two deep scratches on my left arm to prove it—red and tender and don't seem to want to heal. If I get close to that door, she dives on me.

Completely friendly otherwise— Nor do I have anything physically to complain about. Often enough a native comes in with a tray of really quite good food. But I never watch him come in and I never watch him take it away—because Venerians look entirely too human to start with and the more you look at them the worse it is for your stomach. No doubt you have seen pictures but pictures don't give you the smell and that drooling loose mouth, nor the impression that this *thing* has been dead a long time and is now animated by obscene arts.

I call him "Pinhead" and to him that is a compliment. No doubt as to its being a "him" either. It's enough to make a girl enter a nunnery.

I eat the food because I feel sure Pinhead didn't cook it. I think I know who does. She would be a good cook.

Let me back up a little. I told the news vendor: "Better give me two—it's quite dark where I'm going." He hesitated and looked at me and I repeated it.

So pretty soon I am in another air car and headed out over the bush. Ever make a wide, sweeping turn in smog? That did it. I haven't the slightest idea where I am, save that it is somewhere within two hours' flight of Venusberg and that there is a small colony of fairies nearby. I saw them flying shortly before we landed and was so terribly interested that I didn't really get a good look at the spot before the car stopped and the door opened. Not that it would have done any good—

I got out and the car lifted at once, mussing me up with its fans . . . and here was an open door to a house and a familiar voice was saying, "Poddy! Come in, dear, come in!"

And I was suddenly so relieved that I threw myself into her arms and hugged her and she hugged me back. It was Mrs. Grew, fat and friendly as ever.

And looked around and here was Clark, just sitting—and he looked at me and said, "Stupid," and looked away. And then I saw Uncle—sitting in another chair and was about to throw myself at him with wild shouts of glee—when Mrs. Grew's arms were suddenly awfully strong and she said soothingly, "No, no, dear, not quite so fast" and held me until somebody (Pinhead, it was) did something to the back of my neck.

Then I had a big comfortable chair all to myself and didn't want it because I couldn't move from my neck down. I felt all right, aside from some odd tingles, but I couldn't stir.

Uncle looked like Mr. Lincoln grieving over the deaths at Waterloo. He didn't say anything.

Mrs. Grew said cheerfully, "Well, now we've got the whole family together. Feel a bit more like discussing things rationally, Senator?"

Uncle shook his head half a centimeter.

She said, "Oh, come now! We do want you to attend the conference. We simply want you to attend it in the right frame of mind. If we can't agree—well, it's hardly possible to let any of you be found again. Isn't that obvious? And that would be such a shame . . . especially for the children."

Uncle said, "Pass the hemlock."

"Oh, I'm sure you don't mean that."

"He certainly does mean it!" Clark said shrilly. "You illegal obscenity! I delete all over your censored!" And I knew he was really worked up, because Clark is contemptuous of vulgar idioms; he says they denote an inferior mind.

Mrs. Grew looked at Clark placidly, even tenderly. Then she called in Pinhead again. "Take him out and keep him awake till he dies." Pinhead picked Clark up and carried him out. But Clark had the last word. "And besides that," he yelled, "*you cheat at solitaire!* I've watched you!"

For a split moment Mrs. Grew looked really annoyed. Then she put her face back into its usual kindly expression and said to Uncle, "Now that I have both of the kids I think I can afford to expend one of them. Especially as you are quite fond of Poddy. Too fond of her, some people would say. Psychiatrists, I mean."

I mulled that over . . . and decided that if I ever got out of this mess, I would make a rug out of her hide and give it to Uncle.

Uncle ignored it. Presently there was a most dreadful racket, metal on resounding metal. Mrs. Grew smiled. "It's crude but it works. It is what used to be a water heater when this was a ranch.

Unfortunately it isn't quite big enough either to sit down or stand up in—but a boy that rude really shouldn't expect comfort. The noise comes from pounding on the outside of it with a piece of pipe." She blinked and looked thoughtful. "I don't see how we can talk things over with such a racket going on. I think I should have the tank moved farther away—or perhaps our talk would march even more quickly if I had it brought nearer, so that you could hear the sounds he makes inside the tank, too. What do you think, Senator?"

I cut in. "Mrs. Grew!"

"Yes, dear? Poddy, I'm sorry but I'm really quite busy. Later we'll have a nice cup of tea together. Now, Senator—"

"Mrs. Grew, you don't understand my Uncle Tom at all! You'll never get anything out of him this way."

She considered it. "I think you exaggerate, dear. Wishful thinking."

"No, no, no! There isn't *any* way you could possibly get my Uncle Tom to do anything against Mars. But if you hurt Clark—or me—you'll just make him more adamant. Oh, he loves me and he loves Clark, too. But if you try to budge him by hurting either one of us, you're just wasting your time!" I was talking rapidly and just as sincerely as I know how. I seemed to hear Clark's screams. Not likely, I guess, not over that infernal clanging. But once when he was a baby he fell into a wastebasket . . . and screamed something dreadful before I rescued him. I guess I was hearing that in my mind.

Mrs. Grew smiled pleasantly. "Poddy dear, you are only a girl and your head has been filled with nonsense. The Senator is going to do just what I want him to do."

"Not if you kill Clark, he won't!"

"You keep quiet, dear. Do keep quiet and let me explain—or I shall have to slap you a few times to keep you quiet. Poddy, I am not going to kill your brother—"

"But you said—"

"*Quiet!* That native who took your brother away didn't understand what I said; he knows only trade Ortho, a few words, never a full sentence. I said what I did for the benefit of your brother . . . so that, when I *do* have him fetched back in, he'll be groveling, begging your uncle to do anything I want him to do."

She smiled warmly. "One piece of nonsense you've apparently been taught is that patriotism, or something silly like that, will overpower a man's own self-interest. Believe me, I have no slightest fear that an old political hack like your uncle will give any real weight to such a silly abstraction. What *does* worry him is his own political ruin if he does what I want him to do. What he is going to do. Eh, Senator?"

"Madam," Uncle Tom answered tightly, "I see no point in bandying words with you."

"Nor do I. Nor shall we. But you can listen while I explain it to Poddy. Dear, your uncle is a stubborn man and he won't accomplish his own political downfall lightly. I need a string to make him dance—and in *you* I have that string, I'm sure."

"I'm not!"

"Want a slap? Or would you rather be gagged? I like you, dear; don't force me to be forceful. In *you*, I said. Not your brother. Oh, no doubt your uncle goes through the solemn farce of treating his niece and his nephew just alike—Christmas presents and birthday presents and such like pretenses. But it is obvious that no one could love your brother . . . not even his own mother, I venture to say. But the Senator *does* love you—rather more than he wants anyone to suspect. So now I am hurting your brother a little—oh, just a smidgen, at worst he'll be deaf—to let your uncle see what will happen to *you*. Unless he is a good boy and speaks his piece just the way I tell him to."

She looked thoughtfully at Uncle. "Senator, I can't decide which of two methods might work the better on you. You see, I want to keep you reminded—after you agree to cooperate—that you *did* agree. Sometimes a politician doesn't stay bought. After I turn you loose, would it be better for me to send your nephew along with you, to keep you reminded? Or would it be better to keep him here and work on him just a little each day—with his sister watching? So that she would have a clear idea of what happens to her . . . if you try any tricks at Luna City. What's your opinion, sir?"

"Madam, the question does not arise."

"Really, Senator?"

"Because I will not be at Luna City unless both children are with me. Unhurt."

Mrs. Grew chuckled. "Campaign promises, Senator. I'll reason with you later. But now"—she glanced at an antique watch pinned to her gross bosom—"I think I had better put a stop to that dreadful racket, it's giving me a headache. And I doubt if your nephew can hear it any longer, save possibly through his bones." She got up and left, moving with surprising agility and grace for a woman her age and mass.

Suddenly the noise stopped.

It was such a surprise that I would have jumped if anything below my neck could jump. Which it couldn't.

Uncle was looking at me. "Poddy, Poddy—" he said softly.

I said, "Uncle, don't you give in a millimeter to that dreadful woman!"

He said, "Poddy, I *can't* give in to her. Not at all. You understand that? Don't you?"

"I certainly do! But look—you could fake it. Tell her anything. Get loose yourself and take Clark along, as she suggested. Then you can rescue me. I'll hold out. You'll see!"

He looked terribly old. "Poddy . . . Poddy darling . . . I'm very much afraid . . . that this is the end. Be brave, dear."

"Uh, I haven't had very much practice at that. But I'll try to be." I pinched myself, mentally, to see if I was scared—and I wasn't, not really. Somehow I couldn't be scared with Uncle there, even though he was helpless just then. "Uncle, what is it she wants? Is she some kind of a fanatic?"

He didn't answer because we both heard Mrs. Grew's jolly, belly-deep laugh. " 'Fanatic'!" she repeated, came over and tweaked my cheek. "Poddy dear, I'm not any sort of fanatic and I don't really care any more about politics than your uncle does. But I learned many years ago when I was just a girl—and quite attractive, too, dear, much more so than you will ever be—that a girl's best friend is cash. No, dear, I'm a paid professional and a good one."

She went on briskly, "Senator, I think the boy is deaf but I can't be sure; he's passed out now. We'll discuss it later, it's time for my nap. Perhaps we had all better rest a little."

And she called in Pinhead and I was carried into the room I am in now. When he picked me up, I really was truly aghast!—and found that I could move my arms and legs just a little bit—pins and needles you wouldn't believe!—and I struggled feebly. Did me no good, I was dumped in here anyhow.

After a while the drug wore off and I felt almost normal, though shaky. Shortly thereafter I discovered that Titania is a very good watchdog indeed and I haven't tried to reach that door since; my arm and shoulder are quite sore and getting stiff.

Instead I inspected the room. Not much in it. A bed with a mattress but no bedclothes, not that you need any in this climate. A sort of a table suspended from one wall and a chair fastened to the floor by it. Glow tubes around the upper corners of the room. I checked all these things at once after learning the hard way that Titania was not just a cutie with gauzy wings. It was quite clear that Mrs. Grew, or whoever had outfitted that room, had no intention of leaving anything in it that could be used as a weapon, against Titania or anybody. And I no longer had even my coat and purse.

I particularly regretted losing my purse, because I always carry a number of useful things in it. A nail file for example—if I had had even my nail file I might have considered taking on that bloodthirsty little fairy. But I didn't waste time thinking about it; my purse was where I had dropped it when I was drugged.

I did find one thing very interesting: this room had been used to prison Clark before I landed in it. One of his two bags was there—and I suppose I should have missed it from his room the night before, only I got upset and left Uncle to finish the search. The bag held a very odd collection for a knight errant venturing forth to rescue a damsel in distress: some clothing—three T-shirts and two pairs of shorts, a spare pair of shoes—a slide rule, and three comic books.

If I had found a flame gun or supplies of mysterious chemicals, I would not have been surprised—more Clarkish. I suppose, when you get right down to it, for all his brilliance Clark is just a little boy.

I worried a bit then about the possibility—or probability—that he was deaf. Then I quit thinking about it. If true, I couldn't help it—and he would miss his ears less than anything, since he hardly ever listens anyhow.

So I lay down on the bed and read his comic books. I am not a comic-book addict but these were quite entertaining, especially as the heroes were always getting out of predicaments much worse than the one I was in.

After a while I fell asleep and had heroic dreams.

I was awakened by "breakfast" (more like dinner but quite good). Pinhead took the tray away, and light plastic dishes and a plastic spoon offered little in the way of lethal weapons. However, I was delighted to find that he had fetched my purse!

Delighted for all of ten seconds, that is— No nail file. No penknife. Not a darn thing in it more deadly than lipstick and hanky. Mrs. Grew hadn't disturbed any money or my tiny minirecorder but she had taken everything that could conceivably do any good (harm). So I gritted my teeth and ate and then brought this useless journal up to date. That's about all I've done since—

just sleep and eat and make friends with Ariel. It reminds me of Duncan. Oh, not alike really—but all babies are sort of alike, don't you think?

I had dozed off from lack of anything better to do when I was awakened. "Poddy, dear—"

"Oh! Hello, Mrs. Grew."

"Now, now, no quick moves," she said chidingly. I wasn't about to make any quick moves; she had a gun pointed at my belly button. I'm very fond of it, it's the only one I have.

"Now be a good girl and turn over and cross your wrists behind you." I did so and in a moment she had them tied, quite firmly. Then she looped the line around my neck and had me on a leash—and if I struggled, all I accomplished was choking myself. So I didn't struggle.

Oh, I'm sure there was at least a moment when she didn't have that gun pointed at me and my wrists were not yet tied. One of those comic-book heroes would have snatched that golden instant, rendered her helpless, tied her with her own rope.

Regrettably, none of those heroes was named "Poddy Fries." My education has encompassed cooking, sewing, quite a lot of math and history and science, and such useful tidbits as freehand drawing and how to dip candles and make soap. But hand-to-hand combat I have learned sketchily if at all from occasional border clashes with Clark. I know that Mother feels that this is a lack (she is skilled in both karate and kill-quick, and can shoot as well as Daddy does) but Daddy has put off sending me to classes—I've gathered the impression that he doesn't really want his "baby girl" to know such things.

I vote with Mother, it's a lack. There must have been a split second when I could have lashed out with a heel, caught Mrs. Grew in her solar plexus, then broken her neck while she was still helpless—and run down the Jolly Roger and run up the Union Jack, just like in *Treasure Island*.

Oppernockity tunes but once—and I wasn't in tune with it.

Instead I was led away like a puppy on a string. Titania eyed us as we went through the door but Mrs. Grew clucked at her and she settled back on her perch and cuddled Ariel to her.

She had me walk in front of her down a hallway, through that living room where I had last seen Uncle Tom and Clark, out another door and a passage and into a large room—

—and I gasped and suppressed a scream!

Mrs. Grew said cheerfully, "Take a good look, dear. He's your new roommate."

Half the room was closed off with heavy steel bars, like a cage in a zoo. Inside was—well, it was Pinhead, that's what it was, though it took me a long moment of fright to realize it. You may have gathered that I do not consider Pinhead handsome. Well, dear, he was Apollo Belvedere before compared with the red-eyed maniacal horror he had become.

Then I was lying on the floor and Mrs. Grew was giving me smelling salts. Yes, sir, Captain Podkayne Fries the Famous Explorer had keeled over like a silly girl. All right, go ahead and laugh; I don't mind. *You* haven't ever been shoved into a room with a thing like that and had it introduced to you as "your new roommate."

Mrs. Grew was chuckling. "Feel better, dear?"

"You're not going to put me in there with him!"

"What? Oh, no, no, that was just my little joke. I'm sure your uncle will never make it necessary actually to do it." She looked at Pinhead thoughtfully—and he was straining one arm through the bars, trying again and again to reach us. "He's had only five milligrams, and for a long-time happy dust addict that's barely enough to make him tempery. If I ever do have to put you—or your brother—in with him, I've promised him at least fifteen. I need your advice, dear. You see, I'm about to send your uncle back to Venusberg so that he can catch his ship. Now which do you think would work best with your uncle? To put your brother in there right now, while your uncle watches? He's watching this, you know; he saw you faint—and that couldn't have been better if you had practiced. Or to wait and—"

"My uncle is watching us?"

"Yes, of course. Or to—"

"Uncle Tom!"

"Oh, do keep quiet, Poddy. He can see you but he can't hear you and he can't possibly help you. *Hmm*— You're such a silly billy that I don't think I want your advice. On your feet, now!"

She walked me back to my cell.

That was only hours ago; it merely seems like years.

But it is long enough. Long enough for Poddy to lose her nerve. Look, I don't have to tell this, nobody knows but me. But I've been truthful all through these memoirs and I'll be truthful now: I have made up my mind that as soon as I get a chance to talk with Uncle I will beg him, plead with him, to do *anything* to keep me from being locked up with a happy-dusted native.

I'm not proud of it. I'm not sure I'll ever be proud of Poddy again. But there it is and you can rub my nose in it. I've come up against something that frightens me so much I've cracked.

I feel a little better about it to have admitted it baldly. I sort of hope that, when the time comes, I won't whimper and I won't plead. But I . . . just . . . don't . . . know.

And then somebody was shoved in with me and it was Clark!

I jumped up off the bed and threw my arms around him and lifted him right off his feet and was blubbering over him. "Oh, Clarkie! Brother, brother, are you hurt? What did they do to you? Speak to me! Are you deaf?"

Right in my ear he said, "Cut out the sloppy stuff, Pod."

So I knew he wasn't too badly hurt, he sounded just like Clark. I repeated, more quietly, "Are you deaf?"

He barely whispered in my ear, "No, but she thinks I am, so we'll go on letting her think so." He untangled himself from me, took a quick look in his bag, then rapidly and very thoroughly went over every bit of the room—giving Titania just wide enough berth to keep her from diving on him.

Then he came back, shoved his face close to mine and said, "Poddy, can you read lips?"

"No. Why?"

"The hell you can't, you just did."

Well, it wasn't quite true; Clark had barely whispered—and I did find that I was "hearing" him as much from watching his mouth as I was from truly hearing him. This is a very funny thing but Clark says that almost everybody reads lips more than they think they do, and he had noticed it and practiced it and can really read lips—only he never told anybody because sometimes it is most useful.

He had me talk so low that I couldn't hear it myself and he didn't talk much louder. He told me, "Look, Pod, I don't know that Old Lady Grew"—he didn't say "Lady"—"has this room wired. I can't find any changes in it since she had me in it before. But there are at least four places and maybe more where a mike could be. So we keep quiet—because it stands to reason she put us together to hear what we have to say to each other. So talk out loud all you want to . . . but just static. How scared you are and how dreadful it is that I can't hear anything and such-like noise."

So we did and I moaned and groaned and wept over my poor baby brother and he complained that he couldn't hear a word I was saying and kept asking me to find a pencil and write what I was saying—and in between we really did talk, important talk that Clark didn't want her to hear.

I wanted to know why he wasn't deaf—had he actually been in that tank? "Oh, sure," he told me, "but I wasn't nearly as limp by then as she thought I was, either. I had some paper in my pocket and I chewed it up into pulp and corked my ears." He looked pained. "A twenty-spot note. Most expensive earplugs anybody ever had, I'll bet. Then I wrapped my shirt around my head and ignored it. But stow that and listen."

He was even more vague about how he had managed to get himself trapped. "Okay, okay, so I got hoaxed. You and Uncle don't look so smart, either—and anyhow, you're responsible."

"I am not either responsible!" I whispered indignantly.

"If you're not responsible, then you're irresponsible, which is worse. Logic. But forget it, we've got important things to do now. Look, Pod, we're going to crush out of here."

"How?" I glanced up at Titania. She was nursing Ariel but she never took her eyes off us.

Clark followed my glance. "I'll take care of that insect when the time comes, forget it. It has to be soon and it has to be at night."

"Why at night?" I was thinking that this smoggy paradise was bad enough when you could see a little, but in pitch-darkness—

"Pod, let that cut in your face heal; you're making a draft. It's got to be while Jojo is locked up."

"Jojo?"

"That set of muscles she has working for her. The native."

"Oh, you mean Pinhead."

"Pinhead, Jojo, Albert Einstein. The happy-duster. He serves supper, then he washes the dishes, then she locks him up and gives him his night's ration of dust. Then he stays locked up until he sleeps it off, because she's as scared of him when he's high as anybody else is. So we make our try for it while he is caged—and maybe she'll be asleep, too. With luck the bloke who drives her sky wagon will be away, too; he doesn't always sleep here. But we can't count on it and it has got to be before the *Tricorn* shapes for Luna. When is that?"

"Twelve-seventeen on the eighth, ship Greenwich."

"Which is?"

"Local? Nine-sixteen Venusberg, Wednesday the twentieth."

"Check," he answered. "On both."

"But why?"

"Shut up." He had taken his slide rule from his bag and was setting it. For the conversion, I assumed, so I asked, "Do you want to know the Venus second for this Terran year?" I was rather proud to have it on the tip of my tongue, like a proper pilot; Mr. Clancy's time hadn't been entirely wasted even though I had never let him get cuddly.

"Nope. I know it." Clark reset the rule, read it and announced, "We both remember both figures the same way and the conversion checks. So check timepieces." We both looked at our wrists. "Mark!"

We agreed, within a few seconds, but that wasn't what I noticed; I was looking at the date hand. "Clark! Today's the nineteenth!"

"Maybe you thought it was Christmas," he said sourly. "And don't yip like that again. I can read you if you don't make a sound."

"But that's tomorrow!" (I did make it soundless.)

"Worse. It's less than seventeen hours from now . . . and we can't make a move until that brute is locked up. We get just one chance, no more."

"Our Uncle Tom doesn't get to the conference."

Clark shrugged. "Maybe so, maybe not. Whether he decides to go—or sticks around and tries to find us—I couldn't care less."

Clark was being very talkative, for Clark. But at best he grudges words and I didn't understand him. "What do you mean—*if he sticks around*?"

Apparently Clark thought he had told me, or that I already knew—but he hadn't and I didn't. Uncle Tom was already gone. I felt suddenly lost and forlorn. "Clark, are you sure?"

"Sure, I'm sure. She darn well saw to it that I saw him go. Jojo loaded him in like a sack of meal and I saw the wagon take off into the smog. Uncle Tom is in Venusberg by now."

I suddenly felt much better. "Then he'll rescue us!"

Clark looked bored. "Pod, don't be stupid squared."

"But he will! Uncle Tom . . . and Mr. Chairman . . . and Dexter—"

He cut me off. "Oh, for Pete's sake, Poddy! Analyze it. You're

Uncle Tom, you're in Venusberg, you've got all the help possible. *How do you find this place?*"

"Uh . . ." I stopped. "Uh . . ." I said again. Then I closed my mouth and left it closed.

"Uh," he agreed. "Exactly *Uh.* You don't find it. Oh, in eight or ten years with a few thousand people doing nothing but searching, you could find it by elimination. Fat lot of good that would do. Get this through your little head, Sis: nobody is going to rescue us, nobody can possibly help us. We either break out of here tonight—or we've had it."

"Why tonight? Oh, tonight's all right with me. But if we don't get a chance tonight—"

"Then at nine-sixteen tomorrow," he interrupted, "we're dead."

"Huh? Why?"

"Figure it out yourself, Pod. Put yourself in old Gruesome's place. Tomorrow the *Tricorn* leaves. Figure it both ways: Uncle Tom leaves in it, or Uncle Tom won't leave. Okay, you've got his niece and nephew. What do you do with them? Be logical about it. *Her* sort of logic."

I tried, I really tried. But maybe I've been brought up wrong for that sort of logic; I can't seem to visualize killing somebody just because he or she had become a nuisance to me.

But I could see that Clark was right that far: after ship's departure tomorrow we will simply be nuisances to Mrs. Grew. If Uncle Tom *doesn't* leave, we are most special nuisances—and if he *does* leave and she is counting on his worry about us to keep him in line at Luna City (it wouldn't, of course, but that is what she is counting on anyway), in that case every day she risks the possibility that we might escape and get word to Uncle.

All right, maybe I can't imagine just plain murder; it's outside my experience. But suppose both Clark and I came down with green pox and died— That would certainly be convenient for Mrs. Grew—now, wouldn't it?

"I scan it," I agreed.

"Good," he said. "I'll teach you a thing or four yet, Pod. Either we make it tonight . . . or just past nine tomorrow she chills us both . . . and she chills Jojo, too, and sets fire to the place."

"Why Jojo? I mean Pinhead."

"That's the real tipoff, Pod. The happy-duster. This is Venus . . . and yet she let us see that she was supplying dust to a duster. She won't leave any witnesses."

"Uncle Tom is a witness, too."

"What if he is? She's counting on his keeping his lip zipped until the conference is over . . . and by then she's back on Earth and has lost herself among eight billion people. Hang around here and risk being caught? Pod, she's going to wait here only long enough to find out whether or not Uncle Tom catches the *Tricorn.* Then she'll carry out either Plan A, or Plan B—but both plans cancel us out. Get that through your fuzzy head."

I shivered. "All right. I've got it."

He grinned. "But *we* don't wait. We execute our own plan— my plan—first." He looked unbearably smug and added, "You fubbed utterly and came out here without doing any of the things I told you to . . . and Uncle Tom fubbed just about as badly, thinking he could make a straight payoff . . . but I came out here prepared!"

"You did? With what? Your slide rule? Or maybe those comic books?"

Clark said, "Pod, you know I never read comic books; they were just protective coloration."

(And this is true, so far as I know— I thought I had uncovered his Secret Vice.)

"Then what?" I demanded.

"Just compose your soul in patience, Sister dear. All in good time." He moved his bag back of the bed, then added, "Move around here where you can watch down the hallway. If Lady Macbeth shows up, I'm reading comic books."

I did as he told me to but asked him one more question—on another subject, as quizzing Clark when he doesn't want to answer is as futile as slicing water. "Clark? You figure Mrs. Grew is part of the gang that smuggled the bomb?"

He blinked and looked stupid. "What bomb?"

"The one they paid you to sneak aboard the *Tricorn,* of course! *What bomb* indeed!"

"Oh, that. Golly, Poddy, you believe everything you're told. When you get to Terra, don't let anybody sell you the Pyramids—they're not for sale." He went on working and I smothered my annoyance.

Presently he said, "She couldn't possibly know anything about any bombs in the *Tricorn,* or she wouldn't have been a passenger in it herself."

Clark can always make me feel stupid. This was so obvious (after he pointed it out) that I refrained from comment. "How do you figure it, then?"

"Well, she could have been hired by the same people and not have known that they were just using her as a reserve."

My mind raced and another answer came up. "In which case there could be still a third plot to get Uncle Tom between here and Luna!"

"Could be. Certainly a lot of people are taking an interest in him. But I figure it for two groups. One group—almost certainly from Mars—doesn't want Uncle Tom to be there at all. Another group—from Earth probably, at least old Gruesome actually did come from Earth—wants him to be there but wants him to sing their song. Otherwise when she had Uncle Tom, she would never have turned him loose; she would just have had Jojo shove him into a soft spot and wait for the bubbles to stop coming up." Clark dug out something and looked at it. "Pod, repeat this back and don't make a sound. You are exactly twenty-three kilometers from South Gate and almost due south of it—south seven degrees west."

I repeated it. "How do you know?"

He held up a small black object about as big as two packs of cigarettes. "Inertial tracker, infantry model. You can buy them anywhere here, anybody who ever goes out into the bush carries one." He handed it to me.

I looked at it with interest; I had never seen one that small. Sand rats use them, of course, but they use bigger, more accurate ones mounted in their sand buggies—and anyhow, on Mars you can always see either the stars or the Sun. Not like this gloomy place! I even knew how it worked, more or less, because inertial astrogation is a commonplace for spaceships and guided missiles—vector integration of accelerations and times. But whereas the *Tricorn*'s inertial tracker is supposed to be good for one part in a million, this little gadget probably couldn't be read closer than one in a thousand.

But it improved our chances at least a thousand to one!

"Clark! Did Uncle Tom have one of these? 'Cause if he did—"

He shook his head. "If he did, he never got a chance to read it. I figure they gassed him at once; he was limp when they lifted him out of the air wagon. And I never had a chance to tell him where this dump is because this has been my first chance to look at mine. Now put it in your purse; you're going to use it to get back to Venusberg."

"Uh . . . it'll be bulky in my purse, it'll show. You better hide it wherever you had it. You won't lose me, I'm going to hang onto your hand every step of the way."

"No."

"Why not?"

"In the first place I'm not going to drag this bag with me and that's where it was hidden; I built a false bottom into it. In the second place we aren't going back together—"

"What? Why not? We certainly are! Clark, I'm responsible for you."

"That's a matter of opinion. Your opinion. Look, Poddy, I'm going to get you out of this silly mess. But don't try to use your head, it leaks. Just your memory. Listen to what I say and then do it exactly the way I tell you to—and you'll be all right."

"But—"

"Do *you* have a plan to get us out?"

"No."

"Then shut up. You start pulling your Big Sister act now and you'll get us both killed."

I shut up. And I must confess that his plan made considerable sense. According to Clark there is nobody in this house but us, Mrs. Grew, Titania and Ariel, Pinhead—and sometimes her driver. I certainly haven't seen or heard any evidences of anybody else and I suppose that Mrs. Grew has been doing it with an absolute minimum of witnesses—I know I would if I were (God forbid!) ever engaged in anything so outrageously criminal.

I've never seen the driver's face and neither has Clark—on purpose, I'm sure. But Clark says that the driver sometimes stays overnight, so we must be prepared to cope with him.

Okay, assume that we cope. As soon as we are out of the house we split up; I go east, he goes west, for a couple of kilometers, in straight lines as near as bogs and swamps permit, which may be not very.

Then we both turn north—and Clark says that the ring road around the city is just three kilometers north of us; he drew me a sketch from memory of a map he had studied before he set out to "rescue Girdie."

At the ring road I go right, he goes left—and we each make use of the first hitchhike transportation, ranch house phone, or whatever, to reach Uncle Tom and/or Chairman Cunha and get lots of reinforcements in a hurry!

The idea of splitting up is the most elementary of tactics, to make sure that at least one of us gets through and gets help. Mrs. Grew is so fat she couldn't chase anybody on a race track, much less a swamp. We plan to do it when she doesn't dare unlock Pinhead for fear of her own life. If we are chased, it will probably be the driver—and he can't chase two directions at once. Maybe there are other natives she can call on for help, but even so, splitting up doubles our chances.

So I get the inertial tracker because Clark doesn't think I can maneuver in the bush without one, even if I wait for it to get light. He's probably right. But he claims that he can steer well enough to find that road using just his watch, a wet finger for the breeze, and polarized spectacles—which, so help me, he has with him.

I shouldn't have sneered at his comic books; he actually did come prepared, quite a lot of ways. If they hadn't gassed him while he was still locked in the passenger compartment of Mrs. Grew's air buggy, I think he could have given them a very busy, bad time. A flame gun in his bag, a Remington pistol hidden on his person, knives, stun bombs—even a *second* inertial tracker, openly in the bag along with his clothes and comic books and slide rule.

I asked him why, and he put on his best superior look. "If anything went wrong and they grabbed me, they would expect me to have one. So I had one—and it hadn't even been started . . . poor little tenderfoot who doesn't even know enough to switch the thing on when he leaves his base position. Old Gruesome got a fine chuckle out of that." He sneered. "She thinks I'm half-witted and I've done my best to help the idea along."

So they did the same thing with his bag that they did with my purse—cleaned everything out of it that looked even faintly useful for mayhem and murder, let him keep what was left.

And most of what was left was concealed by a false bottom so beautifully faked that the manufacturer wouldn't have noticed it.

Except, possibly, for the weight—I asked Clark about that. He shrugged. "Calculated risk," he said. "If you don't bet, you can't win. Jojo carried it in here still packed and she searched it in here—and didn't pick it up afterwards; she had both arms full of junk I didn't mind her confiscating."

(And suppose she had picked it up and noticed? Well, Brother would still have had his brain and his hands—and I think he could take a sewing machine apart and put it back together as a piece of artillery. Clark is a trial to me—but I have great confidence in him.)

I'm going to get some sleep now—or try to—as Pinhead has just fetched in our supper and we have a busy time ahead of us, later. But first I'm going to backtrack this tape and copy it; I have one fresh spool left in my purse. I'm going to give the copy to Clark to give to Uncle, just in case. Just in case Poddy turns out to be bubbles in a swamp, I mean. But I'm not worried about that; it's a much nicer prospect than being Pinhead's roommate. In fact I'm not worried about anything; Clark has the situation well in hand.

But he warned me very strongly about one thing; "Tell them to get here well before nine-sixteen . . . or don't bother to come at all."

"Why?" I wanted to know.

"Just do it."

"Clark, you know perfectly well that two grown men won't pay any attention unless I can give them a sound reason for it."

He blinked. "All right. There is a very sound reason. A half-a-kiloton bomb isn't very much . . . but it still isn't healthy to be around when it goes off. Unless they can get in here and disarm it before that time—up she goes!"

He has it. I've *seen* it. Snugly fitted into that false bottom. That same three kilograms of excess mass I couldn't account for at Deimos. Clark showed me the timing mechanism and how the shaped charges were nestled around it to produce the implosion squeeze.

But he did not show me how to disarm it. I ran into his blankest, most stubborn wall. He expects to escape, yes—and he expects to come back here with plenty of help and in plenty of time and disarm the thing. But he is utterly convinced that Mrs. Grew intends to kill us, and if anything goes wrong and we don't break out of here, or die trying, or anything . . . well, he intends to take her with us.

I told him it was wrong, I said that he mustn't take the law in his own hands. "What law!" he said. "There isn't any law here. And you aren't being logical, Pod. Anything that is right for a group to do is right for one person to do."

That one was too slippery for me to answer so I tried simply pleading with him and he got sore. "Maybe you would rather be in the cage with Jojo?"

"Well . . . no."

"Then shut up about it. Look, Pod, I planned all this out when she had me in that tank, trying to beat my ears in, make me deaf. I kept my sanity by ignoring what was being done to me and concentrating on when and how I would blow her to bits."

I wondered if he had indeed kept his sanity but I kept my doubts to myself and shut up. Besides I'm not sure that he's wrong; it may be that I'm just squeamish about blood-shed. "Anything that is moral for a group to do is moral for one person to do." There must be a flaw in that, since I've always been taught that it is wrong to take the law in your own hands. But I can't find the flaw and it sounds axiomatic, self-evident. Switch it around. If something is wrong for one person to do, can it possibly be made *right* by having a lot of people (a government) agree to do it together? Even unanimously?

If a thing is wrong, it is wrong—and vox populi can't change it.

Just the same, I'm not sure I can nap with an atom bomb under my bed.

Postlude

I guess I had better finish this.

My sister got right to sleep after I rehearsed her in what we were going to do. I stretched out on the floor but didn't go right to sleep. I'm a worrier, she isn't. I reviewed my plans, trying to make them tighter. Then slept.

I've got one of those built-in alarm clocks and I woke just when I planned to, an hour before dawn. Any later and there would be too much chance that Jojo might be loose, any earlier and there would be too much time in the dark. The Venus bush is chancy even when you can see well; I didn't want Poddy to step into something sticky, or step on something that would turn and bite her leg off. Nor me, either.

But we had to risk the bush, or stay and let old Gruesome kill us at her convenience. The first was a sporting chance; the latter was a dead certainty, even though I had a terrible time convincing Poddy that Mrs. Grew would kill us. Poddy's greatest weakness— the really soft place in her head, she's not too stupid otherwise— is her almost total inability to grasp that some people are as bad as they are. Evil. Poddy never has understood evil. Naughtiness is about as far as her imagination reaches.

But I understand evil, I can get right inside the skull of a person like Mrs. Grew and understand how she thinks.

Perhaps you infer from this that I am evil, or partly so. All right, want to make something of it? Whatever *I* am, I knew Mrs. Grew was evil before we ever left the *Tricorn* . . . when Poddy (and even Girdie!) thought the slob was just too darling for words.

I don't trust a person who laughs when there is nothing to

laugh about. Or is good-natured no matter what happens. If it's that perfect, it's an act, a phony. So I watched her . . . and cheating at solitaire wasn't the only giveaway.

So between the bush and Mrs. Grew, I chose the bush, both for me and my sister.

Unless the air car was there and we could swipe it. This would be a mixed blessing, as it would mean two of them to cope with, them armed and us not. (I don't count a bomb as an arm, you can't point it at a person's head.)

Before I woke Poddy I took care of that alate pseudosimian, that "fairy." Vicious little beast. I didn't have a gun. But I didn't really want one at that point; they understand about guns and are hard to hit, they'll dive on you at once.

Instead I had shoe trees in my spare shoes, elastic bands around my spare clothes, and more elastic bands in my pockets, and several two-centimeter steel ball bearings.

Shift two wing nuts, and the long parts of the shoe trees become a steel fork. Add elastic bands and you have a sling shot. And don't laugh at a slingshot; many a sand rat has kept himself fed with only a sling shot. They are silent and you usually get your ammo back.

I aimed almost three times as high as I would at home, to allow for the local gravity, and got it right on the sternum, knocked it off its perch—crushed the skull with my heel and gave it an extra twist for the nasty bite on Poddy's arm. The young one started to whine, so I pushed the carcass over in the corner, somewhat out of sight, and put the cub on it. It shut up. I took care of all this before I woke Poddy because I knew she had sentimental fancies about these "fairies" and I didn't want her jittering and maybe grabbing my elbow. As it was—clean and fast.

She was still snoring, so I slipped off my shoes and made a fast reconnoiter.

Not so good— Our local witch was already up and reaching for her broom; in a few minutes she would be unlocking Jojo if she hadn't already. I didn't have a chance to see if the sky car was outside; I did well not to get caught. I hurried back and woke Poddy.

"Pod!" I whispered. "You awake?"

"Yes."

"Wide awake? You've got to do your act, right now. Make it loud and make it good."

"Check."

"Help me up on the perch. Can your sore arm take it?"

She nodded, slid quickly off the bed and took position at the door, hands ready. I grabbed her hands, bounced to her shoulders, steadied, and she grabbed my calves as I let go her hands—and then I was up on the perch, over the door. I waved her on.

Poddy went running out the door, screaming, "Mrs. Grew! *Mrs. Grew*! Help, help! My brother!" She did make it good.

And came running back in almost at once with Mrs. Grew puffing after her.

I landed on Grucsome's shoulders, knocking her to the floor and knocking her gun out of her hand. I twisted and snapped her neck before she could catch her breath.

Pod was right on the ball, I have to give her credit. She had that gun before it stopped sliding. Then she held it, looking dazed.

I took it carefully from her. "Grab your purse. We go, right now! Stick close behind me."

Jojo *was* loose, I had cut it too fine. He was in the living room, looking, I guess, to see what the noise was about. I shot him.

Then I looked for the air car while keeping the gun ready for the driver. No sign of either one—and I didn't know whether to groan or cheer. I was all keyed up to shoot him but maybe he would have shot me first. But a car would have been mighty welcome compared with heading into the bush.

I almost changed my plan at that point and maybe I should have. Kept together, I mean, and headed straight north for the ring road.

It was the gun that decided me. Poddy could protect herself with it—and I would just be darn careful what I stepped on or in. I handed it to her and told her to move slowly and carefully until there was more light—but get going!

She was wobbling the gun around. "But, Brother, I've never shot anybody!"

"Well, you can if you have to."

"I guess so."

"Nothing to it. Just point it at 'em and press the button. Better use both hands. And don't shoot unless you really need to."

"All right."

I smacked her behind. "Now get going. See you later."

And I got going. I looked behind once, but she was already vanished in the smog. I put a little distance between me and the house, just in case, then concentrated on approximating course west.

And I got lost. That's all. I needed that tracker but I had figured I could get along without it and Pod had to have it. I got hopelessly lost. There wasn't breeze enough for me to tell anything by wetting my finger and that polarized light trick for finding the Sun is harder than you would think. Hours after I should have reached the ring road I was still skirting boggy places and open water and trying to keep from being somebody's lunch.

And suddenly there was the most dazzling light possible and I went down flat and stayed there with my eyes buried in my arm and started to count.

I wasn't hurt at all. The blast wave covered me with mud and the noise was pretty rough but I was well outside the real trouble. Maybe half an hour later I was picked up by a cop car.

Certainly, I should have disarmed that bomb. I had intended to, if everything went well; it was just meant to be a "Samson in the Temple" stunt if things turned out dry. A last resort.

Maybe I should have stopped to disarm it as soon as I broke old Gruesome's neck—and maybe Jojo would have caught both of us if I had and him still with a happy-dust hangover. Anyhow I didn't and then I was very busy shooting Jojo and deciding what to do and telling Poddy how to use that gun and getting her started. I didn't think about the bomb until I was several hundred meters from the house—and I certainly didn't want to go back then, even if I could have found it again in the smog, which is doubtful.

But apparently Poddy did just that. Went back to the house, I mean. She was found later that day, about a kilometer from the house, outside the circle of total destruction—but caught by the blast.

With a live baby fairy in her arms—her body had protected it; it doesn't appear to have been hurt at all.

That's why I think she went back to the house. I don't *know* that this baby fairy is the one she called "Ariel." It might have been one that she picked up in the bush. But that doesn't seem at all likely; a wild one would have clawed her and its parents would have torn her to pieces.

I think she intended to save that baby fairy all along and decided not to mention it to me. It is just the kind of sentimental stunt that Poddy would do. She knew I was going to have to kill the adult—and she never said a word against that; Pod could always be sensible when absolutely necessary.

Then in the excitement of breaking out she forgot to grab it, just as I forgot to disarm the bomb after we no longer needed it. So she went back for it.

And lost the inertial tracker, somehow. At least it wasn't found on her or near her. Between the gun and her purse and the baby fairy and the tracker she must have dropped it in a bog. Must be, because she had plenty of time to go back and still get far away from the house. She should have been ten kilometers away by then, so she must have lost the tracker fairly soon and walked in a circle.

I told Uncle Tom all about it and was ready to tell the Corporation people, Mr. Cunha and so forth, and take my medicine. But Uncle told me to keep my mouth shut. He agreed that I had fubbed it, mighty dry indeed—but so had he—and so had everybody. He was gentle with me. I wish he had hit me.

I'm sorry about Poddy. She gave me some trouble from time to time, with her bossy ways and her illogical ideas—but just the same I'm sorry.

I wish I knew how to cry.

Her little recorder was still in her purse and part of the tape could be read. Doesn't mean much, though; she doesn't tell what she did, she was babbling, sort of:

". . . very dark where I'm going. No man is an island, complete in himself. Remember that, Clarkie. Oh, I'm sorry I fubbed it but remember that; it's important. They all have to be cuddled sometimes. My shoulder— Saint Podkayne! Saint Podkayne, are you listening? Unka Tom, Mother, Daddy—is anybody listening? Do listen, please, because this is important. I love—"

It cuts off there. So we don't know whom she loved.

Everybody maybe.

Mr. Cunha made them hold the *Tricorn* and now Uncle Tom and I are on our way again. The baby fairy is still alive and Dr. Torland says it doesn't have radiation sickness. I call it "Ariel" and I guess I'll be taking care of it a long time; they say these fairies live as long as we do. It is taking to shipboard life all right but it gets lonely and has to be held and cuddled or it cries.

To Our Readers

You have just read the ending of PODKAYNE OF MARS as Heinlein originally wrote it. However, Putnam's, his publisher at the time, was unhappy with that ending. We thought you might like to see the originally published version.

Postlude

(As Originally Published)

I guess I had better finish this.

My sister got right to sleep after I rehearsed her in what we were going to do. I stretched out on the floor but didn't go right to sleep. I'm a worrier, she isn't. I reviewed my plans, trying to make them tighter. Then I slept.

I've got one of those built-in alarm clocks and I woke just when I planned to, an hour before dawn. Any later and there would be too much chance that Jojo might be loose, any earlier and there would be too much time in the dark. The Venus bush is chancy even when you see well; I didn't want Poddy to step into something sticky, or step on something that would turn and bite her leg off. Nor me, either.

But we had to risk the bush, or stay and let old Gruesome kill us at her convenience. The first was a sporting chance; the latter was a dead certainty, even though I had a terrible time convincing Poddy that Mrs. Grew would kill us. Poddy's greatest weakness— the really soft place in her head, she's not too stupid otherwise— is her almost total inability to grasp that some people are as bad as they are. Evil. Poddy never has understood evil. Naughtiness is about as far as her imagination reaches.

But I understand evil, I can get right inside the skull of a person like Mrs. Grew and understand how she thinks.

Perhaps you infer from this that I am evil, or partly so. All right, want to make something of it? Whatever *I* am, I knew Mrs. Grew was evil before we ever left the *Tricorn* . . . when Poddy (and even Girdie!) thought the slob was just too darling for words.

I don't trust a person who laughs when there is nothing to

laugh about. Or is good-natured no matter what happens. If it's that perfect, it's an act, a phony. So I watched her . . . and cheating at solitaire wasn't the only giveaway.

So between the bush and Mrs. Grew, I chose the bush, both for me and my sister.

Unless the air car was there and we could swipe it. This would be a mixed blessing, as it would mean two of them to cope with, them armed and us not. (I don't count a bomb as an arm, you can't point it at a person's head.)

Before I woke Poddy I took care of that alate pseudosimian, that "fairy." Vicious little beast. I didn't have a gun. But I didn't really want one at that point; they understand about guns and are hard to hit, they'll dive on you at once.

Instead I had shoe trees in my spare shoes, elastic bands around my spare clothes, and more elastic bands in my pockets, and several two-centimeter steel ball bearings.

Shift two wing nuts, and the long parts of the shoe trees become a steel fork. Add elastic bands and you have a slingshot. And don't laugh at a slingshot; many a sand rat has kept himself fed with only a slingshot. They are silent and you usually get your ammo back.

I aimed almost three times as high as I would at home, to allow for the local gravity, and got it right on the sternum, knocked it off its perch—crushed the skull with my heel and gave it an extra twist for the nasty bite on Poddy's arm. The young one started to whine, so I pushed the carcass over into the corner, somewhat out of sight, and put the cub on it. It shut up. I took care of all this before I woke Poddy because I knew she had sentimental fancies about these "fairies" and I didn't want her jittering and maybe grabbing my elbow. As it was—clean and fast.

She was still snoring, so I slipped off my shoes and made a fast reconnoiter.

Not so good— Our local witch was already up and reaching for her broom; in a few minutes she would be unlocking Jojo if she hadn't already. I didn't have a chance to see if the sky car was outside; I did well not to get caught. I hurried back and woke Poddy.

"Pod!" I whispered. "You awake?"

"Yes."

"Wide awake? You've got to do your act, right now. Make it loud and make it good."

"Check."

"Help me up onto the perch. Can your sore arm take it?"

She nodded, slid quickly off the bed and took position at the door, hands ready. I grabbed her hands, bounced to her shoulders, steadied, and she grabbed my calves as I let go her hands—and then I was up on the perch, over the door. I waved her on.

Poddy went running out the door, screaming, "Mrs. Grew! *Mrs. Grew!* Help, help! My brother!" She did make it good.

And came running back in almost at once with Mrs. Grew puffing after her.

I landed on Gruesome's shoulders, knocking her to the floor and knocking her gun out of her hand. I twisted and snapped her neck before she could catch her breath.

Pod was right on the ball, I have to give her credit. She had that gun before it stopped sliding. Then she held it, looking dazed.

I took it carefully from her. "Grab your purse. We go right now! Stick close behind me."

Jojo *was* loose, I had cut it too fine. He was in the living room, looking, I guess, to see what the noise was about. I shot him.

Then I looked for the air car while keeping the gun ready for the driver. No sign of either one—and I didn't know whether to groan or cheer. I was all keyed up to shoot him but maybe he would have shot me first. But a car would have been mighty welcome compared with heading into the bush.

I almost changed my plan at that point and maybe I should have. Kept together, I mean, and headed straight north for the ring road.

It was the gun that decided me. Poddy could protect herself with it—and I would just be darn careful what I stepped on or in. I handed it to her and told her to move slowly and carefully until there was more light—but get going!

She was wobbling the gun around. "But, Brother, I've never shot anybody!"

"Well, you can if you have to."

"I guess so."

"Nothing to it. Just point it at 'em and press the button. Better use both hands. And don't shoot unless you really need to."

"All right."

I smacked her behind. "Now get going. See you later."

And I got going. I looked behind once, but she was already vanished in the smog. I put a little distance between me and the house, just in case, then concentrated on approximating course west.

And I got lost. That's all. I needed that tracker but I had figured I could get along without it and Pod had to have it. I got hopelessly lost. There wasn't breeze enough for me to tell anything by wetting my finger and that polarized light trick for finding the Sun is harder than you would think. Hours after I should have reached the ring road I was still skirting boggy places and open water and trying to keep from being somebody's lunch.

And suddenly there was the most dazzling light possible and I went down flat and stayed there with my eyes buried in my arm and started to count.

I wasn't hurt at all. The blast wave covered me with mud and the noise was pretty rough, but I was well outside the real trouble. Maybe half an hour later I was picked up by a cop car.

Certainly, I should have disarmed that bomb. I had intended to, if everything went well; it was just meant to be a "Samson in the Temple" stunt if things turned out dry. A last resort.

Maybe I should have stopped to disarm it as soon as I broke old Gruesome's neck—and maybe Jojo would have caught both of us if I had and him still with a happy-dust hangover. Anyhow I didn't and then I was very busy deciding what to do and telling Poddy how to use that gun and getting her started. I didn't think about the bomb until I was several hundred meters from the house—and I certainly didn't want to go back then, even if I could have found it again in the smog, which is doubtful.

But apparently Poddy did just that. Went back to the house, I mean. She was found later that day, about a kilometer from the house, outside the circle of total destruction—but caught by the blast.

With a live baby fairy in her arms—her body had protected it; it doesn't appear to have been hurt at all.

That's why I think she went back to the house. I don't *know* that this baby fairy is the one she called "Ariel." It could have been one that she picked up in the bush. But that doesn't seem at all likely; a wild one would have clawed her and its parents would have torn her to pieces.

I think she intended to save that baby fairy all along and decided not to mention it to me. It is just the kind of sentimental stunt that Poddy would pull. She knew I was going to have to kill the adult—and she never said a word against that; Pod could always be sensible when absolutely necessary.

Then in the excitement of breaking out she forgot to grab it, just as I forgot to disarm the bomb after we no longer needed it. So she went back for it.

And lost the inertial tracker, somehow. At least it wasn't found on her or near her. Between the gun and her purse and the baby fairy and the tracker she must have dropped it in the bog. Must be, because she had plenty of time to go back and still get far away from the house. She should have been ten kilometers away by then, so she must have lost the tracker fairly soon and walked in a circle.

I told Uncle Tom all about it and was ready to tell the Corporation people, Mr. Cunha and so forth, and take my medicine. But Uncle told me to keep my mouth shut. He agreed that I had fubbed it, mighty dry indeed—but so had he—and so had everybody. He was gentle with me. I wish he had hit me.

I'm sorry about Poddy. She gave me some trouble from time to time, with her bossy ways and her illogical ideas—but just the same, I'm sorry.

I wish I knew how to cry.

Her little recorder was still in her purse and part of the tape could be read. Doesn't mean much, though; she doesn't tell what she did, she was babbling, sort of:

". . . very dark where I'm going. No man is an island complete in himself. Remember that; it's important. They all have to be cuddled sometimes. My shoulder—Saint Podkayne! Saint Podkayne, are you listening? Unka Tom, Mother, Daddy—is anybody listening? Do listen, please, because this is important. I love—"

It cuts off there. So we don't know whom she loved.

Everybody, maybe.

I'm alone here, now. Mr. Cunha made them hold the *Tricorn* until it was certain whether Poddy would die or get well, then Uncle Tom left and left me behind—alone, that is, except for doctors, and nurses, and Dexter Cunha hanging around all the time, and a whole platoon of guards. I can't go anywhere without one. I can't go to the casinos at all any more—not that I want to, much.

I heard part of what Uncle Tom told Dad about it. Not all of it, as a phone conversation with a bounce time of over twenty minutes is episodic. I heard none of what Dad said and only one monologue of Uncle's:

"Nonsense, sir! I am not dodging my own load of guilt; it will be with me always. Nor can I wait here until you arrive and you know it and you know why—and both children will be safer in Mr. Cunha's hands and *not* close to me . . . and you know *that*, too! But I have a message for you, sir, one that you should pass on to your wife. Just this: people who will not take the trouble to raise children should not have them. You with your nose always in a book, your wife gallivanting off God knows where—between you, your daughter was almost killed. No credit to either of you that she wasn't. Just blind luck. You should tell your wife, sir, that building bridges and space stations and such gadgets is all very well . . . but that a woman has more important work to do. I tried to suggest this to you years ago . . . and was told to mind my own business. Now I am saying it. Your daughter will get well, no thanks to either of you. But I have my doubts about Clark. With him it may be too late. God may give you a second chance if you hurry. Ending transmission!"

I faded into the woodwork then and didn't get caught. But what did Uncle Tom mean by that—trying to scare Dad about *me*? I wasn't hurt at all and he knows it. I just got a load of mud on me, not even a burn . . . whereas Poddy still looks like a corpse and they've got her piped and wired like a crèche.

I don't see what he was driving at.

I'm taking care of that baby fairy because Poddy will want to see it when she gets well enough to notice things again; she's always been a sentimentalist. It needs a lot of attention because it gets lonely and has to be held and cuddled, or it cries.

So I'm up a lot in the night—I guess it thinks I'm its mother. I don't mind, I don't have much else to do.

It seems to like me.